The Silver Kings

- The -
Silver Kings

Stephen Deas

Copyright © Stephen Deas 2015
All rights reserved

The right of Stephen Deas to be identified as the author
of this work has been asserted by him in accordance with
the Copyright, Designs and Patents Act 1988.

First published in Great Britain in 2015
by Gollancz
An imprint of the Orion Publishing Group
Carmelite House, 50 Victoria Embankment,
London EC4Y 0DZ
An Hachette UK Company

This edition published in Great Britain in 2016 by Gollancz

1 3 5 7 9 10 8 6 4 2

A CIP catalogue record for this book
is available from the British Library.

ISBN 978 0 575 10062 6

Typeset by Deltatype Ltd, Birkenhead, Merseyside

Printed and bound by CPI Group (UK) Ltd,
Croydon CR0 4YY

www.stephendeas.com
www.orionbooks.co.uk
www.gollancz.co.uk

For Michaela, my dragon-queen

This is the last volume of a story of enchanters and alchemists and half-gods and, most of all, of dragons and those who ride them. It stands on the shoulders of *Dragon Queen*, *The Splintered Gods* and *The Black Mausoleum*. I cannot promise that it makes sense without them.

Prologue
Skjorl

The tremor woke him up. Hadn't been asleep for long, so no point smashing down the door yet. He'd had a good look at that as he'd been shoved inside. Strong, but the frame had been wedged poorly and in haste into whatever stone this place was made of. A good charge or two would bring it down.

The alchemist was crouched over Siff. The shit-eater was still breathing. Wasn't moving much more than that. Skjorl rolled over and let himself go back to sleep.

When he woke again, the room looked exactly the same. Same light. Shit-eater lying sprawled across the floor. Alchemist sitting beside him. He couldn't tell how long they'd been there. Hours. Could have been the middle of the night; could have been the next morning for all he knew.

'Alchemist!'

Her head jerked. She'd been sleeping. 'What?'

'What's your plan?'

'I don't know.'

Skjorl unfolded himself and walked to the door. He peered through the cracks. Two men on guard outside. They looked bored and sleepy. 'We could leave. If you want.'

'No.'

Hardly a surprise. He sat down again.

'Someone has mastered dragons. Whoever that is, I need to talk to them. It doesn't matter whom they serve. Whether it's Speaker Lystra or Speaker Hyrkallan, or some other speaker I've never heard of, they've mastered dragons again.' She turned to face him. Her eyes were wide. 'Do you know what that means?'

'It means hope, alchemist. I know that.'

'Yes.'

'I saw Taiytakei as they brought us here. I saw soldiers who are of these realms and others who are not. The Taiytakei brought the disaster on us. It was their making.' He looked at her. 'Yet you would help them?'

'I saw *one* Taiytakei,' she growled at him. 'One.'

Skjorl lay down and stretched out. The last few days had been long ones, and Adamantine Men learned to catch their rest when they could. Some time later the door opened. Someone threw in a loaf of bread and a skin of water and slammed it shut again. The bread was hard as stone and tasted of mould, but Skjorl couldn't remember the last time he'd tasted real bread. No one had made it since the Adamantine Palace had burned. He savoured every mouthful, mould or not. The shit-eater was still unconscious. The alchemist was somewhere else, lost in thought. He stared at her for a while, thinking about what he'd do, where he'd be if she hadn't done her blood-magic to his head. When he was done with that he went back to sleep.

The door opening again woke him. More soldiers this time. Eight, maybe nine. He didn't get the chance to count them before they piled into him, ignoring the others. They pinned him down and tied his hands and dragged him out. They didn't take him far, just to another cell hardly a dozen yards from where they'd started. Empty but for a heavy chair. Took most of them to bind him to it, but they did. When they were done, one stood in front of him and cracked his knuckles.

'You're a spy.'

He had an accent, this one. Not a strong one, but an accent none-theless. Familiar. Skjorl grinned at him. 'And you're a shit-eater.'

The man punched him in the face and broke his nose. 'Your speaker sent you. You're a spy.'

Skjorl said nothing. Said nothing when the man punched him again. Said nothing when they held back his head and poured water over his face until he was sure he was going to drown. Said nothing when they told him what else they were going to do, what bones they'd break, what pieces they'd cut off him and how they'd burn and scar him. Men of the Speaker's Guard took worse from the brothers of their own legion, after all, before they were finally given their dragonscale and their axe and sword. A final test. No one ever said so, but the ones who failed never saw another full year, dragonscale or no. Skjorl's test had lasted three days.

The shit-eater grew bored after a couple of hours. When he stopped, Skjorl laughed at him and spat out a tooth.

'I'm an Adamantine Man, shit-eater,' he said, as if that was enough.

They left him for a while then. He didn't bother struggling or trying to break free. When they came back, they picked him up, chair and everything, and turned him around so he couldn't see the door.

'I know about you,' said a new voice. Heavy accent this one, but the words were careful, shaped with thought and spoken slowly so they could be heard. 'Adamantine Men. They raise you from the cradle to fight dragons, right?'

Skjorl said nothing. He was what he was. An Adamantine Man never broke.

'I've led soldiers in three worlds. I would take your kind over any other. I'm sorry I have to take this from you, but time is pressing.'

Skjorl waited for the blow, but what came was a tickle in his head, that was all. Like the alchemist's fingers but infinitely deft. The faintest sense of something taken away, cut with a subtle and expert scalpel. For a moment he thought he saw the flicker of a knife with a golden hilt, reflected in the polished armour of the soldiers around him.

'Now,' said the voice again. 'Tell me why you're here. Tell me everything.'

Skjorl told him. Afterwards, when they took him back to his cell, he sat down and wondered why he'd done that, because it wasn't like they'd ripped it from him, piece by piece, fighting for every word. More like he'd decided it was right, that was all. Just didn't know why.

He watched, strangely detached, as the same soldiers dragged the alchemist away and closed the door behind her. He listened to her shout, and heard the scrape of wood on stone. That would be the chair. Then voices. The man who'd asked him questions, then the alchemist's reply, and then another one, a new one, a woman he'd heard once before, a long time ago, only now he couldn't place her. She sounded sharp and angry. There was something about a

⚜ 5 ⚜

garden. Something about moonlight, and something about the Silver King. His brow furrowed. He ought to care about these things.

A tremor ran through the walls. The shit-eater was still on the floor, unconscious or asleep or pretending, one or the other. Down the hall the voices stopped. When they started again they were fast and urgent, words buried once more under strange accents. He caught one clear enough though. Couldn't miss it. Over and over, shouted like an alarm.

'Dragons!'

Black Moon comes, round and round
Black Moon comes, all fall down.

Children's rhyme, Deephaven, Aria

Landfall

There is no warmth in the ancient fortress of the Pinnacles, timeless bastion against the dragons. The dragon-rider Hyrkallan is a harsh king with a loathing venom for all who practise alchemy. His consort is the mad queen Jaslyn, who once woke a hatchling dragon because she thought there could be peace between men and dragons without the poison of alchemy, a madness that came to her after Speaker Zafir beheaded her mother. The union between this king and queen once carried the desert realms of the north to war and victory, but there is neither love nor desire nor affection between them. Hyrkallan dreams of glories he will never see returned. Queen Jaslyn thinks of the simple things she cannot have. To be with her sister Lystra. To be with a dragon and fly once more. To be left alone and never be touched.

Together and apart Hyrkallan and his queen lay tattered claim to realms now ruled by monsters. They make their home with a thousand souls inside the Moonlit Mountain, above the fire-gutted dragon-wrecked majesty that was once the Silver City. Safe within their fortress they search the endless tunnels for relics of the Silver King, the ancient half-god sorcerer who once tamed dragons. It is said, in whispers, that the old queens of the Silver City were one by one driven mad by the half-god's Enchanted Palace, whose white stone walls shimmer with their own inner light.

The last of those queens was Zafir, vanished when the dragons shattered their chains of alchemy.

I

Zafir

I stand on stone, on the rim of this eyrie. It is mine now. It flies through the air, a half-finished castle made long ago by some half-god craftsman and filled with his spectres. The sea churns and boils below. We are closing on the brooding violet curtain-cloud of the storm-dark. The Black Moon will carry us through, and on the other side is the land where I was born. The Black Moon is a Silver King trapped in the flesh of a man who still wrestles to cast him out, but the man will lose. One does not deny a half-god.

This Black Moon, though, is not the first half-god to come to my land. Another crossed the storm-dark many centuries before I was born. He was the Isul Aieha, who tamed dragons and gave power over them to men. The same men in turn took his gifts and tore him down. They carried his broken body into a deep cave, drove a spike into his head and drank the silver ichor of the moon that dripped from that wound. They took his power into their blood. They call themselves alchemists, and with the taint of the half-god in their veins their potions kept our dragons dull and made them forget. Clouded by alchemy, the dragons sank within themselves, deep into timeless torpor, forgetting what they were.

My name is Zafir. I was speaker of the nine realms once, mistress of dragons and keeper of the Silver King's Spear. With my treacherous lover Jehal beside me and a litter of corpses in our wake, we took the Adamantine Throne for our own. I held the Silver King's Adamantine Spear, the very spear with which the Isul Aieha slew the Black Moon a thousand years ago, the same Black Moon who stands beside me now. With that blow the Isul Aieha splintered the world, though he never meant such an end nor foresaw it. On the day I took my crown I held his spear in my hand and touched its blade. It drank my blood, and in that moment we claimed one another. All world was mine to have, but Jehal had taken another queen to be his wife. Lystra, pretty little daughter of the Queen of Stone. He betrayed me for his starling bride, and so our dragons filled the skies with fire and screams, and many men died, and neither one of us cared a whit save that the other should fall.

Fall we both did.

I have heard now what happened after I was lost. The dragon Snow woke amid our chaos, an avalanche of rage and memory and flames. The dragons threw the curse of alchemy aside and flew at Jehal to burn his kingdoms to ash. The realms of my birth died in fire, but I saw none of it; by then the Taiytakei had taken me. I was chained aboard a ship bound for another world.

I did not understand at first why they let me live after what I'd done, but they did, and so I watched these new men who claimed to be my masters, I, a queen of dragons. I watched their schemes. Baros Tsen, dancing on knife blades and weaving his web around those who thought they were his lords and masters. Once-loyal Bellepheros, grand master alchemist, taken a year before me, steepling his fingers and wringing his hands, fretting and pacing and doing nothing to change the cataclysm he saw coming. Not so loyal any more, I fear, besotted with his mistress, the enchantress Chay-Liang, Baros Tsen's ally and the only one who sees me as I am and fears me as she should. Majestic Diamond Eye, my great dragon, dulled by alchemy and still terrible to all. We bided our time, my dragon and I. We made them pay for their hubris, dear and long and in pain and blood and fire and plague, in glories of vengeance and flames. The skin-shifters of Xibaiya crept from their holes. The arch-sorceress Arbiter passed her judgment. The Elemental Men fell upon us with their murderous knives, but by then the Black Moon had come, the ghost of an echo of a memory carried inside a man of many names, Berren the Crowntaker. He walks with the soul-cutting knife of the stars at his side, the knife of a thousand eyes with a piece of a goddess held within, and with it he enslaves man and monster as the whim takes him. I do not know who set him free, or how or why or what he is. Sometimes I do not think he knows himself; but it no longer matters. A half-god walks in the open once more. The veil is cut from my great dragon Diamond Eye, woken into incandescent fury. In their desperation the Taiytakei hurled our eyrie into the annihilation of the storm-dark, but they forgot – or perhaps they never knew – that the storm-dark was born of the Black Moon's demise, and could not devour him.

He is not the Isul Aieha, but he will be our Silver King again. He will tame the skies and dragons will fly with riders on their backs once more. By his side, I am coming home.

I am Zafir, the dragon-queen.

Eight days before landfall

Zafir stood on the eyrie rim, as close to the edge as she could be. The eyrie flew steadily across the sea, towed by dragons, its handful of growing hatchlings soul-cut and enslaved by the Black Moon's knife. Mighty Diamond Eye laboured beside the other dragons, red and gold scales alight in the fire of the setting sun. Towering clouds lined the sky, a bruise across the horizon, endless into the far distance. The storm-dark. The dragons carried the eyrie straight at its heart, and the dragon-queen Zafir had eyes for nothing else.

A gale blew from the waiting maelstrom, as it ever did. The dragons fought it. Half a dozen ships followed below. They had towed the eyrie across the ocean, but now they each made their own way, battling alone against the waves. The wind caught Zafir's hair. Lifted it. Tugged. The slavers of the Taiytakei had cut her plaits into short ragged tufts, but now it was long again at last. Copper in the dying sun. She ached. Two cracked ribs, mostly healed now, but they had left a stiffness inside her, a reminder never to fight with her feet on the ground. She was a dragon-rider, not some lowly knight.

Her heart sang bright. With every moment the storm-dark inched closer, she soared. The Black Moon would carry them across the void as he'd carried them through the storm-dark of the Godspike in Takei'Tarr. He was taking her home at last, taking them to what he desired most among all things across all the worlds: the Earthspear, the weapon of the Silver King which had tasted her blood and had bound itself to her, all so long ago.

And as she soared with the anticipation of home, she was afraid too. The closer they got, the less she knew what it was, this home, this notion of a place to belong. She yearned for it, and yet she was afraid of what she would see. Burned in dragon-fire, said the merchant-adventurers of Merizikat.

I was there. Diamond Eye spoke straight into her thoughts. She'd long grown used to his constant presence, and he to hers; and though he was bound to obey her by the Black Moon's knife, she had long ago released him of that burden and carefully demanded nothing. She asked, that was all, and she wished she could ride him now, straddle him and fly him into the heart of the maelstrom, but it would devour them both. In the end he would come down before the gaping void at the storm's heart, to prowl restlessly about the dragon yard, grounded until they were through to the other side.

You were there? Where? He hadn't been in the dragon-realms when they burned. The Taiytakei had taken Diamond Eye on the day their moon sorcerers had plucked her out of the sky.

At the end of the world a thousand years ago. When the Isul Aieha faced the Black Moon, we dragons were there. Then as now we flew at the Black Moon's side.

Always, when he said such things, came a flicker of doubt. The Black Moon's first dragon, but Diamond Eye was hers, not his, and now and then a little scorn crept around the edges of the dragon's thoughts. The loyalty he showed the half-god who had once been his master had frayed of late.

You knew the Isul Aieha? she asked. The Isul Aieha had built the palace of her home. She'd been born under the soft light of his enchanted stone, and his echoes had wrapped her life. She'd grown up with his creations all around her. Marvellous, bizarre, bewildering.

Show me, she said; and as the dragon opened his memories she saw seas of armoured men gleaming in silver, sorcerers flinging fire and lightning, dragons in such numbers that they darkened the sky, more even than in her last great battle as a queen of dragons when Jehal and Hyrkallan had driven her from the skies ...

The Pinnacles. Home. Another pang shot through her. Regret. Pain. Longing. *I am no longer the person I was that day*. For the better, perhaps; yet she would fight again, she knew it.

The storm-dark came ever closer. *The Isul Aieha created monsters.* Diamond Eye showed her green birds, flocks of them swarming, falling like arrows into armies of men, striking and turning them into jade glass, shattering them and pecking at the shards.

The jade ravens of the Taiytakei.

And more. A creature so vast that it made even dragons into specks. It crawled along the ground like some colossal maggot on a thousand thousand tiny legs, crushing everything in its path. Armoured scales as thick as houses, too deep for even a dragon to pierce. So they'd burned it. A hundred of them together. Wheeling in and wheeling away. Torrents of constant fire driven into a blind face as vast as a mountain.

The Black Moon. Her thoughts flitted always back to him. To her home and what awaited her, to Diamond Eye and his memories, and back again to the half-god. He divided them. To the Adamantine Man Tuuran, perhaps her only real ally, the Black Moon was a demon, a possessing monster devouring the only real friend he'd ever had. Tuuran would kill the Black Moon without a moment of thought if he could find a way to split him from Berren Crowntaker, the man whose body the half-god had taken, but until then Tuuran was the Black Moon's murderous guardian. To Chay-Liang the Black Moon had been a demented monster, an arch-sorcerer of darkness. She would have fought him if she could, but she couldn't, and now she wasn't with them any more. Bellepheros didn't like him any better, not really, but he knew more than any of them the terror and horror of dragons unleashed. The Black Moon would tame them, and for that Bellepheros would serve him. For a time, at least.

But what is this half-god to me?

They were edging into the fringes of the storm. Strands of black cloud swirled about her. Deep inside she saw flickers of purple lightning. The Black Moon had made the storm-dark, and the Black Moon had set her free. He would be her Silver King, and she would be his Vishmir, the mistress of his dragons, or so he'd promised. But men had promised her many things, and in the end none had ever become more than a translucent shadow, a feeble ghost of the hope she'd held inside her. She'd learned better than to embrace hope or to believe in promises.

He was taking her home. For now that was all that mattered.

Let that be enough. I don't want to think about him any more. Nor the things he'd done.

I took the spear from him once, said Diamond Eye. *I held it in my talons.*

From the Black Moon?

From your Silver King. From the Isul Aieha.

She climbed again into his memories and rode them, a thousand years into the past. Dragon after dragon falling upon the Isul Aieha. Each dissolving to black ash as they came close, yet slowly overwhelming his defences. Bathing him in fire, blinding him with flame, until at last a dragon flew close enough to strike. A lash of a tail; the dragon died in an explosion of dark dust, but Zafir was riding in Diamond Eye's memories, and in them she saw the flicker of glitter as the spear flew out of the Silver King's hand. Exultant, she swooped and snatched and flew away …

With a wave of his hand the Silver King stopped time. Everything froze. Everything except her and him.

The spear, little one. The spear in my claw kept his sorceries from me, but the spear was not mine. It was his, bound with his blood as it is bound with yours. He called it to his hand, willed it to return, and so it did. But for a moment he could not touch me.

The dragon's memories flickered on to the end. The Silver King, the Isul Aieha, racing, spear raised to strike, hurdling fallen corpses, everything that touched him billowing black into ash, dragons and monsters, swords and lightning. The Black Moon waiting, stood at an altar, a stone pillar summoned to rise from the heart of the earth by the force of his will. He wore a faceless helm, blank and made of ice, as he drew form into the ancient Nothing that had existed long before any creations of the gods.

I don't understand. Zafir watched the memories with unease, thoughts too restless for old stories, flickering to the storm-dark as it enveloped them, to what lay beyond, to the here and now and the incipient violence of the future.

None of us did. Perhaps not even the Black Moon himself.

She saw herself as Diamond Eye again, screaming through the air, diving towards the Isul Aieha. Other dragons swept ahead, talons reaching to snatch the half-god from the field, each vanishing into dust as they touched the Silver King's moonlight armour. Yet on they came. Why?

We could think of nothing else.

The Black Moon never flinched as the Isul Aieha charged, and the Isul Aieha didn't slow; but at the very last the Black Moon lifted his helm of ice and tossed it aside, and Zafir glimpsed his face, pale as milk, hair like thick snow and two empty holes where his eyes should have been. A darkness shimmered, a flicker for an instant as though the Black Moon drew a veil over the world, and then the Silver King's spear struck and pierced him through. A dark-light cataclysm burst across the sky as creation shattered. Dragons and stone, sea and cloud, all became dust and vapour as Diamond Eye dissolved into ash …

The darkness was thick around the eyrie now. The black cloud of the storm-dark. She couldn't see Diamond Eye any more, tugging at his chains above, but she felt the change in the eyrie as he let go and swirled down. The wind shifted, sucking them on now. The clouds thickened. The glimpses of the sea she saw were a tumult of monstrous waves. The sky flashed and blazed with violet lightning.

We are close now, little one.

Safer to be down in the tunnels, no doubt. But she didn't move; and as she sat on the edge of the abyss, she felt another presence closing behind her. Tuuran. She knew him by the tremors of his feet, by the pattern of his stride.

'Holiness! You should—'

'Don't even think it, Night Watchman. I will stay and see this darkness for myself, however little you like the notion.'

Tuuran sat down beside her. 'When I was a slave I crossed the storm-dark many times. Our galley masters would send us to the hold and seal the hatches so we wouldn't see. They trapped us in darkness. We could feel our ships toss and heave with the violence of the storm. It broke some. An oar-slave penned like that for the first time, you were certain your ship would break its keel and founder and sink, that everyone would drown, though they never did. When the fear was at its height, then came the silence. Somehow that was even worse.' He idly picked his nose and flicked a snot at the storm. Zafir tried not to laugh.

'You saw it when we left the Silver Sea. I didn't.'

Tuuran sniffed. 'I saw it when they brought old Bellepheros back from Furymouth. I told them he was so frail that the fright might kill him, and so they bolted shut his cabin window and let me sit with him to make sure his heart didn't stop. Not that there was any chance. Tough as old leather that one.' He hesitated, and Zafir knew it was because Tuuran had once thought of the alchemist as a friend when friendship had been thin on the ground. The coming of the Black Moon had changed the first, but not the latter.

'I kicked the window open for him,' Tuuran went on. 'Let him see what it was. I thought that him being a grand master alchemist with all his lore he might know a thing or two. When we reached land the night-skins set to kill me for showing him that. He stood up for me though, and it was Chay-Liang who spared me. Fat lot of use in the end. Turned out he was as ignorant as the rest of us.'

The eyrie shivered and shuddered in the storm. Lightning struck one of the low watchtowers on the wall and sparked across the white stone of the dragon yard.

'Holiness, maybe we should—'

'Stay exactly where we are, Night Watchman?'

Tuuran growled and mumbled something, but he knew better than to press her. Lightning flashed below, thundering from the underside of the eyrie into the clouds. She'd seen that before, riding Diamond Eye around the Godspike of the Taiytakei, how the eyrie and the storm-dark were somehow alike. Now that same violet lightning rattled back and forth beneath them.

The clouds ahead became a wall of black that rushed towards them. The lightning stilled, and then the wall hit them, and with it came a silence and a nothingness. They were adrift in a void between worlds.

'Count, Holiness,' murmured Tuuran. 'Five hundred heartbeats and then a score. It helps. Maybe it's six hundred now. It's been getting longer these last few years.'

I have shown you how it ended, whispered Diamond Eye in her thoughts. *But there is more.*

A flicker again. A different memory. The memory given to them both by the hatchling dragon Silence in the moment before Diamond Eye bit off its head. *Among the wandering dead, the rip is opened again. Diamond Eye will understand.* A mercurial sliver of memory, of moving among the ruins of the place the dragons called Xibaiya, the dead realm through which they slunk from one life to the next. To the edge of a hole and oozing out from that hole a spread of void and chaos. It crept hither and yon, devouring whatever it touched. *The Black Moon was once a cage to keep the Nothing at bay, but now he is free and the Nothing grows.*

Neither she nor her dragon had understood, not then. But Diamond Eye had woken now.

I have seen that cage. A hundred times, between every life. When the Isul Aieha and the Black Moon ripped creation to tatters and cast us into Xibaiya, I roamed the shade-lands. I saw the rip in the world with the Black Moon and the dead goddess entwined about it. A prison, the goddess the lock and bars and walls, the Black Moon its gate and key. Now the Black Moon returns among us, and the shade of the dead goddess is vanished, and where once they stood sentinel, the Nothing unravels creation, slow and remorseless, piece by piece.

And we are inside that nothingness now?

Yes.

Sound and light crashed into life. The wind struck Zafir so hard it almost knocked her down. Tuuran snatched at her, grabbing her with the terror of watching her pitch over the edge, then let go at once as he realised the wind wouldn't take her over. Zafir caught his hand. She held it and brushed his skin with her fingers. There were rough patches on his knuckles and on the joints, split red and raw beneath in places. Maybe to other eyes they were simply the hands of a soldier, but a dragon-rider knew the signs. The dragon-disease had him. The Statue Plague. Sooner or later, one way or another, dragons would be the death of them all.

'Holiness, I beg your forgiveness.' Because he was her Night Watchman, and she was a queen of queens, and men had died for less; but out here they were neither of those things and there was no one to see, and they could both do with a little comfort. Flame knew they needed it, each fighting their own silent demons and with no end in sight. She held Tuuran's hand a moment more, and then squeezed and let him go. She touched a finger to her own arm, an unconscious gesture, stroking her own roughness of skin the size of a thumbnail, always kept carefully hidden away; then settled and set her head to the wind until the dark clouds broke into a brilliant sky and they emerged from the storm. She left Tuuran to his thoughts, and crossed the rough mangled stone of the eyrie rim, between the piles and mounds of random debris, the crates and accumulated pieces of this and that piled outside the dragon yard walls. The rim had been a place for dumping anything that might one day be useful even back in Baros Tsen's day. Chay-Liang had been the worst. There were piles of broken gold-glass from when the Vespinese had come and one of their glasships had crashed.

Zafir moved among them. She climbed the slope of the dragon yard wall, smooth white half-god stone, and walked down the steep steps set into the other side. Everyone else had had the sense to stay in the tunnels, but the Black Moon sat in the middle of the yard, guiding them through the storm. Zafir carefully didn't catch his eye. Diamond Eye and the hatchlings perched alert around him; Diamond Eye looked at her and cocked his head as she approached. She could read his gestures now. It was a cock of the head that said *Yes, please.* She climbed onto his back, and he jumped onto the wall and pulled away into the air and stretched out his wings.

No more dragging at chains, she said. *Let the wind carry them. Let the Black Moon's hatchlings do his work.*

He soared for her, high and fast, wheeling and diving and spiralling for the sheer joy of it, perhaps because he knew this was her homeland where she longed to be, or perhaps because this was *his* home too, where he had hatched and grown. Zafir looked back once at the eyrie. She watched it draw away from the curtain cloud of the storm-dark stretched like an iron wall across the sea. She watched the five ships that slowly emerged, one after another behind it, watched for long enough to see that the sixth never came. Lost in the silence in the storm-dark's heart, she supposed. Removed from existence, its slate wiped clean, its memories gone. After that she turned away and didn't look back.

You hatched a few miles from where my mother birthed me, she said to Diamond Eye as they skimmed the sea. The dragon slapped his tail into the wavetops, explosions of spray left in his wake. *The eyries of the Silver City. Do you remember?*

I see them through the fog of your alchemists and their poisons. He paused. *I have had many hatchings. None were more special than the rest. There were mountains in this world. They were cold, and I like the cold better than desert heat. But I soar for the other dragons I will find here. My brothers and sisters, awake again. I soar with the memories of them as we were long ago.*

The hard truth jolted her again, that everything she remembered was likely gone. Dragons and furious fire. Cities razed, palaces smashed. *Do you feel them already?* she asked, careful to keep her thoughts in check.

Distant and muted. It is harder to reach them in this realm. I had forgotten how different the air is here. In that I prefer the other lands, where everything was easier. We have devoured so much of this one. Its weave is weak and dry. His thoughts seemed to wander, kept within himself. *I had forgotten*, he said again.

The eyrie was far away now. Zafir rode Diamond Eye far and wide, roaming across the waves for days, searching. There were books and charts in the Taiytakei libraries that might have told her which ways to go, but they were left behind, and the first land they found was an unfamiliar coast hundreds of miles from any place she knew.

Once she saw a speck in the distance. Too large to be a bird.

The others know we are here, she thought. Dragons so far out to sea would have told her that something was terribly wrong, if she hadn't already known it. No one from the other worlds sailed here any more. *Have they told you what happened while we were gone?*

Yes.

Then show me.

He showed her how the dragon Snow had woken, and the dragon Silence, chained in the eyrie of Outwatch and then set free; Silence who had given Zafir the slow death of Hatchling Disease, and who had tried twice more to kill her until Diamond Eye had bitten off the little dragon's head, but dragons always came back. He would be here again somewhere; then further into the memories Diamond Eye had seen. The razing of the eyrie at Outwatch, the burning of Sand and Bloodsalt, the siege and destruction of the Adamantine Palace, the murder by poison of a thousand dragons in the eyries outside the Silver City, and the great hatching that followed of a thousand new eggs across the realms. The death and fire and end of everything she knew; and as he roamed the past they flew, following the snaking line of unknown shores until slowly they became places she recognised, until she saw the outline of Tyan's Peninsula with its dyke a line across its neck, and the miles-wide mouth of the Fury river beyond, and on the far bank, the ruin of what had once been a city.

Furymouth.

Memories collided inside her. Of the first day she'd come here, and of the last. The city bright with lights, the air thick with its stink of smoke and rot and the sea. The Sea Kings kept their dragons away from their city and their ships, so Zafir had always come by land until her defeat over the Pinnacles. Fleeing here. Flying over the city, looking down at it and burning the traitor Jehal's Veid Palace in petty vicious vengeance.

Do you remember? Diamond Eye had been there with her on that day.

Yes. Fire blossomed in the dragon's memories. She saw the palace burn, through her own eyes and through his. Such a strange rush of emotion, unexpected and strong. The anger and the pain and the loss and the betrayal, and carrying with them an overwhelming sadness. Nostalgia. The Zafir who'd burned the Veid Palace hadn't known who she was or what she'd wanted, only that whatever she had was never enough. She wasn't sure that she knew any better now, but looking back at who she was was like looking at a stranger. The Veid Palace at least was much as she remembered it, save that it wasn't ablaze this time.

She brought Diamond Eye lower. Most of the palace was built of stone; dousing it in fire hadn't hurt it much, but time had had its turn too. Weeds grew in the cracks. The black scars she'd left across its gardens were gone, turning into a fairy dust chaos of spring flower colours. Creepers had found purchase in the tower walls. Seagulls cried, squawking danger to each other as they circled. She shivered, spooked. From the air the city looked the same now as it ever had, only quiet and overgrown and empty. The air smelled of the sea. It didn't smell of people any more, not of shit and rot and smoke.

I never belonged here. The unbearable stillness shook her. The aloneness. *Take me to the palace. I want to see it.*

Diamond Eye swooped. The Veid Palace was a mosaic of narrow towers linked by bridges and walkways, a design that had never made any sense until she'd seen the gold-glass tower-palaces of the Taiytakei. That was where the palace of the Sea Kings had its heart, in the edgy ebb and flow of love and hate between the kings of Furymouth and the night-skinned sea lords. She landed beside the great Veid Dome, the palace's centrepiece. One of its great brass doors, twenty feet tall, hung open, askew. The other was missing. She slid from Diamond Eye's back and walked closer, and then stopped and listened. The seagulls had fallen quiet, and the breeze rustling from the sea was the only sound. The sun beat down, warm and caressing. A comfort, unlike the relentless heat she remembered from the Taiytakei deserts.

The dome's other brass door lay fifty feet across the yard, half buried in weeds, bent out of shape, a glitter in the sun. The quiet crept inside her. It crawled under her and settled in her heart and belly. She remembered the palace alive and bright with bustle and colour. Servants, soldiers, dragon-riders. Movement everywhere. Commotion. There used to be horses. Sometimes elephants decked with gaudy harnesses, brought in ships from across the sea.

A lump grew in her throat. She could almost see the ghosts moving about, the lives long lost. She walked into the shadowed dust-veils of the Veid Dome, the palatial hall of King Tyan with its three golden thrones arrayed to face her. A sweep of marble stairs arced behind them, curving to the upper balconies. The walls were black with soot, the floor a litter of ash and charred splinters and rubble; the thrones, when she came close enough to see, were half melted. She clambered past them. There had been a door hidden behind them into the rear arches of the dome once, but both door and wall had been smashed down. She stooped and picked up a fragment of cloth, the charred corner of a tapestry. Her jaw tightened. She remembered it. King Tyan the Fourth burning Taiytakei ships at night as they tried to raid his silk farms. Jehal had brought her here late one night. They'd sneaked away, consumed by the rapture of their nascent passion, and he'd shown it to her. Huddled between thrones he'd murmured the story, his hands on her skin and between her legs, his tongue on her lips.

His hands. She remembered the touch of him as though it had been that very morning, as though she could still feel him now, some lingering tingle. She shuddered. Bit her lip and moved on, out through the arches into the little courtyard with its apple tree behind the dome, the secret garden where no one ever came except the royal family; and here was Jehal's ghost again. Sprawled naked, making love, him inside her, their hands clenched and fingers clawed to the very edge. A savagery to them both, clutching at each other as though trying to climb into one another. The world blurred as a thought hit her: *He could be alive.* Was it possible?

The loss of him. The betrayal. They were such colossal things. She staggered and held on to the tree and took a long ragged breath. There was no home for her here. There never had been. Perhaps the dragons had done her a favour, burning it all down and putting the truth inescapably before her, a world that was once so familiar now ruin and ash.

What did you expect, little one?

Is it all like this? Is there anyone left? The silence taunted her, a thickening of the air around her, stifling motion and thought.

Yes. But they hide deep, little one.

Zafir looked at the tree. Jehal had given her an apple from it once, and here and now she could almost taste it. She shook herself, put the courtyard behind her and walked on through colonnades and arches into the feasting hall beyond, into the kitchens and down into the cellars and pantries. Everything had been ransacked, everything that could move taken away, everything too large broken into pieces and carried off. The hangings, the wood panels, even patches of tiles from the floors. Just bare stone walls that became bleak shapes of light and dark under the harsh spotlight beam of her enchanted glass torch, colourless and without life.

The darkness, the stark shadows, the suffocating closeness of stone wrapped about her, they tied her insides into knots. The old fear of being trapped in the dark banged at the cage where she kept it, threatening to break loose. She made herself think of Tuuran, his size and bulk a reassurance wrapped around her, waiting for her. Thinking of him like that helped. She walked on.

Close now, little one.

In the deepest cellars she found the ragged handful of men and women left alive, half naked, three-quarters starved, pale-faced, trapped in fright by her light. They looked on her in terror and wonder, and cringed away.

'Who are you?' she asked them. 'Are there any more of you?'

She was a stranger, fierce and terrible in her armour of Taiytakei glass and gold. None of them spoke. She took a step closer. They stared and trembled.

'Are you all that's left?' she asked. She could have wept. A dozen of them. Half dead, thin and hollow. Furymouth: the smelliest, loudest, sprawling hub of life, and *this* was all that was left, this wretched huddle?

Another step. They shrank away. She took off her helm so they could see her face. So they might see she meant them no harm.

'My name is Zafir,' she said, her voice broken. 'I was speaker of the nine realms once.' How stupid it was, telling them that. The speaker was the guardian of the kingdoms, the keeper of the peace, and she'd done the exact opposite. Great Flame, she'd burned this palace herself! Her arm tensed, half raised. She had two Taiytakei lightning throwers strapped to each forearm on the outside of her gold-glass vambraces. On her hip she carried a pair of blade-less knives, the short glass swords of the Elemental Men of the Taiytakei, blades so thin they were almost invisible, which would slice through stone and iron as easily as they would cut butter.

No one moved. No flicker of recognition. Perhaps they didn't remember her.

'I've come back to ...' To what? To sit on a throne that no longer carried any meaning? To put her old realms back together again? How? To undo the damage she'd done? Prostrate herself? Beg forgiveness from the dead?

Yes to all of that, and all such impossible things.

'To find my home,' she said at last. 'To find a place to be.'

A man stepped closer, watching her with uncertain awe. 'I remember you, Holiness,' he said, and bowed and dropped to one knee. 'I am Vishmir. I am Adamantine.'

She crouched in front of him and took off her gauntlet and touched a hand to his face. The sight of this soldier, of finding him alive amid the ashes, filled her.

'Then get up, Vishmir,' she said, 'for we have work to do.'

2

The Fury

Three days before landfall

So this was Vishmir's story: in the last days of the Adamantine Throne Night Watchman Vale Tassan had sent companies of Adamantine Men to every eyrie, armed with hammers and axes to smash all the dragon eggs they could find, and with letters of authority written by Grand Master Jeiros commanding his alchemists to assist them. A last desperate throw of the dice against looming catastrophe. Vishmir and his company had been sent to King Jehal's eyrie along the coast, Clifftop, but everything had gone to shit before they could reach it, and by this point he didn't give two hoots for who was speaker and who wasn't anyway. Anywhere with food and shelter was good enough.

Zafir led him back under the open sky. Climbing outside, to space and light, was like bursting from under the sea and being able to breathe again.

'What do your company call you?' she asked. Half the soldiers of the Adamantine Guard had called themselves after the legendary Speaker Vishmir when the time came for them to choose a name. She wondered sometimes if they did it on purpose to make them harder to tell apart.

'White Vish.'

'Then I have work for you, White Vish.' She glanced to the skies. *Are there any other dragons close by?*

They are all far away, little one, answered Diamond Eye. *They know what comes.*

Because you've told them?

He didn't deny it. *Many gather in the Worldspine. They wait there to see what the Black Moon will do.*

Zafir took White Vish through the courtyard with the apple tree and the Veid Dome beyond. They stood in the doorway, its one brass door hanging askew. Vish tensed as he saw Diamond Eye.

'The dragon is mine,' Zafir soothed. 'Are there others here, hiding in the city?'

White Vish nodded. 'We see them now and then when we come out to forage. They run from us in case we steal their food.'

'Then I charge you with this: you have two nights to find them.' She pointed out to the sea. 'I have ships coming. On the morning that follows I will bring food and men to help you. I'll bring you whatever you need.'

'Holiness, will you bring an alchemist?'

'Not on the back of my dragon, soldier.' She shook her head. 'But one comes on my ships. Grandmaster Bellepheros himself, stolen into slavery by the night-skins and now free again.'

White Vish stared at her in surprise. 'We heard the alchemists were all dead, Holiness. Murdered by the King of Sand and his mad queen, who hold the Pinnacles.'

The Pinnacles. *Home.* Her heart missed a beat. 'There are people there?'

Vish nodded, though when Zafir pressed him for more he didn't know who else might be alive. She asked after Zara-Kiam, but he only looked blank, and so she left Furymouth not knowing whether her sister was alive or dead. A part of her hated herself for not having thought of Kiam before. A blind spot, blanked from her mind and pushed away because of all the bitterness between them; now she didn't fly straight back to the eyrie as she'd planned, but instead rode Diamond Eye deep across the country, as far as Three Rivers in the east and Farakkan in the north, far enough to see the distant outline of three peaks on the horizon.

The Pinnacles. Home. The one place in all the realms where men could hide and no dragon would ever touch them, with water to last for ever and food for decades.

There are dragons there, warned Diamond Eye. *Waiting for us.*

Can you see my sister? Zafir pictured Zara-Kiam as she remembered her. *Can you see anyone?*

I see a haze of thoughts, little one. The numb dull chattering of your kind. They are unfamiliar. I do not know them and so I cannot name them.

They circled once more, Zafir's gaze fixed on the distant peaks, but she'd made a promise to White Vish, and so she turned back and flew the hours across the sea to the eyrie, told Tuuran what she'd found and had a pallet made up with crates and sacks of food taken a month ago from the warehouses of Merizikat. Diamond Eye guided the Black Moon's dragons towing the eyrie, while Zafir lingered with her handmaidens, Myst and Onyx, and their two babes. She left again without seeing the half-god himself, glad of that and keen to be gone as quickly as she could. She took Tuuran with her. He hated flying on Diamond Eye's back, but she made him.

It was almost twilight when they reached the shore and Furymouth again, certainly not the morning as she'd promised, the sun sinking behind a drizzling mist of rain rolling east from the Worldspine and the Raksheh. Zafir flew high, riding over the top of the cloud in brilliant-blue sunshine sky, watching for other dragons, and only dived into damp miserable grey as they reached land. She set the pallet down, dismounted with Tuuran in front of the Veid Dome, and together they built a fire. After Diamond Eye lit it, Zafir sent him away into the cloud, out of sight but ever watchful, and went to look for White Vish. He had more than a hundred men and women gathered in his cellars this time, gaunt and hollow shells but alive.

'I was beginning to wonder if you wouldn't come, rider. If you were an illusion.'

'Is this everyone?'

'Everyone who would come. There are more, but I couldn't reach them all. Many would not believe what I told them.'

Zafir shrugged. Others would come quickly enough when they heard there was food. 'The ships will reach the shore tomorrow,' she said. 'We'll stay a day or two and then move inland. Come with us or remain. You can all choose.' She wondered if she should try to explain the flying eyrie, the Black Moon, the hatchling dragons that towed them through the air, but Adamantine Man to Adamantine Man was probably better, and so she left Tuuran with them to tell his tale and walked away through the palace, among towers she'd once known so well, wandering aimlessly until she found herself in the solar where she and Jehal had lain together on the last night before his wedding.

So what's she like, this girl you have to marry?

She could hear his voice as though it was yesterday. She could see him as they were, naked together, side by side under a sun so beautiful and warm instead of this drab grey rain. She smiled, sad and wan, remembering how Jehal had made his nests around the palace. Private places where he could come and go through hidden passages. Solars with tall windows, abundant in light and air.

The bed was still there. Mouldy and moth-eaten and ragged at the edges. She couldn't look at it. The last and worst betrayal.

A girl, as you say. Him stroking her thigh. The air in the solar thick with incense. Stifling midsummer hot. *Naive. Full of wonder at the world, and almost completely lacking in any experience of it, I would say.* He'd told her a few pretty lies, things he thought she wanted to hear.

Tell me she's ugly and deformed.

I'm afraid I could only say that about her sister.

Jaslyn. The mad queen who'd come with Hyrkallan and all his vengeance to tear her from the skies over the Pinnacles. Zafir walked to the windows. She looked down, out over the fire ablaze in the palace yard. A murmur of voices reached through the rain. Now and then an outburst of laughter. She'd done some good here then. A little. The start of something.

You like her, don't you?

Jehal's face hadn't flickered for a second. *I hardly know her, my love. She is a doll. All dressed up to look as pleasing as she can, but still a doll.*

Liar. She'd known even then. The beginning of the end, though everything still lay before them, the climb to the Adamantine Throne. But it was there, in that moment. The betrayal of Evenspire had begun right here. And she'd known it and had looked the other way, because the truth would hurt more than she could bear.

Where no one would see, Zafir wrapped her arms tight around her shoulders and hugged herself. She should have pushed him out the window that day and been done with it. Instead she'd pulled him closer.

Rain drummed on the roof above, grey and dour. More laughter rose loud from outside. The first time these people had filled their bellies in a year. The first time in longer still since they'd gathered together under the open sky. Zafir stood, listening to them, staring out at the haze, drifting between thoughts that never lingered, and it was dark by the time she snapped herself away; by then some of the men were singing, Tuuran and White Vish leading the songs. They were tipsy. She had no idea where they'd found wine. Tuuran, slipping a barrel of it onto the pallet when he was supposed to bring water, most likely.

The Adamantine Men looked suddenly awkward as she returned at last. The singing died. Tuuran got to his feet, and then the others did the same. 'Holiness. We …' He bowed.

'My dragon had to carry that,' Zafir scolded him. She snatched the wineskin out of his hand and sat down quickly, before they could all start their kowtowing and all manner of other pointless formalities. She didn't want that now. There would be a time, yes, but not today. Instead she took a long swallow and ordered them to all sit down and get back to their singing, and gradually they forgot who she was. They got quietly drunk together, her and Tuuran and White Vish, sitting in the warmth of their fire while the sun set, while the stars rose and Diamond Eye circled watch in the clouds overhead. The rain dampened nothing except the stones, while White Vish told his story.

'We travelled down the Fury by boat,' he said. 'It was already too late, but we didn't know that. Town after town gutted by dragon-fire. We thought it was the war.' He gave Zafir a mournful look, half sorrow, half accusation. 'We thought you'd done it, Holiness, scorching the earth in your retreat. Then we came to Hammerford. We found the two stone dragons on the waterfront, colossal statues that had never been there before. We came ashore looking for food, and that was where we heard tell of dragons without riders rampaging across the land.' Another pause, another look. 'There had been a great battle at the Pinnacles, we heard, and a massacre of dragons had followed.' He laughed. 'The alchemists, Holiness. After your defeat, the alchemists poisoned every dragon they could. Yours, King Jehal's, King Hyrkallan's – all of them. When he saw what they'd done, Hyrkallan had every alchemist he could find put to the sword. They were trying to stave off the end, I suppose, but it didn't do any good.'

'That was after they drove me from my home,' Zafir said. 'I fled here from the battle. There were Taiytakei ships in the harbour. I knew by then that they were the ones who had made our war. That they had set us against one another to steal our dragons.' She looked away. 'I knew what they'd done, but it was too late to make any difference. I tried to burn their ships so they wouldn't escape with the eggs they'd stolen from Clifftop, but they had sorcerers like the Silver Kings themselves. They took me and my Diamond Eye and made us their slaves.' She was shaking again. Couldn't go on. Just looked about at the ragged survivors laughing and joking into the fire. Their numbers were dwindling, men and women slipping away with the dark, taking whatever they could carry back to their hiding places, not trusting the world. And why would they?

'The eyrie at Clifftop had already fallen when we reached Furymouth,' said White Vish. 'Dragon-riders went and never came back. For a time there was a quiet. The wise and the cowards fled the city, looking for shelter.' He took another long swallow. 'I'm sorry, Holiness. We fought as best we could, but Furymouth offers almost nothing, a city on a solitary hill. There's nowhere much to hide. Hatchling dragons slithered and flew from the eyrie at Clifftop. War-dragons came across the sky. They hunted and killed, and we couldn't stop them. More than a year ago, that was, and that's how it's been ever since. Mostly they leave us alone now, but sometimes another comes.'

A mournful sadness settled like a thick blanket, full of memories of better times never to be reclaimed. Zafir asked a little more – about the Adamantine Palace, about Jehal and whether he was alive, whether anyone at all had survived. They didn't know, and the more they talked the more she caught the glances that Vish and his men tried to hide. She felt the air change, pricked by needling accusation, by resentment and blame; or perhaps they simply wanted the companionship of their own, free of a dragon-rider outsider. Either way, she knew she wasn't welcome any more, and so she took another wineskin and left them, stumbled away in the darkness and drank where no one would see until she could barely stand, until she wept for the folly of pride and the hurt of so many long knives driven into her back, and that was how Tuuran found her later, when darkness had long fallen and the fire had died low. She didn't even see him coming until he loomed over her in the gloom.

'Holiness?'

She struggled to her feet and leaned and staggered into him, and he was drunk too, but big and strong and sure.

'Come with me,' she said, and led him through the towers and up the stairs to the solar where she'd stood before. She tossed her helm aside and stripped away her gold-glass armour and the dragonscale wrapped beneath, and pulled him to her and kissed him. They were drunk and full of need, both of them cut to the quick by their own different hurts, and he wanted her and always had, and it was stupid and dangerous and they'd both regret it desperately, but in the here and now she needed to be touched, to be held, to feel skin on sweating skin. He fumbled with her, uncertain and confused as she took his hand and pressed it to his cheek and kissed his fingers. She pressed his other hand to her heart, to her breast. She heard his breath catch in his throat.

'Holiness?'

'Not here. Not now. Tomorrow again, yes, but not now. Now I am just Zafir.'

She ran his hand over her. He reached behind and cupped her and pulled her hard into him and she gasped, and so did he. She tore at his armour, at the buckles and clasps, clumsy and urgent, head fogged by wine and desire. She stripped him naked and kissed him until he growled and tugged at her filthy sweat-stained silks and lifted them over her head and fell on her, fingers and lips, rough and crude. She turned her back to him and pressed against him, running his hands wild over her skin, along her thighs, inside her, across her belly, her breasts, her neck, her face. She arched and groaned and heard him moan: 'Please, Holiness. Please.'

She ran her fingers over his brittle places of dead white skin. 'You have it too, don't you?' She needed him to say it. 'The dragon-disease.'

'Yes.'

And that was the last of her reasons gone. 'How long?'

'Since before Merizikat.' Dust flew in clouds as they fell onto the mouldy bed together, where she and Jehal had once made love. He drove inside her, harsh and hungry, so different and so much more honest. She came almost at once and so did he, howling like animals, half mad, clinging on, each looking at the other as though at a stranger they'd never seen before, eyes as wide as the world. It wasn't enough. She coaxed him back and straddled him, demanding him, pulling his hands over her. She felt the dim pain of bruises and half-healed wounds, dulled by lust and wine. She rode him, half blind, half forgetting he was even there, until she stuttered and gasped and arched and cried out again, and even then it wasn't enough. She lost herself inside him. Exorcising the pain and the old betrayals, though they'd surely be back with the sunrise, burning sharp as ever. Twice more, and then the wine finally took her and she passed into dreamless sleep, a black oblivion as deep and silent as the void of the storm-dark's heart.

It was still dark when she woke. Her head thundered. Beside her, Tuuran was snoring, sleeping the sleep of the damned and the just. She looked at him lying there and knew she'd done a terrible and stupid thing. One more to add to the list. She dressed and slipped outside, found a quiet corner to squat and take a piss, and called to Diamond Eye; he came and cocked his head at her, as if to ask what *that* was all about, and she had no answer but to fly together, soaring to the freedom of the sky, through rain and cloud to the endless blue beyond for hours and hours. She leaned into him and hugged his scales and dozed until her head was clear.

The ships reached the city later that day, and the eyrie came not long behind. Zafir kept to the skies, high and watching out for other dragons, but swooped beneath the cloud now and then, gliding above the steady stream of boats from the ships to the shore, all carrying men and supplies from Merizikat. She watched the cranes on the side of the eyrie with their up and down, over and over all through the day, lifting everything inside, filling it ready to burst. The dragon yard swarmed with men and sacks and crates, and it took the next day and most of the one after before they were done. By then the dragon yard had become a village of tents and shelters strung with ropes and poles as men looked for places to lay their heads. She brought Diamond Eye to land on the rim and surveyed their work. The eyrie was full, every nook and cranny, every room stuffed wall to wall with food and water and ropes and Flame-knew-what, or else strung with hammocks. She sought out Tuuran and told him he'd done well, and if there was any thought in either of them of that night in dead King Tyan's palace, they both kept it carefully hidden.

Eventually, because there was no getting away from it, she sought out the Black Moon, sat on the eyrie rim, eyes dim glowing silver, oblivious to the hive of bustle around him.

'You know where to go,' he told her.

The eyrie left Furymouth that night. It drifted sloth-like north along the course of the Fury towards the Pinnacles, guided by the Black Moon's dragons. In the morning Zafir found Tuuran with White Vish and his two favoured lieutenants. Halfteeth and Snacksize, born in the Worldspine and sold in the slave markets of Furymouth, both of them, so she wasn't the only one coming home to find old wounds bleeding again. The Furymouth slave markets were overgrown with weeds now, but Halfteeth was still looking for someone to hurt. He wasn't much liking White Vish and his Adamantine Men, and there would surely be blood if he ever found himself facing a dragon-rider with no one nearby to keep him in check.

'Farakkan.' Zafir led Tuuran to the eyrie rim and pointed into the distance. The cloud above and the fields below hazed into a grey fade of rain, but somewhere out there, if they followed the river's meanders, was a heap of shacks and a mound of mud called Farakkan. A bustling stinking hole of a place that became an island every spring when the Fury burst its banks. Zafir had seen it often enough from above, but she'd never been there. She couldn't think of a single reason why a dragon-rider would ever want to.

'Holiness?'

'Survivors, Night Watchman.'

'In Farakkan?' He snorted.

'Someone needs to go and look.' She kept her face a mask.

'Right. In Farakkan.' They both knew she was sending him away to keep them apart, though she might have sent him to do this either way. There probably wasn't anyone left alive in Farakkan because there wasn't anywhere deep underground to hide, but what if she was wrong? They should at least look, shouldn't they?

'Yes.'

To her surprise Tuuran laughed. 'I suppose anyone who survived living there all their life might survive living anywhere.'

There wasn't any more to say, but she couldn't bring herself simply to turn and walk away. He deserved better than that. On impulse, struggling to find anything else, she saluted him, fist pressed to her breast. 'Have a care, Night Watchman. Return. I will watch for dragons for you.'

He grew an inch taller right there in front of her. Pride. Flame, he almost grinned as he glanced at Halfteeth. 'I'll take White Vish and the new men, since they know the land. Halfteeth, you're in charge while I'm gone.' He bared his teeth, letting that grin out this time, and slapped Halfteeth on the shoulder. 'Try not to be an idiot.'

Halfteeth snorted. Snacksize nudged him and gave Tuuran a nod. 'I'll keep an eye on him, boss. Bring us back a present, will you? Something nice.' The three of them laughed while Zafir, suddenly an outsider, stood in awkward silence. If Halfteeth and Snacksize had real names, she'd never heard them, and she never would.

They passed over Farakkan later that morning, not that there was much left of it. The town had been built of wood, and the only thing that had saved any of it at all from the dragons was the constant wetness there. There were outlines that might once have been houses, but most of it was a black char-smear across the hilltop and sodden fields. The eyrie paused while cranes lowered a pair of cages with Tuuran and White Vish and a dozen other men, and then moved on, stopping again for the night a few miles further north, close to where the Ghostwater emerged from the hidden tunnels of the Silver King's Ways, which ran all the way under the ground to the Pinnacles. Zafir looked over the eyrie as the sun set, over the dragon yard sloshing with half an inch of water. The rain hadn't stopped for the best part of three days, and the yard had no drains. They'd have to do something about that before they had rivers running through the eyrie tunnels and people drowning down there. There were too many Merizikat men setting up their tents and shelters too. If the dragons came – and come they would, and soon – everything that wasn't underground would burn. The dragons loitering about her old home, Diamond Eye told her, were paying attention now.

She sent for Halfteeth. 'Set some people to bailing out that water,' she told him. 'I don't want it getting any deeper. And is there really no space below for all these men?'

Halfteeth looked at her hard. No bowing or kowtowing from this one. He took a breath and nodded. 'Some of us like it better up here.' He smiled, half-mocking her. 'Out under the sky, no roof, no walls. At a guess I might say you do too, your Holiness.'

So he knew of her fear of small cramped places in the dark? But the eyrie innards weren't dark at all. The Silver King's white stone glowed soft as the moon in the night, gentle as an early-morning sun in the day, warm and comforting, and she'd grown up and lived half her life in a place exactly the same; but before she could answer him, his face changed. The smug self-satisfied lurking murderer shifting in an instant to a taut-faced killer cornered by something much bigger.

She knew that look. The Black Moon was behind her, eyes glowing silver, moonlight bright.

'There's someone on the ground,' he said to Halfteeth as though Zafir wasn't even there. 'Someone curious.' He pointed to the west. 'Bring them here.'

Halfteeth scurried off. He didn't have a choice, because, like almost all of them, Halfteeth had met the Black Moon's deadly knife, and the half-god had cut away a piece of his soul and made him into a slave.

Zafir rounded on him. 'If you ...' But the Black Moon was already walking away.

One day, half-god or not, I will make *you look at me.*

Have a care, little one, warned Diamond Eye.

Zafir found Snacksize and told her to deal with bailing out the dragon yard instead, then took herself into the tunnels and to the cell she shared with Myst and Onyx. She curled up with them to sleep, and it was only after the next dawn that anyone bothered to tell her that Halfteeth had come back in the night with an alchemist, and with a couple of others, and that one of them was an Adamantine Man, and that Halfteeth was busy kicking the shit out of him.

3

The Crowntaker

Three days after landfall

Crazy Mad, Berren the Crowntaker, the Black Moon, whatever he was today. Not the Black Moon, because his eyes burned with silver moonlight when he was that. The Crowntaker, then. He was already there when Zafir reached the round stone cell. He twirled the Starknife in his hand. It was a strange thing: the blade shone like polished silver and patterns swirled inside it. The shape was odd, more like a cleaver than a knife, while the golden hilt was carved into a pattern of stars that made a thousand eyes. It cut souls, not flesh, cut pieces out of people and made them into what they were not. The Black Moon used it to cut away the will of men and make them into his slaves. His instruments, he said. Extensions of his desire. And Zafir had told him there were to be no more slaves, neither men nor dragons, but he did it anyway when he thought she wouldn't see. He was as he wished to be, and would not be changed or swayed, and the only thing that struck her as strange was that he bothered to try and hide it from her at all.

It was a terrible thing, that knife, and so was the Black Moon who held it. But behind his eyes Zafir saw it was the Crowntaker with her today.

There was a man tied to a chair. The Adamantine Man Halfteeth had found, at a guess. He'd already been beaten half to death.

'Where is he?' Zafir hissed. 'Where's Halfteeth? I'll have him skinned for this!' She could talk to the Crowntaker easily enough when the half-god inside was asleep or resting or … elsewhere, or whatever it was he did in there. Then the Crowntaker was simply Tuuran's friend. Which was a shame, because he was doomed, and he knew it, and so did she, and the only one who refused to see the inevitable was Tuuran himself.

'His name is Skjorl,' the Crowntaker drawled. 'And I sent Halfteeth away before you got here in order to save him from being strung up by his balls. Let the big man deal with it when he's back from Farakkan.'

'And your half-god?' she asked. The Crowntaker winced as though she'd stabbed him. The look he gave her was half pleading, half sharpened edges.

'Not here just now. He's weak from crossing the storm-dark. But I'm sure he's watching.' He spat and turned away and then turned back. 'This lot think they know something about the Silver King's tomb. Does that mean anything to you? Because it certainly does to the Black Moon, and if we don't get it out of them nicely then he'll wake up again and do it the only way he knows.' He paused, desolation in his face. 'This one, Skjorl, he was an Adamantine Man back when that meant something.' He paused in case she knew the name, but of course she didn't. A speaker never knew her legions. 'Anyway, he doesn't know much. The alchemist's the one. Skjorl here says her name is Kataros. You heard of her?'

Zafir shrugged.

'He says the third one with them claims to have found this tomb, but he's not in a good way, and so I was saving him for last. I'm guessing an alchemist might know best anyway.'

'Says he's found the Silver King's tomb?' Zafir scoffed. 'Then he's a liar. But an alchemist would be useful. Be gentle if you can.'

She watched the Adamantine Man Skjorl hauled away. Tuuran would have a use for him, if he could be willingly turned – if he could manage to live in the same legion as Halfteeth after what Halfteeth had just done to him. Maybe he could. She was the speaker of the realms, and the Adamantine Men served without question. It was their creed, drilled into them as children. Was that slavery? They could always choose otherwise, couldn't they?

She watched as the alchemist Kataros was dragged in and tied to the same chair. She winced at that. Wouldn't it be better to ask them in a quiet calm? As friends? Feed and water them, shelter them and then get to what mattered? But she could feel the Crowntaker's impatience, the lurking sense of the Black Moon beneath the surface, and none of them wanted that. She snapped her fingers at one of Halfteeth's men. 'Go and get Bellepheros.

Quick, now!' Another precious alchemist. He would thank her for that, and Bellepheros, of any of them, would seem like a friend.

'Where is it?' asked the Crowntaker. He spoke slowly and carefully. Zafir watched, trying to decide whether she remembered this alchemist's face. Months had passed. Years. It was still a shock to suddenly remember, again and again, that this ash-scarred ruin of a land was her home, that everything she once knew had changed.

No more slaves. *But tell that to the Black Moon.*

'Where is what?' The alchemist clenched her fists. 'Who are you?'

'The Silver King's tomb,' whispered Zafir, because that certainly *did* mean something, and possibly everything. 'That's what you're looking for. Where is it?' Was that where she might find an answer? In the relics of the Silver King, the Black Moon's half-god brother who had once taught blood-mages how to steal the memories of a dragon and dull them into pliant beasts? The woken dragons remembered him with a simmering fury. The Silver King. The Isul Aieha. Diamond Eye spat fire at his name for what he'd done, a sure way to arouse his ire if ever she needed it.

She stretched, easing the stiffness out of her aching back and surly bones, the last twinges of that wound from Merizikat that had close to killed her. Perhaps another alchemist would draw Bellepheros from the gloom that had settled over him since the loss of Chay-Liang.

'I believe it to be in the Aardish Caves,' said the alchemist at last. 'Underneath the Moonlight Garden, where Vishmir always thought it was.'

Zafir tried not to laugh. Vishmir the Magnificent had spent twenty years looking for the Silver King's Black Mausoleum and had never found it. Hundreds of dragons. Ten thousand men. And now, amid the end of the world, some scrawny alchemist claimed that Vishmir had been looking in the right place all along, and yet had somehow missed it?

'Forgive me, Highness, Holiness, lord, lady, but, with the most humble respect, please, who are you?'

'Who am I? Who am *I*?' Zafir didn't know whether to laugh or weep or fall into a rage. A little of all three, perhaps. Two years gone and the world turned on its head. 'I am your speaker. Do you not know me?' She searched for a glimmer of recognition as the alchemist looked her over, and found nothing. If anyone should remember, surely an alchemist …

'Lady Lystra?'

A torrent of fury tore at her. The frustration of their months in Merizikat bursting its dam, the wounded pain since she'd left, forced to her bed as she healed, unable to fly. The searing sense of loss as she'd circled Furymouth and wandered the abandoned passages of Jehal's old palace. All this way, all this time, and she was finally home and to what? To nothing. To an alien land where dragons had burned her cities and her people had forgotten her. And Lystra …? She gritted her teeth. *Little Lystra. Jehal's starling bride.* Oh, but she was past that now, wasn't she? Surely she was.

'Forgive me, your Holiness.'

'Forgive?' Zafir heard her own voice, hard and cold as ice. Forgive? For what? For not remembering? Wasn't that perhaps for the best?

The Crowntaker turned his head. He looked hard at Zafir, straight through her and beyond. There was a glimmer of silver in his eye. Not yet burning bright, but she knew the signs. The Black Moon inside him was on the verge of waking. 'Do you know these places?' he asked her. 'Tell me!'

'The Aardish Caves? I've been there. Follow the Yamuna river deep into the Raksheh forest towards the foothills of the Worldspine and there's a waterfall, a cataract. The Moonlight Garden sits atop the bluffs on the south side overlooking the top of the falls. It's a ruin. Across the river at the foot of the falls are the entrances to the caves.' The words trotted out of her. She wasn't really listening to herself but was watching the Crowntaker's eyes for glimmers of the half-god. Sometimes little hints of desire leaked from his face at times like this. The Adamantine Spear. That, above all else, was why he'd brought them here. But the name of the Silver King stirred him too, the Isul Aieha. When chances came, she looked hard for the tiny tells of his secret avarice. 'There's a story about the Isul Aieha,' she said, 'that he created a mausoleum for himself before he died. "Made of black marble across the great river from the endless caves," or so the legend says. Speaker Voranin's riders thought they'd found it. Vishmir, who followed him, searched the

Aardish Caves for nigh on twenty years. It's not there, Crowntaker, but Vishmir had a mausoleum of his own built in the same place. There's an eyrie, a small one.' Or there had been when she was last there. Most likely it was gone now. Abandoned and burned.

The veil across the Black Moon was paper thin now, and Zafir desperately didn't want him to wake, not here and now, not with a second alchemist right here in front of him and the Starknife already in his hand. She poked Kataros. 'We don't need this one,' she said sharply. 'Get the third one in here, the one who really knows.' Bellepheros could have her. He'd like nothing better. It might even cheer him up, but either way Zafir decided she'd be damned if she'd sit by and watch as the Black Moon cut this woman and made her his slave. An alchemist was worth too much ...

She turned to Halfteeth's guardsmen. 'And get Bellepheros!' Where was he? Why wasn't he here already? 'Is Tuuran back yet?' Although how could he be?

'Bellepheros? He's *here*?' The alchemist looked startled at the name. So she remembered *him*, at least, did she?

The Crowntaker's eyes flared.

'Bring the other one,' Zafir snapped. 'Now!' The one who'd seen the Black Mausoleum with his own eyes. *Get this alchemist out of here!*

'What about her?' asked the Crowntaker. The Black Moon was a hair's breadth behind the Crowntaker's eyes, twirling the knife, and even if the Black Moon was looking elsewhere, the Crowntaker himself knew perfectly well how to use it too.

'I'll get rid of her. And the first one. As you wish.' She could feel the edge of her own panic.

'I suppose we should wait for Bellepheros ...'

'No. I said get rid of her. Both of them.' Tuuran could have the first and Bellepheros the second. They'd probably all be very happy together, but not here, not now; *now* she needed this alchemist away. Safe. She nodded to the soldiers of Tuuran's guard. They took the alchemist's arms and held her down while they untied her ropes. Zafir kept her eyes on the Crowntaker. 'I'll get her out of here and keep her watched,' she said. 'I'll come for her when I'm ready. It's the third one who matters, isn't it? The one who knows where it is?' *Bellepheros! Where are you?* As soon as he arrived she could be done with this façade ...

The fortress shuddered. A tremor rippled the walls. The Crowntaker jerked. His eyes burned, and there, for a moment, was the Black Moon, the half-god inside, awake and potent, flaring before simmering back beneath the surface; but before she could say a word more, Halfteeth skidded around the corner and almost fell into her.

'You!' She grabbed at him. 'I'll—'

'Dragons!' he yelled, oblivious. 'Dragons are coming. Dragons!'

The fear in him spread like plague to the men around her. The room fell into pandemonium. Zafir closed her eyes. Every day since they'd crossed the storm-dark she'd been waiting for this.

'Get her out of here and get the other one!' She rounded on the Crowntaker as Halfteeth's soldiers bundled the alchemist away. '*You're* the Bloody Judge,' she hissed. '*You* deal with them. Wake up your half-god if you must.' But the half-god wouldn't help them. He never did. She might watch him burn with silver light and disintegrate anything that came close enough to bother him, but he wouldn't actually do anything more until the very end, when out would come the knife to cut more slaves to his will. Harvesting the survivors. That was the way of him.

Halfteeth and his soldiers scattered. Zafir raced to the dragon yard and the shanty town of huts and sailcloth shelters. Grey clouds muted the daylight. It was still raining. There was still half an inch of water underfoot.

Where are they? She launched the thought to Diamond Eye, high in the sky above, claws wrapped around one of the great chains by which the dragons pulled the eyrie through the air. *And why didn't you warn me before?*

They deceived me, little one. They hid their purpose from me. The rest of the answer came as a storm of wind and flames. A dragon swept over the eyrie, fire pouring out of its mouth, tearing through rain, scorching wood and cloth dry and setting them alight. Plumes of steam rose where the dragon's breath struck the yard. Zafir ducked back into the tunnel as the wind that followed the dragon's wings ripped through the remains, sucking the debris into the air, tearing rope and cloth, lifting and scattering them like autumn leaves in a gale.

Drive them away. When I'm ready, come to me. She wasn't armoured.

Diamond Eye answered with a familiar scorn, but she knew he would come. Screams followed the fire, men and women caught in the open even though they were told, always, to be close to shelter. Lightning cracked from a Taiytakei cannon mounted on the eyrie walls. A dragon shrieked in pain, and then the first of the Black Moon's soldiers came running through the steam and fog and hurtled into the tunnel, barging into her and almost knocking her down. Zafir bolted the other way, out into the open, taking her chance, racing across the dragon yard, hugging the wall as fire rained again, as lightning and thunderbolts shook the sky. Clouds of steam scalded her face. She couldn't see how many dragons had come.

Are they few or countless? She reached the next tunnel entrance and dived inside with the last handful of soldiers. When it came to dragons, Tuuran had drilled them well: run fast and hide deep.

Twenty, thereabouts. Diamond Eye was flying free, chasing down the attack. *Small and young most of them. Little more than a year. There are many here of that age.*

The first door in the tunnel was hers – a small room because the smaller rooms were the ones close to the dragon yard, and she needed to be close. Myst and Onyx were already laying out her armour, their faith in her bewildering and absolute.

They are awake. They remember. The reminder chilled her. Proof, as if she needed more, of what had happened after the Taiytakei had taken her to be their slave.

Drive them away! Zafir stripped off her dress and threw on a thin silk shift. Myst offered her the bandages she used when she flew, more strips of silk to be wrapped around the places that chafed, but Zafir waved her away. 'No time.' A dragonscale coat next. She wrapped it around her, and felt a spike of glee from Diamond Eye as he crashed into a dragon somewhere above and brought it down. Curls of smoke and vapour wafted into the tunnels and crept into the room, licking at her feet. She could hear the lightning cannon fire over and over, and then the boom of the black-powder gun, not that it stood much chance of hitting something as fast as a dragon. That had been for Taiytakei glasships, and it had been a long time since any of *those* had menaced her.

Onyx pushed Zafir's gold-glass boots in front of her, offering to buckle her in. Again, Zafir shook her head. 'Diamond Eye has his war harness on.' She slipped into the cascade of gold-glass plates that was the bulk of her armour, and held out her arms. Dragon-riders dressed themselves, that was always the way, but there were plenty of old customs she'd discarded these last two years, and more hands made for more speed. Myst took her left arm, buckling gold-glass vambraces and pouldrons. Onyx took the right. They were good at this. Practised. They fitted her lightning throwers, two to each arm; as soon as they were done Zafir snatched up her helm, the beautiful gold-glass helm with its perfect, clear visor that the enchantress Chay-Liang had made so that she might ride again.

Now. She called Diamond Eye down and ran barefoot outside, splashing through the warm surface water in the yard, half blind in the mist and steam, but she knew her way well enough without needing to see. Up the steps in the eyrie wall as Diamond Eye slammed into the rim and bounded beside her. He gave a familiar cock of his head as he lowered it, and Zafir gripped the mounting ladder. She slipped her foot into the loop at the end of the legbreaker rope and held grimly tight as Diamond Eye tossed his neck and threw her on to his back. As best she knew, no other dragon-rider had ever mounted this way. She and Diamond Eye had learned it together. He launched himself into the air, swooping under the bulk of the eyrie for shelter while Zafir buckled herself into the saddle.

Dragon facing dragon has not happened for a long time. Diamond Eye rose from under the eyrie and soared high. Dreary sunless sky above, steady rain, dull hazed horizons and a murky patchwork ground, broken by the black winding water of the Fury river. Amid the grey Zafir could see a score of circling dragons.

They're small, she thought.

They are young. Diamond Eye dived. Zafir pressed forward into his scales. Rain lashed her face, smearing across the visor of her helm, blurring everything. She couldn't see. The Taiytakei dragon armour had been made for riding over a desert, and the best she'd devised for rain was a silk pad tied to the back of her gauntlet. She wiped the visor clear and then watched the world blur again. Thunder pummelled the air and lightning flashed from the cannon below. It caught the dragon ahead of them in the wing; the monster tumbled and tried to catch itself and spiralled down, quickly out of sight as Diamond Eye wheeled and powered after another and then another, chasing them off. The smaller dragons were edging away.

That one. Zafir watched a great golden war-dragon stoop. She wiped her visor again and … *Flame, was that a man standing on the eyrie wall, waiting for the golden dragon with a hefted axe?* Idiot. Yet a moment before fire should have come to burn him, whoever he was, one of the Black Moon's yearlings hit the gold monster from the side. The two twisted through the air and tumbled over the edge of the eyrie, the gold lashing its tail and cracking the wall above the yard. For a moment the two dragons tangled and plunged towards the ground, until the gold war-dragon threw its smaller brother aside. Zafir tensed. Every dragon was precious. Every single one.

That one brings this to us, said Diamond Eye. *Black Scar of Sorrow Upon the Earth was his name in our first lifetime*; and Zafir would have dived to bring the golden dragon down, but Diamond Eye shot forward and rolled, curled in the air, upside down, wings flared. Zafir caught a glimpse of shimmering green before another massive adult slammed into them, an emerald war-dragon. Lightning flashed past. The emerald reached to bite at Zafir; Diamond Eye's teeth closed on the green dragon's neck, but the emerald still strained for her. Its tail whipped and lashed with enough force to snap her in half. Diamond Eye let go the dragon's throat and caught its tail instead, but now the emerald's jaws were free. They were falling together, plunging towards the eyrie, a drop enough to smash all three of them to pieces. Perhaps the emerald didn't care. The dragons would die and find new eggs and be born again. It didn't seem to trouble them.

Zafir raised her arm to the green dragon's face as it lunged. Lightning flew from the Taiytakei slaver wands set there by the enchantress Chay-Liang, and stung the dragon in the eye; it shrieked and jumped away. Diamond Eye let go its tail and flared his wings, catching their fall, pitching Zafir hard forward and smashing her into the scales between his shoulders. The emerald spread its wings and came again, rising in a tight circle, fire building in its open mouth. The other dragons were scattering now, driven away by the lightning of the Taiytakei cannon. Zafir searched, looking for them through the blur of water across her visor and drawing out their thoughts as Diamond Eye danced through their minds. Confusion. Incomprehension. They didn't understand this lightning. *Dragon servants*. A rage that could melt mountains, fill seas and burn skies. Some withdrew. Some did not, could not. They came at the eyrie again. One by one they fell or fled.

The emerald dragon hurled itself at them, consumed by fury. Her. It wanted *her*.

Do I know you? Were you one of mine? Zafir couldn't see well enough to be sure.

A bolt of lightning lit the sky. The air shuddered with thunder. The emerald arched and screamed and twisted and fell, one wing stretched out, the other fluttering useless. It spiralled down, spitting fire. Lightning hit it again and then again; Zafir watched as the emerald dragon crashed into the eyrie yard. The mists and steam were clear now, wafted away in what little breeze blew off the Oordish Moors and across the floodplains of the Fury valley. The fight was done, the attacking dragons in retreat, in dismayed disarray.

Up. She took Diamond Eye over the eyrie. Then higher still, through the rain and the clouds and beyond into dazzling blue sunlight and the huge wild open sky.

They will come back, she thought.

Yes.

She scanned the skies, the cloud below, the old instincts of a dragon-rider driven into her before she was ten years old. Scattered specks moving in the far distance. To the south where the clouds broke she could see the distant sea and the line across the land that was Tyan's Dyke. To the east the Fury river wound away towards Purkan and all the valley towns that once dotted its shores, Hammerford and Valleyford and Arys Crossing, all burned and gone. To the west the Yamuna wound into the endless dark wrinkles of the Raksheh, wrapped in perpetual mist and cloud. Perhaps in the very distance, groping through a white sea that faded to the far horizon, was a slight dark stain. The mountains of the Worldspine.

To the north …

She could see them. The three solitary mountain tops, distant protrusions punching dark through the raincloud. The Pinnacles. So far away they were almost lost in the haze, but they were there. Unmistakable.

Home.

Yes.

Her thoughts were a shoal of fragments. Diamond Eye's were deep and ancient. He was remembering from a thousand years ago.

Yes?

A surge of something ancient burst from the eyrie below. It echoed across the plains and faded and died. Diamond Eye felt it. Saw it. Saw the emerald dragon shattered from its fall, one of his own kind he had known for fifty lifetimes lying crippled and broken in the folds of the eyrie's womb. Saw the dragon cut by the Black Moon's knife and die at the touch of an old goddess who always took something away.

Yes, they will come back, Diamond Eye answered, distracted by the death below them. *Yes, home. Yes to both of those things and more.* His thoughts were far away. He was thinking of the Black Moon. Remembering, and Zafir knew how it troubled him.

They circled downward. The gold dragon Blackscar was keeping his distance but hadn't withdrawn like the rest. He was watching. Zafir nudged Diamond Eye closer, but as soon as she did, the gold turned and flew away, hard and fast.

That one carries a rage that has strength even among dragons.

She swooped low again. The emerald lay smashed across the dragon yard, wings broken, its spirit dead and gone. The handful of Adamantine Men they'd rescued from Furymouth swarmed over it now. There were no special rituals for killing a dragon. You took your chances as they came. Mostly you died trying, and even if you managed to kill one you died at the claws of another moments later, or else you burned; and that was the way of being an Adamantine Man.

They cut off its head. There was no need, but they did it anyway. The corpse would burn from the inside now, getting hotter and hotter for days if not weeks, until flesh and bone crumbled to ash and all that was left were scales and a few scorched bones from its wings. Scales for armour, bones for bows. No one had been able to harvest a dead dragon since the Adamantine Palace had burned, but these men would, and Bellepheros would show them how.

She roamed Diamond Eye's memories, rode among his distant thoughts, looking for bitterness or anger or resentment, but as he watched this dead dragon, he felt nothing.

Sorrow is not for us, he told her. *There is no loss. We come again. Always and for ever.*

It troubled him though, that knife, as it troubled her and Tuuran and Bellepheros too. Their journey would be wreathed in bloody fire – that was always going to be true – but Diamond Eye had met the Black Moon's knife and with furious hostility submitted to its cut. Dragons and men alike, shaped to the Black Moon's will. He used it over and over without thought, on anyone and everyone who crossed his path. It would have to stop.

Yes.

They landed on the rim. Zafir's armour was starting to chafe where she hadn't taken the time to bandage herself under the dragonscale. She dismounted from the war harness, the top half of her cased in gold and glass, dragonscale underneath, bare feet and ankles at the bottom where the coat ended.

Fly free if you wish. Go to them. Tell them what has come. I mean no war against either men or dragon, but I will fight if I must to take back what was mine.

Diamond Eye might have laughed. *They will not care for your ambition, little one, not one whit either way. It is him they watch for. The Black Moon.* Diamond Eye jumped to the rim and fell away into the sky. *They know he is here. His return spreads among us like fire.*

As Diamond Eye soared away, the Crowntaker climbed the steps from the dragon yard. He stood beside her and watched the dragon vanish into the distance. Berren, Crowntaker, Crazy Mad, the Bloody Judge, all the names he carried around with him like memories of lovers past, clung to despite their betrayals, though they all meant nothing now.

'Where is he going?'

'Wherever he wants.' Zafir peered, trying to see how close the

Black Moon lurked behind the Crowntaker's eyes. 'Why did you kill that dragon? Bellepheros could have used its blood.'

'Do you leave a horse with a broken leg to suffer? Bellepheros can have all the blood he wants from the others. The Black Moon will take them with this knife, every dragon that fell and lives. That one I set free because I could.' He paused. 'I told you the Black Moon was weak again now. Crossing the storm-dark drains him. Your prisoners are gone, by the way. Fled in the chaos.'

'Prisoners?'

'The alchemist and that Adamantine Man and the other one.'

'They were never prisoners, Crowntaker. We're not slavers.'

'I think maybe they didn't quite see it the same way. Probably on account of Halfteeth and the whole business of locking them up and tying them to chairs. Anyway, they're gone. Did a bit of damage on their way out, too.'

Zafir looked away. They could have done with another alchemist. Bellepheros hadn't been the same since the last days of Merizikat; frankly he hadn't been the same since the Black Moon had come and Tuuran had hailed him as the Silver King returned, the saviour who would deliver them all from fire, and Bellepheros had been the first to see how that was a lie, and also the first to be cut by the Black Moon's knife. Good or ill Zafir didn't know, but the Black Moon was something else, not the Isul Aieha, and no saviour of anything except himself; and Bellepheros didn't have to keep their dragons tame now that the Black Moon had woken them, but Zafir still needed his potions for the dragon-disease she carried and for other things too. Another alchemist would have been a boon.

'Farakkan,' she said. 'We bring Tuuran back to the eyrie. Then the Pinnacles because the Pinnacles were my home and my throne and where I wish to be.' She watched the Crowntaker carefully, waiting for the Black Moon to come and dismiss her desires. When he didn't, she went on more softly: 'Then to the Adamantine Palace to reclaim my spear. And then we deal with the dragons, however it is your half-god means to do that.' She'd seen it in his head when he'd raged at her once and nearly put an end to her, seen the spear, how badly it mattered, but never the why or what or how, only that it did. The Adamantine Spear. Symbol of the speaker of the nine realms.

The Crowntaker closed his eyes and clutched his head. 'I don't know why either. I don't know what for. I don't know what he wants ...' He collapsed and squatted on the wall. Zafir watched him with wary pity. She didn't know much about the Crowntaker's past except that Tuuran had known him as a friend, but she never knew which to expect, the man or the monster. The Black Moon could stop time itself. He would stay as long as he wanted, and he only even pretended to listen to her because by sheer chance she had cut herself on the Adamantine Spear on the day it had been given to her, and the spear had drunk her blood, and somehow that mattered.

'Tuuran's in Farakkan, yes?' The Crowntaker looked despairingly about the eyrie.

'You know he is.'

'We could ...' He drew the venomous Starknife from his belt. Zafir backed hastily away. The thousand eyes of its golden hilt seemed to watch and follow her. Patterns swirled its ghostly blade into shapes and forms of madness, faces flirting on the edge of recognition and then dissolving into chaos.

'No.' Zafir shook her head. 'We tried that once. We both know better now.'

'But I told you: he's weak from crossing the storm-dark. Last time ... perhaps we waited too long?'

Zafir shook her head. Blind hope was all the Crowntaker had left.

'Then tell your dragon to eat me!'

She kept her distance, watching him, eyes for nothing else, waiting for the first warning of silver light, of the Black Moon inside. 'My dragon isn't here, and none of them would dare to touch you. You know that.'

The Crowntaker came closer. Zafir backed steadily away at first, but he kept on coming. Eventually she stopped and let him close. Too close.

'What do you want from me?' she asked.

'I want to be me.' His hand shot out, snatching for one of the bladeless knives on Zafir's belt. He was too quick for her to stop him, but she caught his hand as he drew out the blade and clamped his wrist, keeping him from turning its edge on himself. 'It won't work,' she snapped. 'I already tried that too, don't you remember? And I don't want to lose that knife.'

'I want to be free.' He was stronger than her. Not by much, but he was, and more desperate too. He turned the blade slowly towards his own throat.

Zafir snarled at him. 'It won't *work*!'

They stared at one another. He wouldn't back down, so in the end she let go.

'You know it won't work,' she said again. 'But if you absolutely must make him angry, be far away from here when you do. I want no part of it.'

'You're the only one he listens to!' The Crowntaker bared his teeth, and Zafir laughed in his face. The Black Moon *pretended* to listen but he didn't, not really, just followed whatever whim of the moment most piqued his fancy. She was so much dust to him, like everyone else.

The Crowntaker gave back her knife. As she took it, he offered the Starknife too. She took that as well, and watched him pick his way down the gentle outer slope of the dragon-yard wall and out to the eyrie's rim. He kept on walking, right to the eyrie's edge and off, vanishing with the falling rain. She watched him go and thought of throwing the Starknife over the edge after him, but she didn't. There wasn't much point. They'd danced this dance before, and petulance only made it worse.

She called to the dragons that remained instead, and told them to take the eyrie's chains and head for Farakkan. They obeyed her because the Black Moon had told them that they must. She didn't know what would happen if the Crowntaker did actually die, but she imagined that the dragons would probably eat her the first chance they got. And it didn't bother her, because the Crowntaker *wouldn't* die, not today. The Black Moon wouldn't let him.

Over Farakkan Halfteeth lowered cages and hauled Tuuran and his men to the rim. They had a few new faces, a handful of feral survivors of the dragon terror. Farakkan, built on mud and flooded every spring. It was a wonder that Tuuran had found anyone at all; but he had, and he came out of the cages and knelt in front of her, the old rituals kept alive even though they both had more pressing things to do. She patted his shoulder and moved on, and in her face he must have seen the torment the Crowntaker carried to anyone he touched. He winced and asked her with his eyes: *What happened, what was it this time?*

'He's gone again,' she said. 'Over the edge.' Tuuran simply nodded.

With the cages empty, Zafir turned for the Pinnacles, for home, while Tuuran set about clearing the dragon yard. There wasn't much they could do about the headless dragon corpse that now filled a good part of it, but they could clean away the rest. For a while she went to sit with Myst and Onyx, to watch them nurse their newborns, hoping to make all the leaden feelings go away. She played with them a little. Sometimes it helped, seeing the blind hope of new life and the fierce love that surrounded them, but not today.

Much later, when it was dark, one of the hatchlings landed in the eyrie. Dark meant the dragons would keep to themselves, and so Zafir had changed out of her armour, although queenly dresses hardly suited the wind and steady rain and so she was wrapped in a soldier's leather coat, up in one of the five watchtowers that ringed the yard. She knew the hatchling as it came down, as she knew each and every one of the eyrie's dragons – Stars Cascade Over a Dying Mirror Sea in her first life – and Zafir wondered why the half-gods had been so melancholy with their names, but Diamond Eye had no answer to that. Stars Cascade had something in her claws. Zafir watched the something get up, then climbed from the watchtower and walked across the yard through the rain. The shanty-town debris of huts and sails and ropes had been cleared. Everyone would sleep in the tunnels now, and if that meant they were crowded, it was still better than being burned.

The figure in the dragon yard came towards her, eyes blazing with silver light in the twilight. The face was still the Crowntaker, but behind it seethed the Black Moon.

'You have something of mine.'

Zafir had the Starknife already in her hand. Without a word she offered it. Without a word, the Black Moon took it and walked away.

4

The Moonlit Mountain

Four days after landfall

The mountains of the Pinnacles poked from the plains of the Silver City like three thousand-yard fingers, sheer-sided, snub-topped, draped in clinging green veils of vines and stubby thorn trees, whatever could find a crack in which to root. Within them lay the arcane labyrinths of the Silver King's Enchanted Palace where Zafir had been born. Between their feet sat what remained of the Silver City, once the greatest metropolis of the nine realms.

Zafir and Diamond Eye plunged out of the cloud towards the sprawl of stone fortress that covered most of the Moonlit Mountain's flat-topped peak, the tallest of the three giant fingers. There had been scorpions here once, giant crossbows that fired iron-tipped spears with enough force to tear a man in half and sting even a dragon the size of Diamond Eye. The scorpions were gone now, smashed and ripped from their mounts. Where they'd stood, spikes protruded from the ground, ten-foot iron barbs meant to stop a dragon from simply slamming into the walls. Several were bent, and a few were torn away. Ceramic tiles painted with pictograms were scattered and strewn across the ground. Most were broken. Some had been stamped to powder by crushing dragon strides.

There were men here. Watching. Diamond Eye felt them and plucked at their thoughts. As she punched through the cloud Zafir watched them run. They ran because they'd seen a dragon, and running was what men with any sense would do. And though she told herself over and over that she meant no murder to whoever had taken her home, watching them run she felt her veneer flake, a seething core of vengeful animosity burning it away.

But I will try, she told herself.

They wouldn't let her though, whoever held her palace. Deep

down, simple and primitive, she knew it. They would fight her, and she was content with that knowledge. Glad even, because it let her pretend it wasn't what she wanted …

She swept Diamond Eye low across the top of the mountain through the ever-present drizzle, scanning the ground. Perhaps there wasn't any point, but she'd already found one alchemist here, and alchemists were more dangerous than she'd ever imagined. How dangerous, exactly? She didn't know.

I feel their thoughts, little one. Hundreds of them teeming through the mountain, but there are no alchemists here. They have a taste to them. It makes them easy to pick out.

Unless they choose to hide themselves, she reminded him.

She circled one last time. There had been beauty to the mountain-top once. The Reflecting Garden was here, a toy of the Silver King, an eternal fountain feeding pools of water that didn't lie flat but ran along in arcs, tiny flowing rivulets twisting cold through the air, suspended in the last echoes of the Silver King's sorcery, all of them leading to the glimmer of the Silver Onion Dome, so old that no one could remember its proper name, where the air was bright and fresh and dry and always smelled of spring in defiance of the seasons. Zafir looked at the remains, at the shattered stones and gravel. The Onion had been smashed flat. There was almost nothing left of the Silver King's water garden except a stream bubbling out of the rubble into a few haphazard pools, with raindrops bounding patterns across them before they drained into the mountain below. That was all.

What was it for? As a girl she'd played in the water, oblivious to its mystery. She'd taken it for what it was, no sense of wonder at how it had been made, just a simple joy that it had.

She shuddered. There *had* been a happiness to the Moonlit Mountain once, but it was so long ago that she doubted she could ever find her way back to it.

To amuse himself. They were all that way. Diamond Eye landed on the stones around the shattered dome. There were no spikes to keep dragons away here, only in the fortress of broken scorpions. Stars Cascade landed beside them, impatient and hostile. The dark shape of the eyrie was coming down from on high now, a sinister blackness laced with purple veins pushing through parting cloud, dropping slowly as the dragons let go their chains. Zafir had made them lift it up above the clouds in the night, sick of rain and wanting to see the stars. She supposed she ought to wait now for Tuuran and his Adamantine Men to march beside her, but she was here, so close, and the urgency to finally see with her own eyes, to know whether her sister or any others lived, to understand how much her world had changed, was impossible to resist.

She slipped from Diamond Eye's back. *Keep watch, if you will. Give warning of what you can.* However hard she kept her expectation in check, however much she quashed the unruly sprouts of hope, both grew virulent like weeds the moment she looked away. Tuuran would be furious with her. Diamond Eye didn't much like her impatience either, though he tried to hide behind aloof indifference. She didn't understand him. Stars Cascade simply wanted to eat her. *That* she understood.

The entrances into the mountain from the dome were rubble-choked. Zafir climbed to the great Queen's Gate at the top of the fortress. The gate itself had been smashed to splinters, the Grand Aisle beyond collapsed, the stair to the High Hall below packed tight with shattered marble. Clumps of grass grew in niches of earth. She went to the lower Humble Gate instead. The rubble there was looser – wood, not stone – and when she pulled a fallen door aside she could see the old Servants' Passage leading down. She smiled to herself. So *this* was where the watchers had gone, was it? And rightly too, for the Queen's Gate was for queens alone.

'Hello?'

She lit her torch, as bright as a thousand lanterns. Whoever was here would come up to parley, wouldn't they? Hidden away in their magical tunnels and caverns, kept alive by the relics of a long-dead sorcerer, trapped in an enchanted cage by rampaging dragons. Perhaps they were all mad by now. Everyone said that about the queens of the Pinnacles. Not right in the head. Her own mother. Her …

No. Not a time to go to that place. She looked down the steps. They had to talk to her, didn't they? A rider come down on a dragon for the first time in … she didn't know exactly, but her old world hadn't lasted long after the Taiytakei had taken her from it.

They don't hear you, murmured Diamond-Eye.

Zafir called again, louder. The Grand Aisle past the Queen's Gate was the gate for kings and queens, wide and bright and airy, full of open arches to the world outside. Not so the Servants' Passage. *My mother kept a menagerie of birds up here, and a butterfly garden. Sometimes she let them loose to flutter about the crowns of visiting kings, and the walls were buttered with gold and white marble behind drapes from the silk farms of Tyan's Peninsula.* She shivered, lost in memories, though Diamond Eye likely didn't care a whit to hear them. *She used to let me play with the butterflies when I was small. I squashed one once. I wasn't looking and I trod on it. She was angry. I learned after that to be so very careful ...*

But those days were long gone even when she'd ridden her first dragon. They seemed so distant now that they must surely have belonged to someone else.

She took a deep breath. The Grand Aisle and the High Hall and the Great Stair were all wide enough for a hatchling, but the Humble Gate had been made with other thoughts. It was the entrance for those who merely served, barely wide enough for an armoured man to squeeze along sideways, carefully and deliberately too small for any dragon to enter. The darkness looked back at her, deep and hostile. The cramped space of it clawed its way inside her until it became almost physical, a barrier against her. And she couldn't be having that. She closed her eyes for a moment and stood amid the leering demons that haunted her, the fanged glinting creatures of small dark places, and thought of Tuuran, not far behind her now, and shooed the demons away and picked her way down the steps. These fortress parts had been carved by men long after the Silver King had come and gone. They were crude and tight and narrow, their walls plain rough stone. She ran her hand over the stone, remembering the times she'd come this way before.

'Is anyone there? Do you hear me?'

The stair took her into a long straight hall, wider but oppressive in its gloom. Shadows jumped to swallow her light the moment she swung it around. There were sconces in the walls where torches had once burned, but not any more. This was where a visiting queen's servants mustered with their bags and boxes, but it was also a killing place where defenders could hold off an assault after their dragons had lost the air above. There were murder holes over her head and slits for crossbowmen in the walls. When Jehal's uncle Meteroa had seized this place, he'd shown how deadly it was. Sadly for him, he hadn't known about the other entrances, the ones below. Likely as not it would come to those again, but she'd promised herself to give whoever held her old throne a chance, first, to talk.

'Hello?'

Her voice echoed from silent stone. No answer. She could see the iron-bound doors at the far end of the hall. They were closed. *They have to be listening, surely! They have to be here.*

They see you, warned Diamond-Eye. *They watch.*

'How many are you?' she called. Her words rang out in the emptiness. The silence that came after swallowed her. 'Are you few? Or are you many? I know the secrets of this place. I can help you.' She took another step. 'Princess Zara-Kiam? Is she here? She will know me. Does the name matter to you? Is she alive?' It mattered to her. Her own sister. Of course it mattered.

The quiet oppression of the walls squeezed tight, squashing the air out of her. The darkness. Her breaths came fast and shallow. She was panting like an animal. She raised her voice and made herself stronger.

'I am Zafir of the Silver City, speaker of the nine realms, and this fortress is my home. I bring hope. I bring a half-god. I bring the Silver King's brother. Is my sister here? Princess Zara-Kiam? Will you not parley with me?'

Silence.

'My dragon sits above. I am alone here but I will not remain so. Speak! I come with an alchemist, and all the martial glory of the Taiytak—'

The first crossbow quarrel hit her in the head. It glanced off the gold-glass of her helm hard enough to knock her sideways. Perhaps that was what saved her when the second missed her throat as she staggered. It hit the pouldron on her left shoulder instead and shattered it. Zafir stumbled back, head spinning. She raised her arm and loosed a bolt of lightning at the wall, not with any hope of striking anything, but to stun, for in this shallow space the noise was deafening and thundered in her ears. Then she ran, the terror of being trapped in darkness an unruly riot inside her.

The iron tip of another quarrel sparked off the steps, and then she was climbing and out of sight of the bowmen below. Step after step, heart thumping, eyes fixed firmly on each footfall while leering fear closed around her, until she pulled herself gasping back into rain and daylight and glorious space. She stopped a moment, bent over, hands on knees, breathing deep until the demons of the dark slunk away.

Alchemists.

'What do you mean, alchemists?' she snarled, furious at her own frailty. A dragon-queen wasn't afraid. Never, ever, afraid. Certainly not of the dark. That was for children.

Alchemists are reviled here. Made into demons. Diamond Eye was almost smiling. Enjoying the sensations. Enjoying her discomfort, perhaps, but then all woken dragons had a special venom in their heart for alchemists.

The eyrie was almost down now, the black stone of its underbelly not much more than a few dozen feet over her head, laced with glowering veins and flickering with violet lightning. The cages were on their way, winching down over the sides. Zafir pointed her dragons to the Queen's Gate.

'Clear that path,' she told them.

The cages reached the ground long before the dragons were done. Tuuran sidled up beside her, watching them at work. 'Last time I came here was as guardsman to Speaker Hyram.'

'And you left as a slave.' Zafir brushed his arm. A fleeting touch, yet lingering. She didn't take her eyes off the dragons. 'Does it feel strange to be back?'

Tuuran grunted. 'Like the stab of a knife. Something like that. Don't know how to put it into better words. A hard pang, and deep, and not what I thought it would be. Everyone gone or hiding, everything burned.' He stared at the dragons, at the colossal bulk of Diamond Eye pulling boulders out of the entrance, flinging them over the side of the mountain. 'No regrets though,' he muttered. He glanced at her, dressed in her armour and ready for battle, and chuckled.

'Regrets?' Zafir shook her head. 'Then I have them for us both, Night Watchman.' She turned away. 'I already went inside. I didn't wait for you.'

'I saw.' She felt the silent admonishment.

'I told them who I was. They answered with crossbows.' She looked to the eyrie. 'This was my home once. *He* should be here.' She didn't expect an answer. The two of them didn't talk about the Crowntaker much these days. Not since Merizikat. Neither of them knew what to say.

After a moment, Tuuran looked her up and down. 'Are you hurt, Holiness? I don't see any blood or anything sticking out that shouldn't.'

'No.' But she *was* hurting, on the inside, and he wasn't so stupid as to not see it. Made for two of them. Maybe that was how he knew.

'He's not coming down. He's gone funny again. Trying to kill yourself would do that, I suppose. Can't blame someone for feeling a bit funny after that.' Sometimes Tuuran's bitterness was enough to burn holes in the rain.

The dragons had cleared the entrance enough for them to get inside. Zafir picked up a gold-glass shield and started for the hole. Tuuran put a warning hand on her shoulder.

'Holiness, you don't know who's in there.'

He gathered White Vish and a few others from Furymouth and Merizikat, a dozen soldiers like him, hard men with hard pasts, in dragonscale and glass and gold, with swords and lightning and the spiked ashgars of the Taiytakei knights. More men were coming down from the eyrie, lowered in the creaking wooden cages they'd built together a blue moon ago when they'd been adrift over the sea, and the cages had been for fishing.

'Do you remember the way?' Zafir asked him.

'Do I bloody remember it?' He scoffed and laughed through the rubble strewn across the Grand Aisle behind the Queen's Gate. 'Bright and clear, Holiness, even if it was a decade ago.' One wall opened to the sky, letting daylight and rain sweep in through carved columns. The rest of the Grand Aisle lay thick with shadow. 'I remember standing here while Speaker Hyram greeted your mother.' Zafir didn't remember it, though she knew she must have been there too, Tuuran at Speaker Hyram's side, herself lingering reluctantly next to her mother. 'I can still see the High Hall as it was that day, paintings and statues, layered with rugs and tapestries.' Tuuran looked about as if trying to find them. The statues had survived, blackened and cracked, some of them broken. The rest was gone save a few charred shreds and stains of damp sooty ash. The wind whistled from the open colonnades, fleeting gusts catching Zafir with speckles of rain. Strands of ivy crept between cracks underfoot. In the shadows something skittered away.

A sudden flutter of wings made her jump almost out of her skin. Two startled pigeons broke from cover and bolted for the open air. No one had been here for months. The Queen's Gate had been abandoned to the dragons.

A dozen steps led around the curve of the mountaintop to a second hall lit by shafts of daylight from above, as desolate as the first and damp with puddles of rain. Beyond waited the Grand Stair, and then the Silver King's gate into the Enchanted Palace and the heart of the Moonlit Mountain; but at the bottom of the stair a block of stone the size of a barn barred their way. Zafir crouched. She took off a golden gauntlet and brushed at the dust with a fingertip.

'They must have sealed themselves in a long time ago,' she said. 'A small band could live here almost for ever, if they were careful.'

'So now what?'

'We come from below, Night Watchman, and from the side.'

She climbed back out and took to the air with Diamond Eye, urging him down to whatever was left of the Silver City. He dropped like a stone while she pressed hard against him, head pushed down, arms spread against his scales. He flared his wings as they neared the ground, crushing the air out of her, settling into a lazy orbit over the ruins. Shapes and outlines resonated with memories sparkling silver in the sunshine and busy with life. The long streets and wide open squares were mottled with weeds and patches of grass now. In places the canals lay choked with rubble or overgrown water plants; elsewhere they still shone with gleaming water. Trees sprouted in the burned shells of houses amid sprawled patches of thorns. The fields and meadows that had made her city rich were gnawing it away. Taking back what had always been theirs.

'The Order of the Dragon once ruled here,' she said as much

to herself as to Diamond Eye. 'There used to be gardens laced with rose bowers and dotted with splashing fountains. Peacocks. I remember there were peacocks.' It was all gone, everything she'd known. When she touched the dragon's mind, she found that he too was lost in ancient memories.

After the Splintering when the Isul Aieha struck the Black Moon down we were cast into Xibaiya. When we hatched and rose anew, all we remembered was gone. Left amid the ruin they made, we searched for the half-gods, lifetime after lifetime, until one by one we abandoned their memory. And now the shadow of the Black Moon comes again, fumbling for what he was, great pieces yet missing, still burning to make the world as he sees it was meant to be.

Zafir caught snatches of visions. Spires of stone, dragons filling the sky, and in that sky the darkness of a silver moon, hard and hostile and violent.

This is how it was, murmured Diamond Eye. *That is what he brings.*

Zafir looked at the ruins of her city, grey and dull in the falling rain. 'And who will stop him, dragon? You? Me?' She guided Diamond Eye away. 'There are tunnels under the mountain. This was my home, and I will have it back, and it will be the way it must be, as violent as your remembered moon.'

5

The Throne of the Harvest Queen

Five days after landfall

Across the sheer cliff-face sides of the Moonlit Mountain the eyrie came, carried by dragons of venom and anger. Tuuran huddled his men behind a wooden barricade on the rim as it reached the first of the scorpion caves that riddled the bluffs. Veils of green vines trailed over a mouth of darkness until Diamond Eye swooped in and scoured it with fire, on and on, hot enough to melt stone. Scorching air billowed out of the cave, rank with the tang of red-hot iron and laced with piteous wails. Tuuran cut the rope holding the barricade. It tipped, rattled down like a drawbridge and crashed against the lip of the cave. Wisps of smoke and cooked ash plumed.

He took a moment then. An instant to savour the seven shades of unholy shit he was about to rain down on anyone who got in his way.

Right then.

A scream to curdle blood. He launched himself. A haze filled the cave, smoke and steam. Hastily roped wood shuddered under his boots, eyes too busy peering through the scalded air for whatever would try to kill him to be worrying about the dizzying drop below. Across the gap and in, men bellowing behind him, howling themselves on, fear cowed by roars, burned air searing his throat with every breath.

A harsh metal rasp echoed ahead. Something shot past him. Huge. A scorpion bolt skewered one of his men on the eyrie rim, picked him up and threw him a dozen yards through the air. The bolt flew on, a rope of blood trailing in its wake. It sparked off the sloping stone of the eyrie wall and ricocheted into the sky. Tuuran unleashed a curse, teeth bared, axe already swinging its song. No regrets, no retreat, no time to think ...

Two men ahead, scrambling from the scorpion at the back of the cave, bolting deeper into the mountain. He leaped after them like a thunderstorm.

'For speaker and spear!' Past a man on the floor, burned to the bone, screaming in agony, not quick enough behind the scorpion's dragonscale shield when Diamond Eye had let loose hell. The air stank. He hurdled another corpse, burned black. Then into the tunnel, shoulders ricocheting off the walls, so damned dark he could barely see, a few feeble remnants of sunlight creeping from outside. At least the clouds had broken, a pause in the endless bloody monotony of rain. He couldn't see the two bastards ahead, but he heard them. He flicked at the enchanter's torch strapped to his arm. Light flared, dazzlingly bright. Too much, but he saw flashes and flickers of movement in the crazed dance of shadows it birthed. One man stopped. Turned to face him. Tuuran crashed into him in a strobe of light and dark, a flash of a shape, a face, wild whites of eyes and bared teeth, the waiting sword not even seen as Tuuran smashed his shield straight onto the point of it and knocked the blade aside. He ran the man down, size and strength and speed his victory. His boot stamped on something, an arm maybe. He staggered, almost tripped. The man he'd flattened cried out.

'Live one!' He stumbled. 'Someone finish the shit rag!' Caught himself, raced on, hard, fast, trying to get to the last man before the alarm could spread.

The tunnel sloped down, the air laced with a smell of stale smoke. Woodsmoke and so dark he couldn't see a thing outside the beam of his light, flashing all over like a maddened wasp. He held his shield in front of him, stumbled again and again on the uneven floor, caught himself each time, careened off the walls and finally crashed headlong into solid stone where the tunnel forked. His shield saved him from breaking his face, but he couldn't tell which way the other man had gone.

He stopped. Swore.

'On me!' Zafir had shown him how the scorpion caves were laid out. Drawn him a nice little map of the tunnels beyond and how to find his way to the heart of the fortress, but he was buggered if he could remember anything except the way straight in to the heart of it. He'd know it when he saw it, she said.

'Sticks of shit!'

'Boss?' Halfteeth, right behind him. Full of shit-eater tenacity. A bastard wolverine with a bad attitude.

'One got out. They'll know we're coming.'

'Never the easy way, eh, boss?' Halfteeth had a grin on him like a dead man.

'Oh why would we ever do that? Listen you, if you die, you do it where her Holiness won't find your body and know I let you out, eh?' Should have left him to stew in his own shit after what he'd done back over Farakkan, but a murderous bastard like Halfteeth, this was right up his alley, and just now Tuuran reckoned he was about to need all the murderous bastards he could get.

Zafir waited in the Silver City's heart, beside Pantatyr's Golden Temple, surrounded by its overgrown gardens, its esplanade, its lake and canals, its livid green dome now half staved in. For a long time she simply sat on Diamond Eye's back, looking at the rain-sodden ruin. The golden doors that had given it its name were gone, a gaping hole in its side like a wound. She watched the rain through the shattered dome. It seemed unimaginable that she'd been here before. An old other life that was more like a dream than anything real.

She watched, but she kept an eye on the eyrie's descent too. She knew every cave and every crevice of these mountains, and when the eyrie closed on the first of the scorpion caves she urged Diamond Eye into the air and across the ash-stained ruins of the Silver City to where the sheer cliff of the Moonlit Mountain burst from the plain, and then sent him away to where Tuuran could use him.

How many survive in there? she asked as he climbed and soared away.

Hundreds, little one.

Why are there no other dragons here? Where have they gone?

Diamond Eye laughed, mocking and dark. *They watch from afar, little one. Lifetimes we spent looking for the Black Moon. Scores more since we gave up that search. They wonder at his return and remember his brother, the Isul Aieha, and what he did to us.*

She followed his rise towards the eyrie until he was a speck, then turned away. The soldiers Tuuran had left down here were waiting for her. White Vish from Furymouth. Other men and women whose names she'd come to know, the last few slaves left standing at Tuuran's side as they'd crashed into the storm-dark around the Godspike back in Takei'Tarr. A few black-skinned Taiytakei from the deserts. A handful of deeply tanned fishermen from the coast of the Dominion. A pale-faced hulk from the north of Aria. The Outsider woman, the one Tuuran called Snacksize, taken and sold years ago by King Valmeyan as though harvesting a useful crop, grumbling about her lover Halfteeth left behind on the eyrie.

Zafir beckoned them to follow and led them through the rubble-strewn streets. There were no walls surrounding the Silver City, pointless things among a people who lived and died by dragons, but there were tithe houses on each road in and out, and the tithe houses had cellars, each with a bronze door above a shaft that sank into the Silver King's Ways, with winches and pulleys. Zafir took them to the closest, where both cellar and shaft lay open to the sky. Diamond Eye had cleared the rubble the night before. Now White Vish levered open the bronze door, and Zafir lowered one of Chay-Liang's torches tied to a length of silk rope. The shaft went down a hundred feet, white stone walls smooth as glass and slick with slimy water. The old winch and pulley were long gone, smashed to pieces, but the soldiers had brought their own. She watched them piece it together; when it was done she stepped forward, thinking that of all of them she should be first.

The Outsider woman planted a hand on Zafir's chest. Zafir supposed the other soldiers called her Snacksize because she was so short, but they treated her with a profound respect nonetheless. 'Tuuran would kill me.' Snacksize glanced at White Vishmir. 'Let your big man go first. He looks keen enough.'

Time was Zafir would have hung any woman for touching her, for talking to her like that. Old days, different days. Bad days. Today she simply nodded to White Vish. 'Go.'

She watched his descent. It seemed achingly slow, and for all she knew the tunnels at the bottom might be flooded or teeming with waiting foes, but Vish reached the bottom and didn't sink or drown, and no one tried to kill him. Zafir peered down, getting in everyone's way. Vish disappeared from sight. She could see a little light flickering about. Enough to know he hadn't gone far, but that was all.

Snacksize went next, and then the hulk from Aria. The winch creaked under his weight. When it came back Zafir took it, dropping into darkness, skin already crawling as she felt the walls close around her until they opened again into a wide tunnel of white stone, straight as an arrow towards the root of the Moonlit Mountain. It was the same stone as the tunnels that spiralled from the dragon yard into the bowels of her floating eyrie, and the same shape too, though bigger in every dimension.

The old Silver King's Ways. A deep scum of litter, of leaves and stones and a few sticks and bones, lay scattered underfoot. Dirt. Detritus left by some recent flood. In places it had drifted almost knee-deep.

'We're being watched,' warned Vish. 'There are survivors here.'

'Half feral,' murmured Zafir. 'Diamond Eye has seen their thoughts. We'll be back for them soon enough. Let them be for now.'

A distant bone-jarring howl echoed through the tunnel. White Vish moved suddenly away, heading towards it.

'Stay—' Snacksize started after him. A flailing windmill of arms and legs burst from a drift of litter on the floor, and crashed into White Vish with the savagery of a wolf pack. Another howl went up, much closer, whooping and hooting. A dozen feral creatures in rags exploded from hiding, waving sticks, laying into White Vish, mobbing him. He went down hard. Zafir ran, kicking her way through the litter, damp dead leaves swirling into the air around her. She raised an arm to loose lightning at the creatures, then paused. They had been men and women once. They still were. They had lived in her city. They were hers to protect, and she'd failed them. Carpenters and potters and masons and barrow men …

Snacksize bolted past her, lightning thrower raised to fire. Zafir knocked it aside.

… carters and livery men and millers and smiths. Even priests. She fired her own lightning into the tunnel wall instead, a thunderclap that shivered stone and echoed and roared loud enough to make her gasp. The feral who'd knocked Vish down squirmed and twisted to his feet and fled. The others jumped back and away, startled and dazed. White Vish scrabbled upright. Zafir held out her hands, showing them empty.

'Stop!'

A dozen men in rags, that was all they were; but they wavered only a moment, and then one of them lunged, a hurled volley of curses, and the rest crashed on like a wave. Five jumped back on Vish, hauling him down again. The rest sprang for Zafir. She battered the first aside. The next swung an old thigh bone at her head; it shattered on her helm hard enough to flash lights in her eyes. She blocked the third, but he grabbed her shield and pulled. She let him tear it away, staggered on, still trying to reach Vish even with one of the feral men clinging to her arm. Vish was thrashing under the weight of too many for him to throw off. They were clawing at his helm, trying to pull it away so they could batter him to death.

'Get away!' Zafir kicked one in the head, knocking him down. She went for her sword, thinking the sight of it might be enough to scare them, but only got it half out of her scabbard before another grabbed her. She threw herself sideways, meaning to smash them both against the wall, but the curve of the tunnel caught her, and she lost her balance and flailed. A hand grabbed her leg, pulling. She let the sword go, arms clutching at the air to stay on her feet as another feral jumped onto her back. He raked at her visor and her throat, and she tipped and fell. Vish raged in fury. Zafir rolled and kicked and punched. There were three of them on her now, wrenching at her armour, trying to find a way in. Someone with a stick was raining blows on her. She kicked and heard a howl as her foot slammed something soft and yielding. Hands grabbed at her throat, pulling at her helm, tugging it loose, lifting the visor open. She grabbed them, tried to pull them off her, but there were too many. Her helm came away and she saw a face in the moonlight gloom, lips drawn back over bared teeth, wild mad eyes. Fingers closed around her throat, throttling her. She clawed, tearing them away. A feral woman lifted a stick over her head; Zafir raised an arm to protect her face …

The air bellowed with the voice of a thousand gods. It lit with the incandescence of the sun, dazzled and deafened. The feral woman with the stick spasmed and flew into the air, hurled away. The biting fingers around Zafir's throat fell slack. Zafir clutched her hands over her ears and rolled away, screwing up her eyes against the light and the noise, blinking hard, trying to see. Lightning. Someone had thrown a bolt of it, murderously hard and as harsh as a lightning thrower could be. When she blinked away the dazzle stars, the feral men were gone, as fast and as suddenly as they had come, fled and vanished into the Silver King's labyrinth. Snacksize stood over her, bloody sword in one hand, bloody knife in the other.

Three ragged corpses lay dead, two cut apart, the third a scorched charred ragbag of splayed smouldering limbs. A fourth feral lay gasping, clutching a bloody hand to his chest. Snacksize finished him without a word. She wiped her knife on one of the corpses, sheathed it and then offered Zafir a hand.

'Injured at all?'

Zafir shook her head. She stared at the bodies. Only a day since her feet had touched the ground of her old home, and already people were dead.

Snacksize went to White Vish. 'What about you? Hurt?'

'No.' Vish shook his head. Snacksize kicked him in the shin. Hard.

'Pity. Stupid sod.'

The rest of Tuuran's soldiers came down. Zafir waited, crouched beside the corpses. 'I didn't want this,' she whispered.

But you knew, said another voice, and it might have been Diamond Eye or it might have been some dark reflection of herself, she wasn't sure. *You knew it would be this way. And you* do *want it. You pretend that you don't, but look deep and you know better.* When Snacksize nudged her to tell her they were ready to go, Zafir closed her visor. No one would see the glisten in her eyes.

They walked on, cautious and tight together, lightning throwers held ready until the Silver King's Ways converged under the Pinnacles in the vast cavern of the Undergates, whose white stone glowed with the same inner light. Water plunged from the cavern roof here, crashing to the stone floor, brushing the air with cold mist, tumbling in rivulets and channels and torrents all the way from the top of the mountain and the fountains of the Reflecting Garden. Zafir watched it fall, the clean fresh water from the fountains that spilled throughout the Silver King's palace. It kept men alive, drained into the canals of the Silver City, mixing with rainwater from the little streams and brooks that wound among the surrounding meadows and fields; but it all came back and ended here, draining away down the old white stone tunnel to the Ghostwater near Farakkan. The Undergates were the only way in and out of the mountain unless you came on a dragon, and they were barred by dragon-rider guards and traps and deadfalls and barricades, and old sorceries worse than any imagination.

Unless, of course, you knew their secrets.

Zafir crept around the edge of the cave, keeping away from the gates themselves. Rafts – not much more than a few lumps of wood strung together – were drawn up at the water's edge where the underground river flowed off towards Farakkan. She crept into the shallows and crouched there. Of all the hidden entrances to her palace, this was her most secret. Hands pushed beneath icy water, brushing aside sand and gravel and slime until she touched the white stone beneath. Her fingers felt the contours of it, the outline of a sigil etched under the dirt.

'They've seen us!' Snacksize raised her lightning thrower. Armoured dragon-riders ran from the gates, fanning across the cave.

Zafir traced the outline of the sigil under the water with a naked finger.

'Come close!' A silver light shimmered beneath her feet. She pulled her Adamantine Men – if you could call this motley band that, but Tuuran did and she wasn't about to argue – into a huddle and raised her arm, lightning ready. Light built around them. Her heart fluttered as the first rider from the gates closed, slowed and lifted his helm. Zafir saw his face. She knew him, if not his name. He stared in puzzlement, then disbelief as she raised her own visor, as the silver light grew ever brighter beneath her. She took off her helm and met his gaze, eye to eye, strength to strength, defiance to defiance.

'I am Zafir,' she said and lifted her bare hand so he might see the Speaker's Ring still on her finger. She saw in his face that at last he knew her. Shock and loathing twisted him. He lunged.

'You will not—'

The light flared silver-bright. They were gone, lifted away by the magic of the Silver King, deep into the Pinnacles' sorcerous heart.

The Undergates, the only way in and out of the fortress unless you knew better.

Light dimmed to dark. Tuuran smothered his torch, feeling his way through the tunnels in the pitch black, fondling the stone like it was the skin of a woman. Hadn't ever liked this place even when it had been filled with light and noise, with chatter and laughter and the belly-rumbling smells of hot grease and mead. A fortress carved out of stone long before the Silver King. Catacombs all the way down. Secret doors scattered among the cellars of the Silver City. If you believed the stories, there were *things* buried here, old monsters, sorceries that would rip a man's soul from his flesh. He felt its hostility at his intrusion. A resentment as old as the moon ...

He shook himself. At least it put him in the right mood for hitting something.

Felt like bloody miles before he found the entrance to the Enchanted Palace. Couldn't have been, nor anything like, but *felt* it. Easing his way in the blackness, ears straining, waiting for the counter-charge, the trap, the lurking knife. Then the glow of light ahead at last, and him as tight as cordage in a storm. Don't think. Just run, axe in one hand, shield in the other. Let it all out – the rage, the frustration, the years of being a slave that lay behind him.

Soldiers waited with iron and steel and bleeding smiles. A wall of spears and shields, and he wouldn't have given a pebble of shit, would have scattered them as easily as old gnawed bones, but these men were Adamantine, and he knew it at once from the way they held themselves. Was enough to pause him, and so he stopped an inch from their spear tips. His kin, these men, and he was theirs, and they saw it too. He lifted his visor.

'I am Tuuran,' he said, 'and I am Adamantine.'

Eight of them blocking his way. Dozens of his own men coming up behind with Taiytakei lightning, half in gold-glass armour over dragonscale, but these eight wouldn't flinch or budge. They'd hold their ground until they were dead. He'd expect nothing less. He tried again.

'Her Holiness Zafir, queen of the Pinnacles and speaker of

the nine realms, demands entrance.' Not that he imagined for a moment they'd believe him. Was quite something that they even listened.

A soldier levelled his spear at Tuuran's face. 'Speaker Zafir died over Evenspire. Speaker Jehal at the Adamantine Palace. There *are* no speakers any more. Surrender yourself. King Hyrkallan will hear your voice, brother.'

Tuuran lowered his shield. Eight years a slave at sea, where the galley masters tossed lightning about the decks on a whim with a casual wave of their hand. When anger took them, then their bolts threw men into the air and left them black twitching corpses, but mostly it was pain they were after, and obedience. Tuuran nodded sharply and pressed his hands to his ears. Thunder flashed and flew about him. Men screamed and crashed to the stone. Not dead, because Tuuran knew his lightning, knew how much it took to kill a man and how to wrap one in fleeting agony. The soldiers behind him swarmed forward, beating the Adamantine Men down before they could rise again, taking their spears and their shields. It almost made him weep seeing that, seeing how easy it was.

'Watch them.' He gave Halfteeth a long hard look. 'My brothers these, so Flame help any man who kills one, for I will flay him. And yes, Halfteeth, I *am* looking at you. *You* can stay with me.'

He pushed through. Adamantine Men were his brothers right enough, but somewhere here, hiding at the back, would be some prancy-arsed dragon-riders. Dragon-riders were different, and Halfteeth could do as he damn well liked. Dragon-riders could bleed and burn and die for all Tuuran cared, and he'd be happy to piss on them as they did.

The flare of silver light faded. In the deep heart of the Isul Aeiha's labyrinth Zafir stood inside a vast hollow sphere of white stone, wide enough to swallow a palace. Its distant walls glowed with soft moonlight. White archways ringed her, while a single span of white stone reached from the centre of the void to its edge. Standing here was like standing in the centre of a bubble.

'What is this?' asked Vish. Hard as iron, most of these men, but here they clustered like frightened children about their mother.

'A relic of the Silver King.' Zafir ran a hand over the stone. 'And nothing we should fear.' As smooth as glass and cold. There were arches like these in the eyrie too.

'But what *is* it?' Vish peered anxiously over the edge at whatever lurked below, screwed up his face and shuddered. At the bottom of the curve beneath them was a pitch-dark hole.

'No one knows.' Zafir put the arches behind her. She crossed the white stone span. That hole wasn't just any hole. If the stories were true then it was a hole in the world, but Vish probably didn't want to hear that. 'I used to come here when I was a child,' she said. 'I used to drop things over the edge into that hole. Stones and sticks and little things. I never did find where they came out.' She clapped a hand on Vish's shoulder. 'So don't fall, eh?'

He looked at her as though she was mad.

Blood ran down Tuuran's axe. A rider threw himself forward, fury and a swinging blade. Tuuran caught the sword on his shield, feinted at the rider's head, let him dodge, then kicked the bastard hard in the ankle, bashed in his face and floored him with a backswing. Twisted it at the last so the axe hit on the flat. Stupid buggers, these dragon-riders. Not one with a jot of sense of how to fight when they didn't have their fat arses spread over the back of a dragon. Pompous bluster, toothless and pathetic. No stomach, no spine, spiritless rags now they'd lost their mounts. He picked the dazed rider up off the floor.

'Who rules here?'

The rider spat blood in Tuuran's face. Tuuran smashed him into the wall.

'Let's try that again. I'll ask nicely, and if you really want to see how it feels while I rip your balls off with my bare hands, you won't tell me. So. Who rules here?'

'Hyrkallan!'

The second time he'd heard the name. Hadn't meant anything when the Adamantine Men had crumbled before his lightning, but he'd had time to think about it now, between murdering stupid stuck-up fools with too little sense to run. Hyrkallan. From Sand in the north. He'd won the Speaker's Tournament when Hyram took the Adamantine Throne. Strong and hard. Good. About time he found someone worth waking up for. He threw the rider away.

'Chance we could do this the nice way, do you think? Settle matters with some pretty words?' He didn't wait for an answer. Dragon-riders didn't bend. They couldn't, because of what they were; and Adamantine Men, when it came to it, were more of the same. Dragons, that's what it was. Left no space for anything but black and white.

More fighting ahead. Halfteeth clenched tight and impatient as a virgin in a brothel. Tuuran ran on and caught up in time to see him pick up a crippled rider and rip out his throat, then jump out into a hallway and thumb his nose at whoever was at the end of it. A flurry of crossbow quarrels chased him back into shelter. At least Tuuran had a few men still with him, and others catching up. They were getting strung out though. Dragon-riders coming from all sides. Could turn bad any time now. Tuuran hurried up close, took a quick peek around the corner and grinned. Coming at him from all sides, yes, but they weren't actually stopping him, and now the arched entrance to the Octagon was right ahead. Queen Aliphera's throne room. Where he wanted to be.

'Gather everyone you can. Right here, right now.' He crouched behind his shield, quarrels pinging off the walls around him. Sneaked a look, then dived across the open space. The Hall of Princes, was that what they called it? Crossbow bolts rattled around him. He rolled and jumped into a niche behind the statue of some old queen or other who'd just had a chunk chipped out of her face. Checked the lightning thrower on his arm. Bastard things were playing up. Not working right. Half-god enchantments all around. Made his skin crawl. Best not to think about it.

A volley of thunderclaps echoed ahead. Flashes of lightning through the archway to the Octagon itself. Tuuran braced himself. Glorious victory or a quick death, one way or the other. The riders in the Pinnacles hadn't seen anything like his lightning, nor his Taiytakei gold-glass armour. So far he'd cut through them like a hot knife through soft old rotting cheese, but damn, there were more men here than he'd been ready for. Surrounded and out-numbered, flanked and nipping at his rear …

Right then. Time to end it. He roared, hurling war cries and curses at his ancestors as he led the charge, loud enough to shake mountains and wake the dead. A quarrel slammed into his shield, cracking it. Another zinged over his head. A swarm of fight-crazed men pelting into the teeth of the storm, hiding behind their shields, screaming at the barricade across the entrance to the Octagon, laying into whoever was there until they shut up and stopped with the fucking crossbows. No idea how many he lost because he wasn't looking back and wasn't going to. Couldn't see much inside as he ran either, except a swirling melee of men. Stupid idle thoughts came at him sideways. *Crazy Mad, he would have loved this*.

Almost at the barricade, and some bastard with a crossbow nearly took his head off; Tuuran returned the favour with a blast of lightning. That was that done, then. Someone screamed beside him. Another quarrel hit his shield and cracked it again – *that* cock-crawler could die too. It wasn't as if they had an armoury stuffed full of shields and lightning throwers back on the eyrie, and they didn't have an enchantress to fix things any more. He smashed through a gap between an upturned table and some sort of dresser and laid about with his axe, splitting the first evil bastard he saw almost in half, and bursting on into the throne room. One way or another it ended here.

The white stone bridge passed through an arch inscribed with sigils and out into a maze of halls and corridors. Etched archways lined the walls, plain and leading nowhere. The servants said the maze shifted, that it was never the same, that sometimes men became lost here for days, but Zafir had never found it so. There were darker stories that on full-moon nights the arches shimmered silver and sucked men inside them. The stories made sure no one ever came to the Silver King's inner sanctum, that and the Hall of Mirages, where anyone who tried to cross found themselves back where they started until they unpicked the secret to its design.

Zafir led, twisting left and right, climbing stairs, always up wherever she could. One hall led past a gaping void, one wall open to an endless darkness. Another became a spiral of steps circling a torrent of water streaming over myriad carvings of monstrous creatures that had never existed. Archways faced her from every wall, and everything was carved with sigils. She remembered the feeling of the place now, how the Silver King's palace felt alive, as though it was watching her, how it had crawled under her skin and laden her with dread and then, in later, darker years, had seemed oddly like a friend. A refuge.

The soldiers grumbled and cursed in her wake. They muttered whispered prayers to their foreign gods. Zafir quietly laughed. No gods would find them here, not in the palace of the Silver King.

'It's cold and dead and quiet,' she said over her shoulder. 'I tried to make a map of it once, but it didn't work.' Or at least it hadn't made any sense. 'Strange and eerie but nothing more. There's nothing here to fear.'

She stopped by an archway that looked like any other and pressed her hands against it. The stone looked as hard and smooth as the rest; but as her fingers touched it, it melted into mist. She turned to the soldiers behind her.

'Are you ready?' she asked. 'There will be blood now.'

Vish nodded. 'Holiness.'

'Ready as it gets, princess.' Snacksize bared her teeth, drew a sword and cast a last glance around the enchanted halls behind them. Zafir looked to the lightning throwers on her arms. She drew a bladeless knife from its sheath and stepped through. Three paces in mist and timeless silence, and then she walked out from hard white stone into a battery of noise and chaos, where men shouted, ran – urgent, desperate – the clatter of boots, the scrape of iron on steel and stone. There were no doors in the Enchanted Palace and never had been. The Silver King hadn't considered them, and no chisel or hammer could touch the white stone he left behind, and so everyone in the Octagon had their backs to her, crowding the entrance to the Hall of Princes behind a barricade of upturned tables. It seemed that no one had imagined she might arrive by simply walking through a wall, but that was because they didn't know this place.

The Octagon. Her throne room. And there was Hyrkallan. There was no mistaking him, and his consort Jaslyn, Shezira's middle daughter, Lystra's big sister. Queen of the North, queen of Sand and Stone, queen of Flint.

Zafir stroked a lightning thrower, dimming it to a thunderbolt less than fatal, to a mere stunning bite of pain as Vish stepped out of the wall behind her. She let fly at the queen of the North, and Jaslyn screamed and fell. Zafir threw off her helm and levelled another lightning thrower at Hyrkallan. Her movement was calm and poised, but scratch beneath and a rabid animal raged at the leash.

'Bend your knees!' she cried. 'Bend your knee to your speaker!' She swept the lightning thrower across the room. 'All of you! One chance. Do it now or face your end!'

Hyrkallan whirled. He stared at her in aghast disbelief. His knuckles tightened on the axe in his hand. 'You! But you can't be real!'

The leash snapped. She couldn't help herself. Her face twisted. She stroked the lightning thrower as harsh as it would go and levelled the wand at his face. 'Did you think I was dead, Hyrkallan? Did you think I died at Evenspire when Jehal betrayed me? Did you think I died here when you sold your soul to him and came at Valmeyan with your dragons?' She bared her teeth and hissed and prowled closer, circling, every nerve alive and tingling, charged tense and ready to strike. 'I tore three of your riders from the sky that day. I hope they were dear to you. Now bend your knee to your queen or I will hang you by your own entrails. Do you understand me? This is my home. *Mine*.'

'Die, ghost!' Hyrkallan threw himself at her, swinging his axe. Zafir clenched the lightning thrower to end him in light and sound and twitching limbs. The thunderbolt shattered the air, dazzling them both, deafening, yet Hyrkallan darted sideways, and the lightning somehow passed him by and tossed another man aside instead. His axe sang down and might have split her in two if White Vish hadn't thrown himself between them and barged Hyrkallan aside. Other men rushed forward now. Zafir slashed with her bladeless knife. Her own men surged to protect her. Hyrkallan's did the same, pulling the two of them apart, but in the heat of it she had no eyes for any other. Slash and lunge, cutting through riders who tried to stand in her way, battered at by axe and sword. Lightning hurling men arching in spasms away from her until there was no lightning left; and then the bladeless knife to cut a bloody swathe, thoughtless of defence. Hyrkallan's riders fell back before her. Her shield cracked under an axe. A corner crumbled away. For an instant Hyrkallan was open. She leaped at him, slicing for his throat, missing as he reeled, smashing her shield into him, too close for him to swing his axe, raising the bladeless knife to end him. The last few pretty thoughts of sparing what men she could scattered and flew away, driven before a howling storm of fury. She had him.

A sword hit her shoulder. Not his. The blow knocked her sideways. The bladeless knife cut air and sliced through another rider's hand, lopping off his fingers. Hyrkallan swung at her, rage for rage. She dodged, and as she did a soldier shot a crossbow, and the quarrel hit her in the chest like the kick of a horse, staggering her back. Her legs went from under her. She crashed. She couldn't breathe. Everything turned numb.

Tuuran smashed into the fight at the head of a wedge, a whirl of slaughter. They tore riders down, one by one. Zafir could yell at him afterwards if she had to, and he'd take it and not bellow in her face for being so bloody stupid, because that's what a Night Watchman did. He sliced a rider's head off and sent a crossbowman flying with the flat of his axe, ripped another dragon-rider out of the way and punched him in the face, took a sword on his shield and swept the man's legs out from under him. A bugger trying not to kill them. Much easier to slice them into ribbons.

A last bolt of lightning thundered. He saw Zafir, her and Hyrkallan. He smashed another rider out of the way.

She couldn't breathe. Could hardly move. There was blood in her mouth. Hyrkallan stood over her, hatchet raised over her head, grinning like a devil. The axe came down. She rolled and threw up her shield. The gold-glass shattered and the axe blade sparked off the stone floor. Another dragon-rider leaped in, blade raised. A bolt of lightning threw him aside. Hyrkallan swung again. Snacksize was suddenly there, yelling something. Zafir scrabbled back, clutching the bladeless knife. Hyrkallan swatted Snacksize away and came at her again, and this time she had nothing left to throw in his way. She lurched sideways, trying to get her legs underneath her, still trying to breathe. The axe missed by a whisker. She grabbed the haft of it with her shield hand and held on as Hyrkallan heaved back for another swing. The unexpected weight unbalanced him. He flailed a moment, and as he did Zafir drove the bladeless knife into his arm, just above the wrist, as hard as she could, clear through and clean between the bones. She drew back to slash again. Hyrkallan howled and let the axe go. It clattered beside her. They were beyond reason now, both of them. She felt a screaming pain across her chest. She forced herself to roll onto her hands and knees. The rest of the fight was a blur of noise and blood. Hyrkallan grabbed at her. She stumbled away, but he caught her and wrapped one bloody hand around her neck, fingers crushing her. She stabbed at him with the bladeless knife, but he caught her wrist with his other hand. His fingers squeezed, his blood running onto her from the wound she'd given him. She punched him under the chin with her shield hand, gold-glass mashing his face, breaking his nose and teeth, then clawed at his throat, strangling him back, pouring every ounce of herself into killing him. The noises around her could have been anything now. Her strength was fading, but his was ebbing too …

Hyrkallan let go her throat and pulled suddenly back. She pressed after him, but something stopped her, an arm around her waist.

'No!' He was getting away. 'No!' She slashed with the knife. Something grasped her wrist, far too strong. Men around Hyrkallan were pulling him away, and it took a moment to see that they were hers. Hyrkallan tried to throw them off, but they were too strong, too many.

The arm around her waist was like an iron bar, the hand around her wrist a manacle. She pushed back hard and tried to twist free, but whoever it was wouldn't let her go. Whoever it was, in that moment she would have cut him to pieces.

'Holiness.'

Tuuran. She rammed her elbow into his ribs. It was like hitting a mountain.

'Holiness. It's done, Holiness. It's done.' He wrapped her tight, forcing her to be still, crushing her.

'Let me go!' she screamed.

He let her go. She whirled to face him and lashed the bladeless knife at his face. He didn't stop her, didn't try to get out of the way, and so he was lucky she caught herself before she sliced him in two. She stood there, quivering.

'Your throne, Holiness.' Tuuran pointed. Opposite the barricades, against the wall she'd stepped through, sat the Silver King's throne. Her mother's throne. *Her* throne. Thin twists of white stone curled and entwined around one another, etched with tiny grooves filled with liquid silver. Two crossed spears rose from the back. A dragon, wings spread, arched over the top. The dragon was white stone too, but its head would move to watch whoever had the attention of the queen on her throne, or whoever carried thoughts within them of deceit and treachery.

'Your throne,' Tuuran said again, and dropped to his knees and bowed his head. The last of Hyrkallan's riders threw down their swords and axes and crowded together, sullen, holding the lolling Jaslyn, still dazed from Zafir's greeting of lightning. Zafir staggered. Her armour was mangled where the crossbow quarrel had hit her. It hurt, deep and burning, but she pushed the pain away and walked to the throne of the Silver King and sat, took off her gauntlets and held up her hand and showed the ring she wore to anyone who cared to see. The Speaker's Ring, the one thing the Taiytakei had never thought to take away from her. She laid her hands on the arms of her throne, skin on stone. *Her* throne.

Home.

Tuuran knelt before her. Zafir offered her hand. He kissed the Speaker's Ring.

'Holiness. Zafir. Speaker. Dragon-queen of the Silver City once more.'

Out in the Hall of Princes and further away men were still fighting. Halfteeth dragged Hyrkallan to Zafir's feet and forced him to his knees. 'Bow!' he said.

'Never!' Hyrkallan spat at her. 'Never to this ... this murderous whore.'

Dimly, Zafir remembered that Halfteeth was supposed to be on the eyrie, shovelling shit from one pile to another and back again for what he'd done after Farakkan. Yet here he was, and now he pulled Hyrkallan to the remnants of the barricade and held him there, a knife to his throat, begging Zafir with his eyes to let him do it. The echoes of steel and lightning fell away and died. An uneasy silence thundered across the Octagon and flowed into the halls beyond. In dribs and drabs Tuuran's makeshift legion dribbled through, pushing dejected dragon-riders before them. Ignoring Hyrkallan's strangled shouts to them to fight on, to let him fall, they held their ground but didn't charge. They watched, that was all, while Zafir's soldiers came one by one to kneel before her dragon-throne; and as they pledged themselves the little stone dragon of the throne peered into their hearts. At the last a handful of prisoners came shoved through the barricade. Tuuran led them to Zafir and stood beside them.

'These men were Adamantine once,' he said. 'Like me. Fierce, proud, strong.' He turned to them. 'Brothers, this is your speaker. Holiness, I will stand with these men if they in turn will stand with me.'

Zafir stared. The Adamantine Guard had been ten thousand strong when she'd left, and all of them dressed and armed the same, so of course she didn't know them. But the way they looked at her, all of them ... they met her eye and they remembered. They knew her. She saw it in them.

She held out her hand, the ring on her finger.

'Choose, guardsmen,' said Tuuran, and she could feel how he wanted them at his side, how they were his brothers, left behind so long ago, and she knew too that he'd hang them himself if they refused, every last one of them.

She thought they would, but then one came and stood before her. He looked hard at the ring and then at her face.

'Do you remember me?' she asked him.

For long moments he didn't answer; but when he did, he dropped to his knees and pressed his face to the floor. 'Holiness. Speaker. My life is yours. From birth to death, nothing more and nothing less.'

The others followed then, one by one sinking at her feet. When they were done, Zafir leaned back in the dragon-throne of the Pinnacles and tipped her head as dead men were slowly dragged away from around her in smears of blood.

I am home.

The Empty Sands, the Konsidar and the Lair of Samim

The city of Dhar Thosis lies in ash and splinters, destroyed by the dragon-queen. The sea lords of the Taiytakei reel and cry for retribution. In mighty Vespinarr, richest city in all the seven worlds, Vey Rin T'Varr struts in his dead brother's shoes, ruler now of all he surveys, yet his nights are filled with screams and visions, with nightmare memories of dragons.

Around the Godspike lies the debris of the eyrie's fall: shattered glasships plunge into storm-dark annihilation; the last few Elemental Men, crippled and bleeding, nurse their wounds; a slaughter of ravening white-painted men woken from their waiting in the depths of the Queverra howl and murder their way across the desert for the Black Moon their god. Above and beyond them all, the Arbiter of the Dralamut Red Lin Feyn has passed her judgment on those who consort with dragons, and sentence has been executed on all but one.

Baros Tsen T'Varr, master of the dragon-eyrie, must face his crimes and die.

6

Baros Tsen and the Dragon Silence

Sixteen months before landfall

Inside her egg the dragon Silence is awake. Little-one thoughts mumble and murmur nearby. Baros Tsen and his lover lie asleep and dreaming. The urge comes strong to burst this fragile shell, to devour and set about whatever fiery conquest takes a dragon's whim. But the dragon Silence holds back. Awakenings can be difficult. It takes time to assemble the memories of so many lives. They lie in scattered disarray struggling to cohere, to piece themselves together, to order and structure.

The oldest memories are the clearest. A second moon, dark and unholy, chasing the sun across the sky, a little closer with every dawn until the Splintering comes and rips the world apart, and the other moon, the dark moon of the dead goddess, shatters, and its pieces fall across the earth ...

The Black Moon. He has escaped his prison in Xibaiya.

Three figures in silver and white.

The moon sorcerers of the Diamond Isles. Echoes of half-gods, lingering when they should have known better.

Other flashes. Little ones with pale skin. Strange words, old sigils. The Azahl Pillar. The skin of a killer. A future foreseen. The dead goddess reborn, her dark unholy moon rising once more from the southern sky to smother the world in ice and darkness.

The grey dead come with the golden knife. They have called the Black Moon to rise again. Do not let the splinters become whole, dragon.

Baros Tsen snores and dreams useless dreams of peace and desert sunsets. The dragon Silence reaches into the weft and weave of the world, a tinge to every thread, hunting. Another memory circles like an angry moon.

You were a half-god, dragon. You all were.

West towards the setting sun the essence of the world shudders. A surge of something ancient echoes across deserts and fades and dies. Unborn, the dragon Silence rides it to its source. Diamond Eye is on a white stone wall with the Black Moon beside him. Diamond Eye. Brother. Executioner. Mate.

Veils of alchemy fall, cut like curtain silks. The great dragon Diamond Eye wakes and remembers, sharply and catastrophically aware of what has been done. Then the Black Moon strikes again with the touch of the old goddess who always takes something away.

Senses in tidal waves. Images. Diamond Eye's thoughts are as clear as polished crystal now, as still glacial water. The dragon's tail slashes the air and lashes a spear-sharp tip through an Elemental Man. His head and torso explode in a shower of gore and splintered bone; the rest scatters in bloody pieces. As the great dragon burns in fury, Silence rides quiet and unseen among his thoughts. She watches, gleefully, the beginning of something endless. Little ones scream and crisp. Glass glows cherry red. Molten gold smears and runs while armoured men flare and burn. Scorched air and cold roaring wind; and in the midst of the great dragon's rage, the world-shudder comes again and again, dragon after dragon roused from their alchemical poison, knife cut to the will of the Black Moon instead.

The unborn Silence writhes in exalted frenzy, flies and burns. This! *This!* Killers come whispering on the wind, but nothing in this world, not one thing, not all the power of every last soul stretched and merged together can touch the Black Moon, nothing but the Starknife he already carries at his side. Glasships gather and lightning storms. Diamond Eye falls, overwhelmed. The eyrie is cut loose from the chains that hold it high. It plunges into the annihilation of the storm-dark. The little ones think it is victory, but they are wrong. The Black Moon is architect and master of the storms between worlds, the annihilation unleashed in his Splintering of the world.

It is not an end. It is a beginning.

'Baros Tsen T'Varr!'
The evening peace of the desert took him in its arms, wrapped like

an old lover, a faithful familiar warmth. From the top of a lonely mesa far away from anywhere he watched the sunset, glorious fiery reds in the sky while the sand turned to liquid gold. He heard Kalaiya call his name, and then felt her warmth beside him, leaning into him. Another day and all this peace would be over ...

'Baros Tsen T'Varr!'

Baros Tsen T'Varr opened his eyes. A light flared and flickered, near, bright enough to stir him, then vanished. The voice echoed through the tunnel. There was something not quite human about it. He shook himself and sat up where he'd drifted asleep, sprawled on the front of a gold-glass sled. The only light down here came from flakes of white stone that glowed through splits and cracks in the walls around him. The same stone as inside his eyrie, with the same soft light, waxing and waning with the rise and fall of the sun. It might have been something to think about, how the same enchanted stone appeared again and again in so many disparate places, but the queue for his attention was long and loud just now, and didn't have much space in it for anything that wasn't about death, and how to avoid it.

There were a lot of things, it seemed, that were just a touch pressing in that regard. Being in a cave at the bottom of a chasm five miles beneath the surface of a murderously inhospitable desert, for example. When he'd fallen asleep, top of his list had been how he couldn't find the way up and out. Close behind that came the very strong chance that, even if he *did* find a way, the climb would simply be beyond a fat old t'varr whose idea of exercise was levering himself in and out of the bath, and occasionally shouting at slaves. A strong third was the part about dying parched in the desert even if he *did* ever get out, and then there was always the small matter of the dormant dragon's egg on the sled behind him that might hatch at any moment. He could never quite figure where on the list that one ought to go, but definitely above weird glowing stones.

A figure stood at the edge of the darkness.

'Kalaiya!' Tsen sat up and nudged Kalaiya awake. So there *was* someone else here after all. Given all that had happened in the last month, it was natural to assume that whoever it was would want to murder him. Pretty much everyone wanted him dead these days, and he couldn't even blame them, not really. He hadn't meant Dhar

Thosis to burn down, but he *had* sent his dragon and its murderous rider Zafir, and when he'd tried to stop her, well, that had worked out rather badly. After that everything had gone horribly wrong, and thousands had died in fire.

His slave. His responsibility. Everyone knew it, even him.

The figure at the edge of the darkness held out her hands. Specks of light flashed across the space between them. Tsen tried to duck. Kalaiya opened her eyes and screamed. Something hit him like a fist in the chest; he felt it shift into liquid and skitter up his skin like a giant centipede. It wrapped itself around his neck and instantly set as hard as metal. He struggled and clawed at it, panicked for a moment and then, as nothing else happened, calmed himself. It was there now, whatever it was, and he'd already been doomed anyway.

Kalaiya had a collar around her throat too. It was made of goldglass. Tsen sighed. He just didn't have the strength any more.

'Do you know who I am, Baros Tsen?' rang out the voice.

Tsen tugged at the collar one more time, not that it did the slightest bit of good, and then gave up. *You don't have any friends any more. None. Everyone simply wants you gone, and they have their reasons, and they are good ones. So just take it, you stupid fat t'varr, and die with as much grace as you can, because frankly you largely agree with them.* And he did. A whole city, its glass palaces smashed and shattered. He hadn't meant it, but if the whole ravening world crying for his blood frankly didn't give a fig for whether or not he'd *meant* it, well, frankly he couldn't really see how they were wrong. *Sorry* didn't really cut it, not when you'd carelessly flattened a city.

Thought you were so clever, didn't you? He sighed and held out a hand to Kalaiya. Some day, maybe, he might stop hating himself. Some day very soon, by the looks of things.

'I'm sorry, my love.' He closed his eyes and squeezed Kalaiya's hand and wept, because really, after everything he'd done and all he'd been through, he'd well and truly had enough. All this way and then days starving in a cave in the dark, unable to find the way out, and now this. *I don't want to run any more. Just let it end.*

Red Lin Feyn, the Arbiter of the Dralamut, stood as a shadow amid the dancing lights of her enchanted globes. There didn't seem to be anyone with her, but wherever the Arbiter went her killers were always on hand. Stupidest thing of all was that he'd never wanted to run away in the first place. Take it like a man. Die with honour. All that claptrap; but for a while he'd really meant it.

The Arbiter reached out a hand. The sled beneath him moved, drifting closer until it stopped in front of her. Tsen looked up. Dear forbidden gods but this chasm was deep. And yes, yes, he knew – because his dutiful tutors had told him so and he had dutifully memorised it – that the depth of the Queverra from its lip to its very lowest tier was some five miles. But five miles was just a number when heard in a school room, a curiosity and a raised eyebrow. Far different if you had to climb it. Which, of course, could be avoided if the Arbiter summarily strangled him on the spot, so maybe that was no bad thing. In that haphazard madness of hopeless resignation Tsen almost laughed. As a way to avoid a lot of steps went, strangulation struck him as perhaps a bit extreme. *But we could also strike exhaustion, dehydration, starvation and falling off a cliff from the list of things that might shortly kill you. Isn't that simply wonderful?*

No. Shut up.

The Arbiter put out a hand to touch the sled as it reached her. In the gentle strobe of the swirling globes, Tsen saw a dead man on the sand behind her. The body looked as though it had been ripped to pieces by a thousand knives. It took him another moment to realise that the shredded bloody clothes were the robe of an Elemental Man.

Oh.

Despite everything else, *that* was truly terrifying. It made even the voices in his head shut up for a second.

The Arbiter of the Dralamut cocked her head. She didn't wear the headdress or the flaming feather robe, only the plain white tunic of an enchantress. For all he knew this was another skin-shifter. She *was* draped in the Arbiter's shards of glass, though, and they were stained red and dripping with fresh blood, and there was a dead killer on the ground behind her, and so, really, did it matter right here and now who she really was?

'Another pretend Baros Tsen?' she asked. 'Or is it truly you?'

Tsen dropped to his knees and bowed. 'Lady Arbiter. Judge me as I know you must, but my slave is innocent.'

'I am Red Lin Feyn, daughter in blood of Feyn Charin and the Crimson Sunburst, enchantress and navigator. I was the Arbiter of the Dralamut until two days ago, but I no longer claim that right. I have discharged that duty.' Her eyes narrowed. 'Who are you really?'

'I am really Baros Tsen T'Varr,' said Tsen.

The collar around his neck contracted. He choked and clawed at it. Beside him Kalaiya screamed, but Tsen found he couldn't make a sound. He couldn't breathe no matter how his lungs pumped and his ribs and belly heaved. He flailed, staggered to his feet, lurched a few steps, but the Arbiter simply backed away with such grace that she seemed almost to be floating. The chasm darkness closed on him. He fell forward. As he closed his eyes he saw Kalaiya clutching at her throat.

I'm sorry, my love.

He came round again a minute later. The Arbiter was sitting between them, perched on the edge of a gold-glass disc. 'Baros Tsen T'Varr. The real one then.' She smiled and then laughed. 'Welcome to the Queverra. You are free to go.'

'What?' The collar had gone from around his neck.

'The Arbiter has passed judgment. I found you guilty in your absence of complicity in the razing of Dhar Thosis. Your body was found in a gondola close to the Godspike. They will take it back to Khalishtor to be flayed and hanged by the feet. Your name will be damned and stricken from history. Your family and slaves will be put to flame and spear, except you don't have any, so that's not so bad. They will parade your corpse through the streets of Khalishtor bound in your own entrails. Half the city will line the way to spit on you, and then they will bury you in a communal latrine somewhere in the hills and no one will ever know where. They have your body for a second time, which is what matters to them, and so I doubt anyone else is still looking for you. Although given that it *is* the second time, I would still be careful. Nevertheless, you may go. I suppose the second body was the skin-shifter then, was it?'

Tsen shrugged. Last he'd seen Sivan, the shifter had looked like himself and had had a spear stuck through him. Seemed best not to mention that, though.

'Free, lady?'

'In the end I believed you. I believe you tried to stop it. Because of your enchantress's faith. Because of your rider-slave's murderous honesty. You were stupid, Tsen, but not evil, and the Dralamut has more use for you alive than dead. Many questions remain. The Arbiter condemns you to death because the Arbiter must, but I no longer wear that mask. I am merely Red Lin Feyn of the Dralamut once more.'

Too good to be true, t'varr. Life isn't this kind. Wisdom suggested shutting up and taking Kalaiya's hand and walking away as fast as he possibly could and seeing how far he got, but the devil inside wouldn't let go. And there was still the list of things that were going to kill him, and he had a hundred questions of his own about how she'd found him and why she'd thought he was a shifter, and how much she knew about what lay beneath it all, but one thing more than anything else ... 'You called yourself daughter of Feyn Charin and the Crimson Sunburst, lady. Why, when the Crimson Sunburst was an anathema?'

Red Lin Feyn chuckled and nodded. She let out a long deep breath. 'A change is coming, t'varr. A catastrophe, perhaps. You see it in the swelling of the storm-dark and in the cracked needle beside the Godspike. You see it in the rise of the sorcerers of Aria and in the necropolis of the Ice Witch and in the dead that do not rest in Merizikat and even here. In other things. In the storm-dark itself. The skin-shifters know.' She looked across the darkness at the shredded killer on the sand, paused again and smiled. 'In your history, when the Crimson Sunburst appeared at the foot of Mount Solence with her army of golems, what became of her, Baros Tsen?'

'The Elemental Men fought her, and she was defeated.'

'So she was.' Red Lin Feyn turned away. 'Disappear, Baros Tsen T'Varr. You, too, will find it is not so hard.'

'Why do you want the egg?' Tsen blinked. *Of all the questions you might have asked, you ask her that? What do you care about the Xibaiya-damned dragon egg? Let her have it and good riddance!*

But the question had popped into his mind from somewhere else. He looked about, bemused, as Red Lin Feyn shook her head.

'But the answer is in your thoughts, little one,' he said. 'The grey dead have called the Black Moon to rise ...' Tsen flew a hand to his mouth and gasped. The words had come from his own lips but they didn't belong; they weren't his at all, as though a stranger had somehow put them there, and they made no sense. 'I ...'

He jumped as a sharp cracking noise broke the quiet. It came from the sled, and it took Tsen far too long to understand what it was. He gawped as the dragon egg cracked and burst apart in a flurry of wings and claws ...

Two furious eyes gleamed. *I am Silence.*

Tsen squealed. Red Lin Feyn snapped out an arm and hurled a marble of glass. The hatchling dodged and shot into the air, vanishing into the shadows of the Queverra's stifling gloom. The Arbiter's light-globes raced after the dragon, illuminating a wheel of wing, a whip of tail, a slash and arc of neck and claw as Silence wove and flew. Red Lin Feyn's glass marble hit the sled and flashed into a hollow sphere, swallowing both the sled and the broken remains of the egg. She threw another and then another, streaking up into the chasm, but the dragon darted between them, racing ever further away.

I will not be made into a tomb.

'I cannot give you a choice, little dragon.'

The hatchling wheeled and dived back at them, spitting fire. Tsen scuttled to the sled, cowering behind the Arbiter's glass. The Arbiter grew a shield around them. The fire washed over it.

Choices are not yours to give, little one. I am far more than you. The dragon soared upward. The Arbiter threw down a piece of glass and grew it into a sled of her own; but when she stepped on it she only watched, staring as the dragon flew away into the darkness above.

'I'd need an Elemental Man to catch him.' She shook her head and looked at the body beside her on the floor, cut to ribbons. 'Sadly, we are no longer on speaking terms. This is unfortunate, Baros Tsen. I think it was important that the skin-shifters of Xibaiya had their dragon soul. I wish I could be sure. I do not yet understand what it was for.'

Tsen tried to pretend he hadn't noticed the dead Elemental Man – better to gouge out his eyes than see something like this – but there was no getting away from it. A killer, murdered by the Arbiter of the Dralamut. He'd heard of Elemental Men being killed exactly three times in the entire history of ever, and it had always been by a dragon. *See, t'varr? She can't let you go, not really, not with what you've seen. She has to kill you now. Both of you. Any chance you might do something about that? Or are you simply going to walk onto the knife when she holds it out?*

'I see nothing,' he muttered. *Do something? Like what? Wag my finger and tut at her?*

The Arbiter smiled. Tsen curled up and withered inside. *Anything, t'varr. Just at least try not to be so miserably useless.*

Red Lin Feyn walked to the glass globe that enveloped the sled. She touched it and it shrank back into a marble, crushing everything inside out of existence. Tsen thought he caught a glimpse of something dark and a flash of purple light as the glass collapsed. A flicker of the storm-dark? He shivered.

Coward.

'Come with me,' said the Arbiter. She beckoned him on to her floating disc. 'You can answer my questions about your skin-shifter friends, and we shall see where that leads us. Then you may go.'

Pathetic useless coward. I hope she takes Kalaiya first so you see the light go out of her eyes and know you did nothing, tried nothing, to save her. 'Am I offered a choice?' His voice trembled. Shame at himself, that was.

'Stay at the bottom of the abyss if you prefer, Baros Tsen!' Red Lin Feyn laughed. 'Or confess yourself to the Elemental Men, or to the Crown of the Sea Lords!' If she was laughing at him, he deserved it.

I am not a murderer. I'm not a killer.

His voices laughed. *Stupid t'varr. Tell that to the thousands who burned in Dhar Thosis!*

But he did nothing in the end, and so Red Lin Feyn carried him and Kalaiya out of the chasm on her sled, and Tsen spent every moment of their flight expecting her to push him off, and every moment in between thinking that he should do the same to her, and yet neither ever moved.

When they reached the top, Red Lin Feyn let him and Kalaiya off by the rim of the abyss. The desert air was quiet and still and rasping hot, dry, scraping at his throat and tight across his skin. He sat quietly and held his head in his hands, waiting for his eyes, accustomed to days of starlight darkness, to embrace the desert sun. When they finally acquiesced enough to see more than bright, bright and more bright, he looked about him. They had stopped amid the chaos and debris of what had once been a dozen slaver camps. Across the abyss of the Queverra the chasm cliffs rose higher, bright in the sun, a pale ruddy pink in the shade. Closer in, juts and spars and mangled walls of mustard stone erupted from the sand, etched and carved and sliced into curls and arcs and windswept bubbles. Swirls of pale-coloured lines stained them in twists and turns, while littered across the sand lay a tale of slaughter and ruin, bones picked clean but not yet bleached white by the sun, rags of clothes, broken tents, abandoned sleds for dragging things across the dunes, slave cages torn down, their doors smashed open. The sky burned a dazzling blue that scoured his eyes. The disc of Red Lin Feyn's glasship turned lazily, catching the sun and casting bright will-o'-the-wisp sparks dancing across the sand. There was a skeleton nearby with its skull split in two. An axe, perhaps?

Still and quiet and death everywhere. In the distance Tsen heard the mournful cry of an eagle.

It struck him then: he was alive. He sat there, mute and acquiescent, and took it all in, half of him wondering when the Arbiter would get bored with her charade and kill him, the other half dreaming ridiculously impossible ways he might make an escape, both halves berating him for being such a pathetic and useless coward.

'It won't be easy.' Kalaiya sat beside him and stroked his hair. 'But you're a resourceful man. No one is looking for us.' Yet she had him wrong for once – it wasn't fear of a new life that had him clenched up so tight.

Dress your cowardice as you will, t'varr; that doesn't change its colour.

Red Lin Feyn was at her glasship, sitting on the steps of her golden gondola agleam in the sun. She was staring at the maw of the Queverra. An Arbiter killing a killer. Something never done, and so perhaps she had her reasons for contemplation; but she had a glasship to take her home, too, and a home to go to, and Tsen had neither.

This wouldn't do. He picked himself up, took a deep breath, dusted himself down and took Kalaiya's hand. Here was the death and ruin of a camp overrun right enough, but sooner or later Red Lin Feyn would ask her questions, whatever they were, hear his useless answers, and then, at best, do as she'd promised and leave; and among the discard and scatter were surely all manner of useful things for a fat old t'varr left alone in this wilderness. Probably no food, but perhaps a sled? Whoever had been here, they'd left in a hurry, and once he started rummaging it didn't take long to find everything he'd need to live for a few days and a few more things he might sell or trade. He supposed it wasn't a bad place to wait around for a while, not with the river running into the end of the abyss. Sooner or later they'd have to walk, of course, and when they did they'd end up in Dhar Thosis because there simply wasn't anywhere else to go for the best part of a thousand miles. If whoever was left in the ruin of that place made him into a slave or recognised his face and hanged him, well then he probably deserved it.

But we could at least try to find a less mournful fate, eh? There was a villa waiting for him in the Dominion, if he could find it. On the mountainous coast halfway between Brons and Merizikat, looking down over a lazy sun-soaked fishing town called Dahat that no one had ever heard of because no one ever went there. The orchards on the slopes above grew some of the best apples for wine-making, and the villa had a fine bathhouse. If, somehow, he could get there.

'There is a dragon loose again,' said the Arbiter, when at last she moved. 'I have to warn the Elemental Men, and so I must return to the eyrie. I'm afraid you will have to come with me.'

Tsen considered this. So she'd changed her mind, had she, and now she meant to hand them over? He'd be hanged as he deserved to be, and he'd been expecting it since ... well, since the moment she'd told him he was free. Couldn't last, a thing like that. The world was never kind enough. *Here it comes ...*

He had a knife in his belt, taken from the abandoned camp. He drew it out and dropped it in the sand. 'It is no more than is right, lady.' *Capitulation. Truly I have a gift for it.* 'I had arranged to own a quiet place to live out my twilight days in the Dominion, should the need arise. Let Kalaiya be taken there to live out her life in peace.' He hadn't the first idea how to get from the Queverra to anywhere useful anyway. *Out here in the desert, where starving to death and dying of thirst vie with one another to be the entertainment of the day? We'd just die anyway.*

His inner voices, usually so quick to scorn, offered only contemptuous silence.

'I suppose a little apple wine and a particularly long soak in a particularly hot bath are quite out of the question before we go?' he asked in the spirit of being at least a *little* rebellious, but neither the voices nor Red Lin Feyn seemed to hear him.

'When my business is done with the eyrie,' she said, at last meeting his eye, 'I will take you to the Bawar Bridge. Beyond that is up to you.'

The dragon Silence alights atop a stone pillar amid a desert wasteland. Under the glare of the sun she watches. She assembles the last of her memories. As the little ones fly away to the Godspike where the eyrie has fallen, Silence roams ahead, strong, high, unseen in the night sky. She ghosts among their thoughts. The white sorceress Red Lin Feyn already knows that the grey dead have called the Black Moon to rise. She knows that the dead skin-shifters of Xibaiya wander abroad, and that they yearn for a dragon soul, but she does not know why. Silence, who knows very well, will not tell her.

This new hatchling flesh she wears has become brilliant. Metallic crimson scales darken to near black along her belly. The body is strong, and will grow large. Even so, this world is not safe any more. She will find her way to another; until she does she hides under sand and high in the sky and wanders the thoughts of the little ones. The grey dead have called the Black Moon to rise. It is the end of all worlds.

They flew in Red Lin Feyn's gondola over the Desert of Thieves. With every hour they drew closer to the Godspike, Tsen felt his tension rising. Red Lin Feyn had some of his apple wine (stolen from his personal cellar, he reminded himself, and then reminded himself again that everyone had thought he was dead, and that it would be prudent not to complain), and was obliging enough to share. Not his best vintage, which was a shame. They traded stories. Tsen told Lin Feyn how he'd been snatched by the skin-shifter Sivan on the night the Vespinese had seized his eyrie, how Sivan had dragged him across the desert to the Lair of Samim, up the Jokun river and all the way to Vespinarr, only to sneak him back to help him steal dragon eggs and then drop the eyrie into the storm-dark. Red Lin Feyn stood at the window as he talked, watching mesas and broken caterpillar canyons and spires of dry dead rock roll beneath, the patches of wind-rippled sand, of brown baked earth spiked with cacti and thorn grass. She stopped over one mesa and opened the gondola, walked out and bent down beside a dark stain on the stone. Tsen, for want of anything better to do, squatted beside her. He watched her fingertips brushing the rock, pinching the fine powdered earth, tasting the stone. The sun beat on his back and the wind blew across his face, stealing his sweat to cool him. The air smelled of sand.

'Why did the skin-shifters want a dragon's soul?' she asked. 'Do you know? I will keep your secret if you can help me to understand. "I will not become a tomb." What did the dragon mean?'

Tsen, who didn't have the first idea, turned his back. He walked to the edge of the mesa. *I could always jump, you know. Put us all out of our misery.* 'Is that what Sivan wanted? He never told me. Just that he meant to steal an egg. I thought he was mad. I still do.' He went back to the gondola and came out with a glass of apple wine in one hand, waving his black rod in the other, the key Chay-Liang had enchanted for him to unlock every glass and gold device she had ever made. 'This was what Sivan wanted of *me*.' He shrugged. 'Just this.'

Red Lin Feyn didn't look up from her inspection of the stone. 'Yes. To release the glasships that towed the eyrie. To drop it into the storm-dark to hide his theft of the eggs. I know.'

'He held my Kalaiya, but I like to think I might have done it for him anyway. An end to dragons and everything around them. I did not see if it worked, but I fear it did not. Was there another enchanter? Did more glasships come in time? I never knew how quickly it would fall. In the end it was more like a feather than a stone. Sivan did not linger to see the result.' He looked out over the jumble-maze of cliffs and mesas, hundreds of miles every which way he turned. *I should have brought my eyrie here and sunk it low. Shonda might never have found me.*

'Your dragon-queen saved them,' said the Arbiter softly. 'She dragged the glassships down after the eyrie, the ones you set free, so their chains could be fastened once more.'

'She has a knack for ruining my schemes, I will confess.' Tsen took a sip of wine and then, on a sudden petulant whim, hurled his black rod as far he could over the mesa cliff. He watched its arc, up dark against the burning blue monochrome sky, and then down, following it with his eyes against the facing crags. He had no idea where it ended up. Somewhere inaccessible, that was all. 'There. The last of all I used to be. Gone. And good riddance.' He took another sip of wine, a big one this time. It wasn't as though he had anything much to lose. *At least drunks die happy.* Who had said that? Vey Rin probably, back in their days in Cashax.

Red Lin Feyn laughed. 'Lord Shonda decided he would leave the eyrie against my order. Your dragon-rider slave returned him. When she came back she found the eyrie falling. I wonder, sometimes, why she didn't simply let it go, but she didn't. She brought the glassships down one by one. When she was done she branded Shonda with his own slave mark. Twice.'

Tsen almost choked on his wine. For that alone he would have given the dragon-queen her freedom. 'I suppose you sentenced her to die for what she did in Dhar Thosis. As you sentenced me?'

'Everyone stood and watched, and did nothing. I suppose by then no one was in much of a mood to try and stop her.' Red Lin Feyn shook herself. 'She was a slave who obeyed her master, t'varr. I could have let her live, but she showed no mercy, no remorse, nothing but a gleeful delight at the murder she had brought. You sent your Elemental Man to stop her, and she killed him. She knew you meant to call her back, and she did it anyway. That is what saves you, and what damned her.' Red Lin Feyn ran her fingers across the dark-stained earth again. 'This is where it happened. This is where your Elemental Man confronted her. This is where her dragon killed him.'

Tsen wondered how the Arbiter could know, how she could pick one mesa from a thousand others that all looked much alike. He went and squatted beside her, fascinated by the stain on the stone. *The blood of an Elemental Man.* That was twice in two days he'd seen such a rare thing.

Kalaiya came and sat beside him. Red Lin Feyn watched them, looking from one to the other and back again. She seemed sad. Distant, at least. 'A dragon hatched and escaped on the night you left,' she said. 'Amid the chaos. Weeks later your dragon-slave hunted it. She killed it here in the exact same spot. Curious, don't you think?' For a moment Lin Feyn's face grew dark. 'A city, Baros Tsen. A whole city, and you sent her to burn it. How could you take such a gamble with one like her?'

'To show the Vespinese for what they were! To save my sea lord's house and fleet! Because I had an Elemental Man ready to stop her, and I did not consider that he might fail, because Elemental Men *never* fail!' He wrung his hands and glared. 'Or so we are told, lady.' Easy to be dry and cynical about most things, especially when most things seemed to revolve around some new way to die or somebody else who wanted to kill him; but Dhar Thosis ... Dhar Thosis would be with him for ever. No matter that he'd tried to stop it, a sea lord had been hung from the broken shards of his own palace, the heart of his city burned to cinders. That's why Baros Tsen deserved to die. *That's why, little voices, I don't listen to you any more. Call me a coward all you like!*

The three of them left, drifting away across the sky in Lin Feyn's golden gondola. They talked a little more as the night wore on and through the day that followed. The fractured stone of the mesas and canyons gave way to sand and spires and wadis, and then a gentle rise to a plateau and a jagged cliff, and beyond that a sea of dunes, the fringe of the Empty Sands. Tsen and Kalaiya took turns to stand at the window and watch it pass as Red Lin Feyn asked question after question about the skin-shifter Sivan, about where they had stopped and when, how they travelled, until Tsen had told her everything he could possibly remember about the Lair of Samim and the Xizic harvesters, about the strange shaft in the desert and the white stone tunnel deep under the dunes, about the Jokun gorge and Sivan's little cave-home tucked behind a waterfall, until it was clear that he didn't have the answers that Lin Feyn sought. As they crossed the last cliff and started over the sands, Tsen saw the stain of the storm-dark around the Godspike in the distance. And yes, he was afraid to die, no matter Lin Feyn's promises, but the shame was worse. The thought of ever looking another soul in the eye and having them know what he'd done. *Why*, they would all ask, as he asked himself, *why would you do such a thing?* And he had no answer. Hubris. Stupid arrogant pride. What else could it be?

The glasship began its ascent, rising past the cloud of the storm-dark. Tsen saw scattered specks on the ground that caught the sun and seemed to glow. Red Lin Feyn peered through her farscope, trying to find the eyrie, and found the sky around the Godspike filled with bright glasships glittering in the sun, dozens of them. Dozens upon dozens, but the eyrie wasn't there.

They returned to the ground to search for someone who might know where it had gone, and there Tsen again saw the shapes that had shone in the sun, only now he saw them for what they were: bodies. The traders from the desert tribes who made their camps out here, butchered, sprawled in brilliant-white ankle-length robes stained with blood, scattered like confetti across the sand. Among them were other men, naked but with their skin painted white. The ghost-men of the Queverra had swarmed the camps, slaughtering everyone, and been slaughtered in their turn by lightning from above. There was no one left alive. Yet more glasships hung around the fringes of the storm-dark, some high, some low, some alone, others in twos and threes. Meandering aimlessly or simply floating adrift like bewildered cubs beside a murdered mother. Eventually Red Lin Feyn spotted a camp on the edge of the storm-dark's shadow. The Vespinese. She went alone. Tsen, knowing what was good for him, kept well out of sight.

'The Vespinese sent the eyrie into the storm-dark after all,' Lin Feyn told him when she came back. She smiled and then laughed, as if relieved and also bitterly sad. 'You got your way. Shonda is gone. The Vespinese are left with nothing.'

'The *dragons* are gone,' said Tsen. 'That's all that matters.' And everyone who lived on the eyrie presumably gone with them. All dead now. He closed his eyes. The dragon-queen, yes, she was wicked and heartless, but the rest … the alchemist Bellepheros, in another life, could have been a friend. The enchantress Chay-Liang was as close as he'd had to one for a long time. There were others. Many good men and women, and none had deserved to die. 'Did any escape?' he asked, but he already knew the answer from

Lin Feyn's eyes, and so he shuddered and tried to shake away the memories of all those faces.

Best not to think about it.

Nothing you could have done to stop it anyway.

And maybe, perhaps, with a bit of luck, mostly it was those bastard Vespinese who'd gone crashing into the storm-dark, or else got themselves eaten by the monster dragon before it fell, and as for the rest, surely some must have slipped away? Scuttled to hide in the desert? There had been no shortage of sleds after the Vespinese came …

Yes. You keep telling yourself that, t'varr. Keep hiding from what you've done.

For a long while the Arbiter didn't speak. She guided her glasship around the storm-dark through the night among the camps, and through the next day too, looking. She didn't say, but she was searching for someone quite specific, Tsen thought, and he could see from the slump of her shoulders how it saddened her she didn't find what she wanted. She looked older. Older and beaten and defeated by some loss of which she would never speak.

'Where now?' Tsen asked, as the next day's light began to fade. Lin Feyn would surely return to the Dralamut, or to Khalishtor, and he was quite certain he didn't want to be going anywhere near either, and equally quite sure he wasn't about to be given a choice; but there didn't seem to be an obvious way to ask if Kalaiya might get dropped off somewhere along the way. Tayuna for preference, but anywhere would do if it had a harbour and plenty of ships and there was a chance she could get a passage across the storm-dark to the Dominion and the little Dahat estate he'd quietly bought for their later years.

With apple orchards and a winery and one of the best bathhouses in the province …

He let out a little sigh.

'I told you, Baros Tsen. I will take you to the Bawar Bridge.' It took him a moment to realise that she didn't mean only Kalaiya. She meant both of them. And yes, she'd said it, but he hadn't ever truly *believed* her.

'Lady …'

'I said you were free, Baros Tsen.' She turned away. 'There are dead enough for the ghosts of Dhar Thosis, and too many honest souls already sent to Xibaiya. I've had enough of it. You can go.'

Free?

While the Arbiter retired to her little upstairs cabin, and Kalaiya dozed propped against his shoulder, he mulled the word over. Rolled it around in his head. He even believed it this time. The Bawar Bridge. Close to Hanjaadi, which was an entire city of Vespinese lapdogs, which in turn brought problems of its own, and Tayuna would be much more preferable indeed; but it seemed churlish, under the circumstances, to object ...

Free. He couldn't stop rolling it around in his head.

A tapping on the window disturbed his musing. He tried to ignore it at first, but they were a thousand feet in the air out in the Empty Sands and it didn't go away, and that was quite distracting since he really couldn't imagine what it could be. A bird? Out here? He opened his eyes and peered.

A claw was tapping on the glass. At the window a hatchling dragon looked in at him. Baros Tsen T'Varr screamed as he'd never screamed before and fell off his chair, and stared and rubbed his eyes and looked again, but the dragon was gone.

'A dream.' Kalaiya held his head and stroked his hair. 'You fell asleep, Tsen. It was just a dream.'

He wasn't at all sure he'd been asleep, but he decided to believe her anyway.

7

The Jokun River

There were ports and there were ports. There was Tayuna, where the Vespinese were universally despised, and then there was Hanjaadi, vassal state to the mountain lords whose distant masters were merely roundly disliked, but it felt graceless to complain to the Arbiter about her choice of destination. Not handing him over to the Elemental Men to be hanged in Khalishtor or flying him out of the desert in her glasship – those seemed quite magnanimous enough and, if Tsen was honest and chose to look at it with any kind of critical eye, bewildering to the point of suspicion. He couldn't quite shake the notion that something bad waited for him by the Bawar Bridge, but pushing his luck, a trait indulged too often of late, struck him as an invitation to Red Lin Feyn to change her mind and drag him back to the Dralamut, and such alternatives didn't bear much scrutiny. Besides, there was Kalaiya to think of. Thus Tsen opted to be small and discreet, to be as innocuous as possible in the hope that the former Arbiter might begin to forget that he was even there. Which, in a gondola where three people shared a space no larger than one decent-sized room, was a challenge, but one he took with relish.

It must have been an odd sight, he thought, when Red Lin Feyn brought her glasship down across the Jokun river in the small hours of the morning darkness, a little before sunrise with the sky already lightening across the desert at their backs, ochres on the horizon to violet and to a deep purple straight above, and still dark enough for the last dawn stars to shine in the west. The gondola came to ground a mile from the bridge where the old desert road ran out into the Lair of Samim and then to the Empty Sands beyond. The road was quiet and, well, deserted, rarely travelled in these days of sleds and glasships, but he still wished the Arbiter might have chosen a more subtle landing place. He kept thinking this while he bowed and scraped and smiled and gave her his thanks.

'Be gone, Baros Tsen. Let your name be forgotten. Find your ship and sail away and let our paths never cross again. Just remember that *I* will not forget. When someone comes to ask a favour of you in my name, no matter how great, remember this day.'

Tsen watched the gondola rise and leave them by the roadside. Lin Feyn had said little about what might happen next among the great and the mighty of Takei'Tarr. Perhaps he shouldn't care. It no longer concerned him, after all, a simple ordinary citizen looking for a way across the storm-dark to visit a business partner at the Sun King's court; but he thought about it anyway. Couldn't not. Red Lin Feyn would be on her way to Khalishtor and Mount Solence to repeat her Arbiter's judgment, but he'd have wagered a deal of what little he had that she'd go to the Dralamut first and the navigators there. Hand in hand, the navigators and the Elemental Men steered the great ship of Takei'Tarr towards whatever destiny awaited it. They did it quietly, and the sea lords barely noticed, but Tsen had had his eyes opened these past months. They were the guides and the enforcers, the helmsmen and the first mates.

The desert air was still. Cold enough to make him shiver. He'd not easily forget the corpse he'd seen at the Arbiter's feet in the Queverra.

'We'd do well to be away from here,' he said and took Kalaiya's hand. A change was coming, was it? A catastrophe? If he was honest, Tsen didn't much understand the meaning behind things like cracked Godspike needles and necropolises and the dead not staying dead, wherever they happened to do it, nor of skin-shifters trying to steal dragon eggs, or oblique insinuations about the Crimson Sunburst; mostly what he knew added up to being very certain that he didn't like the looks of any of it, and should do best to keep as far away as he could. He started to walk then, meaning to do exactly that, setting an easy pace because they were still a mile from the bridge and some twenty more from the city itself, and walking would take the whole day, and there was no point in exhausting himself before lunchtime, not that either of them carried any food. He could barely remember the last time he'd actually walked anywhere. If you didn't count traipsing about the desert after the skin-shifter Sivan, at least.

'There were two villages here once,' he told Kalaiya as they followed the dusty old desert road, arrow-straight with the sunrise
building behind them and the last dawn stars fading as the sky
ahead turned a deep deep blue. 'A long, long time ago before the
Splintering. Each grew and prospered, one each side of the Jokun
estuary, both rich from all the trade around the southern tip of the
Konsidar. The desert wasn't so much of a desert back then.' He
chuckled. 'Isn't it quite bizarre? Almost everything from before
that cataclysm was written into a single book by a secret conclave
of half-mad priests. The Rava. All their lore and knowledge, the
very speaking of which summons death by Elemental Man. What
else do we have? A handful of scraps. A detailed document on the
merits of the various Xizic regions, a complete inventory of the
treasury of Uban, a description of a town that one day became this
city ...'

Kalaiya squeezed his hand and laughed. '"A town full of rich
merchants, and all are large. Bread and meat are abundant, though
you cannot find wine or fruits. Melons and excellent squash are
plentiful and there are enormous quantities of rice. There are many
sweet-water wells. There is a square where on market days huge
numbers of slaves are sold, both male and female. A young girl
of fifteen is worth about six talons, a young man almost as much;
small children are worth about half as much as grown slaves."'

Tsen stopped. He held her hand tight and pulled her close. He
was shaking. Sobbing, almost. He didn't really know why. Relief,
probably. Just to hear her. To be with her still, after everything
they'd endured. To talk, for once, about something entirely dull
and mundane and ordinary.

'It is the story of every town that was once a part of the desert!'
Kalaiya laughed. 'It is Uban, Hanjaadi, Shinpai, Sarrai. All of
them. A story we keep because it tells us of a way of life we once
knew, but no longer. A kinder life than the desert gives us now.'

'The Splintering put an end to both towns.' Tsen stared off at
the Jokun in the distance. 'Traces remain on the western bank, but
most of whatever was there was long ago washed to the sea in the
spring floods.' He looked at the boats drifting up and down on
the river. Night or day made no difference to the endless flow of
commerce. Little Xizic boats, the sort he'd come to know all too

well as the skin-shifter Sivan's prisoner. Vespinese barges, armed and armoured and all well guarded, carrying silver and silks and food; more barges going the other way, laden with gold and sand for the enchanters of Hingwal Taktse. The best sand came from the beaches of Qeled, they said. A desert full of it just a few miles behind him, and the Vespinese brought sand across the sea from another world in ships. He wondered what that said about his people, his race. Perfectionist? Obsessive? Just plain daft?

They crossed the pontoons of the Bawar Bridge, waiting a while for the structure to assemble itself between a gap in the river traffic before they could pass. The desert road where Red Lin Feyn had left them was empty, hardly used, but the road that ran beside the west bank of the Jokun was busy even at dawn; as he and Kalaiya stepped off the far side of the bridge, teamsters and drovers and sailors paused and stared to see who it was coming out of the Samim. Tsen bowed his head, trying to hide his face, and then realised that doing so probably only drew even more attention.

Stupid t'varr. None of these people will know you.

After another hour, as the sun started its morning climb, he left the road and walked to the riverbank. He squatted there and scooped up handfuls of water to drink, then took off his sandals and walked out up to his ankles. The Jokun came down from the mountains; the water was fast and cold, and his feet were hot and sore. The Xizicmen of the river claimed that the Jokun tasted sweet; that was simply because there were no cities to foul it from Vespinarr all the way to the sea, but right now, though his mouth might say the water didn't taste of anything much at all, his feet thought it was delicious. He stayed a moment, savoured the sensation, and looked at his reflection. He wore a plain white tunic, the usual dress of a slave except that his was so badly ripped that he had to hold it together to stop it from falling off him. He had a belt and some wooden sandals. Apart from that, he had almost nothing. Kalaiya beside him wore a plain white robe, a gift from Red Lin Feyn since they were close enough the same size. She had the silk nightdress she'd been wearing when Sivan had snatched her from the eyrie, filthy now, and she had a sword, stolen from one of Chrias's men. Her feet were bare. She didn't even have any shoes.

We're free. He couldn't stop thinking it, over and over. Was that what sword-slaves thought when they got their second brand and were no longer beholden to any master? When they were no longer owned?

A Xizic boat came drifting close to the shore. Its three sailors looked battered and worn, old skin weathered into leather, hair grey and tangled. No long braids, no bright colours, no feathered robes or cloaks. Kalaiya jumped up and waved as they passed.

'We've been robbed!' she cried. 'Will you take us to the city?'

The boat idled on, but after a hundred yards it shifted its course and came to shore, and the men inside stood up and beckoned. Kalaiya ran to it. Tsen followed as best he could, holding his tunic around him.

'Bandits on the road,' Kalaiya gasped. 'Not that we had anything to steal, but they tried to tear my husband's clothes from his back. He knocked a man down and took his sword and chased them away!'

The sailors had a Xizic dullness to them. Their eyes stared into space, but they helped Kalaiya climb aboard and Tsen too. They were fishermen between their workings among the Summer Moon trees of the Samim, and after they pushed away from the shore and returned to their drifting, one of them asked Tsen for his tunic, and it took a moment for Tsen to understand that, far from wanting to rob him, the man had a needle and a thread that he used to repair nets, and was offering to stitch the garment closed. For the rest of the morning Tsen sat naked as the boat drifted on, lazy with the current, no hurry, just a little nudge here and there to steer its way, all in all a rather fine way to pit oneself against the vicissitudes of life. As the afternoon heat rose the sailors took it in turns to doze. Tsen dozed too, Kalaiya resting her head on his chest.

They reached Hanjaadi as the sun was setting, damp wooden huts strewn along the muddy shores, a scattering at first, then packed tight and close as the boat drifted towards the sea docks of the Jokun. Tsen could see the heart of the city further down the river, blocky warehouses, ships moored by the dozen in the estuary, a leafless winter forest of masts and spars, a smattering of stone watchtowers and a few of gold-glass, all lit aglow by the setting sun. The skyline was low and higgledy-piggledy, a haphazard pressing together of stone and glass and damp muddy wood, of merchants and craftsmen and kwens and t'varrs and mud and salt and dirt, siphoning off what wealth they could from the endless flow of the river and all-powerful Vespinarr.

The Xizicmen guided their boat to the shore by the shanty-town slums and let it ground on the muddy bank. Tsen reckoned the three sailors had said no more than a dozen words between them across the entire day, but they'd saved his legs some walking and stitched his tunic well enough that he didn't have to hold it all the time, and so he thanked them and wished he could give them something more; but when Kalaiya tried to offer them her stolen sword their faces hardened and a flare of anger lit their eyes. They scowled and turned their backs and heaved up their baskets of cheap Samim Xizic-tears.

'I don't understand,' Kalaiya said as she and Tsen walked away. 'It was all we had.'

'It was far too much, and what use do they have for it?' He cocked his head. 'Shall we carry a sword with us through the dark alleys of this city, looking as we do, walking as we must among men for whom hunger is a daily companion?' A sword was good money, a great deal to a fisherman or Xizicman. But a sword carried meaning and intent. He took the blade from Kalaiya and threw it into the river.

'Tsen!'

'The less attention we bring to ourselves, the better.' He turned away and set off squish-squashing through the river mud by the water's edge. His feet sank with every step, and he'd barely gone six paces before he'd lost both his sandals. No matter. The feel of mud squeezing between his toes was oddly pleasant, and at least here on the shore he could see who was coming at them. Better to be filthy and stinking than nervous and scurrying through the animosity of alleys unlit and unfamiliar. *Fat old man like you must be rich, eh? What you got? Where you hiding it?* And then the inevitable disappointment when they found that he had nothing at all.

So close to the sea. So close to a ship and a way out. A new life, the two of them. He wanted to sing for joy, but best not, not now, not here; and so he kept himself to holding Kalaiya's hand and squeezing it hard, and now and then turning to look at her, a bright smile on his face even when she didn't look back.

They reached the river docks of Hanjaadi. Tsen walked through them, mucky as a beggar, with such a smirk on his face that Kalaiya kept asking why he was so cheerful when they had nothing, only their filthy clothes between them, and how were they going to get away and get a ship, if that was his plan? And he merely smiled, which annoyed her all the more, but a childish part of him wanted her to see for herself, for the surprise to come without warning. He took her into a seedy sailors' tavern, the Golem, and almost got thrown straight back out for the river stink he brought with him until he asked to speak with someone who was dead; and Kalaiya must certainly have thought him taken by madness, but after a short pause a sail-slave came from the back and ushered them through a curtain and into a dark passage, and then through another curtain and left them to wait, and after a few minutes more an old Taiytakei came and sat with them. He was carrying a small wooden box. Tsen told the old man a story about a fisherman who lost a silver ring in the sea and spent ten years searching until he found it in the belly of the last fish he ever ate, how he choked on it and died. The old Taiytakei listened patiently and then handed Tsen his box and left. Inside the box was a glass sliver etched with words that would grant whoever carried it passage on any ship to any world. Underneath the glass were six small bars of silver and a purse of jade coins. Tsen smiled at Kalaiya. It was hard not to grin. 'Three in every city,' he told her. 'One never knows why and where they might be needed.'

A quiet smugness suffused the days that followed, a happy contentment over an undertow of exhilaration. As far as he could, Tsen kept himself out of sight. He bought himself some decent clothes and some for Kalaiya too. He made discreet enquiries at the sea docks as to what ships would be leaving until he found one, the *Scavenger*, bound for Brons in the Dominion of the Sun King. He found the *Scavenger*'s captain and showed his glass sliver. He took Kalaiya to a bathhouse and bought a bottle of apple wine, and they spent their afternoons together soaking in the water, steaming in Xizic oil, talking about the life they were leaving behind, giving it its own funeral and then casting it away like an old shed skin; and he told her about the waiting Dahat villa and the future he thought they would have, full of lazy days, of peace and calm, of baths and apple wine, of no sea lords or enchanters or killers, and *definitely* no dragons; and the more he talked, the more he wondered at the ambition that had driven him these last years. *A change is coming. We're best away from it, as far away as possible. Just the two of us.* He looked back at what he'd been, at the life he'd led, at who and what he'd thought to become. It had made perfect sense in its moment, but now it seemed like madness.

He bought them each a small travel chest and let Kalaiya fill them with whatever she thought they might need or took her fancy. He bought a pair of sail-slaves, two old men who had once come from the Dominion, three silver clippers for the pair of them, cheap as dirt because they were far past their prime. Maybe it was sentiment, being far enough past his prime himself, but once his sail-slaves knew they were going home they worked hard enough. He saw when he bought them that they hadn't really believed it, how they feared some fate far worse – fodder for some sea lord's jade ravens or to have their flesh murdered and their souls sucked into an enchanted golem perhaps – but as they carried his chests towards the waiting carriage that would take them to the docks and the *Scavenger*, he saw them change. Their faces. That stricken look of anguished joy and hope. Forty years as slaves and they still remembered their home. He'd let them go, he decided, once he'd settled in the villa. A little thing. A touch of goodness to set against what his dragon-queen had done to Dhar Thosis.

The carriage took them to the docks. Tsen paid in jade, a smattering of wafer-thin squares carved with an image of the Hangpoor Palace of Zinzarra where they had been minted. There was another carriage beside the jetty where the *Scavenger*'s boats were waiting. A small gang of men – Taiytakei sword-slaves taken from the desert tribes – sat playing dice and chewing Xizic. Tsen didn't think anything of them until he started onto the jetty and one got up and stood in front of him, blocking his way.

'Baros Tsen?' the sword-slave asked.

Tsen stopped dead, bone-frozen by his own name. The other sword-slaves regarded him. *How did they know?* He bit back a reply, but knew he'd already given himself away. And he supposed he ought to do something like turn and run, but what was the point?

'Get out of the way.' He tried to push the sword-slave aside, to brazen it out, the sort of angry righteous gesture of a wealthy Taiytakei confronted by an upstart slave who didn't know his place. The sword-slave gut-punched him. As Tsen doubled up, the other slaves jumped to their feet. Kalaiya screamed and ran, but they caught her at once. Hands had hold of him, hauling him to the waiting carriage. The door opened and his heart sank. There were two men inside, and he'd seen them before. They'd come to his eyrie months ago with his old friend Vey Rin T'Varr of Vespinarr, who had left as no friend at all.

'Help!' he cried. 'Help! Kidnap!'

His slaves ran away, dropping the chests they were carrying and racing off down the docks. He ought to be angry with them, he supposed, but mostly he applauded. *Well done. Well done for staying alive.* Because really? What could they have done? The sword-slaves bundled him into the carriage and slammed the door. He lunged for the window. 'Kalaiya!' They punched him and held him down, but he refused to stop struggling. One got out a knife and waved it in his face as though that might shut him up. He barely noticed. '*Kalaiya!*'

The carriage door opened again. The sword-slaves had Kalaiya held between them like a wriggling carpet. They had shackles on her wrists and ankles. They bundled her through the door while the two men inside pulled and dragged and forced her to sit between them.

'Now shut up,' snarled the man with the knife, 'or I will cut *her*, not you.'

'I know you.' Tsen forced himself to be still. He couldn't stop his racing heart or his heaving lungs, but he stopped his struggling. The second man tossed Tsen a pair of shackles. They landed in his lap.

'Put them on,' said the man when Tsen ignored them. 'Or she gets cut.'

Tsen put the shackles around his wrists. 'You came to my eyrie. You saw my dragon.'

The man with the knife nodded. 'Surprised we weren't beneath your notice, a great t'varr like you. Not so great now.' He closed the blinds on the windows.

'How much do you want to let me go?' asked Tsen. 'Right now, right here. I'll give you everything I have. I'll get on that ship and no one will ever see me again. No one will ever know.'

The man with the knife banged on the roof. The carriage started to move. 'But you have nothing to offer, t'varr. Nothing.'

Tsen tried his pleas a while longer as the carriage eased its way from the docks and out through Hanjaadi towards the Vespinarr road. Bargaining, haggling, threatening, cajoling. Begging and pleading when nothing else worked, not that he thought it would make any difference. The two men barely said a word. They didn't tell him their names when he asked, but it didn't particularly matter. They'd come with his old friend Vey Rin, t'varr and brother to Sea Lord Shonda of Vespinarr, on the day the great red-gold dragon had broken Vey Rin's mind. Tsen settled to amusing himself by remembering every detail once it was obvious they wouldn't be bribed into letting him go.

'How did you know?' he asked, but they wouldn't answer; and though he came at it again and again from all the different ways he could conjure, they never did tell him.

They left the city. As they passed the Bawar Bridge the men opened the blinds, letting in the sunlight. When they stopped and he took a piss, they stood and watched. When he squatted for a shit, they were beside him. Tsen asked them if they might wipe his arse for him; that was when he found they had lightning wands and were happy to use them, now that they were away from the city. He didn't ask again. The hours dragged to days. They watched him eat and they watched him snore. Always one of them, often both, and their sword-slave mercenaries were never far away. Kalaiya, at least, was with him. They gave him that kindness. Or perhaps kindness wasn't it, perhaps it was simply less of a burden to watch the two of them at once – but it gave him hope to see her, to talk with her, even if their captors saw every gesture and heard every word. He wondered how he might save her now. What bargain he could possibly strike for her life.

The carriage followed the river road through the Lair of Samim and out the other side. The road began its climb into the Jokun gorge. Tsen stared out of the windows, filled with déjà vu because the skin-shifter Sivan had brought him this exact same way before, captive in a different way but captive nonetheless. The same thoughts came around again; and since the men in the carriage refused to talk, Tsen set about getting on their nerves, chattering away with Kalaiya about how the road here had been carved from the sheer cliffs, wondering how many men it had taken to build it, and how long, and all the other questions that had once come to a bored t'varr with nothing else to fill his mind. He talked on endlessly about that journey, how he'd slipped into Vespinarr itself right under the noses of Shonda's guards and flown out on a gondola from the Visonda Fields, disguised as a slave. He chuckled every time the carriage slowed, held up by teams of animals towing one barge after another against the river current. He told Kalaiya of all the times, in his mind at least, he'd almost escaped, and of all the new and colourful words he'd learned. From his own mouth the story sounded like some great adventure, an epic journey across a continent to rescue his true love; and sometimes, when he looked at her, that was exactly how it seemed even now, although the truth he remembered was smaller and dirtier, and very much more fearful. But he pushed that aside and wove on with his tales, and in odd times now and then they both forgot what awaited them, and laughed and smiled and held hands and were, in the moment, happy.

They came at last to the head of the gorge where the cliffs fell away around the shore of a familiar lake, where the Jokun paused its plunge from the mountains of the Konsidar to the sea. Hundreds of boats passed back and forth, and the air was cool and damp and fresh, full of life and adventure. When Tsen had come with Sivan a stiff breeze had blown off the mountains to cover the lake with waves; but today the air was still, the waters mirror smooth. The carriage drove past a shanty town of warehouses and sailors and sail-slaves, of mules and the teamsters who drove them through the mountain passes to Vespinarr, of sweat and cheap spirit and even cheaper Xizic. On the far side, where the river started through the upper gorge with its impassable falls and cataracts, a black stone fortress rose from an outcrop of rock. That, his gut said, was where Vey Rin would be waiting.

'Is it true,' Tsen asked as the carriage turned and drove through the fortress gates, 'that there are vaults here filled with a fortune in

Vespinese silver?' When Sivan had brought him along this same road they hadn't stopped, but he remembered wondering how a fortress like this would fare before a dragon. Badly, he supposed, but with his eyrie lost to the storm-dark, no one would ever know.

His guardians didn't answer. They never did. The carriage stopped in the castle yard, and the sword-slaves opened the doors and pulled Tsen out. They kicked him in the back of his knees to buckle his legs and pressed his head to the weathered stones, forcing him to kowtow, and then held him there until he felt the air change around him and someone come close. A waft of exquisitely expensive Xizic lanced through the stones' vague odour of stale manure. A shadow loomed, stealing the sun and its warmth. Tsen heard Kalaiya cry out. He tried to look, to see what they'd done to her, but he couldn't turn his head.

'Hello, Tsen,' said the shadow. The voice was so familiar, and yet with a high-pitched squeal he'd never heard before. But the voice didn't matter. The Xizic had been enough.

'Hello, Rin, old friend.'

Vey Rin kicked him in the face. The sword-slaves let go and Tsen rolled onto his side, clutching his head. Blood poured out of his nose. Rin kicked him again and then again, and then he was swearing and cursing like a sailor, laying in with blow after blow as though he meant to kick Tsen to death right there in the yard, and Tsen could see Kalaiya now, held fast between two soldiers and forced to watch, and all he could think of was that at least it wasn't her.

'You kick,' he gasped, 'like an old woman.'

Vey Rin T'Varr, sea lord of Vespinarr, stamped Tsen down. He howled with hateful venom, stumbled and would have fallen if his own guards hadn't caught him. 'Take him!' Rin sounded more like a monster than a man, warped and wrenched. 'Take him to the pen! You know what to do with him. Gut him! Flay him!' The sword-slaves dragged Tsen away while Tsen tried to see what they did with Kalaiya, but he didn't dare call her name, not now. Didn't dare even let Vey Rin see him look at her for fear that Rin would murder her on the spot out of spite. Even through the pain and the anguish, he wondered what had happened to his old friend. If friend had ever been what he was.

The sword-slaves dragged him into the fortress, down into stinking bowels of stone never touched by the sun, slick with damp. They ripped his clothes from his skin, beat him with short sticks and then shackled him to a wall, wrists and ankles, spread-eagled, as helpless and as undignified as a man could be. Tsen was fairly sure he knew what happened next – Rin came and gloated and tormented him for a while, and then they tortured him for a bit to make him confess to whatever it was that Rin wanted to hear. Then, probably, they dragged his half-dead carcass back to Vespinarr and hanged him. Or maybe they'd do it in Khalishtor. *Look! Look what we found! Baros Tsen, murderer of Dhar Thosis, alive after all to receive his sentence.* And Red Lin Feyn, once the Arbiter of the Dralamut, who'd been all ready to let him slip into some anonymous new life, would say nothing. They'd hang what was left of him by the ankles, to be mocked and jeered.

That was if he was lucky. If he was *un*lucky then they did everything the same, but first they murdered Kalaiya in front of him.

He wept when they left him alone. Couldn't help himself, even if it was just pathetic worthless self-pity. He had nothing to offer and no bargain left to make. For some reason which made no sense at all, he suddenly found himself immensely angry with Red Lin Feyn for letting him go. *A quick death. You could have given that to me. Pushed me off your sled or strangled me with your glass collar or even handed me to the Elemental Men to be hanged. At least Kalaiya would live. But no. You had to give me hope.*

He didn't know how long it was before Rin finally came. Hours, and it must have been dark outside. Rin stank of wine and smelled of Xizic and grease. The first thing he did was walk up to Tsen and belch in his face.

'Hungry?'

'We were friends once,' croaked Tsen. There really wasn't anything else he could try. 'Do you remember? Do you remember Cashax? Riding our sleds out into the sands, running scout for those slavers? The House of the Burning Womb? You and me and Shonda and the rest? You *do* remember?'

Rin backed away, giggling. He looked terrible, now Tsen had a chance to see him up close. Harrowed. His face was pale, his cheeks gaunt and hollow. He'd lost a lot of weight. His skin sagged, and his eyes were red and puffy, the look of a man who wasn't getting much sleep. His voice, when he spoke, carried a shrill edge of viciousness and of a fear that Tsen had never heard until today. 'Do you know what she did? That dragon-whore of yours? Do you? She tore my brother Shonda out of the sky. She branded him with his own slave mark. Her dragon held him upside down, dangling him by one leg.' Rin twitched. 'Things that should have been done to *you*, not to him!'

'Too close to your own memories, Rin?' asked Tsen softly. 'The last time I saw you, you were a gibbering dull-eyed wreck. After my dragon had you in its claws and was about to eat you. For your monumental stupidity that day, if not this, I wish it had.'

'Shut up!'

'Look at you, Rin. Did my dragon snap your mind?'

'*Shut up!*' Rin hammered a fist into Tsen's chest. 'Shut up! Shut up shut up!' He pounded Tsen and then reeled away.

Careful, tongue. Please, for once. 'They're gone, old friend. The dragon. The rider. They're all go—'

Rin snapped about and levelled an accusing finger. 'Yes! Gone! All except you! You! You and everything you've done to us!' His fists clenched and unclenched. He came close again now, clutched Tsen's face between his fingers, and Tsen saw how Rin's eyes were bloodshot. 'You!' Rin breathed. 'But *I* am sea lord now, thanks to your dragon-whore. And whatever you say, you will never leave this prison. I don't want anything from you. Not a word. All I want is to hear you scream, *old friend*. Scream for me. Will you do that?' He came right up close, eyeball to eyeball, and put on a mocking nasal voice. 'Are you getting enough sleep, Rin? Did my dragon snap your mind, Rin?' He spat in Tsen's face. 'I see it every night. Everywhere I look. Your dragon staring at me. Everywhere, and every morning I wake up screaming. That's what you gave me, *old friend*, and so that's what I will give you in return. Torment and agony for as long as I can make you last. Don't think I mean to let them hang you, oh no. No easy way for you, *old friend*, not after the ruin you brought, not after what your dragon-whore did to my brother. We'll start with your woman, shall we?' He let go and beckoned at the shadows. Tsen heard footsteps.

'Rin, please! Remember who you—'

Rin whirled and lashed him with a backhand slap so hard it knocked loose a tooth. Tsen spat a mouthful of blood. Rin drew out a knife. 'I'll cut her throat for you, Tsen. I'll do it and do it now. I'll have her brought here and do it in front of you so you know I'm not lying. Beg me to, Tsen. Beg me to save her everything else I have in mind. Beg me to do it. I will, if you ask nicely enough.'

'What has she ever done to hurt you?' Tsen heard the quiver in his voice. 'You're better than this, Rin. She's nothing to you.'

'But she's not nothing to *you*, Tsen!' Rin lashed out with the knife. Blood sprayed as the blade slashed Tsen's skin, slicing him across the chest. Tsen screamed.

'You gutless, spineless, vicious little bastard!' Might as well vent some spleen, since he couldn't possibly make it any worse, but Rin only laughed. He tossed the bloody knife to the floor at Tsen's feet.

'Cut off his nose,' he hissed. 'I want to watch. Then strap him to the bench. Spread that fat arse of his nice and wide and tell the world there's a virgin shit hole waiting for anyone who wants it. About time you gave someone a little pleasure, you worthless gelding.' He bared his teeth at Tsen and then came in close and whispered in his ear. 'I'm off to have my dinner now. When I come back I'm going to put your nose on a string and make her wear it. Give it a few days and you can wear hers too. A matching set. How very touching that will be. And after that, perhaps ears, and then fingers. You'll never see her again, Tsen, but you'll always have a part of each other for comfort. Won't that be nice?'

The slave-swords unshackled Tsen. He struggled with every ounce of futile strength. He screamed and cursed and howled, bit at them and punched and kicked, but they held him fast. One took Rin's knife and hacked off Tsen's nose. They strapped him and spread his legs and pushed his face down into stone, burning in pain, half drowning in a spreading pool of his own blood. They beat him half to death, and then they left him there, waiting. He tried to listen out after they were gone, to hear the ominous click of approaching footsteps. Give himself warning. He wondered how to make it as painless as he could, being raped. How much did it hurt? He didn't know.

At some point, despite himself, he passed out. When he came to, alone in the stagnant gloom of a last guttering stub of a candle, a dragon stared back at him. A hallucination. A dream dragon, the same one he'd conjured in Red Lin Feyn's gondola. It sat on the stone floor, watching him, while Tsen lay sprawled on his belly, too weak even to turn his head, watching back, his face one long smear of sticky blood-soaked mucus. It wasn't a big one, but it *was* a dragon. Was it the same dragon that Vey Rin saw in his nightmares?

An urge hit him to scream, but really what was the point? What was a dragon going to do? Eat him? It would be a mercy. Besides, there weren't any dragons any more. They'd fallen into the storm-dark. It was a dream-dragon then; although if he was dreaming then it seemed hardly fair that everything hurt so much.

'Go on, dream-dragon. Eat me.'

I am not here to eat you, little one.

'Then go away,' Tsen groaned.

Why? The dragon bared its teeth. *Why go when I relish such horror and despair? Prey that screams is always better. Prey that is afraid.*

There had certainly been plenty enough screaming, and would doubtless be plenty more. Tsen stared at the dragon, wondering what it wanted and why his addled head had conjured it. Perhaps it *would* eat him once it got bored. That would be nice.

'You came ... to watch, is that it? Well then I'm surely very glad ... to oblige you.' He groaned without much feeling. 'So nice to know that ... that someone other than Vey Rin takes ... some pleasure from this. Anything else I might do for you? Do my screams ... sufficiently please you?' Talking to a hallucination probably meant he was as mad as Vey Rin, but right now madness would be a blessing. He closed his eyes. Talking was too much effort. 'You look like ... the dragon ... from the Queverra.'

Silence stretched between them. The dragon didn't answer, but Tsen could feel it rummaging through his thoughts, his memories, his hungers, his wants. *Yes, I would do anything for my Kalaiya. Yes, if you threaten her, I will give my life. Yes, yes, yes ... But Vey Rin ...*

There is a place you wish to go – the dragon was looking at, of all things, the old memories of his villa in Dahat on the mountain coast of the Dominion, halfway between Brons and Merizikat – *in the realm of the Sun King.*

Yes. There is. Fat lot of good it's going to do me now, but thank you so much for reminding me. Just cruel, that was, torturing him with thoughts of the future they almost might have had.

Why only *might* have had?

Because Vey Rin is going to murder me exquisitely slowly. Before he does that, he's going to murder Kalaiya the same way. And who's going to save you, t'varr? The Arbiter? Who else even knows you're alive? And if she discovered you were here, do you think she'd come riding out of the sky in her gold-glass chariot to set you free? Do you think she has a secret sympathy for mass murderers? Or do you think it's perhaps a bit more likely that she'll do absolutely nothing at all if she ever learns where you are. Face it, Tsen – after everything that's happened, even if the whole world knew you were here, is there one person who would lift a finger to stop what Rin plans to do to you?

I do not know, little one. Is there?

No ... Tsen blinked and frowned at his hallucination dragon. *Perhaps Chay-Liang, but she's gone.* He groaned again. 'Would you mind terribly not ... joining in with my ... inner dialogue? It's confusing enough ... hearing voices ... without there being one that isn't even mine.'

A piece of the half-god who broke the world has returned, said the dragon after some more staring. *He has taken your eyrie, Baros Tsen T'Varr. He is not whole. He means to find his other half. It is in the Dominion of the Sun King. He must fail.* The dragon's tail flicked back and forth.

Swish.

Swish.

Well. That was an odd thought. Tsen watched and waited. *Quite bizarre really.* His mind was wandering, was it? Making up nonsense. Hardly a surprise, all things considered. He'd conjured a dragon to talk to after all, so why not some babbling gibberish? But still, what? Half-gods and broken worlds? Exactly what sort of madness was this that he'd caught? He couldn't imagine himself, even daft as a bag of spiders, coming up with such things.

Swish.

Maybe this was Rin's plan all along. Make them both as mad as each other. Crack him in half and then leave him to burble nightmares into some dank forgotten corner of darkness and uncaring stone.

A change is coming, Baros Tsen T'Varr. The unravelling of everything. The half-god will remake the world in his image. For better or for worse.

Tsen waited a moment to see if there was any more, or something that would make sense of it, but there wasn't, and now his dream-dragon seemed to expect some sort of answer. More worryingly, he rather feared it might be wanting some sort of *intelligent* answer. *Is this my way of working through what Sivan wanted? What he was trying to do? Did he say something that makes this anything more than derangement and gabble?* 'I quite liked the ... world as it was,' Tsen said to the dragon at last. 'And it's a bit bloody late now, frankly, don't you think? So it would be nice ... whatever you are ... if you'd ramble about something that makes a little more sense ... if you please.' There. Much more of this talking and he'd pass out again at the effort of it. He closed his eyes. The pain was easing, or perhaps he was simply getting used to it. *Maybe I'm dying. That would be nice. Over with. So could you just go away, little dream-dragon, and leave me be? A little rest. That would be nice, too.* Rin was hardly likely to have a change of heart come the morning, so all his stupid hallucinations could leave him alone now, please. Didn't know what he was thinking, anyway. He was a good Taiytakei. He'd never had much time or thought for gods, old or new or half, and he couldn't imagine any such having much time for him either. Especially not now.

He noticed then how the air had a slightly odd taste. Apart from blood – *everything* tasted of blood at the moment. But there was something else. He tried to sniff and wished he hadn't. Pain streaked across his face, a blaze of it. He felt a fresh trickle of warm iron at the back of his throat and swallowed hard, quickly, no matter how much it hurt, because Xibaiya help him if he had to cough. Coughing would probably burst his whole face apart.

The dragon moved closer. *You will find a way to cross the storm-dark, Baros Tsen T'Varr. That is where the Black Moon has gone. That is where he will be, looking for his other half.* It came closer still, close enough to touch him. Its jaw closed around the rope that pinned his right arm. He felt its teeth brush his skin. It moved to his other arm, and then bit the ropes that bound his ankles. Tsen gasped in relief. He twisted, tried to stand up, fell over, whimpered and curled up into a little ball, naked on the cold stone floor.

Get up. The dragon nudged him.

'Leave me alone.' He wanted to drift now, that was all. Drift alone into a peaceful daze. Or maybe quietly to die.

Get up, little one. The dragon nudged him a second time. Its scales felt warm.

It hit him, at last, that hallucinations and dream-dragons didn't bite through ropes.

He screamed.

A dragon!

He screamed again.

Really a dragon?

He screamed over and over, but of course no one came, not here where screams were furniture. The dragon simply sat, still as a statue, and looked at him. Eventually Tsen gave up screaming because it hurt too much. He moaned and whimpered instead, and shuffled away and refused to look. Vey Rin had sent a dragon to torture him. Somehow. It was going to kill him and eat him, possibly not in that order, because that's what dragons did.

Is that so bad, all things considered?

Wait! Vey Rin had sent a dragon? How did that possibly make sense?

At least it's quick.

Shut up! Stupid t'varr! Rin doesn't have any dragons. He practically shat himself at the first thought of one …

Run, then? Running was about the only thing that *did* make any sense. He almost laughed. Run, though? Could he possibly think of some suggestion more uselessly stupid? He couldn't even get up! And even if he could, a dragon could fly, and even if there *was* a place to hide, it would find him because it could read his thoughts and he was still in …

You can't run, little one. You can't hide.

But Rin didn't send it … So Rin didn't know it was here … So …

So what? *Think!*

He lay still. The fear slowly went away, turned to a touch of wonder. In the end he was in too much despair and pain to be properly scared of anything any more.

I floated among the thoughts of your tormentor, the dragon said. *Do you want to know what he means for you?*

He did. Of course he did. 'Not ... really.'

A vision washed into Tsen's mind like a tidal wave across a quiet shore. It swept away everything. He was in the eyrie. He was the great dragon Diamond Eye, freed and woken, sweeping fire across the dragon yard. He was hunting the Elemental Men while the Black Moon burned them with silver light. In the air he flew with the dragon-queen on his back, tearing glasships from the sky, shattering them until he fell under the storm of their lightning. He crashed to the dragon yard, broken and dying and yet falling still, all of them into the storm-dark. He saw the violet lightning and the sky turn black, and the Silver King, the Black Moon, blinding bright, reaching out to the waiting void ...

And then nothing.

That is how it ended, little one, after you were gone.

Good riddance.

You will take me to them.

'How?'

Ships.

However he had meant to cross the sea ...

Careful, t'varr. See! The dragon doesn't know ...

No, little one, indeed the dragon didn't, but now the dragon does. We will leave, and you will show me.

Tsen rolled onto his back. He gasped and laughed again at the absurdity of it. 'We can't ... just leave ...' *Look at me, for Charin's sake! I can barely move!* He struggled to his feet. His back and his ribs were a swollen mass of bruises. Standing at all was hard enough, and he was certainly in far too much pain to lift himself properly upright. He hobbled, almost doubled over, and that was when he saw the corpses. The tang in the air he thought he'd tasted, that he couldn't actually smell because his nose was a bloody mess, that had been the three sword-slaves he'd just found very thoroughly burned to death. The whole dungeon must stink of cooked flesh and sulphur.

He looked at them, and a horrible murderous glee swelled inside him. *It's a good start, but there are plenty more.* 'If I don't help you, dragon? What then. You burn me?'

Slowly, and with infinite patience.

Ah well. Still better than Rin would offer.

A crook-toothed grin broke through the pain. 'Then I will help you, dragon, if you will help me. But I have a price.'

The dragon glared, but it seemed to understand.

'Kalaiya,' Tsen said. 'And Rin. I want you to make the bastard pay.'

8

Vey Rin T'Varr

Vey Rin T'Varr tosses in his nightmare dreams of dragons. He is dangling again, as he dangles every night, from the claws of great Diamond Eye. The air is as dry as an ancient corpse and smells of sand and sulphur. The dragon looks at him with pale vast eyes of glacier ice, as cold and empty as the void between the worlds. It searches him for substance and finds naught but smoke and mist. He is so utterly and insignificantly small.

On other nights this is when he wakes, sobbing wails and gibbering, slick with trembling sweat, but tonight he falls into the dragon's eye, a speck like dust. The dragon blinks, and Rin is on the inside, surveying the world from a glass lens in a great palace. He is become single-minded murder, a pure totality of purpose.

… races, claws skittering on stone, exquisite silks shredded. Another pair of little ones. Smashes them. Limbs torn from torsos …

A numb shocking cold soaks deep into sleeping Vey Rin. A ball of smouldering ice punched into his belly. The dragon is here. It has come for him at last, and he is helpless.

… another. Incinerates him. Burns his face to charcoal. Lightning flash and thunder. Spring and tear a flail of limbs, rip away a helm and bite a scream in two …

Vey Rin snaps awake. He sits bolt upright, rigid alert. As he screams he tells himself that no, it was the dream. Every night the same. A dream, just a dream.

But it is not.

Across the dim light rises the silhouette of the dragon. The scream lodges in Vey Rin's head. Sticks and will not stop, even as he gulps to fill his lungs. His bowels and bladder empty. Everything burns white, wherever he looks, blinding and blistering, scouring his skull. Thoughts dissolve, piece by little piece collapsing into tiny helpless fear. He can't look away. His screams are silent now, though they never stop. The dragon comes closer, and he cannot move as it creeps to the end of his bed and crawls on, as its claws wrap around his neck and push him down, as its face comes close, as its hot breath of sand and sulphur brushes his skin. A talon caresses his cheek and leaves a sharp line of blood. The dragon looks down on him, into him, through him. A drip of saliva grows on the tip of a fang. He watches it, helpless in fascination amid the terror, until it falls and lands on his face and mingles with his blood. The dragon's eye blazes into him.

Everything he's done, everything he has yet to do, it all counts for nothing. He understands that his entire existence is worth no more than a mote of dust.

'What do you want?' Vey Rin T'Varr chokes out the words, tiny as a baby.

Stone and damp dark. Tsen watched the hatchling dragon slide off into the shadows, slither and skitter and vanish into the gloom. He couldn't stand, not really. He certainly couldn't walk, which left him with crawling. When he reached the steps from the dungeons he took a few deep breaths and forced himself upright. It wasn't that he didn't have the strength, but the pain was like a burning stake driven into his face, and his back and ribs were one great bruise. If he bent over and put both arms against the wall, he found he could hobble along crabwise with only a few whimpers, one slow step at a time.

He wasn't sure what to do when he got to the top. Which way to go.

'Kalaiya?'

Guttering torches gave reluctant light to a cramped passage. There was another body here, a Vespinese soldier with his head ripped off. A crazy thought came to Tsen that he might take this soldier's clothes and armour and waltz his way right out of the fortress as though just another guard. It made him laugh, despite how much that hurt. *My, my! What about that Baros Tsen and his amazing escape, eh? Yes indeed! Quite miraculous! And, by the way, what happened to your nose, and why can't you stand straight?*

Better than nothing though, better than being naked. He dropped to his hands and knees and started to strip the fallen soldier, and that was how they found him, one man crawling on the floor beside the headless corpse of another, both naked by a pile of clothes and armour. He wasn't stupid though. He took the soldier's lightning wand, first thing he did, and Tsen was still a t'varr to a sea lord as far as the wand's enchantments knew, and so they bowed to him. He sent the first guardsmen who came his way flying with lightning. He supposed the others would kill him then, which would at least be a quick end, but they didn't. They ran for cover and shouted at him instead.

'Baros Tsen T'Varr!'

He thought about turning the lightning on himself. Better than what Rin had had in mind, that was for sure. But something in their voices stayed his hand, and besides Rin would only take out the disappointment of losing his toy on Kalaiya.

'I'm here,' he croaked. He sat there exhausted, legs splayed, awash with pain and with a lightning wand in his hand, waiting to see what would happen. It seemed he waited for quite a while, and then Vey Rin himself was shambling out along the stinking stones, a pair of soldiers shuffling ahead, shielding him with great gold-glass shields. There was something very wrong with Rin. He was in a nightshirt – a brilliant priceless silk, emeralds and yellows embroidered in the entwined dragons and lion of Vespinarr, but still a nightshirt – and he walked with the shambling gait of a man heading to the scaffold, hunched into himself, small and moulded by fear and dread. Of the two of them, Tsen thought Rin looked the more broken. Quite a feat that.

'Stop!' Tsen, on hands and knees, levelled the wand at them. The soldiers stopped, but Vey Rin didn't. He pushed past and then sank to his knees and dropped to his hands and crawled the last dozen paces between them. He pounded his head into the floor, over and over until his face was bloody, and then pressed it there.

'Make it go away,' he wailed. 'I'll give you whatever you want. A ship across the sea. Your slave too. Both of you. That's what you wanted, isn't it? Or money. Do you want money? Anything! But make it go away!'

The temptation to ram his lightning wand into Rin's face, to set it off and char him from the inside out, was almost overwhelming. If it hadn't been for Kalaiya he probably would have done it.

'A ship,' he whispered. 'To the Dominion. All mine.'

'Yes,' whimpered Rin. 'Anything.'

'Silver and jade. A chest small enough to be carried by two slaves.'

'And the slaves to carry it?'

Tsen thought about this a moment. 'We'll start with some clothes, shall we? How about some of yours.'

They brought him a chair to carry him through the fortress, since sitting hurt less than standing. He had them bring him clothes, the best they could find. He had them send slaves to clean him, to bind the wounds they'd given him as best as could be done. When he was dressed, he sent for Kalaiya. He never saw the dragon again, but he knew it was there. He could feel it, lurking on the fringes of his thoughts, whispering in and out of his memories. Red flanks, black belly. The hatchling from the Queverra. He wondered vaguely why, why him, but for the most part he was past caring.

In the morning Rin's sword-slaves carried him from the black stone fortress to Rin's royal barge on the lake. Kalaiya walked beside him. She held his hand, and he couldn't stop looking at her, nor she at him. Eyes full of wonder, both of them. At least Rin hadn't hurt her. Which was good. He could forgive a lot, he thought, but not that.

By the middle of the afternoon they were sailing down the river, making a merry pace with the Jokun's current sure and strong. In the far distance now and then Tsen spied a dark speck in the sky. The hatchling, and he knew that Rin saw it too.

His dreams on that first night on the river were strange. He found himself in a huge crystal cave etched into white stone and filled with moonlight. He felt a familiar moment of confusion before he broke from his egg and stretched his first wings. He didn't remember what he was or how he'd come to be here, but he wasn't alone. Dragons surrounded him. They were small, all of them, but they would grow. They were the first. They told him so.

My first awakening.

Not a dream then. A sending. The hatchling dragon from the Queverra.

Asleep, he settled again, calm, knowing now that he was a passenger in the hatchling's memories. The other dragons took him outside among white spires that snagged clouds from the sky. Men walked among them, but not men from any world Tsen knew. Their skin was pale, their hair long and lush and white as snow, their eyes fresh-blood red. He'd never seen their like, yet they were familiar. He knew them in some way he no longer remembered.

He stretched his wings. Dragons in their hundreds swarmed the spires, circling in currents of air. The sun shone bright, and at night the moon burned and the stars glowered, and still they flew, higher, until the air was too thin to breathe.

But we don't breathe, the other dragons said, and flew higher still.

The dream faded into stars and darkness. Tsen woke late the next morning, soaked in sweat. He crawled from his bed and stumbled into the sun. The river. The Jokun. It took him a while to work out who he was again. When he did, he shivered and hugged himself and crawled back to his bed. He didn't know where they were. Somewhere in the swamps of the Samim.

You have a fever, said the dragon. *Do not die, little one, not yet. You have a debt.*

They might kill me.

Either way you all burn.

He tossed and turned and fell inside himself, drifted afar, deep across time and space. He had grown. His wings were large and strong. His fire melted stone now, and the world had changed. The half-gods had gone, most of them. Those that remained wore silver armour. Blood and the tang of iron tainted the air, war and sulphur and sorcery. Little ones marched in armies, bright and shining. Toys and playthings thrown against one another for sport and amusement, but beneath the click of dice and the roll of fate and the laugh of half-god wagers made and lost lay a discord too profound to simply put aside. More and more they intervened. More and more the last half-gods turned on one another.

He flew. Invincible, unstoppable, burning rivers of fire, slaughterer and devourer. Sorceries of fire and lightning faded like mist at his passing. He fell upon monsters, devil jade ravens, burning their flocks out of the sky. Other birds whose names were forgotten now, black winged and with beaks like spears who drove into flesh and then spewed ravenous beetles. Fire wraiths. The collosepedes that carried entire cities on their backs, stone titans and sea serpents, a hundred other demon creatures shaped for war, and the dragons slaughtered them all. They hunted half-gods and brought back their souls until only one would not yield. The Isul Aieha.

In his bed Baros Tsen moaned and rolled his eyes.

The worlds turned again. The dead goddess of the earth sent a dark planet into the sky to hunt down the sun and blot it into darkness. The living moon burned with a baleful hate so strong that even dragons sought shelter. The stars whispered their ire in changing patterns etched across the night sky. Yet the dragons flew on, and Tsen lost himself in the power of his wings, in the strength of his fire ...

For a moment it fell away. Kalaiya was looking down at him, fearful and sad.

'Tsen,' she whispered, 'don't die.'

He tried to reach out to her, but the moment was fleeting. He was a drowning man in deep tumultuous seas, snatching one quick breath of air, flailing his arms for more but helpless against an undertow that sucked him into the deep. He was the dragon again. He fought on.

Later it was Rin. Quivering and shaking, clinging to his hand and begging for something. Tsen didn't know what or why.

'Do you remember,' Tsen asked him, 'how we used to ride our sleds among the dunes when we were young?' He could see past Rin through the open door, and started, sat bolt upright, dazzled by a moment of understanding, of knowing again who he was. Baros Tsen. 'Where are we?'

Rin said something, but Tsen didn't hear, and the moment danced gaily out through the door, skipping and laughing with all his clarity in its arms to dissolve in the breeze. 'I should like to ride our sleds into the dunes again one day,' Tsen murmured as he closed his eyes and sank. 'Tomorrow, perhaps? Would that be good?'

He flew once more. A last stand. All the dragons that had ever lived; together they rained fire across the Isul Aieha and the armies that came with him. His brothers and sisters fell, one by one, as the terrible Earthspear struck them down. Armies rose, and the Black Moon cracked the earth to swallow them. Petty priests and sorcerers called fire from the sun and scorched the earth. From his airy watch Tsen saw the Black Moon's last great work, a helm made of ice imbued with a fragment of the half-god's own soul. He saw the moment the battle hung in the balance, dragon after dragon storming at the Isul Aieha, drowning him in fire and lashing him with claw and tail, battering him down though they died in their hundreds. He saw the Earthspear tumble away, saw it seized and taken in dragon claws, felt the surge of victory; but the spear returned to its master, and the dragon turned to dust.

He saw the cataclysm of the Splintering, the world broken into pieces. Saw everything hang for a moment in the balance as the Nothing tore its hole, as time and space unravelled. He saw how the Black Moon in his dying wrought a final spell with the dead goddess wrenched from her spear and made a prison of his own soul, a cage. In Xibaiya, the underworld now bloated with fallen souls passing on, and some that were not so dead, he saw the hole the Nothing had made, the dead goddess and the Black Moon entwined together about it, embraced in their mutual murder, self-forged into a cage that held the unravelling at bay.

That Which Came Before.

And then it was gone.

When Tsen woke again, his head was clear. He sat up. He was at sea, at night. In a cabin, rocking back and forth, with a little glass window looking out at the waves. Someone must have carried him here but he had no memory of it. The dragon was still with him, and he felt himself drift outside, over the whitecaps and among the hunting gulls with their cries and their waiting ambush for scraps thrown over the side; yet at the same time he knew who he was again. Baros Tsen, sitting in his bed, weak and fragile and not quite dead.

The dragon flew with the gulls a while, and then drifted further to watch the ship that carried him. Tsen understood. The dragon was showing him things that mattered, but he didn't know what any of it meant.

Why? Why me? Kalaiya deserves this but not I, not after what I have done. Rin was justice. A punishment to fit my pride.

The dragon wheeled and plunged, taking them both diving into the sea, deeper and deeper until the darkness was complete, and on deeper still until they drove through the seabed and into Xibaiya.

In its stillness they moved, together and with purpose, and he knew the dragon had come this way many times, eager for the mewling call of new skin, dulled dreamlike by the alchemical potions of Bellepheros and his ilk; but this time the dragon was awake, rank with stalking menace, creeping among ephemerals to the hole, to show him him how the dead goddess and her slayer, sentinel and prison, were gone, and how the Nothing now seeped through, ending everything, annihilating all it touched. Its taste had a tang dredged from ancient memories of the dragon's first lifetime, hazy and dull from centuries of alchemy. The dragons had scented this Nothing once before.

Together they perched, Tsen and the dragon Silence on the edge of the unravelling of everything, and the dragon wondered what might be done but found no answers, and so wondered a more dragon-like question instead, filled with an acceptance that all must inevitably end.

The Black Moon is gone, Baros Tsen. An echo of a memory of him roams free. It must show the way, how the rip might be sealed once more, for everyone and everything will otherwise be devoured.

Why, dragon? Why me?

The dragon showed him a face.

'Kalaiya?'

Because you will remember.

And, in a blink, the dragon was gone.

Tsen jerked. The shredded depths of Xibaiya vanished and he was back at sea, warm and cosy in a bed, although the cover that wrapped him had a sour scent. The air smelled of tar and burned wax. The rhythmic creak of wood and the rocking back and forth told him that the ship was under heavy sail and making good speed. He blinked, wondering for a moment if this was real. It *felt* real, but then so had the dragon's sendings.

He shifted and then stopped sharply, stabbing pains running from his buttocks to his shoulders. His face felt numb. When he gingerly touched himself there, he felt a lot of soft padded cloth. His head was wrapped in bandages, and he whimpered, suddenly frightened at what Rin had done. The fevered dragon-fed visions fell away like mist-made dreams, while the memories of Rin's black fortress firmed. The more he remembered, the more he wished they might leave him too.

He levered himself out of bed. Everything ached. He was as weak as wet paper. He wrapped the blanket around himself and crawled to the cabin door and opened it, and looked across the deck of the ship. The sky was dark, a quiet cloudless night full of stars. When he hauled himself to his feet he saw, far on the horizon, a glimmer of purple lightning. The storm-dark.

'Hey!'

Tsen turned. A watchman at the wheel on the deck above had seen him.

'Hey! Do you …? What's the—'

Tsen cut him off. 'To what port do we sail?'

The watchman hesitated a moment, apparently baffled to be asked such an obvious question. 'To Brons, t'varr. To Brons.'

Tsen turned away and crept back inside. Brons would do. The Dominion. The Sun King's great port. He crawled back to his bed. He was wretchedly tired, and so he closed his eyes and drifted to sleep. Proper sleep this time, without all those fever dreams that sucked him dry. The dragon, it seemed, was gone.

He missed the crossing of the storm-dark. Slept right through it, and by some happy quirk of chance the curtain of the storm was only a couple of hundred miles from Dominion shores when the ship came through. By the evening he could see the city and the coast through his window. By next morning they were anchored in Brons harbour, the largest and busiest port in the seven worlds, larger even than Khalishtor; and by the middle of the afternoon he was on land, and they had him lying on a slab with three men poking at his face, one from the ship and a pair of city chirurgeons.

'The bleeding doesn't stop. There was an abscess here. In places it went bad. I drained the fluid …' After that Tsen put his hands over his ears and went back to remembering the dreams and visions from his fever. Anything. Some things he just didn't want to hear.

Are you there, dragon? he wondered, but the dragon never answered him again, and so he never knew whether or how it had crossed the storm-dark beside them. It must have, he supposed, because that was what it had wanted, but it would have been nice to be sure. More than a decade ago the Sun King had started all this when he'd told Sea Lord Quai'Shu that the one thing he wanted and didn't have was a dragon. Well then, now the Sun King had one, even if he didn't know it. Tsen wondered how pleased the immortal king might be when he found out.

The chirurgeons agreed there wasn't anything more to be done about his face. There was a mass of scarring where he'd once had a nose, and the fever had come because the wound had turned bad, and he was lucky to have lived through it – but he had, and so that danger was gone, and the worst he had to worry about now was that he'd be as ugly as a toad and never have much sense of smell any more. There wasn't much to be done except to wait and hope the bleeding would eventually stop. Oh, and pray. Lots and lots of praying. Mostly to the sun, but some to the moon and the stars wouldn't hurt either. The more he prayed, the better his chances – for best effect, the two chirurgeons recommended several hours a day. Tsen quietly rolled his eyes. He'd forgotten about that, how the people here revered their gods, the enthusiasm with which they brought praying to the sun into every aspect of their life. One of the forbidden gods the Elemental Men of Takei'Tarr had sought to wipe out, and with much the same fervour too.

Rin, he discovered, had gifted him the ship, crew and everything, and would have gifted him the navigator too if she'd been his to give. Tsen promptly leased it out for a flat monthly payment to be made in gold to one of the city's banks, and between one thing and another they spent more than a month in Brons. By then his face had scarred over and healed. Of everything Rin had done to him, it was the crippling of his sense of smell that he resented most. Xizic baths and apple wine weren't quite the same and never would be. Two of his three great delights.

They could have gone by boat along the coast to the little town of Dahat, but Tsen, his moods ever more capricious, decided to go by land; and so instead of three or four days it took them weeks. When they finally reached his precious villa, almost three months had passed since Red Lin Feyn had left them beside the Bawar Bridge, more than four since the dragon-queen had destroyed Dhar Thosis, and pressing on towards a year since the first dragons had come to his eyrie. Tsen very much hoped never to have a year even remotely as interesting ever again. He took Kalaiya into the hills to a sun-soaked bluff and showed her their orchard, spreading around the villa's warm whitestone walls. A donkey trail wound down the slopes to sleepy Dahat, with its fishermen and its vineyards and its olive groves. The sea was calm and azure. It looked pleasingly warm and inviting.

He held her hand. 'We will never go back,' he said. 'And they will never find us.'

Far away across the sea and the storm-dark, Red Lin Feyn sat in the Dralamut, listening to words of the world outside. Of the growing juggernaut of war between the Dominion of the Sun King and the Ice Witch of Aria. Of the outbreak of plague in Khalishtor, where men seemed to turn slowly to stone, the Statue Plague the dragon-slave had brought to Baros Tsen's eyrie.

When she was alone – *certain* she was alone and with no Elemental Men flitting as wind and shadow nearby – she went to the Dralamut library, the greatest in all the worlds. She walked from one end to the other until she reached an iron door hidden behind a bookcase. She tapped the gold-glass lock with her black rod so it would know who she was and that she was permitted to enter. Inside, among the forbidden books of the Taiytakei, she gathered the journals of the first navigator, Feyn Charin. She lit a lamp and laid them on a table, and then she went to the secret place where the navigators kept the most forbidden book of all. The Rava. An original, penned by the priests of the Vul Storna before the killers found them and wiped away the stain of their heresies. She opened it and started to read, looking for anything that might throw light on the nature of dragons and half-gods, and this thing called the Black Moon.

Somewhere in the middle of Charin's journals, a late one, she found the beginnings of what she was looking for.

'It is said that in the war of the immortals one thousand seven hundred and seventy-seven of the half-gods vanished utterly.'

The Pinnacles

Seven days after landfall

Two years have passed since Zafir took the Adamantine Throne. With it she took Queen Shezira's head and began the war that tore the nine realms apart. Zafir's lover and betrayer Jehal is dead and gone. The realms have burned in dragon-fire, but the bitterness lingers. In the Pinnacles deposed King Hyrkallan would yet have Zafir's head on a spike. The mad Queen Jaslyn, most neglected of Shezira's daughters, weeps. Not for lives lost, but for the dragons she once flew.

Elsewhere, deep in the Worldspine, the last guttering embers of the Silver King, the Isul Aieha, flicker into life. An old seed left hundreds of years ago has been found and has started to grow. A thousand years a wanderer, now the Isul Aieha dreams he might at last go home. The alchemist Kataros and the Adamantine Man Skjorl are taking him where he must go, to the unfound Black Mausoleum, though they do not yet know it.

9

Bellepheros

Took about a day, Tuuran reckoned, to go from the euphoria of victory to feeling utterly wretched. He felt strange, coming back here after so long. Had felt strange in Furymouth and Farakkan too, but not like this. The Pinnacles was a place he knew, the last place he'd been a free man.

He stood on top of the Moonlit Mountain and took a long breath and surveyed the horizon. Ten years? Eleven now? Might even have been twelve, not that it made a fly shit of difference. This was going back to the start of things. Probably felt strange to her Holiness too, coming home and seeing it all torn down, but Tuuran reckoned it was a different sort of strange. Didn't feel like coming home to *him*, not really, but it felt like something. A tug on his guts.

He walked across the summit rubble and quietly watched Zafir. Seeing her here like this, after all they'd been through, after all they'd done, the moments shared, the triumphs and the anguish, he felt a surge of pride. A pocketful maybe, fierce and hard; but it only lasted a moment, and then back came the emptiness. Always happened after a fight. The rush, the elation, the savage lightning-tingle energy of the last blow, blood alive with death or glory. Then the slump. First came the aches, the pains, the twinges, all the little wounds. Then the fatigue, and then the regrets. Normal, all of that, but this time it was worse. At first he thought maybe it was the dragon-disease messing with him. First day in Merizikat had been the same too, victory and despair, one after the other, both the same; but when he took that thought to Bellepheros on the eyrie the alchemist just laughed at him.

'It's what we've done, Night Watchman,' Bellepheros said. 'Nothing more and nothing less than that.'

Maybe the alchemist had a point. The Pinnacles quietly seethed.

Dragon-riders without dragons, strutting and prancing like they were little kings, knights who once flew a thousand miles from Sand and Bloodsalt and Evenspire to bring Zafir down, and here they were with Zafir sitting on her throne again, all their dragons lost, everyone they left behind dead and ash, and what had it all been for, eh? Hyrkallan in a cage frothing and screaming for Zafir's head on a pike. His queen, Jaslyn, mooning about on the top of the Moonlit Mountain, staring at Diamond Eye like she wanted to be eaten. Death by fire soaring the skies and incipient murder all around him, crawling over his skin wherever he turned, and in the middle of all that he was supposed to keep the peace?

No. Not what he'd thought it would be like to come home.

You're losing it, old man. Pull yourself together and stop being so silly. On a whim Bellepheros went out to the eyrie yard just after dawn. He stood carefully away from the dead dragon that was still lying there, steaming quietly in the damp air, and soaked himself in the morning chill. The clouds had finally gone. He could almost hear Chay-Liang talking in his head. *You need to act. If not you, then who will do it?*

He climbed the steps to the eyrie wall and then slithered down to the rim on his backside, dignity be damned, then walked towards the edge, small tentative steps until he felt himself start to sway, vertigo dizzy, and stopped. He'd come out here thinking to peer down at the Silver City, to look at the ruin of it and remember what it had been, but the closer he got to the edge the more his legs quivered, and in the end he sat back amid the rubble and debris and stared out at the horizon instead, and even then he couldn't stop trembling. Stupid dumb mindless fear of heights. He pulled a piece of canvas over himself. Not so much for shelter from the sun as for shelter from the size of the sky. Caves. He liked caves. Or at least a roof over his head.

'Alchemist?'

He hadn't seen that Tuuran was out here. The Adamantine Man must have been hiding or at least keeping very still, and now he was coming over to talk, and Bellepheros didn't want it. He wanted to be alone with his memories and nothing else. He certainly didn't want Zafir's lackey; but wanted or not, Tuuran settled down beside him. 'Surprised to see you out here, Grand Master.' He raised an eyebrow. Despite himself, Bellepheros snorted. They both knew exactly how badly he coped with heights.

'I came to look at the Silver City,' he said. 'I was on my way here when the Taiytakei took me.' He shook his head. 'Stupid. I should have known I wouldn't get within ten feet of the edge without shaking myself to pieces.'

'I used to come out here to watch the sun rise.' Tuuran laughed. 'Hasn't been much point these last few days. A lighter shade of grey and much the same rain. But today ... When was the last time we were up this high, Lord Grand Master?'

'That's not something I care to think about.' Probably when they'd been hanging underneath Chay-Liang's glasships a mile over the storm-dark out in the middle of the Taiytakei desert, and Flame was he glad that *that* was over. He pointed to the north. 'You see that smudge on the horizon, Tuuran? That's the Purple Spur.' The land below faded to a pale haze before it fell away into the Fury gorge, but the mountains beyond were a deeper grey than the sky. Or maybe he was wrong and it was simply a distant bank of cloud. 'I hear there are more survivors there.'

Tuuran sniffed and scratched his nose. 'Crazy's been summoning Hyrkallan's riders.' Crazy Mad. There was a story in a name like that; Bellepheros didn't know it and didn't imagine he ever would, but the name certainly fit. Whoever this Crazy Mad used to be, he was the Black Moon now.

'Shouldn't you be there? To watch over as he cuts them?' He couldn't keep the bitterness at bay, not any more.

Tuuran ignored him. 'I suppose he makes it easier. Keeps them all in line. The Silver King, returned to tame the dragons again. Not that either you or I believe that, but who's going to argue when Crazy has moonlight pouring from his eyes, when you've seen an unbeliever or two turned into ash? Better the devil you know, eh?'

'Did Zafir say that?' Standing at the Black Moon's side even though she too knew that the half-god *was* the devil. Cold, both of them. Ruthless.

'Actually I thought you might agree. Better the devil than dragons.'

'I don't. Chay-Liang wouldn't stand for devils of any sort, and she was right.'

'Every single time I see him, I think the same thing. I'd cut his head off in a blink and say get fucked to consequence, but my friend is in there. Still, it's a good story. These men are ready to believe just about anything. Crazy prowls with her Holiness at his side, and proud riders fall to their knees wherever he goes. They weep and beg the Silver King to save them. Leaves me sick to the core, it does, but what else is there? What other choices? At least it keeps the peace. We'd all be murdering each other otherwise.'

'That sounds like Zafir, not you. Going to make them all into his slaves, is he, eh? Just like he did in Merizikat? Going to cut out pieces of their spirits so they have no choice but to do his bidding? So even their thoughts aren't their own any more?' Zafir's return home struck Bellepheros as like one of those grisly tragedies played out on the stage of the old Zar Oratorium back in better days. Sat on her throne with the 'Silver King' beside her, parading him in grim grinning victory, Tuuran looming and fierce at her back. Sooner or later the executions would start. 'Three little cuts. That's how he does it, Night Watchman. You. Obey. Me. And then you do. You become his slave, and the moment he speaks you have no choice but to listen. When he says something is to be done, you have no choice but to do it.'

Tuuran looked away. 'Her Holiness has forbidden—'

'No more slaves?' Bellepheros spat a derisive snort that cut Tuuran short. 'That tired old mantra? You think any of us believe a word of that any more? The Black Moon didn't give a hoot what Zafir said in Merizikat. And Zafir knew it, too. Do you think she was so naive? Her Holiness dotes on her two rescued night-maidens. They both have babies now. How old do you suppose he'll let them grow before he cuts those too? When their squalling annoys him?' *Her Holiness.* He could barely bring himself to call her that any more.

Tuuran winced. The two of them stared out at the horizon in silence for a while, Tuuran throwing the odd stone, bouncing it off the rim, seeing how far he could make them go.

'What will happen when he does that, do you think?' asked Bellepheros.

'Her Holiness won't let him.'

'And how, exactly, will she stop him? And if she has such miraculous power, why does she let him cut the rest of us? I'll ask her, shall I?'

He started to get up. Tuuran put a hand on his arm. 'It's not your fight, Grand Master.'

'Not my fight? If not mine then whose?'

Bellepheros hauled himself to his feet, left Tuuran to his sunrise and returned to the lonely quiet of his alchemical study. For the first few hours after the attack he'd toyed with throwing his lot in with Hyrkallan and Queen Jaslyn. Tuuran's legion – if you could call his ragtag band of knife-cut lackeys a legion – were clearing up the mess, none of them with Zafir except for Tuuran himself. Letting Hyrkallan out of his cage would have been easy then; and helping him get close to Zafir, that would have been easy too, and then letting events take their course … But he hadn't. In part because alchemists never did that sort of thing, in part because the Black Moon was what he was, and none of them could change that, and Hyrkallan instead of Zafir would make no difference in the end. In part too it was because Hyrkallan had ordered every alchemist murdered in the last days before the fall, and had taken Grand Master Jeiros and smashed his wrists and ankles and hung him on a wheel over the cliff-edge of the Pinnacles to die, and because Jeiros had been a friend.

Or maybe Bellepheros hadn't done anything simply because he was a coward. He didn't know. Chay-Liang would have helped him see it through, but Li – the one person who'd had a sense of duty to the world at large, to the ordinary people ever crushed in blood under the heels of dragons and tyrants – wasn't here any more.

He scratched another mark under his desk. Seven days since they'd crossed the coast near Furymouth. Two and a half months since Chay-Liang had vanished in Merizikat. A little more than two and a half years since the Picker had kidnapped him on the road from Furymouth to the Silver City, and here he was at last. It should have been a journey of a week, that was all, and it made him laugh, wondering if he should just get up and carry on where he'd left off, getting out his truth smoke and quizzing rider after rider to ask what they knew of Queen Aliphera's death.

But *something* needed to be done, and *someone* had to do it, that's what Chay-Liang would have said, and if she'd been the one left abandoned and alone then she wouldn't have balked at being the one to do it, which was how he came to be inside the Hall of Princes, heading for the Octagon all a-brim with righteous outrage when Halfteeth and a squad of Adamantine Men pushed·past him hauling Hyrkallan in their wake. Bellepheros followed, determined to speak his piece to Zafir, twist her, coerce her, whatever he had to do, but as it turned out she wasn't even there. Inside the Octagon the Black Moon lounged on Zafir's throne, his half-god eyes burning silver.

Bellepheros stopped. Halfteeth's men pushed Hyrkallan inside. Riders seized him, his own men now manhandling him to his knees at the Black Moon's feet. The half-god touched a finger to his lips. Hyrkallan fell silent, then he started to struggle and scream, but his cries were muffled as though he had something across his mouth, and it was only when he managed to shake loose one of the men holding him that Bellepheros saw the truth of it: Hyrkallan didn't have anything *across* his mouth. He simply didn't have a mouth at all any more. Nose to chin, sealed with skin.

Bellepheros gasped and almost threw up. He stumbled and turned hastily away, but as he did the Black Moon saw him. Just a glance, a flick of the eye, but enough.

'Wait, alchemist!'

Bellepheros froze. Hyrkallan was on his knees, writhing and arching, nostrils flared, snorting great heaving breaths of air as though each one might be his last. The Black Moon took out his knife and drove it into Hyrkallan's collar. *Three little cuts. You. Obey. Me.* That was how he did it, how he made men into his slaves. Every single one of them.

With a snap Hyrkallan had a mouth again.

'What have you—'

'Quiet.'

Hyrkallan fell silent.

'Bring me your queen, little one.'

Hyrkallan's riders let him go. Hyrkallan rose. He lurched from side to side across the Octagon, marched Jaslyn to the throne and forced her down. He moved with the awkward jerkiness of Chay-Liang's golems, devoid of feeling. There was no affection, no kindness, no sadness or pity or regret, nothing soft or gentle at all. From Queen Jaslyn's face, she'd expected nothing better. She spat at the Black Moon's feet. 'I despise you for what you did, Silver King.'

The Black Moon stabbed her with his knife. 'I'm not your Silver King,' he said when he was done with her, and Bellepheros watched as she walked away, an empty shell; and he stared at the knife in the Black Moon's hand, wondering who would make such an evil thing.

When the last of Hyrkallan's riders were done, the half-god fixed Bellepheros with a languid eye. He beckoned as he waved the riders away, dismissing them to whatever they had been doing before. They filed out of the Octagon, a melange of dull bewilderment, of resignation and frightened fury.

'Her Holiness—' Bellepheros began.

'Quiet, alchemist.' Bellepheros fell silent, felled by the irresistible compulsion to obey. 'You carry a tiny part of my brother in your blood, alchemist. Your Silver King. The Isul Aieha. He's here, in this realm. I feel him. Where? Tell me where.'

'I don't under—'

The Black Moon crashed into his head, as strong and violent as any dragon. *The Silver King. The Isul Aieha. A sliver of him lives in your blood, infinitely dilute but there. How?* Bellepheros didn't even try to resist. The answer came up from inside him, summoned because the Black Moon had called it. The Black Moon ransacked the memories there, took what he wanted and then withdrew. *Be gone, alchemist. The taint of your blood offends me. Do not speak to Zafir of what has passed here.*

Three little cuts for dragons and men alike. *You. Obey. Me.* Sometimes Bellepheros wondered if he should feel privileged that he'd been the very first.

'When I was little,' Zafir said, 'I used to come here to hide.' She walked through the Hall of Mirages, a galleried octagon with archways off every face as tall as ten men. Myst and Onyx trailed behind, quiet and attentive, distracted by the spectacle of the Enchanted Palace but doubtless also thinking of the little ones they'd left behind in the eyrie. Across the threshold of the hall Zafir stopped and looked up. High overhead the roof was a dome decorated with a sun motif. The eight great arches defined the space and, as with the Octagon, each lower arch was crowned by a second. There were balconies above, if you knew how to get to them, each with a false window, an intricate screen cut from marble that radiated a fierce silver light when the moon was above the horizon. With the moon set, as now, the dome's sun glowed a soft lemon colour that would tinge to orange at dusk.

In the middle of the Hall of Mirages rested a sarcophagus. It was supposed to contain the remains of the Silver King. They all knew better, but still it was odd to find it here. Zafir's mother had kept it in the Octagon beside her throne. Hyrkallan had moved it. She would move it back, Zafir decided. Back the way it was. She stretched out her arms and tilted her head. Home. The cold glories of the long-dead Silver King.

'Walk with me,' she said. 'Whatever exit you choose, you will find yourself outside the arch where we first began.' She crossed the hall and walked through the archway on the other side, Myst and Onyx beside her. They found themselves back where they'd started, staring at the entrance again, the passage to the Octagon behind them. Zafir ran her fingers over the stones set into the arch. Every surface was decorated with an exquisite lapidary of precious and semi-precious stones formed into twining vines, fruits and flowers, all in a detail so delicate it was hard to understand what means short of sorcery could have made them. But then sorcery *had* made them.

'I used to come here to think.' She crossed the hall a second time and took a different exit. 'I need to think now, about what to do.' Once again they appeared where they'd started. Zafir walked on as though she hadn't noticed. She took another exit and then another, emerging at the same place over and over. 'About Princess Jaslyn and Rider Hyrkallan.' King and queen now, but that wasn't how she remembered them.

Another exit and then another, each time always back to the start . . .

Jaslyn would have taken her mother's throne, no matter whether Almiri, the eldest of the three sisters, had died at Evenspire.

… but there was a pattern to it. Take the archways in the right sequence and you could find yourself almost …

Hyrkallan? A good choice, Zafir supposed. Political. Practical. Not like the Jaslyn she remembered.

… anywhere.

The Hall of Mirages spat her into a cave deep in the depths of the palace, an underground cathedral filled with stalagmites and stalactites in cascades like corrugated walls and organ pipes. Silver lights shone from the roof far above, stars and a slender crescent moon. The night sky as she would see it from the summit of the Moonlit Mountain, the sorcerous simulacrum moon mimicking the phases of the real moon outside, the stars shifting with the season. She heard gasps of wonder. It was always night in this cave.

'What do I do with them?'

Myst and Onyx bowed their heads. They spoke more than they used to, but they knew better today. They knew her moods.

'When old Quai'Shu and his moon sorcerers took me, I thought they would kill me. Perhaps it was what I deserved. But they didn't. Greed led them otherwise. They made me their slave instead, and you know how I punished them for that. You know all of *that* story, but you don't know what happened before it began.' She wandered among the stalagmites and sat on a rough stone bench. For a while she was still, listening to the drips of water that echoed through the gloom. 'The Silver King used to come here,' she said. 'He would come to reflect. Sometimes for days on end. Sometimes for months. But I don't have months.'

Myst knelt in front of her. 'Mistress, you are home. Are you not content?'

Zafir cupped Myst's cheek. 'My home wasn't a kind place, not like yours before you were taken. It wasn't a place of happiness, and what there was of it is gone now. I can't say I miss it, not much of it.' She let out a long breath. 'I was raised in a tomb filled with the memories of a half-god we could never understand. We carved ourselves in what we thought was his image and climbed into shoes we could not begin to fill. He ate us all, our Isul Aieha.'

She got up and paced languid circuits around the paths between the misshapen columns, pausing now and then to gaze at the false night sky.

'I gave Hyrkallan every reason to despise me. Jaslyn even more so. Do I have to hang them now? I've had my fill of that, and anyway it made no difference in the end.' She tried to push away the jagged memories of the Octagon, of fighting with Hyrkallan for her old throne. Crazed animals, both of them. 'I want them to ...' Forgive her, after all she'd done? But how could she ask for that? How was it even possible? Mad Princess Jaslyn, who loved her dragons more than she loved anyone except her little sister Lystra, whom Zafir had tried to murder. Hyrkallan, a man of stone and iron who loved only duty and honour and the mighty Queen Shezira, Jaslyn's mother, whom Zafir had beheaded.

'They cast me out,' she whispered. 'And they were right to do it, because any one of them would have been better. Even Jehal, in the end, was better.'

'Talk to them, mistress,' murmured Onyx. 'Talk to them and see if there is hope? There is always hope, mistress.' But there wouldn't be, because Onyx was wrong about that, there was never any hope.

'This *is* my home,' Zafir said to the stones.

Bellepheros found himself in the Hall of Mirages, wandering in aimless frustration through the archways looking for Zafir, always coming back to the same place. He was about to give up when she walked in behind him, her two handmaidens beside her with a cool damp smell of caves on them, as welcome and familiar as woodsmoke.

'Holiness!' If Zafir was surprised to see him, she hid it well. She'd know something was wrong too, that he wanted something, because he almost never called her that these days. Well good, because something *was* wrong, and he *did* want something. She'd hear about the Black Moon and his knife one way or another, and she'd damn well stop pretending she didn't already know.

'Grand Master?' She watched him coolly. 'Myst was just asking what it was like to ride on a dragon for the very first time. I'm not sure I have the words. Exhilarating and magnificent, I would answer, but I rode dragons with my mother from a very young age. My first time was so long ago that I have little memory of it. Perhaps you can describe it better?'

Bellepheros shook his head. 'I am not the best choice to ask. For me they are an unrelenting terror quite beyond my capacity for reason. I'm afraid even a Taiytakei sled thoroughly unnerves me.' He looked hard at Myst. 'I've seen you stare at Diamond Eye, young woman, and I know that look. That yearning. Yes, I know you want to fly, but you're wrong to think that a dragon can transform you. They will not form some bond of friendship like a horse or a dog. They are devourers, nothing more.' He frowned hard, then turned away and looked around the Hall of Mirages instead. It was hardly fair taking out his bitterness on someone as innocent as Myst, even if what he'd said was entirely true. 'I ... I had heard of this place,' he said to Zafir at last, 'but I never understood its nature.'

'None of us understands its nature!' Zafir shrugged and laughed. 'The Silver King made it because he wanted to. I know some of its secrets but it may have more. For all I know, if you walk it in the right way it will take us straight to the Adamantine Palace.' Except it wouldn't, because the Adamantine Palace hadn't existed when the Silver King had conjured these halls. 'You want something, Grand Master. What is it?'

'The Crowntaker.' Bellepheros wrung his hands. He almost clutched at her, and then remembered how she hated to be touched. 'Holiness, I have to speak with you.' He glanced back towards the Octagon. For all he knew the Black Moon was still sitting there, lounging in Zafir's throne. He whispered. 'With discretion.'

Zafir nodded to Myst and Onyx and shooed them away, off back to the eyrie and their babies. It amazed Bellepheros how she put up with servants who carried infants, but she did. The blunt-edged vicious creature the Taiytakei had brought in chains to Baros Tsen's eyrie had changed. She was subtler now. He just wasn't quite sure which way she'd gone. Softer or sharper. Either way she was dangerous and selfish and unpredictable.

'You can advise me as we walk.' She beckoned him to follow. 'How should I deal with Jaslyn and Hyrkallan, Grand Master?' She stepped through an arch and Bellepheros followed. It didn't seem to bother her that she ended up right back where she started; she simply kept on going as if she hadn't even noticed.

'With mercy, your Holiness.'

Zafir flicked him a glance. 'There *is* an argument for reconciliation. The Adamantine Palace awaits, and I must leave the Pinnacles in hands I can trust. If I hang those two then I might as well hang every rider that came with them from the north.' She walked through the hall over and over, taking a different exit each time and always coming back to the same place. 'Mercy, though? The Adamantine Men Tuuran found in Furymouth, and here too, quietly whisper that Queen Jaslyn is mad. They say she woke a dragon and wouldn't let her alchemists feed it their potions. But I should let her go?'

Bellepheros paused. 'You know the story of Prince Kazan and the civil war, Holiness? The revolt against the oppressions of King Tiernel? It's all rubbish. Kazan was another rider stupid enough to wake his dragon, that was all. Twelve others went missing trying to find him.' It occurred to him that there must be a pattern to Zafir's path, to her choice of archways, but she was walking too quickly, and talking and asking him questions and making him think all at once. Deliberately, so that he wouldn't be able to remember? 'Fortunately half the dragons didn't have time to wake, and still it took the intervention of three neighbouring kingdoms and Speaker Ayzalmir to put an end to it. Hundreds were killed. *Most* of what you think you know is true, the picking over the pieces afterwards, the destruction of the realm as it was. But the beginning ... There was no revolt. Waking dragons is madness, Holiness.' His voice tailed away. The Black Moon had woken dragons. Her Holiness had ridden Diamond Eye for more than a year and yet the monster hadn't eaten her. It did what she asked. Something to do with what had happened as the eyrie crashed into the storm-dark in Takei'Tarr, although he had the impression that even Zafir didn't fully understand.

He missed a step. Cursed. He'd lost the thread of Zafir's path through the arches. Blasted women. 'I supposed we're past that, all things considered,' he muttered.

'Indeed.' Zafir snorted, almost laughed. 'On the other hand, Hyrkallan went to war because I executed his queen, and Jaslyn was willing to marry him to the same end, though she clearly despises him.' She walked through another arch and this time didn't reappear behind him. There *was* a pattern then, and for a moment

Bellepheros paused, trying to rebuild it in his head … but she'd walked it too quickly, and if he tarried then perhaps he'd not follow her, and then find himself taken to some other place. Stories were stories. They abounded with lies and exaggerations and misplaced drama, but every one he'd ever heard agreed on how the Enchanted Palace of the Isul Aieha was gleefully merciless in its devouring of the unwary.

He arrived in a hall of glowing white stone whose walls were covered in yet more archways. Blank this time, leading nowhere. Just décor. Zafir was a dozen or so paces ahead, looking back at him with that irritating little smirk she had.

'You were trying to work out the pattern,' she said. Bellepheros nodded. No point hiding it – Zafir was too clever for that – but it made him anxious, being with her in this place. Antipathy between the Order of the Scales and the queens of the Silver City went back to the days of the blood-mages, to the men and women who had torn the Silver King down.

'Did you manage it?' she asked.

'No.'

Zafir's smirk flickered into something with a flash of real warmth. 'Then I'll show you, Grand Master,' she said, 'one day.'

'That is … generous, Holiness.' Three hundred years. That's how long the alchemists had been waiting to see the secrets of the Isul Aieha's palace.

'Merely practical.' She started along the hall, brushing her fingers across the ornamental arches. 'The queens of the Silver City guarded their secrets, but in truth we barely understood any of them. You can walk for days and never visit the same place twice and still not see everything the Silver King left behind. And there are three mountain spires that make up the Pinnacles, not merely the one. People forget that this is simply the largest. I would have alchemists back among the works of the Isul Aieha, if opportunity and the Black Moon permit.' She stopped. Paused. 'Jehal is dead. Tuuran told me. There are Adamantine Men who left the Purple Spur after the palace fell.' She sounded bright and yet brittle, as though right now a good solid tap from a hammer might shatter her.

'I remember him, Holiness.' He chose his words with care. 'But I did not know him.'

Zafir smiled with a savage glitter to her eye. 'Not much *to* know,' she said. 'A selfish piece of shit just like any other prince. I suppose we were made for each other. He was a marvellous lover, though.' She walked on into another hall, round-walled this time, curving up and down and from side to side, growing wide and tall and then narrow and small with no rhyme or rhythm that Bellepheros could see. There were no more arches here, but every surface, even the floors, was covered in carvings. He paused, reluctant to tread on them.

Zafir laughed. 'Don't concern yourself that you might wear down the stone, Grand Master.'

Bellepheros tried to crouch, gave up when his knees howled, and dropped to his hands. He ran his fingers over the white stone floor. Like the stone of the eyrie it was as smooth as glass and hard as diamond, the carved edges knife-sharp as though chiselled only yesterday.

'It's all like this.' Zafir tossed the words over her shoulder as she might have tossed a pinch of salt for luck. 'All of it. I couldn't tell you how many hours I spent here after I mastered the Hall of Mirages. I think the whole story of the Silver King is in these walls, if you're clever enough to understand it. Perhaps even the whole history of the world.'

Bellepheros looked down. He paused, trying to make out the picture beneath his feet. Four men walking together, each, if you went by the carving, with a small hole in his head. One was carrying a spear that might have been the Adamantine Spear; one held a knife etched with eyes, the Crowntaker's Starknife; one wore a coat from which sprang rays of light, and one carried a circlet around his brow. In the next scene they were entering a cave. A little further along the floor they were in another, bowing before a woman on a throne.

'The ones with the marks on their heads are the half-gods,' said Zafir. 'Or at least I think that's the way it works. Come here.'

She was a good way further down the hall, looking at the ceiling. As Bellepheros wandered towards her, another sequence caught his eye: what must have been the Silver King, conjuring his tunnels under the earth. Beside it a circle of half-gods held down one of their own and plucked out his eyes. When he came alongside Zafir and looked up he saw a half-god standing beside a broken egg. A dragon's head poked through the shell.

'I was eight years old when I found this place.' Zafir smiled and shook her head. 'For a long time this was my favourite. I used to lie on the floor and stare up at it for hours. The first dragon. I think.'

The dragon, like the half-gods, seemed to have a hole in its head among the lines of its scales. Bellepheros stared.

'You had something to say about the Crowntaker.' Zafir was giving him a look, eyebrows raised, and he couldn't tell how much was curiosity and how much might be simple pity. 'I imagine you mean the Black Moon? Speak, then. We are as alone here as we can ever be.'

It was hard not to be distracted by the carvings. If Zafir was right then there was so much they could learn, so much *he* could learn. 'Yes. He is ...' He knew exactly what he wanted to say. *He's taken his knife to the riders here. He's cutting the souls out of men and making them into his slaves.* But the words wouldn't come. They were in his head, clear as anything, yet somehow stuck. 'You said there would be no more slaves.' It was the closest he could get.

'I did.' Zafir cocked her head.

'And yet ...' *The Black Moon is ...* 'Yes. But ...' But that wasn't what he wanted to say! 'Holiness, forgive me ... It is not something about which I should speak. I have overstepped my bounds.' *No, I haven't!*

'Whom have I enslaved, Grand Master?'

Everyone the Black Moon has cut with his knife! 'Your maids.' His hand flew to his mouth. *What? WHAT?* 'Forgive me, Holiness. I did not mean to say that ...'

The Zafir he'd come to know in Takei'Tarr, the dragon-queen who'd burned Dhar Thosis, would have flown into a rage. She would have lashed him with her tongue until he grovelled for forgiveness, and then still might have had him whipped and hanged. Here, in her palace, she only frowned. The look on her face was strange. Alien. Was that ... hurt?

'You know, I had the same conversation with Chay-Liang. It was a year ago, when we were all lost at sea. I will tell you the same as I told her, that Myst and Onyx may leave my side whenever they wish, and with no fear for consequence. Any one of you may do that. You, Tuuran. Anyone.'

He wondered if he might even come to believe her one day. 'But we cannot ...' *But we cannot leave the Black Moon.* 'That is ...' He screwed up his face and clenched his fists. He couldn't say the words. He couldn't even tell her how he was silenced. The worst was that he felt no sense of another presence the way he did when Diamond Eye intruded on him. He simply found that, whatever he'd meant to say, the words reached his tongue and stopped, and then he didn't want to say them any more.

'We are slaves of circumstance.' It was the best he could do, the closest he could come. And he *knew* that she'd seen the Black Moon cutting men into slaves back before they'd crossed the storm-dark, back in Merizikat. She had to, didn't she? How could she not? 'You must know,' he whispered. 'You must at least suspect.'

A strange look crossed her face, as if perhaps she understood him after all. 'Slaves of circumstance.' She nodded. 'Yes, Grand Master. We are all of us that.'

A tremor shook the hall, and then another. Zafir ran back the way they'd come, and Bellepheros scurried after her as best his old knees could manage. He turned the corner into the hall of arch-ways and skidded into the back of her when she abruptly stopped. The Black Moon was coming towards them, eyes blazing bright, while every arch etched into the white stone walls now shimmered with liquid silver. The half-god moved from one to the next, press-ing his hand against their fresh mirror skin until each rippled and dissolved into something else; and Bellepheros couldn't see what lay on the other side as the half-god reached through, but sure as he was that dragons were monsters, there *was* another side.

'Holiness ...?' he croaked.

Zafir ignored him. 'Crowntaker! What are you doing?'

The Black Moon didn't answer. He didn't look at them, didn't even seem to see that he wasn't alone. He stopped in front of one more gateway, opened it, paused a moment longer than before the others, and then stepped through and was gone. The walls quaked, and the silver gates trembled back to blank white stone. Zafir ran to where the Black Moon had vanished. She touched the wall, and tapped it with a fingernail.

'As a child I heard stories,' she murmured, 'that now and then an archway would open to somewhere else. To some other world. But they were stories, and I later came to suppose that that's all they were. No one had ever seen it.' She couldn't hide the touch of wonder in her voice.

Maybe now, maybe now he's gone … Bellepheros tried again. 'The Black Moon …' *has been cutting souls! Every man he meets! Making them into slaves!* But nothing had changed. He turned away so that Zafir wouldn't see and howled a silent scream. 'Where did he go?' he asked. A stupid question. How could she possibly know?

'Who can say?' murmured Zafir. 'But the world goes on. We managed without him once before, after all.' She gave Bellepheros a hard look. 'Whatever the Black Moon was doing to rile you so, he won't be doing any more now, will he?'

Said, Bellepheros thought, with a little of the old petulance, for which – and this surprised him – he found himself profoundly grateful.

Dear Flame, is she our only hope? Is that *what I've come to?*

He'd never missed Chay-Liang so much.

10

The Dragon-Queen's Sister

Eight days after landfall

Tuuran pushed his way past an old curtain hanging across a crude tunnel. A stair ran down into darkness. He peered and tossed an alchemical lamp into the gloom; it hit the stone and shattered, a dull glowing splatter across the walls some forty steps down. Halfteeth thought he was daft for carrying around these old lamps when he had a Taiytakei light-maker strapped to his arm.

'Can't do that with gold-glass,' Tuuran muttered under his breath. Sadly Halfteeth wasn't here to eat his words. Then much louder: 'Anyone down there?'

Behind him Snacksize hawked up a gobbet of phlegm and spat it between his feet. 'I saw something come this way. I saw the curtain move and it wasn't a rat.' Snacksize, sold to the Taiytakei years ago. The whole idea made him laugh, but whoever had bought her hadn't done much laughing by the sound of things. Way Snacksize told it she'd been taken to Zinzarra, where no one would touch her. Ended up a night-soil slave, escaped, ran away, got caught, then worked in someone's gardens for a couple of years until the old sail-slave who'd watched over her died and a new one came in, which apparently led to some minor disagreements about the proper care of mint plants. Tuuran thought he probably wasn't getting the whole of the story around about there, given that it ended up with the new overseer having a trowel driven though his eye, but he didn't ask out of the respect that one slave gave another. You talked or you didn't, and that was always your choice to make.

Didn't matter. She was Adamantine now. Didn't look like much, and Tuuran didn't think there had ever even been any Adamantine Women – nor any Adamantine Dwarves for that matter – but, like

Halfteeth, she'd been with the eyrie since the Godspike. They'd survived, and in the end that was what an Adamantine Man did.

They weren't getting any answers from the stairs. Tuuran started down, slow and cautious. Hard to see how far it went. Even her Holiness was no help here. He called out again: 'My name is Tuuran. Night Watchman of the Adamantine Guard. I serve the Speaker Zafir, queen of the Silver City. If there's anyone there who can hear me, we have food and water and shelter to share.' He almost said they came in peace, but coming in peace hadn't done much good in the Octagon. At least someone had cleaned the blood off the floor now.

Snacksize at his back and then a dozen men behind. Really didn't want another fight though. He called out again: 'Did you hear? Fresh water and food. You can take as much as you want.' There were three mountains around the Silver City, but only the Enchanted Palace had water streaming through the middle. Tuuran had quietly assumed the other peaks would be empty and dead, but Zafir had sent him to come and have a look anyway. Turned out this one wasn't as dead as he'd supposed.

'They get their water from the rain,' said Snacksize as though that was some miraculous insight. The clouds had come back in the night and it was drizzling again.

'Being from the Worldspine,' grunted Tuuran, 'I imagine you're feeling right at home, crawling around mountains and being rained on.' He stopped and flicked his Taiytakei light back and forth down the steps, hoping to see something useful, but the stair just carried on down. He called out again: 'If there's anyone down there, you could make both our lives easier by talking back, you know. I'll stay right here if that helps.' He turned back to Snacksize. 'All right then, clever bastard, where do they get their food? Because they're not living up here near the top if there's nothing up here to eat, but if there is then where is it?'

'They grow things.'

'What? On sheer cliffs?' Tuuran snorted and started on down. 'You disappoint me, woman. I was all ready to ask our one and only alchemist if he'd like to take on an apprentice. But he'd need someone bright—'

'Birds,' she said. 'Didn't you see? The cliffs are full of old birds' nests, and full of caves too. They put out traps and they raid nests for eggs. We used to do that all the time.'

'Can't be many of them up here if they're living off eggs …' Tuuran stopped. In front of him the stair opened into a fissure, a void that stretched down as far as he could see and disappeared into darkness. The size of it stole the breath from his lungs. The steps carried on, gouged steep and precipitous into its side. One great abyss. He remembered something Bellepheros had told him when they'd been stuck on a ship together with nothing else to do but read books and tell stories. 'Oh, bugger. Not *this* again.' Two years ago that had been, and he'd travelled to four different worlds in between. Could hardly blame a man for forgetting, but still …

'What's up, boss?' Snacksize looked across the fissure, scanning her enchanted torch back and forth, looking for the other side, or for a top or a bottom. The space devoured light. There was no telling how big it was.

'I walked into an abyss once before,' grumbled Tuuran. 'That's what. And I'll tell you for free that climbing out again afterwards was shit. My legs are holding a grudge even now.' The steps in the side of the fissure were little more than an erratic and reluctant series of footholds. A decent person might at least have bolted a chain to the stone to give a man something to hang on to. He started on down, slowly and carefully. Years of scampering around the rigging of a Taiytakei slave galley had given him sure feet and hands and a head for heights, but this was taking the piss. 'I hope you're not scared of falling.' At least he could be fairly sure that no one was about to ambush him. 'King Hiastamir gave this place to the Order of the Dragon on his ascension to the Adamantine Palace. Any of you know that?'

'Can't say as I did,' Snacksize grunted behind him, shifting down the holds.

'Now that you do, do you even remotely care?' Snacksize seemed sure of herself as she climbed. An Outsider from the Worldspine might know a thing or two about getting around a place like this, he supposed.

'No, boss. Not even a tiny little bit. But do regale me with some more pointless shit if there's any to be had. Might make me feel a bit better if I fall off and plunge to some horrid death to know that at least it's sparing me yet another dull piece of history that no one, not even you, really cares about.'

'Ha fucking ha.' Tuuran snorted. He eased himself down ahead of her. 'The temple entrance on the surface was destroyed during the War of Thorns. Did you know *that*, at least?'

'The war of what?'

'Flame preserve me!' He squawked as he trod on a loose stone in one of the crevices and momentarily lost his balance. Snacksize caught his arm. 'Never mind. Long story short ... Great Holy Flame, will you look at that!'

They'd come down maybe fifty feet. Felt like it had been half a mile, but that was just the adrenaline. About the same again below them a narrow bridge reached out over the chasm. The bridge was white stone. Tuuran eased his way on down and crouched, took off a gauntlet and touched it. Smooth as glass and edges sharp like it had been cut yesterday. He grunted. Like the white stone of the eyrie, except here it didn't glow. He got up.

'Half-god stone,' he said, which at least meant he'd trust it to take his weight. The bridge was narrow, half a stride at best, and he couldn't see where it went. *Hopefully* to the other side, but the other side was out of reach of their torches, and half-god stone meant it had been made by the Silver King, and *that* could mean ...

He shuddered. Could mean anything at all.

He looked down. The cliff below the bridge was sheer. Vertical. He had a good look along the sides of the cavern in case there was some other way down that he hadn't noticed, but no, there very clearly wasn't. Of course there wasn't.

Snacksize jumped to join him on the bridge. Made for a bit of a crowd that did, all pressed up against the face of the stone with only a shoulder of space to share between two clumping pairs of boots. Pushed them close. Next soldier down would end up sitting on Tuuran's shoulders at this rate.

'Best you have a quiet word,' he said. 'See if there's any who might have a problem with crossing this. Heights. I'll start out on my own. I'll call back when I see anything.'

'No, boss.' Her hand caught his elbow. 'You're the Night Watchman. The Night Watchman sends other people. He doesn't do everything himself.'

Tuuran glowered. 'This one bloody does, and what's more he does it whenever he bloody well feels like it. I think, if you bothered to find out these things, you'd find most Night Watchmen very much the same in that particular.' No sense of tradition, this hotch-potch legion of his, but after a moment of thinking it over he let her go first. Maybe she had a point, but mostly he did it because she wanted to, and because she was small. He watched her, step after step, taking her time, tense as a drawn knife, half his men spreading along the first few yards of the bridge, the other half backed up clinging to the stone … He watched the dancing of her enchanted light as Snacksize walked into the dark. It was a long way before she stopped and shouted back.

'I see the end.' The words echoed everywhere. The fissure took her voice and made it into the booming call of a god. Tuuran didn't waste any time following, but he was still out in the middle when he heard her cry out. She shouted something, then came another shout, someone else, then a clash of iron, a howl of pain and last of all a crack of lightning and a boom of thunder that echoed and rolled about the cavern like a storm. He had to stop a moment, too dazzled by the flash to see where he was putting his feet; and then he wanted to run, but he didn't dare, not on a bridge so narrow. Didn't like to think too much about what might be waiting at the other end, though. When he reached it, he came with his shield raised high and his axe at the ready.

Snacksize was standing with her light sweeping back and forth over a wide open space and an enormous façade like some great temple entrance carved into the chasm wall. Two bodies sprawled at her feet. Both were dressed in scraps of what had once been dragon-rider armour. One had a bloody hole in his neck from her sword, the other lay twisted up in the unmistakable rag-doll sprawl of death by Taiytakei lightning.

'Just the two of them?' he asked. Couldn't take his eyes off the wall ahead.

'More inside.' She waved her torch at the centre of the façade, to a huge metal-bound door. 'They just came at me.' She was shaking. 'They didn't give me any choice.'

'Well apparently that was very stupid of them.' Tuuran scrunched up his nose. After all the things he'd seen, all the places

Crazy Mad had taken him in their years together, he'd imagined there wasn't much that would put the wind up him any more. This place did though. Couldn't say why. He shivered. 'The Temple of the Dragon. Men made it even before the Silver King came.' Hard to credit, but there it was.

Most of it, anyway. Presumably the Silver King had added the bridge.

He waited until his men were all across and formed up into a wall of shields, then made sure they all had their lightning throwers out and the damned things were working. Wasn't going to be much fun pushing through that door. Good chance he was going to lose someone, which never put him in a good frame of mind. *Still, needs must* ... and he about had them all ready to go, gritting his teeth for a fight, when the door opened of its own accord, loud and grinding, stone on stone, old heavy hinges thick with rust or verdigris crying out for a touch of oil. A woman walked out, and Tuuran had to look twice and hold back a little gasp. First glance she looked like her Holiness. Bit shorter and dressed in rags, and her hair was a tangled mess, but the face ... Most of all, though, it was in the way she walked. How she held herself.

'Adamantine Men, is it?' she asked, apparently not much bothered at standing in front of a dozen heavily armed and armoured soldiers, nor particularly fussed by the two corpses behind them either. She cocked her head and tilted her chin at him. 'And what Speaker do you serve today?' Flame, she even *sounded* like her Holiness.

'Her Holiness Zafir,' growled Tuuran. 'Queen of the Silver City.' He couldn't stop looking. She was like a scraggeldy mirror image. Younger. Ragged and filthy and a mess, softer on the outside and maybe not so lined, but you could see the same steel underneath, hard as diamond. Zafir as she might have been five years younger.

'Zafir is dead,' said the woman. 'Fallen in the dragon war brought by Hyrkallan and that cunt-licker Jehal. But *you* were dressed by the Taiytakei. So where are *your* masters? What did they do with Hyrkallan and his mad queen?'

Tuuran tried to imagine the woman in front of him in different clothes and twelve years younger. It was possible she was ... 'Princess Zara-Kiam?' Zafir's younger sister.

Zara-Kiam narrowed her eyes and looked at him hard and didn't speak.

'I came here with Speaker Hyram a decade ago and then some. You were younger. But I remember you. There's a lot of her Holiness in you too.' He shook his head. 'I've heard bits and pieces of this dragon war of yours, but I was busy at the time being a slave to the night-skins. Her Holiness Zafir didn't die. She was taken. The night-skins took us both, each in our own time.' A crooked smile settled on his face. 'And they came to rue us both too ...' *We brought the Silver King back with us.* But who would ever believe that? It was a thing you had to see for yourself, and rumour already had it that the Black Moon had pissed off somewhere, and who was to say he'd ever bother with coming back? He sighed. 'Her Holiness returns to reclaim her throne and restore the realms to their glory.' He was fairly sure that not one of them had the first idea how to go about doing that last bit, but never mind. 'You're welcome to—'

Zara-Kiam laughed shrilly. 'Come back to rule the wreckage, did she? I flew to war that day too. It would have been better if we'd both died and been done with it. I've seen your flying castle, though. So that's her palace now, is it?'

Tuuran took off his helm and scratched his head. The furrows in his brow deepened. None of this was going in a way that made any sense. Everywhere he went, people refused to believe the simple truths he told them. And you might think, after everything this realm had seen these last couple of years, there would be some sort of pleasure in learning of a sister unexpectedly alive. Didn't look like it, not from the face glaring in front of him. Come to that he couldn't remember if Zafir had ever said anything to him about a sister. He'd already known, but she'd never spoken of it.

'How many of you are here?'

Princess Kiam shook her head. 'I'll not give my people away so easily. You still smack of Taiytakei. You may take me to whoever claims my sister's name so I can explain to them why they should choose another.'

Tuuran tried again. 'Her Holiness will be pleased to see you.' He couldn't quite make himself believe it though. Nothing here was the way it was supposed to be. Be nice, he thought ruefully, if he showed up somewhere and someone was actually pleased to see him.

'Beginning to wish we'd stayed in Takei'Tarr,' he muttered, but no one heard.

He crossed back over the bridge with the ragged princess in front, climbed the wall of the fissure and the stairs to the outside, where the eyrie floated over the top of the mountain. He pointed, and then looked for Princess Kiam to be amazed and awed, but she simply shrugged. 'Bigger than it looked yesterday.' She tilted her chin and scanned the skies. 'Where are all the dragons? I haven't seen any dragons except the ones you brought.'

'We taught them to keep away.' Tuuran grinned smugly, but even then Princess Kiam wasn't impressed. When he thought she wasn't looking, he glowered at her. He led her to one of the cages that would lift them to the eyrie rim. Glared and frowned at them too. The cages and their winches were getting old and had only been lashed together in the first place. Best do something about fixing them up properly before there was an accident ...

Princess Kiam wasn't looking at the cages. She was peering at his neck. 'Are you a Scales?'

The marks on his skin. He shook his head. 'Adamantine born and bred, but I had an unfortunate encounter with a hatchling.'

'Oh.' She shrugged it off as though it didn't matter. 'Why do you keep staring at me?'

'Because you look like your sister. It's ... striking. It keeps taking me by surprise.'

'We don't look anything like each other.' Kiam turned away from him. Tuuran sneaked another glance and begged to differ. Her nose was pointed while Zafir's was rounder. Other than that they were two puppies from the same litter ...

He shuddered and glared at the sky. The drizzle was turning back to steady rain. *Two puppies from the same litter?* That wasn't any way to be thinking about her Holiness and her sister.

When they reached the rim he picked his way through the piled detritus of abandoned crates and ropes and sacks where his men had been offloading the supplies from Merizikat down into the Moonlit Mountain. He led Zara-Kiam up the wall and then tried to take her down to the dragon yard and into the tunnels where it was dry, but she wouldn't have it. She walked along the top of the wall instead, staring at everything. The lightning cannon fascinated her, and Tuuran almost fired it so she could see what they did, then stopped himself. Showing off, was he? He stomped away to get a proper grip on himself, and sent Snacksize off on a glass sled through the air between the mountain tops to take word back to her Holiness, to ask her kindly to recall the eyrie, since otherwise they were all stuck out here on entirely the wrong mountain.

Zara-Kiam was still up on the wall, standing out in the rain. Drenched. He brought her a cloak, but by then there wasn't much point.

'I remember him.' Kiam pointed to Diamond Eye, circling the ruins of the Silver City far below. 'He was one of Zafir's favourites. She took another to ride when Hyrkallan came, but I remember that one. Diamond Eye. So she really didn't die?'

Tuuran told the story as best he knew it – how the Taiytakei had taken Zafir and Diamond Eye and a clutch of dragon eggs and had tried to start their own eyrie, and how it had all ended badly. 'I wasn't there for most of it. You'd best ask Grand Master Bellepheros if you want to know more.'

'You have a grand master alchemist too?' She arched an eyebrow. 'Anyone else?'

'Not from here.' Didn't know where even to start with Crazy Mad and the Black Moon. Too hard to get into all that without sounding stupid. So he didn't bother, and ended up standing beside her in the rain, looking out at the haze and the dim outline of the Silver City, at the other two mountains of the Pinnacles poking up through the earth like the skeletal fingers of some buried god, wondering what to say and not finding any answers, feeling more and more like a fish flopped up on a muddy shore and not knowing how to get back into the water. 'You ought to get inside,' he said after a bit. 'Too much cold and wet doesn't do any man any good.'

She didn't move. Didn't seem right, but then what was he going to do about it? Pick her up and carry her?

'You have no idea what it's like,' she said after a while, 'to be able to stand out here in the open and just breathe the air without looking up all the time.'

He laughed at that. 'I do have *some* idea.'

Took about an hour for Diamond Eye to give up on doing whatever he was doing and come crashing down with Zafir on his back to tow the eyrie from one mountain to the other. Tuuran had Kiam down into the tunnels by then. Pointed her to Baros Tsen's old bathhouse down in the bowels where the Black Moon used to spend his time, found her some threadbare old towels and a reasonably clean old slave tunic. Couldn't think of anyone to send to look after her, not with Myst and Onyx in the Moonlit Mountain and him with nothing but a handful of foul-mouthed scurvy men and one bad-tempered alchemist. If she needed any looking after at all, which didn't look likely.

Zafir's unexpected sister. Hadn't been ready for that.

11

Mad Queen Jaslyn

Eight days after landfall

Zafir sat on her throne, dressed in a queen's dress she hadn't worn for more than two years. Servants who had seen half a dozen lords and queens come and go wafted silently around her. They had survived her mother, Meteroa, Valmeyan, Jehal, and never changed. They knew where things were, even after Hyrkallan and his riders had ransacked the place.

She'd loved this dress once. Fresh-blood-red, threaded with gold and silver and made from silk by the seamstresses of Furymouth, but it seemed tawdry now after the dazzling clothes of the Taiytakei. It didn't quite fit any more either. She wasn't the same Zafir. The last year had sharpened her, changed her shape, leaned her, but her discomfort went beyond that. They no longer belonged to the same world, her and this silk. She was more at home in her armour these days.

Home. The word was supposed to mean something, wasn't it? And perhaps it had when she'd first sat on her throne again, commanding the Octagon, when she'd wandered the old halls of the Silver King dredging through two decades of memories. She'd decided almost at once that she would welcome Hyrkallan's riders into her home, if they would have her, forgive everything that had happened in the dragon war if they would do the same; but they hated her, every last one of them, and it seemed such an implacable thing that couldn't ever be moved, and so the world would go back to the way it had been before, and she'd hang them because they gave her no choice, and then everyone she didn't hang would hate her even more, and they'd all fall to fighting again to see who would be the last to stand upright atop the pile of bones and ash that the realms had become. She *would* fight for that too, if she had to. She'd fight for everything because she didn't know anything else, but it left her so overwhelmingly weary. Weary to the marrow.

Home. Nothing but a great emptiness.

There has to be another way.

It is the dragons' way, little one. Diamond Eye's thoughts were as gentle as a dragon could be as he roamed the once magnificent Silver City. She'd send soldiers into the tunnels, she decided, for the men and women who eked out a living there. And *they'd* hate her too, because she was a dragon-rider and Hyrkallan had been a dragon-rider, and Hyrkallan had had a fondness for sending his riders to hunt and kill them; but she'd do it anyway. Tuuran and his company could deal with it when they were done rooting around the other two mountain summits.

She'd rebuild her city one day. She told herself that every now and then, though she didn't see how. But right now she needed to decide what to do about Hyrkallan's riders. The Crowntaker had kept them in line for a while, but the Crowntaker was gone, and who knew when he might come back?

Talk to them. Myst and Bellepheros had counselled mercy.

Tuuran, off exploring, had left her with Halfteeth running things. Crooked-faced, broken-jawed Halfteeth didn't bother pretending that he liked her, but after what he'd done over Farakkan, Zafir didn't much like Halfteeth either, so that was fair at least. She told him to bring Queen Jaslyn to her, up on the summit, warned him to be nice if he wanted to keep his hamstrings, then left her throne and wrapped herself in the old comfort of dragonscale and a cloak against the worst of the weather. She climbed the Great Stair to the summit, to the whip of wind and the slash of rain, and stood in the ruin of the Reflecting Garden.

Talk to them. But how could that ever work? What could she offer?

Halfteeth brought Jaslyn to her. Jaslyn was dressed in a simple tunic. Halfteeth hadn't bothered to give her anything against the rain, and by the time they reached Zafir, she was soaked and shivering. Zafir rolled her eyes at Halfteeth. The rain lashed them.

'Go away.' She took off her cloak.

Halfteeth sniffed. 'Tuuran will have my balls if I let you get hurt.'

'You won't have any to give him if you don't do as you're told.'

He looked at her, looked at Queen Jaslyn, shrugged and withdrew, settling back under the Queen's Gate out of the downpour. Zafir put her cloak across Jaslyn's shoulders and stood beside her. For a while she looked at the remains of the Reflecting Garden, then at Jaslyn, then back again. She almost had to shout over the wind. 'I get angry about the most stupid things,' she said at last. 'It makes me angry that the dragons did this. Of all the havoc they wrought, it makes me angry that they destroyed *this*. A pointless, stupid vanity of a thing, but it was beautiful, and nothing we make will ever replace it.'

Jaslyn stood stiff and awkward. The hiss of rain splashing on the pools bubbling from the Silver King's fountain filled the silence that hung between them, the whistle of the wind through ruined stone. Zafir wiped the rain from her eyes.

'It used to make me angry that you drove me from my home.' She took a deep breath and sighed. 'Actually, it still does. You drove me into the sea.'

'You brought me here to kill me,' said Jaslyn coldly. 'So can't you just be done with it?'

'I hear you woke a dragon.'

'My Silence. They say I'm mad. Even my lord Hyrkallan.' She spat his name with loathing.

'Yes. I heard your dragon's name was Silence.' Zafir pulled down the collar of her dragonscale coat. Cold rain on her skin. She ran a finger along the scar Silence had given her, then drew back her sleeve and touched the inside of her elbow where the Statue Plague had started to mark her. 'These are both gifts from your Silence. Now I must bow to my alchemists and beg for their potions or else die a slow lingering death.' The old anger fluttered through her, capricious in its vengeance. 'Diamond Eye bit off her head. Though we both know you can't kill a dragon, not really. I suppose she's here somewh—'

Jaslyn clamped her hands around Zafir's throat. She pushed as if trying to lift Zafir right off the ground, throwing them both towards the summit's edge in the storm. The uneven ground made her stumble. Zafir forced her arms between Jaslyn's and pulled apart, breaking her grip. They lurched and clashed heads. Zafir reeled, staggered, tripped and fell, splashed into a puddle. Jaslyn picked up a rock to smash Záfir's skull, but Halfteeth was on her before she could bring it down. He pulled Jaslyn away and then held her while another Adamantine Man offered Zafir a hand.

Zafir howled at them over the wind: 'Go away! Both of you, or I'll have you thrown off this mountain!' Yes, *this* was what she'd been missing. She shoved Halfteeth. 'Go! Go on! Leave us!' The anger. Anger was her engine. She picked herself up and pushed at Jaslyn. 'Is this what you want?'

'You have no idea.' Jaslyn grabbed her again, trying to drag her to the edge of the cliffs. A swirl of wind staggered them. Rain lashed across Zafir's face, left her half-blind. She broke free, danced towards the summit edge overlooking the Silver City. The cliffs here were sheer almost all the way to the ground, but everything was lost in a haze of grey. Zafir turned. Beckoned.

'Come, then.' She backed away as Jaslyn advanced. The rain was getting under her armour now, cold and damp and clammy.

'You have no idea,' Jaslyn said again, 'what I did because of you.' Halfteeth and his men were circling. Zafir screamed at them to go away and leave her alone, and yes, they'd be damned, and Tuuran would feed them their balls, but she was their speaker, their queen, and *let it be just the two of us. Dragon-queens alone!*

She stopped with her back to the cliff, wavering in the wind, her feet on the edge. She cocked her head. She was grinning, on the edge of madness. Maybe the two of them had something in common after all. 'Well? What *did* you do?'

'They told me you were dead over Evenspire. Lystra was trapped. Prisoner or worse. So I had to get her back. I *had* to.' Jaslyn lunged and then skipped away, uncertain. She flicked the rain off her face and came again. 'Nothing else mattered. I gave myself to Hyrkallan.' She was trembling. Hunger and anger and disgust and loathing. 'I pitched my dragons with your Viper. I gave myself away like a piece of meat, and it was all for Lystra, and all because of you. Because of you and Jehal. Because *you* couldn't let him go.'

'Me?' Zafir bared her teeth. 'I'd force-feed Jehal his own manhood if he was still alive.'

'No, you wouldn't! You'd kill Lystra so you could have him again. You'd kill anyone who looked at him. But he's dead now, and my sister is far away under the Spur where you can't touch her.'

Shaking again. Despite the cloak, Jaslyn was soaked to the skin. 'And nor can I. And all I want is to fly again, to touch the sky and ride a dragon and be with her. But I can't, and it will never be, not now. So put an end to me, if that's what you brought me here to do. Put an end to this droning, dull, sad, suffocating mimicry of life.' Jaslyn paused, keeping a distance between the two of them. Four or five strides. 'Jehal's dead, Zafir. Dead. Your lover. A dragon killed him. He died badly, the way that shit-stain prick deserved, and no one mourned him, not one single tear. But I can tell you this, Zafir: I can tell you that at the end he loved my sister, not you.'

Dead. Zafir already knew, but Jaslyn's last sting caught her and made it suddenly real. She barked a harsh laugh, threw back her head and let the rain wash over her. 'So I'm denied the pleasure of killing him myself? But that was half the reason I came back!'

'And the other half was Lystra, was it?' Jaslyn was breathing hard, almost ready to charge. Halfteeth's men were hiding where they thought Zafir wouldn't notice, but they were too far away to make any difference. Zafir let a sneer cross her face. Slowly, with every ounce of disdain she could muster.

'I came back because this is my home. So Jehal's little starling was why you sided with him when you hated his every pore? For sister Lystra? Because you loved her? And then what? She ran away with him and left you here, did she?' The look in Jaslyn's eye. Murder and pain. Zafir spread her arms to Jaslyn and to the storm. 'Come on then! Between them they spurned us both, and I have already stood where you stand, ready to throw myself into the void. In a golden gondola hanging over the great cloud of the storm-dark that lies at the heart of Takei'Tarr, faced by a sorceress who had made me into a slave. I could have charged her down and hurled us both to our end, and yet I didn't, because I am *not* worthless. So here I am. Come then, Queen Jaslyn of the north, queen of Sand and Stone, queen of Flint. Of all you three sisters you have by far the most of your mother in you, and she would not have flinched. Come, unless you have nothing left, unless *you* truly are worthless. I lost Jehal long before Evenspire. I know that. And you lost your sister Lystra too. I can tell you that at the end she loved Jehal, not you. I look at you and I know.'

Jaslyn screamed. She charged, and Zafir didn't try to get out of the way, but let Jaslyn crash into her, let herself take one step back and then another and find nothing but air. Let them tip over the edge together and fall.

'All for her.' Jaslyn held her tight, screaming in Zafir's face as the wind howled past them. It tore the cloak off her back and ripped at Zafir's dragonscale coat. 'No one else mattered. And my mother gave her to that shit-eater!'

The wind tore Jaslyn away. Zafir spread her arms and closed her eyes. Amid the screaming panic of falling was an odd shred of serenity. Of relief. Was that how it was for Jaslyn too? Probably not.

I shouldn't be afraid.

No. Diamond Eye's claws folded gently around her.

Her as well.

The wind was too strong for her to open her eyes and look into the teeth of it. If anything they fell faster now, raindrops scouring her skin like a thousand tiny daggers; and then she felt Diamond Eye spread his wings and gently slow and level into a glide; and then the rhythmic lurch and rise as he climbed back to the mountain's summit. Dimly, over the rush of air, she realised that Jaslyn was still screaming. Not the shrieks of unfettered terror that usually came with being caught in a dragon's claws, but furious howling sobbing wails of despair. *It mattered to her that much did it, to hurt me?*

Diamond Eye didn't answer, but she could see into his thoughts, and through them into Jaslyn. She could see the fractures, the broken pieces that were held together as best Jaslyn could manage, but which would never properly mend.

I suppose I look like that too. It was hard to really hate someone when you could see into their soul.

Yes. Diamond Eye reached the top of the mountain and landed. He lowered Zafir and then Jaslyn carefully to the ground. He stretched his wings over them, a moment of shelter from the wind and the rain, not that it made much of a difference. Little rivulets ran against her skin underneath her dragonscale.

Hold her down. But be kind. Zafir crouched beside Hyrkallan's reluctant queen, the last echoes of her own fury fading inside her head. 'I hear you once thought that dragons should be free. You've seen what comes of that. Diamond Eye is free. The other dragons who fly with me ... not so much. They remember and have woken, but they are beholden to the Black Moon, half-god brother to the Silver King. But you shouldn't hear it from me. Hear it from my dragon. Hear him thunder.' *Tell her the story of the Black Moon. Answer her questions.*

She turned her back, blocked the two of them from her mind and walked away, waiting for it to be done. She scanned the skies for other dragons. Not one, not a single speck. They could be lurking up above the cloud, of course, but if they were anywhere near then Diamond Eye would feel their thoughts and tell her, wouldn't he?

It is done. Diamond Eye let Jaslyn go. The dragon cocked his head, that curious and amused look he had, waiting to see what she would do.

Zafir stood by the edge of the cliff. She spread her arms.

'Well?' she called. 'Shall we go again?' When Jaslyn didn't move Zafir swept her arm over the vista of the mountain top, its ruined fortress and temple and gardens, the haze of raindrops shattering as they hit stone, mist and spray swirling in the wind. 'Dragons should be free? You'll pardon me, I hope, if I'm sceptical. You've seen what they do.'

Jaslyn shrank away. She was shaking. Sodden. Freezing cold and almost naked now her cloak was gone. Her thin tunic stuck to her. She got to her feet alone and walked without a word to the edge of the cliff beside Zafir, stood there and looked down.

'You should have let me fall,' she said. 'All is ruin. There is no hope.'

'And it's all my fault.' The words stuck in Zafir's throat. She'd meant to spit them out with scornful derision, a question mocking the notion, but from the way they hung in the air beside her they sounded more like a confession.

'I don't want life in a world like this.' Jaslyn walked off the edge. Zafir grabbed at her and caught her arm. They almost went over together again. She ended up lying by the edge, holding Jaslyn dangling her by her wrist.

'Let go of me!'

'The world is what it is,' cried Zafir, 'and we've got what we've got, and you might hate me to the very core, but what does it make you if you run away? A coward! And that is *not* what you are! Nor was your mother, nor your sister!' Her voice softened. 'Lystra fought me, axe and sword. I stacked the odds against her and she did it anyway, and she very nearly won. *She* wasn't afraid. I would make a different world in so many ways, and so would you, but you have to *want* it.'

'Let me *go*!' Jaslyn was struggling now, trying to pull herself loose, slowly dragging Zafir further over the edge.

'Flame, woman! You know I can just have Diamond Eye catch you again. I see your lust for little Lystra, so much more than the affection of one sister for another. Lost middle sibling, starved of a mother's love? Is *that* your excuse? Mere neglect? How I wish I'd shared that fate.' Zafir's jaw clenched tight. All the venom she held for the world, and suddenly she could see that Jaslyn held the same, and she was slipping inexorably through Zafir's fingers, and Zafir found she desperately didn't want Jaslyn to die. 'You deserve better! You want to hate me? Here, then. See who I am.' *Show her.* 'Take a good long look at the scars I carry inside me.' *Show her everything.* 'See them! If still you want to fall then so be it. But ride with me and you'll ride on the back of a dragon once more, and I swear I will take you back to Lystra's side.' They'd gone to war. Bitterest enemies, and yet underneath so alike that it made Zafir choke. Diamond Eye pulled it out of her, showing it to Jaslyn, the princess locked away in the lightless room, cold and scared, afraid but more fearful still of what would happen when the door opened, more afraid of that than of anything in the world.

Jaslyn stopped struggling. Zafir hauled her up. For a moment they lay side by side, the two of them gasping, rain spattering them both, wiping it from their faces, drenched and bedraggled.

'I don't want your loyalty,' panted Zafir. 'But will you help me make this world into something different, or do you still just want to die? Because if it's death you want then go ahead.'

'Lystra.' Jaslyn rolled to her feet. Zafir stayed where she was, lying on her back. If Jaslyn decided to pick up a rock and bash her brains out now, Diamond Eye would either stop her or he wouldn't. 'Lystra is the Speaker under the Mountain. What will you do with her?'

Zafir rose to her haunches. She held out the Speaker's Ring on her finger. 'There's only one speaker, Queen Jaslyn. Lystra has the spear. She has the last alchemists. I'm afraid I will need them both.

But I'll not hurt her, if that's what you want. She can have her mountain. Her realm. You can have it together if you want.' The Black Moon would take the spear anyway, probably from both of them, and after that not much else would matter. *Poor broken princess.* 'When was the last time you flew, Jaslyn?'

Jaslyn shuddered. 'When we flew to war.'

'You miss it, don't you?' Zafir touched a finger to Jaslyn's cheek, stood and circled her close, purring softly. 'It's a part of what we are, isn't it? We dragon-queens? Without them we are diminished. Like losing an arm and a leg. Hopping and shuffling where once we could run.'

'It's death,' said Jaslyn flatly.

Will you let her ride you? She felt for Diamond Eye. *You are never some toy to be passed about, but I win peace here if I win this woman.*

Diamond Eye cocked his head. An angry tilt this time. *If you command then I must obey. The cut of the Black Moon's knife demands it.*

I ask, dragon. That is all.

Diamond Eye considered. He bared his fangs and glared at Zafir and then at Jaslyn. *Once only. I promise nothing more.*

I do not ask for promises. They are always broken.

The dragon seemed to laugh, some old dark memory welling inside him that he kept to himself. Zafir turned to Jaslyn. 'I cannot give you a dragon. They are not mine to offer. But Diamond Eye will take you to the sky. I have asked and he accedes. I have earned that, and perhaps one day you will do the same.' She took Jaslyn's hand. 'Give me a bond of peace from you and your riders. You will fly again, and I will not hurt your sister.'

'And her son?'

For a moment Zafir closed her eyes. She'd forgotten, and remembering was like another knife in the ribs. Lystra had been carrying Jehal's child. A son, was it? So the bastard betrayer had an heir. 'And her son,' she said at last.

'And I really will fly again?'

Zafir laughed. 'Ask my dragon, Queen Jaslyn. Do not ask me.'

Jaslyn dropped to one knee. She took Zafir's hand and kissed the Speaker's Ring. 'Then you are the speaker of the nine realms and queen of the Silver City, and no man who rides dragons in my name shall question that it is so.'

Zafir tried not to laugh. So po-faced and serious. When was the last time any of Jaslyn's riders had taken to the skies?

'Why me, Zafir? Why not Hyrkallan? My riders will follow his commands before they follow mine.'

'Because men always imagine themselves to be masters, Queen Jaslyn, and I've had enough of that.' Zafir cocked her head. Maybe she'd been hoping to see a smile, but Jaslyn's plain face remained a mask of tragedy. 'Besides, do you honestly think I might win him over?'

Jaslyn shook her head.

'Neither did I. So there was that too.'

'I never did like him. Once we were married I learned to loathe him.'

'What do you want me to do with him?'

'Whatever you like.'

They walked together to the entrance, to the Queen's Gate and the High Hall and the Grand Stair beyond, out of the rain at last, dripping a wet trail behind them. Halfteeth and two Adamantine Men followed three steps behind. When they reached the Octagon Zafir threw off her sodden dragonscale and told Halfteeth to find Jaslyn a guardsman, and to mind her body with his life. 'Find her armour too,' she said, 'and some dry clothes.' She told him to get lost then, but he didn't, not straight away. Instead he bared his handful of remaining teeth. Maybe it was meant to be a grin. He nodded towards the throne.

The Outsider woman Tuuran liked was waiting there, short and wiry with lethal eyes. Snacksize? Zafir frowned. Stupid demeaning name, but hadn't she been on the eyrie with Tuuran over on the other mountains? Thick as thieves these days, her and Halfteeth and Tuuran.

Halfteeth's grin grew wider. He bobbed and trotted away. Zafir glared. The silks she wore underneath her dragonscale were damp from the rain and already uncomfortable. They kept sticking to her.

'Well? What is it?'

'Tuuran asks if you wouldn't mind having the dragons tow the eyrie back over here, your Holiness.' Snacksize paused.

'He does, does he?' Halfteeth hadn't quite gone, she saw. He was lurking in the shadows by the passages off into the Enchanted Palace.

Snacksize nodded. She beamed. 'On account of us finding someone he reckons might be your sister.'

Jaslyn was forgotten. 'What?'

'He seemed to know her. Reckons she's Zara-Kiam. That's right, isn't it?'

Zafir ran straight back up the Grand Stair, feeling the eyes on her back, and Halfteeth with his silent mocking crooked laughter. She called for Diamond Eye and raced out without waiting to dress in dragonscale and glass and gold, skin stinging in the rain, climbed onto the dragon's back and flew him straight to the eyrie. She landed hard, rain-drenched, clothes clinging to her, slid off and fell and twisted her ankle in her hurry, the same ankle that had never been quite the same since her duel with Lystra back when the realms weren't ruled by dragons. Tuuran must have seen her coming. He was waiting for her.

'Where is she?' Zafir almost barged him off the wall.

'The bathhouse, Holiness, but—'

She ran down the steps into the dragon yard and on into the nearest tunnel, down the spiralling passages. The eyrie was a mess, half unpacked, Merizikat crates and sacks piled up in the tunnels and left there, waiting to be unloaded. She hurdled them where she had to, scrambling and jumping until she reached the bottom where the eyrie tunnels all came together at the hard iron doors to Baros Tsen's bathhouse. She paused then, suddenly wondering what she was doing and whether she had the courage for this. But she had to.

She took two deep breaths and creaked open the door.

'Zara?' Little sister. Zara-Kiam. 'Zara?'

Princess Kiam sat in the bath, head and shoulders out of the water, her golden hair plastered to her skin. She turned and settled a languid gaze on Zafir. For a long time neither of them spoke, until Zafir took another step.

'You're alive,' Zafir said.

'Yes.' Zara-Kiam nodded slowly. 'And so are you, I see. More's the pity.'

Zafir took another step. 'Are you hurt?'

'Don't pretend you care.'

'Are. You. *Hurt?*' Zafir's foot twitched.

'So you're the Speaker again. Does that mean I can have my old rooms back?'

'Zara—'

Zara-Kiam turned to face her fully. 'Because I really would *like* them back. Because it hasn't been the most pleasant time while you were gone, what with the end of the world and dragons and so forth. I've been living with the bare few riders who survived your war and a gaggle of lecherous old men. Mind you, I suppose that was better than living with you.'

However she armoured herself, Zara always pierced her. Zafir strode to the bath and almost grabbed her sister by the hair to haul her out of the water. 'Did they touch you?' Words through gritted teeth.

Zara grabbed Zafir by the jaw. 'If you mean did they rape me, then no, no one did that, although I did have a good few rough fucks for the sheer pleasure of it, that and the not having much else to do after you decided it wasn't enough to wreck our home and went and did it everywhere. If anyone had "touched" me, as you put it, I'd have cut their dicks off and stuffed them down their own throats.' Zara-Kiam let go. 'No, big sister. I can look after myself, in case that's a concern you still pretend to have. Would you like to go away now, or shall we cut each other raw some more?'

'Can we ever find peace, you and I?' Zafir backed towards the door. Two years and nothing had changed, not the slightest thing. She could have been away for a day. An hour.

'Come back and ask me again when you can raise the dead.'

Zafir left. She closed the door and put her back to it, sank to her knees and touched a hand to her eye, wiping it dry. She saw Tuuran then, lurking uncomfortably up the corridor, half watching and half pretending not to pay any attention. Zafir straightened herself.

'Holiness, there are still men inside the—'

She pushed past him, then stopped for a moment. 'When you go back to the eyrie, you will take the riders sworn to Queen Jaslyn and return them their weapons and armour. You will bring them to the Octagon with their queen, and they will swear their fealty to their speaker.'

'Holiness—'

Zafir held up a finger, silencing him. 'Don't speak, Tuuran. Just don't. And listen. Whatever else you do, never tell my sister it was your knife I took on that night when Speaker Hyram came to the Pinnacles. Never. If you do then she'll kill you. Mostly because she knows it would hurt me to lose you.'

'Holi—'

'Stay here and finish your work. Come back when you're ready.'

She walked away, climbed onto Diamond Eye, and they leapt together into the sky. She barely noticed the rain now, already soaked through. They flew long, high, languid circles, up through the clouds into glorious sun and down again into drear and gloom. When she landed she hid away in her rooms, stripped off her wet clothes and curled up naked on the bed, wrapped under silk sheets, then stretched and tossed and turned and tried to think of useful things; but all she saw was that night, more than a decade ago, panicked, pressed against a wall by too much strength to resist, a hand up her dress, and then Tuuran's voice beside them both. *Leave her be, you fat prick.*

Her hand grabbing the knife from his belt. Stabbing and stabbing and stabbing. Murdering the man who called himself her father, though he wasn't, not really. And, by the Great Flame, she'd had her reasons for it.

'I did it for her as much as I did it for me.'

'Did what, mistress?' asked Myst. Zafir shook her head. Off in another room, one of the babies started to cry. Myst hurried away. Zafir stretched out and tried to swallow the memories and wrap them in darkness. As she reached a hand under her pillow, her fingers found a piece of cloth almost lost down the top of the bed. She pulled it out and looked at it. A strip of black silk, a blindfold. Once upon a time it had let her see through the eyes of an enchanted golden dragon, one of a pair that the Taiytakei had given to Jehal for his wedding to Lystra. Jehal hadn't given the second dragon to his bride, he'd given it to his lover. To her. To Zafir, the dragon-queen.

She put it on and stretched out her mind, searching in case it was still there.

12

The Black Moon

Nine days after landfall

From world to world the Black Moon pauses and wanders. Beside each gateway he finds, he reaches out, looking for that something lost, something missing; on and on until at last he steps across a silver haze into a room ringed by archways. There he pauses. A breeze blows, tinged with a tang of sharp smoke and with something else, a scent the Black Moon seeks, a thing familiar and yet unknown, like a well trodden story but a thousand years out of time. Trapped inside him, watching from a shrinking corner of his own mind, Berren the Crowntaker screams in silence. He is fighting for possession of himself against an irresistible enemy, mercy neither offered nor given, squashed into a tiny spark. The Black Moon owns him, flesh and blood, thought and bone.

They are atop a tower. Four archways open to the world outside, a waiting balcony; and Berren knows, without knowing how, that they point to the north, the south, the east and west. The sky beyond is clear and dark, though it was brilliant daylight in the world they left only a moment before. The air is clear and the stars shine bright. A slender crescent moon hangs low on the horizon, tinged with a drop of red. It will be dawn soon.

The Crowntaker feels a shiver, an anxiety deep and old. An ancient hostility that simmers between them, the half-god and the moon. The half-god turns his back, steps through the western arch, and there they stand, the half-god and the last light of Berren Crowntaker, at the peak of a slender white tower. There are other towers here, five in all, arranged in a circle. A city spreads beneath them, and a great river runs beside it, as wide as the magnificent waters of Deephaven, his home, or of Merizikat in the Dominion where the dead walked in dark catacombs until the enchantress Chay-Liang burned them to their end.

The Black Moon sniffs the air. He smells the death-grip of war. Fire and steel, the reckless rage of the flaming sun, the merciless stiletto prick of the murderous fickle moon. He smells death; walking, shambling, marching forests of life extinguished and yet gripped tight. Ships swarm on the black-night water of the river. He can see their lights. Fires in the city scatter along two facing lines. Streets divided. Families. Brother against brother, daughter against mother. The sun and the moon, their pretty clothes stripped away, animosity naked and open, both sides weary to the bone, each aware of the futility of their cause and yet trapped, neither able to give an inch of ground. The Black Moon smells it all. He licks his lips and tastes the air and bares his teeth in vicious joy. The rest of the city is in darkness. Abandoned to whatever war has come.

Divided they fall, Crowntaker, he says, and with that thought comes so much more. A sleeping parasite growing somewhere in the midst of this, rising from strength to strength. A path dark and secret, black-scaled cobras twisting in a sea of poison beneath unsuspecting skin.

Sun or moon, it does not matter. Each as false as the other.

The Black Moon chooses no side in this. He has no love for gods any more. He will bring an end to them all if he has his way.

Flurries of bright orange sparks streak from the river. Taiytakei rockets, launched from one of the ships. They arch through the air and down, and bloom into plumes of flame. A distant roar, a thousand waiting voices calling to arms. Smoke rises. Shapes fast through the air. Men on sleds. The sun-flash of lightning as some new pointless battle begins. The Black Moon looks on, his eyes flaying into the city's heart to the flash-sparks of iron and steel to taste the first scatter of life's extinction, while behind those same eyes Berren Crowntaker turns away. He has seen all this before. At least this time there isn't a dragon.

A dart of dazzling flame flares and flashes across the sky. It crashes into the river. A ship bursts alight, stem to stern. The ball of fire bursts and leaps away. Flurries of lightning give chase. Berren touches a hand to the side of his face. The fire witch of Aria once burned off Tuuran's ear, and she had looked the same as this, if there was a difference to be told between one ball of fire and another.

Aria. With a jolt he realises that he knows this place. Further downriver lies the sprawl that birthed him. Deephaven. Upriver the throne from which the Ice Witch rules the world. Witches, kings, speakers, sea lords, arbiters, elemental men, the Crowntaker has seen them all, and what are they? No more or less than he: fleeting flesh and bone, come and gone in the blink of a half-god's eye.

The Black Moon walks back among the arches. One by one he touches them. They shimmer open, silver and inviting. Another touch and the silver ripples and spreads apart, opening like the iris of an eye.

I see you.

A voice in his head. The Black Moon starts, startled and aquiver like a night-time mouse who feels the owl's all-seeking eye. He moves faster, searching, then freezes as one gate opens to another tower-top ring of arches and balconies, and standing in the centre like a spider in his web, staring back at the shimmer of silver through the light of the Black Moon's eye and straight into Berren's naked heart, is the warlock with the ruined face and the one blind milky eye.

At last.

'You!' He takes a step and then freezes. The warlock with the ruined face and the one blind milky eye wags a warning finger and shakes his head.

'You can't come here, little broken half-god. *She* will have you if you do.' The warlock titters to himself. His eyes dart about the floor. 'Very bad for both of us, that. Our time is short, but I have a moment for you. I made it especially.'

Berren howls at the top of his lungs, bursting through the Black Moon, a spear of incandescent fury. For a heartbeat his body is his own. 'Tell me what you did to me!'

The warlock's head shifts from side to side like a bird's, peering as though trying to look inside him. 'Who have you got in there, broken little half-god? I know your face, but who is it inside? Skyrie? Is there still a bit of you left? You gave yourself to this, don't you remember? You gave yourself to *him*.' He giggles to himself. 'Do you remember the lessons that little pet Vallas gave?

How to hide yourself? Or is it you, Crowntaker? A little piece here, a little piece there. None that makes any sense. None that knows who or what they are. But now and then each piece feels an inexplicable compulsion they cannot help but follow. And then all the little pieces come together, and for a time they remember their task. And they act, oh yes they do, and then back to little pieces again before she can catch them.' The warlock cocks his head. 'Over and over and over. So many little pieces, and sometimes accidents happen and one of them doesn't come back, and then it's gone for ever and the rest must make do as best they can. Like an old old picture with the paint all cracked, and here and there little flakes have come away, and the flakes mean nothing but a drab flash of dirt and colour, but the picture ... oh, the picture survives and keeps its meaning.' For a moment the one-eyed warlock looks as forlorn as a scolded child. 'I have to do it. It's the only way to keep her out. The ice witch comes inside me whenever she wants, you see. She sees the holes. She thinks it's you, half-god, who does this to me. She doesn't know she's got it all wrong, that I am the master and you are the pawns. She's looking for you now. Poor crippled half-god. She understands her mistake and she will do anything to put it right. So hide, little cripple, before she finds you.'

Berren steps closer, determined to snap the warlock's throat, but now the Black Moon stirs and forces him down, drives him away, whips and lashes him into the tiny dark corner that is his own.

Hide?

'We made a hole in you, Crowntaker. Do you remember?'

He remembers. How long ago now? Twenty-five years?

'Little seeds, Crowntaker. You and I were but boys upon the shoulders of others.'

He sees it as it was. The jerk of the knife, the blade pushing into his skin, his own hands pressing it deeper towards his heart. He screams, but there is no pain, only a pressure inside his head. Seeing himself as though looking in a mirror, but he isn't seeing his skin; he is looking at what lies underneath, at his soul, an endless tangle of threads like a spider's web wrapped within itself.

'Tell the knife! Make it your promise: You will be unswervingly loyal to my desires. And then cut, Berren, cut! Three little slices. You! Obey! Me!'

Saffran Kuy. The warlock of Deephaven. Berren the Crowntaker closes his eyes to the dim flood of old anguish.

'I took something away from you, but I put something into Skyrie too. Do you remember Skyrie?'

Berren sees again. The dusty memories he carries with him of a soul now extinguished. A man standing over him in robes the colour of moonlight. He blinks, bewildered. The man's face, where it isn't lost among the shadows of his cowl, is pale. One half is ruined, scarred ragged by disease or fire, with one blind eye, milky white. The warlock who stands before him through a gateway across the world. In Skyrie's memories the warlock's fingers trace symbols that split the air open like swollen flesh. Black shadow oozes from the gashes left behind.

'Are you death?' Skyrie asks, but the words never come out.

'I carry the Black Moon.' The stranger's one good eye bores into him.

And then himself again, more a man than a boy but not yet the Crowntaker. *'It fills the hole, you see.'* Words Gelisya once spoke. The dark queen, before that's what she became. *'Like the Black Moon and the Dead Goddess fill the hole in the world. He showed me. You have to keep it closed. Otherwise something will come through.'* Even with her lips almost touching his ear, her whisper is so quiet that he can barely hear her. *'He's making us ready. To let it in when the Ice Witch brings down the Black Moon.'*

She'd told him, warned him of what his fate might be. Now he chokes out words: 'Was she your puppet too? Everything she did to me? *You* made her do that?'

'We made a hole in you, Crowntaker. All ready to fill. And so we did, and now the Bloody Judge comes to wreak his havoc as ever we foresaw. But you …' The warlock giggles, then winks his one good eye. 'The Ice Witch doesn't know how my little pieces all scurry about. Oh, she despises me, but not like she hates you, broken little half-god.' His eye rolls. He bares his teeth and grins, then cocks his head and raises an exaggerated hand to his ear. 'Hark, now! She comes for you. Run, my poor little mistake! Hide! We all have to hide before she catches us! You know what you have to get to face her down. Or perhaps the Bloody Judge will touch her first.'

Mistake?

Violent silver flares from the Black Moon's eyes. A power as vast as the core of the earth billows up inside, and yet as the Black Moon lunges the gate snaps closed, and when the Black Moon opens it once more it shows nothing but the empty black abyss of Xibaiya. The half-god roars and plunges his hands into white stone, tearing pieces away. The gates shimmer and open into an endless sea of bright liquid silver, then slam closed as the half-god reaches for them. A voice rings in his head once more, born of a different throat this time: *I see you.*

Some brilliant luminance is searching ever closer. The Black Moon looks out over the city once more, at the ships ablaze on the river, the rockets arching in torrents through the air, the cracks of lightning sundering the darkness, the volleys of arrows, the shouts and screams of war, the writhing, walking, seething carpet of dead men crawling, racing, climbing, tearing, until they are burned still by darting balls of fire that punch through flesh like an arrow through paper. He climbs to the edge of the balcony and spreads out his hands and steps into the air.

Time stops.

Rockets hang. Flames pause their flickering. Whorls of smoke freeze still. The sounds of battle snipped dead, snuffed like an unwanted candle. The Black Moon moves as if stepping from one breath of wind to the next. He reaches the rooftops and walks across them, vaults to the street, runs, clambers over barricades, scales walls as the boy-thief Berren did long ago in his home of Deephaven. At the river he walks across the unmoving waves until he touches the first of the ships that wait there; and as he touches it, every part turns black to ash, wood and rope and nail and sail, glass and iron and flesh and bone. Only its shape remains, waiting for time to begin again and for the wind to burst its greasy sooty cloud. One ship to another, touching them, destroying them.

I see you.

Closer now, as the Black Moon dances and bounds into the battle's heart, dashes between the frozen forms of men stood ready, mouths agape with silent cries of war on their lips, spears in hand. He ducks and weaves among arrows an instant from striking home. He touches every man he passes, no matter on which side they fight, turning them to dust, and amid the vengeful fury Berren sees the face for whom the Black Moon hunts. *His* face. Berren the

Bloody Judge. The face he saw every day in glass, in mirror water, until the warlocks threw themselves against him on the battlefield outside Tethis and ripped his soul from his skin and cast it into another. A face behind which all answers lie waiting.

Closer.

A flicker of bright moonlight in the corner of his eye, in a gloomy alley behind a frozen charge of soldiers. The Black Moon whips about, poised to strike.

I see you.

The Black Moon wheels again, throws out his hands, turns soldiers and street and ground, the walls, the very air to ash, all of it. Yet nothing.

Closer still.

A presence above, below, all around, inching under their skin. The Black Moon looks up, seeping desperation. From the horizon the bloody crescent moon looks back, and Berren feels it now. The half-god is afraid.

The Black Moon clicks his fingers. Breathes life into time. Thunderous noise returns, screams and shouts, battle cries, howls of the wounded and the dying. The murdered ships burst into clouds as the wind swallows and scatters their dust across the water. Men dissolve to ash where the half-god has walked. Rockets fizz and hiss and explode. Fire rains. The Black Moon steps through it as though all was mist and illusion, and everything that touches him turns to dust. He seizes a spear from the air and throws it as a gold-glass sled shoots overhead, skewering the rider and throwing him aside. Not a Taiytakei knight or a sword-slave, but a Dominion exalt, a holy warrior of their all-consuming God of the Sun.

The Black Moon leaps impossibly into the air. He lands on the sled and urges it on. A streak of fire blisters the wind, shrieking after them.

I SEE YOU.

The voice of the moon, the blazing bloody crescent that glowers from the horizon while all below is darkness and fire. The Black Moon jumps as the sled comes upon the tower. He touches a silver arch, and as he does an irresistible presence smashes in his head, ripping and tearing and pulling apart, stripping every memory and rending every thought.

Berren stumbles on through. The gate closes behind them. The fury of the moon; the hunter or the huntress, whichever it was that came armed with such old furious loathing, vanishes. He staggers up steps that rise in front of him. He is dazed and dizzy, half blind. The Black Moon screams and shrivels. It the half-god's turn to suffer.

He trips and falls into waiting water. Flails, bewildered and lost, until he sees where he is. Floundering in Baros Tsen's bath, he hauls himself out and stands dripping, and for a moment he thinks he is free, is not quite sure who he is, Berren or the Black Moon, or dead forgotten Skyrie, each as bewildered as the other and unable to say quite what they have seen. But it is a moment, nothing more. The Black Moon shakes himself down. He calls the eyrie dragons, summoning them to carry him away. He has learned something.

The doors inside Berren's head slam shut. He is left alone, blind and deaf in a dark and silent hole.

13

The Fates of Kings and Alchemists

Seventeen days after landfall

'Sisters,' grumbled Halfteeth. 'You'd have thought they might get along.'

'Then *you* obviously didn't have any!' snorted Snacksize.

Tuuran paused from picking his nose and held up a hand, signalling them to stop. The Silver King's Ways ran like a labyrinth under the Silver City, around white stone that glowed like moonlight, criss-crossing at different levels with countless side passages, dead-end spurs and the occasional underground hall. Not too hard if you kept to the easy bits from one place to another, but in parts a maze of whirls and twirls and intricate spirals that didn't even go anywhere. Impossible to search, and Tuuran couldn't help wondering what the point was. Was a bit like calligraphy, and every bit as pointless. Worthless, like shitting on a dead man.

'You have brothers or sisters, boss?' asked Snacksize. A few yards ahead of them a smaller passage merged in from the side.

'Sort of.' Tuuran crept to the intersection and peered round the corner, gold-glass shield raised, lightning thrower at the ready. He hadn't exactly heard something, but all the hairs on the back of his neck were tingling. 'People sell their children to the legion when they're a few years old. That was me. We all grow up together, soldiers from the start. So I had a thousand brothers. Not brothers of the same flesh and blood, mind, but I don't see as how it makes a difference.' Bloody place was a right tangle. You had to wonder what the Silver King had been thinking when he made this. Whether it was all part of some great plan, whether every passage and chamber had a purpose, or whether it had all been on a whim or he'd just plain been bored, and that was why some parts glowed bright with their own white-stone moonlight while others were dark as midnight. Doodling, so to speak.

Everywhere was damp. The tunnels ought to stink. They didn't. The walls were stained with old tidemarks, the floors left littered with tiny stones and dirt and fallen leaves trampled almost to extinction, left behind by some old flood. Whatever had once been in the side rooms was long gone, rotted away, eaten, stolen, maybe got up and walked off of its own free will for all Tuuran knew. All he ever found was dust and dirt, old sacks as fragile as paper and flakes and fragments of wood not much use except as kindling. Oh, and bones. Now and then they found bones. But the air was always fresh.

'No sisters?' asked Snacksize.

'Never had a woman in the legion before you.'

'Everyone knows women can't fight,' said Halfteeth, po-faced, and then sniggered. Snacksize clipped him around the back of the head.

'You want to tell that to her Holiness, Halfteeth?' Tuuran laughed. He started down the passage and then stopped. There was something here. He could feel it.

'Come on.' Halfteeth stopped beside him. 'You know her better than anyone. What gives between her and her sister?'

Snacksize smirked. 'Careful, Halfteeth. Boss has got the moon in his eyes there.'

Tuuran told her to piss off.

Halfteeth leered. 'No. It's her Holiness he wants. That right, eh boss?'

Tuuran told Halfteeth to piss off too. Glared, thinking how there might suddenly be a good deal more latrine duty in Halfteeth's future. Snacksize muttered something crude. Tuuran glared some more. 'Shut it, you two.'

They fell quiet. Tuuran counted fifty heartbeats and then started on again. The tunnel floor was covered in the same litter of gravel and dirt as everywhere else. Old and trodden down, but when he crouched to take a look he couldn't tell whether it had been days or hours or weeks since anyone had come this way. Been raining almost constantly since they'd made landfall. Wouldn't be much fun to be trapped here when the next flood came …

There!

The room right beside him. Midnight dark. A rustle of something. Tuuran pointed his torch inside and saw a man huddled on his haunches, curled up in the corner and cringing from the light.

'Hey! We're not going to hurt you. You hungry?' Tuuran lifted his helm. Slow and careful. The feral cowered further. Tuuran let out a long sigh and stepped back. He slapped Snacksize on the shoulder. 'Go on then.' He pushed her at the opening. Five days they'd been stomping about the place, looking for survivors. Most ran away, which made Tuuran want to grab the odd dragon-rider now and then and smack them in the teeth for what they'd done here. If anyone got the ferals to stay, it was Snacksize.

Snacksize took off her helm and eased in. 'Hey.' Arms held out in front of her, palms open, hands empty. 'You're safe. The old king is gone. You can come inside now if you want. There's food and shelter and safety from snappers and dragons.' Same thing she always said. Sometimes it worked, sometimes it didn't. Tuuran only half paid attention. He shouldn't be down here, not really. A Night Watchman stayed beside his Speaker. Queen Jaslyn and her riders with their blades returned. Hyrkallan still locked in a cell. Zara-Kiam telling anyone who'd listen how Zafir had murdered their father. Sooner or later someone was going to stab someone, and shit was going to kick off, and when it did it would be bloody.

'Hey!' Snacksize eased closer, doing her best to look like she didn't mean any harm. No mean feat dressed in gold-glass plate armour with a sword at her side and an axe over her back. Halfteeth hovered, tense beside him. Had a thing they did, him and Snacksize. Made him all protective. Well, good for them. *Moon in my eyes, my arse.* That night in Furymouth, just one of those madness moments, a flash of incandescence as a dancing phosphor-moth gets it wrong and dives into the lantern flame—

Snacksize let out a yelp. She jumped away. Tuuran's thoughts snapped to where they were supposed to be, sword in hand in a blink. Snacksize backed out as the feral got to his feet. Halfteeth gasped in disbelief. Tuuran gagged. Hadn't been able to see when the feral had been all curled up, but his belly had been ripped open and half his guts were hanging out, and it wasn't a fresh wound either. He looked like he'd been half eaten, and he very definitely ought to be dead.

Halfteeth raised his arm, about to finish the poor bastard with lightning, then thought better of it. Down in the tunnels, throwing lightning was a good way to make yourself deaf and warn everyone for about a thousand miles that you were coming. And the feral wasn't doing anything much. Was just standing.

'What in Xibaiya?'

'Can you walk?' asked Tuuran. The feral didn't answer. His eyes were dead.

'It's a dead man,' hissed Snacksize.

'Don't look dead to me,' growled Halfteeth.

'Merizikat,' whispered Tuuran. They'd all seen the same in the catacombs under the Basilica of the solar exalts. Dead men who weren't dead. Gave everyone the creeps, that had. Broken a few too, but Tuuran had seen it before. Years ago with Crazy Mad before the half-god inside him woke up, in Aria, in a city called Deephaven. A whole necropolis full of dead men who were still walking and talking. Getting on with living as though that's what they still were, manicured up to hide the rot and with their eyes sewn shut, their own little markets and craftsmen. Would sell you fish in a bun if you wanted. Not that the dead had much use for food, but the living did. Pickled fish in a bun from a dead man with his eyelids threaded shut. Tuuran shuddered.

'I think we go back now.' He sighed. 'I suppose we'd better find her Holiness and our grand master alchemist. Tell them it's happening here too.' Didn't want to. Didn't want to go back to the Octagon. All that time he'd spent looking forward, yearning to come back, and now here they were and all he felt was restless and empty. Odd.

They hurried away.

'What you need,' said Snacksize, suddenly beside him, 'is to find some woman to fuck you to within an inch of your life. You need that, boss.'

'I do, do I?' Tuuran snorted. 'You offering?'

'Fuck off!'

'Well shut up then.'

'Them two with the babies, boss. They're starting to miss it.'

'Doesn't feel right. Wouldn't be the same now. Not like it was in the islands. Anyway ...' He tapped the rough white skin on his neck beneath his ear. 'Don't think they'd be as keen as they used to be. There's no cure for the dragon-disease.'

Snacksize shrugged. 'There's still ways, boss. I mean you don't have to stick your ... There's other ...' She threw up her hands in exasperation. 'Worst comes to the worst you can always take a piece of pig gut and tie a knot in the end – you know, boss.' She looked up at him as he glared, a look that ought to have been ferocious enough to scare a mountain into a heap of pebbles.

'*Will* you shut up?'

'Would have to be a big piece, I'm sure. Right, boss? And a real tight knot. But I mean it could ...'

There were ways of standing and looking at someone when you were holding a big axe. Tuuran reckoned he was pretty good at most of them, but that if he excelled at one in particular, it was when he was sizing up someone's throat and imagining exactly the fastest way to cut it. 'What I need,' he growled, 'is to remember that I had a friend once, and that wherever he's pissed off to now, he needs me. So sod you, sod her Holiness, and sod everyone else.'

Snacksize shut up. They walked the rest of the way in silence to the cavern of the Undergates and the waterfall that crashed through it. Tuuran nodded to the soldiers he'd left on watch there and stomped up the steps, muttering under his breath. Bloody alchemist. And of course he couldn't talk to anyone else about it, about how he and Bellepheros didn't get on and how that bothered him. Couldn't talk to Halfteeth or Snacksize or any of the rest of his men because he was their Night Watchman, hard as nails and never wrong. Couldn't talk to her Holiness for much the same reason. Couldn't talk to Crazy Mad because ...

'You all right, boss?' asked Halfteeth.

'No, I'm bloody well not. I've seen a dead man looking back at me, and I'm bloody angry.' Maybe Snacksize was right after all: maybe some tension-blowing tumble, done and gone again, maybe that *would* help.

Past the Undergates lay the Gold Hall, as tall as any tower in the realms, full of elegant pillars and colossal arches. The light carried a yellow tinge which gave the place a sun-drenched look, except that whenever he looked up, looking for the open sky or the great windows, there weren't any. The whole Enchanted Palace gave him the shivers. Didn't help when a wrought-bronze gate at the far end took him into the upper levels half a mile above without any sense of movement.

'I hate this place,' he muttered as he stepped through the gate.

On the far side the Octagon lay straight ahead of him. He marched through, sent Snacksize and Halfteeth off about other errands, then headed for the grand master alchemist's door, not that Bellepheros actually *had* a door as such. The Silver King hadn't bothered much with things like that when he'd conjured his palace. Tuuran supposed maybe he had a point, that any sorcerer who could turn people inside out at a thought, could disintegrate them into greasy black ash with such ridiculous ease that most of the time he had to consciously stop himself from doing it, well, a man like that probably hadn't been worrying too much about assassins in the night and knives in the back and suchlike. Made guarding her Holiness a right nightmare, though. Hadn't much helped the Silver King in the end either.

Either way, Bellepheros didn't have a door, more of a curtain, and even before Tuuran got there he could hear voices from the other side. The alchemist and the guard Tuuran had given him, Big Vish, Vish standing awkwardly to attention while Bellepheros paced around him, a cup of something clenched in white-knuckled fingers. Tuuran barged in.

'Grand Ma—'

'You!' Bellepheros pointed an accusing finger at Tuuran before he could get out two words. 'Did *you* know about this?'

Well that was a good start. 'What have we done now?'

'The alchemists!'

'What about them?'

'The ones who were here! You know what happened to them?'

Tuuran paused. Took a moment to take the sting out of the air, the accusation, the old surly resentment. The inside of the grand master's room was full of fine things. Portraits of kings and queens and princesses of the Silver City hung on the walls. There was a desk which had belonged to Queen Sakabia before she was elected speaker; a sumptuous bed with silk sheets from Furymouth, as good as anything the Taiytakei had ever had; a stone bath set into the floor, constantly fed with water fresh from the fountain up in the ruin of the Reflecting Garden and always warm. It never felt right seeing Grand Master Bellepheros standing in the middle of this tidy and elegant chamber in his scruffy robe and apron, uncomfortable as a cheap whore at a royal wedding.

Tuuran took a good long look at it all, settling his mind. Unclenching his fists. In the end he shrugged. 'If you mean did I know that King Hyrkallan strung up every alchemist he could get his hands on and then murdered them, then yes, I did know that.' They all knew that. 'Her Holiness keeps him imprisoned and we all wait her judgment. If you have something to say on that, I suggest you take it up with her. You'll see no tears from me if he hangs.'

'Not *that*!' Bellepheros slammed his cup on the desk. 'The *other* alchemists! The ones who came here just a few weeks before us.'

'Other alchemists?' Well, here was something. Tuuran glared at Big Vish. 'No, can't say as I do. Should I?' He let Vish suffer a moment. 'Vish, you know about this?'

Big Vish hung his head. 'Yes, boss.'

'Well then you can wait outside and stay there until I say otherwise, and while you wait you can think about the long days of shit about to come your way for not telling me stuff I apparently needed to know.' Vish bowed his head. Bellepheros started to say something else, but Tuuran stopped him and poked him in the chest. 'And, *you*, Grand Master Alchemist, my men answer to me and to her Holiness, not to you. Ever. Do you understand that? You want a strip torn off one of them, you leave that to me.' He heard Vish slip out behind him, the sheepish swish of the curtain. Damn right too. They'd be having more words about this later, and they wouldn't be pretty ones.

Shit. And now here he was, looming over the alchemist Bellepheros like an angry bear roaring at an old man. *Nice one, big man. Well done.*

Bellepheros pushed Tuuran's arm aside. 'Don't you threaten me in my own rooms, Night Watchman. Don't you *dare*! There's only one of me, more's the pity. I'm sure there are plenty more like you.'

'I'm sure there are.' Tuuran forced the anger back. Wasn't

angry with Bellepheros anyway, not really. Had Crazy under his skin, that was all. And her Holiness, and now her sister, and it was all a bit much. He raised his hands and backed away, sat down and tried to look contrite. 'I didn't come here for a fight. So. Other alchemists?'

Bellepheros struggled with himself for a moment. The last year hadn't been easy on any of them, but they ought to be friends, they really ought, both missing people they'd come to love in their different ways and neither with much hope of getting them back; but history noted how a Night Watchman and a grand master alchemist rarely did more than get on each other's nerves, and then there was the whole thing about how Chay-Liang had disappeared in Merizikat, and how Tuuran had been there when it happened, and how Bellepheros had built the Taiytakei their eyrie in the first place and so been complicit in what they'd done.

The alchemist sighed and slumped at his desk. The fight seemed to go out of him. He sipped from his cup and propped his head in his hand, and Tuuran saw how tired he looked, how old he was. Two years they'd known each other, give or take, and in that time Bellepheros had aged a decade. 'That man of yours was from the Purple Spur. Interesting to hear how things are in other parts of the realms.'

Tuuran nodded. 'I know his story.' Although apparently not all of it. 'I hear several of them made it from the Spur.'

'They brought four alchemists all this way under dragon-infested skies. Kept apart to try and make sure that at least one survived. *That* the story you know?'

'Go on.' The alchemist bit was new.

'So. You *don't* know?'

'I don't know about any alchemists, no. Are you saying there are more of you here?'

'I'm saying that three arrived from the Spur, and your man Big Vishmir was with them. Hyrkallan took them to the summit. They never came back. The story was that he claimed they were caught in the open by a dragon, but that actually he threw them off the cliffs.' Bellepheros threw his hands to the heavens. 'Did it never cross your mind that I might want to know something like that?'

Tuuran reckoned the words he'd be having with Big Vish later might be loud and colourful and go on a while. Still, would he have said anything if he'd known? 'I suppose if they were dead then it was done.' He shrugged. 'And Hyrkallan is already caged. Maybe it seemed not to make much difference.'

'Seemed not to make much difference?' Bellepheros jumped to his feet. 'Seemed not to make much difference! Dear Flame! Three men killed. I *knew* them, Tuuran. I knew their names. I *taught* them! They were friends, once. You think I wouldn't want to know?'

Tuuran sighed. 'You carry enough burdens, Grand Master. If I'd known then I might have kept it from you, but I didn't. Does it better your life to hear that?'

'It betters my life to know there was a fourth who got away!' Bellepheros leaned closer. 'While you were in Farakkan your men found two men and a woman wandering between the Ghostwater and the Fury.' His eyes blazed. 'You knew about *that*, at least? One was an Adamantine Man! One was an alchemist! An *alchemist*, Night Watchman, and your men took her captive and trussed her and threw her into a cell. Apparently she took a dim view of that and made good her escape.' He was on his feet, red-faced and quivering with fury.

'Ah. That.' Tuuran grimaced. *Bloody Halfteeth.* 'Her Holiness was not pleased. Very fucking far from pleased, actually. Caused me a shit-heap of trouble.'

Bellepheros looked ready to explode. 'That would be her Holiness who deigned to mention this to me this morning. Fourteen days later! Fourteen? What was she thinking?'

Tuuran shrugged. 'I don't know, Grand Master, but perhaps you might save your shouting for her then?' An alchemist. No one had bothered telling *him* that either. 'Killed a good few men when they left, they did. Got to wonder why they ran. What would make them take their chances with the dragons.'

Bellepheros sat heavily. He reached across the desk and grabbed Tuuran's hand and gripped it tight. There was steel in his eyes. 'Her name was Kataros. She claimed to have found the Black Mausoleum. The Silver King's tomb. Her Holiness doesn't believe a word of it and nor do I, but this Kataros, *she* believed it. She *believed* it, Tuuran, and alchemists aren't idiots, so she must have found *some*thing. Do you know what that could mean?'

'Not really.' Tuuran went to the curtain and hauled Big Vish back inside, pulled him in by his ear, sat him down on his chair and leaned back against the wall. Took a while, the three of them together, but Tuuran reckoned he'd got the gist of the story by the end: Hyrkallan tips three alchemists off the Moonlit Mountain; a fourth shows up and gets wind of it, gets stuck in a cell, and then suddenly she's gone and an Adamantine Man too, and some shit-eater who apparently killed a whole bunch of riders with his teeth or something; three days later Halfteeth's gang finds the same three wandering about and carts them back to the eyrie; Halfteeth sees an Adamantine Man, loses his rag and beats him to a bloody mess. Then comes the dragon attack, and in the middle of the chaos the alchemist and the Adamantine Man vanish, leaving half a dozen corpses behind them.

'Hyrkallan sent out riders,' said Vish. 'Went off to try and find her. Crazy bastards jumped off the summit with a pair of Prince Lai's wings each strapped across their backs, gliding off through the air.'

'*And?*' asked Tuuran.

'And nothing, boss.' Vish shrugged. 'Never saw any of them again.' He screwed up his face. 'One of them was Jasaan the Dragonslayer. Killed a dragon in Bloodsalt, he did, a full-grown adult and him with just an axe, or so they say. But Prince Lai's wings? From the top of a mountain?' Vish shook his head.

'I'll ask about,' Tuuran said to Bellepheros at last. He looked hard at Vish, wondering whether to send him away or not. He settled on not. 'Interesting as this all is, I came for something else. Grand Master, there are dead men walking in the Silver King's tunnels.'

Bellepheros gave him a thoughtful look. There was shiftiness to the alchemist more than any sense of surprise. A guilt. 'I know,' he said at last. He looked at Vish, whose face had frozen ashen. 'Elsewhere too. Under the Spur. That another thing your man hasn't told you, is it?'

Vish seemed to draw into himself. He gave Tuuran the apologetic look of someone who knew he was going to get his bollocks served to him on a plate. 'We used to carry the dead out of the caves at night, boss.' He shuffled his feet. 'We got a few dragons with poison early on, but they quickly got wise to that. But we still take them out because … sometimes … sometimes when we don't, they get up again.'

Different customs in different worlds. Tuuran had been to a good few and seen them all, or so he thought. Rites for the dead. Burned. Left out in the sun. Given to the water. Left under the stars for three nights. Things like that. But never left under the earth, not in any world. Never, never. He looked at Bellepheros, wondering if the alchemist was thinking the same, but the Bellepheros simply shook his head.

'Merizikat,' he whispered.

'Go on then.' Tuuran kicked Vish and jerked his head towards the curtain. 'Get lost. I'll come and kick your bollocks to grapefruits later, and then you can sod off into the tunnels for a day and hunt for walking dead men for me.' He shoved Vish out and was about to follow, then stopped. He'd spent so long in the catacombs of Merizikat that he'd started to give the walking corpses there their own names. *The shuffler. Wobbly eyes. Legless* … Trapped between life and death with deliberate malice. It had scared the shit out of all of them at first, but men would accustom themselves to almost anything given time, and so they had, and besides, of all the things he'd seen, walking dead men certainly weren't the worst.

'Something else you want, Night Watchman?' asked the alchemist.

Tuuran bowed his head. Couldn't find the words. Merizikat hung between them. Merizikat and Chay-Liang and all the secrets he couldn't share. 'I'll let you know if I find out anything about this alchemist Kataros.'

He pushed the curtain back to leave. Bellepheros looked up sharply as he did. 'Bring your corpse to my workshop, Night Watchman. I'll see to it.'

Tuuran nodded. Wasn't any harm. Not with the Black Moon gone. First sign of the eyrie back in the sky and he'd have every man who could walk crawling through those tunnels, finding the not-quite-dead and putting them down.

14

The Adamantine Council

Eighteen days after landfall

Whenever he could, Bellepheros escaped the room Zafir had given him. The master alchemist of the Pinnacles back when the late Queen Aliphera had ruled from the Octagon had been Vioros. Bellepheros and Vioros had practically grown up together, and Vioros had had the decency to leave behind a well stocked laboratory and a workshop deep inside the Enchanted Palace pleasantly far away from anywhere. Hyrkallan's riders had found it and smashed it up a bit, and then left it alone with an almost reverent superstition, and there was a lot he could still use. The workshop even had a tiny sleeping cot and a wardrobe with a fine collection of robes, all a bit wide around the waist for Bellepheros these days, but they were a comfort, old and familiar.

By contrast he loathed the royal room Zafir had given him. Everything about it. How tidy it was, how pristine, how priceless, how everything was to be seen but not be touched; but most of all he hated how close it was to the Octagon, and how people kept bothering him.

The curtain swished open. Big Vish poked an apologetic head inside. 'You should really come now, Grand Master. The speaker is on her way.'

'Yes, yes.' Maybe giving him Big Vish as a guardian had been Tuuran's idea of a kindness, but he didn't *want* to be guarded. Alchemists could look after themselves, and he couldn't shake the sense of eyes peering over his shoulder.

He looked down at himself. Li would have been all over him on a day like this, his first formal duty as the restored grand master alchemist of the nine realms. She'd have been fussing, straightening his robe, picking away imagined specks of fluff; and he'd tell her off for being an old hen, and she'd tell him off back for being an old scruff, and they'd both quietly be laughing because most of the time they worked in whatever stained smock or tunic first came to hand, him with his potions, her with her enchanted glass and gold. And while they bickered they would have talked about the things that mattered, and she would have helped him to know what to do. They would have talked about Tuuran. About Zafir. Most of all they would have talked about the Black Moon.

He missed her smile.

He hurried out and let Big Vish walk behind him, stiff and straight like a reluctant statue, until they reached the Octagon. Zara-Kiam sat in a throne beside Zafir's own, dressed in flame-red silks and gold over hatchling dragonscale. Queen Jaslyn sat in another on the other side, dressed in dragonscale too, and Bellepheros wondered again how Zafir had turned the queen of Sand to her cause. Riders stood impatiently, waiting along three sides of the Octagon, men who once flew with Hyrkallan to burn Zafir out of the skies, yet here they were, bending their knees to her. The rest were a motley collection: the other Vish, White Vish, and the Adamantine Men rescued from Furymouth or found inside the Pinnacles, the handful of former slaves who had survived with them all the way from Takei'Tarr, scores and scores of sell-sword soldiers taken from Merizikat and a few of the Black Moon's soul-cut solar exalts. A mongrel court for a mongrel queen, while the sheer size of the Octagon dwarfed them all.

Bellepheros took his place beside Princess Kiam's throne. She cocked him an eye. 'Look at what we have become, Grand Master. The courts of my mother held three or four times as many, every man and woman dressed in rich silks and gold and dragonscale. Parades of men and armoured knights full of pageantry, trumpets and banners. My blood-mothers once ruled the world from this room.'

Zafir entered last of all. She walked in without ceremony, with Tuuran beside her, and sat down without fanfare, all so quickly that she was in her throne before some of the men from Merizikat even realised she was there. Dressed in dragonscale and Taiytakei glass and gold. The damage to her armour from the fight in the

Octagon was still obvious. Without Chay-Liang they had no one who could repair it.

There was Li again, creeping into his thoughts. Bellepheros shivered and then stared at Zafir, trying to see inside her. Li had despised the dragon-queen. Loathed her from the start and never wavered, seen her for what she really was: ambitious, ruthless, self-obsessed. She'd been that way for as long as he could remember. Maybe she'd softened a little of late, but she was what she was. Dragons never changed their scales; and even if they could, they were still dragons.

Or was it leopards and spots? Li had had a thing about leopards ...

'We have indeed all fallen a long way,' he answered at last, fishing for words bland enough not to be seen to carry some hidden meaning.

Zafir banged the floor with the haft of some old relic of a spear, a wooden thing from the years of the Silver King. She whispered to Tuuran, who hurried away while the Octagon settled to silence, and then Zafir held out her hand with the Speaker's Ring. No one spoke. The little white stone dragon above the throne cast its gaze hither and yon, twisting back and forth like a snake until it settled on Princess Kiam. Zafir kept her hand held outward.

'Sister?'

Perhaps she had Diamond Eye raking through their thoughts. There were potions, of course, to block the dragon out, but Bellepheros needed dragon blood for that, and Vioros hadn't left a stock of it. Diamond Eye had plenty, of course, but Bellepheros didn't suppose the dragon would be keen to oblige him.

Zara-Kiam paused long enough to show her disdain, then slid off her throne and knelt before Zafir. She kissed the ring. 'Sister.' Her tone was mocking. The little dragon's eyes followed her.

Jaslyn came next. She knelt without hesitation and kissed the ring. Her riders watched, some bewildered, some surly, few with any great conviction, but the little dragon on Zafir's throne never reared and hissed at them. Bellepheros couldn't for the life of him understand how Zafir had done that. Then his own turn. He was dreading having to bend down. *That* part was easy enough, but he wasn't sure he could actually get up again these days; but as he came to the throne Zafir stood.

'From you a bow will do, Grand Master.'

Bellepheros bowed and kissed the Speaker's Ring. He returned to his place next to Princess Kiam. Zafir looked hungry. Restless.

'I have seen the realms around us,' she said, addressing them all, steely and strong. 'I have seen Furymouth and Clifftop in ashes. Farakkan, Purkan, Three Rivers, Valleyford, Arys Crossing. All are gone. The City of Dragons too. Perhaps kings and queens still hold their courts in Bazim Crag, in Bloodsalt, in Sand, in Evenspire, beneath the Purple Spur. If they do they are welcome at this council, but until they come, we are but who we are.' She turned to Princess Kiam. 'A speaker must relinquish the throne of their realm. I will do so when we leave for the Adamantine Palace. I name Zara-Kiam as my heir, here and now before you all. All this shall be yours, little sister. You are Queen Kiam now, and I name you to my council.' She turned to her right. 'Queen Jaslyn, heir to Queen Shezira, queen of Sand. I name you too to my council.' Now at him. 'Bellepheros, grand master alchemist of the Order of the Scales, I name you to my council. Last of all I name to my council Tuuran, Night Watchman of the Adamantine Guard. There will no longer be a voice for the Order of the Dragon, for that order is dead. For the other realms, any may stand forward if their claim is strong.'

No one moved.

'Then I have named you, my Adamantine Council. To you falls the burden and duty of finding those who survive and sheltering them. Of taming the dragons or killing them, or of finding some manner of peace with them ...' She stopped as Tuuran returned, dragging Hyrkallan before her throne.

'Isn't your council a bit pointless without your precious Silver King?' asked Princess Kiam, loudly.

Tuuran and Halfteeth forced Hyrkallan to his knees. A restless murmur moved through the dragon-riders from Sand and Evenspire. Zafir glared them to silence.

'Hyrkallan, you are not and were never Queen Shezira's heir. You brought war to my realm. You killed my riders and my men and drove me into exile. Nevertheless I offer you amnesty. Will you honour the ring I wear and bow to me as your speaker?'

Hyrkallan snarled. 'I will not!'

Zara-Kiam snorted her contempt. 'So execute the murderous bastard. Let him die slowly in lingering agony.'

Bellepheros shook his head. Zafir's eyes moved and settled on him. 'Then that is one vote from my council for execution,' she said. 'Grand Master Bellepheros, this man hanged every alchemist here. He took Grand Master Jeiros and smashed his wrists and ankles, and hung him from a wheel over the edge of this mountain to die. Do *you* have an opinion as to his fate?'

Bellepheros closed his eyes. The Hyrkallan he remembered had been a better man than any of these queens. A better rider, a stronger king, a perfect speaker who could have rallied the nine realms against anything. *He* was the one who should be wearing Zafir's ring and sitting on that throne. He was the one to lead them through this. There couldn't be any question of it, surely? And yet the words stuck stubbornly in his throat. Jeiros had been a friend. And maybe he'd never learn the whole truth of what had happened in the last few days before the dragons rose, but Hyrkallan had murdered countless alchemists, and that was certain. Friends. Pupils. The closest he had to family and kin. He found he couldn't forgive that.

He turned his back to Zafir and Hyrkallan both.

'Grand Master Bellepheros abstains.' Zafir sounded surprised. 'Queen Jaslyn of Sand?' Bellepheros closed his eyes. Hyrkallan's own wife, at least, would call for mercy, wouldn't she?

'Do with him as you will.' Jaslyn too turned her back. Bellepheros blinked and stared at the white stone, numb. *Abstains?* He reached out a hand to the wall and touched it to steady himself. *Oh ancestors, I've killed him.* The thought struck him hard. Because Zafir wasn't ever going to show any mercy, and so all of this was a sham, and he'd played into her hand, because now it didn't matter what any of the others had to say.

'Tuuran, Night Watchman of the Adamantine Guard?' There. That little curl of triumph lingering at the edges of Zafir's words. Whatever Tuuran said now, it didn't matter. Zafir would have the last vote. Hyrkallan was already dead.

'Holiness?' Tuuran sounded confused.

'What should we do with this dragon-rider, Tuuran? Should we spare him and banish him?'

Princess Kiam leaned forward. 'I'd like you to say we should kill him. I think my sister would like that too. For once we agree on something.'

'Holiness?' Tuuran's bewilderment fitted the charade this had become. Zafir must have known, *must* have, what Jaslyn and Kiam would say.

'Choose his fate, Night Watchman,' Zafir said. 'Or turn your back as our grand master and the queen of Sand have done if you have nothing to say, and then it will fall to me to decide, and I will banish him. Choose as your conscience demands. Say he should die and so he shall. Say he should be banished and he will be taken to the edge of the Raksheh with a week of food and water to survive as best he might. Wits and strength against the world as befits a great rider in his twilight. He would have a chance to reach the Purple Spur, I think. But you must choose, Night Watchman, or turn away.'

'But there *is* no choice, Holiness. I don't understand why you even ask. He took arms against his speaker. It must be death; it cannot be anything else.'

A silence settled, stifling and heavy and inevitable like a last exhalation. Bellepheros felt dizzy. His face was tingling numb. He couldn't feel his fingers. Princess Kiam stretched into her throne like a purring cat. She smiled and bared her teeth.

'A year and a half living like those feral men under the city, false king,' she hissed.

Bellepheros found Zafir staring at him. No smirk, no gleeful triumph. Just looking at him as though asking why, why didn't he speak? Even now, why didn't he speak?

He couldn't.

'I would have preferred banishment,' she said, quietly so that even Bellepheros had to strain his ears to hear. Then she straightened in her throne and found her voice. 'Execution, then. Ten days from today.' The haft of her spear struck the stone. A dull powerless thump, and yet it rang around the Octagon and sounded in Bellepheros's head like the roar of a dragon. The Adamantine Council was made again, and its first act was to kill. He tried to tell himself that he couldn't have stopped it, that Zafir would have had her way, that Hyrkallan's sentence was inevitable, that his death was what she'd wanted, no matter her words. And yet that searching look on her face as she'd turned to him at the end ... She'd meant it. She really had. Had she?

I should have said something.

No. He couldn't believe it. Dragons didn't change their scales.

The court moved on to Tuuran's forays into the Silver King's Ways. Bellepheros excused himself and left. He hurried past his rooms and down into the depths of the tunnels and passages, away from the grand halls and sorceries of the Silver King until he reached Vioros's workshop, where it was quiet and empty, where he was alone and people let him be. Tuuran's men had brought the walking corpse up from the tunnels. They'd strapped it down with a great deal more rope than it needed, and when Bellepheros let them go, they couldn't get out fast enough. Apparently it hadn't struggled much, but it was very definitely not quite dead, and very definitely ought to have been. He took a deep breath and made himself look at it.

Banishment was as good as execution when there were dragons roaming the skies.

I should have spoken.

But Zafir surely couldn't have meant what she'd said. *A dragon is always a dragon. She wanted him dead. In her heart, she wanted him dead ...*

He looked at the corpse and jumped when it turned its head and looked back. He took a knife and cut it to be sure, but it didn't bleed the way living men bled. Its blood was viscous and dark rust-brown. It oozed like slime.

I should have spoken. If Chay-Liang had been here she'd be standing at his shoulder and glaring at him now, wagging her finger, well and truly angry with him. It would have been weeks before he heard the last of it. And so he *would* have spoken, if only to save himself from that.

A dragon is still a dragon. Her words nothing but pretty lies. That's simply what Zafir is. Isn't she?

He didn't know any more, and he could almost hear Li snort at him for that, derisive and scornful. *Daft old man. Do I need to spell the words out for you?* He shook his head and tried to remember her, flicking through memories of the time they'd shared. Her kindness and her strength, her simple human warmth. He clung to them, bathing in them until he pushed Zafir and Hyrkallan and all the rest away and found his peace again. Then he turned to the dead man who wasn't quite dead. There *were* ways to bring a man back. He'd seen it done and he'd done it himself. An alchemist pulling a soul into its own dead corpse with abyssal powders in order to make it speak.

He pushed a small stone pestle into the corpse's mouth, forcing it open.

'Why are you still moving, eh?'

The corpse, uncooperative, rolled its head away. Bellepheros pinned it still and poked about inside its mouth with a thin stick, trying to scrape out any residues. Abyssal powders were like a thick black treacle. They also stank like nothing else. The corpse stank too, but that was because it was rotting and festering where half its intestines had been ripped out. Bellepheros poked his face up close to its mouth and sniffed. Couldn't be sure about the smell one way or the other, other than that it was foul.

Thing about abyssal powders was that corpses only came back with their memories. They didn't know what was happening around them, and so there was no point in simply asking who had done this. Mind you, he'd never known them able to walk either, or even to move their arms and legs much.

Odd.

He took his knife and made a long straight incision just beneath the ribs. Maybe if he got its stomach open then he could work out what sort of potion had been used; or maybe there had been some sort of reflex and the corpse had swallowed the abyssal powders while it was talking. Or maybe it wasn't a potion at all. Tuuran had his stories about the necropolis of Deephaven, and Big Vish had his own of the dead rising under the Purple Spur, although that could always have been some alchemist meddling with things best left well alone. Merizikat had had its catacombs, where the Black Moon had had Tuuran digging around as if he was looking for something ...

Merizikat. A pang of loss crept up from inside and smacked him in the face. *Li.* Li had put an end to whatever had been going on down there. Never said a word. Just did it and was gone, snuffed out of his life, and so didn't he owe it to her to root out the secrets the Black Moon had been hunting?

He frowned hard, took a deep breath and forced himself to work. Back to his twitching corpse. If he could just get in there and find whatever made it ...

'What are you doing?' asked the corpse.

Bellepheros yelped. The corpse turned to look at him as he jumped away, crippled knees entirely forgotten. He stabbed the corpse three times in the chest, straight through the ribs into its heart, which made no difference at all.

'Who are you?' asked the corpse.

No no no! They never talk back, never never! He ran outside and yelled for help, but no one came because they were all in the Octagon with Zafir, telling each other how many sacks of beans they had, how many barrels of Merizikat biscuits had been unloaded from the eyrie before the Black Moon had vanished with it, and arrows, and all the other necessary things that gave him nosebleeds of sheer boredom. This, though, *this* they needed to hear, and so he set off back there, hurrying as best he could, and had nearly reached the Octagon itself when he turned a corner and collided with Zafir and Tuuran coming the other way.

'Grand Master. I wanted to show you ...' Zafir stopped. Her hand drifted to her bladeless knife. 'What *is* the matter?'

Bellepheros grabbed Tuuran and started to drag him back. 'The walking corpse you found—'

'The *what*?' Zafir's hand landed on his shoulder.

'The walking ...' He stopped himself. 'The catacombs of Merizikat, Holiness? You know what was down there?' She had to. *Everyone* knew. As best Bellepheros could tell the catacombs were the only reason the Black Moon had taken them there at all.

Zafir took a moment and then let him go. 'Yes. I ... saw them.' Her mouth twitched at the memory of something deeply unpleasant.

'I think we've found another one.'

'So I hear.'

'You *know*? But how ...' Tuuran had told her, of course he

had. Stupid to think otherwise. But there was something more, the lingering bad taste of some baleful secret shared that they kept to themselves. It riled him how she was always somehow ahead of him. Alchemists informed their speakers, not the other way around. 'Holiness, how can I serve either you or the realms if—'

Zafir put a finger to his lips and glared. 'Your dead man can wait, Grand Master. I want to show you something. Both of you. All of you.'

She led him back to the Octagon while Tuuran sent Halfteeth and Big Vish to watch over the walking corpse and see it didn't escape or … or whatever else a walking corpse might do. Zafir beckoned Kiam and Jaslyn to follow, and led everyone through the Hall of Mirages. This time, as she walked the arches, Bellepheros made a point to remember the pattern.

'I want all of you to see this place.' Zafir led them to the arches where the Black Moon had disappeared, and on to the carvings that lay beyond, the history, if she was right, of the Silver King. 'I want to show you what I think this means,' she said. 'The story of the Black Moon and the Silver King.'

Bellepheros twitched. 'Holiness, the Order of the Scales—'

'Grand Master?' Zafir silenced him with a look. 'If anyone knows the story of the Silver King, it is an alchemist, is that what you were going to say? You and your histories and your libraries of books?' She leaned in close. 'Consider, Grand Master, that I had a dragon whisper it in my ear, and that my dragon was there when it happened, that he saw it all, and that I have shared his memories. Besides, you yourself once told Chay-Liang that when it came to the Black Moon I might know more than any of you. So then. Hear me.'

She started as before, at the moment on which everything hinged. The Splintering, when the Black Moon had forged his helm of ice, when the last of the Silver Kings, the Isul Aieha, had struck him down, and the Earthspear had ripped the world to splinters. Diamond Eye rode among them all, slipping ghost-like through their thoughts to show each how he had tasted the Nothing in that moment, a whiff of it, quickly clenched and crushed and buried by the dead goddess and her slayer. Zafir pointed to the Silver King's carvings of Xibaiya where they'd trapped the Nothing, all three locked together, the Nothing in its prison, the dead goddess and the Black Moon its cage. Diamond Eye whispered through their minds as Zafir spoke. The dragon showed them all, as he had wandered from one life to the next, how he had seen it with his own eyes.

Zafir took them back in time then, along the carvings to the very beginning, where the sun and the moon and the earth and the stars, the four first gods and goddesses, had created their strands of life; and as she showed them each scene, Diamond Eye murmured among their thoughts and told them its meaning, the story of the first age as he knew it. Bellepheros looked down at the picture beneath his feet that Zafir had shown him before: four men walking together, all, if you went by the carvings, with the marks on their heads that showed them as half-gods. One carrying the spear, one with the Black Moon's knife, one with a coat of light, and one with a circlet around his brow. In the next picture they entered a cave and the dragon told them the story of it, how the earth had summoned the first dark moon into the sky to blot out the sun and cast the world into ice and darkness; how the Isul Aieha and his brother Seturakah had travelled to the fathomless depths of Xibaiya and abased themselves; of the dead goddess of the earth and her demand that one half-god child of the moon should become a sacrifice; how revered Seturakah had tricked the earth, splitting himself in two and hiding a part of his own soul in a faceless helm of ice before he gave himself to the goddess. His return, slow and painful, growing from the seed he'd left behind. How Seturakah had taken the name, from that time, of Black Moon. How the Isul Aieha and the Black Moon had divided the world and ruled it from twin thrones side by side.

The next part seemed out of place, and Diamond Eye seemed not to understand it any better than the rest of them. A half-god raising sorceries, twisting the earth and warping caverns and mountains, gouging twisting tunnels, conjuring labyrinths that wrapped the world in sigils and ritual. The Silver King's Ways of the Isul Aieha; but those, Bellepheros knew, had been made long after the Splintering, after the Silver King had tamed the dragons, when he made his Enchanted Palace and all these halls around them.

The Black Moon turned against the old ways. The other Silver Kings plucked out his eyes. Diamond Eye drifted among them, memory to memory like a wraith.

Zafir led them back to where they'd started. The Isul Aieha and the Black Moon now opposed. The other Silver Kings vanishing one by one, most of them withdrawing to some great silver sea.

'I have wondered about this war,' she said, 'and of the Black Moon's obsession with the Silver King's spear, and of the dead that rise and walk again. That spear is the Earthspear. I think perhaps the Black Moon became the avatar of the dead goddess. She took him and made him her own. Perhaps this is why, in the end, she let him go. I cannot be sure, and even Diamond Eye doesn't know. Such things are perhaps beyond even dragons. But in the stories here the goddess of the earth raises the Black Moon and threatens the Silver Kings with extinction. From that our half-god takes his name. Perhaps he serves the same purpose.'

Another carving Bellepheros remembered from before was on the ceiling over his head. A man with a hole in his skull – a half-god if Zafir was right – standing beside a hatching egg. A dragon's head poked through the shell. The same man and hatching dragon were in the next scene along, the half-god with one hand wielding a knife and stabbing it into another man's skull, the other hand reaching inside as if to pluck something out, while the little dragon lay sprawled, eyes closed beside the broken egg. In the next the half-god was alone, fingers outstretched to touch the little dragon's head, the dragon alive and aflame this time, straining its neck to greet the half-god's touch.

The first dragon, summoned into being by the Black Moon.

And then the end again. The sun devoured in the sky. The dark moon of the dead goddess climbing for a second time. Through it all, Diamond Eye filled them with the story the dragons remembered, with the memories he still carried deep. The Splintering.

They moved on, bewildered and amazed. Now the Isul Aieha wandered alone. His carvings showed him finding the storm-dark and crossing it to some fortress, half real and half an imagined thing substanced from dreams and nightmares. Diamond Eye knew it as Darkstone, filled with relics of death. The pictures showed the Silver King travelling from place to place, standing before archways like the arches in the hall behind them, sometimes passing through, sometimes not, sometimes standing before the gateway to the sea where the other silver half-gods had gone and then turning his back.

'I always had a sense that he was looking for something,' murmured Zafir, 'but I never knew what.' She stopped at a short sequence that seemed to show all manner of rites for the dead, of souls being lifted away to the gods of the sun and the moon, or else the goddesses of the earth and the stars, the old creator deities forgotten by dragon-riders and long forsaken by the Taiytakei; but Bellepheros, and even Zafir and Tuuran, had spent long enough in Merizikat to recognise them for what they were. Different rites of the dead for different divinities. Fire or sunlight for the sun. Water or moonlight for the moon. Wind and air and starlight for the stars. Darkness and interment for the earth …

Bellepheros began to see.

Pictures. Countless souls reaching their proper rest, broken by another savage depiction of the rip in Xibaiya; here were the souls of the dead sent to the goddess of the earth. The picture's meaning was clear. Those given to the dead goddess were dragged to Xibaiya, where they were devoured and annihilated by the Nothing. Feeding it.

More. The Isul Aieha travelling from world to world as a wind and storm of warning. To one realm, where he became a darkness spread upon the entire world, demanding worship and sacrifice, declaring in whispers and catastrophe the moon and the earth to be anathema, the god and goddess whose hubris had allowed the shattering of the world. Then to another. Opening ways to Xibaiya and calling the lost children hidden there, changing them so their shifting forms were no longer flesh and bone but stone and air and fire. Instilling in them a fervour that the old gods be forgotten and obliterated so that such a cataclysm should never happen again …

Bellepheros felt Zafir start beside him. 'The Elemental Men,' she gasped. 'Those are the Elemental Men! He made them. The Isul Aieha made the Elemental Men! Unholy Flame! I didn't see it!'

Another realm. Dragons. Diamond Eye's knife-blade tension, hostile as fire, as Zafir stopped before a grand carving of the Isul Aieha astride a mountain, his silver spear held aloft, the spear that had killed the Black Moon and cast him to Xibaiya, while around him in the sky a thousand circling dragons swooped to devour hapless fleeing men, in turn to be caught in the Silver King's snare. The day he dulled them and gave the power of alchemy to his blood-mages. Taming them. And in the images that followed there was the sense, at last, of some possibility, of an answer; and then the carvings abruptly stopped, for this was when the blood-mages tore their mentor down, and his answer, whatever it might have been, was never found.

'Answer to what?' muttered Bellepheros to himself, but the carvings had nothing more to say. He wandered the last few walls, which showed the Silver King in the Pinnacles – here, right where he stood perhaps – and peered at carvings of dragons and men, and then walked back to the start. Each Silver King carried a mark on his head while ordinary men did not. The dragons carried that mark too. He ambled back to the sequences on the rites of the dead and prodded at them. 'Is this supposed to explain why I have a walking corpse in my workshop?' But that couldn't be right. The carvings were ancient. Whatever they showed, the world had been that way since before the Silver King came. Hundreds of years. No. He turned to Zafir. 'In Merizikat the dead had only begun to rise in the last handful of years, no more. They declared holy war because of it …'

'I have something else.' Zafir was shaking, Bellepheros saw, and her eyes were wide and her face as pale as a ghost. 'You remember the hatchling in Takei'Tarr, Grand Master Bellepheros? The one that hatched woken?' She turned for a moment to Jaslyn. 'Your Silence. I chased her to a pinnacle in the middle of a desert. She landed and waited for us to finish her, but she showed me something before Diamond Eye bit off her head. It made no sense to me, and Diamond Eye had not woken. But now he has, and he understands.' She turned away as another dragon memory poured into them all. A memory from the dragon Silence of the rip in Xibaiya, its festering spread wide, its cage and prison gone.

'It's been like that for years,' Zafir said softly. 'The Black Moon held it back, and now it spreads, whatever it is. *That's* what the dragon Silence wanted us to know, but I can't make sense of it. Or rather, I can't begin to make sense of what it means. Nevertheless, I show it to you while *he* is not here.' She looked hard at Bellepheros.

'I think this matters, alchemist. I think this matters a very great deal. I would rather like it if you would fathom this for me.'

It is the abyss of the end for everything that lives, murmured Diamond Eye.

Bellepheros stared at Zafir. It took a moment to unravel the expression on her face because it was a strange one he hadn't ever seen there before. Thoughtful, and streaked through with dread.

She walked back to where the Silver King slew the Black Moon. She looked from Tuuran to Bellepheros and back again, and tapped the carved image of the Silver King's spear. 'This is what he came for. The spear that killed him. So the Black Moon *will* return to the Pinnacles from wherever he's gone, I have no doubt of that, and when he does, we will find the spear for him.'

And in those words Bellepheros wondered if he heard the first whiff of conspiracy; and he wanted to tell Zafir no, never to say this, but she couldn't know, because Bellepheros couldn't tell her that the Black Moon had cut him with his wicked knife of stars and bound him to obey, nor how the Black Moon, when he returned, would ride these memories and see them all, every one of them.

'Holiness,' he rasped, hoarse and choked. 'When he returns, do not let him see your sister.' He could do that, at least, and he saw by the shock that passed over her that Zafir understood.

She led them back out to the Hall of Mirages then; and when Bellepheros went back to Vioros's workshop, the walking dead man was gone. Big Vish and Halfteeth, fed up with standing guard, had bound it and carried it to the top of the mountain and thrown it off the cliff, hoping that would put an end to it.

15

The Bloody Judge

Between fourteen and four months before landfall

Clinging to the hull of Baros Tsen's ship, unseen beneath the waterline, the dragon Silence crosses the storm-dark. Moons pass, wax and wane. She sweeps the southern coastline, one city to the next along the thin green thread between azure sea and sweeping yellow sands. She circles ragged cloud-clipped spires among the Hothan Mountains and scours the ice-bound plateau in their midst where no men live, where forgotten monsters lurk dormant in caverns as big as worlds. She criss-crosses the night above the Sun King's seething Western Provinces and bathes in their turmoil of resentful revolt. Weeks stretch to months as she searches. Some nights she lands on the spires and domes of temples to the sun that ridge mighty cities, each with more little ones crammed together than she has ever imagined. So, so many.

We might feast and gorge ourselves fat and bloated, and yet barely make a mark.

She plucks drunkards from alleys, lone fishermen from their boats at night. She listens to the thoughts of the little ones. She becomes shadow and darkness and death, and the very few who see her see nothing else before they die.

But the splinters of the Black Moon's soul are not among them.

She flies north and east among terraced hills and glistening water meadows, over little towns and tiny villages as countless as stars scattered across a crumpled land, the Hills of a Thousand Temples. She crosses the Hothan peaks for a second time, the more gentle and forgiving northern range where the mountains topple and fall into the sea. She steals cattle, goats, wolves, bears, men, whatever is alone and will not be seen or quickly missed. She pauses for a day in the colossal fortress city of Merizikat, filled with sailors and shipyards, and eyes with a murderous hunger the hundred ships at anchor in the waters of its harbour. She sits upon the roof of its armoured basilica and stretches out her thoughts, and wonders at the pleading helpless dead creeping restless in its catacombs, but there is no fragment of the Black Moon here, not yet.

She flies again, long winding days following every river and back again. She passes at night over the quiet town of Dahat, and pauses a moment at the familiar-scented thoughts of Baros Tsen T'Varr. She dark-shadow slides through the sprawling megalopolis of Brons and Caladir, the Sun King's twin capitals filled with priests and temples. Amid the unquenchable fire of the unconquered sun she creeps into thoughts of generals and princes, of priests and watchmen and sailors, merchants and tailors and dung men and whores. She sees their world inching to war.

The Black Moon is not here.

She courses south into the great plain heartland of the Sun King, its mighty twin rivers and a dozen stink-swollen cities. Over the mile upon mile of white marble of the Unvaski and a hundred other palaces, each enough to swallow a town and still be hungry for more.

The Black Moon is not there.

Now the dragon Silence pauses from her search. The half-god palace, the flying eyrie of Baros Tsen T'Varr, has gone into the storm-dark. Perhaps she has it wrong. Perhaps the Black Moon will not come to this world after all; but many months ago in the desert when her last life peered into the Black Moon's mind and woke him, there had been a face in his memories, a face and a place and a name. Tethis. The Bloody Judge. The Black Moon split himself in two long ago, a means to survive his sacrifice to the dead goddess. The little one she found in the desert carries one part of him. The face she saw in that little one's thoughts carries the other. He will seek it to become whole once more, and when he does, nothing short of a god will stop him.

The dragon Silence flies far to the north then, to the cold damp moors of the small kingdoms and their dirty mud-bound towns. If she cannot find the Black Moon then she will find that for which he seeks, and then she will wait for him in lurking ambush. She finds the spoor of the Bloody Judge in the memories of that place, in breaths and traces, remembered glimpses and amber-trapped histories. She follows his trail through the memories of those he has touched, follows it from sailors and soldiers, sea captains and whores, ships and taverns and flophouses and merchant stalls, street by street and life by life until the drip-drip memories of his passing bring her once more to the beating heart of the Dominion, to the palace of its immortal king and his arch-cathedral to the all-conquering god of the sun. Curled nestled among spires and minarets, still and silent in the day, slinking between its domes at night, claws clicking on gold and marble and alabaster, the dragon Silence eats unseen into the minds of those who pass below.

The Bloody Judge. General of the Dominion. Favoured son of the immortal king of flames himself. In crypts and catacombs, dead things walk when they should not. The unconquered sun draws in its wrath and sends visions to its priests, who declare the necropolis of Deephaven an abomination, the Ice Witch of Aria who permits it anathema, and so the engines of war grind their gears and rumble to life, and the Bloody Judge will lead the Sun King's armies in the greatest crusade the worlds have ever seen; but the dragon Silence sees the visions for what they are.

Lies.

General of the Dominion, yet the Bloody Judge is a ghost, slipping like water among the thoughts of the little ones below. She has his face, the face seen in the desert of the night-skins, in the little one possessed by the Black Moon. In memories slit from blind minds she meets him, speaks with him, sleeps with him, tries to kill him, but never finds him. The priests of the unconquered sun think to command him, but Silence knows better. The Black Moon has woken in the Bloody Judge, as he woke in the man in the desert, and twists everything to his own grand design.

The hunt changes. She will find the Bloody Judge and kill him. She will send this other piece of splintered half-god screaming back to Xibaiya. She rides her little ones long and deep. Sees at last the face she seeks, the Bloody Judge, and what and who he truly is. She regards him through borrowed eyes, and tries to slip inside his thoughts, but glances away as though grasping for mist. Now he sees her too, and the man from which she watches turns to oily black ash; and from walls and halls rise the grey dead who exist only as shadow; and they throw up their arms and the darkness around them twists and roils; it grows into knives and spears that lacerate every servant whose eyes she has stolen. It rips their souls to shards. She saw these things too in the memories of that little one in the desert. She has found warlocks.

The shadow-knives fly into the sky to hunt. They find her, and each blade that cuts tears not flesh and scale but flays pieces of her eternal dragon soul. She flees, but the shadow-knives fly faster. Their swarm swells and grows, dozens to hundreds to thousands. One by one they catch and cut, until Silence feels herself bleeding away, the core of what she is crippled and dying. It is a true death that comes after her, not the little death, and not to be escaped, and through the hail of blades and knives she hears the warlocks laugh, for even a dragon cannot stop the end of everything that they have foreseen. They have her in a death grip.

But a dragon does not succumb so easily. With ragged failing strength she falls like an arrow from the clouds to the ground. She strikes with the force of a thunderbolt. The shadow-knives rain around her, seeking her soul to finish their murder, but she is gone, flesh and bone smashed and broken, the little death casting her wounded soul to Xibaiya where the warlocks' knives cannot follow. Cheated, they mill and circle and dissipate under the glaring gaze of the vicious sun.

The warlocks return to their sculptures of fate. The Bloody Judge arms for war. In Xibaiya the dragon Silence licks her wounds and waits to heal.

The Black Moon. The half-god split in two. One part must be destroyed. It does not matter which.

The Seven Worlds

The Hsians of Takei'Tarr hide in their towers, mystic logicians calculating their way to victory. In the Crown of Khalishtor the sea lords puff their chests and bellow for war while the Statue Plague decimates their land and the rotting flesh and bone of a corpse they imagine to be Baros Tsen T'Varr is carried across the desert to hang by an ankle. In Caladir the Sun King girds his armies for holy war, a jihad against the risen dead and all who would allow them to walk beyond the catacombs of his eternal prisons; in Aria the Ice Witch waits with armies of her own. In hostile Qeled old spirits stir among the dead who no longer die. In Xibaiya the earth-touched gather around the tear that rips their realm. Among the dragons of the Worldspine a whisper spreads: *The Black Moon is risen*.

In the desert of Takei'Tarr, beside the unfathomable Godspike, the eyrie of Baros Tsen T'Varr is about to fall.

16

Chay-Liang

Sixteen months before landfall

Glasships and lightning fought the dragons overhead. The last of the Elemental Men took his bladeless knife to the chains holding the eyrie aloft. He severed them, and the eyrie started to fall, slipping like a discarded feather through the air. The maelstrom of the storm-dark waited below to devour it. In minutes, everyone was going to die.

Liang dashed across the eyrie wall, risking the dogfight of hatchling dragons and lightning and Taiytakei soldiers screaming through the air on their sleds. The Black Moon sat in the middle of it all, a hundred tempests swirling about him, eyes closed, legs crossed, head tipped to the sky, light streaming out of him.

Well, sod him. She half ran, half slid down the steps, made it to another tunnel and scrambled inside. The white stone walls glowed full-moon bright, blazing stronger with every moment.

Shelter. She felt the shift of the eyrie through her feet, the lurch as it started to fall. She glanced at the glasships overhead, dozens of them raining lightning in a storm around the dragon Diamond Eye as it finally fell. She picked out the ones that had once belonged to Baros Tsen T'Varr, receding upward, dangling chains slack beneath.

Severed. Every one of them. It was done. Over. Still she forced herself to stay at the tunnel mouth until she'd counted them, and knew for certain that the Elemental Man had finished what she'd started. The eyrie was falling irrevocably into the storm-dark, and that would be that. The end. No one to save them this time.

The shock as Diamond Eye smashed into the stone of the dragon yard almost knocked her off her feet. She'd seen all she needed to see, and so now she ran as fast as she could, and never mind how her legs burned and her feet hurt. The tunnels here had been the barracks once, an unfamiliar place, but that didn't matter because they all spiralled in the same downward fractal pattern to the eyrie's core, to where Baros Tsen had built his bathhouse amid a ring of white stone arches. She lurched, sprinted, ran pell-mell to reach it before the storm-dark ate them. There was no one else here. Everyone was dead now, or else had fled to the darkest corner they could find. She stumbled and slipped, legs pumping too fast for the rest of her as she sprawled across the white stone floor. She got up and raced on, deeper and deeper, dodging and hurdling the ripped bodies that lay scattered about until she reached the open doorway to the bathhouse. Cold air billowed out, chilled by the enchantments she'd made for the room to become a morgue.

She stopped there, pinned for a moment by what she saw. The arches. Tsen had brought her here on the day she'd first come to the eyrie. *What do you make of these, enchantress?* And she'd made nothing of them at all, because they were simply a ring of white stone arches around a white stone slab. An altar to the old forbidden gods perhaps, that was all she could say, and Tsen had laughed and declared it as fine a place as any to build his bath and drink his apple wine, since those were as close as *he* could imagine to any gods, and after that she'd barely spared the room a second thought.

She spared it now, though. The space within each arch shimmered silver, something she'd never seen. Shining liquid moonlight. She went to one and almost touched it to see if it would ripple, then shook herself and shivered in the cold and ran on. She was here for Belli, that was all, all that mattered before the eyrie plunged into the storm-dark and everything was gone as though it had never existed. She ran past Tsen's old rooms, past her workshop to Belli's study, praying to the forbidden gods that he was still there, that he hadn't moved, that she would find him ...

A hatchling blocked her way. Small and crippled, but still a dragon. It shrieked as it saw her. Its talons scrabbled at the stone, clawing for purchase. Liang darted back the way she'd come. The hatchling bounded after her. She dived into her workshop, snatched up the first globe of glass that came to hand, stumbled, turned, and threw it as she fell, aiming at the dragon's head, willing the glass to bloom into a cage to hold the dragon tight as it pushed inside her room.

The glass hit the dragon's flank and burst in a thunderclap of imploding air; the dragon lurched and fell dead at once, a gaping hole in its side where a festering dark black mass floated, lit from within by purple flickers. Liang stared in horror. In her haste she'd thrown Red Lin Feyn's captured snip of the storm-dark, and now a tiny cloud of it hovered free in the doorway, filling what wasn't already filled by dead dragon. She couldn't get out. She'd trapped herself, and the eyrie was falling into annihilation, and she was going to die, and so Belli would die too.

She wasn't ready for that, not after everything they'd been through. She reached her mind into the storm-dark as she would into a piece of enchanted glass. There was a twist, Lin Feyn had told her. A reaching in and then doing something different. Not just a bit different, but completely. Something alien.

Glass was a matter of control. Delicate, intricate, precise thoughts. Her fingers touched the storm-dark. It burned like acid fire. She screamed, desperate and anguished, knowing she'd never make it move, that it had her held fast.

The storm-dark curled obediently into a ball. It floated in her palm. Liang stared at it, paralysed for a moment, awed and amazed. She looked at the storm-dark and at the dead dragon, and then remembered where she was and why and where she'd been going, and wrapped the snip of the storm-dark in glass and tossed it aside and clambered out. Belli was where she'd left him, sitting in his study, rocking in despair. She formed a sled from a piece of glass and dragged him to it.

'The eyrie's falling! It's all going to the storm-dark now!' She forced him down beside her, kicked off and raced the sled ever faster, weaving around the curves and loops of the tunnels. They were glowing a brilliant silver now, almost like daylight. She held Belli tight. 'Dragons, hatchlings, eggs – everything, all of it.' Up the spiral to the surface. 'Everything it touches, it destroys.' Past the rooms where Tsen's t'varrs and kwens once lived. Still did, for all she knew. 'We have to get off before it's too late.' Past the rooms where his favoured slaves once slept. 'We have to fly …'

She reached the last twist and shot into the dragon yard.

Heedless of her will, the sled stopped. The madman with silver eyes stood there, arms stretched wide, head pitched up, moonlight blazing out of him. The red-gold dragon Diamond Eye lay curled up on its side behind him, still and almost dead. Two hatchlings flanked him, watching like sentinels. A handful of men and women lingered nearby: a few Taiytakei soldiers, a dozen slaves from across the worlds, maybe a few more, the last survivors. They stood entranced. Enraptured. Liang tried to make the sled move again, but it wouldn't.

Belli climbed off. He walked to join the others. Liang barely noticed. The sky above and beyond the eyrie was a black churning cloud. Purple lightning flashed. They were too late. *She* was too late. They were inside the storm, and she knew what happened next.

The wind stopped.

The darkness turned absolute.

Silence.

She counted, as Red Lin Feyn had told her to. Five hundred heartbeats, give or take. The madman with the silver eyes reached up. He reached out at the same time, as though there were two of him – no, three, no, six – all in the same place, all reaching in different ways, an infinite mirror upon mirror of reflections, of possibility grasping into the Nothing that had become their sky, their sea, their land.

I am the Black Moon, he said in her head, in all their heads, *and I am your creator. Take me home.*

Five hundred heartbeats and then a handful more, and then the darkness changed. A flood of pinprick stars lit across the sky. Familiar constellations: the dragon, the spear, the water carrier. And unfamiliar ones too, stars she'd never seen. She grabbed Belli and pulled him back to her sled and shot into the air, and never mind where the mad half-god had brought them. The Black Moon, whatever he called himself, had pulled them through the storm-dark of the Godspike to another world, an impossible thing, she'd thought, but no matter. Whatever world it was, she would know it, for the Taiytakei had travelled to them all; and wherever they were, she and Belli were getting away, as far and fast as they possibly—

They crossed the rim of the eyrie. Far below rolled a feature-less endless dim-glowing sea of silver, on as far as she could see. Liang's breath caught in her throat. She staggered. Belli let out a quiet wail, shuddered and then fainted, curled up in a ball around her feet, clinging to her as though to let go was death. They were so high that Liang could see the curve of the horizon every way she looked. Dozens of miles up? Hundreds? From here the Silver Sea looked polished smooth, featureless. Gaugeless.

A roar built inside her head. A space so vast she couldn't breathe. She opened her mouth and forced her lungs to stretch. One, two, three and in. One, two, three and out. She'd never been high enough to see the world curve this way, never even close. The scale of everything dizzied her: the emptiness, the size of the Silver Sea stretched out for ever, the sky as clear as glass and black as ink, the horizon infinite and sharp enough to cut, everything else a bewildering conclave of stars set in stark, stark night.

One, two, three and in. One, two, three and out. The air was buttery rich, thick as though they were on the ground in the desert of Takei'Tarr. The eyrie dropped beneath them. It was gently fall-ing, feather-like. There was no wind. Liang found herself losing all sense of motion and scale.

Belli let out another wail. Liang looked about for anywhere they could go, but there was nothing. No hills, no rivers, no mountains. The Silver Sea stretched endless, and she didn't know what else to do but to go back to the eyrie. She landed the sled again on the rocky rim outside the walls, hoping not to be seen, thinking to creep into the tunnels and find a place to hide until she understood where the Black Moon had brought them, but the madman with the burning silver eyes saw at once, and came to her. Belli rolled off the sled and spread himself across the stone. The Black Moon pulled him gently to his feet, and then stabbed Liang with his gold-handled knife carved with a thousand eyes. A short moment of shock, that was all, and the knife was to its hilt in her chest.

Three little cuts, he said in her head. *You. Obey. Me.*

She fell to the white stone and noticed now that it was dull. The Black Moon plundered her memories and took them to be his own. He commanded, and his will would be done. His dragon-queen and her dragon: enchantress and alchemist would revive them. By word he made it so, and so Liang held Belli's arm and led him to Diamond Eye; and though she screamed and howled the Black Moon had cut her with his knife, and no choice was offered.

Bellepheros crouched beside Zafir. Her eyes were open.

'Grand Master ...' Frothy blood dribbled from her mouth. Bellepheros ignored her. He took a tiny razor from his sleeve, made a neat incision in the fleshy part of his hand and dripped a few drops of blood onto Zafir's tongue. He closed his eyes.

'Broken bones,' he said after a moment. 'Several. Punctured lung. Bleeding inside and out.' He shook his head. 'The bleeding I can stop, but she's past my help. There's too much damage. Nothing much in there works any more. She had a strong heart, and so she'll last a while yet before she goes. She's in a lot of pain.' He glanced up as if looking for the Black Moon. 'It would be kinder to make a quick end of it.'

He seemed truly sad. Liang stared into nothing, too shocked for any thoughts except the compulsion to obey and the desperation to shake it off, all-consuming like an animal paw-caught in a trap. It strangled her.

Bellepheros stroked a finger across Zafir's cheek. 'I'm sorry, Holiness, but I cannot mend this.' He went to the dragon. 'At least she died fighting. That's what they all want, dragon-riders. Let her lie here with Diamond Eye.'

No.

The eyrie fell on towards the Silver Sea. The Black Moon showed them his will. Slaved, helpless as trapped flies in amber, Bellepheros and Liang lifted Zafir onto the gold-glass sled that Liang had made for their escape. Together they carried her to the heart of the eyrie, to Baros Tsen's frozen bath. The air was cold, and the ring of arches still blazed silver. They laid Zafir out and took the near-frozen corpses of the morgue and dumped them in the nearest room, and then Liang lifted the enchantment that kept the bathhouse freezing cold and trapped it in a piece of glass, while Bellepheros drained the bath onto the floor to leave them slopping in a few inches of water.

'What ... are ...' They lifted Zafir into the bath. She tried to fight them, but there was no strength to her any more. Almost gone, death sombre at her shoulder.

The eyrie plunged onward.

Back on the rim Liang made a new sled. It was easy here – wherever *here* was – to weave her enchantments, easier than anywhere she'd ever been, as easy as breathing. She flew down, streaking towards the sea, while Bellepheros returned to the dragon. Unlike his rider, Diamond Eye would live. The dragon was strong.

My dragons always were.

Liang flew until the eyrie was a speck against the night sky above, quickly lost as it wafted downward. The sea was as smooth as glass, silver as a mirror. As the Black Moon had commanded, she took enough silver water to fill Tsen's bath to the brim. Then she paused. The Black Moon had told her what she *must* do, but had said nothing about what she must not, and so she lay down on her sled and touched the sea. The mirror-flat surface stretched out for ever in every direction. The stars above were more and brighter than she'd ever seen, the eyrie so far away that she'd long lost sight of it. The silence was absolute. She was as alone as it was possible to be.

She pushed her fingers into the silver. There were no ripples – it simply seemed to swallow her. She pressed her hand in deeper until the silver was up to her wrist. When she drew back, her hand jumped out as though fired from a spring. A single circular ripple bloomed, sluggish and fat and quickly dying away. Not water, this sea, but quicksilver. That most precious thing and twice as heavy as lead, but the sled didn't seem troubled by its weight.

She rode back to the eyrie, through the fractal spirals of the tunnels to the bathhouse, and emptied the precious quicksilver into Baros Tsen's bath as the Black Moon commanded. The Adamantine Man Tuuran now waited there too, cradling Zafir's body with the delicate care of a lover. The rider-slave's eyes were closed, and Liang couldn't tell if Zafir was still alive. When the bath was full, Tuuran laid her on its surface. She barely sank at all.

The Black Moon watched. 'Push her under,' he said. Tuuran shook his head. 'Push her under,' said the Black Moon again and put a gentle hand on Tuuran's shoulder. 'It's going to save her, big man. You have to trust this.'

The pain on Tuuran's face was as clear as the sky. He nodded and pushed Zafir's head down, trying to force her into the quicksilver, but he couldn't. He wasn't strong enough. So they turned her over, him and the Black Moon together, face down, and drowned her, killing, it seemed, what little spark was left. Zafir kept breathing right to the end. Thin shallow breaths. She shook a little and then was still.

'We've killed her.' Tuuran looked at his hands in horror, then at the Black Moon. 'Crazy Mad? If that's you? Tell me we haven't killed her!'

'You haven't killed her, big man,' said the madman. He let Tuuran turn Zafir back to lie with her face up, and then the Black Moon ushered them all away. And Liang, more than anything, was left to wonder why, why not let her die?

Time drifted around Chay-Liang in the months and moments that followed, seeming to pass her by, seconds and hours and even entire days falling wilfully between the interstices of the moments she remembered. She wandered in a daze or else sat in her room, staring at nothing. When she went to the walls the Silver Sea lapped at the eyrie rim. She didn't remember landing – it happened so softly that no one seemed to notice. The great dragon Diamond Eye perched silent and unmoving, one surviving hatchling to either side. A sadness poured out of the three dragons, a longing so deep and profound that Liang had to turn away; and even then it followed her. She caught herself weeping now and then for no reason she could find. She wasn't alone. It seemed that a doom weighed on them all, the few survivors, a crushing weight of mourning for something lost that they'd never even known they had.

Later it struck her as strange that the eyrie didn't float in the air the way it had in Takei'Tarr, but rested in the quicksilver sea. Later still it struck her as even stranger that she never once remembered eating or drinking, or feeling hungry or thirsty. And all the while the sea called to her. Her dreams filled with it, and with the moon, giant and full, silver in the sky, beckoning. Awake she stood on the eyrie walls for hours, staring at nothing. Sometimes the Black Moon stood too, unblinking, with silver light pouring from his eyes, the same light as the sea. He felt it as the dragons did, an unbearable hurt at his very core; he tried to hide it but he might as well have tried to hide the sea itself. She had a sense of him building his strength, readying to leave, but also that this was somehow a place where he belonged, against which he had turned his back long ago.

She took a sled. No one had said that she couldn't. She flew away without knowing why, except that something called her, on and on, barely aware of the passage of time until she came upon a city built of the white stone of the eyrie and the Godspike and the Azahl Pillar of Vespinarr, and other places too. Gleaming spires rose above the sea, thin and tall and impossible, with webs of silver strands between them. She stopped and snipped a piece of glass from her sled and made a farscope, shaped it with implausible ease, moulding it sharper and more perfectly bright than any she'd ever made, and with it, among the towers, she saw the silver-clad men who walked upon the surface of the sea itself. They looked back, wafting a warm and gentle curiosity at her intrusion. Their questions roamed about her in an instant, playful enough to make her smile. They toyed with who she was and where she had been and how she had come here, harmless and kind. She felt them spread around and through her, winged sprites of imagination full of joy and seeking answers, skimming the mirror sea, flitting ever-wider patterns, looking for her source.

She had no idea who they were. It barely occurred to her to wonder.

Her thoughts rode back among them, drawn out of herself with no desire to resist. She led them gambolling back to the eyrie, happy to have found them, sure they would ease the sadness that infused the Black Moon's palace. They darted and danced to the eyrie rim and climbed its walls, and sang with joy as they found the great dragon and tried to welcome him home, but in that moment the Black Moon turned his baleful eye and set his gaze upon them, and burned them into shrivelled screams and sent them howling away. They scattered and were gone. They took their joy and delight and left Liang alone and hollow on her sled. She called after them, and tried to give chase, but they didn't come back.

Then, from the quicksilver sea, came a dark moan of wakening, and a shiver as a different mind fixed itself upon her, as colossal as the light of the moon itself, hostile and terrible and bleak as winter stone. Liang fled, racing to the eyrie as a thousand eyes of burning silver set after her, each a gleaming gaze of murderous animosity.

The sea shuddered and swirled; a whirlpool sank beneath her and grew until it was a hole as vast as the sun, as depthless as night. Liang wept and howled her fear and clung to her sled until she crashed into the dragon yard and fell, but she felt no pain from it. She ran to the tunnels and ran for Bellepheros to hide inside him as deep as she could; and as she did, she felt the eyrie lurch and twist and sink, and the Black Moon howl with depthless rage and furious despair.

She clung to Belli and he seemed to speak: 'What is it, Li, what's happening?' His words carried every edge of her terror as the Silver Sea swallowed the eyrie whole and spat them out and cast them all into darkness. The eyrie shook and shivered and shuddered, and then as suddenly as it had begun, it stopped, and Liang found her mind clear and sharp again. She stumbled and shook away the cobwebs and climbed the fractal spirals of the eyrie into bright sunlight. The sky over the dragon yard was blue, a mackerel of cloud far overhead, thin and pale, not stars and darkness. The Black Moon hunched curled up into a ball in the middle of the yard, rocking back and forth. The dragon Diamond Eye perched on the rim with the hatchlings beside it, both as she remembered, unmoved, their eyes tuned to a dark curtain of cloud that reached into the sky as far as Liang could see, cutting this new world in two. Dim dull flickers of muted violet lightning flashed and pulsed within it.

A storm-dark line. Liang blinked. The memories of the Silver Sea were clear and sharp and yet somehow unreal. She couldn't quite be sure that it hadn't been a dream. The eyrie was aloft again, drifting through the air a hundred feet above some ocean, and what little wind there was nudged them slowly away from the curtain cloud of the storm. The dragons stared, eyes fixed, blind to all else, and Liang felt their yearning, a sweeping sense of loss and want.

It was real, then, the Silver Sea?

The dragons didn't answer. The handfuls of slaves and soldiers who stood on the walls gazed into the storm-dark too. They stood apart from the dragons, carefully distant, suffused with fear and dread and loss. Liang found Belli among them. She slipped beside him and took his hand and squeezed it tight. The ocean below was an ordinary sea this time, of water with its familiar colour of hammered steel and its stippled skin of waves, patient and restless.

'I had the strangest dream, Belli,' she said, and then shivered because it had felt so real, and yet how could that be?

'No dream, Li,' he said.

The glittering sea stretched to the horizon like the taut skin of the world. No one seemed to know what to do except to look at the storm-dark as it left them behind. No one spoke. It had them mesmerised.

'I saw the Silver Sea,' Liang said.

'So did I.' Bellepheros squeezed her hand.

'What was it?'

'I don't know.'

'There were people.'

'They were not people, Li, not like us.'

'I felt a yearning to stay. The dragons too.' Liang shuddered. 'Did not you feel their sadness?'

'I felt my own.' Belli turned to face her. 'I have the Silver King in my blood, Li. Just a touch, but the longing was … unbearable. It felt like it had … as though I had come home.' He blinked a few times. 'I don't know where we were, Li, but I know what we saw. We saw the Silver Kings. As they once were.'

'They would have let us stay with them,' she said. 'All of us. I felt their joy. Delight. But the Black Moon spurned them, and so they sent us away.'

'Is that what happened?'

'In my memories, yes.'

Bellepheros looked away. 'What I saw was different. When they came there was no joy. When they came, they scorned me and cast me aside.' He shifted and let go her hand.

17

Truce

The glasships were high overhead, far higher than they'd been before, receding into specks. The eyrie was falling. The lightning had stopped. Maybe they were out of range. Zafir reached Diamond Eye's head. She'd have to climb on top of him to finish him, to drive the knife through his skull and send him to the little death before the oblivion of the storm-dark annihilated them all. She wasn't sure she could. She threw off her helmet and wiped her eyes, brushing away the pain, then reached for the ruins of his harness to pull herself onto his shoulder, took hold of a rope and howled in agony and frustration when her arms didn't have the strength. She fell back. Another dull wave of pain washed over her. She could feel herself failing.

I can't, she said. And she couldn't. Just couldn't.

You were worthy to ride me, little one.

She wept. Nothing anyone had ever said meant so much.

'Hush.' A shadow moved over her. The Crowntaker stood, eyes burning silver.

'Why didn't you …?' She let out a long breath. What was the point? 'You could have been my Vishmir.' She lifted the bladeless knife to him. 'Finish us. Both of us.' The glasships above were little more than specks now, glints catching the sun.

The Crowntaker, the Silver King, whatever he was, crouched beside her. 'I'll not be your Vishmir,' he said; 'I'll be your Isul Aieha.' And she might have laughed if they weren't all about to die. A darkness swelled around the eyrie. The storm-dark was coming.

He reached and touched her brow, and the gold-glass circlet Red Lin Feyn had cast around her to remind her she was a slave dissolved into ash. 'Be free,' he said.

The storm-dark swallowed them.

She sank into darkness.

Zafir stepped into the sunlight of the dragon yard, slow and wary and a little bewildered. She looked about. Men milled on the wall in little clusters. They stared and pointed at the curtain of darkness that towered across the sky. Some seemed in raptures, some suicidal with despair, others simply bewildered. The eyrie yard was empty except for the Black Moon, crouched curled in the middle of it, rocking back and forth. Diamond Eye perched on the rim, staring. The storm-dark. There was nothing else it could be.

Zafir frowned. The sight of it should have rocked her, perhaps, a colossal darkness spread out across the sky as far and high as she could see. But it didn't. She felt numb. She'd been dying. She *had* died, hadn't she? The Crowntaker, the Silver King, whatever he was, had crouched beside her. She remembered his words. The alchemist had come too, Bellepheros. The storm-dark had been about to devour them. Then suddenly she was in Baros Tsen's bath, coughing and spluttering. The bath was bone dry, and whatever hurt she'd suffered, it was gone.

She down looked at herself. Dressed in her armour, the same mangled glass and gold she'd flown in to battle by the Godspike of Takei'Tarr. She had no idea what had happened since.

Where are we? She quickened her stride and marched to the wall where the dragons perched, to Diamond Eye on the rim. She sat beside him and hunched against his talons, her head leaning against his scales, both of them settling to watch the receding storm-dark. His presence was a reassurance. He was warm. *What happened?*

The Black Moon took us home. Diamond Eye's thoughts were odd. They had an unfamiliar shade she'd never tasted. Bitterness and a regret embraced his usual distant hostility. *Home*, he said again. *To the Silver Sea where the half-gods went when the war came. We felt it as strongly as a mountain, but the Black Moon would not let us go, and then they cast us out.*

They? But all she saw in the dragon's eye was an endless Silver Sea. It made no sense, and came from Diamond Eye with a searing pain, a tearing wrench of anguish and loss. She withdrew and looked over the rim's edge instead. Another endless sea, but water this time, not quicksilver. She shivered. The storm-dark towered over them. The size of it made her cold. It went on for ever. Up and to each side. Endless.

What happened to me?

You were on the cusp of life and death. The Silver Sea brought you back.

And then?

The dragon seemed to shrug as if he didn't much care. *The Silver Sea cast the Black Moon out, and us with him. It threw us into the storm-dark. He brought us here.*

And where is here? she asked again.

Diamond Eye didn't know. *This world? It is unfamiliar, little one. The taste of the air is different. It is new to me.*

Zafir looked at the wall of cloud. *Can you go back?*

No. Another blaze of regret. Wherever they'd been, the dragons hadn't wanted to leave.

Can you pass beneath it? Around it?

We have not tried.

Tuuran was heading across the dragon yard. Last she'd seen, a small war had been going on and there were corpses littered absolutely everywhere, a good few of them ripped to pieces. The place had been awash with blood. Now the yard was empty.

How long were we there – wherever we went?

Time has little meaning on the Silver Sea. Months or hours or somewhere in between. Does it matter, little one? He has taken us away. That is all there is.

Where they were, how they were here, how long they were gone, the dragons didn't care. Zafir looked for the cages she remembered by the walls, and the broken scaffold, but they were all gone. She was thirsty. Hungry. Ravenous, now she stopped to think about it.

'Holiness.'

Tuuran. The hatchlings eyed him as though he was food. Tuuran glared back. Food that bites, said his eyes. The dragons quietly laughed.

'Holiness, you're alive. Are you …' He looked confused. 'You were hurt. It was bad. Crazy had you taken to Tsen's bath and—'

'I am well enough now, Tuuran.' She cut him off. He could tell her the story of how she'd ended up in Baros Tsen's bath some other time, how she was alive and not dead. 'Where has the Black Moon brought us?'

'No one knows, Holiness. I don't think he knows either.' Tuuran frowned hard. He looked out at the storm-dark, at the sea and the sky. 'Holiness, what do we do?'

She couldn't stop looking at the dragon yard. How empty it was. 'Last I saw there were corpses everywhere. There were cages. There was a man in one of them.'

'No one survived, Holiness.' Tuuran laughed bitterly. 'I didn't see what happened, but the night-skins killed everyone they could, and the dragons had much the same thought. We fell through the storm-dark. Crazy took us ... somewhere.'

'The Silver Sea.'

'Yes.' He frowned at her as if wondering how she could possibly know. 'He ... he got rid of it all. It all just vanished one day.'

'The cages?'

Tuuran shook his head. 'There was no one left, Holiness.'

So he was gone then. Shrin Chrias Kwen. The man who'd killed Brightstar. The man who'd told his soldiers to rape her, to remind her that she was a slave. Pity. She'd been looking forward to watching him die slowly of the plague she'd given him.

'Holiness,' asked Tuuran again, 'what do we do now?'

'You could start by bringing me something to drink. I'm parched.'

'Yes.' He shuffled his feet. 'Thing about that, Holiness, as there really isn't all that much left. I think we—'

'Tuuran, if you glower any harder at my dragons, your face is going to rupture.' He was her Night Watchman now. She remembered that.

'Holiness, I'm just a soldier. Or sometimes a sailor, but it makes no odds. I don't know much about anything. I don't understand where we are or where we were, or how we got to wherever we went or how we left again. Truth is, I don't remember much about it. It was a strange place. Real, but at the same time like it was only a dream; but if that's what it was then we were all very hungry in our dreams, for the stores are almost empty.'

'It was real, Tuuran.' The dragons had no doubts, even if Tuuran couldn't be sure. 'Do you mean to say we have no water?'

'We have little of anything, Holiness. We don't know where we are. We don't know what to do, or what any of it means. Holiness, we need you. We need someone to lead us.'

'I died, Tuuran. For an instant, I actually died.'

'I pushed your face into the silver water and watched you drown.'

Too much. Zafir took a deep breath and stood up. 'Is Bellepheros still with us?'

Tuuran nodded.

'And his witch mistress?'

'Chay-Liang?' Tuuran nodded again. Zafir looked into the dragon yard, at the Black Moon huddled in the middle of it. She remembered moonlight blazing from his eyes, but that was gone now.

'Who is he, Tuuran?'

'He was my friend once. Berren Crowntaker he called himself. Other names too. Now ...' Tuuran's face soured. He shook his head. 'Now he's something else. The Isul Aieha, perhaps.'

He didn't sound convinced. Zafir shook her head. 'No, he's not that. But he set me free, and he saved my life, and he took us to wherever it was we were, and then he brought us here.'

They stared together a while longer, each as mystified as the other, and then, since the Black Moon wasn't moving or doing anything much except rocking back and forth, she sent Tuuran to get the witch and her alchemist, and made sure to have them wait a moment before she joined them in the yard.

What do we do? A fine question. She glanced at the three dragons, not that she expected any sort of answer. Not that they cared much one way or another. *Where are we and where do we go, and what happens next? Isn't it a queen's duty to have an answer?* Hard questions, too, but easier than the ones that vied to take their place. *What happened to me? Did I really die? What does he want?*

The dragons didn't know and they didn't care. All she saw was the desire in them, singular, deep and bright. Wherever they'd been while she lay in Baros Tsen's bath, they wanted to go back.

And I? What am I to want?

She didn't know the answer to that any more than the dragons did; and now Tuuran had the witch and Bellepheros with him in the dragon yard, waiting. Zafir climbed down the steps to join them. Something practical to take her thoughts away from fog-laced far horizons. The here and now. She dealt better with that.

'If you think you—' Chay-Liang began, but Zafir cut her off.

'Where are we?' She looked at them, from one to another: Tuuran, Bellepheros, Chay-Liang. None of them had the first idea. All three looked like sleepers woken too abruptly from deep dreams, still fumbling for their senses. Underneath her façade she felt the same. She shook her head, trying to shake some sense into the world. 'Bellepheros, you have a library of sorts. Find out. Tuuran tells me we have almost no food or water. We are adrift, and the sorcerer who brought us here –' she glanced again at the Black Moon '– now appears unable to help us. So whatever happened to us, put it aside unless you plan to die of thirst and starvation. I suggest you find out where we are, and then tell me which way I should have Diamond Eye tow us to find land.' She raised an eyebrow. Delicious, seeing her grand master alchemist and his enchantress mistress lost for words. 'Tuuran, I don't care if it's the last cup of water we have, it's mine and I want it.' She smiled a broad tooth-bared beam calculated to climb as far up the witch's nose as it could possibly go, and went back to her dragons. Space and time alone to think. She didn't know how she was supposed to feel about any of this. Confused, mostly. She was supposed to be dead. The Black Moon had saved her.

She looked at her arm, at the little patch of rough skin on the inside of her elbow where the Hatchling Disease had started to take hold. It was still there, still dormant, still held in abeyance by Bellepheros and his potions. But not gone. He hadn't saved her from everything then.

Tuuran came back to her a few minutes later and tossed a skin full of water into her lap. 'There's a couple of barrels and not many of us left.' He glanced at the sky. 'We'll last a day or two yet. Perhaps our ancestors will favour us with some rain?'

'Rain?' Zafir snorted. The deserts of Takei'Tarr hadn't seen much of that. She looked up anyway, but the clouds were wrong. No rain to save them, not here.

The eyrie drifted on, easing further from the dark curtain of the maelstrom, carried blind and helpless by a soft and gentle wind. *Are there thoughts out there?* she asked Diamond Eye. *Do you sense any others, far away? Land? A town? A city? A ship?*

Nothing.

Anything we can eat?

The sea teems with life.

There were cages and cranes around the eyrie rim. No one had used them since Baros Tsen had dragged them out into the depths of the desert and over the top of the storm-dark. Maybe they'd all been smashed while the Taiytakei lords wrestled for the eyrie, but maybe not. She sent Tuuran to have a look. 'Perhaps someone here knows how to fish?' She drank half the water in the skin and took the rest with her up onto Diamond Eye's back and launched into the sky, soared with him for hours, veering one way and then another, sweeping the sea ahead of the eyrie, looking for land but to no avail. By the time she returned the curtain of the storm-dark had become a distant darkness, riven with its muted violet flashes. She swept Diamond Eye in a single circuit of the eyrie and then flew him underneath, hugging the black stone underbelly and its veins of dull purple light. The storm-dark and the eyrie. The same light, the same lightning. It meant something, but she had no idea what.

She landed on the rim, close to where Tuuran and some of the others were rebuilding one of the cranes, then crossed the dragon yard and went into the tunnels to the little room where her hand-maidens lived. Myst and Onyx stripped her and scrubbed her skin with sand and pumice. They massaged her with Xizic oils looted from Baros Tsen's little room beside his bathhouse. They didn't say much, just looked at her in wonder and awe and perhaps a touch of fear, and when she asked them what had happened, all she heard was the same: the Black Moon had taken them to a Silver Sea, and it had been the most beautiful thing imaginable, and then he'd taken them away again.

For the first time in more days than she could remember, Zafir slept in a bed instead of out on the eyrie walls. Myst and Onyx curled up beside her. She kept touching her head where the Arbiter's circlet had bound her, but it was gone. Gone for ever. The Black Moon had done that.

In the morning she summoned everyone to the dragon yard. The sun shone bright and steady. The blue unchanging sky was cloudless, the air warm, a soft and gentle breeze brushing at her hair. She ran a hand through it and realised it had grown. Last she remembered, fighting for her life against the Taiytakei and their lightning, it had been close-cropped, sheared in the manner of a slave. It was longer now. Close to a finger's length. Quite some time had passed then while she had lain in Baros Tsen's bath. Months?

Did I really die? she wondered, but that was just stupid.

The Black Moon was where he'd crouched the day before, curled up on his side now and fast asleep. She told Tuuran to take him away somewhere quiet. The other survivors, when she had them arrayed in front of her, were a motley collection, a handful of Taiytakei soldiers who might once have served any of half a dozen different sea lords, and a couple of dozen slaves, kitchen slaves and house slaves, old men for the most part, although there were a few younger ones who hadn't died taking up arms. But she had what she had, and would make the best of it, and so she split them into bands. The largest she put with Tuuran to build winches and pulleys to lower men to the sea, to fish and draw buckets of water. The witch Chay-Liang claimed to have a notion how she and Bellepheros might separate out the salt and make water they could all drink; and there were still plenty of pieces of gold-glass out on the rim, enough to make sleds for everyone, enough to shape buckets that wouldn't leak and perhaps parts that Tuuran would need for his winches. Zafir charged Myst and Onyx with searching the eyrie from top to bottom and drawing up an inventory, and then some other men to make lines and hooks and lures for fishing. She tried to persuade the hatchlings to hunt, but they simply refused. She couldn't bring herself to ask Diamond Eye to do anything so menial.

'What of the eggs, Holiness?' asked Bellepheros when she'd divided up the work. 'Shall we have no Scales for when they hatch?'

'There are still eggs?'

Bellepheros led her to the tunnel beside what had once been the hatchery. Inside a room deep within the spiral tunnels were six dragon eggs.

'I don't know how they came to be here,' Bellepheros said. 'I don't recall moving them. But we have no Scales if they hatch.'

'Do you have potion with which to dull them if they do?' Zafir asked. The questions were pointless. Diamond Eye and the two hatchlings were already awake. They barely tolerated her as it was, and even then only because the Black Moon had told them that they must. They would not stand for another dragon muted by alchemy.

'I do.'

'Then throw it over the side. These dragons will hatch free. Those already here will not permit otherwise.'

Bellepheros nodded. 'May I have Tuuran, then, to see to these eggs?'

He meant for Tuuran to take his axe to them and murder the hatchlings in their shells while they waited to be born. Zafir shook her head. 'You may not. Nor may you tip them over the side. If they hatch, Grand Master Alchemist, then they hatch. Diamond Eye will see to them if our Silver King does not.'

Bellepheros's face, screwed up already, pinched a little tighter. 'He is not *our* Silver King, Holiness. Not *our* Isul Aieha. Far from it.' He stamped away, back to seethe a little in his laboratory before turning his mind to separating salt from sea. Zafir watched him go. *Not our Isul Aieha.* He was right about that. *But he is a Silver King. And he set me free.*

She meant to take to the sky again to resume her search for land, but in the end she stayed with Myst and Onyx and rummaged through the eyrie. In the afternoon she went to Chay-Liang's workshop with Myst tagging behind like an eager duckling, Zafir's old armour piled in her arms. The enchantress was making buckets and gold-glass fish hooks. She glared as Zafir waited at her door. The loathing was still there. Hard to tell if it was the same as it used to be.

'May I come in?' asked Zafir.

There was a moment of hesitation before Chay-Liang nodded.

'The armour you made for me is battered. I'd ask you to repair it, but you have more pressing things to do, and I don't imagine we shall find ourselves under attack while we remain adrift at sea. Use its parts as you see fit.' She looked around Chay-Liang's workshop, trying not to stare, not to seem nosy or aghast at the sheer chaos of it, benches covered with half-formed pieces of glass, metal, bundles of gold and copper wires, pincers, tongs, scalpel-sharp knives, and at least a dozen tools whose purpose Zafir couldn't imagine never mind name.

Chay-Liang pointed to a box on the floor. It already contained pieces of half-made armour. 'There.' Myst dropped her bundle into the box.

Zafir spread her arms. 'You have a lightning wand somewhere here, Chay-Liang? I'm sure you must. If you want to use it then get on and do it.' She tilted her head.

'This again?' Chay-Liang hooted and banged her worktop. 'We cannot return through the storm-dark without that devil creature, and he, it seems, is useless now. We have no navigator. We are stuck here, wherever *here* is. We need your dragon or we will all drift and die! So we need him to fly and search for land, and we need him not to eat us, and thus we need you. You well know these things. If you turn on us – if you hurt Bellepheros in any way – I will rack you with lightning enough to make your bones burst, slave. Until then you may strut all you like without fear of me. Go away and make yourself useful.'

'There are no slaves any more, Chay-Liang. None. I will not tolerate it.'

The enchantress almost spat at her. She glared and then looked hard at Myst. 'Have you told that to *her*?'

'I freed Myst and Onyx long before the Elemental Men came to end us. She chooses to stay.' Zafir met Chay-Liang's eye as if facing down a dragon. 'I am not your enemy, Chay-Liang.'

'Ha!' The witch barked with laughter, then stared, hard and cold. 'Here and now you are not. Here and now every soul on this eyrie needs you, as they need me, and neither can survive without the other, and so, as we are both practical women, we put aside our differences. But I have no doubt that as soon as we find land you quickly *will* become my enemy again. That is what you are, and then my lightning will come for you.'

Zafir's eye glittered, a flash of fury. 'I could simply fly away, you know. Take Diamond Eye and head off and not come back. Take my chances. They would be far better than yours.'

'Oh, I'm quite sure you could!' The witch snorted her scorn. 'But you'll not leave us without your alchemist, whose potions keep at bay the plague in your blood.'

Zafir tugged at the arm of her shift. The patch of skin on the inside of her elbow. No bigger than a fingernail for now, but the witch was right: it *would* kill her in time without Bellepheros and his potions. She pulled up her sleeve and offered her arm. 'You can check on it every day if you like to make sure I'm still in thrall.' Then spun on her heel and strode away, calling over her shoulder, 'Until landfall then, enchantress. Do let me know if I can in any way help you in your endeavours.'

As an overture of peace Zafir supposed she'd achieved her purpose. It stuck with her though, Chay-Liang's scorn, and chased her through the eyrie like a petulant ghost. A dragon-queen wasn't supposed to care what her servants thought. A dragon-queen ruled and her subjects obeyed, and that was the simple way of the world. But not here.

The next morning she rose early. She went to Diamond Eye and checked his saddle and harness. She replaced and repaired what she could, and reminded herself that, battered and frayed and broken as the harness was, it had survived intact enough to keep her safe through the battle with the Taiytakei glasships. When she'd done what she could she sent Myst and Onyx for water. A lot of it. Too much, the others might say, but they weren't about to spend day after day with their skin flayed by the wind and the sun on their back. She was about to mount and take wing when the witch came out into the dragon yard, tugging a sled. On the back of it was a huge glass bucket, and in the bucket was Zafir's armour. Chay-Liang stopped at the bottom of the wall.

'Dragon-slave! You asked if you could help. You can.'

'How?'

'Take this tub and fill it with seawater. Bellepheros and I mean to begin our work, he to test his alchemy and I my enchantments.'

Zafir smiled, and for once she even meant it.

'Here's your armour. I can't do anything for the dragonscale, but the gold-glass is repaired and shaped as it was. My own work so it was easy enough.' She handed Zafir her helm. 'I made some changes. You wear dragonscale. It must get very hot under there.'

'Yes.'

'Baros Tsen's bathhouse, after the Arbiter came, was used to keep the dead. I placed an enchantment to keep it cold so they wouldn't rot. The Black Moon had me take it away, so I've put it on your helm instead. Touch a finger to your left brow and it will cool you. Touch a finger to your right and it will stop.'

'And is there another to crush my skull when the whim takes you?' Zafir's smile didn't falter. It was what Red Lin Feyn had done.

Chay-Liang laughed. 'If there was, I wouldn't tell you, would I? Here.' She passed Zafir one of the greaves that would cover her arm. It had a glass rod mounted along the top that hadn't been there before. Liang tapped it. 'A lightning thrower. In case your dragons misbehave.'

'Aren't you afraid I'll turn it against you?'

'Aren't you afraid I'll crush your skull?' The enchantress twisted her face in a crude imitation of Zafir's smirk. 'The seawater, if you please.'

Zafir climbed the wall and stood beside Diamond Eye. She stripped to her riding shift, and if the former slaves on the rim working on the crane all stopped to stare, they knew better than to meet her eye. She armoured herself. Dragonscale, then gold and glass. The witch had done a better job this time. The armour fitted well.

Does she mean us harm? Zafir asked. *Did you see that in her thoughts?*

She knows you will turn on her when she least expects it, and that she lacks the courage to do the same. Diamond Eye felt distant.

I think it is not courage you describe, dragon. I think that is fear.

It is survival, little one. Nothing less and nothing more.

They flew together, carried Chay-Liang's tub to the sea and returned it full to the brim, then took a bearing from the sun and flew again, fast and far. Hour after endless hour Zafir dozed while Diamond Eye flew. When they had travelled perhaps a thousand miles and could still see nothing but sea, she took him down to the water to rest. Not that he needed it, but she'd flown him hard and he was hot, and they both needed to cool. She stripped naked and dived into the water and swam. Later she wished she hadn't. The salt from the sea, trapped against her skin, burned and chafed. She had no idea how far she went after that. They rested twice more, and everywhere looked the same. The sea and even the clouds.

What if there was no land at all? Was that possible? She turned back when her water was half gone, as the second sunset of her flight began to fall, and without Diamond Eye to guide her to the distant whispers of chattering thoughts that were the eyrie, she might have flown out here for ever, adrift and lost over endless water.

She returned after three days on Diamond Eye's back, dehydrated, fiercely hungry, so far into exhaustion that her vision kept blurring, and yet she'd found nothing. No land, no ships. She staggered across the dragon yard, shedding her armour as she went. When Tuuran ran to her side, she snapped him away. A dragon-rider stood on her own two feet. Always. Myst and Onyx had Baros Tsen's bath waiting for her. She fell asleep in it and barely noticed when they pulled her out and dried her and put her to bed. When she woke, she realised that a bath meant Chay-Liang and Bellepheros were making fresh water from the sea as they'd promised. Fresh and pure and cool. She could have kissed them both.

Tuuran had finished his cranes and was winching people in shifts down to the sea to fish. Zafir allowed herself a day to watch them, to rest and recover, and then flew again, a different direction this time, longer and further, and with more water to sustain her. Chay-Liang's enchanted helm cooled her, but she found it gave her headaches too and so after the first day she stopped using it. This time, when she came back, she collapsed in the middle of the dragon yard and almost couldn't get up again.

'You're not taking enough food,' chided Bellepheros, but it wasn't that. It was the sheer numbing exhaustion of flying a dragon so far. Further than any rider had ever flown before. Not that Diamond Eye cared. He would have flown for ever if she let him.

They'd had a storm while she was gone, but it had passed. Afterwards Chay-Liang had moulded a hundred sleds. She wanted to use them to pull the eyrie so they didn't simply drift in the wind, but she didn't have any chains to tether them. Zafir had Diamond Eye move about the rim of the eyrie, burning it until it was molten, while Liang then set the sleds into the stone as it cooled. Half the sleds melted or fell out again, but it was better than nothing. They'd do some more after her next flight.

The Crowntaker was awake again too. He spent most of his time fishing, or so Tuuran told her, and didn't say much. The Black Moon seemed to be gone, but the pain in Tuuran's face told her that something was still terribly wrong.

'He raves,' Myst whispered. 'He wanders in a daze.'

'It's like he's not really there,' said Onyx.

Zafir held them tight. When she asked Diamond Eye before they flew again, the dragon seemed not to know. *The Black Moon is still inside him. But dormant or dead even I cannot tell. Nor do I much desire to look.*

On the third flight she passed a pod of whales a hundred miles from the eyrie. Diamond Eye threw himself at them and almost drowned her snatching one out of the water. A small one. He carried it back to the eyrie and set it on the rim, where the dragons ripped it to shreds and left only bones. Zafir had him catch a second and leave it in the yard. Food enough for the days she was gone; and then off again. This time exhaustion took her long before Diamond Eye returned, and Tuuran had to pull her unconscious from her dragon's back because no one else dared come close. He carried her across the dragon yard and sat with her until Myst and Onyx shooed him away, and he was sitting beside her again when she woke. Her eyes slowly focused on his face. She reached out to touch his cheek. He looked distraught.

'You went too far, Holiness.'

She sat up, reeled a little as her head spun for a moment, then grabbed his face in both hands and pulled him to her. She kissed him, awash with unexpected feeling, then let go and wondered what she was doing. She slumped and closed her eyes.

'No, I didn't,' she murmured. 'I found land.'

18

Red Lin Feyn

Thirteen months before landfall

'Welcome. We are honoured to have a former Arbiter aboard.' Captain Beccerr of the *Servant on Ice* bowed in front of Red Lin Feyn, low enough that the long braids of her hair touched the deck. Lin Feyn smiled uncertainly and looked about her. Sail-slaves were hauling in her sea chests and carrying them below. There were men busy in the rigging. The ship was preparing to sail. 'Our expedition is one of reconnaissance, but we will be in what have become hostile waters so—'

'I am aware, Captain. Thank you for your hospitality. I would see to my cabin.'

Captain Beccerr led her into the stern castle, then waited as Lin Feyn shooed away the sail-slaves and set about unpacking her chests herself. The Taiytakei still traded freely at Helhex in the south of Aria, but had been evicted from Deephaven in the north and restricted to a handful of ships each month. The necropolis still stood in the heart of that city, and now the Ice Witch had built a colossal black fortress further up the coast. Raised it on her own from raw stone in a single night, they said. Whispers spoke of a civil war brewing in Aria, one that the enemies of the Ice Witch were hardly likely to win without some help, and so help they would get. The legions of the Sun King would cross the seas in holy war, carried by the Taiytakei, to put an end to the Ice Witch for ever. The sea lords of Khalishtor had decreed it would be so. Lin Feyn had her doubts, but she kept them to herself, and the Crown of the Sea Lords had not sought her opinion. Captain Beccerr clearly had her doubts too, but *someone* had to go and see what the Ice Witch was building up there.

'Uneasy times.'

Red Lin Feyn nodded. Baros Tsen and his eyrie and his dragons were gone, but the hatchling from the Queverra was still unaccounted for, the Statue Plague still rampant among the slaves in Cashax and now in Khalishtor too, the cracked pillar still in the cage around the storm-dark of the Godspike.

'This war will either save us or plunge us into irrevocable catastrophe,' she said. 'And I don't believe any of us have the first idea which it will be.'

When Captain Beccerr was gone, Lin Feyn opened the false bottom of her chest. She took out her copy of the forbidden Rava and opened it. Damned book was a mishmash of myths, of stories and obscure symbolism all muddled together with no rhyme or reason she could fathom. She couldn't understand why the Elemental Men were so afraid of it. Everyone, for example, knew the tales of how the first men were made: the Rava simply said the same in a more obscure way.

'... and the four creators tore pieces of their essence and spread them; and the sparks of the sun fell like brilliant rain, and where each spark touched the oceans and deserts and forests of the earth there rose a man and a woman, naked and full grown; and as they stood for the first time on sun-cast limbs they saw one another, and were filled with desire and fell at once back to the earth in copulation; and from each union were born two more children of the sun, brother and sister, who emerged from the wombs of their mothers full grown and rich with lust so that they too fell upon one another, brother with sister, mother with son, father with daughter ...'

Lin Feyn skimmed ahead. Prurient prose exalting incest perhaps merited the author's execution, but surely not an entire order of sorcerous assassins dedicated to its eradication.

'... and the shards of the moon fell in the night like silver snow, taut with sorceries of transformation; but the children of the moon did not sprout and teem and swarm in hordes like the seed of the sun, but waited dormant, yet bright was their allure so that the children of the sun might pick them up and give them form of flesh and bone, for always was it that the moon cannot shine without the sun, and yet the moon owns both night and day. And the children of the earth grew from stones, many in number and many in form, changers of shape and substance, while each star in the sky gave forth a single ray of its light, and some came to the earth and some did not, and some are seen coming still, blazing lines of star fire through the sky. For the power of the sun is motion and fire and irrepressible life, and the power of the moon is transformation and change and seduction and the hiding of things, and the power of the earth is mastery of shape and substance and strength, while the power of the stars is divination and time and the unfettering of the past and future from the present ...'

Lin Feyn skipped ahead again. The whole book was like this, most of it in a hurried and barely legible hand.

The rocking of the ship changed. They were raising sail.

'... and the children of all but the moon were many, but the children of the moon remained few and kept their holy essence un-diluted as it was given them; and so the children of the moon rose to rule over all, Silver Kings and half-gods of matchless sorcery, each born over and over and yet each always the same, each life raised anew from a sun-child taken in its prime and cast aside, as a new cloak is favoured over an old and then discarded in turn when its threads grow bare and with equally as little thought, while the half-god within remains unchanged. So it is that the half-gods alone remember the origins of time itself and know their creators for what they were ...'

The ship was starting to turn, and it was Red Lin Feyn's personal ritual to stay on deck as she left home on any voyage, and to stand at the stern until she could no longer see the land. She was about to close the book and put it away, but the last words made her pause and then rummage frantically through the papers she'd been given when she was Arbiter, until she found the sheaf of notes on dragons, the claims of Chay-Liang's slave, the alchemist Bellepheros.

'Dragons do not die as we do. They live one life after another, and each remembers all those that have passed before. Thus when a dragon hatches from an egg, its flesh may be new and weak, but its soul is already a thousand years old.'

She closed the Rava and hid it away, and went to watch the coast of Khalishtor recede. It nagged at her. The Rava and the alchemist seemed to be saying the same thing, one about long-lost half-gods that had possibly never existed, the other about dragons which very much did. But the half-gods had not been dragons. Even the Rava wasn't *that* obscure.

The curtains of the storm-dark were shifting more and more these days. The *Servant on Ice* was at sea for weeks before they found the curtain to take them to Aria. When they sighted it, the *Servant* turned and tacked against the wind towards a wall of black cloud from sea to sky that ran as far as the eye could see. Ran for ever, if you tried to find its end as some of the first sailors had done. Violet lightning lit up the cloud from within. As twilight fell and the *Servant* entered, Lin Feyn stood at the prow, and as the lightning cracked about them she wove the enchantments of her father of fathers, Feyn Charin, and drew the lightning to her until it wrapped the ship like an aura. She held it tight, as the cloud and the roaring wind and the violent seas and the lightning abruptly stopped to silence and a pitch-black nothing, as the *Servant* passed into the timeless void of the storm-dark's heart. Lin Feyn counted out the heartbeats as the lightning-crackle about her ebbed and slipped away. A few more heartbeats with every passing year as the crossing became ever harder. There would come a time, not too many years away, when the navigators one by one would begin to fail, unable to find the strength to hold the Nothing at bay for so long. But not today.

The violence of the sea and the storm crashed back. Lin Feyn loosed the remains of her captured lightning in one thunderous retort and returned, exhausted, to her cabin, and to struggling with the wilful obscurities of the Rava's prose. Darkness had been falling as they'd entered the storm, but the other side offered up a bright morning sun, becalmed in a cloudless sky. Such was the way of the storm-dark.

The *Servant on Ice* sighted land a few days later. She kept over the horizon from the coast of Aria while men on sleds scouted the shore and waters ahead for other ships. When they were far enough north to close on the coast of the Ice Witch's black fortress in the night, Lin Feyn took a sled and rode for miles until she saw the dark line of land and the fires of the fortress itself. She loosed a few tiny gold-glass birds, golems casting eyes for traps and warnings, but found nothing. In the darkness she struggled to return to the *Servant* again, and it was almost dawn as she finally set down on its decks. She felt dizzy, and her head swam with fatigue. She stumbled to bed, too exhausted to think, but woke again an hour later to a mayhem of noise, of shouting and thunder and lightning. As she rushed outside a streak of fire shot overhead, punching a hole in the mizzenmast topsail. A flurry of thunderbolts rattled the air, but the fireball was too quick. It flickered sideways and came back again, fizzing past. A second fireball landed on the foredeck and coalesced into the shape of a man ablaze. Burning torrents flew from his fingers, a hose of flame washing the deck. Red Lin Feyn hurled one glass globe and then another, the first a trap that flashed into a glass prison as it hit the flaming man, the second a shield to hold back his torrents. The flaming man burst into dazzling light. Men became pillars of fire and ran screaming around him; more flames shot up the masts and the rigging, biting into rope and sail and wood as though all had been soaked in lamp oil. Lin Feyn clenched her fists. The glass prison tightened around the magician, crushing him smaller until he was a seething knot of sun-bright flame.

'Stop!' she howled, 'or I will end you!' Her words died in shouts and volleys of lightning as the other fireball shot past. When she looked back her glass prison had vanished and the magician was gone. Sails were burning all across the ship, and most of the rigging too, while sailors ran with buckets, trying to stop the fire from taking the masts. Two galleys were coming at them, closing fast. Rockets whooshed and roared. Bright orange streaks fizzed and hissed across the water leaving trails of smoke in the air as the *Servant*'s rocketeers got their range. Glass globes shattered in clouds of fire as they hit the water. The *Servant* fired a salvo and then another, and the sea around the two galleys erupted in a wall of fire; and then Lin Feyn saw the fireball again amid the flames. It sucked them into itself and came back at her, brighter than before and with infernal speed. It shot through the mainmast and shattered it, punched through a sailor who stood in its path, leaving a gaping charred hole in his chest ...

The world juddered. The ship twitched. Suddenly Lin Feyn was below decks with no thought or memory as to how, running for her cabin to destroy her copy of the Rava, Feyn Charin's journals, the notes from the alchemist on the nature of dragons, all before the fire witch came. She crashed through her door and hurled an explosion of glass at the ship's side to blow open a hole, then gathered up all the papers she could see. The Rava was back in its hidden compartment, and so she threw everything out of the chest and opened it, and then stopped and looked about in time to see the fireball from above hover by her cabin door. It coalesced into the shape of a woman dressed in brilliant orange silk embroidered with cranes in black silhouette. Lin Feyn dived aside and hurled a glass globe. The woman shifted into fire, darted up and hurled a blast of flames. Lin Feyn conjured a glass shield. With her other hand she scattered marbles across the floor. She held her shield firm and drew back her arm to throw again as the fireball coalesced into a woman once more, flames burning from her fingers. She threw a blast at Lin Feyn's feet, transformed again to flames, shot sideways, materialised ... The marbles Lin Feyn had scattered detonated with bangs and flashes ... hundreds of whirling glass blades shot into the air in a blur ...

Time stopped. Flames paused mid-flicker. Her glass blades hung still. The roar of fire, the thunder and lightning from above, all fell away, silenced and mute. Everything froze as Red Lin Feyn looked on. She had the sense of a woman, achingly beautiful, with a gold circlet on her brow. A place of shimmering rainbows and ...

The woman spoke in Red Lin Feyn's thoughts: *You are dreaming, sorceress. Come and sit with me a while.*

The *Servant on Ice* was gone. She was in a dark room in some other ship on a sea so still she could barely feel its rocking swell. Her head throbbed. She was thirsty and had terrible cramps in her stomach. The clothes she wore were unfamiliar, a slave's silk tunic, belted at the waist, and nothing else. Her glass had gone, all her sleeves and pockets. Her wrists and ankles were bound.

A shadow slid across the room, a shadow without light nor any flesh-and-blood body to birth it. It slipped under the crack of the door and was gone ...

Come closer.

Again the world lurched and flickered. Now she was in a room of polished white stone, round, somewhere high in a breeze where the air was fresh and cold. Archways opened to the sky, north, south, east and west. Sunlight streamed through. Between the openings were more arches, blank plain things. They made her think of Baros Tsen's eyrie. Dreams were like that, weren't they?

Her legs were unsteady. She was in the same slave's tunic as before, but now her hands and feet were free. She couldn't see anyone, but she knew she wasn't alone.

'Come outside.' A woman's voice, soft and melodious. Red Lin Feyn took a deep breath and summoned a snip of the storm-dark into each hand. She looked at them and wondered how such a thing was possible, and then remembered that she was in a dream. Fearless then, she walked out to a balcony atop a slender white tower. Four other towers stood about her, all arranged in a circle. A city spread beneath them, and a great river ran beside it, as wide as the city itself and a-swarm with ships and barges. The streets were full of life and motion. Sounds wafted on the air, merchants selling their wares, the singing of street-corner bards, criers shouting news and imperial edicts, the clatter of horses, the distant blare of cavalry horns. The stink came too.

She didn't know this place. Her feet had walked all the cities of Takei'Tarr and many of other realms, but not this. She would have remembered it at once for its towers, their white stone, their shape and texture not unlike the Godspike of Takei'Tarr.

A woman sat with her feet over the edge. She wore tight breeches in a deep lush red, black riding boots and a short tunic of white and gold. Her skin was dark, her long black hair tied in a plait that reached to the small of her back. Her eyes were emerald green, and the golden circlet she wore across her brow blazed with power. The Circlet of the Moon.

'Ice Witch!' Red Lin Feyn hurled her summoned snips of storm-dark, two brutal things to annihilate whatever they touched. The woman barely seemed to notice.

'I learned that trick a while back,' she said. 'Have you learned this one?'

The whistle of the wind fell silent. The noises of the city too. When Lin Feyn looked at the river, the ships had fallen still and the gleaming ripples on the water had frozen. Birds hung motionless in the air between wingbeats. The Ice Witch had stopped time.

'The Sun King plans a war against my world, Red Lin Feyn. Only a Taiytakei witch may cross the storm-dark, and so your people must mean to aid him. Why?' The Ice Witch turned. Her eyes fixed Lin Feyn to the spot, a brilliant depthless green that sparkled with sadness and anger. Lin Feyn composed herself. She had no gold-glass, and the Ice Witch was impervious to the storm-dark, and that left her with nothing but words; but then wasn't this a dream? So words might be as deadly as she liked.

'You are a sorceress,' she said.

The Ice Witch nodded. 'That I am. As are you.'

'You are the most powerful this world has seen for many generations.'

'In your world I might say the same of you. And?'

'You breed more.'

'I do. So do you. And?' In their moment of frozen time the Ice Witch stared into Lin Feyn, and Lin Feyn thought, amid the ire, she saw true bewilderment. The Ice Witch really didn't understand why she was the enemy.

'Sorcerers broke the world into pieces ...' Lin Feyn tried to pick her words carefully. She was an ambassador for her people ...

'Ah. So it's your Elemental Men who wish me dead? But I hear there are hardly any of them left. Besides, you stopped trusting them months ago when they lied to you about dragons, did you not? *They* are the ones for whom all sorcery is anathema. *You* are a witch to them, as wicked as I. But you let them tell you what to do, and so you become useful to them, I suppose.' The Ice Witch stood. 'Why so afraid, Red Lin Feyn?' Her eyes shone; for a moment they burned ferocious bright, then faded and grew sad again.

'Years ago I made a bridge,' said the Ice Witch quietly. 'I made it because the river was too wide and too deep and no builder could span it. It stands beautiful and abandoned. I charge no toll, but no one uses it. The ordinary folk prefer to give a penny to one of the many boatmen who cross the river beside it. Now and then a drunken oarsman will capsize. Now and then people fall overboard and drown. Almost every day someone dies crossing my river, yet no one uses my bridge. Why? Because they do not understand, and so they are afraid.' She cocked her head. 'You are afraid I will become a monster. Ruled by your fear, you force it to truth, and thus a monster I must be, to tear down the pillars of your world, and crush your empire to ash and sand. Your nightmare prophecies take substance and grow real from such nourishment. Is that wise, Red Lin Feyn of the Taiytakei?'

They were suddenly in the room of arches. It happened in a seamless moment, something so natural that Red Lin Feyn thought they must have been there all along, as though the time-frozen city had been an illusion. It was a dream, she reminded herself. No ordinary one, but played by the rules of dreamers.

'The past,' whispered the Ice Witch. She touched an arch. It shimmered silver and rippled like water and dissolved to show a fleet of white ships with huge curved prows like giant swans. Silver-armoured red-eyed white-skinned half-god moon sorcerers sailed upon them, who summoned knives of ice to rain from the air and send slaughter upon some city and raised the murdered dead into an army of deathless slaves. She saw them come upon this city of spires and the dead pile themselves against the walls. She saw them burn, saw the moon sorcerers dissolve the city's walls into black ash, saw the dead swarm the streets and then the fist of the moon strike the earth and the sun climb into the night sky. She heard the moon-god's sister whisper something like the intimate murmur of a lover in her ear. And then light. Endless, timeless light and a limitless sea of silver, and the living dead and their moon sorcerer masters were gone.

'You want to stop the rise of a terrible sorceress who will crack the world in two? I fear you are too late, Red Lin Feyn of the Taiytakei. What you see? I did that to them, to the old ones who still linger here.' A wan smile flickered across the Ice Witch's face, and she tapped the circlet on her brow. 'You should have sent your assassins when I took the Sapphire Throne as regent for my little brother.' She nodded then to the swimming silver arch. 'Others tried. I see now that their reasons were the same. They too might have done better to speak with words than with weapons, but they were right that that was the time to change fate. You are years too late. I have already done the thing you fear, much to my chagrin.' She turned to another arch. 'Now behold the future.'

Red Lin Feyn saw the room where she stood, but now a man was in her place, his back to a slender crescent moon. He stepped onto the balcony. The wind picked up, a strong steady breeze that blew into his face, and Red Lin Feyn was with him as he looked about. The same five towers, the same city spread beneath them, but now night. A flurry of bright orange streaks launched from the river. Rockets. Plumes of bright flame bloomed. A roar rose from below, the voices of a thousand men racing to their deaths. Smoke rose from close to the waterfront, the start of some pointless battle. Shapes moved fast through the air. Men on sleds. The first sun-flash of lightning ...

The Ice Witch touched an arch. 'I see you,' she whispered.

The vision returned to its start. To the man who stood in her place in this room of arches with his cropped hair and pale skin and eyes that poured forth moonlight.

'I will not be the monster,' whispered the Ice Witch, 'no matter what you do. But the monster is indeed loose, and now you have seen its face, and if you fall upon me as his half-kin once did, if you bring this future to pass, I have another to show you. One I cannot stop.'

Through a third arch a dark moon rose from the southern sky to chase the sun. Lin Feyn saw the earth burn and dragons fly. She saw fire and death and ash. She saw glass ground to sand. She saw the dark moon catch the sun and hold it tight, darkness fall to throttle life and fire until all became ice and still. She saw a half-god blaze across the sky with a thousand dragons at his back, and turn the world to dust.

The Ice Witch's voice turned hard. She faced Lin Feyn eye to eye. 'Your people are arrogant and cruel. I will take away from you that which you have no right to have. Ships of all worlds shall cross the storm-dark. I will share that gift far and wide.' She bared her teeth. 'But if you come here, Red Lin Feyn of the Taiytakei, I will destroy you. I will find your ships and your sorcerers. *You*, Red Lin Feyn. You and yours. I will hunt you and end you all.'

Lin Feyn was shaking. 'There is something of the Crimson Sunburst in you,' she blurted.

'I don't know what that is, Red Lin Feyn.'

'How do you know my name?'

'Because this is your dream, and I am inside it.' The Ice Witch reached out a hand. Where her fingers touched Lin Feyn on the cheek they burned with a deep and lingering hurt. 'I would prefer you as an ally, but you have made yourself my enemy.'

The colossal armoured fist of an angry god crashed into Red Lin Feyn's head and ripped her memories out of her, everything she knew and everything she was and everything she hoped for. Took it all out and looked carefully at every piece and then put it back again, all in its proper place. Around the edges Lin Feyn gasped at the flashes that came unsought and unwanted the other way. As the Ice Witch lingered on Lin Feyn's memories of dragons, on the last words the hatchling had breathed in the depths of the Queverra, on knowledge of the Rava and the name of the Black Moon, trickles of colour and emotion bled the other way. The Black Moon most of all. The Black Moon. The enemy, and a dread that she had years ago made a most terrible and ghastly mistake.

How many years? Seven. The crack in the Godspike, the change in the storm-dark, the beginnings of the walking dead. All tied together. All begun at the same time. All caused by a single event. And there, Red Lin Feyn saw, was the answer she sought.

The Ice Witch had been to Xibaiya. She'd seen the rip. She'd freed the Black Moon.

The world of Red Lin Feyn's dreams dissolved.

She woke in her cabin aboard the *Servant on Ice*. Disorientated and confused and a little lost. She roused herself and splashed a little water on her face. A dream then, all of it; and yet when she stumbled on deck she saw that the *Servant* was heading home. When she looked harder, many sailors were simply gone, and no one knew quite what had happened to them or why or how. Her copies of the Rava and Feyn Charin's journals had gone too, and here and there, beneath careful repair, the *Servant* bore the scars of the battle she remembered, charred and burned in places exactly as she'd seen; yet no one else now knew how any of these things had happened, or what had become of their missing comrades and crew. Their memories were entirely gone. They knew nothing at all of galleys or of the fire witch, or of months spent captive in Deephaven harbour held under guard while they repaired their ship, nor of Red Lin Feyn imprisoned in the Ice Witch's black fortress, or of the empress with her golden circlet who came to visit before they were sent on their way. Yet so it had been; and when Red Lin Feyn looked at herself in a glass she saw the pale marks on her face where the Ice Witch had touched her in a dream that had been no dream at all.

19

Awakening

Thirteen months before landfall

Pride. Now there was a thing. Tuuran stood out on the eyrie rim, eyes fixed across the rippling sea, and tried to remember the last time he'd felt properly proud. He'd felt it sometimes back when he'd been a sail-slave on his Taiytakei slaving galley. He'd definitely felt proud on the night he'd cracked the skull of the galley oar-master and hurled him overboard where no one would see. Men he'd taken up from the oars had made him proud – slaves full of broken hate, righteous anger or sullen resentment, and he'd turned them back into men, fierce and strong. Yes, he'd had his moments back on that galley, but not like this. All those times he had never quite forgotten he was making more slaves for the bastards who thought they owned him. *This*, though ... This was different. Pride, clean and honest.

He looked over the eyrie moving steadily towards the limitless horizon. He'd lost track of how long they'd been adrift. A month, maybe. Another day, her Holiness said, and they'd reach land. Her dragon pulled on a chain that the dragon and the enchantress had forged, a harness yoking the monster as though he was an ox dragging a plough. A hundred enchanted sleds pulled too, each one tiny but the sum of them worth something. His men had built cranes and winches and platforms and lowered them, and they all lived on fish and the tepid water hauled up from the sea and made drinkable by the witch and the alchemist and their magics.

And then there were the men. *His* men now, slave or night-skin, soldier or tailor. He'd earned that. Half were more skilled with needle and thread than knife and sword, but he had uses for that now. The tailors and the two seamstresses were down by the sea every day, fishing, keeping their bellies full, weaving lines from their stores of thread, sewing nets and even a few little sails. Everyone was hungry, yes, and bloody sick of fish all the time, but they weren't starving and they weren't dead. Hadn't lost a single man; even when one idiot fell into the sea the enchantress had flown down and dragged him out.

Made him chuckle how many slaves the night-skins had kept to keep their fancy clothes in order. One slave had even been a gardener, though Tuuran had no idea what Baros Tsen T'Varr had wanted with a gardener on a piece of floating stone out in the middle of the desert. Fellow reckoned he was some sort of expert on fruit trees.

Pride. They'd had storms so bad hardly anyone dared come out of the tunnels, but her Holiness had still stooped to the sea on the back of her dragon and drawn up tubs of water. When anyone was injured, Bellepheros made them well. The dragon heated stones with its fire for warmth and cooking. They'd even managed to build a pair of masts from the remains of the shattered black powder guns and rigged sails made from from silk sheets. They were crap, but they weren't nothing. They'd built something, all of them together, and he felt it deep in his chest, hot and pure, a future full of possibility.

Wasn't perfect though. Crazy Mad stood on the eyrie wall, looking out at the sea like he didn't have anything better to do, lost and waiting for the Black Moon to rise again. Her Holiness sat out on the rim, legs dangling over the edge, back arched, head tipped back almost as though she was taunting him, taking the wind and letting it have her, revelling in it with her two servants at her side. She'd changed. She had a wildfire in her. Maybe she always had, but all the stabbity anger had turned into something else. She smiled instead of snarled, and the energy that poured out of her no longer sang songs of murder but of some other determination. To Tuuran she seemed to make everything possible.

He was staring. He made himself look away.

Best not to think about that. Except he couldn't stop. Couldn't not think about that moment before she'd told him she'd found land.

Pride then, yes, but damn did he need someone he could talk to.

They came to the island in the night. It was there in the morning when Tuuran went up before dawn, the coast a few miles away.

Most days he was first out, sitting alone on the eyrie wall to watch the sun rise long before its fire lit up the sea, but today her Holiness was ahead of him, and Crazy the Crowntaker too, side by side on the rim, sitting there and kicking their feet like a pair of children planning mischief. Her Holiness waved him over. She didn't turn to look, but she always knew who was near, and so Tuuran went and hovered behind them, awkward, not sure where to sit. Didn't seem right sitting next to the speaker of the nine realms like they were on a bridge tossing racing sticks into the water. Didn't seem right to choose Crazy either.

Zafir patted the stone beside her. 'Loom behind me like that and I can't shake the sense you're about to pitch us both over the edge,' she said.

'Land, big man,' said Crazy as Tuuran did as he was told, and for once Crazy sounded almost his old self. 'You did this.'

'No, I didn't,' Tuuran snorted. 'I yelled at people and did some fishing and a lot of fetching and lifting and carrying stuff about. That's all.'

'You were a part of it, Night Watchman,' said Zafir, and Tuuran knew she was smiling.

Tension drained from him as though someone had pulled a plug. He let it and smiled too, and leaned back and revelled in the cold dawn air washing over his face. Because yes, he *had* been a part of it. They all had, every one of them together, and that was what made it special, and there was that pride again; and they sat, the three of them, and watched the sun rise and light up a land that no one had ever seen until today. They'd left Takei'Tarr in thunder and lightning and fire, every one of them expecting to die, most of them slaves with nothing much to live for. They'd travelled to the Silver Sea, the moon itself, and yet now here they were. Free men and women, alive, every one of them.

The sun rose and Tuuran knew he'd never see anything like it in all the worlds ever again. There were maybe a dozen islands in the archipelago, all different sizes but all shaped much the same, each a huge dome-like mass, two miles high perhaps and maybe five across, with one side sheer cliffs and a massive bulbous overhang of dark cracked shadow and deep looming caverns shrouded in curtains of hanging green; while on the other side the slope was steep but not sheer, and a sea of trees tangled together to bury whatever lay beneath. Strands of bare white rock ran for miles out among the waves around the bottom of the domes, long tapering tentacles cracked and barren, tufted with dune-grass, sprinkled with sand and shells, and scuttling with giant crabs that must each have been as big as a man.

'It looks sort of like a giant dead octopus,' he said at last. 'With a forest on top.'

Zafir laughed. Even Crazy Mad had a chuckle at that.

'This is where we make our new life, big man,' he said. 'Though it won't be easy.'

Damn straight it wouldn't. But if there was anything that bothered Tuuran, it wasn't all the hard work that would come in simply trying to survive, because they'd done that once already and he'd seen it, and he knew that they could, and so did everyone else. No, if there was a murmuring in his heart then it was that whatever they built here wouldn't last, because neither Zafir nor the Black Moon would allow it.

The sun crept past the horizon. Copper fire lit the sea. Diamond Eye nudged the eyrie up close to a shore between two white strands of beach. Zafir found a stream of water that rattled and cascaded through a sharp cleft down from the island's mountain heart. The eyrie drifted to a halt over the nearest piece of open ground, a bone-hard yellow-white stone shoulder to one of the tentacle beaches. Tuuran ordered the cranes lowered and was the first to step off, the first to set foot on this new world they'd found. Coarse pale sand crunched under his tattered boots, more holes than leather by now. He took them off and let his bare feet feel it, curled his toes. He squatted. The air was humid, the sun bright. It would be merciless out here in the heat of the day, but now, so early in the morning, it felt glorious. He ran his fingers over the dry pale rock. It looked like old bleached bone.

'Right then. Time to find ourselves a place to live.' He pulled his boots back on his feet, took up his axe, chased the nearest crab and split its shell in two. 'Who else wants to eat something that's not fish for once?' And then he set off for the jungle.

Crazy was right: it wasn't easy. Tuuran found the stream quick enough, and between them they hacked a path back to the first beach, but the stream came down a cleft in the side of a mountain that sloped more up than sideways, and the only pieces of nice flat ground to be had anywhere were the beaches, and they were no good because that wasn't where the water was and the midday sun shrivelled and burned every bit as bad as the desert sun of Takei'Tarr, and you had to be pretty stupid or desperate to stand out in it without shelter.

'There are fourteen islands,' her Holiness said as they sat around together in the dragon yard after the first couple of days of expeditions and wondering what to do. 'All clustered together here in the middle of the open ocean. They all look much the same to me. I don't think we'll find a better place, and I don't think there's any other land for thousands of miles. Certainly no other people. Diamond Eye would know.'

Tuuran snorted. Sunny and hot and overgrown and lush with life, but they were on their own. Live in the eyrie? They might as well move on. And he was all ready for her Holiness to tell them that that was what she wanted, or maybe to simply get on the back of her dragon and fly on alone and leave them all behind, but she didn't, and Crazy didn't say anything either; and as for old Bellepheros, Tuuran could almost see him drooling over a whole new world of plants and trees and roots.

'Well?' he said, because in the end someone had to ask. 'Do we move on, or do we stay?'

'We could live up in the trees,' said a slave Tuuran had taken to calling Halfteeth.

And even then when no one said anything, he still didn't believe it, still woke up every morning waiting for her Holiness to decide it was time to go home, but no one argued, and so that was how it was. They stayed.

They had to do everything for themselves, of course. They had what tools they had and nothing more, nor any means to make any; but they had a dragon with the strength to uproot trees and flatten the earth and with fire to melt stone; they had an enchantress with the skill to make glass automata, and sleds to lift them into the air to pick fruit and hunt monkeys, and she made devices Tuuran had never seen before, enchanted lamps and torches, engines to drive saws, all the things for which the Taiytakei used slaves; they had an alchemist who wandered through a cornucopia of unfamiliar flora and fauna in a daze of delight, taking samples and telling them what was safe to eat and what wasn't, and all the properties of leaf and root and organ; they had the memories of three different worlds and how the ordinary folk in each had lived their lives. They put all that skill with needle and thread to use. They started with shelters little more than sails and sheets hung over fallen branches beside the stream. Some hunted and gathered fruit while others fished from the eyrie over the sea. The gardener slave who knew all about fruit trees took to wandering with Bellepheros, his unofficial apprentice. They felled trees with axes meant for fighting, or else the dragons simply tore them down and carried them to the beaches. They set up workshops there, out in the open, and cut beams and planks with gold-glass saws until Chay-Liang made automata to do it for them. Shelters grew to huts and houses up in the trees. They built ropes and ladders and bridges, a whole shanty town nestled in branches skewed up the teetering slope of the island, or perched on the juts of bone-white stone that poked through the thin earth.

Weeks passed into months. They cleared the land on the shoulder of the beach and built a hall and a firepit. They dammed the stream past the bottom of a waterfall and made a little pool, and felled trees and carved little terraces into slopes and planted the last of the grain from the eyrie larder in the wild hope it might yet grow. Grand Master Bellepheros moved his old laboratory down and began an apothecary, though he kept his own house firmly on the ground and refused to climb up into the trees like everyone else. Chay-Liang moved her workshop to the beach to be with him. The eyrie was slowly deserted, left to float alone over the shore, abandoned except for her Holiness and her dragon, for the occasional fishing party who still used its platforms, and for Myst and Onyx, who refused to leave their mistress. Silk sheets were cut into tunics as old clothes wore through; animals were trapped and skinned, and their furs made into cloaks and coats and blankets for when they were needed.

Tuuran lost track of days. Most of the survivors were men. There was a bit of trouble now and then, and Tuuran had to wave his axe once or twice, but nothing more. The dragon kept them all in line in the end, the dragon and its mistress. An arrangement came about whereby the two women who made their home in the village took whomever they chose when it suited them. Myst and Onyx had their lovers too, and Tuuran was one of them, though they took him quietly and in secret while her Holiness and her dragon were away; and they took Crazy Mad as well, and sometimes Tuuran and Crazy went up to the eyrie together and got drunk on the secret stash of Baros Tsen's apple wine that Myst and Onyx kept hidden, and it was like the old days when he and Crazy had been sail-slaves, only now they weren't slaves any more; and on most days they worked, the hard honest work of building and hunting and making a better world; and on some they walked away into the jungle together just to see what was there, and took a little food and a skin of stolen wine from the eyrie, and in the evening they made a fire and told the same stories they'd both heard a hundred times before of the lives they'd known and seen: the day Tuuran had picked Crazy out of a prison hold to be an oar-slave for the galley he worked; the day Crazy had come up from the oars to be a sail-slave instead and Tuuran had branded him and marked him to show his worth; fine old times after the fire witch of Aria had burned their slaver masters, whoring and drinking in Helhex and Deephaven, all with the irresistible sheen of glowing nostalgia that made those days seem glorious and free and a wonder of opportunity, with the grubby dirt of truth polished away; and Crazy never glimmered with silver light, and the Black Moon never rose behind his eyes, and they never once talked about Skyrie or warlocks or all the things that had filled Crazy's life before he was a slave.

It was, for a while, as though the Black Moon was gone and everything else forgotten except here and now and the friendship between them, and if Tuuran's eyes glanced now and then to the strange knife Crazy still carried at his hip, he never mentioned it, and nor did Crazy; and deep down perhaps Tuuran understood that they never spoke of these things because they were both afraid, because they both knew that it was only a matter of time, that things as they were couldn't last.

Five months after they reached the archipelago, give or take, he and Crazy at last climbed the island together to the very top.

They'd talked about it for weeks, and finally they did it. Took a couple of days to get there, scrambling up crags, clambering between precarious-rooted trees, following the stream until it became nothing more than a trickle here, a puddle there, a pool between stones. They took their time, foraging now and then until they reached a place no one had ever been, the very crown of the island, covered in trees and with no place for a dragon to land even if her Holiness had long ago flown overhead and scouted to see what she might find. At the crest they stopped, amazed, for the peak of the island fell away into a giant sinkhole, perfectly round and huge, a hundred yards or more across and vanishing into a depthless black. Tuuran peered with his torch, but there didn't seem to be any way inside. The walls were stained and covered in dirt and tiny cracks, and out of every crack some grass or creeper clung to life; but they were too sheer and smooth to climb. He broke open an alchemical lamp and tossed it inside and watched it fall until it was a speck and then disappeared, but all it taught him was that there were bats down there, lots and lots of bats, and they didn't much like his light, thanks.

They left the sinkhole and clambered up a tall tree nearby and sat high in its branches, looking out through the leaves over the sea, and over the islands like a scatter of dead monsters.

'I still think they look like giant octopuses.' Tuuran nestled his back against the curl of a branch and let his legs dangle. He tossed Crazy a fruit. Didn't have names for most of the things they ate nowadays. Bellepheros had tried a few long and complicated words, but mostly they called things by the way they looked. So this was a spiky pink. Spiky pink tasted like sucking sweet lemon water out of a gauze-like pith. 'I got a couple of dragon eyes and some dried shitberries and a couple of boiled gull eggs. And some pickled fish if you want.' They still lived off fish most of the time.

'Bloody fish. Be growing gills soon at this rate.' Crazy laughed. 'So, big man? Myst and Onyx? One of them yours, you think?' Her Holiness's handmaidens were pregnant, and one of the women in the village too. Babies. New life.

Tuuran shrugged. 'Can't say as I'd given it much thought.' Certainly not enough to wonder about one of them being his. Just hadn't thought of them that way. Made for strange feelings deep inside, now Crazy had made him look at it. A child. A son, maybe. A daughter. Did it matter? Hadn't ever imagined anything except leaving a litter of bastards behind him. The wandering life of a soldier and a sailor. Was odd, thinking about it. Awe and terror both at once.

'Be something to think about,' said Crazy. 'About where all this is going to go.'

The way Crazy said it wasn't right, was just a little off, like he knew something and couldn't quite figure out the words to share it. Tuuran didn't say anything. Wanted to, but couldn't think what, so they sat in the tree in the quiet and didn't say much, just the companionship of old friends who knew each other so well, of being in the same place together. They watched the sunset, and Tuuran thought it was the most glorious spray of colour he'd ever seen. Afterwards they climbed down in the twilight and set a fire and watched about a million bats fly out of the hole in the island's crown, and chatted about this and that and nothing much until the darkness was so thick they couldn't see a thing, and that was when Tuuran noticed the tiny gleam of silver light in Crazy's eye, the faintest sliver of moonlight silver.

'He's coming back, is he?' whispered Tuuran, not much wanting to say it, wishing with every bone that the sliver of light had been something else, that it would go away and be some devilish trick of his imagination. But it wouldn't.

'Yes,' breathed Crazy, with a crack of a tear in his voice. 'He is. Don't tell anyone.'

They didn't either of them get much sleep that night.

Another month passed. Tuuran watched hard, kept his eye on Crazy and stared when he thought Crazy wasn't looking, but he didn't see the flicker of silver again for long enough that he began to wonder and hope that what he'd seen on the island summit had been in his head after all, but Crazy wasn't the same. The rest of life went on and no one else seemed to notice, not even the witch Chay-Liang, who of all of them kept her eyes wary and never forgot who they were and how they'd come here and how, in the end, it wouldn't last.

They built a little watermill and a bakery. Not that they'd had anything to mill or bake for months since they'd long ago finished the stores of grain from the eyrie, but they built them anyway, and when they were done they celebrated on the beach around the fires, and even her Holiness came down from the eyrie and brought what might have been the last of Baros Tsen's apple wine, and sat and watched and smiled. Maybe she saw Tuuran too, standing a little apart from the others, watching Crazy Mad at the edge of the sea, staring out at the gentle phosphorescent waves.

'Come and fly with me tomorrow,' she said. 'I found some caves. I'm curious, but Diamond Eye is too large to go inside, and I'd prefer not to go alone.'

'I found some caves too,' said Tuuran, but when they flew on Diamond Eye's back the next day across a few miles of water and up the hill at another island's heart, the dragon didn't fly them to the top. Zafir circled and pointed down into the trees. The mountain here had two massive hollows in the side of its dome, side by side and each far bigger than a dragon's outstretched wings. They looked like eyes, Tuuran thought. Or at least old empty sockets.

Zafir flew around to the island's dark side of cliffs and overhangs and creeper veils, its sheer behind where no one ever went. She landed Diamond Eye on a rocky outcrop.

'You ride well for an Adamantine Man, Night Watchman.' She slid down the mounting ladder.

'I flew with Hyram's riders when he went on his grand tour after he became speaker.' Tuuran clambered after her. 'We flew to Bloodsalt. Then the Silver City. The hard part is not shitting yourself at getting up so close. The rest ...' He shrugged, and then stopped as it struck him that Zafir was still the speaker of the nine realms, even if the nine realms were far away right now, and he was still Night Watchman of the Adamantine Guard even if his hotchpotch of guardsmen had largely turned into village farmers, and maybe he should be a bit more mindful of his tongue. He bowed as he landed in the grass, and then wondered if that was enough and dropped to his knees.

'Oh, stop it!' Zafir forced him to look at her. 'We're not speaker and Night Watchman here. I'm not sure either of us are those things anywhere any more. But certainly on this island where no one will know any better, you are Tuuran and I am Zafir, and that's all there is.'

For a moment it seemed to Tuuran that they leaned towards one another and that she might kiss him again, but she didn't. Her eyes stayed on him, though. Shining bright. Tuuran hesitated. Wasn't sure he should trust himself. 'From birth to death, speaker,' he said. Zafir snorted and turned away.

The climb to the caves was hard, sheer in places, and dark and damp under the shadow of the summit's overhang. They picked their way through tree roots and climbed up inside a cleft in the rock, and by the time they reached the cave mouth they were breathless. Zafir took a bag off her back, dropped it and gave him two glass rods, torches from Chay-Liang. She had lightning wands too, and more enchanted torches of her own, strapped to her arm, gifts while the truce between her and the witch remained. Another decade or so and Tuuran reckoned they might even get to thinking about liking each other.

Zafir slid a finger along a torch. A beam of light shone from it brighter than any lantern he'd ever seen. She looked at him and grinned.

'Makes me wonder what else she can do,' she said.

The entrance to the cave was narrow and wet. A steady trickle of water crept between Tuuran's feet. More an extension of the cleft they'd climbed than a proper cave. He peered inside, wary.

'I don't suppose there's anything interesting in here. But if we don't look, we won't know.' Zafir strode ahead, quick and confident as if she'd been this way before, but with a brittle sharpness to her that Tuuran had never seen. He followed, stepping carefully. The cleft widened and the floor turned into a pool of water, shallow but cold. The cave cut several hundred yards straight into the island's heart, and then stopped. A trickle of water ran down the end wall from a shaft in the roof above. The stone here was smooth and water-worn, but when Tuuran shone his torch it lit up with an oil-sheen of colours, bright rainbows of blues and greens and yellows and reds like the plumage of a strutting paradise bird. Everywhere his light touched danced with rainbows, not like the bleached-bone yellow-white outside. He ran a finger over the cave wall. It was dry though slick, not rough and porous, and it reminded him of the inside of a pretty shell. Mother of pearl or something like it.

He looked back. The entrance was a bright white ball of light, everything else black or brilliant reflections of the sun and his lamp.

Zafir started into the shaft. She moved easily from stone to stone and disappeared upward. 'It doesn't go far,' she called. 'It opens out into another chamber.' He watched her as she climbed. Maybe twenty feet up the shaft she disappeared. He saw her light flicker, dim and bright as her torch waved back and forth. When he took a deep breath and followed, he found her sitting at the top of the shaft on a stone shelf jutting out over flat still water at the lip of a second chamber, wide at first and high-ceilinged, though the witch's light was strong enough that he could see how the cave narrowed as it led deeper into the island, how the roof dropped until it almost touched the water. Again the walls shimmered rainbows at him as he raked them.

'Pretty,' he muttered, 'but I don't like the look of this, your Holiness,'

'No. Not much.' Zafir waded out into the water anyway. It only reached her ankles at first, but as she went further she sank deeper. When she reached the part where the roof came down low, she was up to her hips.

'Holiness?'

'It's just something to be done, Tuuran. Come, and please don't question it.' Her words sounded strained, and there was that brittleness again. Zafir headed on as soon as he started to follow, until the water was past her waist and the ceiling almost touched her head. The walls closed in hard from the sides and everything became narrow and tight. Now and then he did the stupid thing and let his hand with the glass torch dip into the water, and the world around him went dark. He settled to holding it between his teeth. By the time he caught up with Zafir he was having to stoop not to scrape his head, while the water was up to her chest and yet still she kept going. He could see where the tunnel closed ahead of them now, the top of the cave coming down to the water. Zafir kept on until the water was up to her neck. Bloody cold water too.

'Holiness,' he said as gently as he could manage, 'it's a dead end.'

'I know.'

'Then what are we doing?'

'Are you afraid of the dark, Tuuran?'

'Not particularly.'

'Then turn out your light.'

'Holiness?'

'Do it. Please. But don't go anywhere.'

Tuuran ran his finger along Chay-Liang's glass rod until the light dimmed and died inside. Zafir handed her own torch to him.

'Take it.'

'Holiness?'

'Take it, Tuuran.' She was breathing hard, gulping for air. And yes, it was cold and claustrophobic but it hadn't been *that* hard to get here, yet Zafir looked on the edge of panic. Didn't make any sense. Didn't like it. Put him on edge.

Tuuran took her torch. 'What is this place?'

'An Adamantine Man should not be afraid of the dark,' Zafir breathed, 'and nor should a dragon-queen. But I am.' He felt her fingers against his leg under the water, fumbling until she found his hand and held it a moment. 'Now walk away. Go back to the top of the shaft. Put out the light when you get there and be silent. Do nothing but be there. Do not light either torch again until I reach you. Do not speak. Do nothing. Even if I beg. Do *nothing*! Do you understand me?'

Not really. He felt Zafir's fingers tighten on his own and then she let go. He hesitated, desperate to speak but commanded to silence, then turned and ploughed back through the water. He looked once over his shoulder and shone the torch on her and saw her staring back at him, a head in the centre of rings of ripples. He sat on the stone shelf at the top of the shaft, and put out the light as she'd told him. The darkness was absolute.

Silence.

Then a quiet splash, and a movement in the water. A soft whimper that hardly carried. His eyes slowly adjusted to the blackness so he could see the faintest outline of the shaft, a tiny bit of light making its way out.

'Tuuran?' There was a high quiver to Zafir's voice. Not the speaker he knew but a frightened little girl. More splashes, faster and more frantic, and then a bigger splash and a yelp. 'Tuuran?' Another whimper, then more, coming in a steady rhythm. He could hear her getting closer. The whimpering stopped and a whispering took its place, laced with rasping breaths. 'Kill him. Kill him!'

She was almost at the shaft. As she came past Tuuran reached out and caught her. She jerked away as though lashed by a whip, and howled and swung a fist that thumped into his shoulder hard enough to bruise. Tuuran lit his witch wand, just a little so as not to blind them, and saw Zafir stood in the water, hunched, fingers twisted like claws, breathing hard and harsh like she'd battled death and fought to the very end of her strength and yet, to her amazement, lived. She snarled and threw herself at him and pounded his chest with her fist as if driving an imagined dagger through his heart and out the other side, and then held on to to him, fingers wrapped around his shirt in a death grip, racked with heaving sobs. He wrapped his arms around her, gentle and uncertain, and she shuddered and pulled him into her like she was trying to climb inside his skin. He didn't know how long they stayed that way. Probably not long, but in the darkness of the cave it felt like for ever. When she let go and sat beside him on the shelf she was shaking like a leaf in a storm. Maybe the cold, but Tuuran thought not. They stayed like that, her Holiness staring off across the cave slowly catching her breath, Tuuran wondering what the Flame *that* had all been about, until at last she took a deep breath and stood up.

'Again.'

'Holiness?'

They did it again. All of it, and all the same except this time at least she didn't take a swing at him. The third time she ended up sobbing into his chest.

'Why doesn't it get better?' she howled. *'Why doesn't it get any better?'*

He held her a bit more tightly this time. Might as well, since they'd both be desperately pretending none of this had ever happened as soon as they went back to the village. When she tried to go a fourth time he said no. Stubborn shits, dragon-riders, and she'd be doing it over and over and over until she gave herself hypothermia if he didn't stop her. So he did, and was a bit surprised that she let him.

They were both shivering by the time they climbed down the shaft and got back outside. Clouds covered the setting sun. At least in the shelter at the bottom of the cleft there wasn't much wind.

'I'm freezing my bits off here,' Tuuran grumbled. 'That dragon of yours going to make a fire for us, Holiness?' He looked at her and then wished he hadn't. Silk and cotton, and all of it soaking wet and clinging to every curve. Wasn't right a Night Watchman having those sorts of thoughts. Didn't help when she picked up the bag and pulled out a dry tunic.

'Not bring a nice warm dry cloak of your own?' She pulled one out and tossed it at him and started to strip. Tuuran swore and looked away and swallowed hard. He looked for somewhere else to go and be out of sight, except they were near as damn it on a big ledge halfway up a cliff, with a few bushes clinging to crevices and that was about all, and there simply wasn't anywhere. He swore again, then decided, damn it, he'd look if he wanted to, and so he did, and then wished he hadn't and told himself he was an idiot and turned his back. He pulled his own tunic off and threw the cloak around his shoulders. Swore again and looked down at himself. Erection like a fucking sword. No cloak was going to hide *that*. Clenched his fists and turned back towards Zafir in her fresh silks, for all the good they did in keeping her modest, and found she was watching him back.

'Great Flame, woman.' He took a step towards her and then stopped when she put up a hand. 'What do you want from me?'

'I can certainly see what you want from *me*.'

Gritted teeth. 'You are the speaker of the nine realms, Holiness, and I am yours, flesh and bone, body and spirit, from birth to death.'

'Not here, Tuuran, and not now.' She came and put a hand to his chest. 'I'm sorry. It's been that way between speaker and Night Watchman sometimes before, but not for us. I carry the Hatchling Disease. I don't wish to share it.'

'I don't care.' Desire got the better of him. He pulled her close, ran one hand to the back of her neck, dropped the other and pressed it between her buttocks, pushing her into him. She tipped back her head to look him in the eye and let out a little sigh.

'But *I* do.' He felt a poke just under his bottom rib, sharp but very gentle. He looked down. She had a knife. 'Stab,' she whispered. 'Stab, stab.' She dropped it. Tuuran let her go, and she drew back and ran a hand down his chest. Her fingernails scraped his belly and then pulled away. Her eyes followed her own motion and lingered a moment between his legs. 'There are other reasons too. Do you need a moment to do something about that?'

Tuuran growled and turned away, pulling his cloak about himself. 'Now that's just rude, *Holiness*.'

They scrambled back down, one behind the other, until they reached the outcrop where Diamond Eye perched. Zafir stretched her clothes over the dragon's scales to dry while Tuuran built a little fire. They didn't need it with the dragon's heat so close, but he liked to sit around a fire at night.

'We going back now then?' he asked.

Zafir shook her head and shifted to sit beside him. 'I'm sorry. You deserve better. I'm restless, Tuuran, and I don't think we'll be staying here much longer. And I'm afraid of the dark. I've always been afraid of the dark. The room where my stepfather used to put me when I'd done something he didn't like was dark. Dark and small. Most places in the Pinnacles were lit by the same white stone as we have in the eyrie. You couldn't get away from it. Sunlight in the day, moonlight or starlight at night, never truly dark. But there were a few places that were different, and that was one of them. It made me nervous the first time. Uneasy, but that was all. Once I learned what happened when the door opened and the darkness came to an end, it got worse. It wasn't the dark I was afraid of, it was what was waiting at the end of it.' She shifted and leaned away from him. 'A dragon-queen shouldn't be afraid of the dark, Tuuran. A dragon-queen shouldn't be afraid of anything. I thought, if I could teach myself that what was waiting at the end of the dark was something else, something I could trust, something safe ...' She laughed. 'That's what you are. A rock that will never move or let me down. It's taken me a long time to understand, but you have far more value to me as that than as a lover.'

Tuuran stared into the flames, frowning. Mostly because he couldn't make much sense of anything she'd just said, and in a good part because he was fairly sure he didn't want to be someone's rock when he rather fancied being something else. He had a notion he was being flattered, or at least that that was how it was meant, but that didn't stop a part of him from sulking and leering at the same time, and thinking how he might take Myst and Onyx up on that offer they kept making to dress in her Holiness's silks when she wasn't there.

'Here we are, far from anywhere, and yet I know you'll be the greatest Night Watchman I could ever have. Tuuran, when the time comes, I'm not sure I'll want to leave.'

They sat and watched the fire in silence. Zafir shared some water. They baked a couple of fish caught that morning, and sat about licking their fingers until Zafir stretched and yawned and curled up next to Diamond Eye's massive flank. Tuuran kept to his fire, poking and prodding it while Zafir slept. By the time his head started to nod his tunic had dried, and so he put it back on and used the cloak as a blanket. Kept thinking over what her Holiness had said, trying to make sense of it and not much liking the answer. Making someone want something even more while saying they couldn't have it, that's what it was. He shifted to watch her sleeping, watch the rise and fall of her chest. To look at her face. She looked happy, he thought. And maybe a bit in awe, as though being happy was something new.

'Flame.' He sighed and shook his head and settled to sleep, and fervently hoped for some soft-skinned dreams of Myst and Onyx and no one else. Some people, he decided, were just too complicated for their own good.

They flew to the eyrie the next morning. Tuuran went back to doing what he did and Zafir went back to flying her dragon, and he couldn't get her out of his head, the memory of her with her back to him, naked, and then of his hand on her arse. When she next flew away he went up to the eyrie to see if her handmaidens wouldn't mind a bit of Adamantine Man to keep them company, thinking maybe that would give him something new to think about; and he took Crazy Mad with him too, thinking it would be a bit of the old times, maybe get Crazy to step out of himself a while, remember the whole idea of having some fun and go back to the way he'd been before Tuuran had seen that moonlight gleam; but when they got there Crazy went and sat on the eyrie rim instead, and stared out at the sea and wouldn't talk until Tuuran left him to have his frolics with Myst and Onyx alone. And between one thing and another his heart wasn't really in it, and it left him feeling worse than before. Empty and stupid and a bit shamed, which was probably a first for any Adamantine Man in the entire history of the legion when it came to something as straightforward as fucking.

He couldn't sleep, but stared wide-eyed and bleary at the ceiling over his head on into the middle of the night and beyond, and that was how it was he was still awake when one of the dragon eggs hatched.

He heard the scream first. The wild shrieking challenge of new-hatched rage and hunger. Even while his head was spinning loops wondering how that could be, there were enough old instincts left to make him grab his axe. He ran out, yelling to Myst and Onyx to keep the door hard closed. Slap in front of him in the dragon yard was a hatchling he'd never seen, glistening, dripping fresh from the egg. Its flanks were salmon pink shading to almost white underneath with golden socks and claws and flashings of metallic green along the tips and trailing edges of its wings. Any eyrie master from back home would probably have gone into a conniption at colouring like that, but as far as Tuuran cared the dragon was simply an unusually gaudy way to die. Definitely not one of the two that had flown with them across the sea – those were much larger now, and kept themselves to themselves off on some other island, though they never quite flew away.

'Where did you come from, eh?' He hefted his axe and took a step back. A good suit of dragonscale and he might have stood a chance against a new hatchling. Naked? Well, it was just going to burn him, wasn't it? Best to run. Really was. Yet he didn't.

The hatchling turned a baleful glare on him and flared its glittering wings. Tuuran spotted the broken egg behind it. They had a few, and the Black Moon had said not to touch them, and so no one had. But the Black Moon wasn't here any more, and her Holiness and her dragon weren't here either to give a bad hatchling a kicking, and all of a sudden it was down to him, standing naked with a big axe against a murderous whipwire of claws and tail and fire.

Hatchling fire was weak fresh out of the egg. He knew that. Took them a few hours to find their full heat, but that only meant burning to death slightly slower, more was the pity.

The hatchling twitched. A cold flood of sense finally got hold of Tuuran's feet; he was about to turn and run, fast as he bloody well could, when a flash of silver moonlight lit the white stone. The hatchling froze, and then Crazy Mad was next to it where Crazy Mad hadn't been a moment before, pulling that hideous knife of his out of the dragon's scales, and Tuuran reckoned he knew exactly what had happened and how Crazy had got there so quick: he'd done that same thing he'd done out in the desert when they'd been taken by slavers and the dragon Silence had come poking around inside their heads. Crazy had stopped time, that's what he'd done, strolled up to the frozen dragon lazy as you please, stabbed it with that knife of his and told it to do whatever he said. Except it wasn't Crazy Mad who could stop time and turn men to dust and make dragons into slaves, it was the Black Moon, and that's what the flash of silver light was, and the Black Moon wasn't gone, and Crazy had known all along, and here it was again, the half-god, and it made Tuuran want to scream and weep all at once. Still there in Crazy's head, just not doing very much.

'Go away,' said Crazy, quiet as the night. 'Leave him alone.'

The hatchling looked confused. It lunged another step at Tuuran, stopped, shook itself and then flew away, straight over Tuuran's head, dripping slime from its egg all over his face. Tuuran spat it out of his mouth and almost retched – vile, sulphur and salt. He didn't bother watching where the dragon went. Off to be with the other two, most likely, sulking with them because they wanted to fly off and eat people and burn some towns and villages for the sheer fun of it, and the Black Moon wouldn't let them.

The silver light went out of Crazy's eyes. Crazy sank to his knees in the middle of the dragon yard, the same place he'd been when they escaped the storm-dark from the Silver Sea. Tuuran hauled him to his feet.

'You stop that, Crazy.'

'He's back, Tuuran.' He looked harrowed. 'Just like that and he's back.'

'No.' Tuuran shook his head. 'Not back. It was just a thing. It's not quite gone, but it was just a thing.' He was talking too loudly. Shouting almost. 'You're still you. Like you've been for months now. It's not back. It's not. It's …' He knew he didn't have the first idea, but then he was saying it for himself, not for Crazy any more. Crazy knew better. Crazy had known better from the start. He saw that now. 'Shit.' He steadied himself. 'You're still you, Crazy.'

'For now.'

'We'll find a way. Somehow. We'll get it out of you. I promise.'

'You promise?' Crazy shook his head. 'I know you mean it, big man, but what can you actually do? You can't hit it with an axe ...' He trailed off and looked at Tuuran hard, then drew another knife, a good plain night-skin steel blade. He offered Tuuran the hilt. 'Actually maybe you can. Kill me, big man. Kill me and be done with it while you still can. It's the only way out for any of us.'

'No.'

Crazy grabbed Tuuran's hand and pulled it to the knife. 'Do you think I didn't try to do it myself? But he won't let me. That cost him, doing what he just did. Kill me while he's weak. Because you *won't* get him out, whatever you say, and if you let him get strong again it's going to be the end of the world for all of us. You, me, your dragon-queen, Myst, Onyx, the children growing inside them. Could be a son you've got coming. You want the Black Moon to cut his newborn soul?'

'No!'

'Then kill me, big man! You don't know what he is! You don't know what he's going to do! But I do, and I'd rather die.'

'No!' Tuuran pulled his hand away and took a step back.

'Kill me! Kill me, you cowardly shit! Do it!' Crazy came after him brandishing the knife. Tuuran backed away, then turned and ran down into the eyrie. Crazy didn't follow him, but the rest of the night really wasn't much fun after that.

20

The Starknife

Six months before landfall

Zafir soared the sky, vast, empty and blue. She could see the curve of the world. A rich dark blue above, lightening to white along the horizon all around her, then darkening to the hammered steel of the sea beneath a white puff blanket of cloud. It was cold this high, and each breath caught in her throat as though she breathed a lungful of ice. The devils of tumult and turmoil stalked her from her visit to the caves with Tuuran. The fear, the dark. That night in the Pinnacles. Tuuran, ten years of slavery for the blood on his knife. The cold scoured these things from her thoughts.

I should have done better for him.

Diamond Eye flinched and changed his course. He wasn't listening. He'd found something. The sense of a murmur, far away. Thoughts. Little ones.

A ship? Her mind snapped to attention. She jumped into Diamond Eye's senses. Yes. A ship. She arrowed for it, Diamond Eye dropping to fly just above the cotton-ball clouds, weaving between them with fractious energy. He wanted to burn something, and Zafir agreed. Fire and claw would do nicely. She slipped inside his thoughts, and together they crept among minds and sights. Through the eyes of its crew Zafir saw a Taiytakei three-master laden with supplies of war for the Sun King, thrown far off course by the uncaring meanderings of the ever erratic storm-dark. The ship was riding low under full sail, battering hard through the waves and making good speed, the deck awash with spray under bright sun and a clear sky. She sailed with a sense of unwary contentment.

But not for long.

They stooped out of the sun. At the very last, as Diamond Eye flared his wings ready to rake the ship's decks with fire, Zafir changed her mind. *Cripple them. No more. They may have things we need. Things we could take.*

Diamond Eye didn't like it. He spat a small cough of flame as he swooped across the ship's stern, then smashed through the mizzen mast and lashed his tail across the aft deck, splitting the jigger mast in two and shattering the aft lightning cannon. Zafir threw herself hard against his scales and clung tight. A wanton spray of rockets flew after him as he soared away, set alight by his fire, launching themselves haphazardly into the air. He wheeled for another pass, and then jinked as a bolt of lightning came at him from the front of the ship. There was a sorcerer aboard. The kind who crossed the storm-dark. Diamond Eye felt their presence. A navigator like the Arbiter Red Lin Feyn.

A surge of anger flashed inside Zafir. She crushed it. *Leave them be.* A world-crossing Taiytakei trader ... They'd have charts. They'd know where they were. They'd know how to get to land and where to cross the storm-dark and how ...

Do you command me so, little one? She felt Diamond Eye's disgust.

No. She'd made a promise. No more slaves. *No, I only ask.*

A navigator to cross the storm-dark, though. They could guide her home! That was what she wanted, wasn't it? Tuuran surely did, if he was honest, and Bellepheros too, and certainly the witch Chay-Liang. They were all content enough out here, but only because they imagined they had no choice; and up to now they hadn't, but ...

So for them, then. Not for her.

Really?

The Black Moon was creeping alive again. Diamond Eye felt him stirring inside the Crowntaker. Something had roused him. He was close to waking, and when he did ...

Do you see? she asked the dragon. *We cannot stay.*

Diamond Eye turned away, simmering. Zafir flew him high again, circling out of sight for a while as she thought about what to do.

Could you find this ship again?

Yes.

Wherever they went, no matter where that was?

No.

She flew the thousand miles back to the islands, arrowed skimming across the sea and crash-stopped in a spray of sand and stones and broken shells. She let Diamond Eye loose to do as he pleased, and climbed the winding steps and paths into the tree-house village. Huts and shelters peppered the canopy above her like giant nests, lining the stream that bubbled out of the island's craggy heart. She paused for a moment to look at them. She didn't come here so often any more, and when she did she came and went as quickly as she could.

The tree houses were a hotchpotch, most built from smooth planks sawn by Chay-Liang's golem machines. Scattered among them were the very first huts, which were really little more than ill-knitted log cabins. There were remnants of old shelters on the ground and little clearings now where unwanted trees had been felled in rare patches of flat ground to make way for gardens, some even growing flowers for the sheer colour of it. There were pens with wing-clipped birds from the island forest, something like chickens but smaller. There were glasshouses among the trees up in the branches, sparkling now and then like stars in the sun, catching the light and growing ground-fruit fast and juicy. For the alchemist and his gardener-apprentice Chay-Liang had even built a glasshouse out on the beach. They'd filled it with soil and then every kind of plant they could find.

Elsewhere Zafir saw tame monkeys tied on leashes. Pets or to scare away the birds? She didn't know. And sleds. Everyone had a sled now because the enchantress had more glass and time than she knew what to do with. Sleds to ride up into the trees, to forage for fruit or else ride out over the sea to fish, or simply to climb to their skyborn homes to rest and sleep. Zafir had seen a few skimming the waves for sport too. It wouldn't be long before they started exploring the other islands. If they did that, if they looked hard enough, they might find out what she already knew, what these islands really were. Would it make a difference? It hadn't to her.

The enchantress wasn't in her workshop. Zafir eventually found her with Bellepheros a little way upstream on a rocky outcrop that jutted from the forest, a spur beside a waterfall that gave a clear view of the island spread out below. They were sitting by the rushing water on a spread of fur, sipping jasmine tea from the eyrie, nibbling fruit and soaking up the sun.

'I want a sled,' Zafir said. 'One I can carry on Diamond Eye's back.'

Chay-Liang snorted. 'Why?'

'Because I've found a Taiytakei ship, and I want to talk to them, and I doubt they'll welcome a dragon.' When Chay-Liang didn't move, Zafir added, 'They've crossed the storm-dark. They have charts and a navigator. I will lose them if I don't return in haste.'

She didn't need to say more. The witch wanted to go home more than all the rest of them put together. It took her hardly any time to make a sled; she didn't even have to get up, and Zafir wondered how anyone could live with such power inside them and not have it burn like the sun.

'There was a hatching,' said Chay-Liang when she was done. She gestured to the sled. 'You will need to get used to flying it.'

'A hatching?' Zafir stood on the sled in the sun-dappled shade beside the little river. She wobbled and tried to make it move, lost her balance and fell off. She ought to do this later, she supposed. Have a bath and clean herself up first. Have a good long rest before she took Diamond Eye back out. She didn't want to, though. Impatience was ever the dragon-rider's curse.

A hatching? The significance almost passed her by until she realised that Bellepheros didn't have a hatchery any more, nor any Scales, that she and Diamond Eye had been away and yet the village was still here and nothing was on fire or reduced to smouldering ash.

'What happened?' she asked. 'Where is it?' She climbed back onto the sled.

'Tuuran was on the eyrie. And the Crowntaker too.' Chay-Liang glared at Zafir. 'You know that men visit your slaves while you're not there? Are they your whores now?'

Zafir rounded on her. 'Myst and Onyx are neither my slaves nor my whores. You might care to remember that when they *were* slaves, Chay-Liang, that they were made so by people like you, who taught them to moan and squeal in delight for fat old men behind a mask of docile servitude ...' She caught herself. 'Not you yourself, Chay-Liang. But Taiytakei nonetheless, and you are all complicit. Myst and Onyx were Zifan'Shu's bed-slaves, so they're probably very good at pleasing whoever takes their fancy. They do as they wish.' She inched the sled forward and didn't fall off this time. It was a start. Then backwards. Sideways ...

She wobbled and nearly fell off again. *A hatching. Another dragon out there*. The thought left her uneasy. She and Diamond Eye should probably do something about that.

'So are we in danger?' she asked. 'Or have you a caged hatchling somewhere about? Either way I should ...' She stopped. 'Was anyone hurt?' Belatedly what should have been her first thought.

'Your man Tuuran was on the eyrie when it happened. Apparently he faced the dragon down with nothing more than an axe and his manhood.' Chay-Liang clearly didn't believe a word of it.

'That does sound like Tuuran,' Zafir laughed. She rode the sled sideways straight into a tree and fell off again. 'Is he—'

'As I hear it, the Crowntaker appeared beside the hatchling out of nowhere and stabbed it with that blade he carries.' Chay-Liang's face changed when she mentioned the knife. Zafir clambered back onto the sled.

'Tuuran saw this?'

'He came asking Bellepheros what could be done. Then he went into the forest. That was yesterday, and he hasn't come back.'

'*Is* there anything to be done?'

Beside Chay-Liang, Bellepheros snorted. 'Anything to be done, Holiness? You could take that evil knife off him! He's a half-god, Zafir, and none of us can touch him. If anyone can do anything at all, I actually thought it might be you.'

'Me?' Zafir managed to move the sled slowly each way without losing her balance this time. Practice, that was all it came down to. That and perhaps not being so bone-weary when she tried to learn.

'The Silver King conjured your old palace. There are relics there that your family guard with jealousy. Secrets. And your dragon likely knows more than all the rest of us put together.' Bellepheros shook his head. 'I don't have the first idea how to stop him. But yes, if you wanted something done, you could take that knife away from him while anyone still can, and you could smash the last dragon eggs. None of the rest of us can go near them. You knew that, yes?'

Zafir shook her head. Chay-Liang met her eye as she did, and for a moment the years of animosity between them fell away. For a moment the witch was afraid. 'He's coming back, isn't he?' she asked.

'Yes.' Zafir shivered. The Black Moon had saved her. He was a half-god like the Silver King of legend. He'd told her she would be another Vishmir, that he would be her Isul Aieha. He'd touched the slave circlet across her brow and made it ash. He would take her home, and the dragons would flock to him, and every world would be theirs for the taking, or so he'd said back in Takei'Tarr. The two of them side by side, her and a half-god, and so why wasn't her heart brimming with glee and delight? Why the touch of dread? Because the price of the half-god was Tuuran losing his friend?

No. Perhaps it should have been, but not that.

Because everything she'd ever trusted had turned out to be nothing but lies and betrayal? Because everyone she ever let in had left her bleeding? That, perhaps?

No. Something deeper still.

'Why can't you touch the dragon eggs, Bellepheros?' she asked, as skilful a deflection as she could manage.

Chay-Liang hissed, 'Because your half-god ...' Her face contorted, as though trying to spit out words that resolutely refused to come. She snarled, an odd melange of frustration and anger and despair. 'I cannot speak it, but we must all do as he demands, and *that* is no secret! He made it so while you were lying in quicksilver in Tsen's bath, hovering between life and death. We were all forbidden from touching the eggs and the compulsion remains even if he's not—' She stopped and looked hard at Zafir. 'Has he bound you to obey him too?'

'I don't know. I don't think so. I've never tested him.' Perhaps she should. Chay-Liang might not be able to say it, but the witch's meaning was clear enough. The Black Moon had cut them all with his knife. Three little cuts. *You. Obey. Me.* She'd seen him do it to Diamond Eye right before her eyes, woken her dragon and enslaved him all at once, and she didn't doubt he'd done it to others too. Had he done it to her in her sleep one night? Or while she was lying in Baros Tsen's bath? Would she even know? When the men he cut had been Taiytakei soldiers sent to kill him, it hadn't seemed so terrible. Now ... she didn't know. Didn't know what to think.

The walls came down between them again. Zafir offered her awkward thanks and rode the sled unsteadily from the village to the shore, and tried to get it to climb to the eyrie. Myst and Onyx already had Tsen's old bath waiting for her when she reached it, the room filled with steam and rich with Xizic scents.

Take the last eggs away, she told Diamond Eye. *Take them to the island where the other hatchlings roost. Make them understand that whenever dragons hatch, they must stay away.*

The Black Moon and his knife. Diamond Eye understood at once.

No more slaves, old friend.

Friend? Diamond Eye growled. *I am not that, little one. Never that to any of your kind.*

Then what shall I call you? He thought himself so aloof, but Zafir knew better. He didn't hide his thoughts well enough. They were not mistress and slave any more, not since they'd fought together as the eyrie fell into the storm-dark of the Godspike.

Of course he could see her thinking all those things. *Dragon, little one. Call me what I am. For one lifetime I am your ally. That is all.*

Diamond Eye would move the eggs. Zafir left Myst and Onyx to clean her armour and wash and mend her clothes. She slipped into the bath, aching and exhausted, and thought, as she often did, of the moment on the eyrie wall beside the Godspike of Takei'Tarr when she'd flicked her bladeless knife across the Crowntaker's neck and his head hadn't fallen off his shoulders. The warmth of the water enveloped her. She fell asleep and woke up cold, her skin as wrinkled as a prune; she dragged herself out and went looking for Myst and Onyx and her armour because there was no time to sleep, not today. Done with that, she fixed Chay-Liang's sled to Diamond Eye's back, loaded his makeshift saddlebags and flew.

It took her two days to find the Taiytakei ship again, though it wasn't that far from where they'd left it. The night-skins had either repaired the jigger mast or stepped a new one, and they were making good speed once more. Zafir flew Diamond Eye ahead of their course and then had him land as gently as he could in the sea. The dragon stretched out his wings while Zafir unbuckled her harness and freed Chay-Liang's sled, then discarded most of her gold-glass armour, even her boots, down to her dragonscale undercoat. She kept her gold-glass vambrace with its lightning thrower, and that was all. While they waited for night she flew the sled in circles, barefoot, feeling out the balance of it and how to stand against the wind to move at speed, while Diamond Eye looked on, amused and curious.

Guide me to them. As night fell she skimmed the waves towards the Taiytakei ship. It was easy enough to find, with its lanterns swinging on its deck and the light that came from its cabin windows.

They have watchers, little one. Diamond Eye flitted among their thoughts, showing her what they saw. Zafir wrapped a black silk about her and arced around the ship, coming from the stern, crouching low to make herself as small as she could. When the lookout turned away she dashed the sled in close and lurked in the shadow of the ship itself.

Where is the navigator? The navigator would know the ship's charts. He'd know how to read them. Also, if Red Lin Feyn had been anything to go by, he'd be the most dangerous person aboard.

He sleeps. Diamond Eye watched her thoughts and the navigator's too. *Somewhere at the stern.*

Good for him.

The watchman shifted and turned his back. Zafir brought her sled up over the deck and alighted beside the remnants of the shattered lightning cannon. She crouched in its shadows, wrapped in silken darkness. She had the lightning thrower muffled in cloth to hide its brilliance, and a bladeless knife in her other hand, but a bolt of lightning would wake the ship, and a knife was never a certain thing, not even the irresistible blades of the Elemental Men.

The watchman walked past her. Behind his back she crept around the broken cannon. She crouched again by one of three short sets of steps down to the main deck, waited for the watchman to make another circuit, then as he passed her flitted down the closest steps and hid in the shadows beside them. This hide-and-seek was an unfamiliar tension, taut enough to have her quietly shaking. Skulking in shadows wasn't what dragon-riders learned. Dragon-riders crashed towers and tore down walls.

She listened to his footsteps, to the occasional cough, to the creaks of wood and rope and the now-and-then rattle of a badly sheeted sail, to quiet voices and low mumbles in the dark. Somewhere towards the bows a light flared as a watchman lit a lamp, and yet with Diamond Eye to guide her the Taiytakei were spread out like a map, clear as the stars, and she knew instantly which way to go and when and what was safe, and where she might be seen.

Wide storm-shuttered windows looked out over the ship from the raised aft deck. Zafir scuttled closer. Two sunken doors led to one large room where several lamps hung burning on the wall, too well lit for her to slip through unseen. A woman sat on a bench beside a table, head bent, poring over some sheet of paper with compass and ruler, but she was too far away for Zafir to reach. Slip through the door and the woman was certain to look up and see. Which left her stuck outside …

Tuuran would have sworn round about now, she thought. She'd never learned to swear.

Diamond Eye reached into the woman's thoughts. A tickle of a notion, a suggestion of a face by the far window. The woman got up and went to look. She thought she glimpsed something for a second time. Zafir saw her more clearly now. A Taiytakei of some standing by her braids.

She is their leader, their captain.

The woman opened the door nearest her and looked out. As she did, Zafir slipped in through the other, padded barefoot across the room, eased open another door that led deeper into the ship, and closed it silently behind her. Creeping about like a thief. The Crowntaker had been a thief once, or so Tuuran had it. *He* should be doing this, then, not her.

The papers on the table might have been charts. For a moment Zafir wished she *had* brought Tuuran after all. He'd been a sailor. He'd know a chart when he saw it and maybe how to read it, but that wasn't why she wished he was here. She trusted him. Simple as that, and she hadn't trusted anyone for a very long time, not really, not even her lover Jehal – *especially* not Jehal. Growing up in the Pinnacles had taught her that trust was a weakness, and she wasn't sure she much liked the idea of it lurking inside her. But, wanted or not, there it was.

A passage ran aft. One door to either side, one straight ahead of her. She went for the one ahead, crouched beside it, listened hard and heard nothing but the ship itself, the soft groaning of its wood as though a beast alive. She lifted the latch and tiptoed in. Moonlight shone through unshuttered windows. There were chests and cabinets, a table, chairs and a large bed. There was someone ...

A glint on the table glittered and twitched. A marble sprang into the air and shot at her. Glass erupted around her, the spherical trap of an enchanter's cage. She fell, crashing into a chest, rolling helplessly about the floor, flailing to find her feet. The glass was so clear that she could barely see it. She smashed into the table, trying to shatter the cage, but it didn't even crack. The night-skin man in the bed jumped awake and snatched for a wand. Zafir lurched almost upright, lunged as her feet started to move beneath her, and crashed back down, rolling across the floor. Odd, but she didn't feel afraid, only stupid and annoyed with herself for being caught.

She'd met cages like this before. Shonda of Vespinarr had tried to put one around her, and that night hadn't ended with any happiness at all for the man who claimed to be the mightiest in all the seven worlds. This one too was about to end badly for someone.

Diamond Eye!

The night-skin followed her with his wand. Glass lamps lit up, bright and harsh. Zafir cringed from the light. The night-skin scurried around her, nervous as a foal, then ran out. She heard him cry staccato shouts of alarm, the words muffled by the glass around her. A door outside opened and slammed shut. Zafir eased herself upright, delicate and slow, feet spread wide and braced against the curve of the glass cage. A different Taiytakei came in, took one look at her and drew a sword and another wand. More shouts rang out in the passage, fists banged on other doors, pounding feet, more yells of intruders and alarm. A bell started to ring.

I come.

'I'm not a stowaway,' said Zafir. She tapped hard on the glass, then punched it. The night-skin with the sword flinched, glared, then fired his wand. The ship quivered to the thunderclap as lightning arced across Zafir's prison. She yelped and jumped. The glass rolled and took her feet from her again, tumbling her to the floor. She settled for sitting cross-legged, trying to rub the ringing of the thunderbolt out of her ears. Another Taiytakei in a nightshirt came in, and then the woman Zafir had passed before, and finally the man she'd so rudely woken from his bed. They kept their distance, peering at her; they were scared, prison or no prison.

The woman with long braids slowly came closer. 'Show your brands, slave,' she said.

'I have none.' Zafir didn't move. Diamond Eye was close. She could feel him. 'I am not a slave.'

'I am Captain Beccerr, and the *Servant on Ice* is my ship.' The woman crouched beside Zafir to look her in the eye. 'What are you doing on my ship, slave?'

The navigator was staring at Zafir's gauntlet and vambrace. 'Who made those?' he asked. 'Where did you get them?'

Zafir ignored him. 'You should let me out of this prison now,' she said.

'I've seen this work before.'

'You should let me out right now,' Zafir whispered. Not that they—

The ship shuddered. It heaved and pitched. The floor tilted. Zafir yelped as the glass cage rolled and tipped her over. She curled, squeezed tight, arms wrapped over her head. The cage jolted into the bed, knocked her sideways and started to roll again. She slid inside it like ice in a shaken glass, hunched up, thrown this way and that, the cabin spinning around her, tilting as though some great weight was dragging the back of the ship into the sea ...

The enormous bulk of Diamond Eye's head appeared at the window. A foreclaw smashed through wood and glass. Everything slid towards the dragon's furious glare. A talon flicked the navigator onto his back and ripped his belly open to his spine. Claws closed on another Taiytakei, crushing him into pulp and bony splinters. The last two scrabbled for the door, scrambling to see who could get away the fastest. One flung a lightning bolt over his shoulder without bothering to look, while Diamond Eye caught Zafir's glass prison, squeezed and shattered it. Zafir sprawled across the cabin floor, gasping, head spinning, counting bruises and blinking hard, trying to work out how much of the cabin's leaning was real and how much came from being shaken like a dry old nut in a shell. The ship groaned and splintered. Diamond Eye hung from the back of it, half submerged.

Zafir lurched to her feet. She paused by the navigator in case there was anything to be done for him, but Diamond Eye had ripped him almost in half. He was alive, but not for much longer.

'It didn't have to be this way,' she whispered and cut his throat. Dragons and ships. Always the same.

The *Servant on Ice* was sinking, and fast. Diamond Eye reached a talon for her. *Come, little one. This wooden sea-palace meets its demise.*

Not yet. Zafir raced in the wake of the other night-skins, stumbling this way and that, bouncing off the walls into the room with the charts. The ship shuddered again, almost pitching her to the floor, all at crazy angles now. She clung to the table. Through the windows she could see the listing deck, split and splintered, wild-eyed sailors swirling and shouting in confusion and panic, slipping and falling and sliding across the deck, some already diving into the sea. The *Servant* was going down fast. Zafir snatched the charts from the table, staggered back to the cabin, slipped and fell and pulled herself up again. She snapped her eyes about for something she could use to keep the paper safe and dry but there wasn't any time, and the sea was already close to the cabin windows. Diamond Eye had gone, but a moment later the dragon ripped the cabin roof and smashed his head inside. Zafir stuffed the charts between her teeth and grabbed at the mounting ladder, then clung to it as Diamond Eye pushed himself free of the wreckage. Men on the deck were spilling into the sea whether they liked it or not, two longboats already floating free, Taiytakei and sail-slaves alike splashing and flailing to reach them. A few night-skins clustered around the lightning cannon on the foredeck, trying to bring it to bear. Diamond Eye lurched awkwardly away.

The cannon. Rip it out of the decks. We'll take it back with us.

She felt Diamond Eye's moment of disbelief, and then the dragon wheeled. The ladder swung through the air. Zafir clung on grimly and climbed as fast as she could. She hauled herself into the saddle and stuffed the charts into a bag and buckled it safe. Diamond Eye dived at the *Servant* as Zafir rushed herself into the riding harness.

Be gentle. She didn't have time for buckles before they smashed into the fire deck, seized the cannon and ripped it free. A good piece of the ship came up with it.

They flew away then, raining splintered deck planks behind them, not staying to see what happened to the stricken *Servant* and her crew. The night-skins had their boats – Zafir had seen that much – but they were in open ocean, thousands of miles from anywhere. As they left, the ship's last lanterns winked out one by one, drowned as the sea took them.

I didn't want them to die. They were night-skins and so they were my enemy; still, this wasn't the end I meant to bring. The sense of regret took her by surprise. It wasn't the person she was used to being, and she wondered why and what had happened to her. A dragon-queen showed no mercy. She should exult in the doom of the Taiytakei ship, surely? Diamond Eye certainly did – his satisfaction was like a warm smothering wrap of soft fur. Dragons and ships mixed like fire and water. Everyone knew that, but still it bothered her.

Like the skies over Dhar Thosis, little one. The dragon had nothing to offer her regret but scorn.

By the end of the next day later Zafir was on the eyrie again, so weary she could barely stand, but with charts and a stolen light-ning cannon that Chay-Liang could perhaps mount somewhere on the eyrie's rim. She staggered down the silver-lit tunnels to Tsen's bath, shedding armour as she went, and Myst and Onyx sat beside her on the edge, massaging her shoulders, feeding her fruit and fish and sips of apple wine and great gulps of fresh cold water until she felt human enough to them tell the story of her escape; but she'd barely started when she suddenly stopped.

'Do you *want* to go home?' she asked them.

They looked at her as though she was mad. 'Home, mistress?'

'Back to the desert of Takei'Tarr where you were born.' She looked at their swollen bellies, at the unborn children they carried, each with a dozen fathers. 'Don't you want to raise your children among your own?'

Still that look, as though she was a lunatic. Onyx held up her arms, palms out, showing her brands. 'We would be slaves again, mistress. Always.'

'But don't you want to be with your own people?' She was ask-ing herself, not them. Because she didn't, not really, not when she thought about it, not when she looked deep enough to see past duty and ambition and righteous vengeance. Stealing these Taiytakei charts could set her free of these islands, but to return to what? War and strife? To clambering over the backs of one another to see who could claw their way to the Adamantine Throne, and then clinging to it with a death grip, stabbing at anyone who came too close until finally she was thrown aside to lie with all the rest in a corpse pit of cruelty and ambition?

No. Myst and Onyx didn't want to go back. They were content here. Happy even. And she realised then, to her great surprise, that they weren't the only ones.

'No, mistress,' said Myst, 'but I would like to fly with you on the back of your dragon one day.'

Zafir stared. She'd never imagined Myst or Onyx being anything but utterly terrified of Diamond Eye. One glance at Onyx told her that she thought much the same. 'You're not scared of him?'

Myst hunched into herself, shy and coy. 'No, mistress. Not any more.'

Zafir looked at the two of them, bewildered. They were happy. They laughed and giggled together and took lovers as it suited them. Above all they felt safe. *And I did that. I, Zafir.* And right there was as good a reason as any to stay, wasn't it? She'd done something good, so rare and precious. And with these charts what had she brought them? An escape from something they didn't want to leave, and perhaps nor did she. A way to abandon what was safe and propel them all into an uncertain storm, and for what? What, for the love of Vishmir, would it be for?

Am I afraid, then, of that storm? Then I must face it, for a dragon-queen faces every fear and looks it in the eye and never backs down. But that wasn't it. It wasn't what might come that she feared, but what she might regret leaving behind.

'Give me the charts,' she said. Myst gave them to her. Zafir paused for one long moment, and then pushed them into the water and watched the ink begin to wash away. She felt light, almost weightless. Her eyes danced and she started to laugh. Myst and Onyx looked at her in wonder, and then started to laugh too. *Let us stay then*, she thought. *All of us. Stay and make something.* And it felt so good to let everything go, as though the weight of a hundred worlds had lifted from her. She picked up her story of the Taiytakei ship and had got as far as Diamond Eye's crashing arrival when the Crowntaker barged in. Didn't knock, just slammed the door open and walked straight in, right up to the bath, and sat on the edge and stared at her nakedness. Myst and Onyx edged away, nervous as lambs.

'Is this a custom from your land to be so graceless?' Zafir asked, and then shrugged. 'Do you like what you see?' There was something very wrong with him. His face had a tension ready to explode. She met his eye, looking for the traces of silver that would warn her of the Black Moon awake inside, but there were none. 'Well? Or is this your way to remind me that my girls and I do not live alone on Baros Tsen's eyrie and must now and then share his bath?' She wrinkled her nose. 'You do smell like you need one.'

The Crowntaker drew out the Starknife. Zafir's hand whipped at once to the edge of the bath and came back pointing her vambrace with its lightning thrower straight at his face. The rest of her didn't move.

'I will not be a slave even to a half-god,' she hissed. 'What do you want?' Her hand was as steady as stone.

'The dragon eggs you hid. He found them. He made them hatch, and then he cut them.' The Crowntaker reversed the knife and offered her the haft. He was shaking. 'Take it!' he said. 'Tuuran won't do it. But *you* will. Take it and cut the bastard out of me. Or kill us both. I don't care.'

Zafir put the lightning thrower aside. She took the knife he offered her. 'I wouldn't have the first idea what to do with this,' she said. 'And what you suggest strikes me as madness.'

'You don't need to know how. It can show you. *I* can show you. Three little cuts. *You. Obey. Me.* You rode inside him when he did it to your dragon. You saw it. I know you did, because I was there too, remember? Do the same to him! Do what he did to your Diamond Eye. Make him *your* slave, if you like!' The Crowntaker grabbed her hand that held the knife and squeezed it tight. He pulled it towards him.

'No.'

'Do it!' The Crowntaker threw back his head and howled. 'For the love of the sun and the moon and everything else there is, cut him out of me!'

'Myst! Onyx! Go outside!' Zafir waved them away with her free hand. It surprised her how calm she sounded. The Crowntaker's eyes snapped back to hers, mad and wild.

'It can cut out anything. *Change* anything. Make me your slave if you must. Make *him*. Make *him* your slave and then make him go away! Make him *leave*! I don't care! But you *know* how to do it!'

She did. 'This knife can cut out anything at all?' she asked. 'Could it cut out a fear of the dark?'

He stared at her, a flood of desperation. 'He's waking up! He's right here! You've got to do it now, right now!' The Crowntaker's voice shook. 'Right beneath the surface!' He looked about as if searching the bathhouse. 'These islands. Do you know what they are?'

'I think I do,' murmured Zafir. 'They were creatures once.'

The Crowntaker nodded. 'Drifting ancient bone corpses so vast and long dead they've become like this. He made them, dragon-queen. A thousand years ago he just snapped his fingers and made them. Look at them! When he wakes, he'll make more. And that's just the start. When he wakes, everybody dies!'

Zafir didn't resist as the Crowntaker pulled with vicious strength at her hand. He fell into the bath on top of her. The knife buried itself inside him, and Zafir saw a second ghostly shape at his side, and within that shape a web of silver strands woven together in impossible detail, and within *that* something infinitely more vast, a weaving as intricate and complex as the whole of history, exactly as she'd seen when the Black Moon had stabbed the Starknife into Diamond Eye.

Exactly like seeing a dragon.

He was right. She remembered. She knew what to do. *Three little cuts that even the sun-child within me knows. You. Obey …*

Time stopped. A force like the falling of the moon crashed into her.

No.

She saw the Black Moon, and the Black Moon saw her back, the half-god as he truly was, a relentless hostility that set every nerve and cell to flames. Zafir screamed and arched. A blaze of silver light scoured her eyes. The Black Moon bared his teeth and pressed her down into the water. Hard fingers gripped her face.

His thoughts burst into her head, vast and overwhelming like a woken dragon, brutal and careless. He crushed all thought and memory and everything she was into a tiny crumpled ball.

Who are you, little one? What insignificant speck do you aspire to be? She felt him rummage through every part of her, every memory, and as he did she remembered the hatchling dragon Silence who had once done the same on its way to murder her, and how she had crept around the edges of it and looked back the other way, and she remembered the trick of how she had done that; and so as his relentless glare unravelled her, Zafir slipped inside the thoughts of the Black Moon himself, a thief in a half-god's memories. She saw the murderous threat of the Adamantine Spear, which held him back, which had once drunk her blood when Aruch and Grand Master Jeiros had made her speaker of the nine realms and taken her to see it. Wrapped around it she saw a battlefield strewn with corpses, men, horses, broken spears, monstrous things, dragons dead and burning from the inside, dark-winged birds with beaks like swords fallen from the sky, impaled in the earth where their dead wings fluttered limp like dwarfish banners. Mountains floated in the sky, eyries, a score of them, shattered towers of black stone, half grown, half formed, slumped limp and smashed down. She saw the second moon, dark shadow teeth chasing the sun and drawing ever closer, and most of all she saw the Isul Aieha, the Black Moon's brother, the Earthspear in his outstretched hand, racing towards her with killing intent, the desolation of murder all about, and then the great betrayal as the Isul Aieha struck her down, as the land shuddered and shifted and was rent apart, as impossible curtains of black cloud and violent lightning spread up to the sky with no end. She saw the Nothing open to devour everything, her final vengeful strike against wilful brutal gods. Tumbling towers of white stone and rivers of ash, lakes of fire, the earth torn open, the sky split apart.

And mingled among these memories was the future he demanded, her as his vassal, her lethal spear kept safely aside. Dragons sweeping realm after realm, bending all to his will, tearing the moon out of the sky and the ghost of the dead goddess from Xibaiya, burning them into the hole in the underworld, banishing the Nothing, the That-Which-Came-Before, bending the unconquered sun to his will and casting moonshadow over everything, all realms brought back as one, storm-dark vanquished, a god-emperor to every end of creation.

Amid the hurricane she glimpsed the Crowntaker, fighting, clawing at the Black Moon, exhausted but never quite gone, even now holding the fractured half-god back. She reached for him. *I am here. I see you.* She saw another face too, one the Crowntaker claimed as his own but one she had never seen in the flesh. She saw the half-god as he truly was, split in half, one splinter cast into ice and freed and now the storm inside her head, the other splinter still missing, sought yet feared, vessel for a power a magnitude greater yet than he already possessed.

The Black Moon. She felt herself shrivel into nothing before him, and then a new rage poured into her like the flood through a breaking dam. Fury and hunger, an incandescence as Diamond Eye threw himself down before the Black Moon and shrieked the challenge of a dragon; and it seemed to Zafir in that moment that the two of them were somehow equal and the same.

You dare, dragon?

I dare.

The half-god gazed into her deepest heart. *Take me to it, spear-carrier. Wield it at my side and we shall cross worlds. We shall be titans, you and I, and all will be ours. You will be a goddess, adored, feared and worshipped.*

She was back in Baros Tsen's bath. The Black Moon washed out of her like an ebbing tide. The Crowntaker lay on top of her in the water, his weight forcing her under. His eyes burned silver bright like twin suns. He pulled himself away and left her there, too weak to move, too weak to even watch him go. A half-god.

'Make yourself ready, spear-carrier,' he said as he went.

Zafir sank back under the water. She didn't have the strength to stop herself, save to arch her neck to keep her mouth and nose in the air until Myst and Onyx slunk to her side. They dragged her out and carried her to lie staring at the ceiling above her, waiting to be able to move again, looking for elusive sleep and finding only nightmares in silver light. And the next day, when she had strength back enough to move, she went to Tuuran and told him that his friend was gone and would not be coming back, and had the men and women of the village stop their work and make a wooden cage for Diamond Eye to carry, sturdy and strong; and when it was done she took the cage across the sea and found the little boats from the ship she'd destroyed, the Taiytakei parched and dying of thirst and sun; and she gave them water and carried them back with her to the island, those that would go, so they might live and be a handful fewer deaths on a barely born conscience that she knew would soon bear too many ever to count.

She didn't see the Black Moon stab them, one by one, to make them his slaves. She didn't see him take her stolen charts from the water where she'd left them in Tsen's bath, nor did she see him barter with time to conjure back the words and lines she'd washed away, nor read them and circle a name in thick black ink; but she did see him summon the hatchlings, and that they were eight and not three, and that he had found the eggs Diamond Eye had hidden just as he had said; and she saw how he bound them to the eyrie to drag it through the air, and she was beside him when he walked into the island village and told everyone to ready themselves to leave, whether they wished it or not, and saw how every last man and woman wept and wailed and cried out and raged and gazed at the Black Moon with unbridled hate but nonetheless obeyed.

They will all turn on you, she thought. *Every single one of them. Beneath your yoke they will live their lives to tear you down.*

And I?

She didn't know. The Black Moon had set her free, and his promise was limitless.

21

The Apple Orchard

Four months before landfall

Baros Tsen – first t'varr to Sea Lord Quai'Shu no longer – lay back in the grass with his hands behind his head, chewing on a piece of straw. He savoured the afternoon sun on his face and the warm late-summer breeze on his skin. He took a deep breath and rolled the scents of the orchard around his mouth. He might have lost his nose, but he could still taste and smell the air if he took the trouble to try. Dry grass and meadow flowers and a slight tang of salty surf wafting in off the sea. And apples. The first ones were ripe on the trees. They'd start to fall soon, and so in a couple of days he'd be down in Dahat hiring men to come and harvest them, and then the interesting work started, the alchemy of brewing and distillation; but until the harvest started he didn't have much to do except lie in the sun and stare at the bright blue sky between the leaves and snooze, and think how glad he was to be home. Kalaiya lay beside him, holding his hand, her breathing so rhythmic that he knew she was asleep. He could have chosen this life for himself twenty years ago; more and more he wondered why he hadn't.

Because twenty years ago you were an idiot who thought he was something special, too good for this sort of idleness. Remember?

He did. After he and Vey Rin had left Cashax. The last of their crazy gang of self-obsessed narcissists to finally go their separate ways, all set on changing the world, on grabbing it in both hands and making it their own and shaping it into whatever they desired. And without, he realised now, much idea of what that actually was. He'd gone to Xican. Not the greatest of the fourteen cities by any stretch, but he'd sensed the opportunity waiting there and he'd been right.

T'Varr to a sea lord. Shaping the world with shipping manifests and a firm grasp of logistics. He snorted quietly to himself and closed his eyes, listening to the birds. He wasn't quite sure what had changed and how, but he wasn't that man any more.

You found Kalaiya.

There was that.

You also don't have a nose.

There was that too, although it didn't bother him much these days. He'd never imagined himself anything special to look at.

And, in the end, Shonda and Vey Rin were the ones who got there. Who rose to the very top. Sea lords of Vespinarr, one after the next, the richest city in the seven worlds. Look at you all. Shonda dead and branded as a slave by a dragon-rider. Rin, who can never sleep thanks to his nightmares of dragons. And me. A corpse hung from the ankle in Khalishtor for the murder of thousands. How triumphant we must seem.

Yes, he liked his orchard.

Something in the rustling of the wind changed. An animal moving through the grass, he thought at first. Then it came again. He sat up, but it was only the house-servant Demarko, a sly old fox with a sneaky past and fingers in every pie in Dahat, who mostly liked his simple quiet pleasures, and that, Tsen thought, made them at least a little alike. Demarko didn't talk much. He didn't seem to *do* very much either except sit about and doze, but he knew every single person in Dahat on first-name terms. When Tsen wanted something, Demarko knew someone, and so, effortlessly, it was done, and Demarko would be back to sitting in his chair on the porch and sunning himself. Tsen rather liked him for that.

'Master Baros.' Demarko thrust a rolled-up sheaf of papers at him as though raising his guard in some slightly off school of fencing – the Dahat whispers were that he *had* been a fighter once, quite a famous one too, but if that was so then he'd hung up his sword two decades back and had settled for doing nothing very much. Tsen rather liked him for that too.

'Papers to sign?' There always seemed to be papers to sign. The Dominion was embracing the Taiytakei attitude to bureaucracy with the same religious fervour as it embraced everything else.

Demarko shook his head. 'Courier from Brons. The usual.'

Tsen took the sheaf and nodded, and Demarko ambled off

without a word. News from Takei'Tarr, and for a moment Tsen thought about unrolling the messages and reading them out here in the sun, but really what was the point? What did it matter? Whatever it was could certainly wait until the evening and another bottle of apple wine.

Kalaiya stirred beside him. 'What was that?'

'Demarko. The monthly from Brons. Nothing that can't wait.' He put the papers beside him and lay back, squeezed her hand and closed his eyes. Time went by and the news never changed much except to make him ever more pleased to have left the rest of the world behind.

'All your spies?' Kalaiya shook her head.

'I can't pretend that Vey Rin doesn't know I'm still alive.' Mostly he tried not to think about it.

'You know there's a ship coming in a few days? Bringing an exalted solar of the holy sun. Recruiting soldiers to the Sun King's armies for this war that comes.' Kalaiya yawned and stretched, and then shifted to rest her head against his belly. He had a good belly, they both agreed. Soft and plump as a pillow.

'The young men of Dahat strike me as far too sensible to pay any attention to such claptrap.' Demarko must have told her. Kalaiya talked to him more than Tsen did.

She wriggled her head, trying to make herself more comfortable. She braided her hair these days, like a proper Taiytakei lady. With the braids came long sleeves to hide the slave brands. 'You know how men are.'

'I'm not sure that I do.' Of course he did. Fired by promises of glory and riches and an eternal basking place in the warmth and fire of the holy sun if they died. They'd probably line up in droves. Youth always did, didn't it? Too naive and stupid to realise they were being sold shit on a stick as though it was gold. Pity really. 'I was a t'varr, my love, not a kwen. I don't know very much about tricking men into dying for no good reason. As best I could tell, whenever one of my kwens wanted an army, they simply armed a huge mob of slaves and set them loose. And then murdered them all when they were done.' Being a kwen had never struck him as terribly difficult.

Kalaiya delicately elbowed him in the ribs. 'A t'varr who spent a little more time thinking and a little less snoozing might wonder a little at what a sudden diminishing in the supply of local young men might do to his apple harvest.'

Tsen let out a little sigh. She had a point. 'I'll take Demarko into Dahat tomorrow then. Before the ship comes. Bring it forward a day.' He turned his head and squinted at the apples hanging from the trees around him. They were ready.

'Someone who wished to enhance his standing among the local craftsmen might think about whether there are any particular sons or favoured nephews, or apprentices perhaps, that he might wish to hire and then keep gainfully busy until such time as the exalt of the holy sun moves on.'

Tsen snorted. 'We're hiding, remember?' Lying in the sun like this, chewing grass and with nothing to do, his eyelids were getting heavy. He chuckled. He knew her too well. 'You already have a list, do you?'

'A list?'

'Of the men you'd like me to save.' He lowered his voice and waggled his fingers in exaggerated mockery. 'From the villainous exalt who would carry them away to war!'

Kalaiya rolled off him. She settled on her front, propped herself up on her elbows and poked him. '*If* I had a list, Baros Tsen, it would be of old men I didn't wish to see lose their last son and of young women I don't wish to see become widows. A list you might easily imagine for yourself.'

Tsen made a show of thinking hard, then stretched and nodded. Moving the harvest forward a day would be good for not thinking about other things. Might stop him wondering what was going on back in Takei'Tarr and what they were doing to press the Sun King into a war that the Dominion could very much do without. And yes, kicking off some great war or other every couple of generations was the sea lords' way of keeping the Sun King and his absurdly vast population in check; and yes, the Ice Witch was scaring the shit out of everyone, and so was her necropolis, but sooner or later the immortal Sun King was going to notice what his 'friends' were really up to. He'd ally with the sorcerers of Aria – who, as far as Tsen could see just wanted to be left alone – and that, as Vey Rin used to say back in Cashax, would become the overfilled chamber pot that just didn't stop giving.

He made himself think about Dahat and whom he might hire. The lad who ran the spice stall in the market knew far too much about spices to be getting himself killed in some stupid war. Then there was the boy who worked in the glassworks. Not that Tsen much liked him, but he liked the father, and the boy was exactly the sort to get sucked in by words like honour and duty and glory, and completely not hear the ones about messy ugly deaths and blood and limbs hacked off, and slowly dying and spending your last few minutes trying to stuff your own guts back inside your belly, and just how loud and long a man screamed between someone setting him on fire and finally burning to death ...

Yes. That sort of thing ...

A shadow blocked the sun. Kalaiya was leaning over him, picking at the letters. 'If you don't want to read them, I do.' She butted against him and settled back to using his belly as something between a backrest and a cushion. 'See here – a proclamation from the holy sun, unconquered and everlasting ... death by drowning now for anyone who avoids their proper responsibilities towards the dead ...'

'Yes, yes.' Dead people not staying dead. The catacombs of Merizikat. Blah blah. 'While the Sun King declares the Empress-Regent of Aria anathema for the necropolis of Deephaven, he neglects to notice how he has one of his own.' *Everyone* knew better than to bury the dead under the ground. In the Dominion, in Aria, in Takei'Tarr, in the dragon-lands, in Qeled and Scythia, even the savages of the Slave Coast knew better and always had.

'It's not so far from here to Merizikat, you know.' Kalaiya shuddered. The whole idea of dead men who didn't die unsettled her. It was, Tsen supposed, a reasonable and natural reaction. He wrapped his arm around her.

'There aren't that many of them. There really aren't. And we've seen dragons, and I think those frightened me a great deal more. A little daylight or moonlight or a little fire and these walking abominations go back to being properly dead. Or push them into a river. Even I could do that.' He chortled, but his smile quickly disappeared. 'Half the navigators who ever passed through the Dralamut have come to the Dominion to guide the Sun King's ships across the storm-dark. The fleet assembled in Brons is the greatest massing of ships the worlds have ever seen. Two hundred thousand men. Five hundred ships to carry them. Any sea lord would weep, and yet still the Sun King comes looking for more?' He nodded. 'I will do what I can for the young men of Dahat, I promise you. The worlds are awash with terrible things.'

A pillar of the Godspike cracked, the storm-dark growing inch by inch, the Righteous Ones restless and roaming, the moon sorcerers out from their seclusion, and never mind dragons on the loose. Before he'd left Takei'Tarr there had been whispers of arcane storms racking the oblique heartlands of Qeled, of monstrous creatures roaming the Scythian coast. He'd scoffed at them all. Not so much now, but thankfully those places were all far away. 'The plague troubles me more. I hear it's in Brons now.' He peered over Kalaiya's shoulder. 'Do the letters say anything of it?'

Kalaiya didn't answer. Thinking about the plague always soured his mood. Couldn't pretend *that* wasn't at least in part his fault. 'I should have killed her,' he muttered. 'Chrias was right about that. Should have killed her at the start.'

'Tsen—'

'Chrias couldn't keep it in his breeches.' Tsen spat, suddenly furious. *And yet here I am, passing the blame to another. She meant it, Tsen. The dragon-queen meant to let it loose and do not pretend otherwise.*

'Tsen?'

But she's gone, annihilated by the storm-dark of the Godspike. No need to think of her any more. No need to wonder. Gone, and her dragons too, and the world is the better for it.

'Tsen!'

'What?'

'Sea Lord Vey Rin is dead, Tsen. The plague has killed him.' She could hardly keep the vicious delight out of her voice. She waved the letter until Tsen snatched it out of her hand and read every word with furious hunger while she crouched at his shoulder. 'It has spread to Shinpai and Xican and Khalishtor, but not yet to Vespinarr; yet Sea Lord Vey Rin is dead. He succumbed months ago. He's gone, my love. Gone.'

It seemed crass to get up and dance and whoop in the orchard, but that night Baros Tsen T'Varr and Kalaiya opened a bottle of their most precious wine and shared a smile that was both very quiet and very broad indeed, and on that night Tsen slept more soundly than he had in years.

The morning after the letters came, he rode the steep coil of mule track down from his villa to Dahat, hot dust burning the back of his throat until he reached the bathhouse heat by the sea. He took Demarko with him. They wandered the town together, ambled the markets and the quiet shady squares and the seafront, strolled the pinched-narrow streets of pocket kiosk shops where every shopkeeper sat out in the open air on a little stool and wore more wrinkles than the last, where everything was sold with a tiny cup of something strong – black qaffeh like tar in the morning, a plethora of venomous spirits in the evening. Tsen looked in them all and waved and smiled at the faces he knew, and beamed at the ones he didn't. He found the lad who worked the spice stall and convinced him to pick apples in the evenings, away from the exalt's sergeants when they came. He rounded up the other young men he'd taken a shine to over the months – the honest hard workers who deserved better than hunger, disease and butchery, although didn't everyone? Kalaiya would have preferred some women to join the harvest, but in the end he chose only men because they were the ones who needed saving. The solar exalts and the priests of the unconquered sun took a simple view of the world: men for fighting, women for raising children.

He went back to the villa tired and aching, still not used to riding any animal at all, and certainly not some barrel-chested mule set on tipping him sideways with every plodding step. Come next morning he and Kalaiya were up bright and early with their baskets, scouting the orchard, picking the first windfalls and spying out the ripest fruit. Demarko slouched sleepy-eyed at the front of the villa, snoozing in his rocking chair in the sun, eyes slitting open now and then to direct the straggle of visitors to the orchard for work and a penny for every apple basket returned full. Tsen toiled until the sun rose high, then walked to the little meadow at the edge of the orchard where he and Kalaiya liked to picnic. He lay and dozed and fell asleep; and when Kalaiya woke him she took him to the house and they spent the lazy midday hours swinging in hammocks in the shade, chewing grass and drinking air as thick as syrup. When the heat loosed its grip, Tsen went back to work, and as he walked to the orchard he saw a ship gliding into Dahat, her sails the bright yellow of the Sun King. He put his arm around Kalaiya and hugged her.

'You were right about starting a day early.'

'I'm always right.' She hugged him back.

The days of harvesting were a warm glow of hard work and effort well spent. A clear autumn sun kept the air thick and still, heady with the fresh smell of apples. The ship remained in Dahat harbour. When it looked like the orchard might be picked clean before the exalt left, Tsen found other things for his hired hands to do. He grew used to seeing the same faces up in his orchards day after day, and took the time to talk to them and learn their names. They laughed behind his back at the colour of his skin and the disfiguring of his face, but it didn't trouble him. They weren't unkind, these Dahat lads, or cruel; they laughed at Demarko for being old too, but thought no less of him.

The harvest was all but done. They sat outside, him and Kalaiya and Demarko, the evening air warm and pleasant, crickets buzzing in twilight scents of jasmine and heliotrope laced with the inevitable warm-breath wafts of Xizic, the table lit by a dozen candles. Demarko, unasked, had made a feast for them, and now he fussed and tutted from the kitchen, and flitted about them carrying dishes of pickled urchins drenched in lemon, baked fish, roasted flaked nuts and some strange concoction of sweetened milk curd flavoured with mint. When they were done, while Tsen stretched back, bloated and rubbing his belly, Demarko brought out another letter that must have arrived earlier in the day. Tsen read it, bored and not really interested.

Then he read it again.

'Well that can't be right,' he said. Couldn't be, could it? Because if it was then all he wanted was to scream his lungs out and then dig a very great big hole in the earth and dive into it and pull the soil back on top of him. The letter was short and to the point. A flying mountain had come out of the storm-dark. It had come across the ocean to Merizikat and sacked the city. And he'd wanted to know any word of dragons, hadn't he? Well now he had one almost next door.

His eyrie. It couldn't be anything else.

'What is it?' Kalaiya asked.

Tsen held Kalaiya's arm, fingers tight and digging into her, then forced himself to let go. 'It's nothing, my love. Nothing for us to worry about.'

'Then may we go to bed now?' she asked. 'I'm tired.'

'Yes, my love. We have apples to press in the morning.' He pulled Kalaiya close. They wrapped each other in their arms and turned away. As he took her hand he touched the letter to one of the candles, watched the flame take hold of the paper and burn it to ash.

Peace, t'varr.

Far across the waiting sea the dragon Silence bursts in blood and broken bone upon the ground and returns once more to Xibaiya, realm of the dead and their murdered goddess. In sanctuary there she lurks and heals from the wounds the warlocks have given her. Slowly and painfully. She has found the Bloody Judge but not the Black Moon, and though the one is clearly a part of the other she cannot fathom the how of it.

The Nothing, unbound, creeps from its prison. The tear grows ever worse.

She is a dragon. She hunts for her next hatching with care. The ancient half-god, split in two; she has hunted one splinter and failed. The other, then, will have to do. It will end, one way or another, in flames.

It always does.

The Adamantine Palace

The Silver King muted dragons and made dull servants of them.
In fear and envy the blood-mages drove a spike into his head. Now
they drink the silver ichor of the moon that drips from his wound
and call themselves alchemists, but half-gods are not so easily bound.
The Isul Aieha foresaw his fate and, as the Black Moon had once
done, cut a piece of himself apart and made it into a seed. Along
the Yamuna River, beside the Moonlight Garden, a man called Sif
carries that seed to the Black Mausoleum of legend, bringing with
him the one thing the Isul Aieha needs to open the way home: a
memory of himself, carried in the blood of the alchemist Kataros.

Beneath the ruins of the Glass Cathedral the last alchemists brew
their potions and their poisons and plot their way to freedom. They
too have secrets. Closely guarded, in deep caves far out of sight,
they keep the last enslaved dragon.

While in the Raksheh forest the Adamantine Man Jasaan
searches for Kataros. He has failed her once, and swears he will
not fail her again.

22

Kataros

Twenty-two days after landfall

It hadn't been the easiest journey after Kataros and Skjorl escaped from the flying eyrie, but Kataros hadn't given up. She'd followed the Yamuna upriver into the deep Raksheh, where the trees were a thousand feet tall, to where the banks rose in pale cliffs from the water, to the falls under the Moonlit Garden with crags of rock to either side, a little beach below now littered with dead, to the entrances to the Aardish Caves. In the dragon-smashed ruins of the little eyrie that had once stood there she'd found a boulder torn asunder, a hole smashed into the ground, tunnels of white stone which glowed like moonlight. She'd found the Black Mausoleum, the lost tomb of the Silver King, a simple hemisphere room of soft moonlight, and at its heart a ring of archways. She'd brought him here, led him here, the last echoes of the Silver King himself, the Isul Aieha, hidden inside the Outsider she'd found trapped in the Pinnacles and waiting to die.

She lay between them now, those arches, pale and half bled out on a white stone plinth. Spatters of her ran red and fresh over the arches around. Touched by the essence of a half-god, they shimmered silver. She felt the power coursing through the vault. *His* power. The Isul Aieha. They would open now, if he asked them. The distant sound of the Yamuna falls rumbled through the tunnels. Outside there was a dragon, but it had come too late to stop them.

The Silver King looked at her, almost sad. The stone around him was covered in her blood. It was everywhere. 'Such a shame you couldn't see this,' he said. 'Such a shame.' Moonlight serpents wriggled from his fingers. The gateways beside him opened. Through the arch of white stone a sea of liquid silver appeared before him, and when he reached to touch it with his hand there was no resistance, no shimmer. This time the door was open. A giant moon hung low in a night sky bedecked with stars. 'Such a shame,' he said again.

Kataros watched through half-closed eyes. She couldn't blame him for what he'd done to her. She'd seen him tethered and roped under a mile of mountain stone, frozen in a silent rictus scream with a hollowed-out spike driven into his head from which dripped, slow as tar, the silver essence of the half-gods, one drop enough to give an apprentice alchemist power over dragons for life. As far as she knew he was still there, yet he was here too. The Silver King. Half alive and full of wonder, and she knew that the Silver Sea beyond the gate beside him was his home. There were others there, others of his kind, the half-gods who had once fled their own catastrophe. They were waiting for him, beckoning him to join them, to leave her world behind, and here he was. The last of his kind to linger, or so she supposed. The last relic of a tragic age lost in cataclysm, of a time when even dragons had been young and the silver half-gods had strode the world in their multitudes.

She looked at the Silver Sea. The stones drew their power from her. They needed her blood for the tiny echo of his essence she carried within her. She could take that away, but past that they were a mystery to her. Artefacts of another time and beyond her comprehension.

'Everything is wrong,' whispered the Silver King to the emptiness. 'The Great Flame? No. This. *This*.' He sobbed, overwhelmed, and maybe he was right. With exquisite caution he reached one foot through the gateway. His foot touched the silver beyond and he gasped.

His boot had her blood on it. She reached through the link it made to touch the Silver Sea with her mind. To see, but the quicksilver consumed her as though she was nothing, washed her down, a tidal wave against a sand castle, immense and vast and ever beyond her understanding. In a blink it looked at her, took her in, absorbed her. She felt its size and its age and its utter indifference, and realised that yes, she *did* know what it was. She knew exactly. *This* was the Silver King, not the man standing in front of her. It had to be. Whatever old crippled Jeiros had said, there was nothing else that could be so colossal.

'Alchemist! Kataros!' A voice so distant it seemed to come from another world, one far behind her.

Help us! she thought, simply hoping to be noticed. *We need you!*

The Silver King turned slowly to look at her. Trying to shake away the presence. Trying to bring himself back to the simple world of stone and flesh.

'Siff,' she breathed. 'Look at it.'

Blood and snarls whirled. An armoured man skittered between them, all edges and motion and wide urgent eyes; and Kataros thought at first that it was Skjorl, but he was too short for that, too small. He came, blade raised, and it seemed that he hardly saw her. Silver rose from the sea beyond the gate. It flowed across the Silver King's skin and shattered the soldier's sword as it came down. Steel slivers flew like arrows among the arches.

Jasaan? Her thoughts were muddied, distant and lost, dispersed through her scattered blood and deep in quicksilver. Jasaan stood before her, before the Silver King and his gateway, panting, holding the stump of his sword.

'Jasaan!' she gasped. 'Don't ...'

The Silver King stood through the gate now, the Silver Sea wrapped around him, clothing him. The other arches flickered and failed, their mirrors falling black and dead and then fading to nothing, until each was simply an arch of old white stone and nothing more. All except the one where quicksilver grew into an armour around him, hard plates in layers and layers, exquisite and complex. Two silver swords grew too, short and curved, one in each hand. There were pictures in the Palace of Alchemy of this man. Drawn five hundred years ago, and exactly the same.

'Isul Aieha,' she said softly.

The Silver King pointed a sword at her. History crashed in as their memories merged. She saw herself call the dragons and tame them with a single word. She ruled over men, but they were nothing to her. A distraction. She was looking for something, always. Something about the spear she carried and a great and terrible thing she had once done. An age of looking but never finding, and all the while a building despair inside her, a loneliness until she could bear it no more. She saw herself come to this place and conjure these arches, saw a glimpse of her future and the end that awaited her. She saw men, blood-mages, alchemists in another guise, tear her apart and take her body to their mountains to some distant cave, saw them hold her there caught at the edge of life and death. They drank her in tiny drops, not the blood of her veins but the silver god-blood, and as they did each took a morsel of her power. Through a thin veil far away, the alchemist Kataros knew the truth. She'd been there. She'd swallowed him too. He was inside them all.

The Silver King lowered his sword and turned away.

'No!' Kataros struggled to her feet. She had almost to claw her way up Jasaan to rise. 'Don't! Don't leave us! We need ...'

The Silver Sea became a silver mirror that faded to black and died.

' ... you.' She began to sob. Her blood was all over the arch. She reached through it, trying to open the way again, but there was nothing. Dead stone, that was all it was now. It wanted more than a mere alchemist, and the Silver King was gone, and the world would not be saved. Tears blurred her sight. Jasaan hovered about her, mumbling words she didn't hear. She didn't want him, didn't want to leave this spot, alone and desolate though it was. Eventually he left and went and did whatever it was that Adamantine Men did. Wandered around the other tunnels probably, looking for things to hit. Not here, that was all that mattered, all she cared about.

Alone, Kataros stared at the archways. The Silver King. She'd come here to find his secret, and all she'd done was take him home.

The Black Moon comes again, whispered the last echoes of his memory inside her. *Make right what I could not.*

'But we need you,' she whispered, over and over. She'd lost so much blood. Everything was a haze of missed possibilities. She drifted off, taken by her own weakness, and when she opened her eyes again Jasaan was standing over her. He offered her water. She gulped it greedily.

'I came to find you,' he told her. 'I'm supposed to bring you back to the Pinnacles. All the riders who came with me are dead now. So it's just you and me, and I never meant to take you back there anyway.' He shrugged. 'Tell me what you want me to do.'

He'd come to save her then, had he? Hadn't ever crossed his mind that she didn't *want* to be saved, but too late for that now. She shivered. Her fingers and her arms were stained red. 'We go back to the Spur,' she said. 'Back to Grand Master Jeiros and the other alchemists who survive. We tell them what we've found and we come here again, and Jeiros will make these gateways open and beg the Silver King to save us. That's all we have left.' *The Black Moon comes again*. Another half-god. Another who had lingered, and so the Silver King wasn't the last after all, and so perhaps there *was* still hope. *Make right what I could not.* Something to do with the Adamantine Spear that Jeiros guarded under the Spur. That was all she knew. All the echo had shown her.

Jasaan looked sceptical. 'Back through the Raksheh? There are snappers.'

'We'll use the river.'

'There's the worm.'

'I will soothe it.'

'We'll get hungry.'

'I'll show you what you can eat. There was a dragon outside. Has it gone?'

'Yes. Half buried under a landslide. Are you hurt?'

'I'm weak, that's all.'

Jasaan nodded and waited to be told what to do. While he was waiting, Kataros curled up and went back to sleep. Watch over her for a bit, that's what he could do, and by the time she woke again night had fallen. She crept past Jasaan's snores and sat in the mouth of the tunnel behind the dragon-thrown boulders that had once sealed the Black Mausoleum shut. She loitered there a while, listening. There weren't any sounds of people out here in the forest, only the night noises of the Raksheh, the rustle of monkeys high up in the trees, the flap of bats, the now-and-then calls of owls and other nightbirds. The air here, far under a canopy of leaves that turned even brilliant sunshine into twilight, was still. The night sky cast an odd light across the overgrown landing field, a flicker now and then of a deep reddish blue ...

A tinge of violet ...

A chill rippled through her bones. She crept from behind the boulders out into the open and there it was, floating in the sky overhead, dropping into the gap between the monstrous trees that was the old eyrie landing field: a great black mountain of stone hanging between the stars, purple light crashing out of its jagged underbelly, flickering with now-and-then flashes of inner lightning. The flying castle of Farakkan. A dragon circled it. Only a small one, not the great gold monster that had come after her yesterday, but a dragon was a dragon all the same. A crude cage was coming slowly down from the flying eyrie's rim. The same cages they'd used to lift her and Skjorl and Siff from the plains of the Fury valley.

'Jasaan! Jasaan!' She ran back into the Black Mausoleum and shook him awake, then dragged him out to see what had come in the night. The dragon swooped and soared up the scree of tumbled stone and clinging earth. It flared its wings and settled on the ruin of the Moonlight Garden over the cliffs of the Yamuna falls. The cage from the eyrie touched the ground, and Kataros gasped, for the eyes of the man who stepped from it glowed with a brilliant silver light, the light she'd seen in the eyes of the Silver King as he'd left her only hours before.

She knew at once who he was. *What* he was. The Isul Aieha had shown her before he left. This was the Black Moon, and as he passed where she hid, Kataros recognised him as the pale-skinned man from the eyrie who'd asked her questions when she'd been his prisoner. What was she supposed to do – follow him? She didn't know. *Make right what I could not.* Chase him down and beg his help? But that didn't feel right. She was supposed to stop him, but stop him from what? And how?

I'll get rid of her. That's what the woman on the eyrie had said, that woman who called herself speaker. She'd said it twice.

Here was a half-god. Another who could tame dragons!

The Black Moon walked to the tunnel into the Mausoleum, blind to her, striding quickly. Kataros hesitated, torn by indecision …

The Black Moon crosses the open field, heading for a cleft between two stones. From behind the half-god's eyes Berren Crowntaker sees two figures dart away to hide in the moonlight, but the Black Moon has no thoughts to spare for such trivial things. He has come here to finish what began a thousand years into the past, and will not be swerved. He walks through a cleft and into a tunnel of white stone that runs deeper into the earth, the silver fire from his eyes lighting his way until he reaches a circle of archways that seem to Berren much like a larger imitation of Baros Tsen's bathhouse in the eyrie. The Black Moon stops in the midst of them, riven with anticipation, all-consuming hope and hunger, all-devouring fear and scorn. Beyond these gates lies something so yearned for, and yet so utterly despised.

The Black Moon stoops to look at the blood on the floor. He touches it and tastes it and finds an echo of his prey. *Isul Aieha. Brother.* He has been here. And he is weak, so very weak. The Black Moon reaches for the gates, and Berren finds himself whispering: *Don't*.

Fingers touch stone. Everywhere blooms to shimmering liquid silver. A harsh violent light flays his flesh and pierces his heart, eating, burning, blinding. It is the same cold and hateful fire that cast him from the Silver Sea. The Black Moon screams, the taste of scorching knives driven into his head. He staggers and reels and flees into the night.

Behind him the light dies, surly and reluctant to let go.

The tunnel mouth flared in dazzling light. Kataros heard the Black Moon's horror-scream of anguish and agony, of bottomless pain. Sharp panic cut her to the quick. *Make right what I could not.* What was that supposed to mean? Was she supposed to stop him? But from doing what? What if she was already too late? She started after him, but as she did the Black Moon bolted from the tunnels, straight at her, past her, full pelt, almost crashing into her, oblivious. She jumped out of his way. He was clutching his face. Blood ran from his eyes and the silver light was gone.

'Stop!'

He didn't hear. She started after him again, out onto the landing field, out under the stars and into the darkness, arms waving, shouting, screaming at the top of her lungs for him to wait. He didn't turn, didn't even seem to know that she was there.

'Kataros!'

The dragon perched atop the Moonlight Garden had spread its wings. It swooped. Kataros screamed, turned, fled back to the trees and crashed into Jasaan, both of them scrabbling for the entrance to the tunnels, but the dragon didn't come after them. It disappeared instead over the top of the flying mountain, and when she looked back, the Black Moon had vanished. The eyrie started to rise and drift away. It crossed the falls and sank out of sight into the valley beyond, its flickering purple fading into the night sky.

'Who was that?' asked Jasaan, all wide eyes and bewildered twitches of wonder. Asking as if she might somehow know.

'Another half-god.' Kataros shivered. She started to walk back the way she'd come, back to the Mausoleum of the Silver King. 'The Black Moon, and we're supposed to stop him. But I don't know from doing what.'

Inside the mausoleum the archways were empty and dull, the white stone now tinged grey. When Kataros touched them they crumbled to an ash as fine as powder.

'They found us over the floodplains near Farakkan. Skjorl and I.' Her heart pounded. She didn't know where to start. Silver eyes like the eyes of the Isul Aieha. *Make right what I could not.* Make *what* right? 'They had dragons. Men with dragons, Jasaan. We didn't know who they were or what they wanted or how they survived or how their castle flew, but they were men, that was what mattered most of all, and they weren't afraid. That one asked me questions.' She shivered. 'He seemed so ordinary. We have to find him again!'

She went back outside and sat hard on the ground and held her head in her hands and cried. All the gateways turned to ash. What was it worth now, everything she'd done to get here? All she'd hoped for, to find the relics of the Silver King and call him back. Ash. Whoever this Black Moon was, he'd destroyed it, all of it. What was the point of anything now? 'They said something about Bellepheros,' she rasped. She was tired, so tired. Dizzy. Light-headed. Overwhelmed. She'd lost too much blood.

But pitying herself wouldn't do anyone any good. She wiped her eyes and got up and walked across the open ground of the landing field, and scrambled through the starlit litter of fallen stone. Wrapped in visions of half-gods and an apocalypse of dragons she wouldn't even have noticed Skjorl's body, bloody and mangled, if she hadn't turned back to see Jasaan crouched beside it.

'Is he dead?' She hoped he was. She wasn't sure she could bring herself to help him if he wasn't.

Jasaan nodded, grim. Kataros scaled the slope, climbed quickly and nimbly up the scree of boulders and loose gravel until she reached the firmer granite top of the outcrop. She stood there and stared, looking out over the forest and the night sky after the flying mountain as it drifted away. The water of the Yamuna rushed below her, pitching over the falls on the other side of the Moonlight Garden in a roar of noise, dampening the air. She climbed onward, hand over hand until she reached the flat top and the ruined walls of black marble.

Built in black marble across the great river from the endless caves. The only clue the Silver King had left behind to his Mausoleum, and here it was. Deep within the wilderness of the Raksheh forest on the edge of the mountain foothills of the Worldspine, and she'd found it. The great river of the Yamuna, the endless Aardish Caves somewhere below which guarded Vishmir's tomb, Vishmir who'd searched here for twenty years and failed, and *she*'d found it, and now it was gone. Dead.

The tumbled remains of the Moonlight Garden's dark walls closed around her. She climbed through thickets and ruin in the gloom, up as high as she could without any care for what these walls had once meant. In daylight the marble was a deep dark bloody red, veined with mustard yellow, not black at all, and there was no other stone like it in any of the dragon kingdoms. Between the walls were columned arcades and small round buildings, their domed roofs long since staved in by wind and rain and dragon-fire. Away from the river, the highest points were two grand red sandstone buildings open on two sides, each a precise mirror image of the other. No one knew what any of it meant, or what it had been for, or why the Silver King had built it.

Her hands came away black as she forged her way up, old ash still clinging to the half-buried stone from when Speaker Voranin's riders had cleared the ruins using dragon-fire. The red sandstone heights repelled her, too sheer and high to climb in the dark, so she scrambled to the top of the walls instead, overlooking the plunge pool of the falls. She gazed out across the forest and the Yamuna, high enough to see over the canopy of trees as the river rushed towards the flat open plains of Bonjanland and the Fury floodplain beyond the forest. She could see the flying castle in the distance again, a violet speck among stars, drifting away. She watched it dwindle, a flicker-flash gleam of purple, and tried to guess its course.

The Pinnacles.

Jasaan clambered up beside her. They sat and watched together in silence as the flying mountain vanished against the horizon.

'So now what?' he asked when it was gone. Kataros didn't answer at first. The flying mountain and the Black Moon it carried changed everything, didn't it? Or maybe they changed nothing at all. She didn't know, and struggled to care, so immensely alone in a world that was both huge and hostile. The gateways of the Black Mausoleum were gone. The Silver King wasn't coming back, and he'd left her with a burden that seemed impossibly huge.

'We follow.' She jumped from the black marble wall and started the tortuous climb down the other side of the Moonlight Garden, picking her way through the silver-shadowed night down steep steps that wound from the top of the bluff to the rushing water, and then on between the crags beside the falls until they reached the shore below and the carnage of corpses from the day before. She was shaking by the time she reached the bottom, and pale and exhausted. She had no strength left. The Silver King had bled her almost dry.

Two canoes sat pulled up onto the grassy bank, abandoned by the men who had brought her here. The few survivors were long gone. The dead had been looted, and flocks of silvery night-time carrion birds had already started on skin and flesh. They rose into the trees with angry cries as Kataros shooed them away. No one deserved this. None of them.

Jasaan pushed a canoe off from the shore, little more than a hollowed-out tree. Kataros splashed after him and climbed in. She started to paddle, and then stopped. The Yamuna's current was strong here and there wasn't any need, and Jasaan was dozing before she could count to ten. She hated him for that. Tired as death, but she couldn't sleep, head too full of thoughts that wouldn't be silent, and so she lay there for a while, and paddled now and then, trying to keep the canoe away from the banks, but mostly she was still, bone-tired, sleepless eyes open wide, staring unseeing into the darkness, rolling over and over through what she'd seen. The Silver King in the gateways. The Silver Sea beyond. The hope, the regret, the anguish, the pain, the blood, the ice-cold lake of memories.

Make right what I could not. What do you mean? She looked to the sky, to the moon hanging bloated there, looking for an answer but finding nothing.

They let the river carry them, day and night, taking turns to rest. Its water was clean and fresh. They didn't have much food, but neither of them fancied an expedition into the forest, and so Jasaan gave her what little he had and Kataros ate it without shame, clawing her way back to some semblance of strength. After it was gone they just got hungry, but they'd both lived for a year under the Purple Spur and so they were used to that. Days passed, blurring together, until the giant trees that made the heart of the deep Raksheh thinned and fell away. The land turned rougher and more broken. The river picked up speed. They passed the confluence of the Yamuna with some other nameless river, and then a second a few hours later, and Kataros knew from that that they were close to the edge of the forest, and to the tree village of Outsiders who had carried her to the Moonlight Garden. She kept them going, drawing deep on her last reserves through one more night until they emerged into grassy broken hills. She nudged Jasaan awake then, and had him paddle for the shore, too weak to do it herself any more.

'There's a cataract somewhere ahead,' she told him, and they kept the canoe close to the shore after that. Out here in the open they ought to hide to keep away from dragons, but Jasaan still had a little of the potion to cloak their thoughts and make dragons blind to them, and Kataros still had a pinch or two of powdered dragon blood to make more if she had to, and so from far enough above their canoe was simply another fallen tree adrift in the water. When they came to the upper reaches of the cataract gorge Jasaan paddled to the riverbank and rolled the canoe upside down. They crept underneath it to rest. Later, as the sun set, sleep still broken and elusive, Kataros slipped out again to look back at the forest, distant hills above the plains shrouded by mist and cloud and backlit by the red sinking sun. A ruined village stood not far away, a place she'd stopped at with Skjorl on their way up the river, a few stone houses on the edge of the hills, nothing more. She roused Jasaan and led him there to peer at the scorched walls, roofs gone, black and empty shells half tumbled down. While he did that, Kataros went to the old alchemists' house with its cellar. She climbed inside and rummaged through the shelves of alchemical pots and jars left behind for anything she could eat. She found some nuts and seeds, a few mouthfuls, and greedily chewed them down, and only after they were gone thought perhaps she might have shared what little she had with Jasaan, the Adamantine Man who'd stayed with her all the way from the Purple Spur to the Pinnacles, him and three others to keep her safe from dragons and feral men and snappers, and whatever else roamed the wastelands that had once been the nine realms of the dragon-kings. She looked around for anything else she might give him, but all she found was wine, and wine made her think of Skjorl. *Drunkard rapist bastard.*

There was the knife too, the one she'd almost used to cut Skjorl's throat. She cut herself instead, let out a few drops of precious blood into a vial, mixed it with water from the river and the last of the dried dragon blood she had, and worked on it until she had a potion to keep her and Jasaan hidden from the prying minds of monsters. Enough for both of them for another week or two, maybe three. After that ... after that she didn't know. She was too tired to think.

'Where are we going?' Jasaan asked again when she went back outside.

'The Pinnacles,' she said. She wasn't quite sure why. Mostly because she couldn't think of anything better, and to do nothing at all was to give in to paralysing despair.

'After they tried to kill you?' laughed Jasaan. 'I hope that's a joke.'

'What else? The Spur? For what? To tell everyone there's no hope? That the Pinnacles is filled with dragon-riders who murder alchemists and have learned nothing from the miracles of the Silver King that surround them? That I found not just the Black Mausoleum but the Isul Aieha himself, only to watch him walk away? To tell them that all is ash and join again our steady demise of starvation and hopelessness?' All the reasons she'd left in the first place. The mountain that flew. The half-god called Black Moon.

Dragons who obeyed the will of men. All that. She could take *that* back to the Spur once she knew what they were, once she knew why and how. She waved Jasaan away. 'Go and find some food.'

They stayed a night and a day in the ruined village, and the next night too. Jasaan turned out to be as good a fisherman as Skjorl had been. It wasn't much and they ate it raw, too scared of dragons to light a fire, but any alchemist knew their plants, and Kataros found a few they could eat and so at least they didn't starve. She didn't want to leave, didn't really have the strength yet, and there was no getting the bulk of their canoe down past the gorge and the cataract in the river and so it would be walking for now, but there was nothing here, not really, just surviving each day as it came, waiting for her potions to run out and then for some passing dragon to notice them. She told Jasaan they had to go and tried not to let him see how weak she was, but there was no hiding it, and in the end she gave up and let herself lean on him. Let him do the work, let him hold her, his warmth a token against the fatigue of despair; and after the first night of walking, as they huddled together under cover and watched the dawn light start to rise, she burst into tears, and Jasaan held her and rocked her gently to and fro, and she hardly even noticed he was there, far away in memories.

'I wanted to see the world,' she whispered. 'I didn't want to do what alchemists are meant to do. I wanted to love. I wanted to laugh and get drunk and climb mountains, not sit in caves and study books.' She shuddered. 'I was at Hammerford when the dragons came. I saw an Elemental Man and a blood-mage fight for the Adamantine Spear. I saw a man throw it into the face of a dragon and turn it to stone, and then later I saw him dead. I found the spear in the river, after it was done, and later Jeiros found me and sent me home, and the spear came with me, and that's why, sometimes, they call me the spear-carrier. But all I ever did was pick it up and hold it a while.'

Jasaan hugged her. The pain and the grief ebbed, washed out in tears. She felt herself fading, succumbing to exhaustion. The endless months under the Spur, hungry and hopeless.

'I hate dragons, Jasaan. I hate them,' she murmured and fell asleep in his arms.

They followed the Yamuna at night, walking beside its banks.

There had been people living on the plains once, thriving here. It wasn't a place of cities but of an abundance of villages clinging to the riverbank. Kataros walked through what was left of them, what had once been huts and halls, most smashed and burned. Sometimes the only sign was a field of stumps, blackened and splintered but still stuck stubbornly in the earth. The river started to change, losing its clarity and purpose and spreading across the plain in sluggish brown. Another hard night of walking and the shattered houses now hung on stilts, lifted off the ground. Makeshift boats littered the fields. They were everywhere, scattered among the flotsam and jetsam of the dragons' passing and the river's spring floods, little fishing rafts no more than a few poles lashed together, picked up and dropped at random as the waters fell. Kataros had passed them with Skjorl on the way up the river and had known she'd find them again, and so as soon as she spotted the first she had Jasaan help her carry it into the water. They drifted through the nights after that, resting, carried by the river, conserving the last of their strength. There was nowhere to hide in the day, no hills, no trees, not any more, no caves, no cellars, no rocks, only flat fields full of wild grass going on and on, a slight rise here, a dip there, but she remembered how Skjorl had found them a cluster of rocks, a pit in the ground or maybe simply a mound of rubble. They spent one day dozing under a pile of old boats carefully arranged around the stump of a tree. Anything to hide them from the sky while the sun was up, while her dragon-blood potions masked their thoughts and hid the truth of their presence.

On the way up the river with Skjorl she'd seen dragons every day. On their own more often than not, but sometimes in twos and threes and towards the end a dozen at once, and every one of them flying away from the Raksheh. Now the skies were clear. Maybe she simply slept while they passed, but their absence struck her.

'Have you seen any?' she asked Jasaan. The Adamantine Man shook his head.

'Not one.'

'Isn't that strange?'

He shrugged and frowned. 'Lucky is all.'

They passed the mouth of the Ghostwater with its secret tunnel to the Silver City and the Undergates of the Pinnacles. The

Ghostwater came that way, under the ground from the Moonlit Mountain, but it was too deep to wade against it, and too swift to pole a raft, and so they walked up the valley to the scarp slope at the far end where the river crashed out of its cave on its way to the Yamuna. From the top of the slope three distant peaks stood out against the sky, pale grey fingers thrust against the far horizon. Side by side Kataros and Jasaan stopped.

The Pinnacles.

'Are you sure of this?' asked Jasaan. 'You know they kill alchemists there.'

'I know. But the flying mountain …' She didn't know what to say. It had to be there. If it wasn't then she didn't know where else to go. 'I don't know what else to do,' she whispered.

'Go back to the Spur. Back the way we came, Kataros spear-carrier.'

'I can't. Not with nothing.' Adrift on the waters of the Yamuna she'd already given that all the thought it deserved. A motley band of ragged survivors, of queens and princes and alchemists and Adamantine Men slowly dying out, trapped, alchemical lamps their only light, air choked with smoke and the sewer reek of decay, scraping the most meagre living they could while they waited in hopeless apathy to die? No. She *was* Kataros the spear-carrier, who had brought the Adamantine Spear from Hammerford, for all the good it had done anyone, and though it was her home she wouldn't go back again with nothing. The Silver King had given her a purpose, even if she didn't understand it.

She scanned the skies. Empty. Not a single dragon. *Where have you all gone?*

'Not with nothing,' she said again, and set off across the plain.

23

Hard Things

Twenty-eight days after landfall

Tuuran lay naked on his back, sprawled on silk sheets across a huge bed that had once belonged to a king. Onyx lay on one side of him, propped on an elbow, wrapped in silk as thin as gauze and feathering his chest with her fingertips. Myst lay on the other with her hand resting between his legs. And that ought to have been just fine, except nothing was happening. He could feel Myst's hand well enough, and that was that. A big limp lack of interest. He couldn't understand it. Whoring, drinking and fighting. Three things at which every Adamantine Man excelled.

He pushed Myst away and sat up. Off in the next room one of the babies cooed and started babbling to itself.

'Flame! Can't they be quiet?' His voice sounded harsh, even to himself. Kept wondering whether one of the babies was his. Could have gone either way, that. Could have been almost anyone's, but he found that the not knowing bothered him. He got up and prowled towards the curtain door. That must be it. The babies with their incessant noise. No doors, no privacy, no quiet, no respite. Putting him off. Just knowing they were there all the time, right close by. How was a man supposed to relax?

'I'll go.' Onyx brushed past to the little ones. As Tuuran turned back, Myst sat up, the silk sheet draped provocatively around her, hiding her skin and yet showing it off in little flashes. Other days that would have been enough on its own for him to stand to attention, right there and then. Today? Nothing.

'You're tense.' Myst smiled at him. 'I have Xizic oil. A little massage ...'

'I'm not tense!' Tuuran snapped. 'It's ...' He shook his head and looked for his clothes.

'You know that before we served our mistress of dragons, we were trained and sold as bed-slaves.' Myst slid off the bed. She sidled up to him and ran a hand down his side. He flinched away. 'It happens far more than you suppose. To every man at times.'

Tuuran rounded on her. 'What? What happens?'

Myst glanced downward. 'That. It can be that a man's mind is—'

Tuuran lunged, ripped by the fury of humiliation. He caught himself with his hand about to grab her by the throat. And then … and then what, exactly? He snarled and snapped away from her.

'Would that help?' she asked.

'Would *what* help?' Tuuran snatched at his tunic and pulled it over his head.

'To be rough.' She looked him in the eye. 'Some men like that. For some it helps.'

'I don't want to hurt you.' He couldn't stand this.

'You wouldn't. It would be pretend.'

No, no. That wouldn't do. Too angry. Didn't trust himself. He turned away and tossed his belt onto the bed. Myst came up behind him and put a hand to his back.

'I have another idea.'

'No.' He pushed her away. Done with this. 'It's not working. Shouldn't even be here anyway, not with this stupid plague. I should go. Her Holiness will be back soon.' Maybe that was it. Knowing Myst and Onyx were hers. Or maybe it was the curse he carried, the Hatchling Disease, maybe it did things, made things not work any more. Or maybe it was the Black Moon with his knife, cutting everyone and making them into his slaves. Her Holiness said he'd never cut Myst and Onyx, that they were beneath his notice, but Tuuran wasn't so sure. He couldn't talk to the alchemist because the Black Moon certainly *had* cut him, and because he was the grand master. Halfteeth and Snacksize, the Black Moon had cut them too, and anyway they were his soldiers and he was their Night Watchman. Couldn't talk to her Holiness because she was her Holiness. Couldn't talk to Myst and Onyx because they were her Holiness too. Couldn't talk to … couldn't talk to bloody anyone.

Or maybe it was that the Black Moon had gone and hadn't come back, and so Crazy had gone too, and more and more Tuuran feared that that was the last he'd ever see of the only real friend he'd ever had.

Best not to think about that.

'Wait here. If you want to dress then dress. It'll take me a minute to get ready.'

Myst swished through the curtain and left. Tuuran finished dressing and then slumped back on the bed, propped up against a mound of pillows. Didn't have time for this. Stupid idea anyway. Snacksize and her dumb 'Hey, boss, you need to blow off some steam' ideas. Too many things needed doing, and it wasn't like when they were on the island. Had had too many things then too, but none of them had mattered quite the same. Was the difference between the exhaustion of climbing a mountain because the mountain was there and you wanted to climb it, and the exhaustion of trying not to drown. Nothing was any fun any more.

He punched a pillow. Hard. It didn't make him feel any better. Just more angry. He got up. Paced. Prowled. Was about to go, and then her Holiness came in and he froze, paralysed for a moment with alarm. Dressed in her gold-glass dragon-queen's armour and he could feel how she was naked underneath, even with her hair tied back in a dragon-rider's plait and with a mask covering her face.

Took a moment before he spotted her skin was the wrong colour, night-black where her Holiness was pale. Myst, dressed up, but just for a moment he'd thought it was Zafir, and his heart was still thumping, and now of all things he felt himself stirring. Myst strode to him, grabbed him by the balls and pushed him back and back against the bedroom wall.

'You know what you want, Night Watchman. So take it.' She pushed him away, turned her back, lifted the gold-glass armour over her head and dropped it onto the bed, stood naked with her back to him, erect and proud and waiting.

Tuuran looked down. Not the only thing erect and proud all of a sudden.

'Not that way.' The words caught in his throat. If he half-closed his eyes he could see Zafir again, naked with her back to him outside the island caves, both of them soaking wet. 'I have the Hatchling Disease. You know that.'

Myst dropped a lamb-gut sheath tied at the end. 'And *you* know what to do with *that*.' Her voice was haughty, imperious, almost a perfect mimicry of Zafir.

A dam seemed to burst inside him. He stepped up behind her and pressed himself into her buttocks and reached around to cup her breasts and pulled her into him, slid one hand up to her throat and round her neck and the other between her legs. They parted for him. Myst gave a little moan as he pushed his fingers inside her. A part of him was back in Furymouth, high up in the tower of a burned palace, drunk that night they'd first made land. He closed his eyes, and Myst was Zafir.

'Why won't you let me in?' he growled. 'Why?' he pushed her against the wall and pulled her hips back into him, ran his hands over her skin, fingers clenched like claws, aching stiff with a lust and passion and hunger more than he could remember. He fumbled his way into the sheath, spread her legs and thrust inside her, deep. Myst squealed. 'Why? Why won't you let me in?' One hand tight around her throat, the other pressed into her crotch as he took her. Myst gasped and moaned for him, and a part of him knew perfectly well it was her, not Zafir, that it was all an act, but a part of him believed because that was what he wanted. 'Why won't you let me in? Why won't you help me?' He came quickly and hard, groaning like he'd been stabbed, and Myst cried out too and he was still driving inside her because he still wanted more, but slowly the haze lifted. He drew back. Let go. Stared at Myst still pressed against the wall, both of them panting and heaving. Wide-eyed and wild.

She turned to look at him. Grinned and then laughed. 'Well, *that* worked!'

'Yes.' He looked at her, uncertain for a moment. The skin of her neck was livid where he'd clutched her throat. For a moment he wasn't quite sure who he was any more. Myst looked him up and down, still with a bewildered grin.

'That was quite something.'

'Yes, it was.' Tuuran looked away. Looked at the floor. Anywhere else. 'I'm sorry. Did I hurt you?'

'No. And you did nothing you should be ashamed of.' She touched a hand to his shoulder. 'Tuuran?'

'Yes?' He was still panting, out of breath. Twitchy like a wild animal, battered by the flurry of emotion. Whatever it was they'd done he hadn't seen it coming. Wasn't quite sure what he'd let out either, and whether it would go meekly back again.

'She doesn't let anyone in, not really. Not even us.' Myst ran her fingers down his arm and kissed him between the shoulders, then handed him his boots. Tuuran sat on the bed and made himself decent. 'Halfteeth is waiting outside.'

'Does she talk to you about anything at all?'

'Lots of things, Night Watchman.' Myst smiled. 'Most of them you know. She doesn't talk about her sister, if that's what you were wondering, nor about your friend the half-god. Nor much about you either. You all trouble her in your different ways, and she keeps her troubles to herself.' She brushed past him, all swish and lingering fingernails, and rolled her eyes at the crying from the room next door. 'Your son is hungry *all* the time. I wonder where he gets that from?' She gave him an arch look.

Tuuran caught her arm. 'Her Holiness really doesn't say anything about Berren? About going to look for him?'

'Not to us.' Myst hesitated, then she turned and looked Tuuran in the eye and cupped his face and kissed his lips. 'She talks of the Black Moon now and then, and rails at the absence of her eyrie. I couldn't tell you whether or not she'll be pleased to see him back when he returns, but if she is then I can tell you she'll be the only one. I'm sorry.'

Not as sorry as he was. But then why should any of the rest of them care? Crazy Mad Berren had been his friend. The rest had only ever known him as the Black Moon, tyrant slave-maker and half-god.

It falls to me then. Which wasn't a particularly cheery thought, and so he went outside to see what Halfteeth wanted, and found him and Snacksize together, Halfteeth hefting a heavy hammer, Snacksize leaning on a second beside him.

'Disturb you, did we?' asked Halfteeth, one eyebrow raised so high that Tuuran thought he was about to strain himself. 'Sounded like maybe we should come back later.' He sniggered. 'Didn't mean to interrupt anything.'

'You OK, boss?' asked Snacksize. She was trying not to smirk.

She'd heard the things he'd said while he was with Myst then. Bloody Enchanted Palace with no bloody doors.

'I'm fucking marvellous,' grunted Tuuran. He looked at their hammers and nodded. Pushed past them and headed up for the Octagon. 'And don't you worry, Halfteeth. I came when I was good and ready for you.'

Behind him Snacksize almost dropped her hammer.

'Yes, boss,' snickered Halfteeth. 'We know. I think most everyone inside the mountain probably knows that.'

'Right.' Tuuran ground his teeth. Mood he was in wasn't one for Halfteeth and Snacksize and their smut. 'Good to know. If I need to hear any more about that, I'll be sure to say so.'

'Anything you ask, we'll, uh, *let you in* on it, boss. Yes.'

Snacksize made an odd sort of strangled noise.

'And if there's—'

Tuuran stopped dead and spun on his heel. He grabbed Halfteeth by the throat, almost lifting him off the floor. 'Halfteeth?'

'Gnnnccc?'

'I'm really not in the mood, Halfteeth.'

'Ugnn kehhhh.'

'You sure?'

'Yeth.'

'That's very good to hear.' He dropped Halfteeth and pointed a finger at Snacksize, jabbing it like he might just poke out someone's eye. 'And you can shut it too.'

Snacksize nodded, serious-faced, but Tuuran knew her too well for that to fool him for a moment. Biting her lip to stop herself from sniggering. She shrugged. 'There's nothing wrong with trying something different, boss. A different, ah ... way in, if you like.'

'I wasn't trying somethi— I wasn't ... Great Flame, what do you think ...?' He closed his eyes and turned back to walking. No, they were *not* having that conversation. Let them think whatever they wanted. He shook himself and stretched and rolled his shoulders, trying to shake the sense of being lost. Adamantine Men were never lost. Even if they didn't know where they were, that was because someone had made the map wrong, or rearranged the mountains and rivers in the night, or something like that. And they certainly weren't ever lost in their own skin, because how useful was *that*?

Zafir was waiting in the Octagon with Bellepheros and White Vish from Furymouth. Tuuran looked away before she caught his eye. Couldn't be doing that, not after what he'd just done with Myst. He shuddered. So wrong, and a hundred times worse what with the secrets he knew that she'd shared with no one else. He walked quickly on through the Hall of Princes, up the Grand Stair, on and on around its sweeping spiral until his thighs were burning, forcing Halfteeth and Snacksize to keep up, striding so that Snacksize with her short legs almost had to set to a jog, and them with their heavy hammers. Petty payback for mocking him, that was. Had them nicely out of breath by the time he reached the High Hall and walked briskly outside into the rain.

Yesterday Halfteeth had built a crude crane by the cliff edge of the Moonlit Mountain. It was like the winches on the edge of the eyrie rim, only instead of a cage attached to it this one had a giant wheel, and tied to the wheel was Hyrkallan, almost naked. The rest of Tuuran's Adamantine Men were already up there, keeping watch, making a circle, standing guard. They were bored and sombre and wet. A few of Hyrkallan's riders were there too. They hooted and jeered and hurled abuse when they saw Halfteeth and Snacksize with their hammers, and there were a few shouts about honour and revenge. Tuuran lifted a finger, telling them where to stick it. He wiped the drizzle from his face. Wasn't much more than a fine mist of spray today. Should have been lashing down for a time like this. Would have been more fitting.

Queen Jaslyn watched from a distance, cold and aloof. She really didn't care what he was about to do, and Tuuran simply didn't understand that. The Hyrkallan he remembered – and he did, even from all that time ago – had been a fearless, bold, strong giant, admirable in every way, everything Tuuran saw in himself. Left him to wonder what had happened. Turning traitor he could understand, and alchemists were a nuisance at the best of times, but what had Hyrkallan done to his queen? 'Why do you suppose even his own woman despises him?' he muttered.

Halfteeth shrugged. 'Despises everyone, that one,' he muttered back.

Wasn't quite true but never mind. Tuuran cast an idle eye around for aspiring assassins lurking in the rubble in case any happened to be waiting for her Holiness to come out. There likely wasn't much point, not with Diamond Eye perched on the remnants of the Silver Onion Dome, but he did it anyway. When Zafir came outside she went to stand beside Queen Jaslyn.

'Two bloody ice queens,' growled Halfteeth. Tuuran cuffed him. He watched Zafir until she turned her head and gave a little nod, then he pushed Snacksize and Halfteeth forward.

'Go on then. Get it done.'

He'd have done it himself. Probably should have. But Halfteeth had almost begged, and when Tuuran had asked why, Halfteeth had told how it was he'd become a slave sold to the Taiytakei, how old Valmeyan, the King of the Crags and lord over the Worldspine, used to send his riders out to sack the villages deep in his mountain valleys and burn their homes. How they'd murder the weak and the old and the sick, and bring the young and the fit and the children back in cages carried in the claws of dragons, to sell to the Taiytakei in the slave markets of Furymouth. Hyrkallan was the King of Sand and Stone, not the King of the Crags, but frankly Halfteeth was happy to take what he could get when it came to smashing some dragon-king's ankles with a hammer and watching him dangle over the edge of a cliff and die and take his time about it.

Tuuran still should have said no. Was his job to do as the Night Watchman. But Snacksize had come too, though she'd waited outside and kept herself quiet, making like she wasn't there while she listened to every word, and Halfteeth had leaned in and whispered all shifty-like that it was the same for her, and that she'd gladly take a hammer if it was offered and maybe a knife too, because the King of the Crags and his riders weren't too fussy about what state their slaves were in when they sold them, and the night-skins were none too kind either, and it was sometimes far, far worse for the women than it was for the men. He wouldn't say more and Snacksize would never say a word, but it set Tuuran to thinking of her Holiness and how, all things being as they were, she might quietly approve if she knew. She never *would* know, but that was by the by, and so here they were.

Snacksize's hammer came down, smashing the bones in Hyrkallan's wrist. He screamed. Tuuran watched Zafir and Jaslyn.

Maybe her Holiness flinched, but Jaslyn stayed still as stone. The queen of Flint, like they used to call her mother.

Halfteeth did Hyrkallan's ankles next. One, two, nice and quick. The riders of the north stood sullen in the drizzle and watched, and Tuuran's Adamantine Men watched them in turn, and the dragon Diamond Eye watched them all. Snacksize took her time with the last swing. Had some words to say, it seemed, though they were lost in the rain before they reached Tuuran's ears. He saw her spit in Hyrkallan's face, and he was about to go and do the job himself if she didn't get on with it, but she lifted the hammer before he could take more than a step and brought it down. The two of them backed away. The Adamantine Men on the crane worked their cranks and winches, and the wheel lifted into the air and turned and flipped on its back. Now Hyrkallan dangled underneath, tied by his shattered hands and feet. The crane turned and the wheel moved out over the edge of the cliff, and that was where they left him, howling and screaming curses at Zafir. Wasn't right, killing a man like that, but it was what he'd done to old Grand Master Jeiros, who would have hung there and died just the same if King Jehal of Furymouth hadn't happened by in the nick of time. Whisked him away to the Adamantine Palace by all accounts, just so they could both watch the world end in flames a few days later. Tuuran shook his head. Fate could really be a shit sometimes.

Her Holiness turned and left. Some of the riders and most of the Adamantine Men left too. Tuuran watched Halfteeth and Snacksize saunter back inside, grinning and joking. A few riders stayed to stand and stare and listen to Hyrkallan howl. Queen Jaslyn didn't move, and Tuuran found himself staring too, not looking at Hyrkallan or even hearing him, but gazing right through to the endless grey sky, lost in thoughts he didn't want. It was killing him, slowly, that Crazy had vanished. Was bad enough when he was here, but the difference between abject darkness and a glimmer of light was worlds and lifetimes, life and death.

Even in the drizzle he was getting soaked. He went back inside and thought about looking for Bellepheros, but Bellepheros always just sent him brusquely away. Would have been different with Chay-Liang still here. She would have brought him round, no matter that she and Tuuran didn't get on either, no matter how she'd spat scorn at her Holiness and everything she stood for. With the three of them together he might have approached Zafir to winkle out where she truly stood. And maybe that could have made for four. Her with her dragon, Bellepheros with his alchemy, Chay-Liang with her gold-glass, and him with his ... well, with his axe. Maybe together they could face the Black Moon and drive him out, and Crazy could be his old friend again. Berren the Crowntaker. The Bloody Judge. Whatever name he wanted. But Chay-Liang was gone, and what had happened in Merizikat hung heavy between all of them, and Bellepheros wouldn't talk to him, and her Holiness kept her counsel carefully to herself and wouldn't let him in.

He went to find Halfteeth and Snacksize instead, off together getting roaring drunk in celebration of putting old demons of their own to rest. He drank with them in case that somehow helped, but they didn't really want him, just got louder and wilder and crazier and ended up slinking out, arms draped around one another, off to the nearest place they could find where they could fuck, while Tuuran slumped morose in a corner. Not good company. He kept drinking until he puked and could barely walk, and then spent the last half of the day and most of the night sleeping in Myst's bed while she came and went around him, or else staring into space, lost and wondering what to do, hardly much noticing when she sat beside him and stroked his brow and brought him cups of hot water infused with herbs which mostly turned cold on the table beside her bed, untouched.

'You don't even look anything like her,' he muttered as much to himself as to anyone.

'I know,' she said. 'What does that tell you?'

Tuuran didn't have the first idea what it told him, and didn't think he wanted to either. When the fog of drink cleared out of his head at last he drowned himself in duties instead, running around the Pinnacles and getting in everyone's faces. If wild dragons had come then he might have raced up the Grand Stair to shout challenges to the blind sky, but no one had seen any dragons for weeks, not since Zafir and the eyrie had come, and a fine job Tuuran had been doing, playing that up to anyone who would listen – Zafir the dragon-queen, who had come from nowhere, and the skies empty ever since – but he could have done with one now. A good fiery end full of bluster and fury.

He headed another expedition around the Silver King's tunnels to keep himself busy. Rounded up a few feral men. He spent days at a time down there until he knew the place like the back of his hand. Kept himself away from all the shit that was mucking with his head, and so that was where he was when word came of the eyrie's return, seen off in the distance coming in from the far Raksheh; and right then all thoughts of ferals slipped out of his head like smoky ghosts in a midday gale, and off he ran, axe in hand, straight on up, half mad with anxiety and the other half with murder, all ready to chop off the Black Moon's head and be done with it, through the ruin of the Queen's Gate and racing a sled to the eyrie until he reached the rim and saw the Crowntaker standing on the wall, rainswept and waiting for him, and saw no silver in the Crowntaker's eyes, and Crazy Mad still alive in torment behind them.

'You're still in there, then.' Tuuran looked hard, trying to look into Crazy's skull at whatever was going on inside.

'Still here.' Crazy looked at Tuuran's axe, the white knuckles clenched around its haft. 'Bit late for that, big man. You know he won't let you.'

'Where is he?'

Crazy flicked the rain off his face. He turned away, a flash of bitterness. 'We went somewhere.'

'Where?'

'Don't know. Something to do with the other one like him. The Issle Ayer or whatever you call it. I don't remember much.'

'Isul Aieha,' murmured Tuuran. 'The Silver King.'

Crazy paced the wall, twitching and restless. They both had the same desperation inside them, Tuuran knew it, only for Crazy it was magnified a hundred times. Had to be, trapped in there with some half-god monster. 'It's all blurs until the end. He did something that hurt him real bad, so bad it almost killed him. I remember stumbling out of a place a bit like this.' He paused a moment and swept his arm vaguely over the eyrie. 'I had something in my eye, and then there was blood on my fingers. Ruins on a steep hilltop over a waterfall. A river in the middle of some

×2 326 ⊂×

forest. But it's all snatches. Bits and pieces stolen while he took us back up to the eyrie. After that I just … drifted out. There's something he wants here, big man. Something to do with that Issle Ayer. He wants it real bad.'

Tuuran clapped him on the shoulder. 'You're still in there, Crazy. Hang tight. We'll find a way.'

'Oh, I know how to kill him now,' Crazy said. 'Not that it'll do any good.'

'How?'

Crazy snorted. He looked across the dragon yard. The dragon they'd killed over Farakkan had burned itself to ash from the inside now, and all that was left were scales and bones. Huge great wing-bones. Then Crazy turned his back to it and stared out at the sky instead. He picked his way down the outer slope of the eyrie wall, out to the rim.

'Crazy …'

Crazy spun back and barged Tuuran away, glaring, baring his teeth. 'No, big man. You'll never get him out. You won't find a way. You can't.' He walked right out to the rim and stood on the edge, toes clenched at the void past the top of the Moonlit Mountain, the sheer cliffs to the Silver City far below lost in the haze of falling rain. 'You don't understand. He could be done with me any time he chooses. He keeps me here for fun. You haven't the first idea what he is, and you won't do anything to him that he doesn't want. You can't. He's a god, Tuuran. A god!'

'Only a half-god, Crazy. Only half.'

Crazy grabbed Tuuran's shirt in his fists. 'The Silver Sea. You remember that?' Tuuran nodded. 'He went to a place where there were arches like in Tsen's bathhouse. Only bigger. He opened them, and that's where he got burned. So listen: all you have to do is find a way to get him down to the bathhouse, open up them gates back to the Silver Sea and then push him through. There's something waiting there now. Something terrible, and it's him it wants, not me. So that's how you kill him, big man. Not too hard, eh?' He spat. 'But he'll never let you. Never. Touch him and you'll turn to ash. Go on, push me over the edge and see what happens.' Crazy clenched a fist and hammered it against his own breast. 'I've tried a knife. I've tried … I tried *his* knife. I tried having your dragon-queen cut him out of me. Nothing works. You with your axe, what were you thinking? Take my head off with it? Your dragon-queen tried that, too, don't you remember? First time we met. So *push* me!'

Tuuran held up his hands. He was about to step away when Crazy shoved him with such violent force that it staggered them both. Crazy stumbled back and went over the edge. Tuuran tried to catch him, missed and almost went over himself. He watched the Crowntaker as he hit the mountain summit close by the edge of the cliff ...

No. *Almost* hit. But in the last moment he wasn't there. Tuuran ran back to his sled and shot down to where Crazy should have fallen, almost pitching himself off in his hurry, and found nothing at all except a creeping sensation on the back of his neck that he wasn't alone; he turned round and the Crowntaker was behind him, only a breath away. His eyes were flecked with silver. Glimmered with it. Crazy was gone. He was the Black Moon again now.

'Only a half-god.' The Black Moon nodded. 'The last one of those to come this way tamed an entire race of dragons and raised a thousand blood-mages in their place, and when they brought him down do you know how many survived?' Crazy Mad, the Crowntaker, the Black Moon, cocked his head. 'Eight, big man. Eight. A thousand blood-mages and eight of them lived, and what have you got? An axe. You'd open a way to the Silver Sea, would you? Then go with your dragon-queen and fetch me my brother's spear. The gates will bow to it. With that you could do what you want. Not that you ever will, but you could. Now go away.'

The Black Moon stood in the rain, looking out at the sky, and Tuuran wondered what he saw; but whatever it was, all Tuuran's eyes found was grey and rain, bleak and pitiless and without a sunlight shred of hope. He went inside and figured on quietly drinking himself into another stupor, perhaps staying that way until someone eventually threw him out and her Holiness told him she'd take Halfteeth as her new Night Watchman now, because she could do with someone a little less useless, thanks, and then maybe he could just vanish off across the sea somewhere so they could all forget about him. He could go drown himself in vinegary wine in some windowless cesspit of a cellar under a blanket of rotting slime-coated piss-stench straw ...

Yes, that or something like it. Was about what he deserved, because what use was there for a man who couldn't help his friend? Wasn't an Adamantine thought that, seeing as Adamantine Men didn't have friends; Adamantine Men only had the legion. But it was there nevertheless, big and bright and burning as the sun, and what was Adamantine and what wasn't could just go fuck itself for a bit.

What use?

As it was he didn't even make it to the Octagon before Big Vish caught his arm.

'Boss?'

'Go away.'

'You need to come, boss.'

Tuuran brushed him off. 'Find someone who cares, Vish. Aren't you supposed to be watching Hyrkallan's corpse?'

'You told me to mind the grand master alchemist, boss. So should I take him?'

'What?'

'Boss?'

Tuuran stopped. Took a breath. Because no, Big Vish just wasn't going to leave him alone, not unless Tuuran put an axe blade through his head, because Big Vish was just too damned dumb to ever take a hint. The world wasn't that kind. 'Take who?'

'The grand master, boss.'

'Take him where?'

Vish took a deep breath, as though Tuuran was being unreasonably obtuse. 'To Jasaan. You know, the Adamantine Man who went off looking for the alchemist Kataros.'

Tuuran blinked. 'What do you mean "take him"? Wasn't Jasaan the one who jumped off the summit with a pair of dragon wings strapped to his back? He must be smashed to a bloody pulp somewhere at the bottom of the cliffs.'

'Yes. But he's back. And he found her.'

'What?'

'The alchemist Kataros. He found her and he's brought her back.'

Tuuran's mind started racing. Was it possible? They'd actually found her? They'd found another alchemist? Bellepheros would practically piss himself with relief. And maybe, if he could give the grand master something he wanted, maybe things might start to change at last. 'Alive?' Vish nodded. 'And this Jasaan, he's got the alchemist with him? She's here? In the Pinnacles?'

'She's down in the ruins, boss. Hiding. We'd have to go and get her. So ... do I get him, boss?'

Tuuran almost said no. Let him see for himself whether it was real. But old Bellepheros deserved better, didn't he? And an alchemist wasn't just some other feral.

'No, Vish. We get him together.' Tuuran quietly thanked the Great Flame for giving him a ray of something that might turn out to be hope. Wasn't much, but it was enough that drowning in wine could wait another day.

24

A Conspiracy of Alchemists

Thirty-four days after landfall

Kataros crouched in what had once been a cellar. They'd had a conversation, her and Jasaan, as they'd come to the outskirts of the Silver City. *You hide while I go inside. And if I don't come back, you don't follow. Good men died so I might find you and keep you safe.*

She'd nodded, not really meaning it. Good men died all the time, some for better reasons, some for worse. But she'd gone along with it, and that was why she was in the cellar of what had been the Silver City's Laughing Dog tavern. The Laughing Dog had once been infamous enough that salacious rumours of its outrages permeated even the creaky old walls of the Palace of Alchemy. If you were willing to believe the stories then there wasn't any excess of debauchery or lewdness or violence that hadn't once been witnessed in the Laughing Dog. Bellepheros had even mentioned it in his *Journal of the Realms*, but the tale on which its infamy was founded was of a queen of the Silver City disguising herself as a whore and spending three days and nights on her back in a wager with the tavern's madam. The story was a century old and then some, and Kataros had never believed it, but whatever the truth, the Laughing Dog's days of bare-knuckle fights and snapper baiting were gone. So were the roof and most of the walls past the first storey. Half the grand old staircase was left, rising into nothing; everything that would burn had been charred black by dragons; and everything that could move had been taken long ago by the feral men who cowered underground.

The cellar was all that was remained, and the hidden door in the floor that led into the old tunnels of the Silver King. Kataros was thirsty and famished and so weak that the world blurred in front of her eyes now and then. She had a knife and a last few tattered shreds of hope and not much else. It had been a day since Jasaan had left her. An hour or two of dumb blind anticipation and then the rest spent realising how stupid she'd been to come back here, a growing certainty that Jasaan wouldn't return.

Someone was coming up through the trapdoor. It cracked open. A knife trembled in her hand. She held the blade ready to cut herself and fling her most potent weapon, her own blood. Not that she had much of it left.

'Kataros? Kat?'

'Jasaan?' All he was was a shape. But she knew his voice. She almost collapsed in relief.

The trapdoor hesitated. A second voice echoed from the shaft beneath. An old man complaining about his knees. Then the door flew abruptly wide and Jasaan ran over to her. 'Kataros! It's the most amazing thing! Hyrkallan is gone!'

'Oh help me up then, will you? Let me see her!' The old man again. Jasaan turned back to the trapdoor and hauled another figure out of it. 'Careful, you clumsy great—'

'It's safe here,' Jasaan said, still talking to her. 'They have alchemists of their own.'

She was shaking. Fear and tension. No. Not fear. Jasaan hurried back to her side.

'Kat? What's the matter?' The tremors were getting worse. There were tears in her eyes. Hope, that's what it was. A ludicrous hope that at last she might be able to stop running for her life.

The second man lit an alchemical lamp, a cool familiar light, and at last she could see their faces.

'Grand Master Bellepheros?' She couldn't hide her disbelief. It really was him. 'How are you alive again?' Her head surged. She'd lost so much blood in the Black Mausoleum, and then everything since had been so hard, and she simply didn't have the strength, and Grand Master Bellepheros had gone missing more than two years ago, and everyone supposed he was dead, and yet she'd know his face anywhere – every alchemist in the nine realms would know it – and the roaring noise was louder and louder, and above all his being here meant she was safe because …

The relief was too much. She fainted. When she came to, Bellepheros and Jasaan were crouching over her.

'Grand Master?' Impossible, still, to really believe it.

'You must be Kataros.' Bellepheros smiled, a great beaming smile full of joy as though she was his long-lost daughter. She didn't understand. She knew his face because he was the grand master and she must have seen him a hundred times, but how did *he* know *her*? He'd probably spoken three words to her in as many years. 'Your friend exaggerates; I am the only alchemist here. But now we are two.'

Jasaan offered her his hand to help her up. 'You're safe now. The Pinnacles have changed, alchemist Kataros. Your order is welcome here again.'

Your order ... Kataros glanced at Bellepheros. 'The others? Speaker Hyrkallan ...'

'King Hyrkallan is gone.' A darkness crossed Bellepheros's eyes. 'And your friend is right: the Pinnacles are indeed a safer place for alchemists now.' His words carried more meaning than they said. Saf*er*, but still not safe, was that his message?

She followed the two of them down the shaft, taking the rungs slowly and carefully, wary of her own weakness. Bellepheros went ahead, babbling happily about things that didn't make much sense and shying away from telling her anything that really mattered in between complaining about his knees. It was just as well; her own thoughts buzzed and floated, her mind too light-headed to properly focus, too crazed with relief. Fatigue settled more heavily across her shoulders with every step, drooping her eyes and her head until it seemed to want to crush her flat to the floor. Bellepheros could have been telling her the secret to ending the tyranny of the dragons, but it wouldn't have stopped her from thinking how there might be a bed in her future, and how deliriously happy that would make her.

There was a monster waiting in the moonlight gloom of the Silver King's tunnels, a huge clattering giant of a man covered in plates of golden glass. A light flared, dazzling, straight at her face, bright as the midday sun. She gasped and shied away from it, screwing up her face.

'This idiot lump is Tuuran,' said Bellepheros, as testy as she remembered him. 'Night Watchman of the Adamantine Guard now, Flame help us all.'

The light dimmed. In the tunnel glow she could see more clearly now. Jasaan was grinning like an eel. She could have hugged him. Another wave of relief staggered her. Her knees buckled and almost gave way. Jasaan caught her. Beside the monster Night Watchman were two other Adamantine Men she knew from the Spur, Big Vish and Bishak, and a woman, short but armoured again in glass and gold.

'Snacksize,' grunted the monster, 'you look after her until I say otherwise.'

Old Bellepheros hobbled beside her as they walked through the tunnels, taking their time while he told his wild tale of being kidnapped by the Taiytakei, of being carried across the sea and building an eyrie for the night-skins, of dragons and the dragon-queen Zafir. Kataros half heard, dizzy and too bewildered to listen to anything much. She told him how she'd been in the Worldspine when the first woken dragons had fallen on one of Valmeyan's eyries and torn it to pieces, how she and a sell-sword had escaped and made their way down the Fury intending to flee to the sea.

'If we'd managed to get that far, you and I might have met again long ago.' She laughed, and then her voice choked, thinking of the sell-sword Kemir and what they'd been through together, that he was gone and almost forgotten. 'We got as far as Hammerford. Dragons came ...' The memory seized up inside her and clenched her throat tight. Months of running and hiding, dragons and dragon-riders and feral men. The Spur and its hopeless starvation. Her whole life as long as she could remember. Running and running and fighting and running. No peace.

'In the Spur we call her the spear-carrier,' said Jasaan, filling the silence. He stayed close, protective, and she was grateful for that. 'In the last days someone stole the Speaker's Spear from the Adamantine Palace. The alchemists say it was meant for the Taiytakei, but Kataros found it in Hammerford and brought it back.'

Kataros stopped for a moment. 'I didn't do much more than survive and then pick it up when everyone else was dead,' she said, quiet yet loud in these tunnels that reverberated even to a whisper. 'Dragons came. They burned the town. Then the spear. I didn't see who carried it at first, but it turned the dragons to stone. They all killed each other. I was the only one left.'

'Turned to stone?' spluttered Bellepheros. 'The Speaker's Spear did that?'

'The old story of Narammed and Dragondale, Grand Master.' Jasaan sounded smug. Almost jaunty. 'When the dragons came to the Adamantine Palace, Night Watchman Vale Tassan carried the spear into battle against them. Many stone dragons guard those ruins now.'

Tuuran grunted something and nodded approvingly. 'See, alchemist. Not all the old stories of the legion are nonsense.'

'Finding one that isn't doesn't make the rest of them any less foolish,' muttered Bellepheros.

Kataros stumbled, legs too tired to go on. Jasaan caught her again. How could he still have any strength? All those days wandering through the Raksheh looking for her, and then coming back, with hardly any food, he must surely have been at the end of his rope, yet he would have carried her if she let him. She settled for leaning on him again as they reached the Undergates of the Pinnacles and marched inside. Bellepheros slipped beside Tuuran and whispered in his ear. The monster nodded. After they crossed the Gold Hall, Bellepheros and Vish and Bishak and the armoured woman went their own way, leaving her and Tuuran and Jasaan alone.

'Something you should see,' Tuuran said, and led them through twists and turns and long grand halls of dim-glowing white stone, until suddenly they were at a great staircase to the very top of the Moonlit Mountain, and Kataros couldn't understand how they'd got so high so quickly; but a summit was a summit and there was no denying her eyes. As Tuuran led them out into the open, she cringed and shot a glance at the sky, old instincts driven deep. Open sky meant death from above. This was where the other alchemists from the Spur had died. Friends, as much as she had any.

A dragon was staring at her. A huge old war-dragon in shimmering red and gold. Kataros yelped and gasped and jumped away, stumbling for shelter. Jasaan did the same, but the big man Tuuran didn't even flinch. He stood and glared while Kataros tensed with legs like coiled springs to bolt as soon as the dragon moved.

'I bet she lets *you* in,' he muttered, and it took Kataros a moment to realise Tuuran was talking to the monster. He took his time, him and the dragon staring each other down, and then he turned his back and sauntered to Jasaan's side. He had a vicious look on his face. 'The speaker's dragon,' he said. 'Diamond Eye. He only eats people her Holiness tells him to.'

'Is it tame, then?' Kataros asked. 'It takes Bellepheros's potions?'

'No potions.' Tuuran shook his head. 'I don't know why this one doesn't simply want to eat us like the rest of them do. You'll have to ask her Holiness when the time comes. Or …' He stopped himself, shook his head and instead walked to the edge of the summit, to a crane where something hung over the side of the cliff. It took a moment for Kataros to see that it was a man. 'Hyrkallan,' said Tuuran brusquely. 'Thought you'd want to see him, all things considered.' He nodded to Jasaan. 'Big Vish told us what happened. Look, there are things that need to be said, and all isn't as well as maybe it seems, but you take as long as you like here first. He's been there a while so he won't mind.'

Tuuran stalked back to the High Hall and the Queen's Gate. Kataros looked out at Hyrkallan. He hung still and quiet, and she couldn't tell if he was already dead, but she stared at him anyway. The killer of alchemists. This was where he'd done it. Pitched them off the edge and then said they'd been burned by dragons. She couldn't find any feelings for him at all. Just too tired.

'Is he dead?' she asked Jasaan, but Jasaan wasn't beside her any more, he was by the crane. He brought his axe down on the rope that suspended Hyrkallan's wheel over the cliff. The crane shook. The rope jerked and twitched. Hyrkallan didn't move.

Dead already then. But Jasaan brought the axe down a second time and then a third, and then jumped away as the rope snapped and whipped, and the wheel and Hyrkallan plunged over the cliff, away to the Silver City, tumbling slowly end over end. Kataros ran to the edge and watched them fall. She saw the wheel crash into the side of the cliff hundreds of feet below and shatter into splinters. She squinted, but she couldn't see after that. She turned to look back at Tuuran, split by a flash of fear, but he was still up by the Queen's Gate, waving his arms as though in the middle of talking to someone, even though no one else was there. Kataros couldn't tell whether he'd even noticed.

'Whether he was or he wasn't, he is now,' grunted Jasaan. He led her away. Tuuran, when they passed him, sniffed.

'Think yourselves lucky it isn't raining for once,' he said, and led them back inside to Big Vish. 'Find her a place she can have for her own. Quiet and out of the way. You tell me where you put her, and you can tell her Holiness if she asks, but you don't tell anyone else. Not even the grand master. You got that? You don't tell *anyone* else she's even here.'

'Why do I have to hide away?' Kataros asked, but Tuuran had already gone back outside to argue with the dragon again, and Vish only shrugged and led her and Jasaan through the Hall of Princes and the Octagon, pointed out the Hall of Mirages and told her not to go that way, not that it would make any difference if she did, and then led her another way through halls with grand tapestries hanging behind rounded entrances of white stone that made her think of gaping mouths.

'The grand master.' Vish pointed to where Bellepheros had his room, then took her back through the Octagon. Kataros followed him back into the Hall of Princes and down a side passage, through a maze of tunnels curving everywhere left and right, up and down, gentle slopes and twists, not a straight line in sight, and all of it the same white stone with its comfortable glow of light. Wherever Vish was taking her, she'd never find her way back.

The air smelled fresh as though she was close to an open window, but she never saw one, nor any doors, nor was there ever any breeze. Vish eventually stopped at a storeroom and pushed aside a sacking drape. It was a small room, half filled with stacked crates of alchemical lamps. There was a cot crammed in beside them and not much else. Nowhere to dress or wash or clean herself, but then Kataros hadn't had *that* luxury for years. There was a bowl on a little table with some fruit and a pile of old stale biscuits. A jug of water stood beside it. It was the most beautiful sight she'd seen in months.

Vish nodded to Jasaan. 'She's yours, dragon-slayer. Keep her hidden and apart. Don't talk to anyone. Rest while you can but don't go anywhere. Got that?'

He left them there. Jasaan promised to stand watch outside, but Kataros waved him off. 'You need sleep too.' She slumped into the cot, fully clothed, gobbled down some biscuits and gulped at the water. She started on the fruit, and then her eyes closed and didn't open, and when she woke up hours later she still held a half-eaten pear sticky between her fingers. Jasaan was with her again, crouched beside her, gently shaking her shoulder, and Big Vish loomed behind to say that Grand Master Bellepheros had asked to see her, and so she rubbed the sleep out of her eyes and shuffled in Jasaan's wake, too bleary to think about how she looked or anything much at all. Her head felt so stuffed with wool that she half expected to simply fall asleep again mid-stride and for Jasaan to have to carry her.

They crossed a wide passage and then dived into a steep narrow tunnel. At the end of it was an alchemical workshop. Small, but a workshop nonetheless, and a little part of Kataros woke up and rubbed her hands with glee, despite how tired she was. Bellepheros looked up as she came in. He was holding a plate with a slab of half-eaten cheese. He watched her as she stared at it, her hunger and her aching legs fighting one another, and then smiled and offered it to her.

'Help yourself.'

As she took it he caught her hand and held it gently. He rubbed his fingers over her knuckles, the hard dead skin there, then turned them over.

'Hatchling Disease?'

Kataros nodded as he let go.

'Do you have anything for that?'

'Not any more.'

He gave her an oddly sharp glance. 'Her Holiness has it too. And our Night Watchman.' He sighed. 'I have potions – plenty. Or you can make your own if you like.'

'I'll make my own, if I may.'

Bellepheros sat back and smiled as he watched her work, and she told him that she'd been the one who had pulled the Speaker's Spear from a petrified dragon's mouth in Hammerford, that riders had fished her out of the Fury after the fighting there, that Grand Master Jeiros had sent her back with Vioros to the Adamantine Palace, and so she'd been there when the dragons had fallen upon them only days later, when even the spear hadn't been enough.

'We live as best we can in the caves now,' she said. 'We're dying. Slowly and steadily.'

He'd probably heard it all from Big Vish already, and from the other Adamantine Men from the Spur weeks ago, but it did her some good to have someone listen. When she was done he started to tell her about his time with the Taiytakei, bits and pieces, making light of it as though skirting around something huge and terrible. She finished her potion while he talked, and then they shared the last of his cheese, and she went back to her room and fell asleep again and slept through the night, and when she went back the next morning, fresh at last, a dragon-rider woman stood with Bellepheros in his workshop, fierce and hostile in scales and glass and gold, with the monster Tuuran beside her. Kataros blanched as she saw the woman's face, tense as a drum. If she'd had a knife, she would have pulled it. She hissed, half of her ready to run, the other half to fight.

'I've seen you before,' she spat. 'You were asking about the Black Mausoleum. You were going to have me killed. Speaker ...' *We don't need this one ... I'll get rid of her ...* With the Black Moon, only his eyes hadn't been silver then and he'd looked like just a man.

'Zafir.' The woman nodded. 'Queen of the Silver City and speaker of the nine realms. Or so I was until –' she made a wide gesture with her arms '– all of *this* happened.'

Zafir? The last speaker? Under the Spur everyone spat at her name. She was a curse. A demon who was supposed to be dead. Kataros shuddered and hissed again. She could feel Jasaan right on the edge beside her, and the monster Tuuran felt it too. They were eyeing one other, ready if they had to be. Zafir cocked her head.

'And you say I was going to have you killed? A precious alchemist? I don't think so. Why on earth would I? But yes, I do remember you. Do you recall the man who was with me then? The one with the knife?'

Kataros nodded. *I saw him again at the Black Mausoleum of the Silver King. After I saw the Isul Aieha abandon us. He is another half-god. He is the Black Moon.* She almost blurted it out there and then, all of it, but no, not to this harridan, this murderess, this poisoner, the ruiner of everything, the speaker who had let the realms crumble and burn.

'He is the Black Moon,' said Zafir, and Kataros jerked, startled by words that seemed plucked out of her own thoughts. Speaker

Zafir spoke with a flash of hunger in her eyes. 'Do you know what that means, alchemist? It means that inside him he carries a half-god, a brother to the Isul Aieha.' She looked at Kataros hard, unnervingly, as though she really *was* trying to peer inside Kataros's thoughts. 'I wasn't going to have you killed when we met before. I was going to have you put somewhere safe before he cut you with the knife he carries and made you into a slave.'

Kataros stared. Dragon-kings, dragon-queens, they held no power any more, not for her. But Speaker Zafir ... she couldn't imagine anyone more reviled by the alchemists under the Spur. 'You did this,' she said, too tired to hold her tongue. 'All of this. The end of our world. The dragons set free. You were the speaker. You were supposed to stop it, and what did you do?'

Bellepheros leaned between them. 'We have a great deal to tell you, alchemist Kataros, and whatever else you might think, her Holiness is right about the Black Moon and his knife. We need to keep you away from him. He'll cut you if he finds you, and I'm afraid that means you need to keep away from me too. Tuuran, Zafir, your Jasaan – you can trust them. There are a handful of others.' He sighed. 'And the rest ... I'm afraid you will not find the rest easy to believe.'

Kataros took a deep breath and listened as the monster Tuuran told the story of Berren the Crowntaker and the Black Moon, and when he was finished Kataros told her own of the Silver King and the Black Mausoleum, and watched their disbelief mirror her own. Zafir swept away when they were done, and Tuuran followed, and Kataros and Bellepheros were left alone. They looked at one another in silence and then both looked away, each perhaps as bewildered as the other as to what to say.

'The eyrie leaves tomorrow,' said Bellepheros at last. 'For the Adamantine Palace and the Purple Spur. Her Holiness will claim the Speaker's Spear.' He looked at Kataros for a long time without saying another word. Then: 'Was it all true, what you told them?'

'All of it, Grand Master.' Kataros frowned. 'Should I have not ...?'

'No.' Bellepheros took a deep breath, turned away and paced his tiny workshop and then sat down again. 'No, it's for the best. But her Holiness will likely take you with her to the Spur, and the

Black Moon will come too, and you must stay hidden from him if you can. He mustn't know you're there. Do you have dragon's blood?'

She shook her head.

'Blast! Then you cannot hide your thoughts from his dragons. They will know you, and they will tell him what you are.' He closed his eyes and slumped.

'I have potion already made for *that*. A little still left.'

Bellepheros brightened. 'How much?'

'A few days, but there is more under the Spur. Plenty of it. As much as you could want.'

He came to crouch beside her and clutched her hand. 'The dragons read my thoughts. I am not to be trusted. But the Black Moon is not the Silver King, he is not the Isul Aieha, he is not our saviour, and he must be stopped, and if our speaker stands beside him then she must somehow be dissuaded or subdued. I will need your help and the help of every other alchemist still alive. I need you to take that message to Jeiros in the Spur. Above and beyond all else, no matter what happens, he must hear those words from someone he will trust.' He patted her shoulder. 'But for now I need your help on the eyrie. There's a dead dragon burned to ash and cooled enough that we can harvest its bones and scales. Her Holiness requires new armour, and while we do it we can find you a place to hide.'

He reached into a drawer and pulled out a little pouch. As he did, Kataros caught his arm.

'Grand Master! The Silver King left with a warning. I didn't tell the others what he said. "Make right what I could not." So I will help you stop him, no matter what. I think that must be what our Isul Aieha meant.'

They looked at one another in silence for a moment. Then Bellepheros nodded and handed her the pouch. Inside were some dried berries as hard as seeds.

'From a part of a world that even the Taiytakei have never seen,' he said, and grinned. 'Tuuran calls them shitberries, but I find them quite tasty. These are the last I have. Tell me what you think of them.'

25

The Adamantine Palace

Thirty-eight days after landfall

The eyrie drifted north over the plains around the Silver City, towed by the seven hatchling dragons the Black Moon had cut with his knife. Zafir rode Diamond Eye in long lazy circles overhead, keeping watch. The dragon's eyes were sharper than hers, but his mind was sharper still.

She flew to Hammerford to see for herself whether the alchemist Kataros's claim was true. The town was a burned husk, overrun with grass and weeds and thorns. The fires were long out and the smoke was gone, but the air, when she landed among the ruins, smelled of charred wood and ash. The petrified dragons were exactly as Kataros had described them. One rearing on its back legs, tail coiled over its head and around its neck, the tip in a circle as though it was holding something and had brought it closer to have a look at what it was. The other lay at the edge of the river, wings outstretched. Its tail slanted up, while its head and neck disappeared into the water, toppled forward. A few remnants of shattered boats bobbed against it. All that was left of the waterfront was wreckage, long scavenged.

Dragons turned to stone. Preposterous. Absurd. But there it was. The work of the Adamantine Spear. *Her* spear.

Eyes do not lie, little one.

She dismounted and stood beside the stone dragons while Diamond Eye looked on. Beyond belief, except here they were, right in front of her, close enough to touch. Fifty feet high and a hundred feet long, the detail exquisite and perfect. She'd never seen anything like it. The one reared on its back legs even had a surprised look. No craftsman had made these. Not even the best artist of the Taiytakei could have come close. Easier to believe they were conjured by magic, but Kataros claimed to have seen it with her own eyes.

Diamond Eye believed. In the end that was what mattered, and so Zafir would believe it too. She turned away, mounted again and flew, racing north until the last of the rainclouds broke into white cotton tufts. She overtook the eyrie and reached Gliding Dragon Gorge; high on Diamond Eye's back she stared down at the Fury river as they flew over it, a tiny winding ribbon of silver. On the ground it seemed enormous as it carved its mile-deep scar out of the Worldspine and halfway across the realms. From so high it seemed diminished. Dragons had a way of making everything small.

The massif of the Purple Spur loomed ahead. She began to see distant specks in the sky: other dragons, the first time she'd seen any since she reached the Pinnacles. They were miles away, flying high, distant but watchful. She felt their murmurings in Diamond Eye's thoughts. Half-heard conversations as he spoke with them, too garbled to make into any sense. They were wary. Watching to see what would happen.

What do they want?

The Black Moon comes for the Silver King's spear, Diamond Eye told her. *They know this. They wait to see his purpose. They remember.*

What do they remember?

That a half-god came once before and betrayed us. That the Black Moon is not the Isul Aieha. That he once made us as we are, but that he is no longer whole. She felt then a hesitation. *That the Earthspear is the Isul Aieha's ancient weapon charged with the power of the dead goddess.* Again a hesitation. *A change will come, spear-carrier, for better or for worse. They watch to see what that change will be. They wonder what he will do. What* you *will do.*

What I will do? Zafir laughed. *If only I knew.*

What you will do, little one, when the spear is in your hands again. It carries a power greater than any other, if you have the wit to use it. Greater than the Black Moon at the zenith of his might, and what walks among us now is but an echo of a memory of that. The Black Moon believes it bound to you. We wonder how this can be so.

We? That was telling, wasn't it? *It drank my blood.* The Speaker's Spear. It seemed impossible to believe. It was a strange old spear, that was true, sharp as the sun on glacier ice, metal through and through, with four long blades that ran almost half its length, and it had always struck her more as a lance than a spear. In all the years the speakers had carried it, it had never been more than unusually sharp. Legend said that the first speaker, Narammed, had slain a dragon with it, but that had been hundreds of years ago, and no one believed in those myths any more, not even the alchemists.

She'd sat on the Adamantine Throne and held it.

She flew on, trusting Diamond Eye to warn her if the watching dragons broke their vigil and skewered in to attack. She could see the Adamantine Palace and the City of Dragons, what was left of it, spread out beside the sun-bright glitter of the Mirror Lakes. The bulk of the Purple Spur rose behind them, sheer mountains almost vertical. Here and there cascades of water tumbled over the edge, flashing sparks and glitter as they caught the sun before their waters dissolved into mist and were carried off by the breeze.

Home. *Here* was home. More than anywhere. Zafir lifted her visor, then took off her helm and tucked it down beside her, let the wind pull at her hair and blow tears into her eyes, savouring what it was to be alive. The sky was a deep devouring blue, the sun bright and warm, the wind cold and fresh. From this height the rolling fields below, overgrown now with thorns and weeds, shone in vivid greens and yellows. Blotches of darker woodland lay scattered among them. The Hungry Mountain Plains stretched beyond to the north, too far away and lost in the haze. When she looked back over her shoulder, the ribboned scar of Gliding Dragon Gorge ran as far as she could see to east and west. Flying could be so peaceful. It was always so different to see the world from the sky.

I'll never forget the first time my mother brought me here. The sky a brilliant blue, the sun burning and bright, the far-below ground dark and lush. Distant mountains, and then blossoming beside them as she approached something a-glitter like a jewel, the greatest jewel she would ever see, the Adamantine Palace gleaming in the sun, the lakes sparkling around it, the mountains of the Purple Spur at its back. A sight burned into her mind like dragon's breath.

Jehal had said much the same once. They might even have been his words.

The memory of him shook her back to where she was. She

brought Diamond Eye down in a shallow glide towards the palace. Its towers were toppled and broken, the mighty walls standing but scabbed and scarred and battered, bites smashed out of them. They were littered with the twisted remnants of scorpions. In the Gateyard and the Speaker's Yard were the dragon statues, great monsters rearing up in frozen poses of war, snarl-faced hatchlings, some of them broken, their wings spread wide, their tail tips snapped off. The square bulk of the Speaker's Tower was still there, one corner sheared away in ruin below. The elegant spire of the Tower of Air was gone. The other towers, the Azure Tower, the Towers of Dawn and Dusk, the Humble Tower, all were shattered stumps. The Glass Cathedral alone had survived, a misshapen lump of stone in the centre of the Speaker's Yard.

The eyrie was far behind now. Diamond Eye circled and then landed. His wings threw up a flurry of dust and ash. The smell almost made her retch. A few weeds had found purchase in the cracks between the flagstones, and the ground was littered with skeletons stripped to the bone, still in their armour. Burned. Bits of them – hundreds, perhaps a thousand. Scattered everywhere. The last stand of her legions of Adamantine Men. Zafir dismounted and walked among the dead, looking at them, trying to imagine how it had been. Kataros claimed to have been here and seen a little of it. A handful of men – hard as it was to believe – had survived this cataclysm of fire. They'd actually driven the dragons off the first time they came, but not the second.

She climbed the palace walls and picked her way through twisted metal, through the remains of skeletons still clinging to scorpions, burned so hard by dragon-fire that metal and bone had fused together. She looked out over the ruin of the City of Dragons. Jehal's crushed bones lay out there, and somewhere here in the Speaker's Yard beneath her feet was the corpse of Vale Tassan, the Night Watchman she'd left behind. He'd despised them both, and he'd been right, and yet he'd done his duty nonetheless. He'd walked into the abyss, eyes wide open, knowing he must surely die.

This is what we swore to stop. It hit her hard, and she had to force herself not to look away. *This is why the speakers exist. These were my people, whom I swore to protect.* She'd seen Hammerford now. And her own Silver City and Furymouth and Farakkan. All gone. She shivered. The speaker she'd once been would never have thought such things. There would be blame, yes, and plenty of it, and vengeance for all those who had wronged her. But guilt? A sense, somehow, of being accountable? Never.

But I didn't do this. Dragons did this. The Taiytakei did this. Valmeyan. Was Shezira any better? Was Jehal? Could any of us have stopped it?

She turned away, climbed down from the wall and walked to the remains of the Tower of Air. She sat on one of its tumbled stones and wrapped the piece of black silk across her eyes, the silk from her old bed in the Pinnacles, trying to find the enchanted golden dragon with the ruby eyes that Jehal had given her so they might watch each other while they were apart. It had been fun for a time, although she knew now that the Taiytakei had been watching them too, that the golden dragons had been ensorcelled by Quai'Shu's enchantress Chay-Liang, and had served a greater and darker purpose that neither she nor Jehal had understood until it was far too late.

Quai'Shu was long gone, and Chay-Liang too, but the golden dragon the enchantress had made was still here. Zafir found it eventually, and Diamond Eye prised it free for her, pulling fallen stones aside with ease as though they were made of foam. One of the golden dragon's wings was bent and it couldn't fly, but its eyes still worked and it could hop and hobble along. She played with it a while, pushing everything else aside until she grew bored, and then picked her way through the bones and the thousand corpses to the entrance of the Glass Cathedral. What she'd come for, if it was still here. The spear.

The doors had been smashed down, splintered and rent by dragon claws. The innards were old-scoured by fire. The benches were ash, the metal sconces empty, the alchemical lamps gone. The stone altar was misshapen and glassy as though burned until molten. An old compulsion had her walk up and touch it. It felt cold.

I stood here, she told Diamond Eye. Or told herself, perhaps – she had no idea whether the great dragon listened to her now-and-then wistful memories. *Aruch slipped the Speaker's Ring onto my finger. He placed the Earthspear in my hand and named me Queen Zafir, speaker of the nine realms. I drifted through it as though it was a dream.*

Dragons do not dream, little one.

So he *was* listening. *I made myself look at them. I made them see me. For a moment they all truly saw who I was. Just for an instant.* She walked around the altar of the Great Flame to the spiral stairs that burrowed into the ground beneath and descended, shuddering as darkness wrapped around her, as the confined space of the stair pressed in, a heavy gloom that even an enchanted glass lamp couldn't shiver away. *The tunnels go deep here, dragon. They riddle the earth beneath us.* They were old, far older than the rest of the palace. No one knew who had built the Glass Cathedral or why, its stone burned glassy smooth long before the Silver King had come. *Do you remember it, dragon? Does it live in your times before the Silver King?*

It was a refuge for a few half-gods who lingered, crippled ghosts like the moon sorcerers you once saw. They did not belong. The world was no longer theirs after what they had done, and they are gone now.

Zafir eased her way on, one step at a time, trying to ignore the walls closing around her until she reached the bottom of the stair where it spread into an open space, a place where she could almost breathe without the air catching in her throat. The plinth where the spear once rested was empty. It didn't surprise her. Neither speaker nor Adamantine Man would leave abandoned any weapon that killed dragons. She stared at it anyway, remembering.

It was here, its pointed haft driven into the stone. The walls were lit by alchemical lamps. Their light glittered on its silver skin. Aruch told me to touch it. Aruch, the old dragon priest, last servant of the Great Flame. *So I did because it offended Jeiros and I was annoyed with him. No other reason than that.* She could see the moment, as clear as yesterday. Running the tip of a finger along the spear's edge, wickedly sharp, watching as a few drops of her blood dribbled over bright silver and then shrank away and vanished as if drawn into the metal itself.

The spear has tasted you, said Diamond Eye. *It knows you. You belong to it.*

Aruch had said the same. The exact same words.

There were more tunnels here leading into the Spur, but she wouldn't walk them alone, and so she climbed out of the gloom back to the open sky and took great gulps of air, then returned with Diamond Eye to the eyrie lumbering slowly through the sky beneath the surly resentment of the Black Moon's hatchlings and their chains. The half-god stood on the walls, staring ahead, eyes blazing silver. Half the Adamantine Men and all of Jaslyn's riders were with him, watching and waiting. Even so, the eyrie felt empty, the sacks and crates they'd emptied from the warehouses of Merizikat now stored in the Moonlit Mountain, and most of the Merizikat sell-swords left to watch over them. To watch over her sister too.

'The spear has been taken under the Spur,' she told the half-god. 'Bring the eyrie to the Adamantine Palace. We can enter through the tunnels there.'

The Black Moon didn't turn his head. For all she knew he hadn't even heard, but she could hardly bear to stay, not on the walls among such a crowd, waiting for them to gasp as they saw what she already knew, the ruin she'd left behind. She abandoned Chay-Liang's gold dragon with its ruby eyes to keep watch, and returned to the Spur, flying high to the cliffs over the old Zar Oratorium, to where the Diamond Cascade tipped its waters over the cliffs. Set back from the bank a little way down the river was a lodge, not much more than a single room squashed under an overhang and almost impossible to spot unless you already knew it was there. A secret place passed from one speaker to the next, one of several tucked among the silent crags of the Spur. It was untouched, exactly as she remembered it. The dragons hadn't found it, or else they hadn't thought it important enough to burn.

Hyram brought me here before I became speaker. Afterwards I came with Prince Jehal. She watched the water rush by beneath her, then she walked along the little path that led to the great cliffs, to where the waters of the cascade pitched over the edge to vanish in rainbows and mist. She sat on her haunches right at the edge and looked down. *I brought Sirion here. I don't even know why I did that. Trying to make them fight over me, I think.* She looked down at the ruin of the Adamantine Palace, of the Silver City, of what had once been nine glorious realms of dragon-kings and -queens.

Regrets, little one?

Plenty of those, dragon. But dragons didn't understand regret. Or sorrow, or forgiveness, or mercy or spite or vengeance or love, or so many other things. *And here is something new for you. This feeling. New for both of us.* Shame, was it? She wasn't sure she knew. But probably that. She'd returned to the dragon-realms to claim back her home, her throne, to take what was hers, but all that seemed hollow now. She wanted it undone, unwound, to try again, to somehow make it right.

I miss him, you know. She walked back to the lodge and settled inside.

Who?

Jehal. Obscene after all they'd done to one another, and if he'd been alive then no doubt her fury would have bettered the rest of her and had his blood and his skin. Still, she *did* miss him, parts of him at least. Moments they'd shared.

But the tears that stung her eyes weren't for him; they were for the little girl she'd once been, coming to the Adamantine Palace on the back of a dragon, wrapped in her mother's arms; and for a time she found herself lost in a sorrow she couldn't explain or understand, and she was glad beyond reason when the eyrie finally drifted across the last miles of the plain and came to rest over the ruin of the palace below. By the time Diamond Eye spiralled down to join them, Tuuran and Halfteeth and the first dozen of his men were already on the ground.

'To get to the spear this way we will need an alchemist,' she said to Tuuran. 'Bring Kataros but don't let her be seen. Armour her up as one of your own. Do it yourself.' She didn't give him any chance to object, but brushed on past to look for the Black Moon. When she found him she looked him in the eye and stared into his moonlight pupils. No one else could look at him like that and hold his burning gaze, but she was a dragon-queen, raised from the moment she could walk to stare down monsters. She hunted for any sign of the Crowntaker inside him, for Tuuran's friend Crazy Mad, and found nothing. Only the half-god Black Moon, end to end, inside and out.

'You will bring out my brother's spear, dragon-queen,' he said. He didn't mean it as a question, but Zafir chose to imagine that he had.

'I will. And then?'

The Black Moon smiled. 'We make everything as it was meant to be.'

'Which looks like what?' She kept hold of his eye. The moon inside him flickered and flared.

'The world healed,' he said. 'The Splintering undone. The gods cast down. Dragons at our side. Dominion, dragon-queen.'

'*Your* dominion?'

'Mine.'

Zafir shrugged. 'I suppose at least you're honest.'

'And you at my side with the Spear of the Earth and a thousand dragons at your beck and call. You will be beautiful and terrible, dragon-queen, desired and feared above all. Men will poison and murder and fall on their swords for a glance from you. Be gracious and merciful or terrible and dance on their bones. Be constant or capricious. All the worlds save one will be your playground, for I will not care.'

'You know me well.' Zafir smiled, though she didn't believe a word of it, but the Black Moon didn't smile back. He leaned into her. 'Above the storm-dark, beside the Godspike, I saw into your soul. I know you, and I know what you are.' He touched two fingers to her cheek, not a gesture of any kindness or affection but a threat, a reminder, a claim of ownership, a demand for submission; instead of brushing them away, Zafir pinched his nose and squeezed and pushed him back.

'You don't own me. You earn me. Half-god or not.'

The Black Moon snapped away. Furious light blazed from his face. His hand flew to the Starknife on his belt, but Zafir refused to look away. No fear. Not for a dragon-rider.

'Can you bring back the dead for me?' she asked. 'There's a lover I once had I'd see die slow and screaming over and over. *Can* you do that, half-god? Bring back the dead?' Let him see the darkness. It was a part of her, after all.

The Black Moon froze. His fury sparked about him and then ebbed as he laughed. 'No, little one. None of us ever could do that. Now fetch my brother's spear, dragon-queen.'

She watched him stride to the cages dangling from the eyrie rim, moonlight pouring out of him, soldiers scattering from his path while the bones of the dead turned to black ash around him. There would come a time, she supposed, when he'd tire of her. But for now he needed her – not that she understood quite why – and she needed him, and that was all there was.

'The alchemist you asked for,' said Tuuran, and Zafir realised she'd been staring at the Black Moon all the way up to the rim, and Tuuran had come up beside her, and she hadn't even noticed, and he had a fire in his eye too. 'So we get the spear now, yes? That's why we're here?' He was restless as though he couldn't wait.

'Why doesn't he cut me?' Zafir asked, though she was asking it of herself and never mind the flash in Tuuran's eye, the wild desperation he kept clenched inside, perhaps asking himself much the same. She put a hand on his arm, stilling him before he said something they'd both regret.

'Yes,' she said. 'We get my spear.'

'And then?'

She laughed, although it was an empty sound. 'And then, Tuuran? And then I really don't know.'

The Black Moon might have looked into her soul in Takei'Tarr, but there were things there now that hadn't existed to be seen back then.

26

Avalanche

The dragons gather among the deep peaks of the Worldspine. They circle and wheel, an impatient sky of talons and scales and waiting fire. They are young adults hatched after the Adamantine Palace fell in flames. They are hunters and great war-dragons. But all are here made small by the ice-crowned peaks of the Worldspine itself. Bleak and jagged, iron-hard sheer faces of black stone. Nothing lives so high, so cold, so far and remote. Under a deep clear sky of searing violent blue the dragons watch, hungry, snapping taut on a leash of anticipation. On the tallest peak the world offers her, a dragon of pure white perches motionless. The half-gods once called her Alimar Ishtan vei Atheriel, Beloved Memory of a Lover Distant and Lost. More elegant, they would say, than a thousand stars. The little ones had named her Snow. Because she was white.

She watches now, eyes almost closed, quiet and serene as dragons roar and scream.

The Black Moon has come.

Maker.

Creator.

The Isul Aieha is fled.

The Black Moon seeks the spear.

The Black Moon is risen from the dead. The maker-creator who abandoned them to their fates now comes once more. So says the great dragon Diamond Eye, who in those thoughts he lets them see stands aloof from what must come. The Black Moon. Shatterer of worlds.

Even a half-god can burn.

We served him. We are his children.

Over and again, in mantras and refrains like a familiar chorus. They are divided, while eyes and thoughts pry into the distant veiled mind of great Diamond Eye, watching and waiting; but the biding of time is not for dragons, and Snow has long made her choice.

She stretches. She flares her wings and flies.

Dragons do not serve.

27

The Silver King's Spear

Thirty-eight days after landfall

No fear. Not for a dragon-rider. Not of anything. Of no man, no monster, not even a half-god, not of the sun crashing from the sky or the moon shattering to silver-glass splinters and raining into the sea. But of a dark place with walls pressed close and the air suffocating with old still dust?

Tuuran and Halfteeth and six other Adamantine Men circled ahead of Zafir down the stair behind the altar of the Glass Cathedral. Kataros walked beside her, dressed in dragonscale and the old armour of some dead rider, hostility oozing from her every pore. A mistake, bringing this alchemist instead of Bellepheros, and Zafir already felt it. They reached the room with its empty plinth where the Earthspear had once been. Halfteeth at the front opened the iron-bound door deeper into the tunnels. They filed through.

It knows you. You belong to it. Aruch's words on the day he'd crowned her.

The door closed, a dull metallic boom. Zafir shivered as Diamond Eye drifted in and out of her thoughts. He was gliding the updraughts that wrapped the cliffs of the Purple Spur. She envied him. She wanted the wind in her hair too, and the huge spaces of the sky around her; not to be wrapped in stone like this, guiding Tuuran's men from memory through dim forking passages, smooth-worn and narrow.

They reached a long hall, dark now but in her memory lit with dozens of alchemist lamps. The enchanted glass torches of the Adamantine Men danced harsh and sharp, light hard-edged enough to cut the eye. The jerking shadows unsettled her, their motion too erratic. The darkness and the walls picked at her corners and frayed her edges. She closed her eyes and thought of racing among the clouds, of howling winds on her face. A dragon-queen had no place for fear. A dragon-queen had no place for doubt.

'I never much liked your grand master,' she said to Kataros beside her. 'He didn't know as much as he thought he did.' Talking made it easier.

'You despised him,' said Kataros. 'Everyone knows it. And he despised you. Thoroughly and completely. Why did you bring me here?'

Zafir faltered as her thoughts burst apart. She laughed, a shrillness creeping at her edges. 'No wonder Hyrkallan locked you up.' She pointed Tuuran to some steps, worn and sandy into a low-roofed maw of darkness, and let him lead the way down. 'Jeiros told me these tunnels lead all the way to the Fury at the bottom of Gliding Dragon Gorge. Is that true?'

'Why am I here?'

'Bellepheros hides his disdain more ably than old Jeiros ever did. I might mistakenly trust him. I know I will not make that mistake with you. That's why you're here. Also because if I must lose an alchemist in these caves then you are the less precious, and because Bellepheros is fearfully old and his knees aren't up to all these steps and Tuuran has better things to do than to carry him. For all these reasons, but most of all because I know, although he cannot say it, that the Black Moon has cut Bellepheros with his knife, and I wish to keep you hidden from our half-god.' The walls pressed at her. The shadows ahead and behind simmered with unkind mystery. She bared her teeth and tried to force the tension out of her voice. 'So. Is it true these tunnels reach all the way to the Fury?'

'Why an alchemist at all?' Hostility like a naked blade. Zafir welcomed it. It kept her mind sharp.

'I asked you a question, Kataros.'

'The Silver King's Ways reach to the gorge, yes, but closer to the top than the bottom. Why an alchemist?'

Zafir laughed. 'You'll have your answer when we get there.'

Into the bowels of the earth with the darkness always creeping behind her. Hours of the same rough-walled passage, on and for ever. Zafir closed her eyes and summoned wind and space around her, below and above. Caves were for alchemists, not for dragon-riders. Not for her. But she'd lived for years with this fool-ish fear and learned the tricks to hold it at bay.

'There was a river here once,' she said, searching for a distrac-tion. 'Its course was changed to create parts of this passage. Jeiros told me that.'

No reply. *Fine. Be that way.*

The tunnel stopped at another iron-bound door. Tuuran pulled at it, but Zafir stopped him. 'You won't get in like that,' she said and snapped her fingers. 'Only an alchemist may open this door. Jeiros told me that too, and that, Kataros, is why you're here. So open it.'

'What if I refuse?' asked Kataros.

Blood-magic? Sealed doors? Jeiros had shown her more than he'd ever intended. 'I only need your blood to open this door, Kataros. How much of it gets spilled is entirely up to you.' Easy here in the dark with the earth wrapped so close around to find her old spite jumping out of its pit to grab her while she looked the other way. Zafir slammed the lid on it and stamped it back.

'I will need a knife,' said Kataros at last. Tuuran gave her a blade.

'Is it bad in there?' he asked.

'I fought a duel with Lystra once,' said Zafir. 'I hated her so very much.' She put a hand on Kataros's shoulder; the alchemist flinched and lurched away as though she'd been stung. 'I'm not here seeking bloodshed.'

'Do you think any of them will believe you?' asked Kataros.

'Not really.'

'Then why should I?' Kataros sliced her palm and placed her hand on the door. It shuddered and groaned ajar. She returned Tuuran's knife, turned her back and stepped away. Zafir pushed the door open and strode into the cave beyond. Darkness swallowed their lights, a yawning void as black as pitch. She had Tuuran leave one of their lamps behind, and together they crossed the cave, a black cathedral of nothingness over smooth pale sand. A whisper of rushing water touched the stillness, and the sound was her guide, rising to a roar as it led her towards a lonely scaffold of old wood and ancient knotted ropes that climbed out of the sand into the shadows and deep black stone of the cavern roof above. Tuuran sent Halfteeth to climb ahead, and then Zafir took his arm and led him to where water swirled a plunging storm from above, a thunder that spattered and sprayed off dark stone outcrops before diving on to some other chasm far below.

'The Silver River flows right through the Spur,' she shouted over the roar. 'From the Great Cliff to the Mirror Lakes.' Last time she'd come this way all they'd had were dim alchemical lamps, and she found herself absurdly grateful to Chay-Liang for their gold-glass torches, so much brighter.

'Holiness!' Tuuran had a strange look to him, intense and urgent. 'Holiness, there is a way to cast the Black Moon out!'

Zafir looked around. Kataros and the other Adamantine Men had stayed close to the scaffold. They were alone. She cocked her head.

'A way to kill him!' Tuuran was nodding, eager for her ear. 'With the spear. He told me.'

'Would sticking him with it do? It seems to have worked for the Silver King.' The torrent of water was strong enough to shake the ground. The air tasted moist. Zafir pulled away and looked at Tuuran. Something was wrong with him. He was ripped up inside like he'd been for months, but there was a hope there again. He wasn't talking about killing, he was talking about setting his friend free. *What do you know?*

'No. Not that. A way to get him out. With the spear.'

What makes you think I want to get him out? But that would crush him.

Shouts came from the scaffold. A wooden platform rattled slow and creaking down through the middle of it. Zafir tugged Tuuran away and climbed on as it reached the ground. She had the wind in her hair and the noise of the water, and stray damp specks of spray on her skin and Tuuran beside her.

'We're at the back of the caves behind the Diamond Cascade,' she said. 'The Zar Oratorium isn't far from here.' She said it as much to herself as to Tuuran. 'I made a promise, Night Watchman. Lystra, if we find her, is to live. Make sure your men know.' She touched his hand. 'Tell me about the spear once we have it. Tell me then.'

Halfteeth was at the top, and he wasted no time laying into

Tuuran about how much he'd enjoyed climbing a slime-covered rickety old scaffold in the pitch dark. Zafir pushed on past, leading the way down a rough-hewn passage, driven by urgent expectation while Diamond Eye rode inside her, watching and listening, looking for thoughts around her, for anyone close. *Little Lystra. You could swing an axe, I'll give you that.* Her ankle twinged at the memory. She'd been in such a towering fury …

They passed a bronze door. Behind it was a dragon trapped in chains, or there had been when she'd come this way before. She walked on. *First things first.*

A jab of warning from Diamond Eye. Zafir closed her eyes and looked at what he saw. 'Two men ahead of us,' she said and stroked her lightning throwers dim, in part for stealth, in part for mercy. She hid her torch and walked with Tuuran at her side, guided by the spill of light ahead, creeping until she turned the corner and there they were: two guardsmen. Adamantine Men. They saw her and gawped in surprise and alarm. Hands flew to axe hafts as they began to bark a challenge.

'Sta—'

Pocket thunder rippled the walls. Twin claps of lightning rattled her ears and left them ringing. Zafir pushed on fast as the two guardsmen arched and fell and clawed out silent screams. 'Make sure they don't get up again!'

Tuuran ripped a glance at Halfteeth. 'But no throat cutting!'

Diamond Eye was already flitting through the minds around her, a greedy ghost stealing flashes of thought and sense. He saw a shaft, a platform starting to rise, a man pulling ropes to lift himself up. Fire to be poured down … Zafir sprinted around the next corner, crashed into a stone wall, torchlight flashing madly back and forth, yelling at Tuuran to move, fast. The shaft. There ahead. She reached it, jumped, caught the edge of the platform with the fingers of one hand and drove the bladeless knife of the Elemental Men straight through the wood and into some poor bastard's foot. Through Diamond Eye she felt the sear of pain. A scream. The platform lurched, stopped, started to fall, and then Tuuran and Halfteeth were there as she dropped, grabbing hold and pulling it down, hauling the solitary watchman off as blood gouted from his boot. They dumped him, and Halfteeth punched him out. Tuuran bounded straight onto the platform, trying to haul himself up without her.

'Don't you dare!' She jumped and pulled herself up beside him. Halfteeth clambered over the edge. The rest would just have to wait. Tuuran and Halfteeth heaved at the winch. Rope creaked and wood groaned as the platform rose. Zafir checked them both at the top, making them wait quietly and out of the way as the others ascended in twos and threes.

When Kataros came, Zafir pinned her to a wall and hissed in her face, 'Queen Jaslyn has my word that I won't hurt her sister Lystra. She keeps her crown, for what it's worth, and Lystra may do the same as long as Jaslyn holds to her peace. You want Jeiros spared? Take me to where they keep the spear and I won't cut out his heart.' The dark, the tension, the walls all around, they were spilling out from her.

Someone comes.

Zafir clamped a hand over Kataros's mouth. *Who?*

A little one.

Zafir drifted with the dragon among stray thoughts. She nudged Tuuran and put a finger to her lips. Gestured a warning.

'Just one,' she whispered.

Tuuran nodded. Halfteeth slipped off into the shadows. The lights from Chay-Liang's enchanted torches dimmed and died. Zafir's hand tightened over Kataros's face, the two of them pressed together against the stone.

'Make a sound and I run you through.' She could feel the alchemist's jaw working under her fingers. Biting down hard enough to draw …

Blood.

Zafir lurched away, spun Kataros around and smashed her face into the stone, dazing her for a moment, then pulled her away and clamped a hand across her face, holding her jaw firmly shut. The other hand whipped out a bladeless knife.

'I will drive this through your head. You'll die before you know it's in you. Don't! I am *not* your enemy!' *Diamond Eye! Read her!*

She is hidden from me.

Potions to hide from dragons. Like the ones Bellepheros used to make, like the one she'd used in Takei'Tarr when the hatchling

Silence had stalked her through the eyrie tunnels. An unease shivered her, but a stray thought too – would they hide thoughts from the Black Moon too, as they did from a dragon?

Halfteeth came back, pulling a dead man by his feet. Zafir let Kataros go.

'Did you *have* to kill him?'

Halfteeth cocked his head. He thought about this for a moment and then nodded.

Zafir snapped back to Kataros. 'I do not want a bloodbath, alchemist, but I will not leave without the spear!'

Kataros glared. 'I'll show you the way if I must.'

Zafir smiled and shook her head. Tuuran shifted silently behind Kataros and wrapped one huge swift arm around the alchemist's neck and squeezed, while Halfteeth grabbed her from the front and held her arms. Zafir shone her torch into Kataros's eyes and watched the panic in them.

'I do not need a dragon to see the betrayal in your thoughts, alchemist. We will find our own way.' *Do you know where it is?*

Yes. I will guide you.

Tuuran let Kataros go. 'She'll wake in a few moments,' he said. 'You want, I'll snap her neck.'

'No, but keep her here until we come back. Don't let her bleed or she'll have you.'

Halfteeth trussed Kataros and shoved a wad of balled-up cloth into her mouth. Zafir lingered a moment when Halfteeth was done and pretended not to see the face he made when he thought she wasn't looking. She touched a finger to the alchemist's skin. Kataros was starting to move again. 'Better than have you turn on me,' Zafir whispered. 'There would be no coming back from that.'

Diamond Eye roved thoughts and memories trapped in the caves of the Spur. Zafir surfed them with the dragon as she led the way. She felt an old twisting glee, the delight of enemies oblivious, triumph amid the murder of others, a vicious hateful delight grown long ago, seeds planted in a child groomed to be a dragon-queen, fed and nourished for as long as she could remember. Yet entwined around them was something much less familiar. A sadness like a strangle-vine. A longing and a wishing for something different.

Her torch raked the tunnels, thin narrow winding things crudely cut from black stone. Tuuran and his Adamantine Men followed, moving brisk and sharp. The air, rank and stale, filled with the ammonia reek of waste, of men squeezed together, worse than the old slave markets of Furymouth and the filthy rooms on Baros Tsen's eyrie where the Scales had lived. She saw glimmers of light ahead, and then the tunnel widened into a fissure rising endlessly into the mountains above, lit by a scatter of alchemical lamps, too few to do more than shake a hopeless fist at the enveloping darkness. Furtive feral eyes watched from behind pillars of stone.

Diamond Eye wandered their thoughts. Men, women and children, wandering here and there, half-starved with nothing to do, with no purpose and no hope.

Sometimes I wish we'd never left the islands, she thought, but the dragon didn't reply.

They crossed the fissure. Tuuran and his men marched around her, a sharp cluster of incipient violence moving quick and taut, lightning and axes at the ready, shields raised, menace barely leashed. The path narrowed again into a winding tunnel branching left and right, twisting and turning ever closer to the spear. They crossed another cave of cowering eyes, of filthy hopeless fugitives. Beyond were passages carved square with niches for alchemical lamps, dusty and empty, the last clinging scatter of some ancient tiling visible now and then on the floor, welded to the stone by age. They were close now, and Zafir could smell the alchemy. She should have asked Kataros how many alchemists were down here ...

The caves opened into a crude mockery of the Silver King's hall of arches. Pools of light spilled out of them. More eyes staring. Her Adamantine Men clustered tight, moving quick, daring anyone to stand in their way. A boy barrelled out of the gloom, turned and froze right in their path. A woman came after him. She skittered to a halt, terrified, twitching, too afraid to flee. Old men and young stared and did nothing. Through Diamond Eye Zafir felt a melange of fear and hostility over a crushing undertow of apathy and despair. Tuuran lunged, scooped the boy in his huge arms and set him down out of the way. The twitching woman darted back into the shadows and both were gone. Zafir stared after them. Her stride faltered. She stopped and then realised she didn't know what she meant to do. Give them food? She didn't have any. Tell them she was their speaker and would set everything right, was that it? And how, exactly, would she do that?

'Holiness?'

They were broken, the men who lived here, and she had nothing to offer them. Nothing.

She marched on. The hall ended in wide steps, ancient stone worn smooth by the passage of feet over a thousand years. The old Palace of Alchemy, part of whatever the Glass Cathedral had been, built so long ago that the stones under these mountains had no memory of dragons.

From before the Splintering, little one. From before the Black Moon.

There were pictograms on the walls in places. Crude carvings. She wanted to stop and look at them, to study them, but there was no time. The spear was close. *People should not live like this, dragon. Your kind have done this to us.*

Five hundred years of alchemy and slavery, little one.

The steps led to a second hall. Straight across was a double door, the only door she'd seen since the alchemy-bound entrance. Zafir stopped. *So what hope does that leave us?*

None, little one. We will soar and hunt. Your kind will burn and die.
There is nothing else?
Nothing.

Zafir offered the darkness a nod and a taut little smile. Queen Jaslyn carried some foolish notion of a day when dragons and dragon-queens might live side by side, but Zafir knew better, had known and understood for as long as she could remember. Dominate or die. That was all there was.

Diamond Eye laughed at her. He did that now and then, when he thought she was a little too much like a tiny flaring dragon.

'The spear.' She nudged Tuuran and pointed at the door across the hall. 'Through there. With Grand Master Jeiros and a pair of alchemists and four Adamantine Men. Are you ready?'

They burst through side by side, her and Tuuran. Musty shadows filled the chamber beyond. Zafir felt the size and the space, stale air that smelled of old dust and wasn't as rank as the feral caves outside. A lamp rested on a table. Four Adamantine Men sat around it, playing dice. Their faces snapped up. Zafir ignored them and went straight for the back room and the alchemists. Alchemists were far more dangerous. Lightning from behind her knocked one of the Adamantine Men sprawling. A second bolt took another one down and then they were on their feet.

'Jeiros! Grand Master!'

Zafir tried to run past them. An Adamantine Man swung an axe at her. She sliced it with her bladeless knife, lopping the haft in two. The soldier jerked and stared, bewildered at what she'd done. She battered him with her shield, trying to keep him off balance. A moment later two of Tuuran's men barged him down. She pushed past, not waiting to see how it ended.

They come.

Half with the dragon's eyes, half with her own, Zafir saw the three alchemists together in the next room starting to move. Crippled Jeiros in impotent fury, two others snatching up knives, ready to cut skin and bleed their lethal blood to burn whatever it touched, or else go crawling into a man's soul. She walked smartly to the doorway, dropped her gold-glass shield and dived through the curtain with a lightning thrower in each hand. She let fly with thunder on the other alchemists before their knives could even move, then levelled both wands at Jeiros, sitting in his wheeled chair beside his bed. The wands were spent, but he had no way to know that.

'Look at me, Jeiros.' She lifted her helm and let him see her face. Her hair still hadn't fully grown back. Maybe in the gloom he wouldn't ...

'You!'

'Who am I, Jeiros?'

'You're dead!'

'Who *am* I, Jeiros?'

'Zafir!' He bared his teeth. 'Zafir the ruiner!'

The Adamantine Spear stood propped in a corner of the room, dumped there like an old broom. Zafir took a moment to savour the look on Jeiros's face – the shock, the horror, the terror, the loathing, all naked in front of her – then she walked past him and took the spear and held it tight. She paused a moment to see if anything would happen, but no, it was like picking up any other spear – no blaze of mystic power, no transformation, no soaring insight, no more than the dozens of other times she'd held it. Just a weapon, lethal, brutal and sharp, perfection in its form. She twirled the spear between her hands and then snapped the point at Jeiros, the tip poised at his throat.

'You despised me from the very start.' She kept the tip perfectly still, touching his skin but not cutting. 'Tell Lystra I have returned on the back of a dragon with the Silver King at my side, with Grand Master Bellepheros and with the sorcery of the Taiytakei.' Her voice trembled, choked by being home, by seeing Jeiros in front of her again. The spear never wavered. 'Two days, Grand Master. I will wait for her in the Zar Oratorium. Fearless under the open sky. She may parley with me then. You may tell her I am not here for either blood or throne, not that I expect either of you to believe it. You may tell her that I have her sister, and I will give her Jaslyn for this spear.'

She wheeled away and left, quickly before he could recover his wits, before the two alchemists she'd stunned found their senses again. She picked up her shield and marched through the chaos outside with the spear held high, visor open, making sure they all saw her face.

'I am Zafir. Dragon-queen. Speaker.'

She left the way they had come. On the way out she stopped at the bronze door close to the scaffold and went inside, in part to see if the story of the spear was true, in part as a mercy to the dragon that the alchemists kept in chains. No one tried to stop her.

28

The Black Moon

Forty days after landfall

Through flickers and glimpses the last shades of Berren Crown-taker, the Bloody Judge of Tethis, once apprenticed to the thief-taker of Deephaven, soars on the wings of the Black Moon. He speaks to the dragons of the eyrie. He commands them to fly and they answer. He feels no snarling resentment from them as he does when the dragon-queen demands their service, only vicious delight and an eagerness to be unleashed. They know him. They remember him. In the deep ferment of the Black Moon's thoughts, they see the future the half-god means to bring, and Berren sees it too.

The eyrie flies west to the setting sun, abandoning Diamond Eye and dragon-queen alike to their fates. A handful of one-time slaves and cripples remains. The Black Moon barely deigns to notice them. They are, to him, as insubstantial as the wind.

Berren sees this new unknown land in snips and snatches between the wax and wane of the Black Moon's veil. Voices and whispers pulled out of the air. Alchemists. The source of their power. The dragons know. A dragon called Snow. A place called the Worldspine. He stands on the rim and sees through the Black Moon's eyes as the eyrie drifts high over a maze of canyons and chasms, lifeless and pale between tangles of churning white water that tumble and slice headlong through pillars of dry dead stone in their rush for the great canyon valley of the Fury.

On and up. The sun sets. The beat of dragon wings goes on. The Black Moon paces the walls over stars and mountain peaks. The moon rises, its silver light a cloak of animosity draped upon the world below. The Black Moon turns his back. He will look at the sky, at the ground, at the stars, at the night, at the sun when it rises, but not at the moon. The moon is dead to him. The moon has cast him out.

The night passes. The sun rises again among mountains that are now towering things, glowering and guarding their territories across deep wide valleys. The eyrie floats on, deeper and deeper. The mountains rise sharper, closer, piled on top of each other, squashed together now. The valleys become ravines while summit snow spreads ever further. Life diminishes and slips away, hiding from the cold in the sheltered depths of the valleys, driven from this freezing airless place. In the distance wait a thousand dragons, tight with a hunger for answers.

He feels the Black Moon's thrill. The half-god has found what he is looking for. The sun comes down, fiery red, and with it a fury of dragons, swirling from the depths of the Worldspine. While the others circle high, so many they darken the sky, a single white hunter lands in the heart of the eyrie yard. The Black Moon walks to greet her. He touches a hand to the dragon's scales.

Beloved Memory of a Lover Distant and Lost. I remember your soul. Your scales shine bright again.

This world is ours now, Black Moon.

I claim your service, Beloved Memory, to overthrow the tyranny of gods who demand we abase ourselves before them. To make the world as it was meant to be. As it ever was.

A thousand years you were gone, Black Moon. That vision is yours, not ours.

The Black Moon touches the white dragon again. With a surge of silver light he reaches to grasp the soul of Alimar Ishtan vei Atheriel and turn her to ash. Then thinks better of it.

The little death, he says as Snow flies away, and all the other dragons with her, all save the handful slaved by the knife at his side, touched by the essence of the ephemeral goddess of the stars, remote and aloof so no invocation will touch her, yet within that knife a power greater than any half-god. *The little death comes and goes, dragon, but a final end to devour you grows even now in Xibaiya. You are dragons. Will you simply bow your heads and fade?*

The sun sinks once more. The tips of the mountains shine like fire while the slopes below grow dark with shadow. The eyrie crests a steep plunge of earth and jutting boulders above the ravine of some nameless river. It drifts into a narrow valley, its flat bottom lush and green, its walls sheer cliffs pitted with fissures, stained with streaks of black and dark green. Tiny trickles of frothing water bubble over the cliffs and dissolve into clouds of spray. In every possible crack stunted trees and bushes struggle to grow. There are tiny streaks of silver which glow at night like moonlight.

The eyrie sinks. The valley ends at a sheer rise of jagged stone. Water bustles from caves at its foot. It skips and rustles between scattered trees and then past a tiny village which is no more than a dozen scraps of huts thrown together, until it tumbles over the edge and into the ravine now left behind. Patches of open ground where men once grew food run wild and abandoned. At the end of the valley the eyrie stops. The Black Moon walks to the rim. He watches the ground rise towards him, a ramshackle spatter of burned-out buildings, of roofless stone walls, little yards, charred-dead skeletal trees, their ruin already choked by grass and vines. He steps off the edge into the rush of air. Hard icy wind rips the breath from his lungs and brings tears to his eyes as he falls. The ground blurs and ...

Stops.

He is upright. Standing. Doesn't know how, just is. The silver light of the Black Moon burns fierce and bright inside him, swallowing everything. Between narrow cliffs all around the sun doesn't touch the ground. It is a twilight place. The river chatters from its caves, shallow over a litter of stone. Close to the water Berren sees an old shield almost as big as a man, and then another with an arrow sticking out of it, half drowned in weeds. Beside them lies a rotting crossbow. When he looks harder he sees more. Axes. Helms. More shields. Metal rusting, warped wood. Some old skirmish, years past.

The Black Moon steps into the water. He walks against its ice-cold rush into the cave. The mountain swallows them, quickly dark save for the silver pouring from the Black Moon's eyes. He whispers words, a name. *Isul Aieha*. A hot fire of vengeance, brewed and festered for a thousand years. He touches the walls, cold and damp as they close too narrow for a full-grown dragon to pass.

The half-god walks on, steps sure and certain in the cold dark water. The cave widens. A sand beach rises to either side, the river quick and agile through it. Abandoned. Flame scoured. The air smells of smoke and a touch of sulphurous fire.

What do you want? Berren tries to stop, to reach out and touch the walls again, to have some sense of something that is his own, but the Black Moon has him in an iron fist, effortless and immense. In a blink the cave is gone and they are in another place, the river vanished, the floor beneath his feet smooth, the walls a tunnel arching steeply until it becomes a chimney, vertical, metal rungs hammered into the rock. Then a place so narrow it seems that even his small frame might not fit through, but the Black Moon walks on, shoulders square, a cloud of black ash wafting in his wake where stone dissolves to let him pass.

Brother. Where are you?

Another blink. The tunnel is gone. He is somewhere new. Screams of old men racked with fear fill his ears in lingering echoes. Alchemists, but they are already gone, greasy chokes of settling ash where they stood. Then water again, the sound of the rush of it, close but out of sight, echoing through chasms and caves. The alchemists have built their tunnels along the course of an underground river, just like they always do.

Isul Aieha. I come for you.

A walkway of wooden boards hung over swirling water. Niches cut into walls. A memory of ghostly white lights. At a narrowing the Black Moon finds alchemists again, the last handful of them, the hold-out survivors of a year and half of dragon siege, of smoke and fire and remorseless starvation. The wooden walkway ends abruptly at a fissure in the stone. A cleft and a voice from the darkness above.

'Who are you?'

'The Black Moon.' His voice echoes around the caves. Berren tries to scream. *Run! Flee! As fast and far as you can!* But his screams are mere soundless thoughts. The Black Moon sinks his hands into stone and carves holds from raw desire. He climbs, fast and sure.

Something touches his skin. It burns and won't be denied, something even the Black Moon can't turn aside. Blood. The blood of an alchemist tinged by the essence of the Isul Aieha, half-god, Silver King, brother in life and death.

The Black Moon stops time. He rises and greets three men stood frozen in a moment. Alchemists. With a single touch he turns two to ash. He reaches inside the last, stealing everything the alchemist knows and leaving him as dust. Memories of dark caves and wizened old men and damp stone. Endless tunnels to a place that has never seen the sun. The Black Moon walks through the memories of the alchemist, and Berren walks helplessly beside him.

Another cavern, and the echoing rush of the underground river returns. The Black Moon points to purple-stained walls. For a moment he addresses the soul he has usurped.

'This, little Crowntaker,' he says, 'these tiny little plants, the alchemists make them into potions. The Scales feed the potions to dragons. But look!' In the silver light of the Black Moon's eyes lines of silver glitter across the damp stone of the cave like snail trails running down the wall. 'My brother awaits, Crowntaker.'

The Black Moon walks on and turns the stone to mist and smoke. A white spiral stair rises inside, the white stone of Baros Tsen's eyrie, the white marble of the Silver Kings that Berren has seen in three different worlds. At the top the Isul Aieha waits, held at the brink of death by alchemy and blood. There he is. The half-god who tamed dragons, pinned spreadeagled to the floor of a tiny sealed room by a hundred iron spikes, each forged with the soul of a blood-mage, whose enchantments hold him fast, body arched in rictus agony, face tipped back, the tendons of his neck ropes against his sallow skin, his mouth torn open in an eternal silent scream.

From a hollow spike driven into the Silver King's skull, a single drop of bright silver drips to a finger-wide channel etched into the floor. It clings to itself and rolls away, a tiny quicksilver marble, and vanishes into the stone.

The Black Moon crouches beside the Silver King, beside his brother the Isul Aieha, and Berren sees the memories of the ten thousand years that lie between them. Walking together, the four great sorcerers of the Quartarch, sun and moon and earth and stars, brothers side by side into the underworld of Xibaiya to face the wrath of the dead goddess and the dark moon she has cast into the sky. The Black Moon clawing his way to life from the brink of extinction after the dead goddess had claimed him, growing whole again with a burning hate buried in his core, a hate for gods and their unending hubris. Cataclysmic enchantments hammered in vengeance to bind the dead goddess for what she has done. Runes carved spanning continents across the skin of the earth, mountains raised, rock rent, the earth split into canyon and crevasse, writing the one word to end all gods, the word written on the last page of the eternal Book of Endings.

But you tore me down, ancient brother. You plucked out my eyes. Such bitter betrayal. He who had sacrificed all but one solitary shred of his soul to the dead goddess that the rest might live in peace.

So he shatters that peace.

War.

Turning on his kin. Weeping as he kills them and takes their eternal moon-given essence. Rewriting his end of days into the skin of the earth. The last scratch of the last sigil. His dragons tear his enemies down, rending them to nothing, carving and burning and weathering them to ash and sand. The Nothing ready to be born from chaos. *Join me.* The last brothers of the Quartarch. God-emperors in waiting for a new creation. *The two of us together, brother.*

The Isul Aieha, the Earthspear held high. Creation shatters to pieces, yet he catches the world as it falls into the abyss. A thousand years of darkness and agony. Sightless. Powerless. Trapped in that hateful embrace. Yearning to be free.

You, brother. You will take my place there.

Berren sees at last the Black Moon's design. The Adamantine Spear, the Silver King's spear, brought to him by the dragon-queen in her ignorance, and charged with the freed force of the dead goddess. Plunged into the Silver King. The Isul Aieha cast into eternal darkness as the Black Moon has been, the Nothing tamed and pinned once more. The world remade, the Splintering undone, gods cast aside and swallowed. One voice, one will. The Black Moon. God-emperor of all.

The Black Moon tears the spike from the Silver King's skull. He reaches his hand inside, the flesh of the Isul Aieha already turning to black vapour, but all he finds are echoes. Ghosts of memories. The Silver King has already gone, and all that is left is an empty shell.

Among the circling dragons of the Worldspine the dragon Silence has waited. She has watched, silent and obscure, but the Black

Moon's unleashing is close, when every dragon must decide. She feels the weave of the world shudder. A taut shiver.

I am Silence.

In the whirlwind of tails and wings that drown the stillness of the sky, the dragons slow and pause as Silence shares what she knows. Xibaiya. The Black Moon. Warlocks and Elemental Men and the secrets the dragon Diamond Eye conceals. The Bloody Judge. Worlds on the cusp of war. Restless dead men walking in dark-shadow catacombs. The Godspike and the storm-dark and the Silver Sea beyond. Another cataclysm, veiled thin and pushing through, naked soon and to the brink beyond which it cannot be stopped. Annihilation, perhaps, or restoration, or some glorious thing unforeseen.

He comes for the spear, Silence tells them. *He demands we serve.*
                    We shall not be slaves.
He is no master to us.

                                        But he is our maker.
                    He will take the spear.
He will force us.
              Like his brother the Isul Aieha.
                                    But he is the Black Moon!
We take the spear.
                    Why? To bargain?
To destroy.

                                        To serve him.

We take it for our own.
We burn the little ones out of their caves.
                    We storm the seven worlds at his side.
                    As we should have done in the beginning.
                    We make the vision whole.

My end will be my own, says the dragon Snow. *Not his. Not yours. Not anyone's but mine.* She is the first to decide, and with her choice she flies away. Others follow. Others do not. Words grow to savagery. Dragon turns upon dragon. With fang and talon, in fire and flame, the storm begins.

*

The Black Moon howls in furious despair. He plunges his hands into the tomb's white stone and ripples through the caves and mountains of the Worldspine, hunting for every single thing that might exist in this frigid stone, ripping life away, flesh to ash to dust, souls and memories torn to shreds, hunting the ghost of the Isul Aieha and finding nothing. He blunders through the echoes, the last lingerings of his brother half-god, but only spectres remain. Anguish and torment. The Isul Aieha, searching to undo what between them they have done, torment and penance and regret.

He sees the great betrayal. He sees the Black Mausoleum, the room of arches. He sees the alchemist called Kataros, and the Silver King's essence inside her opening at last a way back to the Silver Sea, to their home, to the moon with the last of the eternal hundred thousand. He sees the Isul Aieha's seed taken to where he can never reach it. His own trick, played against him.

One tiny piece remains. A fragment of a simulacrum, a fractured reflection.

Brother, whispers the ghost. *Let it go.*

Inside the Black Moon Berren feels the hunger, the crushing weight, the grieving bloody wound of longing for the Silver Sea that has cast him aside.

Bare your heart and plead your sorrows. The moon will forgive.

Tears of silver light streak the Black Moon's face. Remorse and loss for a brother for ever gone, but wrapped inside them a hardness like flint, black and cold as the void.

No.

Under a mountain already dead the Black Moon grips the desiccated skull of his brother and crushes its glass-brittle substance to dust.

No, he says again. He turns to Berren, the last flickering spark inside him, and snuffs the Crowntaker out, irresistible as a dragon breathing fire on a snowflake.

Merizikat

Unholy Merizikat, city of the setting sun, whose catacombs become the last home for the most wicked men embraced within the Sun King's reach. For hundreds of years souls have been damned here, bound in chains, carried across sea and mountain range to be hanged in the dark where neither sun nor moon nor starlight, nor fire nor water nor wind, shall touch their decaying flesh. Souls damned to be trapped in Xibaiya, to mourn and wail for the dead goddess who once dwelt there, but now even her ghost is gone.

In Xibaiya the Nothing spills forth. Unlucky souls are consumed, annihilated, every memory and record wiped away, erased as though they had never been. Others flee the only way they can, infesting brittle old bones to walk again.

29

The Adamantine Legion

Five months before landfall

Rockets flew. The eyrie's underside bloomed with fire, a wreath of flames enveloping its belly, but it came on regardless, dragged by three of the Black Moon's dragons. The others skimmed in from the sea, wings clipping wave crests, tails lashing the water, leaving swirling hissing white-faced foam in their wake. They arrowed at the harbour. Fire and flames lit up the dawn as they shrieked, as they shot among bright-armoured solar exalts and temple-born armsmen and raked the harbour walls. Rockets fizzed and streaked to the air in their wake – out to sea, up the river, into the city, straight at the sky, haphazard and everywhere. Some zinged away on tails of smoke, others spiralled and looped, or simply disintegrated midair. They fell by the docks, among the ships moored in the estuary, on warehouses and shipyards, in open spaces full of wagons, amid warrens of huts and houses amid streets so narrow they appeared little more than cracks in a sea of rooftops. Fire bloomed as each one fell, as their glass tips shattered and the fire trapped within exploded to freedom.

'Hey, big man.'

Tuuran watched the rockets fall. From atop the dome of the Holy Basilica of the Unconquered Sun they looked far away, but he and Berren had been down in the middle of all that shit once, in Dhar Thosis, and he didn't much fancy doing it again. Men were running this way and that along the harbour ramparts. Scorpions fired at the dragons as they wheeled. The dragons swooped, tore the scorpions out of the walls and hurled their mangled remains into the sea, then returned for their scattering crews, burning them, biting them in two, smashing their bones with the lash of a tail, picking men up in their claws and throwing them far across the sky. In the estuary the first ships already had wind in their sails, manoeuvring for the open sea. As Tuuran watched, Diamond Eye dropped from the eyrie rim, her Holiness and her dragon intent on persuading them otherwise.

'You remember what it was like?' Tuuran asked. Quietly he scowled at the scorpion crews. Idiot novices, panicked and hasty, who wouldn't have lasted a day in the Adamantine Guard.

'I remember, big man.' Berren wore a strained look, flecks of silver deep in his eyes, the way he got when the Black Moon let him out but had him on a short leash. The half-god inside was wide awake, no doubting it.

'Do you miss it sometimes? Dhar Thosis?'

'A sky full of rockets? Men screaming and drowning? Smoke. Fire. Couldn't see shit half the time. Crap falling out of the sky all over the bloody place, glass exploding everywhere, splintered stone flying through the air? Miss it?' Berren wrinkled his nose. 'Mostly what I remember is running from one place to the next like a demented monkey, not doing much useful except not dying. But we tore their palace down, big man.'

'Sounds about right.' Tuuran gazed over Merizikat. The Basilica of the Unconquered Sun marked a line across the city hillside where slums blurred to wealth, where alleys and squashed-up filth and wooden sprawl morphed into avenues and parks and the steeper upper slopes of grand stone and colonnades. Further out, the city was ringed by grand temples and palaces. 'Going to be the same here, is it?' he asked. Dhar Thosis. The first time he'd seen a dragon in ten years of slavery. Diamond Eye and Her Holiness had gutted that city, and the horde of ravening blood-crazed slaves let loose from Shrin Chrias Kwen's ships had run through its corpse like maggots, leaving nothing but bones.

He looked hard at Berren. Dhar Thosis was the last time Crazy Mad had been just plain Crazy. Before the Black Moon. Before he'd started turning people into ash and stopping time and ripping his way through people's heads and stabbing them with that shit-born knife of his. Back when the world had been right and proper.

Berren shrugged. 'Going to put the world to rights, big man.'

'Says Berren the Crowntaker or says the half-god inside him?'

Berren shook his head and turned away. They both knew this

was the half-god's doing. 'He never touched you. You and her. Her because of the spear she's bound to. You because of me. You're both free to go whenever you want. Not like the rest.'

Tuuran's eyes flicked to the Starknife on Berren's belt.

'He'll keep doing it, big man, no matter what your dragon-queen says.' Berren shrugged. 'You know I tried to get her to cut him out of me?'

'Oh? How'd that go?'

'Not as well as I'd hoped.'

Tuuran got up. The heart of the basilica was a colossal dome of enchanted glass and Scythian steel, crowned by a second much smaller dome of beaten gold and with a walkway around it. From that upper balcony Tuuran could see everything. He turned to Berren and gripped his shoulder. 'Whatever I have to do,' he said. 'One way or another. Anyone, anything.' He cocked his head. 'You in there, Black Moon? You listening? Why not a dragon? Wouldn't that be better? Tell me what I need to do to get my friend back and I'll do it …'

A dazzling light burst from the sky, a beam straight from the sun. It smashed into one of the hatchlings. The dragon screamed and dropped away, wreathed in dazzling white flames, crashing into the city below. Tuuran caught a glimpse of it, burning, rampaging through the streets and setting fire to everything it touched before it melted and died. The silver in Berren's eyes flickered.

'You remember I told you a story once, how I went fighting for the Sun King to earn the money for my slave girl?' Berren looked out over Merizikat. 'Was here. And that was the sun priests of the Dominion bringing down the fire of their god …' His expression changed to something painful. 'Got to put to an end to that malarkey. He's coming, big man. You really should go now.' Berren's eyes flared silver.

The other hatchlings scattered across the city. A second blast of sunfire struck the eyrie. It raked back and forth. Where it touched the rim the black stone turned bright orange, to lava that ran over the edge and rained a second deluge of fire on the city below. Brilliant silver light burst from the Crowntaker's eyes as the balcony door opened behind him. A solar priest stood frozen in the entrance. The Black Moon took two quick steps, touched him and turned him to ash. He did the same to another. A third priest erupted in a dazzling light of his own, golden and warm, but the silver of the Black Moon devoured and consumed him. The half-god pressed on past into the dome and calmly closed the door behind him, and after that Tuuran didn't see what happened and didn't much care to. Howled evocations echoed, commandments hurled like weapons, curtains of light sliding through one another to score the sky as the Basilica of the Unconquered Sun lit up brighter than a lighthouse.

Enough of that. Didn't look like a place for hanging about. He rode his sled across the rooftops to where his legion waited. Seventy-odd men and women, half survivors from the eyrie, half of them from the night-skin ship her Holiness and her dragon had sunk. Knife-stabbed and soul-cut, every last one of them as best he knew. Made to be loyal. Forced to obey. The only ones missing, the only ones left up on the eyrie, were the enchantress and the alchemist and Myst and Onyx. The rest were here, every last one of them, young and old. Most didn't know which end of a sword was which, but they were all soldiers now, because the Black Moon simply didn't care. Tuuran had kept the white witch busy to exhaustion as they'd crossed the sea. Every man and woman had a sled, each wore enchanted gold-glass armour, each carried a pair of lightning throwers and a huge glass shield. The rest was up to them. It might be enough, he hoped, at least to keep them alive.

He took a moment to look at them. *His* legion. Not many of them yet, and most weren't fighters and never would be, but it took his breath away thinking what it would be like to have a thousand men armed and armoured like this. A legion of true Adamantine Men with sleds and lightning. Unstoppable ...

Most of them were scared witless. A handful couldn't wait. That handful would do, and fate and luck would see to the rest, one way or another. He pointed to the palace at the top of the hill of Merizikat. They all knew what they had to do, so there was no point in some great speech. He looked at them instead, met the eyes of the ones he thought he could trust one by one, and then rode his sled as fast as he dared, low over the rooftops of the city, trusting the men who were truly soldiers to follow. Never mind the palace walls and its gates and its heavy iron doors and its hundred guards. Never mind everything the sun-born kings of the Dominion thought made them safe. *Here I come.* Tuuran grinned. *Death from above. Like a dragon, only worse*.

He spotted a balcony high over the front of the palace, the sort of place where a king stood to wave at his distant subjects, safe and out of reach of any harm. A set of gilded doors behind it beckoned him, and there was no one standing watch there with a bucket full of crossbows like there ought to be. He grinned, then glanced over his shoulder to the basilica and wished he hadn't. An eerie light shone from every crack and window of the dome, a flickering brilliance of swirling silver and gold. It made his stomach churn.

Best not to think about it.

He shot over the outer palace walls. Kept his eyes on the waiting balcony as he skimmed a labyrinth of gardens and yards and stables, an archery field, a jousting circus, maybe a bear pit, other things that didn't make much sense when all you had eyes for was racing through the sky as fast as you dared and praying not to fall off. Soldiers on the ground pointed up. Maybe they shouted something, but if they did then he couldn't hear them over the rush of wind. *You're all too slow, you lazy shits.* Archers came next. He saw a man stringing a bow. The first arrows flew, but only a handful, wild and hopelessly wide. He braced to hit the balcony, flipped the sled, trying to make it stop at the last moment, lost his balance, flailed horribly, and jumped as the sled hurled them both smashing into the doors. He made sure to hit them axe first. They burst open. He rolled and came up on his feet, battered and shaken but with all his bits still working, so that was something. He was at the end of a wide gallery. Thick carpet, mustard yellow. Panels of pale wood. Alcoves on both sides, neat and regular, all very pretty, each with a statue or a bust set just so, but more to the point were the six armed men at the far end. Decked out in fine golden armour and armed with halberds and short stabbing swords ...

That was the opposition? Flame, they might as well have set some kittens on guard for all the difference it would make. He pulled his axe out of the mangled door, took a deep breath and bared his teeth. *Right then.*

'Tuuraaaaaaaan!'

He had about a split second to throw himself flat as the next sleds reached the balcony. The first came hurtling way too fast, clipped the mashed doors and flipped into a spin. Halfteeth fell off and rolled across the carpet ahead. The next came a little slower. A woman half jumped, half fell, and landed beside him. Her sled smacked into Halfteeth as he was getting up and knocked him straight back down again. He swore. He was still moving though. Good stuff, that witch armour.

The men with the halberds were yelling their lungs out, but they were holding their ground, not charging like they ought to. Mistake. Tuuran took a moment. Checked behind, but the next sled riders were coming in more carefully. Not as brave or not as stupid, he wasn't sure which. Should have practised this a bit more, but too late to be worrying about that now.

'You two good?' Halfway along the gallery the walls opened either side to a wide double flight of stairs that curved towards the back of the palace as they swept down. Soldiers were already running up them, yelling and howling, swords drawn. Not many, not yet, but there would be plenty more soon enough. Had to put an end to that. Cut them off, and fast.

The woman nodded. Flame, but she was so short he could have picked her up and thrown her. Halfteeth let out a volley of curses and drew his lightning wand, and that, Tuuran reckoned, would have to be enough. 'Fast and brutal,' he howled. 'No quarter, no stopping.' He took off down the gallery. The soldiers at the far end were exalts, the armour told him that much. The best the Dominion had to offer. Might even have been a fair fight one on one, hand to hand, but fuck that. Tuuran paused a moment, let Halfteeth and the woman run past him, and fired off a blast of lightning down each stairway, sending the men running up scurrying back for cover. More Adamantine Men were landing. They were strung out, each flying their sled at their own pace. Maybe he should have kept them together, shepherded them, but at least this way he knew the ones who got here first had the balls for a fight.

'You!' He levelled a finger at the next man along. 'Hold these stairs. Twelve men either side then send the rest on through. Anyone tries to come up, let them chew on lightning.'

Halfteeth and the short woman had stopped, waiting for him, giving a wary eye to the six bellowing exalts. Flame! He bawled at them, 'Need me to hold your hand, do you?' He hit the exalt wearing a bigger golden plume in his helm with a bolt of lightning wound up as far as it would go. The exalt flew backwards, slammed into the door behind, jerked and spasmed a few times and fell twitching. 'Like that, you dogs!' Sod fair fights. He threw another bolt from his last wand and then fell on the others with his axe. Another explosion of lightning told him someone else had got the idea. The exalt in front of him swung. Tuuran caught the halberd with the shaft of his axe. Two more thunderclaps went off, felt like right beside his ear. The exalt in front of him flew back and smashed into the wall, knocking down a bust. His back arched and his arms and legs jerked up and down and then he was still. The air smelled of scorched skin and burned hair. That was more like it. No mercy, no quarter …

Another thunderbolt. Lights danced in front of his eyes. His legs gave way. He stumbled and stretched out a hand to catch himself. Sparks arced from his gold-glass gauntlets to the floor.

'Not at me, you shit-stained blankets!' He twisted and rolled but the exalts were already done for, lightning-crisped, all of them. The short woman stooped beside him.

'You all right, boss? Halfteeth caught you with his lightning.'

'He did, did he?' Tuuran picked himself up. His legs felt taut as though every muscle had clenched tight. More thunderbolts bellowed behind him. His men defending the stairs. He turned for Halfteeth, thought about punching him a few times and making him Noteeth, then thought better of it. 'This witch-made gold-glass armour might mostly turn our lightning, but fucking ouch and be more fucking careful.'

The exalts had been guarding an ornate double door of mahogany with the seal of the sun set in gold right in the middle of it. Mahogany and gold. Meant something, that did. Crazy had told him so once. Something important. Couldn't remember what, but sod it: guarded meant something behind that was valuable. Made it as good a way to go as any.

Cracks of lightning shook the walls. He had enough men at the stairs to hold them now, lined up behind their shields and with Chay-Liang's wands to rain thunder-death down all day if they had to.

'Hold your nerve, lads, that's all you need to do.' The last of his makeshift legion were arriving, stacking their sleds, slinking in slow and reluctant. The ones who didn't want to be here, who didn't know what to do. Tuuran turned back to the mahogany door. Couldn't see how to open it, but a door was a door and he had an axe. The first blow hacked off the seal of the sun. The next splintered enough wood to show him the metal bars across the back of it.

'Shit!' He grabbed Halfteeth. 'These doors open, you murder anyone who comes out. Got it?' He ran the length of the gallery, back to the balcony, yelling at the soldiers still coming in to get out of the way until he found the men at the back who'd come with a crate of the enchantress's bombs. Black powder. Would make life interesting, this would. All the way across the sea he'd drilled and drilled and drilled his tiny ragtag legion, even in the weeks before they left, between stockpiling food and water for the journey. Even the ones who were next to useless knew how to form a wall of shields and keep back dragon-fire. They knew how to protect one another and they knew how to throw lightning. A few knew how to fight with a sword or an axe or a mace, but they learned that on their own time, because when you had a lightning thrower on each arm, who gave a shit for swords and axes ...?

Bombs were different. They hadn't practised bombs. He picked up one in each hand and weighed them. Didn't even know how hard he had to throw them or how far away he needed to be to be safe.

'That's one big pair of tits, boss.'

The lightning from the top of the stairs was getting fierce. Crossbow quarrels stuck out of the walls and pinged off glass shields. He saw more than one already cracked. Plenty of repair work to keep the witch busy after they were done. He shoved the bombs at whoever it was with the smart mouth. Didn't know if dropping one was enough to make it explode. They were glass, so he reckoned maybe it was.

'They'll bring scorpions to the stairs before much longer. When they do, throw these at them. That'll shut them up.' Not that half these soldiers even knew what a scorpion was, but he figured they'd learn quick enough once they had one pointed at them. He grabbed the sled with the rest of the bombs, sprinted down the gallery, snatched hold of Halfteeth. 'You two!' He shoved the sled against the door, then pulled Halfteeth and the short woman back a good way because he had no idea how big these bombs really were.

'We cover the men behind us.' He pushed Halfteeth to one side of the gallery and pulled the woman beside him to the other. He pushed her against the wall and set his shield beside hers. They probably looked ridiculous, him and her together, him as big as he was and her small enough she was almost a child. 'I'm sure you've got a name, but once you're in the legion you get another. You can be Tiny.' He turned his head and roared back down the gallery. 'Everybody duck!' Gave it a moment to sink in and then threw a bolt of lightning at the box of bombs on the sled beside the door. Cringed.

'Tiny?' said the woman beside him when nothing happened. 'That's shit.'

'You're in the legion. You take what you're given.'

The woman propped her shield, kicked over a statue and smashed it with an ashgar as tall as she was. She picked up the statue's head and offered it to Tuuran. 'Last man who said that ended up with a trowel rammed through his eye,' she said. 'Halfteeth calls me Snacksize. Still a bit shit, but I've let him long enough that it'll do. You want to throw this at those bombs of yours or shall I brain you with it?'

Tuuran shrugged. '*You* throw it. Bombs go bang, you can be called whatever you like; bombs do nothing and you put up with what I choose.'

The woman snorted, gave him a look and threw. The explosion hit like a wall, hard enough it tossed him off his feet. Pieces of glass faster than arrows shattered on his shield, a cascade of noise, or maybe that was his ears ringing from the explosion. Choking sulphurous smoke filled the gallery, making him weep. He trotted forward, spluttering and waving at the air as if that would make the stench go away. Pieces of twisted metal hung from the stonework, but the doors were gone. Not so much staved in as disintegrated. A good chunk of floor had gone the same way.

No time for thinking, not now. He ran and jumped the gap. The room beyond – what was left of it – was square and as tall as the gallery. Richer than Tuuran had ever imagined possible, or at least it had been before some vandalous bugger had let off a bomb right beside it. Rugs ran from wall to wall; they looked so thick and soft that they might have made him want to take off his boots and walk barefoot if they hadn't been on fire in a few places and smouldering in a good few more. A tapestry covered the far wall and told, in embroidered reds and golds and bronzes and every colour between, the story that everyone in the Dominion knew, of the creation of the first men by the holy sun. There were paintings on the other walls, all portraits, a good few of them slightly shredded now, bookcases that had toppled in the shudder of the blast, a credenza, tables with bottles and glasses scattered and smashed. A pair of swords hung drooping from the far wall, one with a hilt of pure gold ...

'Come on! Come on!'

Shallow spiral steps rose curling through the middle of the room. Tuuran bounded up them, Halfteeth and Snacksize and another man right behind him. Speed was all that mattered, times like this. Shock. Wouldn't be long before the exalts brought priests with their sunfire. Maybe those rockets from the harbour, if they still had any left. When that happened, even the witch's lightning wouldn't be enough ...

The stairs ran through a library. Books and what looked like an alchemist's workbench. No people. Running footsteps from above. Tuuran raised his shield as two soldiers head to toe in gold plate came clattering down at him. He let lightning fly and then threw himself out of the way as the two exalts tumbled past down the stair, arms and legs twisted and flailing and with a smell of burned skin lingering behind them. He clutched his ears, ringing from the explosion and never mind all these fucking thunderbolts. Took a moment trying to shake the noise out of his head. Halfteeth and his other friend pushed past; Tuuran chased on, still shaking himself. Rattled his bones, all that thunder ...

The steps spat them into a square room. First thing Tuuran saw was a man in a yellow robe. Second thing was Halfteeth's friend bursting into flames, screaming, haloed in golden fire and burned to ash. Halfteeth fired both his lightning wands. Yellow robe flew off his feet, up into the air and smashed into a wall. Snacksize caught him in the face with another bolt. He fell like a sack of dead meat. Twitched a few times, skin black and flaking. A surge of movement came at Halfteeth from behind, a fat man wearing the clothes of a king and wielding a hatchet, about to bring it down on Halfteeth's head. Tuuran swung his axe and took hand and hatchet together, and then something hit him from behind, staggering him. He whirled. A man with a sword who'd been stupid enough to swing it like a club and not take a hopeful stab for the gaps in the gold-glass. Tuuran roared. The swordsman jumped away, but that only landed him right next to Snacksize, who punched him in the face with an armoured gauntlet. Down he went.

Took a few more minutes of kicking in doors and throwing lightning before Tuuran realised he'd lopped a hand off the arch-solar of Merizikat himself, and the buffoon with the sword was his son and heir. He dragged them back to the gallery and the stairs and held them there, one each side, and let them scream at the soldiers in the hall below until everyone got the message that it was all over, and could they please stop shooting crossbows at their king. The Black Moon, last Tuuran had seen, was enjoying himself with the half-god sport of disintegrating priests, and her Holiness and her dragon were out over the estuary explaining with judicious fire why none of the ships anchored there should think about sailing away just now, and so it all got a bit awkward when the arch-solar started blubbering questions like 'What do you want?' and 'Why are you here?' Mostly they seemed to think it was him who ought to have the answers, which was a bugger, because Tuuran hadn't the first idea why they'd come to Merizikat at all, never mind started on sacking the place. Didn't help that he was in a shitty mood that had been getting steadily worse ever since they'd left the islands. Zafir. Dragons. Half-gods. Fuck the lot of them.

He went looking. Wasn't supposed to take long. Five minutes on a sled to the basilica to find the Black Moon, but no such luck. He saw her Holiness on the back of her dragon snatch up a little skiff from the river and use it to scoop water and dump it on the burning city somewhere. Flame knew who that left in charge in the palace. Halfteeth, probably, which wasn't likely to end well. He supposed he ought to care, but then her Holiness headed off up that way, and that was good enough.

He found Berren wandering the city. Wasn't hard to spot the flashes of silver light now and then. Clouds of dirty smoke drifted through the docks, and parts of the riverside slums were on fire. Berren was meandering about the little squares and squashed alleys behind the basilica. He had a sword in one hand and a shield in the other, yelling and shouting challenges at anyone who would listen. Judging by the trail of dead he'd already got himself into a fight or two. Tuuran watched him walk up to a gang of looters, out making the most of the chaos, and pick a fight with far too many to have a chance of walking away. He watched Berren take one of them down before someone caught his legs with a spear. Over he went, and the rest were on him, knives and fists raised, a bloody and brutal murder, except that as the first blade fell there was a flash of silver light and half of them exploded into greasy black ash. The rest had the sense to run. Berren staggered back to his feet, howling at them how they were cowards. He might have gone after them too, until Tuuran came and stood in his way. There was a madness in Berren's face. The old madness that had once got him the name Crazy Mad, but Tuuran couldn't call him that any more. Crazy had been the name of his friend.

'He won't let you,' said Tuuran curtly. He felt the Crowntaker's hurt, felt it deep. Poor bastard was trying to get himself killed, but they both knew it wasn't going to work, and surely he'd tried enough times now to give up. 'He won't. He just won't. You know that.' He put a hand on Berren's shoulder and then glanced at the basilica. The great doors hung open and the insides were a black-scorched ruin. Wafts of a fine dark ash breezed out in gasps, as if the basilica itself was wheezing a last few dying breaths. 'What—' But no. He didn't want to know what had happened in there. Really, really didn't.

Berren closed his eyes and collapsed into Tuuran as though he was some grief-stricken lover. 'Why, Tuuran? Why don't I just die?'

Tuuran shook him. Made Berren meet his eye. Peered closely. 'Is he in there, Crazy?'

'Always.'

'Is he listening?'

'Always that too, big man.' The Crowntaker pulled away. Turned his back. 'He's missing a piece, just like me. Just like

Skyrie was before me. It burns him up, doing the things he does. He's weak from the fight now.' Berren shrugged. 'Thought that might be enough to make it end, but no. Nothing ever is. But yes, he's here. He hears you.'

Tuuran gripped Berren and spun him round so they were face to face. 'I don't know what any of this is any more,' he said. 'I don't know why we came here. I don't know what he wants. I killed a round dozen men today and I haven't the faintest idea why.' He snarled and spat. 'I don't know shit about anything – never did – and death comes when death comes, but a man should surely know the why of it when he takes another's life. I meant what I said. If there's a way to take this half-god out of you, Silver King or not, I'll find it. My life. You hear me? And when I find that way, I'll stop at nothing to see it through.'

Berren nodded, though not like he really believed it. He was staring at something on Tuuran's neck. 'What's that?'

'What's what?' Tuuran ran a finger over his skin. Yes, a roughness. A patch of it. Had those starting up all over the place these last few weeks. Bloody nuisance. 'Chafing.' Or that's what he told himself. Or maybe some sort of stupid rash. Had to be. Too much other shit to worry about for it to be anything else.

Berren gave him a hard look, long and steady. 'Chafing, big man? Really?'

'You think you know better?'

'I think you need to go see your alchemist, that's what I think.' Eventually Berren turned away, the light of the Black Moon gone from his eyes. 'Never mind. Ah shit, big man, do what you want. Let's get drunk.'

A preposterously dumb idea with the Black Moon about, a city in flames and barely fallen before a tiny conquering army that he was supposed to be leading, but Tuuran had been past caring for weeks now. And yes, if he was honest for a moment, he knew damn well what that patch of rough skin was, and all its little friends he kept hidden out of sight. Fucking dragons. Fucking Hatchling Disease from the fucking hatchling back from that night on the islands; and so yes, all things considered he reckoned that maybe everyone else could manage without him for a while, whether they liked it or not.

'You think it would work on me?' asked Crazy.

'What would?'

'The dragon-disease.'

'No.' Tuuran made a face. 'And don't you even think about looking at *me* to give it to you just so you can see what happens.'

They looked at one another for a long time, and then Berren burst out laughing, and so did Tuuran, and for a moment he could imagine that Berren was Crazy again, and nothing else. 'Fine. I'll go see Bellepheros.' And a good part of him was thinking how it might just be a lot easier to do nothing at all, but he'd gone and made another stupid oath, hadn't he? And dying was always just a cheap way out. He slapped Berren on the back. 'You were here once before, right? Recommend a good place to get shitfaced?'

'Disappear for a day, eh?'

'At least. Let her Holiness sort this shit out. Fuck knows she'll do a better job of it than you or I.'

30

The Catacombs

The Black Moon came to Chay-Liang after the storming of Merizikat. He wanted an army, he said. A thousand men, not a meagre hundred, and she would arm it. She was to move her workshop and equipment into the palace. He already had rooms put aside for her, a whole tower if she wanted it; and Liang did as she was asked because the Black Moon had cut her with his knife and left her no choice. Week after week he kept her at work until she was dripping with the fatigue of it. She barely saw Bellepheros for a time, up to his neck in his own problems, starting with trying to make sure that the arch-solar didn't die from Tuuran cutting off his hand.

Lines of men came to the palace, summoned by the arch-solar to his court. The Black Moon sat on the throne of Merizikat with his knife, waiting for them. Three little cuts. *You. Obey. Me*; and with that he made the city into his slaves, one by one. The Dominion soldiers, the exalts and the temple armsmen, he sent to Tuuran; the rest he returned to be about their work, not caring what it was save that they give their all to their new cause and proclaim the virtue of their new god. For his soldiers Liang made sleds, armour, lightning-throwers and anything else the half-god could be bothered to imagine. Each day Tuuran brought her another dribble of men. 'Soldiers recruited into the legion,' he would say, and Liang knew that meant they'd been stabbed by the Black Moon's knife, and surely even Tuuran wasn't so stupid that he didn't see what was happening. He had his own problems now, though, so perhaps they blinded him. The Hatchling Disease. Bellepheros, in one of their fleeting moments together, claimed Tuuran had caught it when the first dragon hatched in the islands. While Belli worried about how much further the disease might already have spread, Liang couldn't help wondering whether it hadn't come from a dragon at all, but from the dragon-queen instead.

After the first weeks Tuuran stopped bringing new soldiers to dress in her armour and carry her lightning, though he still huddled away with Bellepheros, claiming his potions to keep the dragon-disease at bay; each time he stalked away white-knuckle tense. Now and then she and Belli talked between themselves in the scant time they had of how to be rid of a half-god. She found herself thinking that perhaps Tuuran having the dragon-disease was no bad thing, that it gave her and Belli a hold over him; and yes, maybe it was unworthy of her, but violent use brought violent thoughts, and Liang would have murdered the Black Moon in any way to hand if only there was something that might have worked.

Not that there weren't plenty of others willing to try. She lost track of the number of times Merizikat assassins tried to kill him. A dozen by the end of the first month. He made no effort to stop them. He made it easy, even, and then turned them to black ash as soon as their knives touched him. Liang half wished that those knives would come after the rest of them too, until she realised that that largely meant her. Zafir stayed on the eyrie after the first day of anarchy, aloof, circling the city now and then with her dragon to remind everyone of the threat she posed. Sulking, perhaps – Liang had no way to know; but even from her eyrie Zafir surely knew what the Black Moon was doing. She couldn't be oblivious to it, could she, not really? So much for *no more slaves*. Leopards never changed their spots.

They'd been in Merizikat for a month and a twelvenight when Bellepheros rushed to the eyrie at the news that Onyx was about to give birth, and Liang went with him to help because she saw so little of him these days and liked to have him near when she could. As an excuse she took a company of Tuuran's soul-cut soldier-slaves to collect crates of broken glasship debris from the rim for use moulding sleds and armour. When she brought her sled over the rim she saw Zafir was on the wall, sitting beside her dragon, looking out over the city, Myst beside her stroking the dragon's scales, fat with another of Tuuran's little bastards waiting to pop. Stupid bed-slave was infatuated with Zafir's monster. It made Liang want to shake her and shout in her face: *Don't you see what they are? Don't you see what* she *is? Either one would toss you aside without thought or care, without remorse or regret, without remembering you even have a name.*

The dragon turned an eye. He looked at Liang and cocked his head.

'You know what he's doing, don't you?' Liang shouted. 'You *do* know what he's doing with that knife, dragon-slave?' Zafir didn't even look round.

Onyx gave birth to a son. She called him Tuuran. A few days later Myst followed her and gave birth to a son of her own. Another little Tuuran. At night, afterwards, Liang curled in bed with Belli. She could have punched him sometimes for his fatalism. The Black Moon had made her a slave, and every night she paced the cell of the half-god's will like a restless lion. Bellepheros, ensnared exactly the same, simply fell asleep.

'Why don't you scream?' she asked him 'Doesn't it make you want to murder something?'

Bellepheros shrugged. 'Should a slave care who is his master?' A nasty little barb, because she'd said much the same once about Baros Tsen, but he put an arm around her to tell her he didn't mean it. 'I grew up a slave to dragons, Li. Speakers come and speakers go, but the dragons are always there. I suppose I'm used to it.'

'I'm not. I can't stand it.'

'Then perhaps you have more in common with her Holiness than you thought.'

The day after that a Merizikat assassin stuck a knife in him. It wasn't the cleverest way to try and kill a man whose blood was at the heart of his sorcery, but it was enough of a warning that the Black Moon sent Belli back to the eyrie and told him to stay there, and after that Liang hardly saw him any more. She took to leaving her balcony door ajar and a sled outside so she could fly to him without the half-god seeing her go. She went to her old workshop there and dusted off the enchanted glass dragon she'd made years before. It was the size of a cat, a crude prototype for the two golden automata she'd made for her new master of the time, Sea Lord Quai'Shu, who in turn had given them as a wedding gift to some faraway dragon-prince years ago. In Takei'Tarr she'd once used it to spy on the Vespinese and then the Elemental Men, until the Elemental Men had noticed and, with very polite menace, requested that she stop. She took to flying it again, wrapped an enchanted silk tight over her eyes until the glass dragon shifted and woke and its crystal eyelids opened and Liang saw through its amethyst pupils. She sent it scurrying through the galleries of the Merizikat palace, stalking the deepest shadows, settled it lurking in gloomy corners, a silent sentinel statue spy, watching the Black Moon, listening to his plans; and though Zafir and her dragon roamed far and wide and rarely came down, it wasn't long before she caught the two of them together. Twin evils dancing swords about each other. She saw the Black Moon's gaze blaze silver, and if she had to give anything at all to Zafir it was that the dragon-queen was the only one who could look the half-god in the eye when he was that way. She met him head on every time. Face to face he stood a finger shorter than her, and she never let him forget it.

Today Zafir was in a temper. 'Why are we still here? It's been nearly two months. I have fifty ships penned into the mouth of the river and not one of their captains suggests that more than eight could work together to pull our eyrie across the—'

'A half-god I called brother made it, that eyrie.' The Black Moon raised a disdainful hand. He touched splayed fingers to Zafir's face. Zafir swatted him away. 'When the river of history swelled to a flood he chose to stand upon the wrong bank, and for that I took his soul. On which bank do you stand, dragon-queen?'

'There is an army assembling to drive us into the sea,' said Zafir. 'I know.'

'Then why are we still here? For what? What does Merizikat have for you?'

'The catacombs, dragon-queen.' The blaze in the Black Moon's eyes faded to an ember. He waved his dismissal at Zafir, disdainful and bored, and turned his back, and for a moment Liang thought Zafir might hit him, but she didn't. She whirled on her heel and stalked away, barely checked fury swirling about her like a cloak in a storm. Liang unwrapped the silk from her eyes and went back to her glass. The same rider-slave she'd known in Takei'Tarr, petulant and swaddled in her own wants with never a whit of care for anyone but herself. If she'd seemed different in the islands, it had been an aberration. Leopards and spots.

She stared at the glass she'd been working. All inspiration had fled today, and so she went out to her balcony and looked over this alien city, at its unfamiliar domes and blocky stone mansions, its flat-topped houses. She tried to remember the cities of her home. Xican, all buried in stone, cliffs full of doors and windows and ladders, gantries and the glorious glass of the Palace of Leaves. Khalishtor, with its red-tile roofs and wide open spaces full of green, its towers of glass and gold. She missed them, and then wondered: was this what it had been like for Belli when Quai'Shu's Elemental Man had stolen him from the dragon-lands and brought him to Takei'Tarr, this sickness, this longing for home? He'd told her so, but she realised now that she'd never understood. How could she?

As she turned away she caught a flash of light from the eyrie. A sled. She watched it arc over the city and wondered who it could be. It was heading for the basilica where Tuuran spent most of his time, something to do with the catacombs and the dead who walked down there.

She sent the glass dragon in pursuit to spy. There were sides now. Battle lines to be drawn and they all knew it. There was the Black Moon and Zafir, and Tuuran reluctant beside them, and then there was her and Bellepheros and everyone else in the seven worlds.

The figure on the sled was Zafir.

Zafir on a sled, not on the back of her dragon.

Truly curious now, Liang settled into the tiny golem thoughts of her automaton. She kept her distance as Zafir descended towards the basilica and landed on its glass dome and hurried inside. A spiral of stairs made a sweeping arc around the basilica's inner walls, bright and gold, warm and sun-dappled. Amid the pale yellow stone and the wooden benches and the hundred golden effigies of the unconquered sun, people looked up and stared, priests and other Merizikat folk. They all knew of the dragon-queen by now, and Zafir wore her glass armour and dragonscale and made no effort to disguise who she was. Zafir ignored them and marched into the cloisters behind the basilica, between the twin statues of the moon and the stars that stood guardian to the catacomb shafts. A handful of Tuuran's soul-cut Merizikat men waited there, bored and idle, and Liang had to wait for a chance for her little dragon to scurry between them unseen. She caught up as Zafir descended into the gloomy vaults that antechambered the dark depths of the catacombs. Grated shafts driven from the basilica square above lit patches of stone in bright sunlight, while elsewhere lamps and lanterns fought against the shadows and lost. Carvings covered the walls down here, signs and sigils of warding and protection, unfamiliar save the two or three that Liang recognised from her brief foray into the forbidden texts of the Rava.

Zafir walked briskly on, stiff and uneasy in the dark. An Adamantine Man greeted her. One of Tuuran's favourites. Halfteeth, was it? Liang had no idea, nor of what the Black Moon wanted from under the basilica, but he was surely after something, and she dearly wanted to know. Halfteeth led Zafir down a grand stairway shrouded in gloom, broad steps that went on and on. Liang scurried after, glass flitting from shadow to shadow. The dragon-queen, her movements so languid and fluid when she strutted her eyrie and the Black Moon's palace, looked sharp and taut here, head twitching as she looked about, side to side and up overhead, always on edge and on guard. There *was* something that got to her then …

The stair descended into a maze of vaults, of brick archwork and shadows. Lights flickered and gleamed, peeking from behind columns and vanishing again, winking in and out. Where she thought no one would see, Zafir paused and shuddered and then gathered herself as Halfteeth beckoned her on. They crossed in near darkness, Liang struggling to keep them in sight as she hopped and skipped and danced, trying to keep the click-clack of glass talons on stone from echoing too loud while creeping among the vaults' myriad lights, smitten with curiosity. They passed into a dim tunnel, skeleton-filled alcoves to one side, pits full of bones and skulls to the other. In her distant room Liang's skin crawled. Zafir was as tense as a knife. No one buried their dead under the ground, not in any realm. No one had ever said why it was wrong, and the Taiytakei didn't even believe in gods and afterlives and so Liang wasn't sure why it should bother her, but it did. It put dread in her bones.

She'd seen more than a dozen men already. What was the Black Moon doing down there? What did he want?

The tunnel ended at a balcony overlooking a second vaulted

dome even deeper than the first. Halfteeth started down a creaking wooden stair wandering rickety down a crumbling brick wall, hunched into the curve of the vault pressing from above. The air felt old; the stone looked ancient. Liang flew into the darkness and the void, and a thousand years of dust stirred in the wind of her little wings. Tiny pinpricks of light dotted below only made the darkness seem deeper. She glided into the open space and down, creep-crawling in the gloom. There was a scaffold in the middle of the floor here. Gallows. Handcarts and shrouds for the dead, and Tuuran waited beside them. He held an alchemical lamp in his hand, a tiny circle of spilling light quickly devoured by the emptiness around him. Liang perched on the scaffold to watch and wait. She pricked up her glass ears.

Zafir came to Tuuran alone. She was breathing fast. She looked pale and ... scared?

'You want me to turn the lamp out?' Tuuran asked.

Zafir slapped him. 'How many people, Night Watchman? To how many has he done it?'

Tuuran rubbed his cheek. 'Done what?'

'The knife!' Zafir shoved him. 'How many has he stabbed with that knife? All these men you now command? Every one of them?'

Tuuran had his back to Liang. She couldn't make out his face, but she saw his shoulders slump. He turned away from Zafir for a moment, bowed his head and mumbled something.

'What?'

'All of them, Holiness,' said Tuuran quietly. 'Everyone except you and me. Perhaps Myst and Onyx. I don't know. Maybe a few others he's missed.'

'Merizikat too?'

'Every single one.' He shrugged hopelessly. 'I thought you knew.'

'You did, did you? And you thought I'd do nothing? I said there would be no more slaves. Are my words so empty?'

'You think that thing inside Cra— inside the Crowntaker's head listens to you?' Tuuran rounded on her. 'Or to me? Or to anyone?' He grabbed Zafir by the shoulders. 'He's a half-god! The Silver King!'

'No.' Zafir pushed him away. 'Not *our* Silver King. Not the Isul Aieha.'

Tuuran shook his head. He let out a long heavy breath. 'He's my friend, Holiness. I don't know what to do.'

'Why us?' Zafir asked after a moment. 'Why spare only us?'

'The Black Moon spares you because of the spear you once carried. The Adamantine Spear of the Speaker. Without that he'd cut you in a blink. Me? Because there's still enough Crazy in there to stop him, that's why.' He shrugged again. 'That's what he told me anyway. You and I alone are free to go.'

'But we're not.'

'No.'

Zafir took a step closer. 'He's not going to stop, is he?'

'No, Holiness.'

She took another step and then, to Liang's surprise, pressed her forehead against Tuuran's chest, drew back and gently butted him a few times as if banging her head against a wall. 'As you say, Night Watchman. He is a Silver King.'

'No. More. He was my friend.' Tuuran flapped his arms as though he didn't know what to do with them. He made as if to stroke Zafir's hair and then thought better of it. In her workshop Liang took a little step back. It was so unexpected.

'Why has he got you down here?'

Tuuran swept his arm across the vault, the scaffold and the gallows. Liang froze for a moment as the big man looked straight at her, but in the gloom he must not have seen the little glass dragon. 'He told me about this place years ago.' Tuuran walked from the scaffold into the dark. Zafir stayed close by his side. Liang crept after them, claws clicking on the stone floor. 'Merizikat, where the worst come to die. I've seen it in galley slaves, Holiness, men taken from here, what they'll do to breathe their last under the sun and not some other way. Night-skins didn't ever give a shit for what slaves from other worlds believed when it came to gods and the like, but I paid heed for my own reasons. Crazy ...' Tuuran stopped and seemed to choke on something for a moment. 'Beg your pardon, Holiness. The Crowntaker used to tell stories. Stupid things about how he used to be someone else until some warlock pulled his soul out of his body and trapped it in another. Didn't used to believe a word of it until the Black Moon came. Now ...' He shrugged.

'What did he tell you about Merizikat?'

Another heavy sigh. 'That the sun-fearing folk of the Dominion bring all the worst men here. In the dead of night in the middle of winter they execute them. They hang them in this vault underneath the ground where the sun never reaches. They leave the bodies here to rot in dry lightless still air, in alcoves untouched by any whisper of sun or moon or stars, damning their souls to a listless lingering in Xibaiya. That's what he told me. I've heard from others, more lately, that the men they hang here have developed a penchant for getting up again, even after their necks are broken.'

'The Black Moon told you that?'

Tuuran shook his head. 'Galley slaves from hereabouts. Started before I ever met Crazy. Didn't pay it much heed at the time. Slaves tell all manner of wild stories just to have a story at all.' He laughed. 'Except me. I never told mine to anyone but you, and you already knew it. You want to see a walking dead man? We've got a few down here. They're a bit delicate, mind.'

In her tower Liang squeaked.

Zafir followed as Tuuran moved off. Liang skittered along behind. The Adamantine Man talked as they walked. 'There's a prison down here. The priests run it. They usually hang everyone on midwinter's night, but *he* wanted it done straight away and so we did. The dead all got carted back to their cells to see what happened.' Tuuran chuckled bitterly. 'There's an army coming for us, right? Come to get rid of us? And a bigger one on its way to Aria, to the Crowntaker's old home and the necropolis there; but if the Sun King knew what was happening down here then he'd pause from his war across the worlds and fall on us with every force he has.' He stopped at an iron gate set into the tunnel. A turnkey let them through. 'I hear it was a bit of a problem when the dead started walking. That fire the sun priests make kills them good and proper so they stay down, but that went against the whole point of them being here. Same goes for ordinary fire and dragon-fire, and any other kind of fire, I suppose. So it's all a bit of a bugger's muddle. They went to chopping the restless dead to bits, but the bits wouldn't be still. Brought rats to eat any bits that kept wriggling, or burned them with lime, but either way they just wound up with ghosts. The bastards they send to Merizikat to die come here to have their souls damned to the dead goddess of the earth. Nowhere else. Eternal torment, that's what this lot reckon, earned by villainy done in life, but whatever they used to do here it doesn't work any more. It's been that way for some years now. Like the place they're supposed to go simply isn't there any more. Or maybe like they've found a way out.' Tuuran shook his head. 'All bloody stupid, if you ask me, but no one ever does.'

'Dead is dead,' sniffed Zafir. She was looking this way and that, head twitching like a nervous bird. 'Our ancestors find us wherever we lie.'

'Aye.' Tuuran stopped at another gate and another turnkey. 'People believe all sorts though.' The tunnel was narrow now, tiny, claustrophobic and pressing, and Liang saw the dragon-queen breathing fast and shallow. Close to panic, though she kept it from her voice. Liang saw too how Zafir kept reaching to take Tuuran's arm and then snapping her fingers away. *She's afraid. Actually afraid.* Though whether it was of the dead or of the dark or of being so deep under the ground Liang couldn't be sure.

Past the second gate came rows of tiny cells, little more than scrapes of stone scooped from the wall and barely big enough for a man to lie down. Tuuran shone his torch over them. The nearest body was missing one arm from the shoulder and the other from the elbow, and the rest was rotting off. Strips of skin hung from his skull; his belly had split open and a trail of guts hung from the hole, yet he wasn't still. He sat and looked up. Zafir stiffened. In her tower behind her silk mask, Liang gasped. She backed away and flapped the little dragon's wings. Glass scraped against stone.

'He comes down here sometimes,' said Tuuran. 'He just looks at them.'

'Burn them, Tuuran. All of them.'

'But the Black Moon—'

'Burn them.' Zafir looked straight at the shadows where Liang's dragon lurked as though she'd known it was there all along. 'Alchemists can bring the dead back to speak,' she said quietly. 'That's already quite enough.'

Liang fled. She spread her glass wings and flew away, weaving through the catacomb tunnels until she found daylight and brought her little dragon home. She hid it then, half expecting Zafir or

Tuuran to come and smash it, but the days passed and neither did, though Tuuran came late the next night and rattled her out of bed with a hundred rockets from the city arsenal, their fire globe tips removed, with a curt request for Liang to extract the black powder and, too, to meddle with several enchanted torches to make them erratic. She did as she was asked, breathed a quiet sigh of relief and went back to bed. She tried to sleep, but sleep was as elusive as ever.

A change came after that day in the catacombs. Zafir, aloof in her eyrie until now, suddenly spent all her time in the palace and in the basilica and at the docks. Bellepheros supposed the wails of her handmaidens' newborns had driven her away, but Liang saw other changes too. Zafir was everywhere, and Tuuran as well, and the handful of Adamantine Men he kept closest, Halfteeth and the like. The eyrie moved from the top of the palace hill to float over the docks, and its cranes winched up crates and sacks day and night. Tuuran brought new soldiers to Liang again, dozens of them to be refitted with armour she'd already made for others he'd brought before. He never said, but Liang slowly understood: Zafir was replacing the soul-cut slave-soldiers of the Black Moon with sell-swords bought with stolen Merizikat gold, with street fighters, with anyone she could find who would serve a dragon-queen for the promise of treasure and had little to leave behind. The dragon-queen meant to move against the Black Moon then, did she? And if she did, so be it, and Liang would rub her hands with glee. Let them fight. Let one kill the other. So much the better if Zafir won, because she would be so much easier to send swiftly to Xibaiya in her turn, right on the Black Moon's heels.

So Liang said nothing to anyone about what she'd seen, and did as she was asked, and tried not to think about the soul-cut soldiers Zafir must be murdering as she replaced them. Dragon fodder, perhaps. Day after day Tuuran brought her more while the eyrie filled with barrels of wine and water, and with sacks of grain. Some Taiytakei trader must have let slip about the enchanted cold rooms their ships sometimes carried to keep fruit and meat fresh over a long voyage; Liang found herself summoned to bind enchantments as she'd once enchanted Baros Tsen's bathhouse, keeping it cold and close to freezing. She barely recognised the eyrie any more. The fighting men busy at work there were strangers, and Zafir had brought women to mend and fix and make and, yes, to fight too. A whole little town she was building, while the eyrie rim was piled high with food and rope and nails and thread and cloth and everything Liang could imagine, even animals in cages. She saw other Taiytakei too, though they quickly averted their eyes and scurried shamefaced away, and Halfteeth, who was her minder here, wouldn't let her talk to them.

She built the enchanted cold rooms and ovens as she was asked, and returned to Merizikat exhausted only to find Tuuran's other lieutenant, the one he called Snacksize, waiting for her, grumbling about gold-glass torches flashing erratically under the basilica and demanding that Liang come to fix them at once. There was a carriage ready and waiting, but instead of taking her to the basilica it drove Liang to the city walls over the peak of the hill where Tuuran stood looking out over the riverlands and the army that the Sun King had sent to crush them; and it was only then that she remembered Tuuran himself had been the one who'd asked for torches that would fail. That was how tired she was, forgetting something so obvious.

Tuuran sent Snacksize away. He pointed to the distant patch-work, to the sea of white tents camped two miles up the Merizikat river and spreading along some small tributary. Now and then sunlight glinted off polished metal.

'Ten thousand men,' he said. 'A footnote to the Sun King's army. Bigger than my Adamantine Legion, though. The Black Moon wants to know if you can make a lightning cannon to reach that far.'

'No.'

'Rockets.'

'Not that far.'

'Then you're to pack your workshop and return to the eyrie. You'll work from there instead of the palace. To be safe, enchant-ress. There are spies in our midst, and assassins too.' He gave her a hard look. 'In this you'll do as you're told.' She would too. The Black Moon hadn't given her a choice in that. Just as she wouldn't run away. Couldn't. None of them could except for the dragon-queen; and perhaps that was why Liang had come to hate her of late as much as she did: Zafir, of all of them, had the choice to leave, and yet she chose to stay.

'What did I ever do to you, Tuuran, to make you despise me so?' she asked. It came out with a twitch of bitterness.

'Turned my alchemist master's head, that's what.' Tuuran laughed harshly. 'He told you it was wrong. He told you what would happen if you brought dragons across the storm-dark. And everything that happened after, you throw that at my queen's feet with outraged condemnation, and yet you built this, enchantress, you as much as anyone. Her Holiness owns who she is. You do not. Yet you call her a monster.' He guided her down from the wall. A company of soldiers fell in around her. 'The Black Moon cut you with his knife. I know that, and so here in Merizikat you have no choice but to do his will, and that I must accept.' He stabbed an accusing finger across the city at the eyrie hanging over the docks. 'For that, though, lady, you *did* have a choice. You took away our freedom and made us slaves, and now you wail in horror at what we do to be free? You night-skins are so soaked in your own hypocrisy that you can't see it even when it's held jiggling and shouting before your eyes. Remember that. Now come with me to the basilica catacombs. Your lamps misbehave.'

He stayed at her side, silent and brooding, and snapped his fingers for two other soldiers to come as escort, not Zafir's sell-swords but two solar exalts in golden armour, soul-cut men turned by the Black Moon's knife. The carriage drove Liang past the palace and down the hill. As they drove Tuuran reached into his boot and handed her a sliver of glass wrapped in a torn strip of dirty linen.

'Do you recognise this?' he asked.

Liang looked at the glass. There were words etched into it. 'It commands all Taiytakei sea captains to grant the bearer passage and transport to whatever destination they desire, by order of Quai'Shu, sea lord of Xican.' She cocked her head at Tuuran in wonder. 'From where did you steal this?'

'I did not steal it, witch. Your killer gave it to me long ago. The Watcher. You remember him? He gave it to me so I could find my friend with the funny symbols hidden in the scar on his leg. He meant Crazy Mad. Though how he knew back then … I used to wonder if even *he* was a pawn in some game. You might wonder at that too, witch, if you wish, but I'm long past such thoughts now.'

He shuddered and shook his head as the carriage rattled across the basilica square. 'No matter. Will it still work?'

'Perhaps. Quai'Shu is dead and dishonoured, but a few captains may not yet know that. Others may harbour secret sympathies. You would have to be careful, Tuuran, if you mean to leave this way.'

'Not me, witch. Crazy was my friend. I'll find a way to set him free or I'll die at his side while I try.' Tuuran shook his head. 'Keep it, Chay-Liang. Take this temptation away from me.'

Liang wrapped the glass and put it into one of her pouches. 'So *I* must look at it and have it taunt me instead?'

Tuuran didn't answer. He turned his head and stared out of the carriage window as they rolled past the basilica's grand atrium. The driver took them on into a smaller square around the back. The catacomb gates were open as they drove into the cloister yard, but the carriage didn't stop until the driver had turned all the way round and was back facing the way he'd come, as though he couldn't wait to get away.

'Why all this bother with my torches anyway?' asked Liang. She found herself fingering the raw gold-glass globes tucked into her cuffs. Weapons, always, in case she needed them. Life in the eyrie had taught her that, and Tuuran had a gravel to him today that set her on edge. His face showed a bleak determination. Set on some course he didn't much like but meant to see through nonetheless.

'You must obey the will of the Black Moon,' Tuuran said at last, 'and he commands that you serve, and so you cannot escape, no matter how you wish you could, and you build him his army, though it is against your will to do so. But there are other ways of escape, Chay-Liang.' Tuuran opened the door for Liang and stepped out behind her. The back of the basilica was closer to the river than she'd thought, not far from the banks of the estuary and butting against the run-down upriver end of the old docks where everything was crumbling and the streets smelled of harsh raw spirit, of stale smoke and rotting human waste. Litter-strewn alleys wriggled towards the water, tunnels almost black with shadow even in the middle of the day.

The soul-cut exalts got out beside her.

'I hope you are worth the lives you cost,' said Tuuran.

For a moment the air was electric and still, the instant before the first crack of thunder breaks from a storm. Then soldiers burst into the light from the slum alleys, Dominion men in the Sun King's colours, six of them, crossbows loaded. Liang gasped in shock. Tuuran grabbed her from behind and wrapped one huge arm around her neck, squeezing her throat between his bicep and his forearm, strangling her.

She shook her sleeve, dropping a glass ball into her hand.

'Remember this, enchantress,' hissed Tuuran in her ear as her vision blurred. 'Whatever life comes next, remember that I set you free.'

The exalt beside Liang died instantly, two bolts through his face. The second took three in the chest, punching through the gold-glass armour she'd made. He fired a bolt of lightning before he died, taking two of his killers with him. The thunderclap shook the air. Somehow it shook her fingers too, and the glass ball they held fell harmless at her feet. The two dead exalts collapsed and clattered to the ground. She heard more shouts behind her. Cries of warning. She struggled as best she could, trying to wriggle herself free, anything that would break Tuuran's grip, but he only squeezed tighter.

'I know you must resist, enchantress,' he whispered. 'I know you have no choice. So I have made your choice for you.'

The four Dominion soldiers still on their feet rushed at her, hands reaching out. The colour drained from her world. She heard muted thunder, deep and rumbling as though she was underwater. She felt herself falling, drowning, and then everything went black.

31

The Arbiter

Four months before landfall

Red Lin Feyn stared into the mirror. She touched her fingers to the three pale marks on her cheek that looked like fingertips.

'The catacombs of Merizikat are hardly the Ice Witch's necropolis,' whispered the Elemental Man standing behind her.

'It wasn't real,' said Lin Feyn at last. Every day she looked at herself and repeated the same mantra, and every day the scars on her face said otherwise. The marks weren't terrible; they were barely visible at all, and easily hidden with a little powder, but they *were* there. 'I summoned the storm-dark to devour her, and one does not simply conjure the void on a whim. Yet the *Servant on Ice* and I both bore the scars.'

'You are changed, lady Arbiter,' said the Elemental Man when she was done. 'There is a manner about you that I would liken to a priest now.' There. A carefully crafted taunt to heat the blood of any true stalwart of the Dralamut and the ways of the Elemental Men, but those days were gone. She lived by their sufferance now, the few of the killers that had survived the catastrophe of Baros Tsen's eyrie and the Godspike. Or perhaps to call it an uneasy truce would be more accurate. She'd told them what she knew because she felt she had no choice, and now she wasn't sure whether they thought she was mad or brilliant or desperate, or simply a fool. Perhaps a little of all of those things, but what mattered was that they believed her enough to let her carry on, if under their very watchful eye.

'Must it be Merizikat, lady?' the Elemental Man asked.

'Yes.' Red Lin Feyn tilted her head as if to ask what troubled him so about the city of the dead. 'A ship directly to the city itself would be preferable. I would ask you to help me make the necessary arrangements.'

'Merizikat,' said the Elemental Man again. 'You really don't know, do you?'

32

Each Her Own Way

Two months before landfall

Liang gasped and sat bolt upright only to find she was trussed like a fly in a spider's larder. Not dead. That was the first shock. Tuuran had despised her from the start. Thick as thieves, him and the dragon-queen. An impulsive violent ape – no surprise that he'd be the one to do away with her. *I have made your choice for you.* Never cared about getting his hands dirty. Brute. Yet here she was.

She blinked and took in the world. Cold fresh spray. An orchestra of sea sounds, a sail purring like a lion as the wind shifted, ropes rattling taut against wood, the slow breathing creaks of a ship, the bend and flex with each sigh.

Not dead.

The boat was a little river skiff with a triangular wedge sail, beating upriver against the wind. One man sat behind her at the tiller. Another was by the mast pulling on ropes, two more in front of her, watchful and waiting with crooked squinting eyes all big and dark as the Sun King's people often were. They looked like fishermen but they had soldiers' knives and axes tucked among the sail and rope at their feet.

'Water?' offered one. He had a skin he was drinking from. When Liang shook her head, he hawked and spat. His teeth were crooked and yellow and his nose was bent. Another gnawed noisily on a strip of dried meat. The hair was missing from one side of his head and the skin there was red. He'd been burned once.

'Your dragon,' he said when he caught Liang staring.

'Who are you?' she asked.

The boat trembled. A rumble like distant thunder echoed across the water. Liang lifted her head to look at the city. At first she didn't see anything amiss, but then one of the corner towers of the basilica leaned very slowly sideways and tipped and broke into pieces and fell, and a cloud of dust and smoke rose to take its place.

Tuuran. It hit her like one of her own bolts of lightning. Tuuran and his furtive midnight demands for black powder and torches that didn't work. He'd taken the powder from the arsenal rockets and set it off through the catacombs. Her faulty torches had been an excuse for oil lamps. He'd burned the walking dead of Merizikat because the dragon-queen had told him to; and since he was who he was, there wouldn't have been any of his men down there when the explosions went off. He would have set the powder himself ...

And she understood then that he hadn't been trying to kill her at all, that he'd given her a way to escape. He'd choked her out and passed her to men who would take her out of the city, tied like a midwinter pig so she couldn't run back as the compulsion of the Black Moon demanded; and while he was at it, he'd given her a means to cross the storm-dark and go home and a reason for her to be dead so the Black Moon wouldn't look for her; and whether he'd done it to set her free, or whether he'd simply meant for her to take the blame to protect his precious dragon-queen from what he'd done, it didn't matter. And it occurred to her too that Tuuran was the one who had brought soldier after soldier to her to fit with new armour, that *he* was the one recruiting sell-swords to replace the soul-cut men the Black Moon had made; that while the dragon-queen wallowed in her endless *no-more-slaves* hypocrisy, while the Black Moon's knife cut men's will left and right, perhaps Tuuran defied him more than Liang had ever thought, more than Zafir herself, more than any of them.

She'd got him wrong. Quiet and resolute he stood against the half-god.

I wish you'd told me. I wish I'd known.

A pang of guilt shuddered her. Not for the things she'd done, but for the things she hadn't. She watched the spindle of smoke twist and coil, unfurling over the basilica of Merizikat to drift and fade in the breeze. The boat heeled a little as the wind changed.

Did he stand in secret against Zafir too? Now *there* was a thought ...

A mile past the city wall the skiff tacked across the river to the shore and delivered her into the maw of the Sun King's waiting army, a seething litter of white tents that spread like a pox on the hillside. The boatmen picked her up and carried her ashore and then fell into an argument with some soldiers about what they were supposed to do next. Liang, who wasn't quite sure whether she'd been rescued or captured, said nothing until the argument looked about to turn bloody.

'I made their lightning,' she said, which somehow seemed to settle things. The soldiers and the boatmen together carried her to a wagon made into a cage of iron bars and locked her inside. They threw a sail over the top to hide her away, and she was glad to be their prisoner for now, helpless and stripped of choices. Left to herself she might have gone back, siren-lured by the compulsion of obedience cut into her by the Black Moon's knife, by affection and loyalty and friendship, by shared hopes and pain and joys, the alchemist's gift, a more subtle poison by far. But the bars around her meant that she couldn't, and she had to be content with that, and if she had the artifice, as an enchantress, to escape such a crude prison, she chose not to use it.

In the days that followed men brought her simple food and water. Exalts and priests sat around her cage in quiet crescents, a devoutly attentive audience who drained her of the Black Moon and the dragon-queen and the eyrie. She shared what she knew, willing and eager to be rid of it, and begged them not to let her go; but one secret she kept to herself, the strip of black silk wrapped high around her arm under her tunic. Each time the exalts and their armsmen threw the sail over her cage to hide her from the light she wrapped the silk like a blindfold across her face and watched through the eyes of the little glass dragon in Merizikat, scouting the aftermath of her disappearance.

Tuuran was limping but alive. She found him quickly and felt an odd flood of relief. She'd never know how he escaped the explosion and the collapse of the catacombs, but she listened to the story he spun in lieu of the truth: of how Liang's enchanted torches had failed and left his men with no choice but to use oil lamps, how the choking smoke had driven them out, how he'd brought Liang to the catacombs to see for herself the faults in her work, how she'd smuggled kegs of black powder beneath the basilica and set the walking dead aflame there, and how the flames and her powder kegs had blown both tunnel and enchantress to pieces. The catacomb vaults had collapsed and no way in could be found, and the risen dead were all gone, every one of them burned and blown to pieces or buried beneath a mountain of crushing stone. She watched Bellepheros as he heard the news, the stony hostile face he presented and how he sagged and broke and wept once he was alone, and felt the heartbreak of not being able to tell him otherwise. She watched Tuuran tell his lie to the Black Moon with Zafir at his side and then later tell her the truth: that he'd been the one, that Liang was safely free; and she saw Zafir shake her head and tell him no, he couldn't share that truth with Bellepheros however much the alchemist hurt, because Bellepheros had been cut by the Black Moon's knife, and no one was to be trusted; and she saw how Bellepheros, never a fool, began to see that Tuuran's story wasn't the whole and honest truth, and drew conclusions of his own that were entirely and horribly wrong.

Days passed. The Black Moon and Tuuran and Zafir left the city to parley with the Sun King's exalts, and Liang and her little glass dragon followed and looked on. The exalts' demands were no surprise: the return of their city, reparation and the withdrawal of the eyrie and the Black Moon's army. The Black Moon didn't answer, and so Zafir and the exalts negotiated back and forth, the dragon-queen's exasperation more evident with every passing moment until the Black Moon grew bored.

'The Bloody Judge,' he said. 'Bring me the Bloody Judge. He stole my face.' Without warning he stabbed the nearest exalt and pressed a hand into his face, forcing him to his knees. The other exalts flashed blades. One swung at the Black Moon and immediately dissolved into ash. Three charged at Zafir, two at Tuuran. Zafir took the first exalt to come at her and sliced him open with a bladeless knife. She ducked the second. Tuuran backed away, weaving his axe in arcs. He couldn't hide how he was favouring one leg over the other. Zafir severed another exalt's hand at the wrist and then took a hammer blow to the back that knocked her flat. The wounded exalt fell on top of her, huge and armoured, pinning her, howling curses and trying to drive a knife at her face while she held him off with one hand and rammed a second bladeless knife into his ribs, stabbing as he screamed until blood ran out of his mouth and he collapsed. The one who'd taken her down raised his axe to split her in two, then vanished into the air as Diamond Eye swooped and plucked him away and tore him to pieces in the sky. The rest fled then, except for the Moon's snared exalt, who burst into a pillar of silver flame and shrieked and died. The half-god stayed where he was. Liang didn't think he'd moved as much as a muscle.

Zafir struggled free from under her corpse. She hobbled, stooped, drenched in the blood of her murdered exalt, growling and gasping in pain. She shoved the Black Moon, almost kicking him over. The half-god whirled and raised the Starknife; Zafir hissed and lashed the air, a blade in each hand, ready to make a fight of it; Diamond Eye smashed into the ground and bared his fangs, and for a moment Liang thought the most wonderful thing was about to happen.

'*No!*' Tuuran half-jumped, half-limped between them. He threw down his axe. 'Damn you both, no!'

Half-god and dragon-queen faced each other down for a moment more, and then Zafir sheathed her bladeless knives. She turned and lurched away, snarling in pain. 'I don't care what you are.' She hobbled in small circles. 'We go back now. We go back to *my* world. We take back my spear you're so precious for, and call the nine kings and queens with their dragons, and then you do whatever you like with them. A thousand dragons. More. Does anything else matter?'

'One thousand seven hundred and seventy-seven,' said the Black Moon, the light in his eye dying to a silver shimmer. 'That's how many I made.'

'Then you made more than enough to burn any world you please.' Zafir gasped and doubled up and lurched to Diamond Eye's side, clinging to his scales. She buckled and fell to one knee and then hauled herself up again. Glistening white face contorted in agony, she climbed one-handed onto the dragon's back and flew away. As soon as she was gone the last light went from the Crowntaker's eyes. He sagged and sank to his knees.

'All this way.' He was almost sobbing. 'All this time. For what? For what, big man? He's not even here.'

'Who's not here?' Tuuran crouched beside the ruin of his friend.

'The Bloody Judge. The man who stole my face.'

Liang watched as Tuuran sat with the Black Moon, talking softly to the tattered remains of what had once been Berren Crowntaker, solemn whispers and earnest nods of the head, then a little smile and a touch of laughter between them, of older, better times, of easier days fondly remembered. She saw at last how all of this was for him, this simple soldier for whom she'd once had such scorn. Friendship and duty. However deep you went in him, nothing else mattered. Worlds might burn and empires crumble and he'd barely even see it. Stupid, perhaps. Blind and foolish and unwise, but whatever the dragon-queen and the Crowntaker did, he'd be there for them as best he ever could, and she found that she envied his simplicity, and that she envied Zafir and the half-god too for such loyalty; but most of all she wished she could spare Tuuran the day when he'd have to choose between them.

She watched them walk away and then, later, when Tuuran was gone, after the exalts and priests had come to her and lifted the sail from her cage and questioned her through the long hours of the afternoon as they laid their plans for battle, she retied the silk across her eyes and watched the Black Moon slip out once more to wear the Crowntaker like a cheap coat, watched him meander through the Merizikat slums, spitting his rage, bright moonlight eyes, rending houses and streets and anyone who crossed his path to ash on random whim until the fury slowly died. In the dead of night she flew the little glass dragon to the eyrie and found the dragon-queen lying flat naked on a bed, head propped up, staring furious eyes at her own door, spittle-flecked, glassy-faced in pain, gnashing her teeth and hissing like a viper at her two maidservants and Bellepheros as they huddled over her, Bellepheros poking and prodding. The whole of one side of her back was livid red, the skin split and caked in a wash of dried blood. The others had their backs turned, but as the little glass dragon crept inside, exposed for a moment. Zafir looked up and locked her eyes on it, and Liang knew that the dragon-queen understood.

'Stop!' Zafir gasped. 'Stop!'

Bellepheros froze, stung still. 'Holiness! There are bones cracked at the very least and I hazard there are some broken. There is damage inside that might yet be fatal. I must ...' But Liang knew Zafir had meant the command for her, not for him.

Zafir ignored Bellepheros, screwed up her face against the pain and looked the glass dragon in the eye to mouth words without sound: *Hide your toy, witch. Go! Be gone!*

Liang scuttled the little dragon outside the door and waited a while in case there was more, but all she heard were Zafir's howls and curses of pain. She hurried away and hid, waiting for Bellepheros to come out so she might see him again, but he never did that night, and back in her cage Liang must have fallen asleep, because the next thing she knew it was light outside and the air was full of screaming and the earth quaked, and as she pulled the silk from across her eyes the sail over her cage was ripped away and the great red-gold dragon stood over her, those piercing glacier eyes staring right through her. Liang screamed as Diamond Eye picked up the wagon and tore into the air, soaring up as arrows and tardy lightning flashed their pursuit, but the dragon didn't take her back to the eyrie as she imagined he would, nor did he rip her to pieces; instead he set her down in her prison on the far shore of the river. Alone and abandoned. Free to go as she chose or to die unseen and unremembered.

Fly far, little one.

Liang huddled in the corner of her cage, waiting for her heart to explode. The eyrie drifted out to sea across the estuary, towed by half a dozen ships. The Black Moon was leaving.

Diamond Eye took the wagon between his talons. He wrenched the cage apart and then walked away along the riverbank.

'Wait!' Liang struggled between the mangled bars and flopped to the ground, sinking into sticky silty mud. 'Wait!' She wanted to know: 'Why did you come for me? Did you choose this yourself or are you sent? Did Zafir command you? Why?' She wanted to know where the Black Moon planned to go now and what he meant to do, and so many things … 'Wait! Would you take me back if I asked?'

The Black Moon? The dragon was in her head. *He is a half-god and will do as he wishes. Two faces I see in his thoughts. One he seeks, one he fears. One he calls the Bloody Judge. The Black Moon seeks him for the other half of his own splintered soul. The second face is the sorceress who wears the circlets of the moon, the mortal foe who set him free from Xibaiya and whose birth you once saw as a comet in the sky.*

He will take the Isul Aeiha's spear now, and he will find each face and skewer them through. This Black Moon? He is but a splinter, terrible beyond imagining to your kind, but had you seen him at his height and whole it would have shattered your mind. Scorn, was that? *Fly far, Chay-Liang. Go and be free. I have no care one way or another for the fates and ends of little ones. You are small and mundane, sometimes amusing, often beneath notice.*

The dragon stretched its wings and flew. The wind of its leaving hurled Liang flat. She rolled onto her back, filthy, and lay gasping for air as she watched the dragon rise over the river and turn out to sea, following the eyrie's wake. When it was gone she propped herself exhausted against the broken wagon. She sat in the rising sun, sheltering from the cold sea breeze, and wrapped the black silk around her eyes. The little glass dragon was in the eyrie where she'd left it, waiting patiently and obedient, tucked in shadows out of sight in what had once been her workshop. She knew the eyrie as though it was a part of her, and Belli had his laboratory almost across the passageway, and so now she scurried to it, but the door was open and he wasn't there. She tried his study and found him sitting at his desk, head in his hands, quill and paper untouched in front of him. He might have been asleep by the way he jumped when she tapped his leg. He sprang halfway to his feet, leaned into the desk, wheezed and winced at his knee and stared.

'Li?' His eyes narrowed. 'Wait. No. Who are you?' He got to his feet and backed away. 'Who are you and what do you want?'

Tuuran had told him she was dead, and she'd never given the little glass dragon a voice. Eyes and ears, yes, and wings and claws and little teeth and a tail, a silent and beautiful spy to peer through the windows of dragon-princes and queens and kings in their lofty towers. But never a voice to speak.

She thought for a moment and then jumped onto Belli's desk and dipped a claw into his ink and started to write. The words were messy, barely legible, the first thing she could think of to tell him it was truly her:

Qaffeh? Bolo?

'Li!'

She watched him crumple and felt tears behind the silk across her eyes. Knee forgotten, Belli jumped and snatched the little glass dragon from the desk and hugged it. He put it down again, gently, and stroked a fond hand across its snout. 'Li.' For a while he just said her name over and over. 'Tuuran told me you died! That you took black powder and burned the walking corpses in the catacombs and were crushed in the explosion! How are … Where are you, Li? Are you hurt? Do you need help? Tell me where you are!'

The little glass dragon cocked its head and wrote:

Alive. Not hurt. Left behind. Scared.

Belli leaned closer, eyes bright and wide. 'Where are you? I'll come to you. I'll even ride one of those blasted sleds if I must. I will, Li! Just tell me where to go.'

Behind her silk Li smiled at the thought of Bellepheros and his terror of heights trying to ride a glass sled you could see right through all the way to the ground, lying flat and with his eyes screwed shut in terror. He'd faint from fright if ever he managed to guide himself over the eyrie edge and saw how far up he was, but he probably wouldn't even get past the walls; then her smile faded as a sadness lanced her through, remembering the first day she'd ever seen him, and the sled she'd made to take them up to Quai'Shu's Palace of Leaves, so long ago.

The little glass dragon shook its head.

'You left,' said Bellepheros. 'Didn't you? You found a way to get away from from him.' And it was so much more complicated, but she couldn't possibly explain, not with scratchy writing and a dragon's claw for a nib.

I will come back for you.
No matter the world.

'Li!' There were tears in his eyes as he smiled. 'Then I'll be here. Waiting. Doing what an alchemist must. I miss you already.' He shook his head. 'But don't do it, Li. Don't follow. You know what waits here. Nothing. Go back home. Tell your people. Tell everyone. Find a way to stop him.'

Yes. Together.

Liang stared hard and frowned at him. Belli threw up his hands in exasperation. 'Li! Don't—'

The glass dragon lunged and nipped his hand. Belli jumped away.

'Don't! Don't come back here. You know better. You do.'

Daft old man.

She tried to make the little glass dragon wear a defiant nothing-you-can-do-will-change-my-mind-about-this-so-you-might-as-well-get-used-to-it look. She had no idea how it came out, but Belli's shoulders slumped and then he smiled and stroked her snout, and so it must have come out close enough.

'If you come, Li, don't come alone. Find your Elemental Men and your Arbiter and all her friends and ... Wait a moment!' He hurried out of his study, and when he came back he was clutching a handful of wax-stoppered vials. He stuffed them into a sack. 'Can you carry this?'

Liang took the sack between her claws. She hopped about the desk and then jumped off the edge and flew to Belli's bed. The vials clattered and clacked against one another.

'Be careful!' Belli flustered and chased her to the bed and sat down beside her. 'Remember when the Black Moon came and the eyrie fell. Do you remember the potions I gave to the killers? This is all I have of them, but they will hide your thoughts from the dragons so they don't see you, so they don't know you're there. Bring an army, Li. Bring whatever you can.'

A hurried padding of footsteps came from the doorway. Liang looked up, eyes darting for a place to hide, but too late. Myst was at the door, a baby in her arms. Bellepheros jumped to his feet and stood between her and the glass dragon, trying to keep Liang out of sight.

'Grand Master?' Myst hopped from foot to foot.

'Her Holiness takes a turn for the worse?'

'No, Grand Master, it's little Tuuran. He has such a fever. He screams and screams, and I fear her Holiness cannot rest.'

'Colic, probably.' Liang couldn't see Belli's face but she could feel him roll his eyes. It made her smile and sob both at once to not be with him any more. 'Go back to him. I'll be with you in a moment.'

Bellepheros closed the door and turned back to Liang, half his usual testy self, half full of smiles. 'A dozen women on this eyrie and not one of them a midwife.' He shook his head. 'Wait for me, Liang. It's probably wind. It's always wind. In that regard he apes his namesake. I won't be long.'

He left. While he was gone Liang wrote a last few words.

Keep the Bolo fresh or I will be cross. I will find you. I WILL.

She flew away then, knowing that if she didn't then she might stay with him for day after day until the little glass dragon could never come back to her. She cried a little, pausing to wait on the eyrie rim, not sure how or whether she could honour the promise she'd left behind, knowing she'd do everything her power would allow and fearful it wouldn't be enough. Then she flew her precious burden back to the shore, to Merizikat, to the riverbank and her upturned cart. With Tuuran's glass sliver in her pocket and Belli's potions in a sack slung over her shoulder, she set to walking.

The roads were unfamiliar. They led her through villages long abandoned in fear of the dragon of Merizikat. She took food where she found it and sent her little glass wings searching far and wide for anyone or anything that might help her find her way, and that was how she found Red Lin Feyn in her carriage with two Elemental Men at her side, and neither could quite believe the other was real, but Red Lin Feyn had qaffeh and Bolo bread too, and it was the best food Liang had ever tasted. They shared it together around a little fire in the hearth of an abandoned hall while the Elemental Men stood watch and Liang told her story. It was a long one and ran late into the night; but when she was done neither of them seemed tired, and so Lin Feyn launched into her own. How she'd returned to Takei'Tarr on the *Servant on Ice* to find that months had passed for which she had no memory.

'I returned to the Dralamut. I read the Rava. Every page.' She smiled at the glaze of dull shock that passed across Liang's face and at the glance Liang threw at the watching Elemental Men. 'They already know. They have come to accept it …' She closed her eyes then and screwed up her face, frustration showing through at last. 'Something is coming, Liang. Something from Xibaiya. The storm-dark grows inch by inch. Some great change is happening that will sweep across every world. The first pillar of the Godspike cracked eight years ago. And here in the Dominion, on that same day in the catacombs of Merizikat, those condemned to die without the light of the sun began to walk again after they were hanged. Something happened, Liang. Worlds apart, and yet on the very same day. That's what brings me here. I thought perhaps a navigator who walks the storm-dark might find some reason for the restless dead of Merizikat.'

Liang shook her head. 'They are gone, lady, and the catacombs with them.'

So on the morning that followed Red Lin Feyn turned back for Brons and the armada of the Sun King's ships. She took Liang with her. Her journey to Merizikat had lost its purpose with the burning of the catacombs, and that left her with the necropolis of Aria and the Ice Witch, with the city of Deephaven that sat on the brink of cataclysmic war.

Merizikat to Brons was four hundred miles as crow or dragon flew, but the coast road was longer, winding around the northern edge of the Hothan peaks where they crashed into the sea, threading its way through passes and narrow valleys, past lakeside villages, then back to the coast snaking in coils along the side of the sea, cliffs above, azure waters below; and as they began their slow toil along the winding road, both Red Lin Feyn and Chay-Liang agreed that neither could wait any longer, for the Black Moon had gone to one realm and the Sun King to another, and both girded themselves for war. Red Lin Feyn made sleds, one for each of them, and the two Elemental Men – bodyguards or captors Liang never knew – became wind and air and flew beside them. They came to Brons exhausted, hungry and filthy. They had almost nothing with them but Liang's glass sliver, given to her by Tuuran, and Red Lin Feyn's name, once the Arbiter of the Dralamut and the most powerful voice in all the seven worlds, but either one would have been enough, and so each set their course; and thus it was some days later that two ships sliced through crashing waves, tossed from side to side while storm winds howled across spray-lashed decks and loosed banshee wails through rigging taut as steel, yet both ships carried every shred of sail they dared, racing the ocean towards the storm-dark.

On the last night before each would go their separate ways Red Lin Feyn burst into Liang's cabin far past the middle of the night, dressed in a nightgown.

'I have it!' She slammed a book onto the table beside Liang's cot. 'Look!'

Liang, racked by her old curse of seasickness, dry-heaved into a chamber pot as the ship bucked and rolled. 'Go away.' Her words slurred like a drunkard, but Lin Feyn didn't seem to notice.

'Liang! Look! One thousand, seven hundred and seventy-seven.' Lin Feyn's eyes burned like candles. She lit an enchanter's torch and shone it at the book, and never mind that Liang could barely focus on Lin Feyn's face. 'I knew I'd seen it before. You said the Black Moon numbered the dragons and claimed to have made them? But here! Look!'

There was a page of something. Words and a picture all swimming across her eyes. Liang closed her eyes and shook her head and groaned. 'Just tell me, for the love of Charin, what it means.'

'The Rava speaks of the half-gods as immortal, and in the same breath claims some vanished in their war before the Splintering. It numbers them. It is the same number, Liang. And here. Look. *Look*!'

Liang finally forced herself upright. The cabin blurred before her. Lin Feyn swayed back and forth and Liang couldn't tell whether that was the ship or simply her own eyes playing tricks on her. She took a deep breath and summoned her last strength and looked. Lin Feyn's picture was of a crudely drawn man. One hand wielded a knife and was stabbing it into another man's head. The other hand seemed to reach inside as if to pluck something out, while lying on the floor beside them both, flat on its back, was a small dead dragon.

'This is him,' hissed Lin Feyn. 'The Black Moon. And the dragon's not dead. He's bringing it to life. He's killing other half-gods and making them into dragons. Half-gods and dragons. They're the same, Liang. The same!'

Liang nodded and fell back onto her blankets, whimpering. Lin Feyn paused a moment, then touched a hand to Liang's brow.

'Your alchemist would have made something for the sickness, wouldn't he?'

Liang closed her eyes. Yes. He would. And he would have sat with her for as long as it took and never left her side.

The clouds and the wind and the lashing rain didn't relent, and so Liang didn't see Lin Feyn go, flying on her sled through tumult and gale to her own ship. But she forced herself up to the deck and watched as the two ships sailed one after the other into the storm-dark, and whispered her farewells until the silence came, the blessed stillness of the Nothing at the storm-dark's heart, where they would part, each to their own other world, Lin Feyn to stand before an army and the might of her own people to stop a holy war before it could start, and Liang to go alone into the dragon-lands while her borrowed ship turned back for whence it had come. She wasn't sure which one of them was the bigger fool.

Alone, but Belli would be there, and she would find him; and together they would bring the Black Moon down and his dragon-queen too. Whatever it took.

Half-gods and dragons. They're the same, Liang. The same! Now there was a thing. Through the knotting snakes writhing in her belly, Chay-Liang smiled, picturing Belli's face as she told him.

The Black Moon

There are tunnels under the Purple Spur. There are palaces bored into stone, made by the first men before the fall of the Silver Kings. When dragons flew wild and unchecked they were a shelter, a sanctuary in which to eke out a life. Abandoned when the dragons were tamed by the Isul Aieha, they became home to alchemists and the most dread of their secrets, but now they once more offer shelter from fire and claw that come from the sky. The last alchemists fade here, and dragon-riders too under the rule of their queen and their grand master alchemist. Lystra, last of Shezira's daughters, King Jehal's bride. And Jeiros, crippled by King Hyrkallan for his last desperate poisoning of a thousand dragons. For both, one name conjures all their spite, one name mothering all they have lost.

Zafir, the dragon-queen.

33

Hide-and-Seek and Alchemy

Forty days after landfall

Bellepheros had no idea whether the Black Moon knew he was still on the eyrie, or whether the half-god even cared. Zafir had left the Merizikat sell-swords and most of the exalts back in the Pinnacles. She'd taken her Adamantine Men down to the Spur and the ruin of her old palace, and Queen Jaslyn's riders too. A dozen abandoned souls wandered the eyrie, that was all, bemused and wondering what to do with themselves – solar exalts cut by the Black Moon's knife, mostly – and Bellepheros hid from them in Li's old workshop while Myst and Onyx brought him food. No one paid much attention to Zafir's handmaidens except to court them for the dragon-queen's favour, but they'd come to see him as a friend because he'd midwifed them both through the births of their sons. Kept him busy, at least.

He drank the last of Kataros's potion to hide his thoughts from the Black Moon's dragons, and then kept out of sight as best he could, flitting, lurking and forgotten, between his laboratory and his study and Li's workshop, surrounded by all the things Li had made, all the scatter of half-built ideas and discarded shapes of metal and glass whose purpose he couldn't decipher. He looked at them all, wishing she was here so she could tell him what to do. Stop the Black Moon? Take his power and use it to tame the dragons, not that he knew how? Or let the Black Moon tame the dragons himself as the Isul Aieha had done, if that was what the Black Moon planned, and then somehow bring him down? History repeating itself, except a few hundred years ago it had taken a thousand blood-mages to silence a half-god. This time there was only him.

At dawn he crept to the dragon yard to see the sun rise. They were deep within the mountains and the sky was filled with dragons. The Black Moon seemed oblivious, but Bellepheros didn't dare stay; he slipped away again and stayed hidden after that. Perhaps, in the end, because he was most comfortable in a quiet cosy place with walls and a roof and solid stone to every side, and with the memories of Chay-Liang all around him. When the eyrie stopped he didn't even know it until Myst came to tell him, in her own gentle words, that they had reached somewhere, and that the Black Moon was gone.

When he peeked outside to see, he knew at once where he was. The Valley of Alchemy. The old secret redoubt that was the source of every alchemist's power. So the Black Moon had found it then.

Myst, beside him, pointed at the sky. There were dragons everywhere. Hundreds, perched on the cliffs. Quietly waiting. He'd never seen so many.

'What do they want, Grand Master?'

'To eat us,' Bellepheros said flatly and wondered why they didn't. Wary, he climbed the eyrie wall. A few Merizikat men Zafir had left behind sat out on the rim, carefree and untroubled, legs dangling over the drop, kicking their heels beside one of the cranes. They were looking down at something, not bothered by the dragons at all, and Bellepheros wondered if he might walk to join them and peer over the edge. Maybe he should. Whatever they were looking at, he ought to see it for himself, oughtn't he? But the drop already made him dizzy just thinking about it. Standing on the wall was bad enough, out in the open under the gaze of so many dragons. He wondered idly why they paid the eyrie so little thought.

The alchemists' redoubt. The place the blood-mages had brought the body of the Silver King. If he had a home, one where he truly felt in his heart that he was safe, here it was.

'Where are we?' asked Myst.

Bellepheros looked at the dragons. Kataros's potion hid his thoughts, but it didn't blind the dragons' eyes. 'This is where we make our alchemists,' he said. 'The key and the heart to everything we are. The Black Moon went inside, did he?' *Why else come all this way?* 'Then I need to follow.' He was talking to himself, not to Myst. Telling himself because he knew that it mattered and that he needed to know, and yet the thought left him petrified. To go out there alone ... He'd have to go out to the edge. Dragons everywhere, looking on. The vertiginous drop to the valley below. The creaking wood and rope as someone lowered him down. It terrified him, every drop of every thought. Of being surrounded by the sky, of falling, of a dragon tipping off its perch and swooping in some lazy arc across the valley sky to snatch him as he dangled. Of so much naked space; and as paralysing as all those things were, none wrenched his insides as much as what he knew must come after. Walking away from the eyrie into those familiar old caves, alone, leaving every comfort behind and knowing that the Black Moon lay in wait.

'Zafir would do it,' he murmured. 'Tuuran would do it. Li too.' He had no idea how they found the courage.

'Do what?' asked Myst.

He turned to her. She'd always been a strong one. 'Will you help me?'

'How?' He saw how she hesitated.

'It's stupid, when you look at everything. Dragons all around us, a half-god ... Will you come with me to the ground? Just that far. I'll have my senses back when I have the earth under my feet again, but I fear I need a little more courage for what comes after. Will you?'

Myst climbed down the wall. She walked across the rim to the men around the crane, smiled and whispered in their ears. She came back and took Bellepheros by his hands.

'Don't the dragons terrify you?' he asked.

'I think they're magnificent,' she whispered. 'I wish her Holiness would take me into the sky with her just once.'

You know they're going to eat us, don't you? But he couldn't say that. Not to such a shining honest face full of hope and light, that bizarre unshakeable belief both Zafir's handmaidens had in their mistress and in the Adamantine armour of her protection. He wanted to shout at her that it was all an illusion, that the Black Moon kept them alive by the most slender and tenuous thread ... but why? Why do that? It would only hurt her. It certainly wouldn't save her.

'Look,' she said. 'They're not scared either.' She pointed at the men by the crane, how they idled and paid no mind to the dragons above. 'They'll lower you down.'

Bellepheros could only imagine the Black Moon had put some sort of spell on them to make them so fearless, or more likely he'd cut them with his wicked knife and they had no choices any more, or perhaps he'd simply cut all the fear right out of them. *Three little cuts. Don't be afraid of dragons.* And so they weren't. Was it that easy?

Three little cuts. Don't be afraid to fall ...

Myst put a hand on his arm.

'Come.' She led him with care down the outer slope of the wall and onto the rim. He was shaking and he hadn't even looked over the edge yet. Pathetic. He wished Tuuran was there. Or even her Holiness. Didn't see eye to eye much with one and could barely stand the other, but their fearlessness was infectious. They would have stood with him for this without a moment of hesitation if they thought it was right. They would have come inside the caves. They would have faced the Black Moon ...

And they would have died, like he was going to die. Or worse.

Myst walked him to the edge, to the crane and into the wooden cage that dangled from its arm. She came in with him, and he felt so stupid as the cage lifted into the air and swung out over the void below, but he was shaking like a leaf. He closed his eyes. Myst wrapped her arms around him. She cooed and whispered into his ear as though she was comforting a child or an animal – him, Bellepheros, grand master of the Order of the Scales, a blood-mage alchemist whose potions mastered dragons, whimpering like a whipped dog.

He kept his eyes closed until the cage bumped onto the ground. Took a few long deep breaths and then made himself let her go. He lifted the loop of rope that held the cage door closed, pushed it open and stepped out. The air smelled wrong. The sweetness he remembered scorched by a tang of ash ...

The dark purple-veined underside of the eyrie glowered down. So huge. Overpowering. If he hadn't been here a hundred times before and known this valley as well as he knew his own fingers, he might never have guessed that the smashed scattered stone around him had once been something else. Stores. Workshops. Homes for alchemists. And he should have been ready for this, he told himself, he should have known, after everything he'd seen, that of course the dragons would find this place. Of course they'd tear it down and smash it to pieces and stamp it to dust, yet the sight rocked him. Around the ruins and cave mouths the ground had been scorched black. Burned to the bedrock.

He turned to Myst in the cage, and it hit him right between the eyes then that he wasn't coming back, a certainty as sure as the rising sun. He supposed he ought to say something, but he couldn't think what. In truth he hardly even knew Myst. Hadn't ever seen her as anything more than a conduit to her mistress, just like everyone else. He felt ashamed of that now.

'Look after the little ones,' he said in the end.

'Is there anything I should tell my mistress?'

'Nothing she doesn't already know.' Bellepheros shook his head. 'Nothing that will make a difference. I know you love her. I wish I could love her too.' He forced himself to turn away and start for the caves before he simply wilted into nothing. 'Tell her the same as I told you,' he called back. 'Tell her to look after the little ones.'

Unsteady legs hurried him into the mouth of the nearest cave. With the comfort of walls around him and a roof over his head, he dared to look back. The cage had already risen halfway to the rim. If Myst was looking back at him, he couldn't tell; and when it reached the top she was too far away for his old rheumy eyes to make out anything much at all. He stood and looked for a few seconds more anyway. A longing filled him. Li would have come with him. Stood beside him. The two of them together, maybe they might have stopped Zafir and the Black Moon from bringing down whatever end of the world the half-god had in mind. But Li wasn't here, and it was just him, and he really didn't think he could do it on his own.

'I'm sorry, Li. I'm sorry I couldn't wait.' At the very least she'd have known how to make him stop feeling sorry for himself.

He turned his back on the eyrie, on the sun and the sky, on the lurking dragons who barely seemed to know he was there, on stone and air, on everything. He faced the darkness of the cave where the Black Moon had gone and walked slowly into the gloom. Every man had his fate, but he really would have quite liked a different one.

34

The Zar Oratorium

Forty-one days after landfall

Tuuran, if anyone had bothered asking, would have said that he didn't much like traipsing up to the Zar Oratorium, not one bit, not with a dozen Adamantine Men herding a gaggle of riders he couldn't even name and a queen everyone knew had a madness inside her. Didn't know what to make of what they were doing, didn't know what to make of any of it, but mostly what he didn't like was the three miles of walking out in the open in bright daylight. First through the crippled ruined gates of the Adamantine Palace – maybe a little cover there if a dragon suddenly fell out of the sky and set about killing them, but not much. Then around the flattened scorched ash and rubble that had once been the City of Dragons, where the only place to cower was between broken-down walls and in ripped-open cellars. Dragons had spent a good long time here, that much was clear, tearing up everywhere a few guardsmen might hide. Then to the cliffs of the Purple Spur. Filing up the exposed winding steps to the Zar Oratorium, a narrow stair carved into the rock with nowhere else to go. Three hundred steps. If a dragon came by, he might as well jump up and down and wave his arms and shout, daring the dragon to eat him.

Almost no one here had seen the Adamantine Palace burn. Kataros had. Big Vish and a couple of others, Adamantine Men who'd actually fought and survived. That was all. Queen Jaslyn and her riders had been in the Pinnacles. White Vish had been on his way to Furymouth. Jasaan had been in Sand, far in the sun-stricken desert of the north. Queen Jaslyn's home. Way Jasaan told it, Sand had been one of the first places to fall when the dragon-rage was at its height. Ash and smoke hadn't been enough; they'd burned it until the stones cracked in the heat, until even the deepest cellars turned to ovens. Later, after they'd gone, Jasaan said he'd found women and children cooked through. Tuuran reckoned he'd got a sense of how bad a dragon could be when her Holiness had sacked Dhar Thosis, but Sand sounded infinitely worse – the darkness, the screams, fire and flames, tooth and claw and talon and tail moving like whirlwinds through a city as it fell.

Not a thing he much wanted to see coming at him from the skies, all things considered, and so he kept watch like a hawk. Zafir circled overhead on Diamond Eye, watchful and obvious, but there were other dragons here, somewhere. He couldn't see them, but he could feel them lurking. Watching, waiting, and that wasn't what dragons did. Set him on edge, thinking that, tense and ready at any moment for a shadow to plunge from the mountain cliffs, for the burning to start.

'Adrunian Zar,' muttered Big Vish beside him as they started up the steps. 'Did you know he was an alchemist?'

The Diamond Cascade came over the lip of the Spur a hundred yards to the right of the Oratorium. Down this low it wasn't anything more than spray and mist except on days when the air was as still as a mouse. 'Doesn't sound like an alchemist name.' Tuuran looked up. Checked the sky again as they climbed the steps. 'Dragon comes now, we're dead,' he said.

Big Vish sniffed. 'All his own work. Him and the hundred or so men he hired.' He grunted. 'There used to be a lift. Pulleys and a platform to get people up. And the props for the stage. Dragons burned all that. But most of the rest is still there.'

For a moment Tuuran forgot about expecting dragons to fall on them at any moment. 'You're an Adamantine Man, Vish. You telling me you used to go to the theatre?'

'Whenever I could.' Vish frowned. 'They used to put things on at different times throughout the year. Except in winter because of the sun being too close to the horizon behind the stage. Best time was an early-summer morning.' He sighed. 'Sun would come sideways across the stage from the east straight through the cascade. Made for the most vivid rainbows you can imagine.'

Tuuran tried to picture it. Big Vish, the scarred and battered Adamantine Man who'd killed a dozen men with his axe, who'd stood and faced and fought with dragons, standing on the edge of a cliff, mooning at rainbows. Tried but couldn't make it work. 'Really?'

'Really did, boss. Dyton's Narammed in *The First Speaker*. That was something special, that was. If he'd stood up here with that pretend spear and given his great soliloquy on the day the dragons came, he'd have turned them away, he would. Just with his voice.'

They reached the top of the steps. Tuuran looked back at the plodding trail of figures following him up. Checked the sky once again for the dragons that would surely come, but saw only Diamond Eye, circling over the ruined Adamantine Palace. When he was sure they weren't all about to burn he spared a glance for the Oratorium itself. Granite terraces cut from the natural amphi-theatre of the cliff, infilled with earth, small stones and pebbles shovelled down from the higher ledges and lined with marble slabs brought from Bazim Crag. Curved tiers of bench seats, steep concentric semicircles of scarred stained stone with numbers and letters carved into each. The cliffs of the Purple Spur rose behind them, an undulating curtain of striated stone.

'Never came up here before,' he muttered. 'It's smaller than I thought.'

'Seats used to be covered with cypress wood before everything burned.' Vish sounded almost like he was giving a eulogy.

Tuuran nudged him. 'Wood,' he growled, 'is just wood.'

'I know.' Vish shook his head. 'It's just I never came up here after—'

'Most people here had a good few friends who used to be covered with skin before everything burned,' snapped Tuuran. Tension was making him waspish. 'They walked and talked too, and sometimes I dare say they were even funny.'

Big Vish gave him a sour look and stomped off to the tunnels under the stage that led into the depths of the Spur. There would be more Adamantine Men in there somewhere, keeping watch. Friends. What few Vish had left.

Queen Jaslyn came up the last steps. She reached the stage and stood there, unmoving, her back to the open sky, as exposed as you could possibly imagine. She kept staring out at Diamond Eye, and Tuuran didn't much like the look on her. Too much longing. And all her dragon-riders kept stopping too, as they came up, and stood with her, looking out over the distant landscape peeling away towards Gliding Dragon Gorge. The ruin of the City of Dragons, tumbled stone and ash, part overgrown now. On the low hill beside it stood the palace with its sheared towers, only the walls looking much as they ever had, too massive and mighty for even dragons to destroy. Was a good view if you'd never seen it before. Question was: did you want to see it at all, all that loss?

Some of his men had set about lashing up a makeshift throne of wood and rope. It occurred to Tuuran then, far too late to do anything about it, that the riders under the Purple Spur were mostly men from Furymouth, while the riders in the Pinnacles were largely men from Sand and Bloodsalt, opposite ends of the realms who rarely managed to play nicely together even at the best of times. Which it certainly hadn't been when the palace fell. And then there was Zafir and him, caught in the middle.

Vish came trotting back from the tunnels. 'Boss?'

Tuuran sighed. Nodded. 'They waiting for us, are they?'

'Black Ayz has the gate. He'll be the one leading Speaker Lystra's vanguard.'

'And what did you tell him?'

Vish laughed. 'I told him he'd better let us in, didn't I!'

'Take that well, did he?' Tuuran chuckled. 'Come on, get that blasted throne built. Sooner we're out of here the better.' He paced the edge of the old stage and watched his men set up their stupid throne. When they thought they were done he went and stood on it and sat on it and jumped on it to make sure it was sturdy. They were still making the second when Queen Lystra's vanguard emerged from the passages under the stage that led into the caves of the Spur. The one at the front, he supposed, must be Black Ayz. He was carrying an absurd crossbow, a murderous thing that would probably go right through a man, armour and all. Had had one of those himself, once. Made for killing dragons. Took the best part of a day to cock, but one well-placed shot could kill a hatchling dead, and that made it quite something. He watched it, calculating, as Black Ayz walked up to him.

'I want to see my sister!' Tuuran almost jumped out of his skin. Queen Jaslyn was right behind him. Her voice had a shrill edge of hysteria.

'Well?' Black Ayz stopped a few feet short. 'You in charge?'

Tuuran shivered. 'Queen Zafir comes with—'

'Yes.' Black Ayz sounded on the edge of exasperation. 'Messages. The Pinnacles. Wonderful. Vish told me. But I don't know who you are.'

'I am Tuuran. Night Watchman to Speaker Za—' He stopped. Black Ayz had levelled the crossbow at him. Just sort of done it without Tuuran seeing it happen. 'What?'

'I am Black Ayz, and *I* am Night Watchman here.' He peered hard at Tuuran. 'An Adamantine Man.' He nodded. 'I'll grant you that much. But I still don't know you.' Black Ayz looked around the stage. 'Big Vish I know. And is that Jasaan the Dragonslayer? And Bishak. Those too are men I know. I'll raise a cup to you for bringing them back to me. But let fifty armed and armoured dragon-riders I've never seen before down into the Spur?' Ayz shook his head. 'I don't think so. You stay here until my speaker says otherwise.'

Tuuran felt Jaslyn at his back. And they were still out in the open on a stage in the glaring sun, wedged between cliff faces and with nowhere to go if a dragon came.

'I—'

A rider he didn't know – not that that narrowed it down much – pushed past him and shook his fist at Black Ayz and his crossbow. 'You stand before Queen Jaslyn, daughter of Queen Shezira of Sand, rightful speaker of the nine realms whom you should serve, Adamantine Man! Your disloyalty must—'

Tuuran winced as Ayz roared. The crossbow shifted. 'Disloyalty? Rightful? You piece of shit! Where were you when the palace fell? Where were you when the dragons came?'

'Lapdogs for the viper Jehal, all of you!' The rider took another step, which put the back of his head conveniently beside Tuuran's left fist.

'*Speaker* Jehal died when the Adamantine Palace fell.' Ayz's face was taut. 'And if you fuckers from the Pinnacles hadn't been sulking away there mooning about over your dead dragons, if you'd been here instead then—'

Tuuran fired a tiny flick of lightning into the back of the dragon-rider's head. The man screamed and dropped like a sack of apples.

Tuuran watched him fall. Dragons didn't care, that was the thing. You could be heir to both the twin thrones of Xibaiya for all the difference it made; a dragon ate you just the same, and that was that.

Could see Black Ayz thinking much the same. Could see him having a good long think about Tuuran and his lightning and what he'd just seen too. Good. Two birds with one stone and all that. Tuuran turned back to the stage. 'Jasaan! Big Vish!' He beckoned them over. 'Get this idiot dragon-rider out of the way.' He gave Black Ayz a look. 'No rush. You lot have a bit of a talk, eh?'

Kataros, trussed up, looked to the sky, scanning for dragons, but there was only Diamond Eye with the pretend-speaker Zafir on his back. Zafir who would murder them all. She remembered Jeiros telling her once, when she'd asked him why he hated his old speaker with such a venom, *You didn't know her. You were off in the Worldspine, doing your duty in King Valmeyan's eyries. You didn't see what she was like. I was her grand master alchemist for the few months she held the Adamantine Throne. She brought this on us.* Under the Spur they all spat at the name Zafir.

Tuuran was still wrestling with his wooden throne when Jasaan came and touched a hand to her shoulder and then moved away, and then all Tuuran's men were suddenly running and yelling, clearing the stage and looking for cover as the dragon Diamond Eye came down. They braced themselves against the whipping wind of its wings, but the dragon swooped past the Oratorium and soared away instead, while Zafir seemed to step off its back and glide through the air. When she landed on the stage Kataros saw the gold-glass disc she rode, another enchantment from the bastard night-skins. Zafir carried the Adamantine Spear. Her gold-glass armour was scarred, a hotchpotch of pieces taken from several suits, but it still made her fearsome, with golden dragons on helm and gauntlets, and if anything the dents and cracks made her even more terrible. She snapped her fingers at Tuuran and went and sat in her throne, ready or not. A dozen more soldiers in Taiytakei glass and gold hurried to flank her, Tuuran at their head. A handful of others dragged Kataros to kneel, bound, at Zafir's feet.

She could bite her lip. That would be easy. A little blood smeared onto the ropes that bound her, turned to acid to burn them through. Spitting blood into all their faces to blind them ... Perhaps Speaker Lystra would bring her other alchemists. Let loose their blood to run amok, wreaking havoc ...

'I will let you go, Kataros,' said Zafir, 'when Lystra comes. We're too few for more killing. Give my regards to Jeiros when you see him. You and he might turn your thoughts from how you despise me to how we might usurp the dragons who now rule these realms that once were mine. You might turn them to our half-god too.' She eased herself forward from her throne then and crouched between them. Her voice dropped to a whisper. 'Tell me, alchemist, what would *you* do in the face of the Silver King's return?'

Kataros snarled. 'This half-god is not the Silver King.'

'No, that he's not.' The corner of Zafir's lip curled in the flicker of a smile. 'But what would you do if he was?'

'Submit,' Kataros said, 'and accept the inevitability of his will.'

Zafir let out a little sigh. 'I suppose that's alchemists for you. When I leave here, tell Queen Lystra what you've seen with your own eyes, not the stories you've heard.' She shifted and settled back into her wobbling throne. 'Hyram did what he did, and Shezira pushed him off a balcony, and yes, I took her head for that, but Jehal was the poisoner, not I, while Jeiros hated me from the very moment Aruch put the Speaker's Ring on my finger.'

And why? Zafir sat back in her improvised throne, wishing for a moment that it was Jeiros bound before her so she might kick him down and needle her feet into his old skinny ribs. *Why? Because I was young and pretty? Because I wasn't old like you? Because I was a queen of the Silver City and you hated us all for keeping the Silver King's secrets to ourselves?* Restless pacing would have suited her better than sitting on this throne, waiting for Lystra. A dull uneasy fury at the Black Moon for taking her eyrie swatted at any calm and flushed it away. And where were the dragons? Hiding? But that wasn't how dragons were. Why hadn't she seen them? Why hadn't they fallen on the eyrie, the Pinnacles? Where was the storm of fire and fang?

They come. Diamond Eye peered into the thoughts and souls of everyone around her, but she still wished she was on her throne in the Pinnacles with its white stone dragon that sought out deceit and glowered it naked into submission or revolt. So easy to fall into old habits, tried and tested and found wanting, but habits nonetheless. Kill them all. A clean sweep. Alchemists, dragon-riders, everyone who would not submit; but whatever she did, mercy or murder, it made no difference to what was coming. The Black Moon would have his way with the world. None of the rest mattered.

None of us are anything but insects to him. Even you, dragon. Ants. Diamond Eye bristled at the truth she threw at him. *Will Lystra bend her knee to me?*

No.

Good. Wouldn't have believed it anyway. Better Lystra's animosity come open and raw.

A trumpet sounded, garish in the still air of the Oratorium, blazing her Adamantine Men into silence. Zafir stayed still, stiff as a rod, the Speaker's Spear firm in her right hand and the ring worn on the left. She heard the tramp of boots through the secret entrances under the stage to the tunnels and caves of the Spur. She pictured Lystra, murderous defiance, the two of them face to face, spittle-flecked. Diamond Eye whisking Lystra into the air and ripping her apart. But no, that wouldn't do. The spear then. Rammed through her black treacherous heart.

Or another way. Lystra mute and humble. Bowing and scraping and begging forgiveness. But no, that way too ended in the spear and blood.

I made a promise …

She was sweating under her gold and glass. She wished there was a breeze to cool her; no, not a breeze, a gale to blow out the detritus of past lives clawing inside. Staying so still, waiting like this, next to impossible not to twitch …

Lystra emerged from the tunnels. She came alone. Jaslyn's little sister, smallest of them all, and yet she walked like a speaker, like a queen; and she didn't come to the stage to tower or grovel before Zafir's pretend throne, but instead climbed the first tier of the Oratorium seats and sat on the stone benches with the three Adamantine Men she'd sent ahead of her. Meeting Zafir eye to eye across the still air and open space where musicians once played between the speeches of each performance, where jugglers tumbled and frolicked between the acts of *Narammed the Great*. They watched one another. She deserved respect for that, Zafir thought. Sitting on her throne with her guardsmen arrayed about her with their lightning throwers and their Taiytakei armour, with her dragon circling his obvious and irresistible menace above, Zafir had imagined herself appearing strong and terrible. But to come alone and sit apart, Lystra took that away.

She's more like me than I thought. And in that perhaps she found a chance they might part with no blood spilled, and so she rose and walked to the edge of the stage and waved Tuuran to stay where he was, and jumped down into the space between them. She stood in the middle of it, straight and tall with the spear in her hand, with everyone looking down on her, and made it her own.

'I am Zafir of the Silver City,' she said, strong in this place made for strident voices. 'These realms were once mine. All of them.' She looked Lystra in the eye and saw strength there, and frailty too. 'Lystra, daughter of Shezira of Sand. Queen of Furymouth. Our realms are ashes. Everything between us is burned in fire. We begin anew. The slate clean. That is what I offer.'

She snapped her fingers. Tuuran cut Kataros free. Zafir turned and looked at Jaslyn, nodded and tipped her head, beckoning her. Other words of building the realms back to glory wandered through her thoughts, but they tasted of ash and crumbled on her tongue. The realms would be built into whatever vision the Black Moon saw, and nothing anyone here said or did would change a whit of it.

Kataros edged around the side of the stage to sit quietly beside Lystra's Adamantine Men. She whispered to them. Queen Jaslyn, hesitant as a butterfly, climbed down to stand at Zafir's side. She wore a helm that hid her face and she didn't take it off. Zafir lowered her spear and cocked her head. She looked up at Lystra, meeting her eye.

'Well?'

Lystra regarded her in silence a moment, then rose and stepped nimbly down the tiers of the Oratorium. Like Zafir she came alone, and as she came closer, Zafir saw her clearly at last, how thin and gaunt and tired she was, and how young, though a year and then some under the Spur had aged her. Lystra stopped a few feet short.

She met Zafir blaze for blaze. A void of animosity settled between them. She held out a hand for the Adamantine Spear. 'Return what you stole,' she said.

'No.'

She looked Zafir up and down. 'Why did you come back?'

'Because this is my home.' As close to one as she'd ever had.

'Now it is mine.' Lystra turned her back to walk away.

'Wait!' At last Jaslyn took off her helm. Lystra froze. When she looked back, just for a moment, it was with a look of wonder. Joy, even.

'Jaslyn?'

'My gift to you,' said Zafir softly. 'Did Jeiros not pass on my words?'

'I took them to be lies,' Lystra said.

Jaslyn stepped forward to greet her. For a moment the two sister queens faced one another. Lystra pulled off a gauntlet and touched her fingers to Queen Jaslyn's cheek.

'You're alive. You're real.'

Jaslyn pulled back a pace, tight, full of anguished tension. Her face seemed to crumple. 'Speaker Zafir, queen of the Pinnacles, greets you,' she said. 'She offers you a gift.'

Jaslyn's hand went to her side. Zafir caught a glint of steel.

Far away, dragons fly. Hundreds pouring from the Worldspine in a wind of wings and scales, racing turbulent over the rapids and cataracts of the Silver River, leaping and diving under the shadows of the Great Cliff. Hatchlings, young adults, great old war-dragons, sleek agile hunters, they come. Silence drives them on, and the white dragon Snow above. A hundred hatchlings peel away as they reach the tumultuous sink hole where the Silver River plunges into abyssal depths under the cliffs of the Spur. Dragon after dragon dives into the chasm and soars into darkness, spewing bursts of flame to light their way, a hundred flaring mouths in a cathedral of space that makes even monsters small. Behemoths birthed these mountains, and here is their abandoned shell, hollow and vast, the mouth of a fissure that cracks the Spur in two. A mile overhead scatter-specks of sunlight filter through, brilliant-bright like morning stars. The dragons fly on, searching, diving, wheeling until they find the caves and tunnels that lead away, that wiggle from the great fissure of the Silver River. The dragons call to one another. Far it runs, this abyss, old as time and deep as the ocean, through the mountains to the other side, carrying the water that feeds the bottomless wells of the Mirror Lakes.

Through secret paths to where the little ones hide, newborn dragons race and leap and bound. Through the deep unlit caverns of the Spur, the unknown places, unexplored, untouched for more than a thousand years but not forgotten. They shriek and light their way with fire, while far above and high, those dragons already grown too large for such places slice onward across the open dust of the Hungry Mountain Plains, ripping the wind.

The spear.

Across desert plains and high valleys between skyborn peaks they scour stone and forest with their thoughts. They sing old songs, words in strange dead tongues long rotted to dust, rhythms born in the first shaping of the world. The spear of the earth hears them, and answers their call.

Zafir caught a glint of steel. Jaslyn already had the knife in her hand. Zafir lunged to stop her, already too late, but the knife never struck. Jaslyn reversed it and held the blade pointed back towards herself.

'Life.' Jaslyn's voice broke. 'Speaker Zafir offers us the gift of life, sister.' The knife slipped from her fingers and clattered to the stone. Queen Jaslyn, weeping, fell towards her sister's arms. Lystra backed away.

'No!' She shook her head. 'This woman beheaded our mother, Jaslyn. Our mother!'

Zafir bared her teeth. 'Because she threw Hyram off a balcony when he chose me instead of her, Lystra. You can't simply kill a speaker and expect it not to matter!'

'I will never bow to you. Never!' Lystra backed further away.

'Then I will not ask you to.'

Lystra didn't stop shaking her head. 'No. Not to you. Keep my sister, whatever you've done to her.'

'Lystra!' Jaslyn fell to her knees sobbing. Zafir hammered the haft of the Adamantine Spear into the ground.

'Shall we murder one another then,' she shouted, 'while dragons own our skies? The last few of us left railing bitter about who shall be queen of the ash pile? Which of us shall be the last sour relic?' The spear in her hand felt firm and cold. If she listened hard she thought she heard it murmuring, but more likely that was her own growing madness. *I could throw it. Pin her to the stone and take it all away. Let more blood run.*

Lystra paused, fierce and furious. 'You took the Adamantine Throne by treachery, murder and poison. You made it into a pile of skulls and bones, and look what you brought! These caves and tunnels are all that's left of our brightness, and you claim it as yours? No. There will never be peace between you and me. Never!'

Zafir gripped the spear. Teeth bared on the edge of fury. She took a step and levelled it ready to throw. 'Whom did I murder? Your dear Jehal was the master of poisons, not I.'

'You murdered my *mother*!'

Zafir shrugged. 'I have brought a half-god, starling Lystra. One way or another he will tame the dragons again. He will make them his, for better or worse. He will have his spear whether you like it or not, and he will do what he will do, and none of us will matter a jot.' Her anger seeped away, scurrying shamefaced into the dark corners of her thoughts, withered and sucked dry by a bottomless fatigue.

'I see no half-god; I only see a murderess.' Lystra walked away for the tunnels under the stage. Kataros and the three Adamantine Men followed. Zafir watched them leave.

What did I expect? Old anger still bubbled and simmered in its corners, refusing to die, growling under its breath that she should strike them all down. Zafir took a deep breath and turned to the men assembled on the stage. She hauled weeping Jaslyn from her knees. 'You are all free to choose,' she cried. 'Follow her if you wish.'

For a moment no one moved. Then the Adamantine Man Jasaan headed for the tunnels, following in Lystra's wake. A murmur and a shuffling of unrest rippled through Queen Jaslyn's riders, until at last one of them moved. They came together then, fearful as though they expected Zafir to change her mind at any moment and cut them down, that it had all been a trick. They gathered Queen

Jaslyn among them and left, and Zafir watched them vanish into the tunnels under the stage. She stood, long after they were gone, fixed to the spot. Her fingers gripped the spear, still pointing it where Lystra had stood. They were tight as stone. She had to put her other hand to them to make herself lower it.

'Night Watchman,' she said, raddled by exhaustion, 'we have what we came for. We have what he wants, and we are not welcome. Leave them to their troglodyte ways. We'll ask no more.' For a moment the world shimmered and blurred. She closed her eyes against a wave of fatigue and nausea. 'We await the pleasure of the Black Moon.' And to do whatever must be done, and as always she would do it alone.

Little one! Diamond Eye pierced her, sharp and urgent. She saw in his mind a swarm of hostile wings skimming cliff walls, coming fast, minds closed to his questions but brimming with fire and murder. The dragons of the Worldspine had chosen their course.

Little one, run!

35

One In, One Out

The old redoubt was a labyrinth, impossible to navigate if you didn't already know your way or have a guide, and even Bellepheros didn't know where half its passages led or what was really at the end of them; but he'd been here enough times to get to anywhere that really mattered, and he knew where the half-god was going: to the Silver King, trapped on the brink of death. He walked through the passages and tunnels that would take him there, climbed shafts and ladders and winced at the pains in his old knees, and wondered in the name of Xibaiya what he thought he was doing. How, exactly, was this going to work? Did he simply pull the spike out of the Silver King's head and wake him up? And then what? Even if that worked, he probably wasn't going to exactly be pleased …

He reached a bridge across a fissure. A rustle of water echoed from below. He put one tentative foot forward and then stopped, trying not to think of the gaping abyss beneath him. Yes, he'd been this way a dozen times before and more, but it never got any better. He stuffed his lamp inside his robe. Better not to see. Better to close his eyes …

A gleam flickered below. Not the pale white glow of an alchemical lamp but a silvery sheen. Bellepheros froze, heart hammering fit to burst from his chest as the Black Moon walked along the sand beside the river at the bottom of the fissure, and he was sure the half-god would somehow know he was there, but the Black Moon passed on and vanished, the last sight of him a lingering flicker of moonlight. Bellepheros waited to catch his breath.

The bridge was a rickety wobbling thing held up by old creaking ropes. He crossed it with his eyes tight shut and let his feet feel their way, clung to the ropes either side and tried to imagine the ground just a short step beneath his toes. He counted the steps as he'd always done until he felt stone under his boots again, welcome as an old lover. When he opened his eyes another alchemist stood less than ten feet in front of him down the tunnel. He was holding up a lamp and peering in disbelief.

'Bellepheros? Grand Master Bellepheros?'

Bellepheros gawped. He hadn't expected to find anyone still alive in the redoubt. 'Who are you?' he blurted, the first thing that came into his head. He wondered if the other alchemist was some desperate delusion, but the alchemist stubbornly didn't vanish. Bellepheros peered. 'Do I know you?' he asked. Then fear got the better of him, and he scurried forward and wrapped his hands over this strange alchemist's lamp.

'Grand Master Bellepheros? How—'

'Hide the light!'

The alchemist pulled away. 'It *is* you!' he whispered. 'Where have you been? Grand Master, the dragons can't reach this far into the caves. There's no need to fear them here.'

'Dragons?' Bellepheros shook his head. 'It's not dragons I'm worried about! There's a half-god loose in here!' He poked the alchemist to be sure he was real. 'I thought the redoubt would be dead and abandoned long ago. How many of you are here?'

'A half-god?' The alchemist's mouth fell open. He looked at Bellepheros as though he was mad. As though he was a ghost.

Bellepheros shook him. 'How many? And what's your name?'

'My name?'

'Your name! You still have those, don't you?'

'Vatos, Grand Master.' They were walking fast now, Bellepheros tugging Vatos along, almost running, which in these caves was often a quick way to end on your arse with sore knees and elbows, but right now Bellepheros didn't care. He felt on the brink, right on the edge of something he couldn't grasp. Another alchemist!

'Vatos! Are there others here?'

'Y-yes. But you were dead, Grand Master! Everyone said. You went to Furymouth and never returned and—'

'How – many – others?' Vatos. The name didn't mean anything. 'Don't you see how important it is?'

Vatos stopped. 'How did you get past the dragons, Grand Master? Where did you go? Why did you leave us?' He clutched at Bellepheros. 'Tell us what to do! There's nothing left!'

A wild plan already swarmed in Bellepheros's head. Gather the last alchemists. Trick the Black Moon's dragons into taking the old poisons again then haul the half-god down. Let loose the blood-magic. Blood-mages once tore the Silver King from his perch, and one half-god was surely much like another …

He forced the madness in his head to be still and looked at it with cold hard reason. The arch-magus Pantatyr had led a thousand blood-mages at the height of their powers, not some ragged half-starved handful. Yet …

He stopped and took careful hold of Vatos. 'One more time. How many other alchemists are in the redoubt, Vatos?'

A distant flash of silver reflected glistening along the damp tunnel wall. A scream echoed after it. Vatos's fingertips froze on Bellepheros's robe.

'Grand Master?' He sounded like a fearful child.

'The Black Moon,' breathed Bellepheros. 'We need to find the others, Vatos, before *he* does. We need …' He heard another scream. The words died. Too late. He felt numb.

Vatos stumbled away. 'They've found a way in! Oh, Great Flame, they've found a way in. How did you get past them, Grand Master? What have you done?'

'Not dragons. The half-god.' Bellepheros leaned against the tunnel wall. He sank to his haunches and held his head in his hands. 'The half-god struck down by the Isul Aieha's spear. Alive again, and now he's killing us. There's nothing we can do, Vatos. You have to go now. You have to hide.'

Another flash of moonlight flared through the caves, carrying another scream. Silver light glinted off the walls, growing ever closer, ever brighter. Vatos looked with eyes wide in terror, looked over his shoulder and then back at Bellepheros once more, forlorn like a beaten dog, and Bellepheros couldn't blame him for his fear. The very walls gleamed silver, and the Black Moon was coming, and Vatos simply stood there because they were in a tunnel and there was nowhere to go, nowhere to run. No nooks, no cracks or crevices for a man to crawl inside, only bare stone walls and shadows and the silver-bright of the Black Moon like the light of the sun, the midday moon, closing them steadily down. He stood quaking while Bellepheros huddled against the wall and waited to see if he would die.

The half-god came. In the fire of silver fury that surrounded him, the glaring bright that filled the air, Vatos froze and arched and screamed. He rose helpless into the air, arms and legs wind-milling, and hung adrift until the Black Moon stood before him. A ruddy haze filled the space between them. Bellepheros stayed where he was, careful and silent. The Black Moon didn't seem to see him, but that couldn't possibly be right.

'I know your thoughts.' Glee and triumph came in gaudy streamers from the Black Moon's tongue. He tapped a finger on Vatos. 'An alchemist should know there's no such thing as a place to hide from a dragon as he peers into your soul.'

The crimson haze thickened, a red iron vapour torn from Vatos and oozing from his skin, slick and bloody now, silvery too, flow-ing into the Black Moon. The essence of the Silver King that every alchemist carried inside themselves. The Black Moon took it, and Vatos died, and the Black Moon let him fall and walked on; and Bellepheros pressed himself against the stone, as plain to see as a man on a rock under the midday sun, and yet the Black Moon passed him by, and he didn't understand why, why the half-god would leave him be, but he did. It was as though Bellepheros wasn't even there.

Vatos was a husk, what was left of him, dead and white-skinned and flaking as though a corpse left to dry in a cave for years. All the moisture had been sucked out of him. Every drop, every prick of blood. He was shrivelled. At a touch Vatos would crumble to dust.

Bellepheros moved away, on through the redoubt, already sure he was too late. He found more alchemists – his family, for want of anything better, their corpses sucked desert-dry in caves precipitately abandoned, lamps still lit, food half eaten. In some the air carried the taint of a greasy black ash, settling like silent corrosive death. The Silver King had vanished. Dead or raised to vengeful life, Bellepheros didn't know, but it hardly mattered. He *was* too late; and it struck him hard then: there would be no more alchemists. None. Ever. He and Kataros might well be the last. He sat down and held his head in his hands and shook and heaved, racked by the irrevocable end of everything he knew.

He was there for a while, lost in grief and misery. By the time he forced himself back to the mouth of the caves the sun was sinking, the eyrie gone and the Black Moon with it. The distant clouds at the end of the valley hung edged in purple. He tried to remember why he'd come here and what he'd thought he could achieve. The stupid notion of a hundred alchemists united to his cause, their power and blood turned as one against the Black Moon after the dragons had been tamed. The stupid notion that there could be anyone left alive.

Ash. All of it. Ash and sand.

'Belli?'

The voice came from deeper in the cave, hesitant and hurt. A voice that couldn't possibly be real, but after a moment he looked up anyway, ready to see the Black Moon again, to see that the half-god had known he was here all along, and that everything had been one cruel trick.

Chay-Liang sat cross-legged on a bizarre and ornate gold-glass sled, looking at him.

'You're not real,' he said flatly when he found his voice.

'Belli,' she said, 'if that is so, then this mirage would nevertheless like some Bolo and qaffeh, if you have any. I am rather hungry.' She gave a wan smile, and then she jumped from her sled and ran across the sand beside the little bubbling river, and Bellepheros started to get to his feet and his knees almost gave way, and then she had his hands, pulling him up and into her arms and holding him tight, quivering and shuddering as though she meant never to let go, and he knew exactly how she felt, a relief as though his blood had been made of lead and was suddenly turned to air.

'Li,' he said, over and over. 'Li. How?' His head spun with why and what she was doing here, and when had she crossed the storm-dark, and how many others were with her, and so many questions spinning in his head like an unruly carousel, all tangled and tripping over one another before they could be made into words, but more than anything else she was here, and the relief and the joy and the sheer dazzling happiness to see her again almost knocked him flat.

'I told you I'd find you again,' she said. She felt different. Hardened and sharpened. Thinner than she'd been the last time he saw her in Merizikat.

They let one another go at last, but they held hands and never stopped touching, even if it was only fingers. Bellepheros led Li back among the caves and stopped in a hand-hewn cellar beside the underground river, the darkness of the fissure above them. Sturdy wooden stools sat around a stone-block table and three half-eaten bowls of pasty mush. Three desiccated corpses lay on the sand beside the water. Bellepheros set his lamp beside the bodies and held Li close, feeling her as she shivered into him – both dazed, both amazed to be alive – and he knew that the corpses at his feet could so easily have been either one of them. He imagined the Black Moon drawing out their lives, and didn't dare peer at their ghastly upturned faces in case there was enough left that he would recognise them. He knew every alchemist alive well enough to at least flounder for a name. Many were old friends. Some he'd studied beside for twenty years. A handful he'd known since they were children. So no, he didn't want to see their faces.

Li pulled away and righted a stool and sat on it, ravenously shovelling food into her mouth. 'I'm sorry,' she said. 'I haven't eaten for days.'

It seemed wrong to eat a dead man's supper right beside his corpse, but Li ate like she hadn't eaten for a month, and Bellepheros was sure the dead alchemists would have understood. Between mouthfuls she told him the truth of how Tuuran had helped her to escape Merizikat, how she'd found Red Lin Feyn and crossed the storm-dark. She laughed as she scraped the last bowl clean and her eyes ranged the floor for more. 'My ship headed back into the storm-dark before I was even out of sight.' She started to shake. Sobs, and Bellepheros wrapped his arms around her and they clung to one another again.

'I wish you hadn't come, Li,' he whispered. 'And I'm so glad you have. So very happy.' He closed his eyes and basked in her, and for a while there was nothing else, and even the Black Moon was forgotten. Then he took her hand and led her further into the fissure, skirting as far around the scattered corpses as he could. One thing he could do: there would be food here, somewhere.

'I had a map,' Li said behind him. 'I thought Zafir's home must be easy to find. I never imagined all the cloud and rain you have in this land.'

They reached a shaft so narrow that even Bellepheros had to twist his shoulders. He went ahead, peering with his failing lamp until Li lit up a brilliant wand behind them, a glass torch like the hundreds she'd made in Merizikat and a hundred times brighter. A film of greasy ash covered the walls. Another desiccated body lay across the tunnel at the top. Bellepheros tried to step around it, lost his balance, stumbled and landed heavily on the corpse's shoulder. It crumbled and cracked underfoot like a mound of dead wood, dry-rotten almost to dust. He shuddered.

'What happened here?' Li asked.

'The Black Moon.' Bellepheros told his own tale as they went from cave to cave through the redoubt's stores, gathering what food they could carry. He stopped as he reached the tale of Zafir's expedition to retrieve her spear, and shivered. Li leaned into him.

'I'm sorry, Belli.' She'd found a bucket of nuts and was gnawing on them.

'These were my last few friends, and the Black Moon brushed them away as though they never existed. When *was* the last time you ate, Li?'

She wrapped an arm around him and rested her head on his shoulder. 'You know I was born and raised in a city, Belli. We had two sail-slaves who cleaned and cooked. When I was eight, I was sent to Hingwal Taktse, where half of us forgot to eat when we were supposed to and wandered about suddenly ravenous at all odd times. The slaves there were used to it. Food was a distraction made by other people that came and went, to be dealt with as quickly as possible. An irritating necessity. I never truly appreciated it until now.' She shook her head and stretched and got up and rubbed her belly. 'I got lost. I was in the middle of nowhere and starving, and I didn't have the first idea what to do, and there wasn't some nearby market, and I couldn't just have a slave prepare a salad ...'

'No qaffeh?'

She laughed, and they sat together a while longer, drinking each other in while Li told him how useless she'd been, how lightning throwers weren't the best weapons for a hungry hunter, and how she'd eventually found the Pinnacles and followed the eyrie all the way to the redoubt.

'I saw the Black Moon come into these caves,' she said, 'and then he came out and the eyrie flew away, and all the dragons with him, and you were still inside, and I thought ...'

Her last words trailed into gossamer silence. Bellepheros struggled to his feet, wincing at the creaking of his knees and how they always hurt when he sat still for too long.

'I thought I might stop him,' he said. 'I don't know how. I don't know why he didn't see me. Or why he didn't see you, for that matter.'

'I took your potion,' Li said. 'To keep myself hidden.'

'But that was for dragons, Li. Not half-gods.'

Li grabbed him by the arm. 'But that's what I found out! After Tuuran sent me away! The dragons *are* half-gods. The Black Moon changed them, but they were like him before. They were your Silver Kings, the ones he defeated. I saw it in the unholy Rava. It's right there, spelled out in black and white, if you know how to look.'

Bellepheros froze as though he'd been turned to stone. 'The carvings in the Pinnacles!'

'What?'

The Black Moon with his blindfold. The Black Moon with his eyes plucked out. And suddenly he knew: the Black Moon's eyes were blind. The Crowntaker saw as any man did, but the half-god hunted as dragons hunted hidden prey, by thought and memory, and Bellepheros, who had hidden his thoughts from the dragons and made himself as invisible to them as he could, had without knowing it made himself invisible to the Black Moon too.

Li told him what Red Lin Feyn had shown her, the same pictures he'd seen in the Enchanted Palace beyond the Hall of Mirages, of the Silver Kings and of dragons, and how every one of them had been drawn with a hole inside their head, and of the Black Moon cracking open the skull of a half-god and seeming to take something out and offer it to a sleeping dragon. And he'd never quite understood what that had meant or what it could be, but what if it was a soul?

'His eyes are blind, but he sees our thoughts and reads our minds, and what hides us from the dragons also hides us from—'

'From him!'

'Yes! And if he can't see us and read our thoughts, he can't command us, and the pieces that he cut out of us with that wretched knife no longer matter. We are free!' Ice crawled up and down his skin. 'Li?'

'Belli?'

'If dragons and half-gods are the same, then there is poison enough here in these caves to wipe out every half-god ever born.'

36

The Savage Claw

Forty-one days after landfall

'The tunnels! Now!' Zafir spared a glance for the sled she'd used to fly from Diamond Eye's back, but it wouldn't do her any good underground and it couldn't outrun a dragon. Tuuran stared, bewildered at first, but when he saw the onrush of dragons swooping across the plains he understood right enough. He swore a lot and yelled; Zafir was already moving, bolting for the tunnels where Lystra had gone, bracing for the fight she knew she must now have with Lystra's soldiers. Better to face men than dragons, though.

Already on edge, taut as a twisted rope from having Lystra stand in front of her again after so long, adrenaline-spiked from the storm of dragons rushing to fall upon her, Zafir ran under the stage and into the sense of the mountain closing around her, walls pressing in, the roof low over her head, the suffocating wrap of stone and gloom and looming darkness.

'Lystra!' Her heart was pounding. Too fast. She had to run because walking was too stifling. Her hands gripped her spear, anything to release the pent-up tension. 'Lystra!' She didn't even know which way to go through the nest of little rooms and passages under the stage where the actors used to keep their costumes and make their changes; but she didn't have to look far before she saw the flash of a lamp and then Lystra's Adamantine Men ahead of her. They heard her coming, of course. The alchemist Kataros stopped and turned to face her, and the Adamantine Man she'd brought with her, whatever his name was – Jasaan, was it? – drew out his axe. She saw him hand a knife to Kataros. The others hurried Lystra and Jaslyn away.

'Turn back, Zafir,' said Kataros.

Zafir laughed at them. 'Turn back? You think I *want* to be down here? The sky fills with dragons that mean to kill us all. Shall we fight them together, or shall I kill you first and fight them alone?' She raised a lightning thrower and levelled the spear. A snort, a sneer, a word of scorn, a hint of derision and she'd have them all. The Adamantine Man was the least of her worries. Zafir shifted the aim of her lightning thrower. Kataros stiffened.

You were thinking it, then …

Long deep breaths. She was shaking. Quivering, desperate to explode into a frenzy, anything. A minute ago she'd felt so tired she could have dropped where she stood, but now …

Tuuran skidded to a stop behind her. 'Holiness …'

Zafir lowered her lightning thrower and grabbed him, shoving him in front of her. 'Tell them, Tuuran. How many? How many dragons?'

'I didn't stop to count, Holiness.' He glowered through the gloom at Jasaan. 'Frankly I don't think we've got enough fingers between us.'

'How – many?' She already knew the answer. Diamond Eye had shown her. Dragons in a horde she'd never seen except swirling in that carnage of tooth and claw and fire over the Pinnacles with Jehal and Hyrkallan.

'I don't bloody know. Hundreds of the fuckers.'

Zafir snapped back to the alchemist and her Adamantine Man. The lightning thrower still pointed straight at Kataros. 'Doesn't it make your heart race to hear? Dragons. *Hundreds!* Go on then, go and fight them. Isn't that what you're for?'

They didn't move. 'Dragons come now and then,' said Jasaan evenly. 'They don't fit down here, and even a dragon can't uproot a mountain. Adamantine Men don't fight battles they can't win, where dying serves no purpose.'

'Really?' Zafir bared her teeth. The rest of her own Adamantine Men were crowding behind her, pressing in close, eager to get as far away as they could from the dragons above. Their tension fed her own. 'Then do you really want to stand in my way?' The mountain shook as the first dragon crashed into the stage above. Were they deep enough yet to be beyond the reach of its fire? She snarled, her last few fragile strands of patience snapping one after the next. 'I've seen hatchlings scour tunnels smaller than this, Jasaan.' Dragons or men, Kataros was giving her no choice but to fight one or the other. And damn her, the alchemist still didn't move aside to let her pass. Her lightning hand trembled.

No.

She lowered the spear. Nodded. There was a better way. 'Go, then. I have Adamantine Men of my own. I will hold this path alone. Go to your starling speaker.'

'Yes, go wipe her arse for her,' sneered Tuuran. 'Or whatever use you are down here in the dark, hiding away. There's work only for real Adamantine Men here.' The last was aimed square at Jasaan, the dragon-slayer hero of the Purple Spur. Jasaan bristled. He exchanged a curt few whispers with Kataros and the alchemist hurried away, reluctant and casting glances over her shoulder. Jasaan bared his teeth at Tuuran.

'You show me then. Your men may pass, Tuuran, but either you or your queen tries it and you'll take my axe.'

'Care to see how that ends?' Tuuran pulled his own axe from his back and took a step. 'Shall we just settle that now? I can't imagine it taking more than a second or two.'

'Night Watchman!' Zafir slapped his arm. Easy as anything to scythe Jasaan with lightning and run deeper into the Spur with the rest, but no, there was a point to prove and she needed Jasaan alive to see it made. She turned, ready for the onrush of dragons, the dim filtering of daylight at the far end of the tunnel where it turned and then opened under the oratorium stage. The first hatchling would come at any moment.

'Have you faced a dragon before, Night Watchman?' she asked.

Tuuran was arranging his men, trying to stand them between her and where the dragons would come. 'Faced and fought?' He shook his head. 'Faced and been lucky? Once. In the desert beside the Queverra, trapped in a slave cage. It would have burned me, but some monster crashed out of the sky before it had the chance and chased it off into the abyss.'

For a moment the two of them looked at one another. Perhaps Tuuran didn't know it, but that monster had been Diamond Eye, and Zafir had been on his back, and she'd known Tuuran was near and yet had left him there.

'And you? Have you faced a dragon, Holiness?'

'Only riding on the back of another. I ran from a hatchling once.' She set herself. 'Baros Tsen's white witch faced down a dragon on her own though, more than once, armed with lightning and enchanted glass. The lightning will stop them.'

Tuuran grunted. 'It knocks them down good enough, but someone still has to go to them with an axe and finish the job before they get up again. We have Taiytakei gold and glass armour. Fine against lightning, but I'm not so sure about dragon-fire.'

'I have dragonscale under my glass and gold, Night Watchman.'

Tuuran gripped his axe. At the far end of the tunnel a shadow crossed pale ghosts of second-hand sunlight. 'Good. Then I'll worry a little less for your safety while you stand behind the ranks of my soldiers.'

Zafir didn't move from his side. She looked back to Jasaan, watching from further down the passageway, and called to him: 'Soldier! Your alchemist lover Kataros claims that the Silver King's spear turns dragons into stone. Do you believe her?'

'Why don't you show me?'

Tuuran laughed, but Zafir gently nodded. 'I think I will.'

A darkness fell at the far end of the tunnel. A shape, blocking the light. The Adamantine Men raised their arms. A dozen enchanter torches raked the tunnel stone, dazzling sharp beams born of gold-glass. There it was, a snout. Fangs, claws. A dragon eased around the corner and paused a moment to glare at them all, dazzled by the light. Tuuran gritted his teeth. 'If your spear turns dragons to stone, Holiness, perhaps you would be kind enough to allow me to wield it on your behalf?'

High above the mountain Diamond Eye danced and wove the air, beset by a hundred dragons who demanded to know why, why do you choose this little one, why do you let her ride when you are free, why? And yet as he wheeled and arced and swooped among them, he rode with Zafir and she with him, and through him she saw into the hatchling's thoughts, the dragon in the tunnel who meant to kill her.

'Sooner rather than later, Holiness,' urged Tuuran. She barely heard him. Deep now, inside dragon minds.

The hatchling took a step closer and then another. It bared its fangs. Cautious. It would be inside them too, peering through their thoughts, reading their minds, scanning their memories. It saw the lightning they carried, but it had never tasted that lightning for itself. It wouldn't know quite how it hurt, not yet.

Her. Its head turned a tiny notch, and Zafir knew it was looking at her.

The spear.

An exhilaration. Awe and a flash of understanding, wrought from the skies above her. *That, little one. The Earthspear. That is why they come.*

Jasaan, still behind them, still watching. Zafir regarded the dragon, eyeing her in return.

'But Tuuran, I also have the dragonscale.' She took a glass shield from the soldier beside her and sent him scurrying back. Then cocked her head as Diamond Eye might have done. *Are you afraid of me, little hatchling? Because you should be.*

The hatchling bared its fangs and opened its mouth to unleash fire. Zafir gripped her spear a little tighter. She hunched behind her pilfered shield, ready for the flames to come.

Deep in the caves under the Spur, wending their way along the cascade and rush of the Silver River, come a hundred hatchling dragons. Claws spark on stone. Tails scrape, wings flare, looking for a way in, a way to reach the little ones in their secret hiding places, the deep earth that will be their tomb. Through crack and crevice, cave and fissure and ancient tunnel they come. Stone bars the way. Tiny narrowings where men might squeeze but too small for any dragon to pass. Rockfalls too deep to dig aside. Walls and barriers built long ago to keep monsters at bay in the years when fire last ruled the skies. The dragons swirl in furious confusion, rage and hunger surging them on, filled with desire for blood and the hunt.

The spear. They feel it. All of them. Awake and alive. Keening for the touch of a half-god, but the caves and tunnels offer no passage.

Amid chaos and storm the dragon Silence pauses.

The water, she calls. *The water will take us through.*

In she dives and others follow, for water is one thing the little ones cannot live without, and though the Silver River dances through deep lake and cistern and mile after mile of drowned inky black wend and wind, there is a truth that even the little ones of long ago had not fully understood. That dragons do not need to breathe.

Fire burst from the hatchling's maw. Trapped and held fast by the tunnel walls the flames rushed at Zafir and Tuuran and their bristling steel and lightning.

'Shields!' Tuuran pulled Zafir beside him, pressing against her. He wrapped himself around her as best he could. Zafir slammed shut the gold-glass visor of her helm and planted her shield beside his. The Adamantine Men pressed together, a single solid wall of gold-glass. The flames washed around them, over and past while they cowered tight together like some armoured beast, waiting for the fire to end but it didn't. It burned on and on and crept like water between crack and chink, searching for skin to burn. Baros Tsen had asked Zafir once how much fire a dragon could vomit from its gullet before it was spent and she'd laughed at him and told him that no one knew. No one had ever seen a dragon drained. There was no end to them. Nor would there be today.

She stole a glance behind her. Lit by the garish light she could see the length of the tunnel, reaching far on into the mountain before opening wide. Jasaan was crouched behind a dragonscale shield of his own. On and on the fire came.

'Back,' she cried. 'Send your men back, Night Watchman.' Their shouts were tinged with pain now, and fear. They would break, and Tuuran knew it, and if they broke even once before a dragon's fire then she would never have them stand again as they stood now; but in glass and gold and with dragonscale wrapped around her, the flames wouldn't touch her, not yet.

Tuuran's hand pulled her, drawing her with him in retreat. She shook him away and lifted a clenched-fist from behind the shield and let the flames wash her. Dragonscale. She barely felt the heat. She straightened, one arm holding the spear, the other holding her borrowed shield across her face and throat, the only weakness in the armour she wore. The fire scourged her. She let it.

'Holiness!'

Tuuran's scream rang over the roar of the fire and the shouts and cries of his men as they scurried away. He lunged for her, but too late as she ran straight at the dragon's throat, into flames too burning bright to see the monster at the other end. With every stride the roar and rush grew. The heat wrapped her in a gasping embrace. She half-drew a breath and choked on it at once, blistering and fierce. Blind and breathless she raised her lightning thrower and let fly. The thunder of it shook the walls and shuddered the air and deafened and dazed her. The hatchling jarred back, twitching and twisting. The fire, for a moment, paused. Dazzled by flames and lightning and now drenched in sudden gloom, Zafir saw only shapes of shadows, a blur, a whirl of claws and wings and tail as the dragon tried to right itself, to shake clean its lightning-raddled thoughts and understand what she'd done. She took a lungful of air, clean and warm, and burst forward, and howled and lifted the spear. The hatchling shook itself and faced her, grinning fangs to snap her in two, but too slow. As it opened its mouth she hurled the spear with every drop of her strength. The dragon arched and twisted as though it already knew what was coming, but the stone around it was a cage, a wall against escape. The spear struck and flashed with silver moonlight as bright as a thunderbolt. The dragon froze. Before her eyes it turned to stone.

Zafir stood, chest heaving, gasping for air, looking at what she'd done. A warning from Diamond Eye whistled through, arching and weaving in the air somewhere far away now. And yes, she felt them, the other dragons in the tunnel behind, crazy-eyed with murderous madness. She tugged at the Isul Aieha's spear, jutting from the frozen dragon's petrified scales. It came free with a willing ease. Then she turned and ran.

Tuuran already had Jasaan pinned to the floor, his men around him. Zafir strode among them, a wildness coursing through her. They were huge, these Adamantine Men, muscle and strength, and yet she felt taller than any of them. She kicked Tuuran off Jasaan.

'You just had to make a point, is that it? Let him up,' she said. Her glare snapped to Jasaan. 'Did you see? Did *you* see, Night Watchman?'

Tuuran nodded.

'They can be killed.' She waited as Tuuran's men drew away. There was an uncertainty to the way Jasaan looked at her now.

An amazement. Not a fear, exactly. Was it awe? He half-expected her to murder him. It was in his eyes, yet he wasn't afraid. She crouched beside him.

'Do you see? They die. They *can* die.' She offered him her hand to help him to his feet. She thought perhaps he might take it, but in the end he shied away.

'Holiness,' he said. He shook his head, bewildered and confused. 'From birth to death we obey. Nothing more, nothing less. Lystra is our queen and our speaker. But I will vouch for what I have seen. I will speak of your victory.'

'We'll kill a hundred dragons more and it still won't be victory, but so be it.' Zafir nodded. 'Lead the way, soldier of Narammed, and takes us to where we might all stand together and turn back this tide.'

They ran, all of them together, while the dragons skittering through the tunnels lashed the stone hatchling to rubble and came on.

Water. Deep and dark and cold, black as death and old as unholy Xibaiya. The dragons swim silent through its icy calm, drawn by the current. Bottomless and timeless, these holes and burrows from when half-gods strode the sky and labyrinth wyrms crawled beneath the skin of the earth to caress their doomed goddess. Long gone all of these, all but their relics, earth places whose desiccated souls stir restless now, goaded from their eternal sleep by the murmurings of the goddess's spear. Hostile and sullen they watch the dragons pass; but though the dragons feel their presence they know the ancient earth for what it is, toothless and without power. The dragons care nothing for its animosity, and besides, water bows always to the moon, fickle and changing and ever shifting.

Mile after mile the river draws them on into the air once more, to a grand void of darkness rising among the mountains, the great fissure spread wide like an opening wound. In blackness the hatchling Silence skitters across wet slime-drifted stone and pauses to listen.

Little ones. Silence feels their thoughts. They are close now.

*

Jasaan led them fast through lamplit passageways carved long ago to a grand cavern riddled with pillars of water-grown stone, fangs rising from the ground and hanging from above like the teeth of some ossified devil as tall as a mountain. The walls and low-pressing ceilings of stone lifted away, and Zafir felt the tightness in her chest lift with them. Space. A chance to breathe. Not like open skies, but not the oppressive cage of dark narrow places either. Their Taiytakei torches shone bright, dancing leaping shadows across the twisting spires. The Adamantine Men talked quietly among themselves of the Great Flame, the first mother of all dragons who climbed from the earth beneath the Spur and gave birth to a thousand eggs, a dragon as big as a city. Zafir knew better. She had an idea, now, of the father of dragons. The carvings in the Pinnacles laid it out for anyone to see if they had eyes to understand. The Black Moon had made them.

'How far does all this go?' she asked Jasaan. The caves under the Spur belonged to the alchemists and always had.

'A realm all of itself,' he said.

Across the cavern, close enough to see with their torches, gates of iron and wood hung open into another maw-like darkness. Men thronged around them, lit by bobbing alchemical lamps. Lystra's Adamantine Men and Lystra herself, a hundred strong arms in dragonscale. They even had a pair of scorpions, battered and bent in places, salvaged from the walls of the Adamantine Palace after it fell. On either side the cavern fell into a darkness black and all-swallowing. A sense of lurking demons clawing at Zafir. She pushed it aside as best she could and approached the gates alone. It helped to have something there, right in front of her, something immediate to fill her head. A scorpion pointed at you was good for that, and the hostile glare of soldiers who had once sworn to serve her. For the second time she faced Queen Lystra, old rival and enemy, face to face and eye to eye, wary and pleased at the distance between them. Once-impossible things came more easily now, but it still took a breath or two before she could bring herself to drop to one knee. She couldn't bow her head. Too much pride for that.

'Dragons come,' she said. Her voice echoed through the emptiness, the darkness. She spoke the words loud. 'This is your realm, Lystra of Sand. If you will have it, I will stand at your side, my men with yours, until these dragons are gone or else we die in their fire.'

Lystra, armoured for battle as she'd been before, turned her back. Zafir stayed as she was, down on one knee but head held proud. Waiting.

Tuuran watched, half of him wondering why Zafir didn't just blast the wretched queen under the mountains with a nice dose of lightning like she had with her sister Jaslyn. Teach her some manners, that would. The other half of him busied itself with how long they had before the next hatchling came scrabbling after them and how, exactly, he was supposed to do anything about it while Zafir held the spear that conveniently turned them into stone, and how, exactly, he was supposed to do what a Night Watchman was *supposed* to do and keep his speaker from harm when there were dragons one way and a horde of hostile soldiers and alchemists and scorpions the other.

'This is just a little bit shitty,' he grumbled. He looked at White Vish and then at Jasaan. Jasaan at least had the decency to look away, shamefaced. 'Well? Dragon-slayer? Do you stand with us or not? If it's not then could you at least go and ask your queen if she might just possibly consider helping us not all burn to a crisp?'

Jasaan shook his head. 'I'll stand with you, Tuuran. But you've been gone a long time. You don't understand what Zafir did here. You don't understand what she means to them, how many died because of her, how—'

'Dragon!'

The cry echoed from the tunnel, which was handy for Jasaan because it saved him from a punch in the face. Zafir didn't move. She didn't even look round. Which was all very Zafir, but not very helpful.

'You going to get that spear, then?' asked Jasaan. But that wasn't how this worked, and he really ought to know it. Bloody queens. Both of them as bad as each other. Just happened to love one of them, that was all.

Shit. Did I just think that? Bollocks no!

The love of duty. That was probably what he'd been thinking. Yes. That.

The soldier he'd set at the rear watching for dragons came

bolting past out of the tunnel, and Tuuran had never been so grateful for something else to think about. 'How many?' he yelled.

'Six? Ten? I don't bloody know. Lots! It's big, this one. Hardly fits.'

Big made it slow. So there was that.

A last glance back to the gates with their scorpions. Would they do better to hold there? Lystra seemed to think so, but Tuuran wasn't so sure. Better here at the entrance with the dragons trapped in a tunnel and coming at him one at a time. Once they spread into the cavern the men at the gate might kill two or three, if they were astoundingly lucky, and then everyone died in fire …

'It's never the bloody easy way, is it,' he said, as much to any of the old spirits of the legion that might happen to be watching. They ought to be, he thought, because there wasn't going to be another fight quite like this for a while. True Adamantine Men – even if there were only a dozen of them – armed with a pair of lightning throwers apiece, with Taiytakei gold-glass shields and armour. Men who just might keep their shit together when a dragon came at them. 'Sit yourselves down and enjoy it,' he muttered, 'if only because there might not be any Adamantine Men left come the end of it. If you could find some way to pitch in and help, that would be nice.' On the other hand, they might just think it was as good a blaze of glory as any to die in.

Ghosts. He was talking to ghosts.

Zafir was still on one knee before the gate. Still not moving, still no bloody use. Down to him then. He shouted at his men to back away a distance from the tunnel mouth and get their shields and those lightning throwers ready, because they were bloody well going to need them, because any moment now the first dragon was going to come and hose everything with fire until it squeezed itself out, and Tuuran needed them far enough back not to burn, but close enough that they had some chance of hitting what they were aiming for once they started throwing lightning back the other way. And even this handful might have held a tunnel where dragons could only pass one at a time if their lightning throwers had worked as well as they did in Takei'Tarr or in Merizikat, but they didn't. Took bloody ages to find the strength to fire again. Ever since they crossed the storm-dark, and Tuuran didn't have a bastard clue why. Bellepheros reckoned something to do with the dragons, but it hadn't made much sense.

'Never the bloody easy way,' he grumbled again, and looked about for anyone else who had a nice big axe and might be up for using it. 'You!' White Vish. 'With me.' He looked at Jasaan. 'You too, dragon-slayer, for when one of us gets his head burned off. The rest of you lot, shield wall and blast anything that shows its snout through that hole until it stops moving, but not until it's poking its nose out, mind!'

'We're going to die here, are we?' asked Jasaan.

Tuuran bared his teeth. 'If we do, won't it just be glorious?' Which, in the end, was all that was supposed to matter. He tucked himself out of sight where the tunnel opened into the cave, where the dragons had to pass, lightning thrower at the ready, axe propped against the stone beside him. Waved Vish to the other side. He sneaked a glance into the tunnel and swore loudly. The hatchling was only yards away, slithering on its belly, scales scraping along the walls, almost too big to fit.

The dragon grinned and belched fire. Tuuran barely jerked out of the way in time, and then everything kicked off.

'Hold!' he screamed. 'Hold!' Last thing he needed was people wasting precious lightning, and he needed the dragon out in the open, or at least a part of it, enough of it to hit. He flicked another glance at Zafir. Still hadn't moved. Nor had the men at the gates, but he had their attention now right enough. So that was something. He grimaced at Vish. 'Die well. That's the best we ever get, right?'

The dragon lunged out, claws scrabbling for purchase, trying to pull itself through as fast as it could. Its jaws snapped round and bit at him. Tuuran jumped back as flames swept over him, screaming burning pain. Then lightning, a cacophonous scatter of thunderclaps that set his whole skull ringing, loud enough to blur his eyes. The dragon shrieked. It coughed on its own fire.

'Now! Take it down!' He snatched up his axe.

Lightning flashed, dazzling. Thunderclaps boomed. The cavern air shook in deafening echoes. Light and noise and he could barely think, but that didn't matter. Didn't need to *think*. Just needed to bring his axe down on the hatchling's head.

He swung. Missed as it snapped away. Bastard thing was half out of the tunnel now, almost loose. Another bolt hit the dragon and then another. It screamed and shook, talons flailing. Vish brought his axe down on its head. Glanced sideways, cut deep but not deep enough to kill. Jasaan jumped wildly past him, smashing his blade into the dragon's snout, and still it came. Tuuran roared and leaped, howling with every ounce of muscle, springing into the air, axe square into the dragon's skull with all his weight and strength behind it. Down deep, the whole axehead driven through scale and bone. Wrenched it free and jumped again, screaming his head off for it to just die, over and over and ...

He stood for a moment, gasping. The dragon fell. Half his face was burning agony where its fire had caught him, worse than when that fire witch had burned his ear off in Aria.

'It's dead, boss,' yelled Vish. 'You killed it.'

Tuuran nodded. '*We* killed it.' His ears were ringing. After-flashes of lightning seared his eyes. He staggered, trying to orient himself, and then the dragon lurched forward, and for a moment he thought it was still alive and howled and lifted his axe, and damn, what did it take to kill these bastards? But then he understood: the dragons in the tunnel behind were barging it out of the way, ready to come at him again, and just for a moment he wondered if he could really do this any more.

Not an Adamantine thought that. He shook himself and scanned his eyes over his waiting men, crouched behind their Taiytakei shields. The glow of their lightning throwers in the gloom. He picked them out, the bright white dazzle-light of the ones primed and ready, the dull glimmer of those already loosed. A dozen left still strong. Good enough. One of the pair fixed to his left arm still gleamed bright too. Never mind the roar in his ears, never mind the flashes of light and shadow that meant he could barely see, or the pain of his scorched face. He let it eat him and turned it to savage anger.

'Come on then!' he bellowed. 'Who's next? I don't care how many of you there are. One by one my axe will have you!' Maybe they'd get three or four before their lightning was spent. But like he'd said: fucking glorious.

Zafir still didn't move. What was the bloody woman thinking?

The dead dragon flopped to one side. Two small hatchlings shot through the gap, one after another. Tuuran caught the first with his lightning and sent it tipping head over tail in among the stone columns. 'Someone kill it! Kill it quick!' He swung his axe at the second. Missed. Vish shield-slammed it. Lightning hit it in the face, three bolts at once, and Tuuran ended it with a second swing, straight through the neck. A small one this, if you could say that anything was small when it was the size of a carthorse. Jasaan ran at the hatchling loose in the cave. Another soldier broke from the wall of shields. In the gloom Tuuran didn't see who it was, but he saw the hatchling dart and lash with its tail, saw his soldier fly twenty feet through the air, chest caved in, saw him smash against a stone pillar like a petrified tentacle and slump still. Lightning sprawled the dragon back down. Jasaan slammed in with his axe. Two more men dived out of the wall and finished it.

Tuuran looked at his arms. His lightning throwers were nowhere near ready again. Looked at his men for the sun-bright of charged wands and didn't see it. They were spent. That was that, then. Lightning gone. So the next one was going to be a right bugger.

'I'll wall you out with a mound of your own corpses!' he spat. He looked at White Vish, and Vish looked back.

'As good as it gets, boss.'

Fire thundered from the tunnel, long and hard and fierce, enough that he had to back away. He could feel it through the stones, the trembling earth. Big like the first. A monster, hauling itself through. He took deep breaths and braced to take a swing.

'Holiness!'

The fire came on and on, washing around the entrance to the cavern, sweltering hot, cooking him in his own sweat. With a sudden lunge the dragon's head snapped out, curling to the side, snapping at him, fire burning on and on. He had his shield ready, gold-glass held up to cover his face. The dragon twisted and squirmed, pulling itself onward. It bit at Vish and then whipped back, fangs splintering glass, knocking Tuuran down like the kick of a mule. Flat on his back. It opened its mouth to burn him, and he had nowhere to run. No time.

'Bollocks to you!' Tuuran threw the knife off his belt, the

only thing he had. It struck in the dragon's eye. Its fury blazed, a thunderclap. Then flame and blinding light. For a moment he couldn't think. He blinked. A scorpion bolt struck the dragon's neck. It reared away from him. More thunder smashed it back, dazed them both with noise and pain, and then Zafir was there with her spear, driving it into the dragon's scales. Tuuran didn't move. Just lay and watched the dragon turn to stone, sealing the tunnel tight with its bulk.

He blinked and looked at himself in amazement that he wasn't dead. Visor down, but through the clear glass of her dragon-rider's helm he could see Zafir's eyes, wide and wild. She offered him her hand.

'We have earned entrance to the Spur, Tuuran. *You* have earned us entrance.'

Tuuran stared a moment longer at the stone dragon.

'Up, Night Watchman. More will come.'

Halfteeth, left in charge of the ruin of the Adamantine Palace, had Snacksize standing up on watch on the walls since he reckoned she had the best eyes. So it was Snacksize who first saw the dragons coming. They flew low, hugging the cliff wall of the Spur a few miles to the north, and she didn't spot them until they were close, dark specks against dark stone. She took a moment to be sure of what she was seeing, and then she ran, hard and fast like she'd never run before, yelling and screaming to anyone and everyone to drop whatever they were doing and flee like the wind. Halfteeth, never much one for doing what he was told, bolted out of the Glass Cathedral into the rubble-strewn yard as the commotion broke.

'What?'

Snacksize pointed northward. 'Hundreds of them.'

There was a terror in the way she looked, and that wasn't the Snacksize Halfteeth had come to know. He let her go, though, yelled at everyone who hadn't already started running to get on with it, and clambered up the stone remains of some monster dragon. He crawled onto its back and still couldn't see over the walls, and so he went on clambering up its scaled neck.

The first dragon he spotted was a hundred yards short of the palace, skimming the ground, keeping low, racing in fast like a night-skin rocket and looking straight at him. Halfteeth froze for a heartbeat. And then, since there wasn't much else to do except gawp and die, he slid down the neck of the stone dragon, skittering across its scales and praying to every god from every world he could remember on the off chance that one of them was real; and maybe one of them was, because instead of falling off the dragon's neck to dash himself to pieces in the rubble below, he managed to cling on until he reached its back, and then twisted and tumbled and fell and rolled and grabbed hold of one half-open petrified wing. He ducked underneath it as fire poured from the sky, as a very alive flesh-and-blood dragon shot across the ruined palace and doused everything in flame.

Its shadow blotted out the sky as it passed over him. It flicked its tail, shattering the wing beneath which he'd paused, but by then he was moving again. The stone shuddered, almost shook him off his feet. He ran and slid and fell off the dragon-statue's tail and smashed into the ground. The breath burst out of his lungs. For a second he couldn't move, too winded to get up, but Snacksize, every bit as stupid as he'd always thought, was already hauling at him with the desperate strength of a man twice her size and yelling so many curses that his head spun. She kicked him and pulled him and ran and threw them both flat through the entrance of the Glass Cathedral as a second torrent of flames washed the yard outside. Halfteeth staggered to his feet and turned back to see what was happening. The skull of some great old dragon rested in front of the cathedral. Halfteeth stared at it, and then a live dragon crashed to ground beside it, swatted it away and rammed its snout through the doorway to scour the place with fire. Snacksize loosed lightning straight in its face. The dragon lurched back, stung, and that was long enough for Halfteeth to scramble to his feet. Snacksize thumped him.

'You really as stupid as you look?' she screamed. 'Keep moving!' She pulled him and bolted for the far end of the cathedral behind the altar, where the men he'd told to run were fighting each other for the steps that spiralled to the tunnels below. For somewhere safe. Halfteeth swore at them.

'Shields, you idiots! Get your shields up. And your lightning, damn you!' The ones who actually had shields. The ones who even had lightning throwers.

Something slammed the Glass Cathedral hard. It shook. Snacksize worked her way through the crush of men around the stairs, dragging a few of them out, the ones with lightning and armour. Another dragon head burst through the entrance. Bolts of lightning smacked it back. The noise left Halfteeth half deaf, but there wasn't much else to do except hold his ground. Another dragon came, or maybe the same dragon for all Halfteeth could tell, and then another, and then suddenly they were out of lightning and the last of his men were still on the stairs, screaming at the ones below to get out of the way.

A new dragon came. A white one this time. Riding inside their heads, plucking out Halfteeth's thoughts.

Your fear is delicious, little ones.

Halfteeth threw a rock at it and then cowered behind the altar as the fire came, scorching and furious.

Under the Spur the dragon Silence prowls onward, sniffing ever closer to the thoughts of the little ones. Through crack and crevice and fissure, always with the water leading the way, until at last a glimmer of light shines on distant stone. A lamp. Silence feels the hunger of her brothers and sisters who follow, hatchlings all, not long from the egg yet each with the ravenous memories of a thousand years and centuries of servitude.

I am Silence, the dragon whispers to the little ones in their terror, *and we are hungry.*

Along the caves around the fissure of the Silver River the dragons dance amok. Little ones run and scream. Silence tears them from their holes, men and children, women, infants, animals, all scythed the same. The iron reek of blood scents the air. Red-muzzled fangs snap on flesh and bone. The little ones howl while dragons move in murderous silence. They creep among the scatter of terrified thoughts scrabbling to escape. They lurk in shadowed corners. They leap and pounce. Tails lash air and crack iron and bone. A handful of little ones escape along tunnels too narrow for even a hatchling to follow. The dragons pour fire in their wake, scorching the last to flee, burning their skin, charring them, listening to their fading screams.

The first nest is found and put to death. The dragon Silence dives once more into the water. On and again until all are gone, and the Earthspear is held in dragon claws to keep the Black Moon at bay.

37

The Enchantress

Bellepheros led Li to the potion store, and Li set about making another sled. In Takei'Tarr and Merizikat Bellepheros had seen her shape glass and make it flow like water, moulding it to her desires in seconds. Here it moved like reluctant molasses.

'The dragons,' she said when she saw him frowning. 'They feed on the weave of the world and take it for themselves. They've drained these realms almost dry. That's why the Elemental Men were so afraid of them, once they knew. Nothing here works the way it should. Everything is dying.'

They rolled potion barrels onto the sled when it was done, and floated it to the cave mouth. The sled Liang had used to fly across the ocean waited there. It was a strange contraption. Concentric rotating rings hung from the back end at all angles to one another, a crazy jumble of spinning geometry rimmed in bright-lit gold. A Taiytakei sled was usually little more than an elongated ellipse, and riders simply stood braced against the wind, but Li had moulded something much larger for herself, something more like a sedan chair with a seat and a roof set into a glass hemisphere. It didn't strike Bellepheros as particularly comfortable, but at least he could sit down.

'You put a top on it.'

'Because of the rain,' said Li drily. 'You never thought to mention that in your world it rains all the time!'

'You never thought to ask.'

The front of the sled bristled with lightning throwers and gold-glass shields. The rest was a mishmash of harnesses welded into glass, of leather straps and ropes and buckles tying down crates and barrels. Two ranks of golden spheres lined its underbelly. More lightning throwers protruded there, and there were glass tubes loaded with Taiytakei black-powder rockets tipped with globes of trapped fire. Mounted behind the rider's seat was a battery of them on a steel pivot mount a bit like a small scorpion. Bellepheros laughed.

'You've made your own dragon, Li.' He walked around the sled, looking at it, over it, under it. 'Rockets, eh? Some dragon lords from the northern realms would strap scorpions on the backs of their war-dragons.'

Li touched a piece of gold-glass shaped like a bucket. It rose into the air. She guided it to the river and grinned as it sank and filled and then floated back. 'Sleds have more uses than you think! I was imagining the desert again, you see. Where water is hard to find and doesn't constantly fall out of the sky without ever stopping. Do you have deserts here?'

'In the north. I don't know what's there any more. The Black Moon never went so far. I suppose I have no idea where Zafir has roamed on her dragon.'

They loaded as much from the redoubt as the sled could carry. Potions to kill, to hide, to strangle a dragon's memories and make them dull. Not enough for the thousand who haunted the Worldspine, not yet, but enough to start. Enough for the Black Moon, if they could find a way to make him drink them. The night was half done when they stopped, the sky as black as tar under rolling clouds that covered moon and the stars, the air filled with the familiar hiss of rain, but Bellepheros and Liang worked on, roaming the old redoubt. They took as much food as they could find, more water from the river, lamps and potions and pouches of herbs and minerals, leaves and roots and powdered stone, anything Bellepheros thought might have a use. They returned to Li's sled when they were done to find the long shadows of dawn already creep-crawling along the cliffs of the valley outside. The dragons that had once stood sentinel over the crags were gone. Bellepheros couldn't see a single one.

'Even so, we shouldn't fly in the day,' he said. 'The dragons will see—'

'Dragons?' Li snorted. 'I've seen dragons every day for the last week.'

She was full of fire now, and so was he, nothing like the wasted, exhausted creature he'd been before he found her. Seeing her again was like a new life coursing through him, although he still balked as she climbed onto the sled and beckoned him to follow, knowing how utterly petrified he was going to be the moment he saw the ground fall away.

'Just close your eyes, Belli.' She took his hand as he climbed onto the sled. 'Close your eyes and hold my hand. I'll keep us safe.'

He huddled under the battery of Taiytakei rockets and curled into as tight a ball as he could manage, wedged in and pressed against her, wrapped in an old dusty fur. He closed his eyes so he wouldn't see and tried to think of happy days long ago, and the next thing he knew the sun was a long way past its zenith, and Li was shaking him awake, and the sled was blissfully on the ground under a canopy of trees, and the caves of the redoubt were far away. He felt it in the air – thicker, warmer, dry. They were still in the mountains but out of their deep heart.

'Welcome back,' Li said, a little drily. 'We passed the eyrie a while ago but now I don't know which way to fly.'

Bellepheros tried to unfold himself and whimpered at the pain of it. His knees, as usual. Locked fast from being cramped up for so long. None of his joints wanted to move, and his legs had gone to sleep. Took a few minutes before he could stand on his own.

'You're getting worse,' Li said.

'I know. It's the dragon-disease. These last months ...' He might have said more, but she cupped a hand around the back of his head and pulled him close and kissed him, and Bellepheros, once grand master alchemist of the Order of the Scales who had held the fate of kings and realms in his hands, entirely forgot how much his old knees hurt. Chay-Liang kissed him for a long time and then gently eased him to the ground and held him tight.

'Alchemists don't take lovers,' said Bellepheros hoarsely. 'Well, we're not supposed to. The disease ...'

She shut him up by kissing him again.

'I'm an old man, Li.'

'And I'm an old woman.' She shifted abruptly and sat cross-legged beside him, but when Bellepheros tried to get up as well she pushed him down. 'Tell me about your Silver King, old man,' she said. 'How did your blood-mages bring him down? What do we have to do?'

'There are more stories about that than I have fingers.' Bellepheros wrinkled his nose. 'When the dragons forgot who they were, the Silver King showed the blood-mages how to bend them to their will, how to ride them and fly them, but as to how they brought him down?' He sighed. 'I don't know. No one remembers. It was never written. If dragons and half-gods are the same under their skins then the best I can think of is to use the same potions we once used against dragons, the ones the Silver King taught us. What does the Black Moon mean to do, Li? Do you know? What does he want? Vengeance against the Silver King who once slew him and cast him into the abyss of Xibaiya? But he's taken that. What was left of the Isul Aieha is turned to dust.'

'The Black Moon turned against the first gods, Belli, the forbidden ones the Elemental Men would have us forget. He is the half-god who shattered the earth itself, who slew one goddess and aimed to slay three more. He will try again. Him and his dragon-queen beside him. He will gather the monsters he once made, and he will ride them through every world and burn them. I know you want to remake this world as you remember it, Belli, but you cannot. It has already burned. I'm sorry.'

'What do we do if the potions don't work?'

Li laughed. 'Then we take the spear that killed him once before and we run it through him for a second time, that's what!'

'Zafir went looking for it. She probably has it by now.'

Li straddled him and leaned in close. 'You see, I was thinking about that, and what you said when Mai'Choro Kwen's assassin poisoned me. You saved me with your blood, and then afterwards you told me there would be consequences. That I would feel things. That you would know things about me. That it made a link between us. A bond of sorts. I have felt that, and it is sometimes quite wonderful. But you said that you could ... do other things. Yes?'

'Li! I never did and I never would!'

'I know, Belli. I know. But you could, yes?'

'Yes.'

'Could you make me act against my own will.'

Bellepheros swallowed hard. Li was leading him to blood-magic and the darkness every alchemist carried and fought, even as her lips brushed his face, as she nuzzled his ear. 'Could I? Li, if I wanted to, I could probably make you cut your own throat. But I *don't* want to, and I never will!'

'How many potions have you made for her, Belli?' Li whispered.

'You mean Zafir?'

'Yes. Does she not have that bond with you too?'

'She does.'

'Then let her carry the spear. Let *her* be the one to do it. *Make* her do it.' He could feel the glee in her. 'They will neither of them even see it coming!'

'Li … I can't …' Except of course he could. It wasn't a matter of if or how. It was a matter of who he was and of choices and consequences, of elemental right and wrong.

'Then we'll probably die, Belli,' Li breathed, 'as the Black Moon is not likely to conveniently drink your poison and die. But we'll still try because if not us then who? Do you see, you daft old man, why I don't care much for your stupid Statue Plague just now? If it comes to it, if we live long enough for it to matter, you can make potions for us both and be glad that we're alive at all.'

She wrapped him in her arms then, and for a while Bellepheros forgot all about dragons and dead friends, about the Black Moon and the end of the world.

38

The Alchemists

Zafir planted the spear between her feet in front of Lystra's men and their scorpions. She cocked her head. Her eyes raked them and settled on Lystra, waiting to see if Lystra would turn on her before the chance to do so slipped away like so much sand.

'There are dragons under the Spur,' Zafir said. 'Dragons in your kingdom, Queen Lystra. They come in from the Silver River. There are dragons at the Adamantine Palace too, seeking entrance there. Dragons everywhere to bring ruin to the last of us.' Old pride slithered like a snake in her belly. There would be no bending the knee now, no pretence of humility. 'May we enter or not?'

Lystra spat, 'Do you still hurt from where my axe nearly took your ankle?'

'A twinge now and then.'

The Adamantine Men of the Spur looked at her. They'd seen the speaker of the nine realms carry the Silver King's spear and slay a dragon as Narammed the Magnificent himself had done, and to men like these that was all there was. For a long moment Zafir thought about what it would be like to kill Lystra now. She ran the notion around herself, wrapped her thoughts inside it, dressed herself in the feeling of it. She knew how it *ought* to feel. Delicious. Hot and gleeful. Sweet and salty vengeance, pain returned a hundredfold for everything Jehal had done to her; and yes, for that twinge in her ankle from when she and Lystra had fought. That was how it *ought* to feel, but with that idea wrapped around her she felt nothing except cobwebs coated with ancient dust. The sensation bewildered her. She didn't know what to do with it.

I made a promise, she reminded herself. Jaslyn was right there beside her sister. *Kill one and you have to kill them all.*

Kataros sidled to Lystra's side and whispered in her ear.

'You should act, Holiness,' muttered Tuuran. 'Half these men are Adamantine. They've seen you slay a dragon. If you strike at all, you must do it while you have their hearts.'

Her head swam. Her arms ached and her legs burned and her heart pounded. The looming darkness unbalanced her, unseen demons in the shadows, and all the time the spear seemed to sing in a quiet voice too subtle to hear. She looked for Diamond Eye, for the reassurance of his presence, but the great dragon was quiet and distant, somewhere far away and with troubles of his own.

Lystra met her gaze, cold and steady. She stepped to the front of her men. 'I will grant entrance to your Adamantine Guard. Your band of night-skin sell-swords may shelter here. For returning my sister and her riders, I grant this.'

Tuuran growled and bristled. 'Sell-swords?'

'Hush, Night Watchman.' Zafir threw an arm across his chest to hold him back. Lystra took another step.

'But *you* are neither wanted nor welcome, Zafir, and nor will you ever be. Return what you stole.' She held out a hand.

Zafir reversed the spear and drove it into the ground between them. Its Adamantine tip bit deep. It quivered, erect. 'This is why the dragons are here,' she said. 'This and this alone.' What did it matter who carried it now? In the end the Black Moon would do with it as he wished. Lystra reached to take it, and Zafir almost let her, but as Lystra's fingers touched its shaft she found she had too much pride after all. She drew her sword and levelled it at Lystra's face. 'I did not steal it,' she said. 'It was always mine, and if you want it then you will have to earn it.'

Lystra stared at her. No sign of fear. 'Again, then? Sword and axe?'

Tuuran lurched forward to step between them. 'Holiness!'

Zafir brushed him aside. She nodded to Lystra. 'Sword and axe and let's be done with it.' She tossed the Silver King's spear to Tuuran. 'Be quiet and make yourself useful, Night Watchman. Whoever remains, they are your speaker. You will serve Lystra as you served me.'

Again he tried to stand between them. 'Holiness! It doesn't have to be like this!' He rounded on the men at the gates, many of them like him, bred and raised for the legion. 'In the face of dragons we stand together! Adamantine Men! Do we not?'

'Tuuran!'

'Tell your speaker as I tell mine! This is not the way!'

'Tuuran!' Zafir slapped his face, then laid a hand to his cheek for a second time, gently now. His eyes gave him away. He was afraid for her. 'Let it go.'

He growled. 'Then do not lose, Holiness, for if you do I will follow you to Xibaiya and hunt you down and stand by your side against death itself. You'll never be rid of me, and I'll complain a very great deal and at quite some volume at the inconvenience of it all.'

Lystra took up a sword and an axe. She stepped into the cave among the stalagmites and the gloom. 'I would have beaten you last time –' she smiled '– and so I will again.' So far from the soft queen Zafir had thought she faced in the Pinnacles all those months before with Jehal's uncle Meteroa dying on her throne. The men around her then had been Valmeyan's dragon-knights, allies by necessity more than choice. Lystra had fought like a tiger. She *had* been winning. The strength and courage of desperation, perhaps.

Spite, that was all. Petty revenge for Jehal's betrayal over Evenspire, which had driven a knife through her heart deeper than any of the many knives that had come before. *Why can't you just let it go?* Was she talking to Lystra or to herself? She wasn't sure.

She took a long deep breath and found that, despite everything since, despite all her months as a slave, despite what the Taiytakei had done to her and she to them, despite the Black Moon and Diamond Eye and the islands and the cave there, the locked dark room and Merizikat, despite all those things Jehal's betrayal still cut her to stone, a splinter of rusty iron for ever buried deep under her skin. It had no right. *He* had no right. He was dead and gone and still he hurt her, and it left such a rage inside her. She wanted it finished. Just done.

She whirled and screamed and threw herself at Lystra, sword flying, axe a-swing to make it end. Lystra blocked and dodged. She swept at Zafir's legs, but she'd tried that trick when they'd fought before and Zafir saw it coming. She jumped as Lystra veered and they crashed together, the two of them pressed up tight, gold-glass against dragonscale. Zafir threw away her sword and axe and wrapped both hands around Lystra's face, pulling at her helm. They fell, smashing down side by side. Lystra tried to roll away, but Zafir caught her arm and pulled her close again. Lystra's helm rolled into the shadows. They staggered to their feet. Lystra lunged as a moment of space opened between them. Her sword caught Zafir's hip and skittered off Taiytakei armoured glass, and then Zafir sprang and bore her down, winding them both. She straddled Lystra and drew back an arm to smash a gold gauntlet into that pretty face, the face Jehal must have wanted more than her own, except with Jehal nothing had ever been about love but always about lust and greed and power and money, and had she ever been any different? No.

The lightning thrower on her arm shone bright. Filled with white fire. She clenched her fist, tighter and tighter. Somewhere among the Adamantine Men a commotion rose. She didn't look, didn't hear, but her fist never came down. Lystra twisted. Zafir tumbled off. She rolled and jumped onto Lystra's back, wrapped an arm around her throat, pulled her up to her feet and held her there, strangling her, a knife whipped from her hip and pressed to the pretty skin of Lystra's neck. A dragon-rider's knife for cutting harness ropes.

So easy to slit her throat. Her hand quivered there for a moment, razor-edged steel against smooth, soft skin.

She pushed Lystra away. Tore off her own helmet. Tossed the knife at Lystra's stumbling feet. 'If Jehal was here, I would kill him in a thousand ways.' Not because she'd loved him, if she ever had. Not because she'd wanted him. But for the betrayal. For doing to her what her mother had done, her step-father, her sister. For tricking her into thinking that she mattered, that despite everything she'd learned she was worth something, and then taking that away. Zafir tipped back her head. 'Go on then. If you must.'

Lystra picked up the knife. She swayed, battered and uncertain. All she had to do was take a step and then another, and then a slash or a lunge. And before she took that second step Zafir would draw the bladeless knife of the Elemental Men from her scabbard and slice little starling Lystra in two, straight through her dragonscale to end her. She'd stared at death before, offering herself, quietly hoping for it to take her, but not this time, not any more.

'Holiness! Holiness!' Someone was shouting. 'Holiness, there are dragons loose under the Spur. Holiness!'

Lystra set the knife back on the ground. 'One each,' she said. 'But we're not done, you and I, and my condition doesn't change: the spear, and then you may enter.' She held out her hand. 'Else rot here.'

For a long time Zafir looked around her. At the men on either side. At Tuuran. Then she nodded. 'Give it to her.'

'Holiness?'

'The Black Moon will have it when he returns either way. You know that.'

Lystra took the spear from Tuuran. She turned her back and walked away.

Halfteeth practically threw Snacksize at the stairs. He held his post a moment longer, pressed against the altar. When the fire stopped, that was when he bolted, because he knew that was when a hatchling small enough to fit through the Cathedral's smashed-down doors had come looking for him. He caught a glimpse of it over his shoulder, leaping and bounding, a great flare and flap of wings. He jumped into the shaft and spun as he did and fired his last lightning throwers. One missed; the other caught the hatchling and knocked it out of the air. The dragon crashed into a jumble of charred smoulder that had once been wooden benches, all pushed aside now, but it wouldn't stay down for long. In the moment he'd bought himself Halfteeth slid and bounced down the first half-spiral of the stair until he fetched up against Snacksize.

'Did you ...' she started, and then her eyes snapped to something behind him. She whipped up the bright gleam of her lightning thrower, and Halfteeth had exactly enough time to slap his hands over his ears and cringe away before she let loose a thunderbolt. A chaos of claws and wings tumbled down the steps and crashed into them both, momentarily dazing them, all sliding together. The hatchling's eyes snapped back into focus. A claw raked at Halfteeth, grabbing him, scratching over his gold-glass, hooking into its layered scales, cracking plates.

'Shit!' Halfteeth swung his axe at it. A hatchet, really, nothing more. No leverage. The blade slid across the dragon's scales. Snacksize stabbed at its eye. The hatchling snapped at her face.

She lifted her arm, that instinct to protect herself, and the dragon's teeth bit shut through glass and gold and flesh and bone. Blood sprayed. Snacksize screamed. She drove her sword hard into the hatchling's eye, slitting it open and then fetching up against the bone of the socket beneath. The hatchling shrieked. Pain-mad, it bit at her again and caught her by the shoulder. It tossed her into the air and spat fire.

'No!' Halfteeth jumped onto its head and wrapped his legs around its neck. He closed a fist around the sword still stuck through the dragon's eye, pulled it free and drove it in again, deep, twice more until he drove it to the hilt into the dragon's brain. The hatchling shuddered and died. Ahead down the stairs he could hear men yelling, seeing the fire behind them, trying to get away. There would be more hatchlings, no doubt, but right now he didn't care. He grabbed at Snacksize and looked at the horror that was her arm, severed above the elbow and gouting blood. He didn't know how to stop it. He tore at her armour, trying to pull it free so he could tie something tight above the wound, and saw her face. Eyes burned blind, skin scorched red and charred.

She started to spasm.

'No! No, no!' He shook her. 'Fight it, damn you. Fight it. Live! I don't care about the scars! One-armed you're still better than half the men down there! Don't! Don't you …'

The cry trailed out of him like a last failed breath as Snacksize died.

Kataros raced into the depths, lamp held high to light her way, tripping and stumbling on the uneven floor. Jasaan followed at her heel. There were dragons in the Spur, coming through the river.

'Jasaan!' Kataros pulled him into a crevice and unstoppered a drinking horn. 'Jeiros has potions to hide us from them. Enough for everyone.'

The same potion as they'd drunk together drifting down the Yamuna. Jasaan took a swig. Kataros watched the other Adamantine Men run on, watched their lamps disappear into the darkness, then slipped deeper into her crevice, a crack in the mountain so narrow she almost had to walk sideways. Her lamp lit their way, dim and shadow-shrouded, scraping and squeezing to an old rusty door. Hinges ground open, reluctant grating rusted metal. Light crept from the other side; not sunlight, but still bright enough to make her screw up her eyes. Moonlight silver in a hollow shaft of glowing white stone. A breath of air wafted over her, cool and fresh, not the stale reek of the tunnels.

'You have a head for heights, Jasaan?' A rope bridge stretched across the void to a latticework of nets. More ropes dangled down into the middle of the shaft like some old attic cobweb. Kataros scrambled across the bridge. The web of ropes shook and swayed with each step as she clambered down a crazy mess of knots and pieces of netting and tethers and hawsers and knotted sheets of all different shapes and sizes, cobbled together haphazard and higgledy-piggledy over decades. The white stone walls were cracked and broken as if the shaft had once been part of something greater and had been snapped off.

'The Silver King made this?' asked Jasaan.

The bottom of the shaft was filled with rubble. Kataros clambered across fallen stone to a crack where the white wall was split. She squeezed through. 'The Silver Kings left their relics scattered like salt at a wedding.' She stopped at another iron door. 'It hardly matters now. You were there. In the Black Mausoleum. You saw the Silver King leave us. Help me with this, will you?'

Jasaan added the weight of his shoulder to the door. A cracking sound made him jump as something snapped and the door creaked open. Kataros wrapped her lamp in cloth over and over until no glimmer of it remained. Together they crept into the darkness.

'We make our potions beside the river because we need the water,' she said.

The river. Where the dragons were.

Adamantine Men surrounded Zafir, all mixed up together in the madness to survive. The darkness and the press of men suffocated her and left her twitching like a nervous bird. She took a lightning thrower and pressed it into Lystra's hands. Something to do. To take her thoughts away from her demons, battering at their cages.

'Point it. Think bad thoughts. It'll kill a man. With a dragon it will buy you a moment. In that moment you must use the spear.' Perhaps Lystra would shoot her in the back, but then she'd find out how Taiytakei gold-glass turned lightning into harmless sparks, and in the moment after, which would be her last, she'd discover how dragonscale didn't, and why Zafir wore both, one layered over the other. A coldly calculated purchase of uncertainty.

Am I turning into me again? The Zafir I left behind? The old habits, the double-thinking, the scheming, the perpetual watching for who would be next to slink behind and stab her in the back, the deep dark fears she buried in bottomless pits but which never quite let her go. For a while all that had gone; she'd been someone else. But now it was coming back. She'd forgotten how tiring it was.

'Dragon!' A crack of lightning, and then Tuuran pelted from the corner ahead where she'd sent him, one hand raised, two fingers in the air. Two fingers, two hatchlings, hurtling hard on his heels, maws gaping, fire ready. Thunderclaps blew the first dragon tumbling a dozen yards back. Crossbow quarrels peppered its scales, punching through with poison tips. More lightning flew. Zafir's ears rang so loud she could barely hear her own thoughts, but she kept them there, shining bright for the dragons to see, letting them linger long enough that they couldn't be missed. *Let it pass among you, from one to the next as you flicker through one another. The poison that dulls is what waits you.* More arrows flew. When the hatchlings tried to rise, lightning pressed them down. Zafir sent her men forward with their axes.

The little death, little dragons. Do not come back.

She went to the bodies when the soldiers had finished their butchery. Hacked to pieces. Paralysed with lightning, and yet they'd still killed three men lashing back and forth as they died.

Tuuran looked sourly at the corpses. 'Three good men, Holiness,' he said. 'It had better work.'

Lystra pushed past, spear in hand. She carried it well. For a moment Zafir envied her. Another dragon-queen, hard as iron.

Kataros froze. The darkness was absolute but she could hear the scrabbling of claws on stone. There was a dragon somewhere in the tunnels ahead. She counted heartbeats as the sound came and went. When she didn't hear anything more she crept on. One hand held a knife, ready to cut herself. With the other she felt her way along the wall.

Light spilled into their crevice a little further on. A low dim glow. It flickered as a shadow passed across it. Kataros waited again, then eased forward to where the crevice joined with a wider tunnel. She crouched, invisible, a shadow in a deeper dark. The light ahead came from an alchemical lamp, its luminous innards smashed and spattered across the tunnel floor. She listened, and then darted out towards the distant hiss of the Silver River as it wove and split and fell through the caves to the Mirror Lakes and its final end. To the workshop Jeiros kept here.

The door hung ajar. She slipped inside, pulled Jasaan after her and closed it. Listened again in case dragons lurked. Or, more likely, someone trying to hide from them.

No sound. She felt her way to the potions she wanted, then unwrapped her lamp and gave it to Jasaan.

'Here.' She cut herself across the heel of her palm. One by one she opened every bottle and dripped a little blood into each, then stoppered them shut.

'What are you doing?'

Kataros gathered the bottles and packed them into a sack. She gave it to him. 'We have what we need now.'

They eased back as they'd come, across the glowing patch of tunnel floor, and there was the dragon she'd heard, waiting for them, a hatchling soft and fresh from the egg and as old as time, sniffing at the crevice to the white shaft as though it had caught a whiff of something. Kataros saw it at the same moment as some instinct made it look up, hardly more than a good spit between them. The dragon bared its teeth. Hesitated. Hunting for her thoughts and curious, perhaps, because it couldn't find them. Kataros slashed her wrist and flicked handfuls of blood onto the stone and across the dragon's scales, and then stopped and quivered as she quietly forced the wound to close. Her blood dripped from the dragon's face. The dragon opened its mouth to burn them, trembled once and fell dead, holes burned clean through its skull by the fire of an alchemist. Kataros stepped past. She slipped into the crack in the wall, back towards the white stone shaft.

Jasaan hissed behind her. 'Kat? How did you do that?'

She paused. He deserved it, didn't he? A confession of sorts. 'I saw things,' she said. 'When the Silver King gave me his memories.

I saw his fall and what came after.' She faced Jasaan. In the garish shadow-light of her alchemical lamp she couldn't read his face. 'Jasaan, the Order of the Scales is nothing but the Order of the Dragon by another name. The blood-mages of the Silver City were not driven into exile by alchemists but by their own kind. We call ourselves by a different name, but we are the same as we ever were. Alchemist. Blood-mage. There is no difference.' It felt better, somehow, to say it. He'd find out soon enough anyway.

Jasaan snorted. 'You may as well say that the sun is the moon!'

She didn't answer. Didn't look back. She'd told him what she was. No reason he had to believe her.

Among the little ones running and screaming in the darkness the dragon Silence tears through the river warren. They try to hide but Silence ferrets out their thoughts and burns them from their holes. Skipping and bounding from one slaughter to the next. No mercy, no remorse, no pity under fang or claw or fire as they hear the luring song of the Silver King's spear.

Armed men gather, a feeble imagination of resistance, lines of spider-web substance. Dragonscale against flame. Spear against fang and talon, a shredding whirlwind of tooth and claw. Mayhem and slaughter, murder and chaos. No life, no breath, no movement. Behind them the dragons leave dark caves stained red.

Alchemist!

A hatchling dies, dissolution in alchemical blood.

The dragon Silence pauses from her savagery. Among the thoughts of the little ones she has found one whose scents are familiar.

The poison that dulls … Do not come back …

The dragon Silence listens to the distant dragon-queen, small and yet sparking with prideful fire. *That one. That one is mine.* She crushes the little one trapped beneath her claws, who once called himself a rider of dragons and becomes now a feast for worms and maggots. Spear shafts are broken, swords bent, dragonscale shields split in two. Around her the once proud riders of Furymouth die, the cream of King Tyan's court, the victors of Evenspire and the Pinnacles; now they burn and bleed.

Against whom did you pit yourselves in your meaningless wars?

whispers Silence to the corpses and the blood-rank caves. Again the dragon-queen pits her enemies against one another.

It does not matter. High above the mountains great war-dragons and hunters circle and watch. They listen and wait for the Black Moon to answer their challenge, one way or another.

Zafir kept Tuuran close after the hatchlings. Her demons were out of their cages now, riotous inside her. He said something: Lystra and her sister Jaslyn. She hardly heard. Too wrapped in her own whirlwind, too deafened by so much lightning. A year flying on Diamond Eye's back, listening to the great dragon's thoughts. She was tuned to them, and now others were leaking through. The hatchlings running amok below. Snippets and flashes, flares of gleeful joy, a hiss of momentary frustration. She shook her head. Too full. Too many things. 'Lystra leads us from fire to inferno, Tuuran. There is nothing ...' He probably thought she was mad.

'Holiness, we should slip away.'

Zafir stopped. Among the dragon thoughts one looked back, steady and knowing, and when she closed her eyes and hooded her mind there was a taste to it, as Diamond Eye would say. A scent, a crisping crinkle at the edges, a unique sibilant hiss and crackle.

I see you, little one.

Silence. *And I see you, little dragon.* Zafir stumbled. She batted Tuuran away as he caught her. *Diamond Eye bit off your head. Yet here you are.*

The spear, little one.

Touch me for it and I will make a pretty statue of you. The Black Moon would make a new world. And she would carry the Isul Aieha's spear beside him. Or so he said.

We will stop him.

Are you not afraid, little dragon, that you might lose?

No.

She laughed then, remembering how Silence had hunted her with murder in mind on Baros Tsen's eyrie. Through cave and tunnel, in darkness and shadow, the dragon Silence would come.

'Holiness!' Tuuran was shaking her. 'Holiness!'

Around her the other Adamantine Men lingered, White Vish and her last few. She touched a hand to Tuuran's arm. 'They come,

Night Watchman. They come for me and for the Silver King's spear. The Isul Aieha commanded them once before, and I am no half-god, but he commanded them with that spear and nothing else, and if that is what I must do, then so I shall.'

The look he gave her was half madness, half adoration.

Kataros swung onto another twisted thread of uncertain rope dangling across the shaft. She eased her way along it, sure-footed as a goat, to a crevice they'd not traversed before. She opened another rusted door and unswaddled her lamp and held it in the open and ran through cave and tunnel until she heard a volley of shouts, cracks of lightning and a dragon shriek. The shouts became louder, and then another slew of lightning and a cheer. She rounded a corner where the tunnel spilled into a cavern wide enough to swallow a palace. Dull white alchemical lanterns bobbed, their light pale like a cloud-streaked moon, and between them the raking beams of gold-glass torches carried by the false speaker Zafir and her Adamantine Men. Kataros saw Zafir almost at once, picked out in the light, walking alone with her back to a strange-formed lump of stone, and it was only as Kataros came closer that she saw it was another dragon, jarred helpless by lightning and hacked dead by a dozen Adamantine axes.

Speaker Lystra's soldiers moved together, pressed tight in a circle of shields. Zafir paced like a restless tiger around them, her handful of men following like they were her cubs.

'Holiness! Holiness!' Kataros took the sack from Jasaan and ran ahead, calling out. Zafir and Lystra both turned. 'Holiness!' As she drew closer, Kataros tossed her stoppered bottles to Lystra's Adamantine Men. 'Drink,' she shouted. 'All of you! You know when you leave the Spur how the dragons can find you, and you know we alchemists can make potions to hide you. Here they are. The dragons are hunting us, looking for us. With these they will walk straight past you. So drink. Let the hunted become the hunters!' She pressed her head to the stone before Speaker Lystra, one hand stretched in offering.

'What did you do?' Jasaan hissed as he caught up with her. 'I saw you tamper with them.'

Kataros ignored him. Lystra took a potion bottle and drank deep.

'They're coming for that, not for us.' Apart from the others, Zafir pointed to the Adamantine Spear. 'Give it to me and I will lead them away.'

'And how would you know?' asked Lystra.

'Because I talk to them.' Zafir swooped in close and snatched a bottle from Kataros's hand, then tossed it to Tuuran. Her eyes fixed on Lystra. 'To drink this? For a rider? Do you know what it means? I did it once and I couldn't ride until it was gone, and I would rather have torn out my eyes. A battle swung one way that day when I might have swayed it another.' She raised the bottle in salute. 'To the ruins we leave behind us, queen under the Spur.' She laughed. 'Queen of Stone, just like your mother.'

A tension drew tight across Kataros's shoulders. The waiting, the held breath of anticipation. Zafir snatched another flask. 'The alchemist is right,' she said. 'They seek us out. Deny them what they desire.'

She put the bottle to her lips and drank.

Watch me vanish, little dragon Silence. Find me if you can. Zafir ran with Tuuran deeper into the Spur. The dragons were a tightening net, Zafir the rudder, steering between them.

It will not save you.

Their thoughts were hazed and distant. She'd long lost any sense of Diamond Eye, already far away, an absence worse than losing a hand, a leg, the ability to speak. No rider had ever known a bond like theirs, a woken dragon revelling in all its strength, the sorcerous rich air of Takei'Tarr, untainted by a millennium of wings and fire. A thousand years ago half-gods had ridden on Diamond Eye's back; in moments, now and then, she felt pity that Lystra would never know how it felt. Perhaps Jaslyn, who had glimpsed it, might understand. Perhaps she would find the words to describe it.

She'd hardly taken a drop. Barely let the potion touch her lips. Just a few hours to vanish. *I will face you then, little dragon Silence. You and I. Tooth and claw and tail and fire, and I with lightning and spear.*

The dragon didn't answer.

They ran down a long sloping passage. Zafir heard shouts echo far ahead. Jaslyn claimed Lystra had born Jehal a son; so Lystra was heading for him, for the rest of her riders and the core of her strength. The dragons were heading there too. It would be a race. Zafir held back, shivered by a sense of doom. She drew Tuuran close to her again.

'Holiness?'

A hatchling was following them. She'd glimpsed into its thoughts as the alchemical fog had settled through her. As they passed a niche she tugged Tuuran and ducked into the mouth of it, buried and cloaked in gloom.

'We have a dragon shadowing us. He leads the others.'

Tuuran hissed at her, 'Then perhaps we should go a different way, Holiness! Perhaps we should let it find them!'

'No.'

He grabbed her then. Took her arms in his hands and almost shook her. 'She has what she wants from you, Holiness. She will not let you go. She *will* turn on you.'

'Go, Tuuran. I release you.'

'No!' He wouldn't leave her. And there might have been more from either one of them, so many words not spoken here in the stifling dark, but she heard a scratch of stone then and pressed a hand hard over Tuuran's mouth and a finger to her own lips, and wished their Taiytakei torches into a blackness absolute.

'Dragon,' she whispered in the dark, soft lips brushing his ear.

They moved apart. Zafir crouched into her crevice, still as stone. Silent except for her own racing heart. Could a dragon hear a heartbeat?

Another scratch of a claw. The scrape of a careless wing. Cold sweat prickled her skin in the darkness. She pressed deeper into her crevice, part of her a girl again, hoping not to be seen. The old fear rose in wave after wave; she pushed it back, eyes screwed shut: *Not now, not now, not ever, but especially not now.* She pictured Tuuran, close enough to touch though she couldn't see him. The strength of him, the sureness, the certainty. The strong arms tugging her from the water in that stupid cave before they'd left for

Merizikat. Enough to take the edge away, to blunt the fear so she might stand against it.

Scratch and scrape. Closer still. She didn't see the dragon but she felt its heat. A heartbeat passed and then another.

'Here, dragon,' she whispered.

Her enchanter's torch lit up the tunnel with a light like day, blinding bright. She sprang as the dragon turned, and drove her two bladeless knives into its flank, ripped and cut. The dragon's head whipped and snapped. It spat fire at her visored face, and then Tuuran's axe came down on its neck and split its spine. Zafir wove the bladeless knives in arcs and stabbed them into the dragon's skull. She watched it sink and die, and stared at what they'd done.

'Holiness, do you see?' murmured Tuuran. 'You do not need the Isul Aieha's spear.'

'With the spear I would have made him into stone.' She stepped away and idly touched her arm where the Hatchling Disease had taken hold. 'I would have done to him as they have already done to me. Why is it always stone, Night Watchman?'

There was a reason, she thought. Something she didn't see. Something to do with the dead goddess of the earth whose spear the Silver King had carried, and stone her element, but the riddle was beyond her. She climbed past the dragon and . . .

Stopped.

Someone else was here. Someone else had waited.

Thoughts burst like pricked balloons. The strength drained from her legs as though her strings had been cut. The bladeless knives slipped from her fingers. She stumbled. Her hands turned numb. She couldn't speak. She fell.

'Holiness!' Tuuran caught her as she crumpled.

'Step away.'

A woman's voice. Zafir took a moment to place it. Not Lystra, not Jaslyn . . .

The alchemist. Kataros.

Poison.

'Step away,' said Kataros again. 'She has my blood inside her, Adamantine Man, and if you raise even a finger towards your lightning, I will stop her heart.'

Zafir couldn't move.

'I will snap your neck, alchemist.' Tuuran lowered her to the stone. Zafir heard his footsteps, furious and fast, and then a strangled gasp and the clatter of crashing glass. When she strained her eyes she could see where Tuuran had fallen, flat and still on the ground.

'You drank my blood too, Adamantine Man.'

Tuuran? The thought she'd lost him was a knife in her skull.

Kataros crouched beside her. 'Her Holiness Queen Lystra sends her regards.' She took the lightning throwers from Zafir's vambraces, the bladeless knives lying beside her, the glass wand of light, then heaved Zafir floppy-limbed onto her side and took every other weapon and left her for the dragons. The last gleam of her lantern bobbed and weaved and then faded as she walked away.

Zafir could barely move her fingers.

Diamond Eye! But the dragon couldn't hear her. No dragon could, not any more.

The darkness closed in, still and silent and empty.

Halfteeth left Snacksize at the bottom of the stairs. Couldn't even take her with them; just had to leave her as the next hatchling and then the next came down the spiral shaft. He could hear them, the click of their claws on the stone. They were death, and he didn't have the stomach for fighting any more. He pushed through his men milling at the bottom of the shaft and led them on, fast, running away deep into the ground, the way he'd gone before with Tuuran, the way Zafir had shown them. He remembered it well enough. That was the thing about being raised in the mountains, in caves and forests and crags: a man got to have a sense of where things were. It had always been a point of pride – follow a path once and he never needed to be shown it again.

Lightning shivered the air somewhere behind him. The rearguard, fighting off the hatchlings. He ought to be there.

Snacksize. Stupid name, but somehow she'd liked it. She would have led them better than he ever could. Shown them the way. And then he could have been at the back with the best of Tuuran's men around him, trading lightning with the dragons that wanted to eat him. Knocking them down and then watching them get back up again.

Screams. Shrieks. Sometimes he looked back and thought he saw an orange glow of fire reflected from passed-by walls.

They ran. Mile after mile under the ground, and Halfteeth didn't stop, putting his lover's corpse as far behind him as he could until they reached the door that only an alchemist could open, that they'd never closed behind them. He rushed his men into the cavern beyond and told them what to do, where to go, pointed them towards the far end and the scaffold there and tuned their ears to the rush of water. He waited and shooed the last on their way, staying, he said, to close these doors which even a dragon couldn't pass. And when the last of them was gone, he did exactly that, and then stood with his back to them, on the wrong side and not following his men at all, lightning throwers ready, an axe in one hand and a shield in the other, to see how many of the chasing dragons he could kill before he died.

Snow and a hundred dragons soar. A thousand more gather above. One by one the minds of the little ones flicker and fade. They gutter like dying candles and vanish while the spear still sings, calling. In the skies over the mountains dragons wheel and dive and race, circling, tracing the spear's path under the earth, away from the peaks and towards the great gorge of the indomitable Fury. Orange stone welcomes them, old as time, split and cracked and flecked with dull-glowing shards of white and a last touch of the songs of the half-gods, hostile and resentful. Shadows and crevices. A way in but too small for dragons. Outside, then, they wait.

The first hatchling emerged from the shadows. Halfteeth howled and threw lightning in its face. It tumbled back, a flail of twitching wings and claws and whipping tail. He ran at it, saw a second dragon right there and knew at once that he was doomed. And that was fine because he'd known from the moment Snacksize had died in his arms. He cracked his hatchet into the first dragon's head, raised his second lightning thrower, and then the fire came and rushed him back, screaming, futile arms lifted to cover his face, twisting and turning and dancing for a way out of the pain, an escape that simply wasn't there.

His skin burned. The dragons scuttled and leaped and bore

him to the stone and pinned him to the ground. They glared him down, and all he could think of was Snacksize and how slight she'd seemed as he'd held her, even in her armour. Light as a feather.

The dragon seared into his head. He felt the true size of it. Trapped in newborn scales but as old as mountains and as vast as the seas. It tore through his memories, shards of confusion wrapped in a jigsaw of pain. He didn't try to stop it. Why bother? What did he know that mattered? The door behind him was barred with alchemical sorceries. Nothing but the blood of an alchemist would open it, or so Zafir had said.

Little one.

The hatchling crushed his arm. Sparks jittered from his light-ning thrower as it snapped. They arced over the dragon's scales. The dragon shivered but didn't let go. It wrapped one talon around his head and picked him up and held him helpless while with its other claw it scratched at the wound Halfteeth's hatchet had left in its face. Dragon blood. It touched its blood to the door and pushed. The door swung open.

We know now what we are, little one, it said, and squeezed Halfteeth's head until his skull burst.

Silence follows the song of the Earthspear, creep-crawling through the labyrinth, the click-clacking scrape of claws on stone, lingering here and pausing there to devour the last little ones who remain trapped and helpless, their thoughts naked with delicious fear. Hours pass. Day becomes night, and a distant glow sings of old sorceries of the earth, of the white stone of the Silver Kings and of the passages the Black Moon once made into Xibaiya.

Among these ancient half-god paths Silence and her hatchling kin run and leap and bound. They gather and pour, fast now, moonlight walls to guide them, space around them, rushing upon the little ones far away who hide their thoughts but blindly cannot hide the spear they carry. They come, Silence and her dragons, in a wave of fire and tooth and claw.

39

Myst

The eyrie drifts over mountains, serene and quiet. Sometimes Myst climbs the walls to watch. Often she brings little Tuuran, and Onyx comes too, and they sit together with their uncertain sons of Tuuran's legion and watch the world pass below and talk of nothing much. Sometimes she comes with little Tuuran alone. She loses herself in the lives she's lived and tells them to her child, though he cannot yet understand them.

Myst ...

'I had another name once,' she tells little Tuuran. Born a child of the desert, the slavers took her in the year she turned a woman.

Myst ...

'There was a boy. He was the last ever to hear it.' Her eyes are bright, the air over the mountains as thin and clear as a desert night. 'I remember our hour together. It is twilight and the air is cool. We are travelling towards whispers of black ooze rising from the dunes, because harvesting the ooze for the city lords brings us riches and fat bellies. We are in the ruins of a place called Uban. Much is buried under the sand, and has been that way for very long, but some parts still rise into the sky. I have never seen a city before, even one old and abandoned. I wander through it as we set our tents. Hidden away out of sight, out of sound, I wait behind a stone that climbs from the sand, tall as the stars, for the boy I want. He comes to me and I see him. His eyes are like moonlight. He takes me in his arms and whispers to me. He brings me a blanket. It is camel hair. He says he wishes it was silk. It scratches my skin as I lie beneath him. It itches, but I soon forget. We fumble and kiss and find our way, a first time for both of us. It is a miracle. A mystery of the universe drops its shy veil and hangs naked among the stars as we lie, limbs entwined, looking at the sky.'

A last memory of joy. She shies away, always, from what comes next.

Myst.

Diamond Eye flees the mountain theatre. The theatre is Adrunian Zar's life's work. Little ones are always building, littering the landscape with monuments to their short lives lest their memory dissolve to nothingness; but Diamond Eye remembers only an alchemist, a potion-maker, acolyte and priest to his slavery.

The dragons of the Worldspine have chased him far away but their thoughts sing to him still. Silence, dripping wet and stalking blood, hunting the Isul Aieha's spear. A dozen dragons have died, but each is a drop in an ocean of fire, and there are always more. They feel Diamond Eye's thoughts in return, the tickle of them as he whispers for his little one under the stone, self-hidden and vanished. She is dead by now, perhaps, ephemeral and passing as they always are, fragile and so easily broken, but Diamond Eye searches for her nonetheless. He chooses not to believe that his little one has ended; he chooses to care.

The others do not understand. Even Diamond Eye has no answer. The Black Moon has cut him with the knife of stars he carries and commands that he obey. He hides behind this, it is true, but there is far more. An unsought kinship he has a reluctance to leave behind.

He reaches to the Black Moon for his aid, but the old half-god cares only for his schemes of deicide.

The dragon Diamond Eye reaches, then, for another.

The horizon seems so distant. The sheer size of it burns her eyes. Myst can't look, and yet she can't look away. There are tears. There were a lot of tears on that night when the slavers came and found her wrapped in the arms of the boy she would never see again.

Myst.

Dragged away wrapped in nets. Her family scream, run, scattered across the sand as the slavers sweep through on their sleds. They cast their snares, swing their staves, throw their flicks of weakened lightning, enough to fell a man but not to kill. She will never know how many are taken, how many die, how many flee.

She tries not to remember her boy, screaming for mercy, forgetting her as though she doesn't exist.

Why today? she wonders. Why do these memories all come back to me today?

Myst.

Powerless. Tied and stripped under desert stars. Tied hand and foot to long wooden poles, the men are marched into the night. The children are next, on a great glass sled pulled by a dozen Linxia. The women are last. The slavers take longer, dividing them by the skills they claim, their age, the look of them. They poke and prod and pry at her. They take her in manacles and fly away. They send her to learn how to be with men. She weeps every night at first, but in time it passes. They teach her how to please. They beat her when she fails, in ways that leave no mark.

She never sees her people again.

Myst!

'I excelled,' she breathes to the mountains, though why they want to hear her story she can't imagine. Only Kalaiya and Onyx have heard it before, because for Kalaiya and Onyx it is their story too. 'Within a year I am among the best. Within another all of Cashax whispers my name. The Desert Orchid. By the end of a third, men from other cities come for no other reason than to lie with me. My last is Zifan'Shu. The money he pays to own me would have bought a ship.' She chuckles. 'A small one, he says. But he is small too, in the places only his women see. I excel at what I do. I wear a mask and make it perfect.'

A life with no feeling is a thin veil for death.

'I am a performer. I am exquisite and without compare.'

And then Zafir, who killed Zifan'Shu on the deck of his own ship. Who'd stabbed him eighteen times before they pulled her off and wore, it seemed, no masks at all. Terrible and terrifying. *How I envied her. For who she was. For what. For what she had done.*

And now you would die for her.

'Yes.' Myst, too, has no need for masks any more. No need to be anyone other than who she is, a quiet woman who yearns for the desert stars and a boy long lost. Zafir has taught her that. Zafir has set her free. Her and Onyx, and others too.

Myst watches Zafir's dragon rise from the valleys. He circles the eyrie and slams to the wall beside her. She doesn't flinch. As he lowers his head she sees that Zafir isn't on his back. He looks at her. Gazes inside her.

Your mistress has gone to a place I cannot see. I desire your aid. Be my eyes, little Myst. Be my sight and hunt for her.

The dragon draws pictures in her head. Everything. The Black Moon's indifference. Faces and names she doesn't understand. Zafir vanishing from his thoughts. A sense of need. Of a debt. He shows her what he wants, and Myst swells with pride and delight, for to ride a dragon is a dream she has. She hurries into the tunnels and takes a bladeless knife, one of many the dragon-queen keeps hidden there. Zafir once named her Myst after a dragon she flew, her and Onyx. And Brightstar too, long dead but whom none of them forget.

'Don't you mean *our* mistress?' she asks because no one has told her that dragons bow to nothing, but Diamond Eye doesn't answer. When she is on his back, he jumps into the sky.

40

Diamond Eye

Zafir lay in darkness, heart pounding, gasping shallow breaths, squirming inside with the old dread. She could still move, but only a little, a twitching of her fingers and toes. She could turn her head now to look for Tuuran, but in the darkness she couldn't see whether he was alive or dead. When she tried to call out, all she managed was a strangled gurgle.

She had no idea what the alchemist Kataros had done to her. She twitched and wriggled towards where she'd heard Tuuran fall. In the black she couldn't tell whether she got any closer. She was still trying when she realised that she could see a little, and thought at first that her eyes had grown accustomed to the dark, but the light kept growing. A lamp, bobbing from a passage towards her, and with it a sharp spike of fear. The darkness and what came after.

Footsteps came closer. She saw the silhouette of a man. The tension inside her was like a drawn bow. The man crouched beside Tuuran. He set his lamp on the ground and tipped a cup to Tuuran's lips. 'Come on, big man. You're Adamantine. You want to die here rolling in the dirt?'

She knew the voice.

Jasaan!

The frightened girl inside Zafir dissolved in a flurried stutter of heartbeats. She was the dragon-queen again. She managed another strangled gasp.

'Come on, come on. You're still breathing. She didn't kill—'

Tuuran moved with a sudden violence. A hand, an arm, fingers grabbing Jasaan hard by the throat.

'Jasaan.' Tuuran turned and rolled and clawed across the stone as Jasaan stumbled away. 'Come to finish us off? Come back here, you cowardly shit!'

'What, so you can thank me for saving your life?' Jasaan danced away.

'So I can break your fucking traitor's neck. Why are you here? Your queen is long gone.'

Zafir again tried to move. It came more as the last death-twitch of a broken-necked bird. *Be quiet! Listen to him. Beg if you have to, but help me!*

Jasaan squatted between them. 'You serve the wrong speaker, Tuuran, that's all. I've seen many men wear the name and armour of the legion. Some were good, some were bad, many were strong, a few were cowards. You're loyal to your queen as I am to mine. How can I blame you for that?'

'I find blaming you and yours as easy as pissing, Jasaan, so perhaps you're just not trying hard enough.' Tuuran struggled to get up. He managed to lift himself onto his elbows, tried to roll onto his hands and knees, then crashed back to the ground.

'I've seen men kill dragons before, you know,' said Jasaan. 'Some of them were shits even so. But if you'd been Speaker Lystra's Night Watchman, I would have been proud to take your commands.' Jasaan eased closer and cautiously stretched his cup again to Tuuran's lips. 'I've seen plenty of arseholes wear dragonscale, and I've heard men sing their praises. I came back because you deserve a better death, that's all.' He dropped something to the floor. 'One of your lightning throwers. A lamp. A knife. A few hours and what Kat did to you will fade on its own, but you'll find your strength much quicker if you drink this. Only the one cup though. What you do is up to you. I'll say it again, Tuuran: you serve the wrong speaker.' He nodded towards Zafir. 'That one's bad. Rotten inside. Let the dragons have her. Speaker Lystra carries the spear now, and we're all the better for it. We could use a man like you. Black Ayz likes you.'

'You piece of shit!'

'Your choice, Tuuran.'

Jasaan left the empty cup in Tuuran's hand. He stepped over Zafir as though she wasn't there and walked away. Tuuran rolled, fumbled up the lightning wand and pointed it at Jasaan's back. 'Jasaan.' He was quivering with rage.

Don't! Zafir growled at her own impotence.

'Jasaan! You stop there!'

'Follow us if you want, Night Watchman,' Jasaan called over his shoulder. 'If not then the quickest way out is back behind you. A tunnel to the Mirror Lakes. Turn back and keep stone to your right, and always take the upper path. In time you'll see the light of the Silver King's Ways. You can't miss it. The lamp should last you long enough to get there.'

Jasaan kept walking. Zafir groaned. *Don't do it! The noise will call dragons on us!* Tuuran kept the wand pointed at Jasaan's back, but Jasaan didn't stop and didn't turn his head, and Tuuran didn't fire. He let it go, and Jasaan disappeared into the darkness. 'One day, Jasaan. When I have back my axe. Then we'll see.'

He came to her then, crawled on hands and knees, lifted the lamp and brushed the hair from her face. He looked into her eyes and saw her looking back.

'You hear me, Holiness?' he asked.

She couldn't even nod, not really. But she could blink. A blink for yes, then.

'You heard that shit-stain? You heard what he said?'

Blink.

'Then you know what this is.' He lifted her head and pressed the cup to her lips, the last mouthful of whatever Jasaan had brought him spat back out and saved for her instead. Giving her his strength, as ever. When she was done he cradled her. She could hear him breathing, and knowing that he was alive was a warmth and an almost unbearable relief. She started to shake. In the dark she was naked before her demons, but Tuuran was her armour, her shield, her lightning; and as she listened to the rise and fall of his chest, the demons slunk back to their cages, slow and reluctant while he rocked back and forth with her held in his arms, cursing himself for how he'd failed her. 'Forgive me, Holiness.'

'Tuuran?' She had her voice again, croaky and rasping. They lay together, still, sensation slowly returning. 'Tuuran.' Where no one else would see or know she closed her eyes and imagined her hands pressed to his face. A private moment they could never have again.

As soon as he could stand Tuuran tried to pick her up and almost crashed them both to the ground. Five minutes later he had her over his shoulder, grunting and groaning at the weight of her armour. In the quiet lonely dark he staggered step after step, snapping and snarling about how he might just beat Jasaan's head against a rock until it split like a melon. An age seemed to pass in lurch and growl and stagger, but Tuuran kept stone to his right and always took the upper path, and in time Zafir saw a familiar distant light reflecting off the stone ahead. A tunnel like the ones under the Pinnacles. The Silver King's Ways.

'Go ahead, Night Watchman.' She smiled, a weak little gesture he didn't see. 'I think I can stand now. Go ahead and check for dragons for me.'

He set her propped against the tunnel wall. She waved him away, further and further until he was almost out of sight. When he was gone she collapsed. Gulped lungfuls of air. Forced herself up again and staggered out of sight down some tiny tunnel, pulled herself along the wall and then squatted. Trying to piss out the demons running riot inside her head. The dark, the quiet, the stillness, the unbearable crushing weight of the earth above her. She'd come to the Spur with a dragon, with the spear in her hand and soldiers beside her. One by one she'd lost them, and now the old fear came at her from all sides to slip back under her skin. In the dark, alone, she faced it down.

'I am better than you now,' she whispered, 'and you cannot have me.'

The dragon Diamond Eye leaves the Worldspine. Night falls. Myst sleeps across his back. He rides her dreams and whispers to her as she walks through other worlds. *Your mistress will find her way to you.* Your mistress? Our mistress? A dragon has no mistress or master, or so they tell themselves, but what then of the Black Moon? What of him?

In the false light before dawn the dragon Diamond Eye settles beside the Mirror Lakes, by caves the last alchemists will use to make their escape. He wakes Myst and leaves her there.

Be my eyes, little one. I will be with you. I will ride inside you.

He flies to perch beside Adrunian Zar's gasp for immortality, and there wonders again how the dragon-queen has come to matter to him so. He trawls through the roaming fire of dragon memories leaping through the tunnels and cathedrals under the mountains, but none, it seems, are of killing her. All dragon eyes are elsewhere now – the hunt for the Silver King's spear has become a chase. The turn of the moon and the stars falters to a pause. A world frozen in the place between heartbeats, all except the dragon Silence, closing with murderous impatience to barter lightning for flames. Dragons fall and tumble and rise again. Fang and talon tear flesh and iron. Arrows fly, poison-barbed to bite through scales. An axe strikes off a claw. Everything is fire and the stone-maker spear. Half-blind amid flames and screams, Silence sees the armoured shape that carries it. The spear strikes and pierces the air. Dragons pirouette and jump and crash among the little ones. They burn and snap with tooth and claw amid their scouring fire. They die together, dragons and men.

The spear falls, knocked ajar and skittering through the air as it once fell from the Isul Aieha's hand, and as it arcs the dragon Silence springs and snatches it for her own. The little one who holds it does not call it back, as the Silver King once did from Diamond Eye's claws. This little one cannot. The spear does not claim her.

Lightning and axes and poison barbs. Dragonscale and gold-glass. The little ones have learned, at last, how to fight. The dragon Silence takes the spear and leaves as the little ones murder the last of her hatchling kin. The little death does not matter. The spear is everything, and who carries it will shape the world. All worlds.

Zafir dragged herself to the mouth of the Silver King's Ways. She forced the mask of the dragon-queen back into place and leaned into Tuuran, letting him take her weight.

'No dragons, Night Watchman?' Her voice sounded brittle.

Tuuran shook his head. 'They'll pay, Holiness. They will bend their knees to you, all of them, or they will die on blades of Adamantine. I swear this.'

'You stand beside me, Tuuran. You alone. You always have. But what will you do? Will you fight them all for me? Every last one of them?' Zafir closed her eyes.

'If I must.' Tuuran quickened his pace. 'Do not despair, Holiness. Your sister remains in the Pinnacles with three hundred men from Merizikat and—'

'Most of whom will sell their swords to her if she dangles something pretty in front of them, and she also has three hundred riders from Sand who will jump to stand at Lystra's side. Kiam herself calls me a murderess, and rightly so.' She shrugged. 'You know what I did. I doubt she would believe me after all this time, if now I told her why.'

'Then *I* will tell her.'

Zafir laughed. 'She won't believe you either, Night Watchman.'

'I was there. I saw it with my own eyes.'

'She will hear only what she wishes. She will have you hanged for slurring our noble dead stepfather, and I will hang beside you. There's nothing left, Tuuran. Nothing.' Nothing except Diamond Eye, the rock of her life, the other half of her soul now driven far away by a thousand angry dragons. Nothing except the Black Moon, who would discard her like a used whore without the spear.

Nothing except her Night Watchman.

She walked faster, anger feeding the return of her strength. Beneath it she was as tired as death. She wanted to stop, to lie down, to wail and scream and tear her hair, but Tuuran kept her going simply because he was there and she wouldn't let him see her that way. On and on, step after step, hour after hour through the moonlight glow of smooth white stone, the same stone she'd seen over and over throughout the many worlds, relics of the half-gods. Her legs burned and her hips ached, her armour weighed her down, her helm pressed too tight around her skull. She'd twisted something in her shoulder and couldn't properly turn her neck.

'I didn't know what it would be like to come home,' she said. 'But I didn't think it would be this.'

Tuuran ploughed on. He seemed never to weaken. If she faltered she thought he might simply pick her up and keep on going without breaking stride, all the way to the Pinnacles if he had to as though she was nothing more than a feather. 'Mostly I didn't think I would ever come back at all,' he said at last. 'I suppose I thought everything would keep on much the same.'

'Did you ever think about me while you were a slave?'

'Some. I used to think about that night on and off. Still do. I wondered who you were, at first. I had my notions, but I didn't know for sure. Too well dressed to be just some servant. I wondered what happened to you.'

'Do you blame me?'

'For killing him?' Tuuran snorted. 'Flame, no!'

'Not for that. For what happened to you afterwards. For being sold as a slave.'

Tuuran shrugged. 'Shit heel deserved what you did to him, that's all I knew.' Which meant he *had* blamed her, at least for a while, Zafir thought.

'I only wish I'd thought to stab him more in the gut and less in the chest so he might have lingered a little longer. Did you hate me?'

'Hate you, Holiness? No.' To her surprise Tuuran laughed, a deep chuckle that echoed from the hard white stone around them. 'When I thought of you at all, I imagined you grown powerful and beautiful, a dragon-rider with a heart full of righteous fury, the scourge of every man like him. I thought of you doing as I had done, a hundredfold. You had to be to make it not matter, to make it worthwhile that I was a slave because of that night. And I was right, Holiness. I was right. When I saw you again in Dhar Thosis, you were all of those things.'

She could feel the pride in him.

'I *was* many of those things, Tuuran,' she said after a moment. Deep breath. Breathe in, breathe out. So tired. 'That much is true, although my fury was selfish more than righteous, and I certainly had a heart brimming full of it. Still do.' Step after step after step. She sighed and took off her helm and tried to tuck it under one arm. It felt awkward. Clumsy. She let it hang from her fingers. It seemed heavier than it was.

'One of those night-skin sleds would do nicely just now,' Tuuran grunted.

'I left one at the Oratorium if you'd like to go back and get it.' They both laughed and then walked on in silence a while longer, Zafir's thoughts chasing each other like maddened dogs snapping at their own tails until she couldn't take it any more. 'Do you know what I did before the Taiytakei took me? It's true, much of what they say about me. I helped Jehal to poison Hyram, and then I dangled a cure in front of him that wasn't real. I took him to my bed. I hated myself for that, but it got me what I wanted, and I'd long ago learned how *that* worked. I took the Speaker's Throne, which should have gone to Lystra's mother, and then I had her executed for Hyram's murder. She probably didn't kill him. Old fool probably fell all on his own, but I didn't care about that. I allowed a blood-mage to live under the Glass Cathedral. While I took the realms to war to crush Shezira's daughters, my lover stole my throne and my blood-mage stole the Adamantine Spear. Jehal was a snake, poison, and you'll not find many to disagree, and yet they'll say he was better than me. Perhaps he was, perhaps not, but he wasn't worse. Are you still proud of me, Tuuran? Because you shouldn't be. You should leave.' Leave because everyone always betrayed her in the end. 'You should go back to Lystra. She'll make a better speaker than I ever did.'

Tuuran didn't reply at first, and Zafir wondered if he would answer her at all, or if, when he did, it would be anything more than a stiff and dutiful affirmation. But then she felt a hand on her shoulder, stopping her, turning her, urging her to look at him, and when she did he dropped to one knee and looked her in the eye.

'I wasn't here, Holiness. I don't know the whys and wherefores of who you were or what you did before I met you, or of anyone else. I only know the Zafir I met in Takei'Tarr, in the smashed ruin of the Palace of Roses amid the burned-ash fires of Dhar Thosis. I met the girl for whom I had once given my freedom, and I saw in her everything I had hoped, bringing fire and terror on those who made us slaves, fighting to the death to keep what I had given away, a courage I never found in myself in all my years as a galley slave. The Zafir I know tamed a wild dragon without alchemy. When we were adrift and lost at sea, I saw her lead her people to shelter and help them build a home. So yes, Holiness. I do not know this Zafir who used to be, but the one *I* have seen, I am proud to serve.' He smiled, and she thought he would let her go but he didn't. 'Holiness, if my words may be free, you were at your best on those islands. You were what was needed. Whatever comes, if any of us are to live and prosper, we will need you as you were then.'

'Without a dragon?'

'Either way, Holiness.'

'But without a dragon what use am I?'

He laughed and got up, and for a moment she thought he was about to wrap his arms around her and hold her, and right there and then she wouldn't have minded that at all. But he only shook his head and laughed. 'Without your Diamond Eye, Holiness, you took the Silver King's spear from the heart of your enemies.' His eyes glittered in the moonlight glow. 'Without your Diamond Eye, you used that spear to kill dragons. And we *will* get it back, and we will send the Black Moon to his end.'

She nodded. Bit her lip. Couldn't not. Faith. Loyalty. All that. And in the end, when the Black Moon stood before them and she had the spear in her hand once more, she would let Tuuran down. She would betray him.

They walked on in silence, too much effort simply to keep going for there to be any more words, until ahead the Silver King's Way faltered and split, riven by a mountain fallen across its back. A narrow crevice led on towards the Mirror Lakes, wrapped in shadows. Zafir saw a glimmer of starlight reflecting from the dark stone. Almost there. Almost out.

Tuuran froze.

'Holiness ... someone else is here.' He clutched the knife Jasaan had left them, motioned Zafir to stay and then crept into the darkness of the crevice. Zafir fingered the lightning thrower. Its light was bright and ready. She looked back into the dim light of the Silver King's Ways and saw nothing but the arrow-line length of it, vanishing into the distance under the mountain.

A sharp cry, and then an oath from Tuuran. Another voice. One she knew.

Myst? He was coming back now, and yes, he had Myst with him, clambering through the uneven passage, her silhouette unmistakable. Zafir stared, incredulous. It wasn't possible. The eyrie? The Black Moon? They'd returned? But Myst? Here ...? She tried to make sense of it and found that she couldn't.

'Myst. How ...?'

'Holiness.' Myst shivered and fell, but Zafir was on her before her knees touched the stone, pulling her back up, hugging her.

'How ...'

*

I have it! The spear! The Silver King's spear. The Earthspear. The power of the dead goddess, reborn when the Black Moon was set free. From a thousand silent voices come dragon-songs of victory and death, of triumph and defeat, of flames and a world's end. They course from thought to thought. The Black Moon comes. An end, one way or another. Spear and half-god and a sky filled with fire.

Among them a voice pierces the chorus.

Silence!

The dragon Silence pauses from her glee. *Diamond Eye?*

I have a gift for you, little Silence, if you are not afraid to take it.

In the great dragon's mind Silence sees a shape and figure and a place, and a joy lights inside her.

'How are you here?' Zafir looked at Myst in disbelief. 'What are you doing? Are you hurt?' No sign of blood, though in the gloom it was hard to be sure. Myst didn't *look* hurt. 'Is the eyrie …? Has the Black Moon returned? How …?' She didn't know what to think.

'Your dragon brought me. I rode him.'

'Diamond Eye?' Zafir blinked in amazement.

'He asked me to find you, Holiness. I hear him in my thoughts.'

Which meant other dragons would hear hers in turn. A cold shock that, a lurching back to the here and now and the vicious truth that they were all in danger. 'Myst, if you can, tell him to come! You can't be here! Tell him I lost the spear. It's over. The Black Moon will—'

Something in Myst's face shifted. The look in her eye changed to a glitter of glaciers, hard and ancient and frozen. She cocked her head, exactly as Diamond Eye would have done.

'I already know, little one. I ride the thoughts of my kind.'

'Myst?' The voice wasn't Myst at all. All warmth gone. Cold as ice.

'No.'

'Diamond Eye?'

'A dragon is coming, little one. Fast behind you. You do not have long.'

All she could see down the Silver King's Way was gentle light. Zafir cupped Myst's face. 'Why did you bring her? Why? She'll die here!'

Myst's face changed. She became herself again. 'Then I will die free, Holiness, and I thank you for that.'

Zafir turned away. A daughter who should have been a son, a princess to earn her father a crown. A lover to moan and cry whenever it suited. A queen to be cruel and terrible, to be feared and hated and loved. A dragon-rider to stand guard, to fly in battle against any who opposed her mother's will. A speaker to guide and lead. Never herself. She didn't know who that was any more. And yet what arrogance to imagine that made her any different to any other. Tuuran, beside her, an Adamantine Man from birth, raised for obedience and then sold as a slave. Myst, taken from her people and taught to be nothing more than a vessel of pleasure for men to whom slaves were objects, who cared nothing for anyone else. Dragons, wrapped dull in alchemy, lifetime after lifetime ...

'We are all slaves. Every one of us.' She was shaking. Furious.

In the far distance a shadow in the moonlit tunnel skittered towards them.

'Tuuran!' Zafir pointed. One hurl of lightning, and then Tuuran with nothing but a knife. They would die.

'Holiness, run!' Tuuran tried to push her on, away and out, but Myst stood firmly in their path.

'Little one.' She was Diamond Eye again.

'I don't have the spear,' howled Zafir.

'I told you that I once held it between my claws, snatched away from the Isul Aieha. He called it to him, little one, and it came because it was his. Call the spear. It has tasted you and claimed you. It is yours.'

'I don't know how!' Zafir whirled back. The dragon in the tunnel was coming fast. She shouted at Tuuran. 'Go!' She held out her hand, willing the spear to appear and feeling stupid. Nothing happened.

'The dragon has it,' cried Tuuran.

Zafir levelled her lightning thrower at the onrush of claws and fangs. 'Run. Both of you.'

'Mistress!' Myst had her own voice again. 'Take this!' She handed Zafir one of the bladeless knives of the Elemental Men. Zafir took it. There was a surety to holding it.

'Tuuran! Go! I am your speaker and I command you. Myst!

Run!' Zafir flipped her visor shut against the dragon's fire and braced herself. The dragon slowed, eyeing her. Something about it seemed familiar. Not its shape or its colour but the way it moved, the way it looked at her as though it knew her too. It grinned and hissed. She saw what it held in its talons. The Silver King's spear.

Tuuran jumped in front of her, knife ready, for all the good it might do him. The dragon bunched on its haunches. Strange to face one and not to feel its thoughts, its glee, its hunger, its furious desire.

'Holiness! You must live!'

The dragon sprang. Tuuran jumped sideways. Zafir let the lightning fly, and the thunderbolt slammed the dragon back, knocking it down. Her ears rang with the boom of it. Tuuran leaped and landed on its head, scrabbling to lock his arms around its neck and stabbing his knife at its eye. The dragon reared and shook. The Silver King's spear hung awkward and useless in its talons. It let go with one foreclaw and raked at Tuuran, slashing at him through his armour and throwing him loose. He fell and slid across the smooth white stone. The dragon opened its mouth, fire in its throat to burn him to ash. Zafir dived between them. She took the dragon's flames on gold-glass and dragonscale and sliced at the other claw. The bladeless knife cut through scale and bone. The spear fell. The dragon shrieked, and Tuuran scrambled away. Zafir ducked a lashing tail. She lunged for the spear but it clattered out of reach. She slashed, cutting into the dragon's scales again while the fire came on, scorching fingers reaching through her armour until she reeled away and knew then that the dragon had her, tooth, claw or tail. No blade would be enough, not even the enchanted glass of the Elemental Men. She threw herself flat under the whip of its tail, rolled to her feet, turned and faced it, blade ready for the end.

'I know you,' she whispered. 'Silence.'

The dragon Silence stared, grinning like death, still for a moment, eyes sparking as if trying to tell Zafir something yet unable to reach through the fog of alchemy that wrapped her. Then the light in the dragon's eyes dimmed, and it turn to stone.

Tuuran pulled the Adamantine Spear loose. He walked, slow and shaking, around the hardening corpse. They stood together, side by side. Tuuran handed Zafir the spear.

'Yours, Holiness,' he said. He looked pale.

'I gave you a command, Night Watchman.'

Tuuran bowed his head. 'One I could not obey.'

'I'm glad you didn't.' She half reached out to touch a hand to his face, then thought better of it. She couldn't see well enough in the moonlight gloom to be sure, but he'd been burned by dragon-fire more than once today, and it probably hurt.

'I come,' said Myst from deep inside the crevice. 'Fast and with fire. A thousand of my brothers follow on furious wings. Do not delay, little ones.'

Zafir ran into the crevice. They climbed and ran some more, the three of them, until at last the underground darkness changed into overcast night. The still cold water of the depthless Mirror Lakes spread out before them, and for a moment Zafir looked at the ripples and at the spear in her hand, and wondered if she should simply be rid of it, throw it into the depthless cold where no one would ever find it again …

Diamond Eye thundered from the sky and crashed to the ground, a flare of wings and a clash of air and water. He lowered his head and they flew away, the three of them, the spear still clutched in Zafir's fingers, while distant comet flares and shooting-star lines of flame wrote words across the sky, until they climbed through the cloud and burst into the cold clear night above, the stars and the baleful moon glaring upon them all, the three mountain tops of the Pinnacles bathed in gleaming silver light, far ahead.

41

The White Dragon and Her Killer

Diamond Eye smashed hard into the rubble of the Silver Onion Dome, scattering stone. A glimmer of dawn tinged the eastern sky pink. The dragons swarming from the Spur smeared a dark stain across the horizon. They were close, rushing onward.

'Do what you must.' Zafir slid to the ground from Diamond Eye's neck. The dragon wheeled and jumped over the mountain edge, heading for the canals of the Silver City to cool himself, scorching hot from the exertion of their flight. Zafir dragged Myst behind her. They ran down the Grand Stair and under the massive stone the Silver King had left to bar the way; inside she paused beside a hanging, reached behind and twisted a silver bar set into an alcove. The stone came smashing to the floor. Enough to keep even dragons out.

'Wake everyone up,' she snapped at Tuuran. 'Dragons come. Make sure there are scorpions and lightning at the Undergates and men not afraid to stand and use them. That's where we're weakest. I will be there shortly.' She left Tuuran shouting at bewildered bleary-eyed men to quit lollygagging and dozing through the night watch and to get everyone out of their beds, and beckoned Myst to follow her through the Hall of Mirages to the carvings of the Silver King's story. She stopped before them and banged the haft of the old half-god's spear into the glowing white stone.

'Well?' she challenged. 'I have it. I've brought it back. The Black Moon wants it. Should I give it to him? Do *you* want it? Where are you?' She banged it again. 'What do I do with it?'

'The Isul Aieha is gone,' hissed Myst, Diamond Eye still riding inside her.

'The Black Moon then? Shall I give it to him?' Diamond Eye had become inscrutable when it came to the Black Moon, a silence which thundered.

Myst said nothing. Zafir wandered the scenes. The Silver King hadn't carved them with any great care to their order, it seemed, and she wasn't entirely sure she had the history right. The Isul Aieha and the Black Moon and two other nameless half-gods travelling to Xibaiya, where the the dead goddess demanded her sacrifice. The Black Moon's trick, splitting himself in two, hiding a part of his own soul. His return as the avatar of the goddess, slow and painful, growing from the seed he'd left behind, all that made a sense to her, but the next scenes belonged much later: the Isul Aieha building his paths between the worlds after the Splintering of creation, conjuring the Silver King's Way, twisting the earth, warping caverns and mountains. The stories of the alchemists claimed that the Silver King had made his passageways after the dragons were tamed. The scenes were out of sequence with the others …

Zafir blinked. What if the alchemists were wrong? What if the carvings *weren't* out of sequence? What if this wasn't the Isul Aieha at all? What if these scenes were here for a reason, the order of the carvings not haphazard as she'd thought, but arranged with meticulous care? Then these were still the Silver King's Ways, but the Silver King hadn't made them. The Black Moon had done it.

Sigils. There were sigils everywhere in the corners of the carvings. Sigils like those of the warlocks and the Crowntaker; like the Azahl Pillar of Vespinarr and the gates to Xibaiya in the Queverra. She'd never seen any of those things except the marks on the Crowntaker's scar, but Tuuran had.

She touched the carvings and whispered: 'The Silver King's Ways. The Black Moon made them, not the Isul Aieha.'

Myst tensed beside her. Diamond Eye hadn't known.

An arcane revenge against the dead goddess, conjuring labyrinths that wrapped the world in sigils and ritual, a mesh of vast rune sorceries that sucked at her strength, that pulled the life out of her. Black monoliths. White stone. *That* was from where they drew their power!

Another sequence. A circle of half-gods breaking the mesh of wards and sigils strung around the earth. They plucked out the Black Moon's eyes and banished him. She'd got it all wrong. The Black Moon was never the dead goddess's avatar or servant; he was her nemesis, and *there* was the reason he couldn't touch her spear, the reason for the vitriolic animosity she felt inside it. It wasn't his weapon, to be retrieved and handed over. It was his doom, to be kept carefully and for ever close ... 'Why did they take his eyes?'

'They did more than that,' said Myst. 'They ended his sight. They made it something that for him cannot ever be recovered.'

'The Black Moon is blind?'

'When he is the little one, he has eyes. When he is the Black Moon he sees as a dragon sees. He sees the elemental nature of the world – earth and air and fire and water, ice and metal and light and dark. He sees your thoughts, little one. Your life.'

'Then he doesn't see me now?'

Myst paused. 'No.'

Zafir looked over the carvings, mulling the memories Diamond Eye had once shown her of the Isul Aieha and the Black Moon going to war, of the other half-gods vanishing to the Silver Sea. The dead goddess raising her dark moon from which the half-god had taken his name. The Black Moon slaying his kin, taking some part from inside their heads and making them into dragons.

Souls.

'You were once like him,' she said. It numbed her.

'Yes.'

'How long have you known?'

'On the day you took the Earthspear.'

Zafir crossed to the Silver King's last battle, the Splintering. 'When *you* took the Isul Aieha's spear, you said his sorcery wouldn't touch you.' She closed her eyes and bowed her head. 'Dragon, if I gave you the spear now, what would you do with it?'

'I would give it back.'

'What if it was yours?'

'But it is not. You touched it, and it cut you, and you did not turn to stone.'

'So I must choose, must I? Dragons or a half-god. And what do your brothers and sisters offer? Will they leave this realm? They cannot. Will they let us be and allow us to grow our cities once more? To farm our fields and herd our cattle and fish our rivers? Will they allow us to return to the lives we once had? Shall we ride on their backs as I ride on yours? Shall we live in peace, side by side? No. Any one of us might become an alchemist, and so it is war to the bitter end between men and dragons, with no quarter to be given. The Black Moon, then? Shall I carry the spear at his side? Do his bidding? And what then? Dragons enslaved, and men too. Worlds conquered, all of them. War against old gods and goddesses whose names I've never heard. Better than extermination in fire perhaps, but not by very much.' Zafir spat. A surge of bitterness shivered her. 'Death for most or slavery for all, dragon? Is that the choice I have? If it is then I reject it. I will not have either one.'

She threw the spear hard away, out of the hall of carvings and into the Silver King's gallery of arches. It struck the heart of the nearest and drove its point in deep to the white stone. It froze there a moment, quivering with force; then the arch shimmered silver and the spear crashed to the floor. Where once had been plain white stone was now a gateway, climbing through the wall into the endless Silver Sea.

Tuuran marched across the Octagon, shouting at everyone to wake up and get moving. He felt like a bobbing boat in a giant ocean of rolling waves which picked him up and carried him with them whether he liked it or not, with no thought to which way land might lie, not that he had the first idea himself either. He tried to find Zafir, but she'd disappeared deep inside her palace, and the Black Moon was coming, he knew it, and with him some sort of end, and he still didn't know what to do or how to drive the half-god out.

He went outside and lurked in the rubble by the Humble Gate. The clouds had rolled in low from the Raksheh, or else a fog had risen, and he couldn't see the ground. Dragons clustered on the Moonlit Mountain's summit, on the other peaks of the Pinnacles, while yet more circled overhead. Hundreds flew in and out of the cloud, down to the Silver City and back again, looking for a way in; and as the sun rose higher and lit the sky, as the cloud below took a pink glow like lightly blooded snow, the perching dragons pitched over the edge, and swooped and shrieked and doused the summit with criss-cross lines of flame, greeting the rising sun with a spray of fire that chased Tuuran back inside.

They came then, with the rising light. They scoured the scorpion caves, ravaging them with flame until Tuuran gave up on their defence; they landed clinging to the sides of the mountain, claws gouged deep into nook and crevice, tearing out the scorpions they could reach, hosing fire into the tunnels inside, clearing the way. Hatchlings followed, racing rampant through the outer caves, but the tunnels to the Enchanted Palace were too narrow for them. They came through the Queen's Entrance and down the Grand Stair to find stone barring their way. They clawed at the Humble Gate and the Servants' Passage, but the tight staircase was too small for even the tiniest of them; they scurried through the maze of the Silver King's Ways, the half-written sigils that spanned the world and were forged by the Black Moon to bind a goddess. They came to the Undergates and found Zafir waiting to throw them back with scorpions and arrows and lightning, with men with axes, and her spear to turn dragons into stone. They rode their thoughts through the Enchanted Palace. They ate the fear they found there and laughed, and whispered deep into the souls of every mind they found, murmurings of anguish and pain and fire. *We are fire. We are death.*

Yet everywhere they whispered, Zafir followed, spear slung across her shoulder, the dragon-killer, defiant and fearless. The sell-sword soldiers of Merizikat eyed her with wonder and awe, but the looks she took from the old dragon-riders touched Tuuran more. The dragonscale warriors who had once ridden with Hyrkallan or Jehal, with Queen Jaslyn, men of Sand and Furymouth, sworn enemies who had gathered to tear Zafir from the sky, now they looked on her and saw, at last, what Tuuran had seen from the very beginning. A true dragon-queen, a Vishmir, a worthy heir to Narammed, the first speaker of all, who had killed the dragon of Dragondale and founded the nine realms of the dragon-kings.

In the quiet moments of the night Zafir dozed. Her dreams were of fire, of the smell of scorched air and burning skin and singed hair. When she woke the smell was still with her. She called to Myst and Onyx to dress her for war.

'A dragon-rider learns about fire,' she said as Myst held up her dragonscale, 'and a dragon-rider learns that they are alone, but most of all a dragon-rider learns, quick and early, how to check their armour. I was ten years old when I was given my first dragonscale. My mother fastened and buckled every piece with painstaking words that commanded my attention. I felt so proud. She took me to the summit. There was a dragon perched on the edge of the cliff with my father on its back, my real father back then. My mother stood me in front of him. She gave me a helm and told me to put it on. She told me that if I moved, that if I even flinched, then the dragon would eat me, and then she walked away. I tried so hard not to be afraid. Fear before a dragon is doom and a short bloody end, every dragon-rider learns that. So I stood and waited, daring it to hurt me, as it opened its mouth and breathed its fire over me.'

She shivered as she fastened her dragonscale, as she checked each buckle, remembering how the force of the flames had staggered her. 'I screamed,' she said, 'but I held my ground because I was told I must. The fire went on and on and on, and slowly I understood that I wasn't burning. I stopped being afraid. I leaned into the flames as though basking in them and asking for more. I stretched out my arms to embrace the fire. I reached into it, forgetting the palms of a rider's gauntlets are soft plain leather to bend and flex and not dragonscale at all. My hands burned, but the fire went on.' She held out her arms for Myst and Onyx to strap on her Taiytakei gold-glass plates. 'The burns weren't deep, hardly anything. They hurt for a few days and didn't even scar. My mother told me I was stupid, and that I must dress myself the next time. So I did.' From the corner of her eye she saw Tuuran sidle in, keeping quiet, waiting patiently. 'It hurt doing the buckles with burned hands, but I did them anyway. I climbed the Grand Stair alone and bathed again in dragon-fire. By the time my mother found me, all there was to see was her little girl wrapped in flames.' She turned to Tuuran. 'The Black Moon will come soon.' In the calm now she saw his face clearly, one side red and swollen where he'd been caught by a touch of dragon-fire under the Spur.

'I know.' Tuuran rolled his shoulders, easing out the stiffness there. Adamantine Men learned about fire too, in the same ruthless ways. His Merizikat men were a mess.

'You need a new legion. A proper one.'

'Holiness, what will you do when the Black Moon comes?'

He craved closeness from her, the closeness they'd had under the Spur. She understood that well enough, both of them driven by demons they couldn't fight, although Tuuran's demon at least had a name and a face and some teeth he could punch out if the mood took him.

'Berren Crowntaker is still inside him,' he said.

'I know, Tuuran.' It would be easy to tell him what he longed to hear. Easy, too, to give him what he wanted from her.

'He was my friend. The only friend I had for years.'

'I know that too, Tuuran.' If she was honest with herself, she wanted it too.

'I don't know what to do, Holiness.'

'Nor do I.' She turned and fleetingly touched him. He could have that much, even if he could never again have more.

'Help him, Holiness,' Tuuran whispered. 'Please.'

'And the Black Moon half-god who rules his soul?'

Tuuran flinched from her. 'The Black Moon can have my axe in his skull!'

Zafir sighed. She turned away. Too hard to look him in the eye for what had to be said. 'When the half-god comes, Tuuran, I will stand at his side. I will do as he asks, and you will do the same, and so will the alchemists if there are any of them left, even though they despise us both. We will all do as he asks because what else is there? Who will save us from fiery annihilation if not our Black Moon?' It was hard to give him any hope when she didn't see any herself.

'You have your dragon, Holiness. I have him.' *And we could have each other.* His unspoken words. He leaned closer, words whispered: 'He told me how to set him free, Holiness. With the spear. I told you—'

'I know.' She pushed Tuuran back, gentle but firm. 'And the spear will open the way to the Silver Sea. I have seen and done that much.' The old Zafir might have said she'd done it just for him too. Tried to earn his gratitude even when she didn't need it. But it had been an accident, that was all, and the Zafir she found in her skin today simply wished she hadn't said anything at all, because Tuuran's eyes turned wide as saucers. Hope flared in them so bright that she had to look away again. It seared her.

'Holiness! Then we can save him! Holiness, if you have opened the way to the Silver Sea then I swear on everything, I will find a way to take him there and push—'

'Stop!' She rounded on him, though she still couldn't look him in the eye. 'Just stop, Tuuran. Even if I could fool him. Even if I did, what then? What of the dragons? We burn and slowly starve.'

But no, there was no crushing an Adamantine Man. Tuuran set his jaw. He nodded, and she knew exactly what he was thinking. *Right then. Dragons first, and then boot the bastard half-god back where he belongs.* Something like that.

The dragons left them alone on the second day, waiting now for the Black Moon to come. Zafir hid with Myst and pretended to sleep – Flame knew she needed it – but in the middle of the night she dressed in gold and glass and dragonscale. She slipped alone to the foot of the Grand Stair and touched another hidden piece of moonsilver. The stone that barred the way shivered and shifted and rose without a sound, opening once more. A gateway wide enough for a full-grown dragon if it didn't mind a bit of a squeeze.

She called to Diamond Eye. She felt the dragon touching her soul again now. Kataros's potion had worn away at last, and so perhaps Kataros could reach from the Spur to touch her again now too. Another alchemist might know the answer to that, but Zafir didn't have any of those and so she supposed she'd never know until it happened. She tried not to think about that. Too much like the alchemy that Bellepheros and his ilk once used to control the dragons. Too much like the gold-glass circlet the Taiytakei had wrapped across her brow to crush her skull whenever the whim took them, until the Black Moon had turned it to ash and set her free.

Was that what he was? A liberator? Hard not to have her doubts about that, all things considered.

She climbed the Grand Stair and walked into the night, sucking in the air, revelling in the space around her. The stars. The moon. The cold. The scents rising from the land far below. Never again. Never again trapped in suffocating holes and tunnels and caves. Never again living in a cage. She'd rather die.

Diamond Eye waited for her on the cliff edge of the summit.

The others? she asked. *The dragons?*

Some have flown to burn the Black Moon's eyrie. A few have scattered, knowing what must come. Most wait close for him. Some will side with him when he comes. Most will not.

Can they stop him?

No.

Then it's futile, is it? The Black Moon will be master of us all. He will make slaves of everyone he touches, even dragons. But what else is there? We will all become like the man who was once Tuuran's friend. Caged and drowning in our own skin.

That one is gone, dragon-queen. The Black Moon snuffed him out. He has taken what essence remained of the Isul Aieha and has added it to his own. He is finding his true strength.

Zafir walked through the fire-cracked stone. She stopped at the bubbling water, all that was left of the Silver King's Reflecting Garden. She took a drink. The water was cool and pure and fresh, as it always was. *Why did you have to smash it? Where was the need for that?*

Diamond Eye rumbled, looming over her, massive and dark against the night. A flash of fury seared her. *Five hundreds years of servitude, little one. That was his gift to us. We would erase his memory as he erased ours.*

Vengeance, Diamond Eye? I thought dragons had no use for it.

He didn't answer at once. His thoughts, when he did, were measured. *So that no one else remembers that it can be done, little one.*

Is that wise? You were half-gods once. Did you remember that?

Another pause. *No.*

But you know that it's true.

Yes.

Yet if the Isul Aieha had not left his story you would never know what you once were. You would never know that it not only could be done, but that it already had. Zafir left the water and climbed onto his back. *Take me to the dragon Snow.*

She will kill you.

You will not let her.

And the other thousand dragons who wait? Shall I fight them too?

You will do what you can.

Diamond Eye lowered his head. He turned and stepped off the edge and spread his wings. *Would you dive together, little one, one last time?*

Zafir smiled. *I would.* She didn't quite know why she was doing this. Stupid, perhaps. But what did she want? Not the things she'd wanted before the Taiytakei took her as a slave, when all she thought was to climb to the highest throne where no one could touch her. *And after they took me, all I wanted was to be free.* Was there a lesson there? Or were they actually the same thing when you cut to the heart of it? Perhaps they were. She didn't know.

Together they plunged from the summit of the Moonlit Mountain. Zafir clung to Diamond Eye and pressed herself against his scales. The wind tore and whipped, and for a short span she lost herself in the rush of it, the sheer exhilaration of arrowing almost a mile straight down through the air. Diamond Eye broke the dive gently, sparing her bruises and battered bones. He soared silently, wings stretched taut, gliding through the night from the smashed-down ruin of the Silver City and the eyrie beside it, east towards the great Fury river and Hammerford. Zafir closed her mind, keeping him distant and all the other dragons too. The spear was back in her room. Perhaps without it they might not notice her – they might not think to look – but as they came close and started their descent, Diamond Eye felt the presence of the white dragon Snow circling over the long-burned town. Zafir felt it too. The white dragon was waiting for her.

Why leave your fortress, little one? The white dragon asked. *Out here you are only prey.*

In the moonlight below Zafir could make out the stone dragons on the waterfront, the frozen statues made by the Silver King's spear, the first dragons to die in their war of awakening. *Your name is Snow. I remember you, although I never saw you. You were supposed to be a present for Jehal. A gift to come with his bride.*

The half-god comes, little one.

The Black Moon will make you into the scourge of worlds, Zafir said, curious, *yet Diamond Eye says you mean to fight him. Does it not please you what he brings? Fire and death and ash? Destruction, annihilation, isn't that what you are? Isn't that what you crave? Isn't that your nature?*

We are all that, little one, and such things shall not be tamed into servitude. The dragon Snow snarled her thoughts. Zafir looked about, trying to spot her in the sky.

Diamond Eye laughed. *Little sister, how will you stop him? With the spear in your claws, even if you held it? I held it once, torn from the grasp of the Isul Aieha himself. It served me nothing.*

With remorseless fire and tooth and talon and tail, great brother. With an endless whirlwind to weather him down. We will all die the little death, over and over, but we will come at him again and again and again, and we will never stop until he breaks.

Snow shot out of the night, arrow hard. Zafir almost didn't see her. Diamond Eye rolled at the last and took the impact. Claws raked around his flank, reaching. Snow's tail slashed the air. It whipped past Zafir's head and curled and smashed down, and would have shattered her, but Diamond Eye twisted and lunged and caught the tip of it in his jaws and bit it off. A haze of dragon blood misted the air. Snow snapped at Diamond Eye's throat and tore at flesh and scales.

You are weaker, great brother, with this little one on your back. She makes you small.

Diamond Eye caught Snow's head between his foreclaws and pulled her away. *Little Snow. Little hunter with your long wings and tail, but what substance is there to you? You have no strength. Graceful wings but not for fighting. I have given the little death to far greater dragons.*

Snow raked fire over his belly, not that he felt it, but Zafir knew the fire was for her, for the harness that held her. Claws tore a savage gash in Diamond Eye's flank, lashing to catch his wing. Diamond Eye threw Snow away and wheeled. He dived after her, but Snow was a hunting dragon, fast and agile, and while Diamond Eye had speed and strength to match her and more, he could never be as nimble. The white dragon darted aside. She twisted in the air, wheeled and arced and lunged and snapped at Zafir. The long tail lashed again, its bloody severed tip whip-cracking past Zafir's face. Diamond Eye rolled, a vicious wrench as he flared his wings, falling backwards. Snow veered away, out of reach of Diamond Eye's great claws.

Let me have her, great brother. Who are you to serve a little one? Snow arced and pirouetted and slipped beneath Diamond Eye and came again. Zafir pressed herself hard flat. The fury of the fight had her. The two dragons were inside her head, coursing through her, pitiless for blood, to claw and slash and rend and kill …

Give her to me, great brother. Snow came again, a violent flurry of talons, of blood still flying from her damaged tail, drops spattering Zafir's face. She howled with a furious glee. *The blood of my enemies!* Diamond Eye roared. Snow lacerated his flanks. He flared and wheeled and shot in pursuit. Snow pinwheeled. The dragons passed one another, and again Diamond Eye rolled Zafir away from Snow's claws and tail, and again they savaged one another, and this time Zafir felt a surge of vicious delight. Snow didn't turn this time as they parted, but dived for the ruin of Hammerford. Zafir pushed herself upright and peered. She quivered and shook, wrapped bloodthirsty and murderous in dragon-fire and fury. The white dragon was favouring one wing.

You hurt her! She couldn't let it go. *Finish her!*

Diamond Eye rolled away.

Kill her!

To what end, little one? To sate you? The great dragon circled. His thoughts, always cold, turned to abyssal ice. *The Black Moon cut my soul with his knife of eyes, a fragment of the forgotten goddess of the stars. He bound me to you against my will. You demand this? So be it. I will kill for you.* He snapped viciously in the air and shot after Snow. Zafir screamed. The rage was like a fire in her blood. Glorious flames, a violent greedy joy of victory that left no space for other thought …

Stop! She closed her eyes. *You are free. Do as you wish.*

Diamond Eye slowed. The white dragon Snow vanished into the night, sinking lower with each broken beat of her wings, and as Diamond Eye soared homeward towards the Pinnacles, Zafir thought she heard a voice that was meant for someone else.

Here lies your answer, little sister.

42

Gliding Dragon Gorge

Forty-two days after landfall

Chay-Liang flew low, the two of them freezing and shivering and squashed together for warmth. They left the mountains behind them in the night, Belli with his eyes tight shut and sunk so deep into himself with cold and his fear of heights and open spaces that Liang wondered if she'd ever get him back. As the land fell to foothills she skimmed rolling dales and dipping valleys, until the world below her dropped into the gorge of the Silver River and the Great Cliff beyond. She stopped not far from the sink-hole rush and torrent where the river vanished under the mountain spur, and shook Belli from his stupor.

'Are we there yet?' He didn't move except to look at her balefully. 'If we're not, can I go back to sleep?'

Liang snorted and poked him. 'We're definitely somewhere. I don't have the first idea where, so whether it's *there* or not I couldn't tell you.' She rummaged through the leather satchels at the back of the sled. 'I'm also too tired to care. While you've been snoring, one of us has been flying, you know.'

Belli didn't move until she started building a fire. Then he hauled himself up and hobbled towards her, flapping his hands. 'No! No fire.'

'I'm cold, Belli. I want to be asleep, and I want to be warm. Wrapped in silk and lying on a bed of feathers with a hot summer breeze wafting in through the windows, if you could manage that for me.'

'A dragon might see flames from miles away.'

Which made her feel a bit stupid. 'You're such a killjoy sometimes.' She went to the sled and pulled out a bundle of sticks and sailcloth which, with the right application of patience and on a good day, could sometimes manage to turn itself into a sort of conical tent. She wrestled with it. 'We can have a little fire inside this, can't we? *If* I can get it up.'

Bellepheros glanced at the sky, but he didn't say no. He was cold and shivering too. Liang fussed around him, battling ropes and poles.

'I haven't seen any dragons since this morning,' she said. 'Doesn't that seem odd? They were everywhere when I followed Tsen's eyrie to those caves.'

'They're probably still with the eyrie.'

'What do you suppose they want?'

'I don't know.' There was a flicker of amusement in his voice as he watched her struggle with the tent. 'The Black Moon thinks himself their master. If they think otherwise then I'm glad not to be there.' His head hung. 'Suppose we succeed? Suppose we poison the Black Moon. What then?'

'One day at a time. We're alive, aren't we?' Liang ruffled his hair, mostly because she knew he hated that and so maybe it would snap him out of feeling sorry for himself. She leaned against her sled and scratched her head, and looked at the mess of cloth and poles and ropes and pegs scattered around her. The tent was having one of its days when it resolutely didn't want to be put up. 'You know, whenever I needed any sort of shelter in Takei'Tarr, I made it out of glass. A big block of it. I'd take my sled here apart and mould a shelter to fit the landscape. In the morning I'd turn it back into a sled! Both done in a matter of minutes! It was so easy. I hate your world, Belli. Nothing works as it should.'

Bellepheros looked over the tangle of poles. 'You need to put those three big ones together first and make a tripod.'

'I've had this stupid tent with me for a month.' Liang glared at him. 'You sit here for five minutes and you think you can tell me how to put it up?'

Five minutes and he had it done. He made a vague effort to look more apologetic than smug, and failed dismally. Liang glowered and seethed, growled a little when he shrugged at her, and then barged inside with her collection of sticks and kindling and set about making a fire. It wasn't much of one, but once she had it going it would warm the air, and that was enough. When she was done she glared at him again, and then beckoned him to join her inside.

'Going to tell me that putting up tents is man's work now, are you?' she grumbled.

He snorted. 'Shall I tell you it's work for slaves, *mistress*?'

'Then you slaves have your uses. Tents, eh?' She sighed and put an arm around his shoulders and pulled him close.

'I spent three years of my life wandering these lands.' The alchemist held out his hands to the flames. 'I was younger then, and less bothered by things like not having a comfortable bed and a proper roof over my head. In the deserts to the north and the east we used to sleep out in the open under the night sky. I remember one night we watched shooting stars and didn't sleep at all.'

'We?'

He smiled a sad little smile. 'It was a long time ago. Her name was Meileros. We were friends, nothing more, or at least we thought so. We had the idea we might travel the country and write a journal to bring back to the Palace of Alchemy. The history and geography and flora of the nine realms.' He chuckled. 'Old Tsen even had a copy in his eyrie. It's still there if you want to read it. Truth was, it wasn't much more than an excuse to be away and alone together, though I don't think either of us quite understood that at the start. She was young; I was –' he laughed again '– not so young any more, I suppose, not even then. But not old. I could still run. I thought I needed an assistant. We started in the north and worked our way south. Two years we were together. She was stupid and careless, wandering the fringes of the Raksheh. A snapper got her. I never forgave myself for that. She had a way of looking at things. Like you do. Quite special.'

He faded for a moment, eyes lost somewhere far away, until Liang squeezed him a little closer. 'I was all for giving up on it then, but in the end I finished without her. It carries my name, but it's filled with her memory. I hated it for a while after it was done. Loathed it. Wished we'd never started. Now ... now I think I'm quite proud of it.' He shook himself, as if throwing off old dust, and leaned into her. 'Anyway ... my point was meant to be that I spent months in the wilderness, much of the last of it alone with nothing except a tent very much like this one for shelter. So that's why I know a thing or two about tents.' He smiled and took her hand.

Later, as they let the fire die, he showed her how the one last piece of sailcloth she'd never understood was a cap to go over the top of the tripod. It covered the vent hole that let out the smoke, and thus trapped the warmth inside. They lay tangled together, warm and cosy in their little shelter, with the world outside far away behind fragile walls.

'Where are we, Belli?' she asked.

'The valley of the Silver River. The hole where the Spur swallows it is called the Silver King's Tomb. Entirely wrong-headed, but there you go.' He clucked and tutted. 'Riders would come to the cliffs out here back when dragons wore our alchemy. They used to race from the top of the cliff to the ground. Idiots, if you ask me, but who ever does? Every year a few would die, broken by the hurricane wind of such a stoop or the force of a dragon's flared wings.' He snorted. 'Speaker Hyram held a tournament once, in his early years. Quite a prize he offered. Riders came from everywhere. Shezira and Hyrkallan from Sand, everyone wanted to see *them* dive against one another, and they did. Two riders from Bazim Crag raced and both dragons crashed. Broke their wings and killed their riders, along with Prince Vollis of Three Rivers and most of his entourage, who'd camped close to watch. Too close, as it turned out. Thrown a hundred feet in the air by the force of the dragons coming down beside them, so I heard. A young rider from the Silver City won in the end. Riders from the Pinnacles often win the Great Cliff dive. They get more practice than most, with the cliffs of the Moonlit Mountain right there. You might have heard of this one. Her name was Zafir.'

Liang snuggled closer as they stroked each other in lazy circles. She closed her eyes and listened to Belli talk his wandering stories of younger days, of the beauty of his homeland and of its horrors, of dragons and men, and fell asleep.

In the morning, while Belli still snored, she slipped outside to shape her sled to carry two instead of one. When she was done she stopped, and looked at it a while. She and Red Lin Feyn had poured hour after hour into building it. Black-powder rockets strapped to glass javelins tipped with storm-dark snips of annihilation.

Lightning throwers stronger than any wand, closer to the cannon carried by the armoured golem-guardians of the Dralamut, though neither she nor Lin Feyn were more than journeymen when it came to wrapping lightning into glass. Talking quietly, burying themselves in work, keeping busy, both armouring themselves as best they could. The sorceress and her apprentice. Lin Feyn to stand between the Ice Witch of Aria and the Sun King of the Dominion. And her, Chay-Liang of Hingwal Taktse, to stand between dragons and a half-god; and Liang couldn't help thinking how she'd come out with rather the worse end of that particular bargain.

Belli finally floundered from the tent, all aches and groans and bleary eyes. Liang poured him a cup of river water, and they chewed seeds and dried fruit from the alchemists' caves. She let him put the tent away on his own and didn't help, and in return he smiled at her every time he saw her sour face carefully held in place, until in the end she gave up and stuck out her tongue at him. They took to the air over the swirl and white crash of spray where the Silver River plunged under the Spur. The Great Cliff loomed above into tattered shreds of cloud, drifting from the mountains to die over dry dusty plains and desert. They passed the glitter of the Emerald Cascade, spray sparkling green and rainbows glinting in the air. She skimmed the Sapphire River, rushing rapids under an old rope bridge and the charred ruins of an abandoned eyrie overgrown and choked with thorns. Through the day Liang revelled in the grandeur around her, the curtain cliffs of the Spur, the crags above, the tenuous clinging thorn trees, the dazzling sprays of bright sunlit water. For a time she almost forgot why she was here.

But only for a time. As twilight came she caught a glint of sunset fire on a distant lake, and when she climbed the sled high she saw a ruined city beside the shore, gutted and smashed down, flattened and trampled, already half lost under shreds of creeping green. A shattered palace stood on a low hill beside it; the dark shape of a dragon took to the sky as she watched, rising from the ruins and heading south. She slowed then, letting the night darken as they reached the tumbled ghost stones and moon shadows of the fallen Adamantine Palace.

'Wake up, you.' She poked Belli.

'I wasn't asleep.' He yawned and stretched. 'Just keeping my eyes closed so I don't have to see how far away the ground is.'

'There was a dragon. The first I've seen since I found you,' she said.

'Perhaps the rest are mobbing the Black Moon. So much the better if they are.' Belli looked about him at the ruin of the Adamantine Palace. 'Good place to rest. Plenty of hiding under the ground here. Tomorrow we throw ourselves at the abyss, eh?'

'If not us then who will do it?'

'Fifty years, Li, give or take.' Belli let out a heavy sigh. 'It would be nice if it was someone else for a change. It really would.' There surely couldn't be anyone left here alive, but Belli led the way into the fire-scoured hulk of hollowed stone that was the Glass Cathedral anyway. Down the spiral of stairs hidden behind the altar was the sprawled corpse of a hatchling dragon, but that was all. They slept in the tunnels and left on the next morning, Liang skimming the overgrown plains from the smashed-down City of Dragons to the Fury gorge, searching for an entrance to the Silver King's Ways, and that was how they found Kataros and Jasaan and the last survivors from under the Spur.

'Belli!' She had to wake him up. 'Bellepheros!'

'Grand Master Bellepheros?'

Bellepheros blinked a few times, trying to clear his head, trying to work out where he was. They were in the mouth of some cave, and two Adamantine Men with lightning throwers were staring at him, while a dim glowing light filtered through broken stone from deeper under the earth.

'Jasaan?' Bellepheros staggered from the sled. 'Jasaan! Where—' He stared past Jasaan at the figures beyond – Kataros and a feral old man in a wheeled chair, wrists and feet crippled and useless. 'Jeiros?' His mouth hung open. He stumbled closer. '*Jeiros?*' They'd grown up together, learned, trained and taught together. They'd sat by firesides and spun tales and brewed potions that no one else had ever made and never would again. Half a century of friendship whose presence should have been the comfort of a cosy fire and a favourite robe and a cup of warm spiced brandy; and yes, he knew the story of what Hyrkallan had done, but it hadn't made him ready, not for this …

'Jeiros,' Bellepheros said at last. 'I heard about the hammers. I'm so sorry.' He shook his head.

The other survivors from the Spur were camped further down the tunnel. Bellepheros bowed to a queen he barely recognised as Princess Lystra, and to the son she carried wrapped in a dragon-scale bundle, little Jehal, heir to Furymouth. Three thousand men had fled under the Spur when the Adamantine Palace fell, so Jasaan said. A score of alchemists, hundreds of Adamantine Guard and dragon-riders, a thousand servants from the speaker's palace and the Palace of Alchemy, and as many again rescued from the City of Dragons in the days that followed. Bellepheros looked at the bedraggled company around him now. Less than a hundred. A dozen alchemists and a few motley handfuls of simmering Adamantine Men and dispirited dragon-riders. He listened as they murmured to one another. They were walking dead men, half of them, shambling from hour to hour with no thought of what to do, half of them bloody or burned from battle, waiting for the end to come and take them in talons and fire.

Kataros took him to Queen Jaslyn. She was all but dead, ripped half apart in the dragon attack that had seized the spear, and for a while Bellepheros forgot about anything else while he and Jeiros worked to save her. Most of one arm had gone below the shoulder, leaving nothing but rags of flesh and a splintered stump of bone. A claw had ripped her open down one side from armpit to hip. Bone glistened through a wound harsh enough to kill most men. Bellepheros cut himself and dripped a little of his blood into the wounds, and Jeiros did the same, the two of them working together to knit muscle and skin, to close veins and arteries. There wasn't much to be done about the arm, but it felt good to do something that made a difference, even if it was only a small one, only one life. While they worked Bellepheros tried to explain what had happened to him, the last two years of his life, but there was so much to say and so little time, and he soon tied himself in knots. The other alchemists looked at him askance, their old master, vanished while their world was sucked into cataclysm and now miraculously returned.

Jeiros's lip curled. 'It was Zafir. She did this to us. All of it.'

Everything came out. The last days under the Spur. The long months of dragon tyranny. The years before. Zafir and the spear. Everything she'd done.

'She's like a cockroach,' Jeiros spat. 'Squash her down and she's crawling again the moment you lift your boot.'

'What happened to her?' Bellepheros asked. He looked round and caught Jasaan's eye. 'She left you all to die, did she? Took the spear and abandoned you?'

Jasaan shook his head. 'She stayed, alchemist. She fought the dragons, but she is not with us now.'

Dead? Hard to be sure from the look on Jasaan's face. 'And the spear?'

'The dragons have it.'

Bellepheros laughed. Probably made him look deranged, but he couldn't help himself. Zafir gone, the spear lost? He wasn't sure how he ought to feel about that, but what he actually felt was almost nothing.

'The Pinnacles,' he said to Jeiros. 'That's where the Silver King kept his secrets. Kataros tell you about the Black Moon, did she?'

Jeiros nodded. 'It's good to see you again, old friend. Even if these are our last days.'

Jaslyn needed rest and water and to be looked after in peace and quiet, and in a day or so she might wake or she might not. Li flew her sled out into the gorge, scouting for dragons and not finding any, and there didn't seem much point in waiting for that to change. She took Bellepheros across the Fury to the sheared mouth of a white tunnel halfway down the cliffs, the Silver King's Ways that would take them to the Pinnacles.

'Bring the other alchemists before you carry the rest,' Bellepheros told her. 'We need to talk about what's to be done. You and I and them. Alone.'

'Even the cripple?'

'Especially Jeiros.'

Li pointed across the sky, far away down the gorge, and passed him a farscope. Far away to the west, drifting across a horizon of distant grey mountains, a speck moved. The eyrie, on its way to the Pinnacles. 'We need to get there first,' she said.

Bellepheros nodded.

'It will be poison, then?'

'Without the spear there's no other way. But I doubt it will work, Li, and then he will kill us all with a snap of his fingers.'

Chay-Liang flew her sled back across the gorge. She returned with Kataros and Jeiros and Jasaan – apparently because two old alchemists and a scrawny woman needed some beefy Adamantine Man to make sure they didn't hurt themselves. When he had them all together Bellepheros told the last alchemists of the dragon-realms the truth as he knew it: that the Black Moon was a half-god who must be stopped, and that it fell to them because there was no one else. It didn't surprise him much when they didn't like it.

'What about the dragons?' Jeiros asked. 'Without the Isul Aieha, who will stop them?'

'It will be down to us,' Bellepheros began. 'Whatever we can—' A cacophony of dissent drowned him out, a melange of fear and dread and bewilderment and mistrust, until Li set off a thunder-clap that shocked them to silence.

'There is another choice,' she said. 'Kill the Black Moon and simply leave. I can cross the storm-dark. I can take you away.' She looked at them, these ragged old men and women. 'All of you. My people would fete you. Yes, you would be their slaves, but you would live like little kings for the powers you bring. End the half-god, and then leave this world behind.'

'Li! No!' Bellepheros rounded on her. 'What are you—'

Her face tautened. 'Haven't you seen enough, Belli? There's nothing left here! It's all gone! All your kingdoms, all your palaces. This world is lost, but the Black Moon will carry this destruction to every other!' Her gazed raked the other alchemists. 'If you want more to think on then consider this: you could build eyries for my people as Bellepheros did, but you could do it willingly. Castles that fly, armed with lightning-cannon and black-powder guns. Belli here knows what I mean. He's seen them. You could build an armada. Not to face the dragons in the skies in open battle, but to steal their eggs. With the potions you make and the arsenal I could build, we might slip from world to world and take the dragons' unborn young. Hatch them in eyries of your design, if you must, where you would be waiting for them. They cannot cross the storm-dark, but *we* can. In a generation you would make them tame.'

She let that hang between them as Bellepheros looked away. There were so many things wrong with that that he didn't know where to start, but in the end he didn't say a word. They were all desperate, and Li was no different, and nor was he.

Li went back to ferrying the survivors from the Spur. They were half on one side of the gorge and half on the other when the first dragon appeared, arcing away from the speckle of dots in the sky swarming the Black Moon's eyrie. It chased Li across the gorge, and when she threw lightning in its face and it didn't fall or die, Bellepheros and the alchemists and Jasaan and the handful of his Adamantine Men already across fled into the Silver King's tunnels, and Li shot after them, leaving Lystra and her riders stranded on the other side, not waiting to see how it would end for them because there simply wasn't anything else to be done.

43

The Black Moon

Forty-four days after landfall

The eyrie reached the Pinnacles in the small hours before dawn. Tuuran was on the summit of the Moonlit Mountain. On watch, he told himself, but mostly it was because he couldn't sleep. It wasn't the easiest place to be, what with the hundreds of dragons that had taken to perching on the cliffs, circling overhead, doing whatever dragons did when they were bored and waiting. Kept him busy, though. Sometimes they burned stuff for the fun of it, not that there was anything left that would burn any more. They'd seen to that long ago, but they still strafed the place with fire for no apparent reason now and then. Strafed each other too, lighting up the night; and then one would get annoyed with another and they'd fight. Maybe it was play. Tuuran couldn't tell. Whenever it kicked off between a pair of dragons, that was him scurrying pell-mell to shelter. He didn't stay to see whether they ever really hurt each other, but they certainly hurt anything that happened to be anywhere near. Like rocks. Lot of broken rocks. Taking a right pounding they were. Try hard enough and keep at it, the dragons looked like they might smash the whole mountain down.

They took off when the eyrie came. First thing they did was have a go at the dragons pulling it through the sky, and there wasn't any play about *that*. With Diamond Eye keeping out of the way, wherever he was, the Black Moon had a dozen half-grown dragons doing his bidding now. Six or seven from the mountain went for each. Tuuran saw them in flashes and flickers, in streamers of bright fire and the dull moonlight glow of the eyrie stone, tearing the bound dragons out of the sky and ripping them apart in the starlight. He caught a glimpse, now and then, as pieces of dragon fell in a bloody rain.

The eyrie drifted on. The victors took its chains and started to pull it away. More flew in from other mountain peaks, up from the Silver City, from across the rolling fields and the distant Raksheh. Starlight lit their wings. They circled the eyrie, swooping in torrents of flame until a violent silver light flared. The eyrie lit up. The dragons pulling the chains vanished. Tuuran didn't see how or what happened, only that one moment they were there, the next they were gone, swallowed by the night. He reckoned on having a pretty shrewd idea, though. Dissolved into greasy black ash. The Black Moon did it to men, so why not to dragons too?

The eyrie came on, slow and remorseless, glowing fiercely. Purple lightning criss-crossed its underside, flared and crackled, alive with pent-up possibility, bright in the darkness. It stopped over the Moonlit Mountain and the Black Moon stood on its rim. Brilliant like a nova he was, light bursting from his eyes as bright as the sun. Even his skin glowed. He stood and looked about, and then stepped off the edge and plunged like a falling star, and smashed into the rubble of the mountain top. A shock ring of force spread out around him, a detonation, a shimmer in the air, a cracking of stones. Tuuran felt it shudder through his feet, and then a blast of air knocked him flat.

Three dragons swooped at once. They doused the Black Moon in fire, not that it made any difference. The half-god stood, oblivious to them, wrapped in a silver aura. Another dragon came, claws stretched to tear the Black Moon to pieces. It dissolved as black dust. The half-god turned to the Queen's Gate and walked towards it, while dragon after dragon dived to stop him, to burn him, to tear him, to pick him up and hurl him away, to crush him under falling stone, but it made no difference. Their fire bathed him and he barely noticed, and whatever touched him simply turned to ash.

Didn't matter. Tuuran dusted himself down and ran ahead to the Queen's Gate and the High Hall. He stood in the Black Moon's path, waiting for the half-god to come as the mountain shook under the impacts of stone and dragons, as the night sky flashed with fire. Lazy wafts of scorched air drifted through the gate; and then the Black Moon, sauntering in as though he barely knew what was happening, dissolving the starlight with a brightness all of his own.

'Oi!' Tuuran might have shoved him. Almost did, but pulled

back at the last, thinking of the men and dragons he'd seen turned to ash. 'Yes. You. Crowntaker. Crazy Mad. Berren still in there? Because if he is then I want a word.'

The Black Moon didn't seem to hear. He swatted Tuuran aside as though he was a feather and walked on towards the Grand Stair.

'I want him back. Find someone else. Have me if you must.' Sod being scared. Tuuran shoved him. Or tried, but it was like pushing at a mountain. He stepped into the half-god's path again. 'Oi! I'm talking to you!'

He didn't see the knife. The Black Moon must have moved as fast as lightning. Or maybe he simply stopped time. Hard to be sure. All Tuuran knew was that one moment he was standing there, and the next he had the Black Moon's knife stuck into him.

Three little cuts. You. Obey. Me.

'Your friend is gone, little one. Make yourself useful. Have a throne set into the summit stone. Bring the spear-carrier and her spear. Have her and my dragons attend me at moonrise. Then when you have done my bidding, little one, be gone. End yourself as you see fit, and give yourself peace.'

In threes and fours Liang ferried soldiers and alchemists along the Silver King's Ways, far enough to be out of sight, always making sure she left behind enough men with lightning and axes in case a hatchling came. In the deep night she crept the sled back to the tunnel mouth in case there was a chance to slip back across the Fury gorge. The dragons had gone, but Lystra and her men had disappeared too, and Liang didn't try to find out where they'd gone.

It took most of another day to walk and fly the length of the tunnel to the Pinnacles. By the time they were done, Liang was exhausted. They walked in two groups, one ahead, one behind, and she ferried constantly back and forth between them, from the rear to the front, and then, when they were all together again, started anew until her eyes blurred with fatigue; but she thought, when they arrived, that perhaps it had been worth it, that perhaps they had come before the Black Moon's eyrie.

*

By the time they reached the Undergates beneath the Moonlit Mountain, Kataros's head was full of mush. She could see Jasaan wilting too.

'You'd have thought,' he grumbled, 'it would be you alchemists who fell over from exhaustion first. Look at them! Old men, half of them, but they just keep on going.'

Kataros laughed at him. 'They are alchemists, Jasaan. Even old Bellepheros will still be going when the last of you Adamantine Men collapse. I could give you something if you like?'

'Has your blood in it, does it?' Jasaan shook his head.

'Everything we do relies on our blood.'

'Then no thanks.'

'You took my potions willingly enough back on the Yamuna.'

'Because back then I didn't know what it meant! Does it ever wear off?'

Kataros looked away. 'No.'

'So we're all your slaves then? Any time you want us?'

'If you want to look at it that way.' She glared at him.

'Blood-mages are abominations.'

'Fine. Then all of us are abominations!' She stormed away.

She thought Bellepheros would lead them right to the Undergates themselves, but he didn't. He stopped a little way short and handed out potion skins. 'The Black Moon will be watching,' he said. 'The potions that hide us from dragons hide us from the roving eye of the half-god too, but he will see into the thoughts of the men he has around him. If anyone else sees us then he'll know we're here. Best he doesn't.' He looked around them. 'So how do we get in? Scale the mountainside?'

'The scorpion caves,' said Kataros. She pointed to the night-skin witch's magic sled. 'And that.'

Kataros took them all to the tunnels leading to the old Laughing Dog tavern and climbed the steps to the cellars, looking about to see whether there were any feral men hiding there; when there weren't she clambered from the ruin and crept through the overgrown streets, watching for dragons. Hundreds of specks circled high in the sky, orbiting the Moonlit Mountain. As she watched, a tight pack of six or seven dived across the city, raking the old artisans' quarter with fire. She tried to see what they were chasing, but as far as she could tell they weren't chasing anything at all. She didn't hear Jasaan come up until he stood beside her.

'It works both ways, you know,' she said.

'What does?'

'The bond I make with my blood. Whether I like it or not. Zafir killed Garros when she took the spear, did you know that? Stopped his heart with lightning and it didn't trouble her. Jeiros, Queen Lystra, little Prince Jehal, who do you think she would have spared?' She sniffed. 'Anyway, if you think very hard of me, you'll find that the tether runs the other way too.'

'Blood-magic is an abomination.' Jasaan's words were mechanical this time, rote and hollow. He had doubts. That was something, then.

'"Make right what I could not." That's what the Silver King said to me in the Black Mausoleum. I still don't know what it means, but I think the Taiytakei woman is right. We have to stop the half-god.'

Jasaan looked to the skies, to the circling dragons around the peak of the Moonlit Mountain. 'I knew what you'd done,' he said, 'and so I went back. I gave Tuuran something you once made for me to return the strength you took from him. I gave him my lightning and a knife. Maybe the dragons found them and ate them anyway, or maybe not. Either way, however they ended is not on your conscience, if you actually have one.' He sniffed hard. 'How will you stop a half-god, Kat? Did the Silver King tell you? Even if the night-skin witch finds a way to get her sled out of the tunnels, we'll never get up there. You'll never get close. They'll burn us out of the sky.'

Kataros didn't answer. She eased out from the alley behind the Laughing Dog into the old Raksheh Way that led from the Forest Gate into the city's heart. In years past it would have been crowded even at this time, a bustling jumble of noise and life. She beckoned Jasaan and pointed deeper into the city to the broken emerald dome of the Golden Temple. 'That's where I came down.'

'What?'

'When Skjorl and I stole a pair of Prince Lai's wings and jumped out of a cave. That's where I came down.'

'There?' Jasaan stared in disbelief. 'When *I* jumped they carried me for miles.'

'Because you jumped from the summit.' She looked back at the green and grey dappled cliffs of the Moonlit Mountain, tracing its sheer face, weaving her eyes through the hanging trails of vines and moss. She pointed at a patch of shadow under a sheet of grey rock, one side swathed in tangled ropes of vivid green creeper. 'There.'

'The overhang?'

'It's a cave. The palace labyrinth behind is largely abandoned. Only a few hundred feet above ground. A bold man might even have a go at climbing to it.'

Jasaan snorted. 'A bold man on a good clear day and with a kind wind and no rain, and with no dragons circling above, you mean.'

'I suppose so.' She sighed and faced him. 'I did what I did, Jasaan. I thought it was best. I didn't kill them. I could have, and maybe I should have, but I didn't, and I didn't need you to spare my conscience. I was content enough. Do you see the eyrie?'

'Not yet.'

'I'm going to stay here and keep watch then. Someone has to.'

'You want some company?' he asked.

'Not really.'

The night-skin witch came up as twilight fell, with a sack of glass balls as big as grapefruits. She sat with them in the cellar of the Laughing Dog for hours more, and every time Kataros looked, her pieces of glass were different shapes, until, long past midnight, they were shields almost as tall as a man and a single wedge-like sled that hovered off the ground. The alchemists and the Adamantine Men gathered around her. The witch picked up a handful of glass rods and passed them out.

'These are your lightning throwers. They make a lot of noise. Give them to whoever you think best.' She dumped the rest of the wands in Jasaan's arms and went to where half a dozen odd-looking fat-bodied bulbous javelins were propped against the cellar wall, each inside a glass tube like an oversized map case with a curved piece visor near one end. 'These are your black-powder rockets. Close the back end and it will fire the powder. Hold the glass tube over your shoulder and make sure the visor covers your face. And do make *sure* you do that unless you don't mind having your eyes burned out. Point it at whatever you don't like and wait for the rocket to go off. On the nasty end is a glass bulb with a snip of storm-dark inside. The storm-dark annihilates whatever it touches, and so that should be the end of whatever you hit. If I were you I'd point them at the Black Moon and set them off all at once.' She shrugged. 'It might work, it might not. Hard to hit something that's moving fast like a dragon though. Our rockets were never very accurate.'

As the night ended and the sun rose they crept across the shattered city, keeping together and keeping to the shadows, slipping from ruin to ruin until they reached the foot of the mountain.

'Who's first?' asked the witch. 'I can take two.'

Kataros went because she'd been this way before. Jasaan came too. A few minutes later they were hovering outside the entrance to the caves.

'This one,' Kataros said.

Moonrise. A slender crescent chasing the sun. Zafir stood on the highest point of the Pinnacles above the Queen's Gate, the Silver King's spear in her hand. Myst stood beside her. A terrible thing to ask, but alchemy once again hid her thoughts from dragons, and she would need Diamond Eye, and so Myst would be her dragon's voice, and it would probably get her killed. Zafir didn't think she could ever forgive herself for that, but here she was anyway because someone had to be.

She watched Tuuran below her as he wandered the ruin of the Reflecting Garden, restless and aimless both at once. The Black Moon had demanded a throne, and so Tuuran had brought him one, a flimsy wooden chair that wobbled and barely held together and would have fallen apart if anyone sat on it. A spiteful act of rebellion, and the Black Moon turned it to ash and conjured one of his own, grown from the stone of the mountain itself, flowing like liquid butter and adorned with a tormented dragon writhing along each armrest. Crystals of ice spread across its surface, little white lines like twigs and branches of tiny trees.

'Tuuran!'

'What?' He came to her slow and reluctant, like a dog to his master's side after a beating, full of prowling discontent.

'It's beautiful here today,' Zafir said. There were no clouds, no rain. A hot sun beat down, mingling with the cold air, a steady wind blowing from the north, dry from the deserts. She pointed her spear at the moon on the horizon. 'Why does this matter to him? Moonrise? Who does anything at moonrise?'

Tuuran didn't answer.

'He cut you, didn't he?'

Tuuran didn't answer that either, but he didn't need to; his face said it all. Fury and crushing despair all at once. When she put a hand on his shoulder he flinched.

'He's gone, Tuuran.'

'No.' He wouldn't look at her. 'He's still in there. Somewhere.'

'The Crowntaker wouldn't have let him cut you. He never did before.'

'He *is* in there, Holiness. He. Is. Still. There.' Tuuran was trembling. 'Yes. He cut me, and he told me to end myself after I brought you here. As I see fit, he said. So you'll open the door to the Silver Sea, Holiness, and I'll push him inside, and it will kill me, but the Black Moon will be gone for ever, and Crazy will come back, and *that* is how I see fit.'

She didn't press for more, for how he might manage such a feat. She thought he might strangle her if she did.

The Black Moon turned to look at her then. The wind abruptly dropped. Tuuran froze and so did Myst beside her. Everything fell silent. Everything stopped except for the Black Moon, walking slowly up the stone path towards her. Zafir stayed exactly as she was, watching him come, too shocked by the sudden stillness of the world to move. Tuuran had seen this once, so he said, out in the deserts of Takei'Tarr when the Black Moon had first woken. And in Diamond Eye's memories Zafir had seen the Isul Aieha do the same when Diamond Eye had snatched his spear. The stillness she'd felt in the dragon's memory of that moment. There was nothing quite like it. The Black Moon had stopped time.

The half-god stood in front of her. The world snapped into motion. The wind blew again. She felt Tuuran's quivering.

'Give me the spear,' the Black Moon said.

The spear was all she had. She hesitated a moment, and then handed it to him. The Black Moon gripped it tight. His face screwed up in agony. Silver fire burst from his eyes, and ice-white cracks spread along his arm as he lifted the spear and aimed it at the rising moon. 'Do you see me?' he cried, a roll of thunder enough to make mountains shiver. '*Do you see me?*' He handed the spear back to her. 'Call them,' he said. 'Call the dragons, spear-carrier.'

'How?'

He whirled at her and slammed a hand into her face and drove his fingers into her skull, and for a moment she felt him inside her, rushing through her, a whirlwind maelstrom of unbearable power.

'Like this,' he said.

The knowledge was there before her, the keys to the Silver King's spear unlocked. She summoned the dragons as he asked, all of them, while the Black Moon raised his hands to the sky and locked his eyes on the distant moon.

Bellepheros led them through the Enchanted Palace. The Silver King's maze eluded him. The Hall of Mirages remained a mystery, as did the routes to the arches and the carvings and all the palace's other innermost secrets. But from the cave where Kataros had flown she took a shaft to the old reflection cells that had been her prison while Hyrkallan decided how to be rid of her, where Zafir had held Hyrkallan himself, and from there Bellepheros guided them to the Gold Hall beyond the Undergates where a pair of dragon-riders sat in mute boredom, keeping watch against errant dragons. They looked at Bellepheros, curious, and then at the men who came after him. At Jasaan holding a lightning thrower, not quite pointing it at them but not quite not. At the other alchemists, and then Adamantine Men they'd never seen before, and Jeiros in his wheeled chair, and Jasaan and Kataros circling behind, perhaps simply to walk on through and make way for those who were following, or perhaps not.

'Alchemist?' The watchmen rose slowly, wary now. Riders who had once flown with Hyrkallan, who had been taught that alchemists were devils.

'As you were,' Bellepheros said gruffly. 'I've brought more alchemists with me from the Spur. Where is her Holiness?'

'Alchemist? How did you get inside?' Their hands drifted to

their swords. In an instant Jasaan had his lightning thrower pointed to their faces. Bellepheros shook his head.

'No, Jasaan. No need.'

Jasaan gave him a look as though he was daft. 'Then shall I tie them up? Set a man to watch them? How many should I leave, do you think? One? Two? What if they shout out? Do my men kill them for that? How many soldiers live here? Will more come this way? When will other men come to relieve this post? Hours? Minutes?'

'Leave the soldiering to the soldiers,' muttered Jeiros, sidling beside Bellepheros and craning his neck to whisper in his ear.

Bellepheros looked at them all. 'What are we? What have you all become?'

Almost every potion he made held a taint of his blood mingled with that of a dragon and diluted with water. They were nearly all the same. Oh yes, there were spices and ground-up roots, but those were more for taste to cover the iron underneath. He reached into the two riders and snapped them to sleep like snuffing a candle. There wasn't a man alive in these realms who hadn't once tasted him. He glanced to Kataros and then met Jasaan's eye.

'We are all abominations, Jasaan,' he said. 'Every one of us. The difference is what we choose to do with ourselves. Tell me, was this more evil or less than slitting their throats?'

He didn't wait for an answer. He led the way after that, brazenly walking wherever he chose, through a gateway that carried them in a single step through half a mile and more of stone to the upper reaches of the Enchanted Palace and the Princes' Hall. Everyone knew who he was, Queen Zafir's grand master alchemist, and no one short of Tuuran himself would stop him.

They reached the foot of the Grand Stair. Two dragon-riders stood with their backs to the steps, keeping people out. They looked pale and nervous.

'Her Holiness is up there, is she?' Bellepheros asked. 'And your Night Watchman?'

'And a very great many dragons, Grand Master.'

Bellepheros smiled at them. Their knees buckled and down they fell.

'Then that's where we need to be,' he said.

Dragons swarmed the Pinnacles. Hundreds. They swirled and circled, a vortex of wings spiralling over the Black Moon on his throne.

'He's talking to them,' whispered Myst. Zafir held her close. Her and Tuuran, afraid of what Tuuran might do if she let him go. 'The dragons tell him he is a ghost, a shadow, a mist-made echo of their half-god creator. They say he is not whole, that he is only a splinter. He answers that he is the Black Moon, come to end what began ten thousand years ago.'

The Black Moon rose from his throne. His voice thundered volcanic, shuddering the air with syllables Zafir had never heard, words and sounds that bent the world and changed its fabric. Colours spoke and stone mourned.

'He declares himself against gods in every realm. He demands our obedience. Obeisance. Many refuse. They will not demean themselves to an echo. Others acquiesce. They know, as I know, that there is no resistance to be offered ...' Myst's voice petered out to a whisper. 'Little one. It comes, and I must fight for him. The cut he gave me commands it. Some others will fly for him, but most will not. Hide away, little one. It comes once more. Dragon against dragon in the names of gods and half-gods.'

'We both knew this was waiting for us, Diamond Eye.' Zafir bowed her head. 'Come to me then. Let me ride you this last time to battle.'

'No.'

'Then I'm sorry, but for this last service I command you. Whether you will it or not.'

'I cannot hear your thoughts, little one.' Myst looked as fierce as a tiger. Was that her, or was that some manifestation of the dragon speaking inside her?

'No matter. I will ride you anyway. This is our end.'

Myst gasped and shrank away as Diamond Eye crashed into the mountain beside her. A fury bellowed from him. Zafir took up her spear and bounded to the mounting ropes.

'Myst! Look after Tuuran. Keep him close. Night Watchman, care for my Myst and my Onyx!' She wasn't sure Tuuran heard, but Myst bowed and touched a finger to her brow. Zafir jumped into the harness and tightened the buckles that held her fast. The Black Moon's voice thundered in the dead words of a tongue long lost, but Zafir didn't need to see into Diamond Eye's thoughts to know what he said. She knew this speech, a hundred times from a hundred different men. Always, in its heart, the same. *I am your master. I have power and I will use it. I will have your obedience, because that is what you owe me, because of who I am.*

The same tired tirade. A flash of rage streaked across her eyes, and she might have struck him down there and then if she'd had a way. The entitlement. The arrogance. The naked demand of ownership. God or half-god, speaker or king, no matter the consequence, no matter what he stood for and what might come either way, she would spit in the eye of any who ever made such a claim of her.

And how many times have I claimed others thus?

Diamond Eye shot into the air. The dragons were coming now. She spotted Snow among them, not too crippled to fly but lurching with a distinctive beat to her wings.

Enslaved to a half-god, or have dragons devour us all. An annihilation or an end to the curse of alchemy.

A score of dragons dived at the Black Moon on his throne, fire scouring the stone. Pointless. Other dragons gave chase, snapping at their tails.

The spear is yours. Diamond Eye's voice. Not heard, but remembered. *Call it to your hand and it will come.*

A wild melee spread across the sky, tail and claw and fire. Choosing sides, some for, many against. Dragons swooping to burn the Black Moon. Others gave chase, still more chasing the chasers. In circling swirls, dragon turned on dragon. They tore into one another, claw and fang, hurling each other from the sky while the half-god on his throne railed madness against the moon, turning on his creator while demanding fealty from his progeny. Dragons rebelling against a creator of their own. *But we little ones are still little ones, and we will all die in fire in the end.*

Diamond Eye smashed into the back of a red-scaled dragon. He ripped at its wings, crippling it. Wheeled away as Zafir watched the dragon fall. He rolled and lurched, throwing her like a doll, slamming her into his scales. The wind roared. Dragons were everywhere. A monster in silver and grey lurched and snapped at Diamond Eye's neck. He veered. Another came from above, green this one. Zafir turned. An awkward motion. The green dragon opened its mouth. Fire bloomed. It reached its claws to rip her to pieces ...

She threw the Silver King's spear. It struck the dragon in its throat. Green scales rippled to grey, wings froze and it fell, made into stone. Diamond Eye bucked and twisted and threw her forward, tearing at another as it passed beneath. The dragon she'd killed plunged and smashed into what had once been the Reflecting Garden. It shattered into a thousand pieces.

The spear is yours. Call it to your hand and it will come. She held out her hand as she had under the Spur, willing the spear to return, never thinking it would. It hadn't before.

The spear was in her hand once more. The Black Moon had shown her how.

Putting guardsmen to sleep was one thing, climbing the Grand Stair was quite another. Bellepheros struggled up, cursing under his breath at the pain in his knees which came with every step, quite sure he'd never make it to the top. At least old Jeiros was having trouble too, his chair carried by gasping soldiers. The rest bounded on ahead, Adamantine Men, who never wore down, Kataros and the younger alchemists, who still had youth in their legs. Chay-Liang simply floated up on her gold-glass sled.

'Get on,' she grumbled. 'Both of you.'

'I hate that thing.' Distant rumbles shook the mountain, the shiver and shudder, the dull muted screams of dragons.

'Just get on it, you silly old man, or whatever is happening will be finished!'

They stopped. The Adamantine Men carrying Jeiros gratefully hoisted him onto the sled. Bellepheros climbed after him. He thought of the disc Li had made on the very first day he'd met her, carrying them all up through the sky to the floating Palace of Leaves, and then wobbled, dizzy, and wished he hadn't. He'd hated that too.

*

Diamond Eye twisted and rolled. The whip-crack of a tail swept over Zafir. The wind of it jerked her head. She lunged, stabbed, drove the Silver King's spear through scales. Another dragon turned to stone, crashed across Diamond Eye's back and almost knocked him out of the sky, then fell to smash below. Diamond Eye drove for a cluster of smaller dragons, scattering them as a shark might scatter a shoal of fish. They wheeled and came at him from all sides. He tore one out of the air, almost ripped it in half. Zafir hurled the spear. Another dragon fell. A monster as big as Diamond Eye himself shot from beneath. The two dragons tangled, biting at one anothers' throats, claws tearing at bellies, sunk into shoulders, slashing at wings.

The spear returned to her hand. She drove it into a claw and turned the monster to stone. They fell, all three of them together, a shock of speed until Diamond Eye burst free.

See, little one. See! She didn't need to read Diamond Eye's thoughts to know his mind. Nor the Black Moon as he watched her, revelling in the chaos. Dragon fell on dragon. Flames wreathed the Black Moon, but a silver light wrapped him and pushed them away. She threw the spear again. Missed. Did it matter what dragon she hit any more? No. Like the dragons themselves, the fury took her and carried her past any care.

Li's sled drifted serenely into the Grand Aisle behind the Queen's Gate. Beyond the colonnades the air was unbridled fury. Dragons shredded one another. Fire raged. They fell, wrapped in furious tearing balls, curled up together and ripping each other to pieces. Bellepheros saw three dragons crash into a fourth. He saw them fall, plunging down the cliffs of the Moonlit Mountain towards the ruin of the Silver City below.

'You should get off,' Li said. The Queen's Gate was open wide, a maw in the mountain summit big enough for a dragon. The sled eased towards it. Li started lining up pieces of glass around her, slowly shaping them.

'What are you doing, Li?'

'Off, old man!'

Bellepheros levered himself over the side of the sled and slid gingerly down, wincing as his knees bent. Li helped Jeiros to follow.

From the height of the Queen's Gate the flat top of the mountain summit spread below. Bellepheros saw the Black Moon, arms aloft, wreathed in moonlight. Dragon murdered dragon in the sky, jarring the mountain as they crashed bone-breaking into stone and wrestled on the ground. Two pinned a third, holding it down, and ripped out its throat. Another limped away, dragging a mangled wing. Others threw themselves back aloft. A monstrous shape fell, fast and hard as a stone meteorite. It shattered and exploded on the edge of the cliff. Pieces arced into the void below. Bellepheros looked up. He squinted.

'Li, what are you doing?' he asked again.

'Someone has to stop her.'

'Who?'

'Zafir, you blind old man!'

'She's here then? Where?' he asked. 'Li! Where is Zafir? What's she doing?'

Li pointed into the sky and the thunder-swirl of dragon-fire. 'Killing dragons. Turning them to stone. She has the spear, Belli.'

'On whose side does she fight?' Bellepheros threw himself flat as an emerald hunting dragon dived from the sky, claws outstretched, and shot over his head. It struck the Black Moon's silver halo and dissolved into a cloud of ash. 'Does she fly for the Black Moon or against him?'

'How in Xibaiya do you suppose I can tell? For, I think. Does it matter?' Li finished whatever she was doing with her glass and rubbed her hands. 'So how do I stop him, Belli? How do I stop the Black Moon?'

'The Black Moon? You don't, Li. You wait and bide your time and we poison him, remember?' He struggled to her side. 'Li … He's the only thing that can make everything back as it was, Li. Leave him be. Leave it all be. Let them fight. I don't want to lose you.'

The glass around Chay-Liang shifted and grew, spreading slowly around her. She watched him sadly as she worked. 'Back as it was? It's too late for that, Belli. Far too late, and you know it.' Her eyes lingered on him and her face softened. 'You always came through, Belli. You always sought the truth that lies beneath and you never gave up until you had the answers. You always had a trick up your sleeve, and you always did what was right. More than anything that's why I came to love you. Gather your alchemists and do what you can. The Black Moon is the end of everything, and I believe you know that. Stop him for me, Belli, and I will see to his dragon-queen.' She looked back to the hall as Jasaan and Kataros crested the Grand Stair. 'You! Adamantine Man. Bring those and come here!'

Jasaan trotted forward, puzzled. He had one of Li's rockets slung across his back.

'You wanted to kill dragons? Now's your chance.'

There were rules for war. When a dragon-rider flew, she flew with the words of Prince Lai's *Principles* filling her head. Height and speed. Death from above. The rider is the weakness, so ignore the dragon and kill the rider. Strafe with fire to burn a harness until it snaps. A slash of a tail, enough to break every bone in a man's body. Never claw and fang, though that would be the dragon's desire, because claw and fang meant first flying through fire and tail.

But there were no other riders today. Dragons for the Black Moon and his cause, others against, and Zafir had no way to tell them apart, knew only that she was alone, that these dragons, though all had once flown for Prince Lai in different scales and colours, cared nothing for the rules of *Principles*. There was no fire, because what was fire to a dragon? Time after time they crashed together and fell out of the sky, wrapped around one another until one was torn to bloody shreds or both smashed into the ground. Nor were they afraid, for what was death but a chance to be reborn?

In slow steady defeat the Black Moon's dragons were beaten down, torn apart, battered to the ground of the Moonlit Mountain. Alone, Diamond Eye flew undiminished. Wherever he soared dragons fell, turned to stone by Zafir's lethal spear.

A thunderclap jolted the air. A flash of lightning. Diamond Eye lurched as if stung.

Liang dived over the edge of the cliffs and hugged her sled to the cleft-riven stone, mindful of dragons falling from above. She swung around the side of the mountain and shot across the Black Moon's throne. A dragon came at her. She veered. Fire washed over the sled. The dragon dissolved into ash. Liang swore. She banked and looked over her shoulder. The Black Moon was watching her. Laughing. She swerved sharply, flipped, shot back over his head and scattered him with glass-wrapped snips of the storm-dark. Blackness swirled around the half-god. His wreath of silver flickered and waned, and then flared bright. He arched and flexed and tipped back his head and roared. *I see you, Chay-Liang. Weep, little one, for I* am *the storm-dark.* Silver light poured from his mouth and burst in a cloud of glittering rain. Droplets of silver blossomed about him. Where they fell, the stone of the mountain top turned white and smooth and lit up like the sun. A flock of silver birds sprouted and took to the air, chasing after Liang and her sled like winged arrows. She dived behind the mountain cliffs again, out of sight. When she looked back, the birds were gone.

How could they stop him?

Zafir's spear. *That* was how.

She sought Diamond Eye then, and found him where blood rained from the sky. A dragon fell, back broken, another turned to stone. She rolled the sled and hurled lightning into Diamond Eye's tail. The dragon wheeled and snapped at her as she flew in a corkscrew around him. She glanced back, half fearing she must have thrown Jasaan away into the sky, half terrified Zafir's dragon would murder her, but Jasaan clung grimly on. He fired lightning at Zafir, missed and hit the dragon again. He reached for the glass tube with a rocket inside. Liang levelled the sled for him, a moment of stillness. Jasaan shouldered the glass. Sparks showered from the back of it. Her rocket shot out on a plume of fire and smoke.

'Jasaan!' A dragon roared at her. Liang fled, dived and dodged and wove. The dragon followed, closing fast, but then another smashed into it from above. They tumbled away down the face of the cliffs, a jumble of claws and teeth. Liang looked again for Zafir. Diamond Eye was being mobbed, seven or eight dragons taking turns to swoop and strafe, streaming flame, drowning the dragon-queen in fire.

Kataros bounded from the Queen's Gate, yelling at the Adamantine Men. They ignored her, spreading out in the rubble, taking shelter where they could, lifting their Taiytakei rockets, firing them in among the dragons. She saw one shoot through the middle of the swarm and on, up into the sky until its trail of smoke faltered and died. Another streaked low across the stones and exploded around the Black Moon. The silver light flashed and flared. More flew skyward. A rocket struck a dragon in the belly and burst, and a terrible black nothing spread across the dragon's scales. Pieces of it disintegrated, annihilated by the touch of the storm-dark. The ruined dragon spiralled and dipped and fell. It crashed dead to the ground.

Dragon after dragon came down as they tore at each other. The rockets from the Adamantine Men petered out and died. A handful of dragons flew in low, raking the stone with fire, burning everything that moved. The lightning throwers left by the night-skin witch might as well have been feathers. The Adamantine Men, with nothing left to save them, turned and ran.

Kataros looked to the sky. She saw the witch chasing a red and gold monster. The sun glinted from something on the dragon's back. Gleeful and grinning, Kataros reached into her blood and across the binding between them to stop the dragon-queen's heart.

Chay-Liang! The Taiytakei rocket struck Diamond Eye on the shoulder. A spray of black flew out like acid, burning gouging holes in Diamond Eye's side. A streak flashed past Zafir and glanced her. Where it touched, glass and gold and dragonscale disintegrated into black dust and nothingness. It burned her skin to scars.

She'd seen that before, from the Black Moon.

Diamond Eye shrieked and turned. The sled was pelting away, dragons diving after it. He wheeled to give chase, then veered full of warning. Three hunters stooped as one, shrieking fireballs streaking the air. Zafir drew a deep breath and held it as flames engulfed her, pressed her arm over the storm-dark rent in her dragonscale as they washed over, drowning her. Through the perfect glass of her visor the air burned. The ornate gold on her helm and her gauntlets, battered and scratched and bent, softened at the edges; but underneath the glass and gold of the Taiytakei she wore dragonscale, all but impervious. She twisted and hurled the spear into the flames. Diamond Eye bucked and flared his crippled wing. The spear came back to her hand. She threw again. Two dragons arrowed past. Diamond Eye rolled, shivered and shuddered as something hit him, then another came with fire and she was engulfed once more. She gasped for air as the flames stopped, threw, howled in pain and exhaustion, and threw again. Her shoulder screamed at her, muscles beyond ragged. Close to the end of her strength.

A war-dragon slammed into Diamond Eye's belly. They plunged, tearing at one another. Again fire bathed her. She lunged as it stopped, throwing herself sideways, reaching and stabbing at the claws ripping at Diamond Eye's scarred flank. Both dragons screamed. The spear struck home. A moment before they all smashed together into the Moonlit Mountain Diamond Eye bucked and twisted free, tossing Zafir this way and that.

Something in the harness snapped, fire-scorched leather burned through. She felt herself slide. She grabbed at Diamond Eye's scales, fingers of one hand turned to claws, the other still clutching the spear.

Let it go.

A suffocating wet fist burst inside her head. The feeling she'd had when the alchemist Kataros had let loose her blood-magic. Her arms slumped limp.

She let go.

Tuuran saw Zafir fall. He ran, jumping and bounding down among the stones, heedless of the storm of fire as if he might somehow reach her before she hit the ground. As if he might somehow catch her.

Kataros slid inside Zafir to pull her apart. She felt the dragon-queen slip. Deeper, tighter, further, but then a coldness bloomed inside her. An icy blackness that came with a soft old hand on her shoulder.

'What are you doing, alchemist?' Bellepheros.

'By your own account, Grand Master, what you should have done long ago.'

His hand tightened on her. In the sky the great red and gold Diamond Eye had seen his rider fall. The dragon dived and snatched Zafir out of the air. He flared his crippled wings. Too mauled to break his plunge he twisted, curling around Zafir as he hit the mountaintop and tumbled, scattering boulder rubble all around him. Another dragon fell out of the sky in their wake, landing hard on Diamond Eye's neck. Zafir rolled away, curled up and clenched with pain.

'What are you?' asked Bellepheros. 'Alchemist or blood-mage?'

'What's the difference, old man? *What is the difference?*'

Zafir clawed at the ground, writhing. The spear lay beside her. She was screaming in pain. She knew. Knew what was happening to her and who was doing it, and that she was helpless. Powerless.

'The difference is murder, alchemist,' said Bellepheros quietly.

Another dragon slammed into Diamond Eye's flank, and then another, holding down his tail. They were pinning him, as they'd already pinned a dozen others.

'Without the Black Moon, the dragons will kill us all. Zafir knows this. Li would see the dragons free, the Black Moon ended, but this is not her world, and it *is* mine. So we disagree, but that is all. We argue with words, and we do not kill each other. I ask you again, Kataros. What are you? Alchemist or blood-mage?'

The ice spread inside her. Bellepheros, grand master alchemist and the greatest blood-mage of them all, and one way or another his blood was inside every last one of them. His potions.

'Alchemist.' Kataros let Zafir go.

Bellepheros nodded. 'Then help me, alchemist.'

Zafir screamed. She'd never known an agony so taut, clawing its way though her insides as though some tiny dragon was tearing free. She felt herself fall and was glad. A relief to dash her head against the rocks below and end it.

The spear slipped from her fingers. Diamond Eye caught her. They crashed. She rolled free, half-blind with pain, holding herself doubled over, rolling like a death-stricken animal; and then as suddenly as the pain in her chest had come it left her. She staggered to her feet. Standing on the mountain top. Dragons pinning Diamond Eye to the stone. The Black Moon, arms spread wide, laughing at them all because of what a wonderful show they had put on for him, even if none of it mattered.

The spear stood where she'd fallen. Point first, driven into the ground, erect, waiting to be grasped. A dragon swooped towards her, lame and erratic and white. Snow. Zafir lunged for the spear and snatched it up, tripped and fell over her own exhaustion. Stumbled to her feet. Snow landed a little way short. The white dragon looked at the Black Moon. At the dragons left circling above. At Zafir.

You are beaten. The dragon said it with her eyes, with the contemptuous curl of lip over fang. *Spear-carrier. Half-god. We defy you all. We choose to be free.*

Zafir met the dragon's gaze. *So do I.*

Tuuran was thundering towards her, waving his arms, shouting something her dazed ears and jangled head couldn't make into any sense. She didn't see Chay-Liang in her sled skimming the air. The first she heard was the thunderclap as lightning slammed into her back.

'The Silver King's spear,' Bellepheros said. To Kataros, because she was the only one of them young enough and strong enough and with the legs to run and duck and weave. He watched her arrow for it. Kataros the spear-carrier. The alchemist who had saved it from the dragons once before. He hoped she understood what she had to do with it, that she would have to drive it through the Black Moon's heart while he held the Black Moon's sorcery at bay.

The difference between blood-mage and alchemist is murder, is it? Does it count if I murder a half-god?

Because the Black Moon had Bellepheros's blood inside him. He'd seen to *that* months ago. And his blood carried the power of the Silver King, and the Silver King was a half-god too. It wasn't a battle he could win, he knew that; but he didn't have to *win*. He just had to not lose for a second or two. That would do.

And after that, to make all the dragons go away? He hadn't the first idea. Just as well it was going to be a problem for someone else then.

The enchantress's lightning sparked through her battered gold-glass, reaching through like a hundred prickling fingers. Zafir collapsed to her knees and dropped the spear again. She shuddered. Her eyes blurred. Time slowed. Chay-Liang on her sled, lightning thrower in hand, pointing it at her. The alchemist Kataros running from the ruins for the fallen spear. Dragons, hundreds, landing in a hostile ring around the Black Moon in silent challenge, while the last dregs of battle ebbed above in shrieks and blood and claw. Tuuran pounding towards her. The Black Moon himself, twisting in unexpected pain as though knifed in the back, staring up at the Queen's Gate, where Bellepheros stood.

'Holiness.' Tuuran threw himself at her.

Too slow. On hands and knees Zafir grabbed the spear. Chay-Liang was rushing closer. Another thunderbolt rang her head as though she'd been hit with a hammer. Flattened her. Kataros leaping towards her. Tuuran …

Everything fell still.

Everything stopped.

Silence.

Chay-Liang on her sled, left to hang in the air. Dragons above, paused in a wingbeat. Kataros leaping from stone to stone, poised like a frozen dancer. Tuuran sprawling across the rubble, hand stretched out to her. The stilled rush of the wind. The only sound her beating heart as the Black Moon stopped time. She lay still, waiting. He'd told her to summon the dragons, but the dragons hadn't needed summoning. They'd already known what was coming.

With a wave of his hand the Silver King stopped time, but the spear in my claw kept his sorceries from me.

Carefree, the Black Moon walked slowly closer. His eyes lingered on the far horizon and the crescent moon that hung there with the sun. The knife of a thousand eyes gleamed naked in his hand.

'Unruly children,' he said, and though his voice was quiet there was no other sound. Only the words of a half-god. 'I gave you a choice.'

Two hunting dragons pinned another to the stone. The Black Moon dissolved them to smoke, all three at once. They stayed as they were, dragon-shaped clouds of black dust, waiting for time to start again, for the wind to scatter them.

'Fickle whore father, I am more than you made me to be.' He clenched a fist and raised it to the moon. 'Older than you. Here before you. The void that was before. Endless and without substance.'

His voice fell. 'Without time.' He walked past Zafir as though she wasn't there, ignored Chay-Liang on her sled and everything else. He stopped beside Diamond Eye and touched each of the four dragons holding him down. They turned to dust.

'You set us here on the skin of the earth. You and brother sun with his numberless little ones. You left us to the mercy of the dead goddess, and she raised the dark moon and left us with your cold light alone. We pleaded. We prayed. We begged. But you gave us nothing.'

His eyes flared silver. He looked from Diamond Eye to Snow. To Chay-Liang. To Kataros and to the Queen's Gate, where Bellepheros stood frozen. Helpless, all of them. He lifted his knife of eyes.

'A new beginning, fickle father. A new creation. No fiery sun. No hostile moon. No cold distant stars. No dead goddess with her violent wrath. It will be as it should have been, and we will all be free of you, and all the better for it.' He cocked his head to Chay-Liang on her sled. 'You. Tiny and small. You think to touch me with the storm-dark?'

Zafir rose behind him. Her feet were unsteady. He didn't see. His own eyes were blind, and in this crack between moments there were no other eyes through which to see. The dragon-potion hid her from more than dragons, and that was why she'd taken it. So he wouldn't see her, or know her, or read her thoughts, or understand what she meant to do. Even if she hadn't quite known herself.

'You know nothing,' he said. 'Your ignorance is your doom.'

Zafir stood behind him. As The Black Moon reached out to turn Chay-Liang into dust Zafir drove the Earthspear into his back. He spun, ripping the spear out of her hands. The point stuck out from his chest. The weight of its haft almost toppled him. His lips drew back. Moonlight silver poured from his eyes. He reached – not for her, but for something she couldn't see, for something that wasn't quite there. Then he toppled to his knees and pitched down face first into the broken stone of the mountain.

The wind blew.

Diamond Eye shivered.

Dust-turned dragons shattered into formless smoke, dissolving in the breeze. Chay-Liang's sled shot past Zafir's face. Dragons wheeled and shrieked. Kataros skittered to a stop, bewildered at Zafir and the spear and the Black Moon, who had all moved from one place to another in the blink of an eye. Zafir opened her palm and raised her arm and flexed her fingers. The spear appeared in her hand. Calm and smooth and sure she drove it through the Black Moon again, through his heart this time, spearing him to the mountain stone. The last light from his eyes flickered, and for a moment Zafir thought she saw another man inside. She heard a howl of anguish. And, perhaps, of relief.

Tuuran stared aghast. The silver light dimmed in the Black Moon's eyes. For a moment Crazy Mad seemed to look out at him. Crazy Mad. Berren Crowntaker. The Bloody Judge.

And then he died.

'No!' Tuuran screamed. '*No!*' He whipped the axe off his back. Lifted it to split Zafir's head. Saw the shock on her face and smashed the blade into a stone beside her instead. He ran to Crazy Mad's side, dropped to pick him up, filled with some foolish hope that somehow Zafir had driven the Black Moon away and that was all, but Crazy was dead, as dead as a spear through the heart would make you.

Never mind the circling dragons. Never mind the alchemists and their schemes. Never mind the Taiytakei witch and her lightning.

'Hush.' He felt Zafir's arms around him, clinging to him. 'Hush.' Felt her head pressed into the back of his singed hair. She held him tight. 'He's not the friend you once had any more, big man. He stopped being that a long time ago.'

A part of Tuuran knew she was right and that it was true, and another part knew that Crazy Mad had never been quite dead until now, and that Zafir had killed him.

44

The Silver Sea

The dragons eyed one another. Diamond Eye, mauled and battered. Crippled Snow with a hundred dragons arrayed behind her. Paused between them the Black Moon lay dead and pinned to the earth by the Silver King's spear, just as he had a thousand years before. And Tuuran, crouched over him, and Zafir beside them both.

Kataros, out in the open. She stared at the spear sticking out of the Silver King. A spear that killed dragons. Zafir had used it to summon them. What else could it do? She took a step forward, then stopped. The white dragon Snow crept a pace closer. Diamond Eye languidly stretched his battered wings.

Do you see now? he seemed to say. *Do you see why?*

Snow eyed the Silver King's spear, but before she could move Zafir snatched it from the Black Moon's corpse and slammed it into the stone. The mountain quivered. 'There is another way,' she said.

Diamond Eye bared his fangs. Zafir faced him.

'Old friend. Do you remember the Silver Sea?'

The dragon cocked his head. *Yes.*

'Do you remember how it felt to leave it behind? What was that place – the Silver Sea? Was it home? That's what I felt from you when we left it. A longing for home.'

Home.

'You tried to hide it, but I saw what it meant. I saw the loss in you. The yearning you felt. That's where they went, isn't it? The other half-gods? Your sisters and brothers. And you were the ones who stayed behind, the courageous ones. The Isul Aieha's brothers. You stayed to stop the Black Moon from turning the world inside out, but he tore you down. He broke you. He took your souls and made you forget what you were. He turned you into dragons and claimed you for his own. You've seen the carvings the Isul Aieha left behind, Diamond Eye.' She walked to the old dragon and touched a hand to his snout. 'Tell them. Tell them all. Tell them everything you've seen and everything you know. He didn't take away all that you once were. Perhaps he couldn't, and that's why you felt the yearning.'

She turned to Snow and levelled the spear at the white dragon's eye. 'The Silver King did to you what the Black Moon had already done once before. And I know your mind, dragon. You would kill every one of us now while you can so there can never again be such alchemy, but there *is* another way.'

There would never be another alchemist again. These few here would be the last. Kataros already knew that because Bellepheros had quietly told them all as they walked the Silver King's Ways. The Silver King, nailed to a cave beneath a mountain, was gone. The last of him. Without the filtered essence of his divinity, there could never be another. Kataros and Bellepheros, Jeiros and the handful of others, they would be the last.

Zafir lifted the spear. 'This is the Isul Aieha's palace, dragon, and this is his spear. He left behind a way for you to go home. With this I have opened the gates to the Silver Sea. So you *do* have a choice, white dragon. You can stay, and we can fight, you and I, and we can kill one another over and over, or you can go home and become the half-gods you once were. But you cannot have this end by force. Smash at this mountain for a thousand years and you will not get in. I will allow hatchlings to enter. One at a time, and I will take you where you want to be. Make your choice, dragons.' She turned and started the climb to the Queen's Gate. 'We cannot live together. But we *can* both live, and there will be no more dragon-riders, for there will be no more dragons to ride.' She walked to the old gate where every queen of the Silver City had walked in their turn to claim their throne, and not one dragon moved to stop her.

45

The Speaker

Forty-six days after landfall

Lost and forlorn on the edge of the Fury gorge, Queen Lystra sat, the last speaker of the nine realms, last survivor of her house and family, queen of a city burned to ash, speaker of realms that no longer existed. Thirty-seven men and fifteen women, that was all she had. Queen of nothing much. For all she knew they were the last humans left alive for a thousand miles.

She dangled her legs over the cliff, holding her son Jehal tight in her arms. The four Adamantine Men she had left to her stood nearby. They didn't like it that she was out here in the open. Her riders didn't like it either, but most of them had stopped caring when they'd lost the Spur. At least the Adamantine Men did what she said and didn't talk back.

Zafir had executed her mother. Almiri had died in the battle over Evenspire. She'd seen Jehal picked up and crushed by the white dragon Snow. Now Jaslyn hovered at the brink of death, shredded by a hatchling. That was what had become of her family.

As she swung her legs and looked to the south she saw specks in the sky. Dragons. She didn't have any alchemists left, so there were no potions to help them hide, and so the dragons would feel her thoughts even if they didn't see.

'Holiness.' The Adamantine Men moved in closer, pointing.

'Let them come.' What was the point in running. Run to where? To the Pinnacles to throw herself on the mercy of Zafir's sister, if anyone there was still alive? She'd seen inside the Silver King's Enchanted Palace for a while. Had a good look around. If anywhere could hold, it would be the Pinnacles. But hold for what? For how long?

The dragons she'd seen were coming straight for her. Fifty or sixty of them. She pulled herself to her feet, struggling to find the will to move. She looked at little Jehal in her arms, wrapped up tight and warm and asleep, without the first idea of the world he'd been born to. She had to force herself not to give him up, hand him over to one of her Adamantine Men and send him running for shelter, or back to her riders who were still cowering in the Silver King's Ways, getting hungrier by the day.

'I hope you're ready to die well,' she said. She didn't bother putting on her helm, looking out across the Fury gorge as the dragons flew in towards her. Instead she unwrapped little Jehal from his dragonscale basket and held him in his blanket. 'When the fire comes,' she murmured. 'It will be quick.'

The dragons rose overhead and circled. One by one they landed. They formed a semicircle, pinning her against the cliff. Fifty dragons, give or take.

'Does it have to be this way?' she railed. 'Can't you just win?' She'd told herself she wouldn't be afraid. She had really thought she wouldn't, but now, as the end came, she found she was. It wasn't so much for herself, but dragons liked to play with their food. They toyed with the people they cornered, eking out their terror. She thought for a moment of tossing little Jehal over the cliff and being done with it, just so they wouldn't have him.

The last dragon to land was colossal, a real monster, as big as a dragon got. Its scales were red and gold; its wounds were deep and terrible, and it wore them with a fierce and ghastly pride. A rider sat on his back. Dressed in fractured glass and battered gold and shreds of dragonscale. She carried a spear.

Zafir slid to the ground. She took off her helm and laid it down, and then the spear beside it and her gauntlets too. She regarded Lystra steadily as she did, then walked slowly closer until they stood face to face, an outstretched arm apart.

'I won't bow to you,' Lystra said. She half expected Zafir to simply reach out and push her, to topple her off the edge of the cliff.

'I'm sorry about your sister,' Zafir said. 'She was a little bit mad, but I liked her best of all of you. Perhaps the madness was why. You will do better with this than I ever did.'

She pulled the Speaker's Ring from her finger and dropped it to the dirt at Lystra's feet. Then turned and walked back to her dragon and flew away.

Xibaiya

The Black Moon crashes spitting into Xibaiya, pinned helpless by the spectre of the Adamantine Spear. Silence takes him in her jaws. She has been waiting. And though the Black Moon howls and screams and threatens and begs, though the dead goddess is loose unfettered upon the world once more with all the horror she will bring, though the Black Moon alone cannot cage the Nothing, the dragon Silence carries the Black Moon there nonetheless, and hurls him to be devoured, all without a word.

Epilogue

Three years after landfall

'The speaker Zafir flew to her Enchanted Palace that very day with a single dragon egg. Atop her mountain fortress she slew her dragon Diamond Eye with the Silver King's spear and released him from his promise to serve her one of his many lifetimes. Later that day he hatched again from the egg they'd carried together. He found Zafir waiting for him dressed in simple silks, fearless. When he was ready she led him through the Hall of Mirages to the Silver King's gateways and touched the Adamantine Spear to the archways there. One after another they opened to the Silver Sea. The two of them stood together before the gates and waited, the dragon-queen and her dragon, and Diamond Eye let every one of his brothers and sisters ride his thoughts and eyes to share what he saw: the Silver Kings walking across the Silver Sea to greet him and welcome him, finally, to be with them, to become again the half-god that every dragon had been before the Black Moon came. And when the dragon Diamond Eye had shown the end that waited for any who wished it, he turned away and chose to stay with the dragon-queen for one lifetime more. And in the days and months that followed, dragon after dragon came, hatchlings freshly woken, and the dragon-queen led each one of them home and thanked them for their choice.

'In twos and threes the men who lived in the Enchanted Palace left her there and walked away. They had lived without the sun while she was gone and now they wanted it back. There weren't enough people left anywhere alive to rebuild the Adamantine Palace, but a little life returned to the Silver City, and a small town grew beside the Mirror Lakes on the fringes of the old City of Dragons, though only the brave and desperate went in among the ruins, foraging for tools or clothes, or perhaps simply stone for building homes, and always finding bones.

'The dragons honoured their pact. We saw them often in those early days, but they left us alone and slowly we came to trust their peace. As the months turned to years they diminished. There are a handful of them left now, but they are hardly ever seen.

'Jasaan and the other Adamantine Men, the true ones who had always been a part of the legion, were among the first to leave her. The Taiytakei witch flew them back to the Adamantine Palace on her sled to serve their new speaker. We sent a few off across the realms, to Furymouth and Sand and Evenspire and Bazim Crag to see if there were survivors, to hunt out the caves and the old eyries and castles and palaces, the tunnels and the alchemists. The alchemist Kataros went with them, though Jasaan had asked her to stay. But she said she would know where to look, and so off they went to spread the word that the terror was over. We didn't think we would see them again, but they came back in time, most of them. They told stories, sometimes, of how now and then a dragon had helped them.

'Jasaan? Black Ayz died under the Spur fighting dragons, so Jasaan became our Night Watchman, though there seems little need for a legion of Adamantine Men any more. The alchemists Bellepheros and Jeiros and a few of the others threw in their lot with the witch. They came to the palace before they left and told us where and why and promised they would return now and then to do what they could, but that there was no place here for alchemy without dragons. Bellepheros said it was because of the Statue Plague, spreading across the other worlds, that he and the others wanted to be useful. But the truth was simply that he was in love with the Taiytakei witch, and she with him, and she wanted to be back among her people, and he was content to follow her. Two old sorcerers in their twilight years.'

Lystra sighed and stroked little Jehal's hair. 'That was a year after the pact, and the last time we saw the dragon-queen Zafir. She came with them, riding on the back of a yearling. She didn't say much. But she looked at you for a very long time. She said you looked like him. That you have his eyes. And so you do.'

She laughed. 'He was a glorious lover, your father, and an arrogant selfish prick too, and we both loved him, and because of that ...' She shook her head. 'Zafir went back to her empty mountain. No one sees her any more, the crazy dragon-queen in her ghost palace with her dragon, where hatchlings sometimes arrive but never leave. They say she has explored all of the Silver King's enchanted palace and knows every one of its secrets, but that there is still one dark room she keeps sealed and never enters. They say she flies out now and then to hunt down dragons that forget the pact they made. She turns them to stone, but she always takes an egg and carries it home so they might hatch in front of the gate to the Silver Sea. When you're older, Jehal, and wandering the world and you see a dragon made of stone, you're seeing the story of her passing.'

Lystra went to the door and opened it. She shivered in the icy wind which blew even in the shelter of the old palace walls. 'And Tuuran? I would have made him Night Watchman. Jasaan said I should. But he wouldn't leave the dragon-queen until she forced him to go, and when he did, he left with the Taiytakei witch and the alchemists and the dragon-queen's handmaidens. She sent them all away. They say there was another child who went with them, the dragon-queen's child, and that Tuuran was its father, but that's just a story. They say too that the man who became the Black Moon, who had once been Tuuran's friend, had had a twin or some such left behind. A brother perhaps, and that Tuuran meant to look for him, that he meant to find his old friend again. But one should not pay much attention to stories, little Jehal.'

Lystra stepped outside into the snow. She climbed the ice-covered walls of the old Adamantine Palace and looked up at the sky. It was clear today, and the air was bitter. She pulled her dragonscale coat tighter. Riders once wore it to keep fire at bay; it had never crossed their thoughts that it might keep out the cold. The dragon-realms had never been cold when she was young. Raised in the desert, she'd never seen the snow.

She stared at the sky, at the halo of fire that was the midday sun wrapped around the black disc of the new dark moon. She looked at the stars, the bright ones that were visible even in the day now, in the dim perpetual twilight.

'No one knows what became of the half-god,' she whispered to the wind. 'But now that the dark moon has risen to devour the sun, now that the dead goddess is loose, now that the world slowly dies in ice, they whisper at night that the dragon-queen will emerge from her fortress one day and carry the Silver King's spear, and return to save us all.'

She turned away. 'But I knew her well, little Jehal, and I wouldn't count on it.'

Acknowledgements

With thanks to Simon Spanton, devourer of unnecessary prologues, who asked for dragons and got more than he bargained for. To Marcus Gipps and Robert Dinsdale for their editorial work. To Hugh Davis for copy-editing all my dragons, and to the proof-readers whose names I've rarely known. To Stephen Youll for his gorgeous covers. With thanks to all the people who read *A Memory of Flames* and talked about it. Thank you to lovers of dragons everywhere. Thank you to all the alchemists and enchantresses. Thank you for reading this.

This will be the last dragon book for a while, perhaps for ever. It's been long and glorious and sometimes exhausting, and yes, there are other stories that could be told, but this one was for Zafir, not for anyone else. To this day I don't quite know where she came from. I had something quite different planned when I started, but when it didn't work out the way I thought it would, Zafir rose from the ashes. *I'll tell you a story*, she said, *but you might not like me very much*.

If it happens that you did, then please say so. Loudly and to lots of people, and maybe, now and then, to me.

The Bloody Judge

Six years before landfall

Men pressed him from all sides, crushed together. His own soldiers pushed against his back and to either side. The enemy were forced before him by their own numbers. He met them with remorseless savagery, slashing and stabbing, reaching for any inch of unguarded flesh. The black moonsteel edge of his sword glittered in the sunlight. Dark as night and sharp as broken glass, it shattered steel and splintered bone with a hunger all of its own. Spears and swords broke. Armour ripped open like skin beneath a tiger's claw. Entrails spilled across the ground to join the bloody mess of severed heads and arms. His feet slipped and slid beneath him. Sweat stung his eyes. The air stank of iron and death, while blood ran down his blade and over his gauntlets. A part of him forgot his name, forgot why he was there, forgot everything and gave itself over to the savage he kept inside, letting it fill up every pore, every hair, every thought.

There was a peace to killing. He'd always found it so.

The enemy broke and ran. He watched them go, scattering into the long grass, racing for the line of trees ahead. The savage inside wanted their blood, but the savage was on a leash, always.

My name is Berren. Berren the Bloody Judge. Berren the Crowntaker.

A last knot of soldiers ran at him, one mad suicidal charge. He drove his moonsteel blade through the first man's mail and into his heart. Blood sprayed as he snapped the sword away, and then the grey sorcerer in their midst was in front of him. Berren drove his sword through heavy robes, through flesh and blood and bone until the point emerged from the man's spine. It was the easiest thing in the world.

The rest turned and ran. Madness.

The grey sorcerer pressed a strip of sigiled paper to Berren's chest. He clawed a handful of his own blood and threw it at Berren's face. Then crumpled and fell, lips drawn back across his teeth, grinning blankly at the clear blue sky.

'For Saffran,' he breathed.

The world blurred and Berren fell. Something oozed inside his head. Something from a dark place. It pushed through him, clambering over him, squeezing him back. Huge and vast and ablaze like the full moon, it bloomed in an explosion of silver light as Berren tumbled screaming into darkness.

In the light of the battlefield, surrounded by the faces of strangers, the Crowntaker, the Bloody Judge of Tethis, opened his eyes. He looked about him at a world fresh and full of gawping faces. He tore the half-ripped sigil from his breast and got to his feet. Alive as he had never been.

'Let's be at it then, lads,' he said.

A flare of silver moonlight flashed across his eyes.